The Innkeeper

and

The Cannibal

THE INNKEEPER
and
THE CANNIBAL

Jacob C. Sadler

Auberdine Publishing – Fort Collins, Colorado

Printed in the United States of America
First Printing, 2022

ISBN: 979-8-9859095-0-0 *(paperback)*
ISBN: 979-8-9859095-1-7 *(ebook)*

Auberdine Publishing
2519 S Shields Street
Suite 1K #612
Fort Collins, CO 80526

To my mother, whose experience inspired me to write this story.

Your faith in me has always given me faith in myself.

To my aunt, whose advice helped guide the editing and rewriting process.

To my wife, who has given me strength when I had none for myself.

And finally, in this age of self-hatred, insecurity, and anxiety—I think it important to recognize oneself from time to time. So here's to you, me. Good job.

Prologue

Arthur eyed his men suspiciously, keeping his backpack close to his chest. It did not matter that the remains within belonged to their old captain. The soldiers' hunger blinded them to honor, to loyalty. If they knew he had his brother's remains, if his fellow soldiers caught even a scent of the rotting foot within his bag—Arthur would have a mutiny on his hands.

"Captain," Gerald said with a revolting salute. "The Muhali are all around us now."

"I can hear their drums," Arthur growled. All day and all night, he could hear the *dum da da dum dum*. He tightened his hold over the backpack. He felt all that remained of his brother, Auldwine, at the bottom of the fraying cloth. "Reinforcements will come."

"And until then?" The soldier questioned.

Arthur raised a brow and answered, simply, "Find a rat."

Kristoff coughed, "Ain't no meat on 'em."

Arthur argued for his brother's sake, "They've been eating our dead for three years. They have meat."

Gerald scoffed, "Ain't none anyhow. All's left in this mudpuppy hovel is burnt bones."

"Barbecue is a fine tradition," Arthur said, staring out the ashen ruin at a line of lanterns. The enemy had now surrounded the blackened village.

Kristoff sniffed the air, "Y'all smell that?" He waved his nose in the air like a beast. "Somethin' rotting in here."

Arthur leaned forward, covering the backpack with his torso. He pressed Auldwine's remains up to his thumping heart. The Muhali war drums began to beat faster in no-man's land. The enemy was simply taunting them now.

"Listen to them," Darius shook his head. "They aren't even shelling us."

"Don't need to," Gerald stated. "They're doin' just fine starvin' us."

Three other soldiers shuffled into the crumbling barn. Upon approaching Arthur and the others, they paused. One of them looked around, his nostril twitching. "We find some food?"

Arthur licked his lips. He glanced at his white knuckles and wished dearly that they had. He tried his best to sound optimistic, like how an innkeeper ought to sound. "Only a little while until reinforcements arrive."

More of his men began to filter into the makeshift bunker. Arthur repositioned himself and his pack at the far corner of the ruined barn. He faced his men, back to the wall.

"No," Darius whispered, hopelessly. "And there's no more rats."

Several soldiers groaned, one rubbed his stomach, and the other looked down the barrel of his rifle with contemplative eyes.

Arthur decided to complain as well. It was not hard. He was starving, too. The only difference between him and the men he now led was he had made a promise. He would not start his tenure as innkeeper by breaking his word. Especially not to his brother. He looked at the ground despairingly, "Never thought I'd miss the trenches." He added a snort and peaked up at the troops.

His men eyed him strangely. Several heads were tilted. The distant war drums grew louder.

Arthur steadied his speech and prayed his voice did not crack. "When all this is done—" he paused when Gerald inched forward. The big bastard's nose was twitching like a rabid dog. He finished, "We will have the biggest feast Auberdine has ever seen."

He should not have mentioned a feast. Kristoff and Darius encroached, looking around with narrow, thoughtful eyes. Meanwhile, Gerald raised his chin and stared at the officer's pack, "What ya got in there?"

Arthur's throat swelled. He tugged at his collar. He told a half-truth, "Rounds." The other half, however, was that his brother now rotted at the bottom of the bag.

"Mmm," Gerald hummed. He picked his nose and flicked his fingers. The brute shrugged, "I'm low. Think I could borrow your pack?"

The two men stared at each other. Arthur rubbed his lips together and after a moment, smiled, "What's that one take? 75 mil? I'll get you some."

Kristoff and Darius crept closer. Gerald's gravelly voice echoed, "Not a lot of clanking for an ammo pouch."

Arthur knew what needed to happen. As he watched his soldiers surround him, even as they themselves were trapped, he set the backpack down. Then, he stood up. The distant drumming got even louder. *Dum-da-da-dum-dum. Dum-da-da-dum-dum.* Arthur smiled jovially and extended his arms, "Is this how you treat your officer? Your new innkeeper?"

"You ain't been an officer very long," Kristoff spat.

"Ain't been innkeeper that long, neither," Gerald added.

Arthur rolled his upper lip toward his nose. "True," he put his arms behind his back and frowned. *And if any of you come any closer to Auldwine, I will make sure your body is never found.* Arthur took a deep breath. His chest rose and fell. He clicked his tongue.

Kristoff raised his hands and pleaded, "We've been chewing on tires."

"I know," Arthur replied through gritted teeth. "I have been chewing them with you."

Darius drooled, enthralled with the rotting smell coming from the corner. "What are you hiding from us? Rat? Raccoon?"

"I bet he's got rations still," said some young idiot in the back.

Arthur chewed on his cheek. Finally, he risked the truth, "I have Auldwine in there. What's left of him, at least."

Most soldiers froze. Some stepped back out of respect for the fallen. Only Gerald kept moving. He snorted like a bull before the charge. "It's been two weeks since they shelled your brother."

"I am bringing his bones back home," Arthur declared. He watched the massive man greedily stare at the backpack. He slowly coiled his finger around a hidden trigger. When his hand slipped comfortably into that familiar, lethal position, Arthur widened his eyes. He raised his nostril in disgust, "But Gerald… If your fat fucking foot comes any nearer, I promise *your* bones will stay right here."

The mutiny started with a footfall; it ended with a thud. Blood and brains soaked the faces of the starving soldiers. Gerald's hollow skull spurted like a drinking fountain. His legs writhed and bounced like popcorn. His eyes rolled back like dumplings in a soup.

Arthur again took a deep breath. Then, he pointed his pistol at every ravenous man, one by one. "Now. Do you want to die over a foot, or?" He stretched his neck. "Gerald was a big son of a bitch, wasn't he?"

Bayonets were removed from rifles. Flesh was removed from limbs. The war drums of the Muhali beat on through that lightless day and into the starless night.

Arthur watched his men sate their hunger but he no longer trusted them. The moment Gerald's generosity waned, he would have a similar uprising to put down. He shook his head at the gruesome sight. *As long as we are pinned down, we will be animals.* Arthur watched as the men divvied up the organs. *When they next get the itch—with whose flesh will they scratch?*

Arthur shuddered. He opened the backpack and retrieved a rusty knife. He had made a promise and he would fulfill it. *But there is always a promise in compromise.* He then took out his brother's rotting foot. His stomach growled. "I will get you home," he whispered. While his troops butchered Gerald, Arthur turned his back on them and began carving the flesh.

1

Eastmont

Blackness blanketed the barren battlefield. Charles gazed into no-man's land. He glanced at the gashes and slashes gutting the rock, where men had created holes from which to kill one another. The landscape was charred and chiseled by billions of bombardments. Smoke obscured the sun. Gasps of mustard gas seeped up like volcanic fumaroles. Oozing mud slowly swallowed a hollow automobile. And—far in no man's land—burning mounds of corpses were penciled into the scene as if a painter's afterthought.

Charles Eastmont watched the pallbearers of the dead. An army of ants arrogantly marched beside the trains. Several raccoons chased each other atop a ruined tank. A wolf rested its head atop a trench, its tail hidden in the wastes of war. Rats leapt to safety as a trench caved in. Birds fluttered away as a line of barbed wire sank into the mud. *We did not win this war. Nature did.*

He shivered, glad the Great War was over. *I made the right choice joining the navy.* He turned his back on the bubbling quagmire and boarded the train for home.

All the windows were shut and all the curtains closed. Green and blue wallpaper coated the walls. Loaves of bread and jam were lined up on a table, as well as several slices of fruit. Charles approached the modest buffet and reached for a slice of bread. He realized quickly that the bread was harder than bone. The jam had flies in it. The fruit was overgrown with mold. Charles shrugged. He had gone without before.

A lone window had its curtains sprawled open. A hooded man stood in front of it. Charles grunted a cough to alert the stranger to his presence, but he did not stir. The train bellowed a five-minute warning and the train jolted forward slightly. The man placed his hand on the window. He looked like he was waving. He stood so close, his breath was beginning to obscure the glass.

"Morning," Charles said. In truth, it could have been dusk—he could not keep track of the passage of time when all things were dark. The haze around the Tanglewood permitted no passage of day or night, just one perpetual gloom.

The stranger removed his hand from the window and grunted. His voice had humor attached to it, "One word… That's all you have for me?"

Charles' eyes widened. He had never dared hope for such a reunion, not after Auldwine. Yet there they both were, heading home from the bloodiest war in history. Charles spoke as if he had just finished running a marathon, "Arthur Gardner."

The man removed his hood. His skin was as pale as moonlight. He raised his cheeks slightly, but his eyes precluded a smile. Fatigue wore his gaunt face. His left eyelid twitched uncontrollably.

Charles rushed to greet his friend. In that moment, he counted himself the most fortunate man in all Auberdine. He hugged the man tightly and slapped his back. He towered over the pale figure like a great, dark oak. Realizing his embrace was hurting him, he let go.

Arthur burped, shrugged, and looked at his feet. He blurted out what seemed a confession. There was pain in his friend's voice. "I always thought it would be Auldwine to survive. Not me."

Charles looked into Arthur's eyes, though the veteran did not seem able to return his gaze. He patted his friend's back again, but the action was more for him.

Charles leaned against the window. His voice was unsure. His dark skin casted a shadow over them both. "He was… The most honorable man I ever met, your brother."

Arthur's brow twitched and he opened his mouth to speak. The thought faded from his mind and he shut his mouth again.

He is morose… I don't blame him, Charles Eastmont thought. Small talk was nearly impossible now. For his part, he had not had a normal conversation in almost four years. The Great War had always loomed over his words. Now that it was over, it was clear both had to relocate their voices. Charles offered his widest smile and stuttered, "Guess you, uh… You're the…uh-"

Arthur shifted uncomfortably and interrupted his statement. "Yep. Innkeeper. More's the pity."

Charles nodded and sat down beside Arthur.

The man's eyes stared ahead but Charles knew he was seeing only memories. The new innkeeper's eyes glazed over. A slight smirk flickered across his lips. He gazed off into his memory and scratched his finger nervously. "My brother was only ever good at growing things. Should'a known he'd get himself blown up."

Charles debated not responding. Arthur's brother, Auldwine, was fifteen years his senior and by all accounts—the most loved man in the entire town. "He was the only one to ever treat my mother kindly. And you, of course."

Arthur's smile became more pronounced and it lasted long enough for him to finish his sentence. "He was born to keep the inn. He treated all the world as his guest." Arthur paused and Charles noticed a change in his voice. The man seemed to lament his next words, "Love came so easily for him."

Arthur's brother had been a great friend to Charles and his mother. While everyone else in the town gossiped and laughed at them, Auldwine gave Cora and her infant son a place to live. He folded his arms and covered his heart, "He was like a father to me."

Arthur nodded and a silence ensued. Charles knew only a minute had passed, but every second felt like an eon. Arthur had never wanted to keep the inn. He had told Charles as much in their younger days. In those times, Arthur only wanted to make people laugh.

Finally, Arthur sighed and sat down next to him. He crossed his legs and began to tap his foot rapidly. He bent over and gently pushed his backpack under his seat.

Charles noticed how anxious his friend had become. Was it their talk of his brother, or had the war changed him permanently? He shifted the topic, "Have you heard anything from the kids?"

Arthur nodded. He looked at Charles for a moment and then glanced to his side. "Aeric thinks I'm some damn war hero…"

Charles' sense of humor let out a chuckle without his consent.

Arthur faced Charles again and after a pause, chuckled too. "And Emilia is only happy around her dog. Otherwise, everything scares her."

Charles nodded, "I can see why. She grew up during the war. Good thing she has the dog."

"Until that dies," Arthur replied grimly.

Charles stretched the side of his lip into a half-frown. The train ride was sure to be a depressed affair. *How could it not be?* He asked himself. Of course his friend would be sad. He had not seen his wife in half a decade, his daughter grew up without a father, and his son retained the patriotic idealism that had gotten most young men in their town killed.

'*I heard what happened to your sortie. In that village,*' Charles was about to say. He could only imagine being the only person left of his company when reinforcements came. "I heard what happened—"

"How's your mother doing?" Arthur rubbed his hands together as if a great chill had settled into him.

Charles lifted his shoulders aloofly, "The wildflowers were overgrown, last I heard. She said she wasn't going to do anything about it… She is still mourning Auldwine. I want to get back as quick as I can. I bet she is smoking again." Charles stopped and his voice broke, "He was the only man she ever trusted. After me, of course."

Arthur sat straight in his chair and rubbed his chin, "My brother loved everyone. But your mother, especially."

Charles nodded. Auldwine cared deeply for the broken, and his mother had been the epitome of shattered when the old innkeeper found her. '*The inn will be a different place,*' he was about to say.

Just then, however, the doors to the carriage swung open and a man with caramel skin leapt aboard. He pointed at Arthur and yelled, "You liar!"

Eastmont's head swiveled from the stranger to his friend. Arthur's face grew a devilish grin and he giggled. Charles was glad his friend could still laugh, albeit with reservation. *His laughter used to be deafeningly contagious,* he reminisced.

The man strode confidently over to them, "I ended up pissing behind one of the trains going toward Aubourg." He acknowledged Charles and said to him with a smirk, "This bastard led me on a fool's errand for a bathroom." He turned back to Arthur, "Well, I hope you are happy, because some of those city folk saw a rainbow of yellow and orange from their seats."

Arthur's laughter trailed off as he sighed an exasperated, breathy 'Whoo.' He motioned to his left and introduced the man. "Galahad."

The man named Galahad saluted Charles. "And yourself?"

"Charles Eastmont."

Galahad's face contorted in a mix of surprise and confusion. Then, it settled back into relaxed confidence. "Cora's boy?"

"Yes," he answered coldly, though he did not intend for his tone to be so biting.

Galahad did not seem to notice. The boisterous soldier wrapped his arm around Arthur, "Well boys, we did it. The captains did their best to kill us off… But damn them, we did it." He mimed a toast, "To not being rat food!"

Arthur promptly chastised the soldier, "You're an ass."

Galahad folded his hands toward his face and gave puppy dog eyes to Arthur. He assumed an innocent expression as he declared, "What? A man can't be happy he is not carrion?"

Charles glared, "Show some respect."

For a second, their vision locked. The man's eyes flickered with enmity and then, Galahad shrugged. He declared, "Ah, hell. I hated it as much as the rest of you." He pointed a finger and shook his head like a disappointed parent, "Arthur, you can't let yourself be a captive to suffering. War's over. Don't be a prisoner of war."

Charles did not expect to agree with the loud man, but his words echoed long in the silent train. He looked down in his lap. He still did not like this Galahad but he would rather not be a hypocrite. He scolded himself. *How many people have judged you from afar?*

Charles sighed and tried to start anew, "Tell me about yourself, Galahad."

The younger man had been busy looking at the food with repulsion. After reorienting his body away from the food, Galahad spoke. He had long black hair and moved his hands rapidly as he spoke. "Well," he began, "I come from the outer ring. My father owns a liquor store there."

Charles knew quite well the man was from the outer ring. People who looked like Charles and Galahad lived in the Overgrowth of town, in the shadow of the forest.

The train whistled and steam surged past their windows. Galahad sat back down and yawned as the train began to move, "Well boys. Back to the home-front." He closed his eyes and said, sarcastically, "Off to paradise."

Charles could see Arthur looking intently at him and widened his eyes in expectation. Arthur frowned and asked with insecurity in his fluttering voice, "I need a grove-keeper at the inn."

Charles' eyes darted away from Arthur. He looked as the Tanglewood faded from view. Green shapes were beginning to reemerge.

Arthur also glanced out the window. "I haven't seen that color in over half a decade…Still, I can't grow green things. That was always Auldwine's job. Hell, he planted the grove."

Arthur was right. When Auldwine would take them planting, it was always Charles that ended up playing in the dirt. He expressed his regret, "I am nowhere near as good a gardener. I mean, look at my last name."

Arthur Gardner shook his head firmly, "Look at mine. Last names don't mean anything. My thumbs couldn't be green if I dyed them…" He closed his eyes and prepared his breath. His chest rose slowly and he added, "You are as much his family as I am."

Charles smiled and furrowed his brow. He shook his head slowly and put his hands up. He folded them placidly, "I have my mother to look after."

Arthur nodded. He looked around the carriage for a moment. Then, he pulled several pages from his pockets. He went toward the end of the locomotive and knelt before a small fireplace. He tossed the paper into the fire.

"What are you doing?" Charles asked.

Arthur let the smoke kiss his face. He stared at the embers for a minute and when he returned to Charles, he declared with a bittersweet smile, "They were my death letters—to be delivered to Hanna and the children when I died. But, every time the captains blew their whistles and we vaulted over the trenches, I survived."

Charles swallowed and his voice cracked, "You don't seem too happy about that."

"No." Arthur rubbed his eyes until they were red. He sat silently with his hands dangling limply from his seat. Then, just as Charles was trying to remember how to whistle, Arthur let out a yawn. The new innkeeper closed his eyes and joined Galahad in deep sleep. Charles thought they were competing against one another to see which could snore the loudest.

Charles Eastmont would have liked to join them in their rest. Yet despite his weariness, he was giddy. It had been too long since he strolled along the springtime streams with his mother. It had been years since he talked late in the night with Hanna Gardner about philosophy and life, too long since he had any friends at all. His legs began to bounce and his breathing intensified as the familiar landmarks of Cottonwood came into view. The overgrown homes of the outer ring began to coalesce. *Even those look beautiful,* he decided. Eastmont stared out of the window with tears in his eyes.

2

Auberdine

Hanna clenched her daughter's clammy hand as she hurried down the Hill. Her son, Aeric, was racing ahead. He yelled,

"Come on, come on. He's going to wonder where we are!"

Hanna encouraged her daughter, "Let's go, Emilia. Your brother is going to beat us."

The little girl at her hip hastened. Her face swiveled left and right as they walked down to the town. Emilia hated leaving home. The child squeezed her mother's hand. Instinctually, Hanna Gardner reminded her, "Don't you worry, sugarbear. Isabelle's right here."

A large hound trotted happily beside them. Isabelle was Emilia's truest friend and the only thing that made the small child feel safe. Her daughter looked at her hound, which stood a head taller than the girl. The animal smiled at her and its tongue drooped lazily to the side. Hanna felt her child's hand relax.

They came to a gate carved out of hedges. The only people at the hedge gate were Evelyn, Yao Yang, and a young Muhali boy. Hanna knew the first two. Evelyn was a widow like so many others. Yang was an aspiring young doctor.

"Good morning, Yang." Hanna then addressed the woman with a smile and a nod. "Evelyn."

The Pale woman rolled three fingers in her hand as a type of wave. She was dressed all in black to show she was mourning.

Yang wasted little time asking about Hanna's headaches. "Are your pains going away, Misses Gardner?"

Hanna shrugged and brushed her hair behind her shoulder. She answered, "No," and followed with a reassuring, "Though I took a few of those pain pills you told me to try. They seem to work."

Yang did not share her optimism. She could see it in his downcast eyes. The young doctor took her continued headaches to be a personal fault. He looked at his feet and muttered a few indeterminate words about his uncle, Yu. Then, he looked off to the east and said, "I will keep studying. Do not worry, Misses Gardner. I will help."

"I am sure you will," Hanna beamed. She wished he would stop losing sleep over her headaches. *That poor boy*, the innkeeper's wife thought. *His uncle shattered his self-image like a cracked mirror.*

As the sun began to rise, deep and dark shadows cascaded down tall buildings. The group's footsteps were the only noise coming from the Inner Ring. The silence unnerved Emilia, who clenched her mother's hand tighter. She did not like leaving the inn. Hanna did not like leaving much either. When they walked Auberdine, they were reminded of the war's true toll.

The town had been bellicose about fighting at first. When half their men were wiped out in a single artillery barrage, however, the town's morale plummeted. From that day on, the veil of a good war was never worn again. Instead, the women wore veils of mourning and nobody hoped for dawn, nor sang patriotic songs in the streets.

Hanna suddenly realized she had forgotten her courtesies. She beamed at the Muhali man and asked, "What is your name?" She had thought she knew everyone in her small town.

The brown-skinned boy spoke with a thick accent. He must have been in his late teens. He answered her with a quivering voice, "Momed, my queen."

Evelyn chuckled. Yang grinned and nodded to himself. Hanna's own children looked at the Muhali and then at her, expectantly. Hanna forced out a gust of air from her nostrils as a sign of flattery and put a hand on the man's shoulder. "I am not a queen. We don't have those here. Especially not in a little town like Auberdine. I am just the innkeeper's wife. Call me Hanna, Momed."

The Muhali blinked. He turned toward Yang. Momed seemed more comfortable speaking to him. "Will I insult her husband if I do not kiss her feet?"

Yang shook his head and began to say, "Not at all," when Hanna answered for herself. "You would offend me if you did. Come on, then. I miss my husband and it is his kisses I am concerned with."

Momed laughed awkwardly. His cheeks flushed red. He followed the small company as it continued through the Inner Ring. The charming houses watched them with shut doors and closed curtains, as was tradition.

Hanna looked over at her son, a tall boy of sixteen. Aeric's back was straight and he did not sway. Every step he made was deliberate. He marched as if he were already a soldier and saluted any crippled veteran he saw. She hoped there would not be a war for many years, because her son would surely enlist.

Despite her trepidations, she was proud of the boy. Aeric's father would need his family today. He had been around so much hate. Hanna shivered to think of the many times her jolly, funny husband had been made a killer. Arthur had told her enough to know he had, indeed, ended a life. Several. She looked down at her daughter.

"All smiles today for daddy, okay?"

Emilia nodded and Hanna pinched her cheek. She turned her attention to the villas of the Inner Ring. They were grown like individual mountains beside the brick road. Aside from the Yao Yang and his uncle, only Pale folk lived in the Inner Ring.

Each stone estate housed a family. Between each house was a fence and behind that, a small yard. Most lawns were barely big enough for a dog to do its business. The homes were made of long-lasting marble, decorated in ever-changing fashions. Trees were placed in a line along the sidewalks, planted in squares of mulch and rock. Nothing else was permitted to grow. Anything else was a weed. There were cracks in the large road from where the more prosperous homes parked their automobiles. Laborers were paid to salt the cracks and not a single succulent sat in the salted breaks. Automobiles parked on the road, but plants were thought unfashionable.

Hanna had always found the Inner Ring lacking and much preferred the Overgrowth. People only *dwelled* in the Inner Ring. There may have been living—but Hanna could not tell. She saw and heard nothing. Nothing ever happened in the Inner Ring. The rich merchants with happy houses knew as much, too. They kept homely market stalls in the Overgrowth.

Hanna felt a tug on her shirt.

Emilia was looking up at her, "Mama…" The girl whispered. She looked around her and began feverishly petting Isabelle's fur. The child squeaked, "What if he doesn't come back?"

"He's coming back, baby girl. Constable Goodwind assured me."

Emilia played with a long strand of hair. No amount of reason or assurance could ever help for long. Emilia scooted closer to her mother and leaned on her, as if suddenly consumed by great weariness. She opened her mouth to speak, but the child seemed unwilling to let the thought come to fruition. Finally, she asked, "What if the train derails… What if he chokes on a biscuit when the train is taking a turn too fast?"

Hanna wrapped her arm around her daughter, "The army can't spare biscuits. You know that." The girl recoiled and Hanna knew her tone was not loving enough. Often, Emilia retreated into her mind if she thought she was being talked down to. And it was precisely her mind Hanna wanted Emilia to come out of.

She tried again, "The probability a train derails is less than one in ten thousand. Daddy would have to ride ten thousand trains before he would have a chance to get hurt." Hanna knew her simplified explanation of chance was wrong, and in truth she did not know any probability for a train derailing. Still, she knew her child had a healthy respect for numbers.

"Yeah…" The child admitted, "You are right."

Hanna kissed her forehead, "That's mama's girl."

With her daughter's anxiety quelled, Hanna returned to her own. She could not deny her husband's letters had grown darker of late. *Arthur did not even seem happy about the end of the war...* Refusing to despair, she called to her son.

"Aeric, do your impression of papa's laugh."

The boy turned around and suddenly became an actor. He was always ready to fulfill an order. Aeric spat out a hacking cough and stretched his head forward.

Emilia began to giggle.

Aeric's exasperated cough turned into a rhythmic, dry heaving. His laughter grew and the boy bent his back and rested his hands on his belly. The cough died away and booming laughter filled the silent street.

Hanna pointed at her brother and said to Emilia, "You were too young to remember that—but he's dead right. You'll be able to tell where papa is from the laugh alone."

Yang joined the reminiscing. He recalled, "And when he sneezes, he roars."

Aeric looked at Isabelle and roared like a lion. The great hound licked his face.

"What a kissbug," Emilia glowed.

Hanna leaned back and observed her surroundings. They had entered the outer ring. She glanced to her right. A man living in his pockets was strewn aside a wall, sprawled about in a urine-stained blanket. A derelict stable devoid of horses was decorated with climbing pillars of vine weed. Cracks had formed along the road, and weeds found residence within them. Hanna looked up and saw the branches of a mighty tree growing over a house. A rogue, low-hanging branch looked like it was knocking on the door.

The man in the soiled blanket saw them staring. "Meeting someone?" He questioned. His voice was gruff and groggy. Stains coated his beard. His ebony skin was blotched with bruises, bandages, and cuts. His accent was strange, but his skin reminded Hanna of Charles Eastmont. *A Redfeather. I wonder if he fought on our side.*

Hanna blinked at Isabelle and then smiled at him. *He must be a newcomer to town.* Hanna answered the man formally, "My husband. He's coming home from the war."

"Took him long enough," the man replied. Hanna realized he was missing a leg. His crutch was leaning against a moss-laden post. The tool was full of splinters. The amputee murmured, "He must have been an operator."

Hanna said nothing and smiled placidly at the man. She put her hand behind Emilia's head and stroked her hair. She looked over at Aeric. He was leaning forward, like a panther ready to pounce. She patted his back. He relaxed his fists. Hanna had a mother's instinct and her son had a boy's. He thought he wanted to be a man, but he was foolish. Being a man had gotten all the other boys killed.

Aeric had no wrinkles on his face, no crow's feet. His skin shined white with not a single freckle on it. He had no blemishes or tan, as if he had not yet lived a single day. *He doesn't know how lucky he is that he was too young.*

A Fall breeze brushed over the company. Leaves rustled against the sleepy, stone ruins. Clusters of leaves gathered in gutters and laid in piles, waiting to be plucked up for trespassing. Hanna leapt into a pile and savored the satisfying sound of the leaves as they crunched beneath her feet. Promptly, everyone in the Gardner household deviated from the path.

"Look at these leaves," she said to Emilia as they stomped forward.

Hanna then glanced at her boy. He was crunching through the leaves, too. Aeric was actually playing. That surprised her. When the war started, he had sold every toy he owned. He wanted to be ready when he *too* went to war. Hanna wondered if her son had figured out being grown was not something to aspire to. She calculated not. The boy was happy to see his father. That was all.

Eventually, their paths led over many slightly submerged bridges. Instead of the crunch of autumn leaves, their feet splashed in the last of the summer runoff. The cool mountain water tickled Hanna's toes. Emilia, Evelyn, and Hanna held one another's hands to avoid slipping. Evelyn commented, "The outer ring is so charming. Like taking a trip to some ancient ruin."

Hanna raised her brow and thought, *Except it is not a ruin. People live in the Overgrowth. Quite enough to warrant some bridge repairs.* She kept her comments to herself. Evelyn was predisposed to liking anything foreign. It was a refreshing quirk in those days of prejudice.

The Overgrowth was separated by many streams. The waterways acted as natural dividers of very artificial neighborhoods. The largest embankments had grown to be islets of cultures. The tiny, pebble-filled tributaries from the west mountain formed two silty streams which encircled the neighborhood, partitioning the people of the Golden River into their own part of the Overgrowth. Hanna felt certain those people thought the rivulets were pathetic compared to their canyon-carving course. Still, they made a nice home in the Oleander Wash.

The poor, Pale families of Auberdine were interspersed throughout the Drowned Anchorage. Once, when the rivers of Cottonwood had been tamer, a river-port had stood on the banks of a tranquil lake. Now, the docks were submerged.

Those that remained lived their lives on makeshift houseboats; Anchorage folk were the poorest of all. And still, the residents never sought to rebuild and spited the inn's aid. So, they lived in squalor and hated their sunken circumstances.

Adjacent to the Drowned Anchorage, the waterways dispersed and formed an islet. The Muhali people inhabited that section of the outer ring. Hanna gestured at the houses and asked Momed, "Where do you reside?"

The Muhali pointed down a nearby row of vine-strangled buildings. Several men were pulling their donkeys out of her company's way. "A liquor store—I am assistant of the shopkeeper there, at least until tonight."

"Why until tonight?" Hanna inquired.

"My employer's son is returning from war. He sent me to fetch him."

Evelyn was aghast. "He sent you to get your replacement? How cruel."

Evelyn had not told a joke. Momed laughed all the same. He stuttered, "Not so bad, it isn't. Galahad is sweet."

Hanna glanced to her side. Momed's eyes *were* happy. Something in his voice seemed happy, too. "You know him, then?" She asked.

"He trained me before going away... He was always kind to me."

"I don't care what my neighbors say, you Muhali are all so very nice." Evelyn's light skin shined brightly in the afternoon sun. "So very polite."

Feeling a tinge of embarrassment over Evelyn's fawning, Hanna assured the Muhali, "If you find yourself without employment, I am sure my husband will offer you a bed. Maybe a job, too. What are your strengths?"

"I have none. I played music, but music... That is woman's work."

And my professors professed math was man's work. Hanna's eyes glinted with a glare. No doubt some awful man had filled the boy's head with insecurities. Evelyn interrupted her annoyance.

"War aside, I just adore your culture's music. You must play for us sometime."

Momed nodded shyly, surprised he was not being ridiculed.

Hanna inquired about Evelyn's late husband., whose shadow had loomed even after death.

Evelyn replied like a mouse, quick to say, "I still mourn Gerald."

Hanna saw she was picking at an old scar. "Nobody would shame you if you were no longer mourning."

Evelyn stared silently at the Oleander mountain.

The company slowed as they entered a circular, domed structure. The center had collapsed long before Hanna's time. The entire roof would have caved in had it not been for a huge, spiraling willow growing in the building's hollow belly. The willow branches like pillars supported the remnants of the roof, creating the façade of a complete building.

Hanna waited eagerly. *We are right on time,* she knew. A mighty whistle came from the north lobby of the ruin. Isabelle's head jolted upright. She was terrified of loud noises. The hound tried to squeeze her massive body between the bottom of a bench and the cold brick. Emilia called after her, but she was muted.

The whistle blew again. The innkeeper was home. The sound brought Hanna to tears. As the locomotive neared, her mouth fell open and she covered it with both hands. The stenciled shape of a train began to fill in with detail. Despite her resolute hope all those years, she could not believe it was happening. Outlined in darkness no longer, her husband's train came into the light. Her eyes darted to the windows, trying to catch a glimpse of the man.

Her hope had not allowed joy, yet now she wept with happiness. She bent her knees and bounced with anticipation. It seemed as she spoke there was no air in her lungs, "Daddy's home."

Her daughter was the first to spot someone coming down the steps. She shrieked with unbound joy. Emilia ran toward the doors and as they opened, she jumped into a figure's arms. Hanna laughed as Charles Eastmont came out of the train, carrying Emilia.

"Daddy's home," Emilia echoed happily.

Charles looked at Hanna and laughed, "I'm not your father, sweet thing. I *am*, however, your old uncle Eastmont."

"Oh," Emilia replied with a giggle. "Hi, uncle." She pointed at him and said to Hanna, "Look mama, Uncle Eastmont."

"I know," Hanna replied. Charles walked up to her and put a hand on her shoulder. She smiled at him, not taking her eyes off the steps.

Charles put Emilia atop his shoulders and asked the little girl to fill him in on all that had happened.

Hanna beamed as her daughter relayed all of Isabelle's shenanigans. She spared a glance toward them before quickly gazing back at the carriage. She could catch up with her old friend after reuniting with her husband. Her son must have felt a similar way, as Aeric was frozen beside her.

A man Hanna did not know came out of the train. She and Aeric sighed simultaneously.

Momed stepped forward and whispered into the man's ear. The soldier raised his hand, "I am here half a minute and my father is already ordering me around." The man seethed and eyed Momed. He snarled and repositioned the luggage on his back, "Tell him I will return once I've had a drink."

"Supreme gratitudes," Momed bowed clumsily.

The soldier glared toward the west. "Enough with the formalities." He sighed and rubbed his face of its anger. He grabbed the boy commandingly, touching his hips. "We should catch up. I have missed you." He chuckled like an angry bull snorts. "Now get on back to Cambyses before he beats us both."

The young man skittered away and looked back at the soldier. The scene reminded Hanna of a dog with its owner. As he left, Hanna was sure there was a slight skip in Momed's step.

There was still a meeting to be had. Her attention went back to the steps. Hanna walked hesitantly toward the door. She heard the steps first. Then, she saw his boots. A uniformed man entered view. A familiar face descended the stairs. Hanna raced toward her husband and nearly knocked him over.

He was stronger than she remembered. Arthur wrapped his arms around her. So tightly did he hold her, his fingernails dug into her back. She hardly noticed the pain. She had waited so long for this moment. She buried her head in his chest and rubbed her cheek against his uniform.

Arthur relinquished his grip. Hanna took a step back and looked at him. He looked frail, and his eyes—those eyes. They were bloodshot, with one of his eyelids twitching wildly. She raised her hand and grazed the back of it against his face. His eye sockets were deep and tired, as if all the youth had been drained from him. He was barely middle-aged, but his hair was starting to turn a shining silver.

Hanna felt the urge to speak to the man like he was her child, to coddle him and sing to him. He looked aged and old, but she knew there was a man who needed to be held. She could see it. It was time for her to be a wife again. Like a ghost he had come back to her. She hoped this pale, frail figure still liked blackberry jam.

Hanna trembled, "I have your favorite foods waiting for you at home. We've got to fatten you up, and fast."

"That's what feasts are for," Arthur tried to smile. His lips seemed too weak to raise themselves up. Hanna could tell from the arch in his brow he meant to be joyful. She smiled for them both.

As if not wanting an answer, her husband asked, "How much did the feast cost?"

Hanna put a finger to his lips before he could say anything more, "You don't worry about that now. Today is about you."

Arthur froze and his lip began to quiver. His eyes twitched. Hanna saw it before it happened. Arthur fell into her arms once again. He pulled her as close as he could, putting his hand against the back of her head. Hanna felt his tears falling. He pecked a thousand kisses upon her forehead before surrendering her again.

Aeric stood beside his parents. He swayed as he waited for his father's attention to turn to him. He did not interrupt their reunion, and soon his father saw him from his periphery.

"Who is this handsome man?" Arthur peered, readjusting the straps of his backpack. He acted as if he did not recognize the boy.

"Welcome back, sir," Aeric replied, courteously. Her son expressed no emotion except reverence.

Arthur seemed taken aback and shook his head. "Don't call me sir. Call me anything else."

Hanna saw a mischievous grin appear on their son's face. "Okay," he said. "You get lost or something, old man?"

Arthur pulled his son close and ruffled his hair with his fist, "You better just get lost." He squinted at his son, "Winning a war is hard work."

Aeric looked at his father and quietly said as he suppressed a rogue tear, "Welcome back, dad."

"Good to be back," Arthur answered. Hanna thought the statement sounded more like a question.

Hanna noticed Yang eyeing the train suspiciously. On any other day, she would have beckoned him over or spoken to him. Yet today, she was fixated on her husband. Yang's troubles washed from her mind as she saw Arthur step toward their daughter.

The innkeeper wandered over to Emilia and Charles. His steps were cautious. He paused when a loud clamor echoed farther down the station. Hanna observed Charles and the other soldier; they too seemed jittery. Arthur sighed and bent down to greet his daughter.

"I see you remember Mister Eastmont," Arthur said to her.

I doubt it, Hanna mused. Emilia had just started speaking when the two men went to war.

Charles seemed beside himself with joy. Emilia nodded excitedly and said, "I was telling him about Isabelle. Come here, come here!"

Hanna beamed at her baby girl. She had learned to appreciate her daughter's moments of happiness, as they had become rarer of late.

Arthur knelt and stared at the dog, "She's almost as big as your brother. How old is she?"

"Four!" Emilia yelled excitedly.

"Four!" Charles shouted with surprise. He slapped his thighs like a judge with a gavel. "You must be seventy then!"

"No!" Emilia giggled. "I'm not that old!"

Arthur stated casually, "I don't know. Seven is damn near middle-aged these days."

The other soldier laughed at the grim humor. Hanna was sure that was Galahad. Her husband had mentioned him in his last few letters. '*A real free spirit,*' he had said of him. '*Laughs at anything and anyone.*'

Emilia was indignant and grabbed Charles' hand. "I'm eight," she protested.

Hanna had not noticed her husband's slip, but when he turned toward her, she had to nod. She raised a half-smile, noting the sting in Arthur's stare. Their girl was eight and at the realization, Arthur grimaced. He had forgotten.

She saw Arthur's shoulders rise and fall. He got up and looked down at his daughter. He shook his head and for a moment, Hanna thought he might cry. Instead, he chuckled. The laugh was nothing like her husband's. She remembered booming bellows and cackling hacking. His reserved hiss startled her. Even his laughter was melancholy.

"Eight," Arthur corrected himself.

Charles pinched the girl's chubby cheeks. "Look at you," he said, "You still haven't grown into those."

Emilia looked worriedly at her mother. Her chipmunk cheeks reddened, "You said I wasn't fat!"

Hanna scowled at Charles but before she spoke, she bore a guilty smile. She argued, "You aren't fat. You've just got some baby blubber."

"As we all do," Galahad interrupted. Emilia seemed to forget her qualms with her mother, because she stared in awe at the man. She analyzed him curiously. The Muhali addressed her playfully, "You'll need that for your growth spurt. Else you'll look as thin as your dad here."

Emilia ignored his comment and pointed at Galahad's flowing black hair. It dangled halfway down his back. With a bluntness only a child could possess, she asked sincerely, "Are you a doll?"

Hanna had to brush off her smile and quell her laughter. She wondered how such a man could survive the Great War with all that beauty intact. She decided he must not have a care in the world, or far too many.

Arthur remarked, "He's the prettiest man I've ever met and that's the truth."

Galahad rotated his shoulder blades and scoffed. He raised his chin at Arthur and said, "Prettiest man? I'm prettier than most women and *that's* the truth."

The man's vanity struck her. Galahad seemed to notice she was staring at him and approached. He bowed and begged her pardon, "Of course, you are the diamond of us all. Hanna, I presume?"

Hanna smiled formally. "And did you flatter or flatten your enemies?"

"A healthy mix of the two," Galahad assured her with a wry smile. She did not like how his teeth poked out of his lips.

Her husband shifted his footing and began to say, "Well…" He paused and from his tone, Hanna knew he meant to get on with things. She became his voice and said hastily, "Gardners. Shall we?"

Galahad saluted Arthur and bowed once again to Hanna. "I'll see you lovely innkeepers for my feast. I have many months of hunger to sate."

Hanna heard a hint of longing in Galahad's words. Anger, too. He leaned upon his last remarks like an old man with a cane. Many were the silent sufferers she had seen in her life, and Galahad seemed the most stalwart of that unhappy group. The man departed. It took some time before his shadow also disappeared.

Arthur inclined his head and tossed a regard at Eastmont. "What about you? Coming to the feast?"

The idea seemed to nip at Charles as he began to bite his lip. "I suppose I can't make it to my mother's before nightfall." He breathed in and looked wistfully toward the east. "One more day won't do mama in."

A lump formed in Hanna's throat. Hanna disliked spending time with women, but Cora was different. Even still, Hanna had been so busy with the inn, so worried for Arthur's safety, she had not given much thought to Cora Eastmont. As Charles looked in the direction of his mother's lonely mountain, Hanna felt glad. Cora had suffered much in her life, she deserved all she had gained with Charles. He was without a doubt the brightest and most caring man she had ever met.

She jogged up to Charles and gave him a hug. He wiped his brow and beamed down at her. She raised her chin proudly at him and tapped her foot. She eyed her husband and then grinned at Charles. "Are you two going to ask how I fared running an inn all by my lonesome? Or should I just go ahead and begin?"

Charles and Arthur shared a humored look. Then, each man bowed his head and let Hanna Gardner speak.

3

Good and Properly Drunk

Charles found the inn almost magical. It seemed fabulously extravagant and charmingly impoverished at the same time, depending on where you liked to lie your head. There was a bathhouse for the tired, a library for the studious, and a great feasting table for the hungry.

Charles approached the hedge gate. Interlocking bushes, vines, and branches formed a sloping gateway. He passed through, admiring the late innkeeper's gardening skill. *Everything Auldwine loved, he made better. And he loved everything.*

Charles hastened to see the orchard. The trees had been no taller than Arthur's children when he last saw them. It seemed several springs and summers had done the saplings well. Now, the trees dwarfed even tall Aeric. *Beautiful,* Charles remarked. Only the faintest trace of fall was found in infrequent flecks of yellow. Of the dozens of trees, one was dead. That too, though, looked beautiful in its own way. Many birds, rodents, and other squatters were clearly living in the dead wood's bones.

Charles had been so lost in thought, he was unaware of Yao Yang standing beside him. He also was looking at the grove, his eyes fixed on the skeletal tree. "My uncle was not on the train," Yang remarked.

"He was directing the last flows of traffic. He'll be several more days."

Yang laughed. "He just wants to be the last man home from war. He thinks that is a great honor."

Come on, Charles complained silently, *this is a happy night.* "How was school?" He wanted to know.

Yang sank into an old accent, as if mimicking his uncle who could not be parted of it. "Dread-a-ful." His cheeks reddened.

"It took me a while to acclimate to the Castle Rock," Charles said lightly. "It was so hot and humid. Damn near failed my fieldwork."

"I did not fail," Yang corrected with a defensive tone. He acknowledged his pride with a passing quip. "I was second in my class."

Charles knew the source of Yang's defensiveness. Some days, the markets heard doctor Yao Yu, with his protégé in tow, crying in his shrill accent, *"Keep up. You feet are so young. Lazy."* Or, if Yang had done something of note, Yu would boast. He would say, as if drunk from some intoxicant, *"My-a boy is number one nephew. I am-a so proud."*

Charles encouraged, "You don't need your uncle's approval."

Yang looked at him for a while before turning back to the forlorn cottonwood. Had it been anyone else, Charles might have thought the action rude. But Yang was a thinker. Nobody received an answer or action from Yang until the boy had made up his mind. That was just his personality. Indeed, he played chess with himself every morning. The board had not been moved from his uncle's dining room in nigh on twelve years, since Yang took up the game. The boy had not lost. Nor had he won.

Yang ended his silence and responded to him. Charles listened. "The old make way for the new. Eventually, anyway."

Charles stared at the fallen tree, surrounded by many struggling saplings. *In time, it will have to be cut*, he figured. Or else, trees would not grow there ever again. He pointed up the Hill and said, "Should we finally join the festivities?"

Yang shook his head, "No, you go ahead. I want people to be more drunk. That way, I don't have to try as hard to seem like I am enjoying their company."

Charles could not help but cackle. Even Yang's bluntness was sharp. "They aren't the worst humans, our fellow townspeople."

"No," Yang admitted reluctantly. "Quite average. Always trying to find common ground with you." He began to mimic his interactions with the townsfolk, '*I heard the Golden King was executed. I am so sorry.*'"

"They see my face or hear my name and speak in the lowest common denominator. *Your people are so wise. Best mathematicians around, would you calculate my taxes if I paid you? I would love to see the Golden River before I die.*'" Yang coughed slightly and tried to kick a stone, missing the pebble entirely. "I can't even remember my parents, let alone the river. Speak to me like any other young man, damn it."

"And how do young men speak?" Charles asked, bemused.

Yang paused and flicked his eyes. "Crudely, I suppose. With conversations about big breasted women and prior bad decisions."

Charles mimicked a proud parent, "You've learned so much from university." He said his goodbyes to the aspiring doctor and climbed the Hill. The redwood door was left open. The tavern glow pierced the dusken sky like rays of sunlight, inviting everyone in.

The loud ambience of a full tavern greeted Charles. Down the length of the hall ran a single, petrified log. Some claimed it was older than the two mountains. A hundred could easily fit at the innkeeper's table. However, so many had come from home and abroad, circular tables were scattered like islands across the expansive tavern. At the tables, guests chose from an array of colorful foods. They ate luscious pears and golden apricots. There were peaches and plums, apples and peppers. The sauces were hot, sour, sweet, bitter, and everything between.

The smell and sight of so much food overwhelmed his senses. Charles scanned the petrified table for an open seat. At the head of the table was Hanna. She was looking directly at him with eyes which waved him over. As he approached, he realized she was alone amongst the commotion of the crowded table. The petrified log was peopled to full capacity, save the seats at the head of the table. No other Gardner was present.

"Where's Emilia?" Charles sat in her brother's empty chair. "Aeric?"

"Emilia had a panic attack seeing all the people. I sent Aeric to tuck her in."

Charles frowned. "Her hound was no help?"

Hanna chuckled, "Isabelle was scaring the orphans. Neither she nor Emilia understand how intimidating she is."

Charles glanced down the petrified table. Farther along, the heads blurred into bobbing blobs. Closer to the table, he espied the orphans of the war. Josephine and Virginia had been reduced to floating heads, hardly reaching the tops of the table. They had a splatter of food around their mouths. Currently, a Redfeather woman was turning Josephine's cheek toward her, trying in vain to wipe away the mess.

"She has been doting over the orphans."

"Hmm?" Charles asked, turning his attention back toward Hanna.

"Laverne. She and her boy came here after the child's father died."

Charles watched Laverne wrestling with the girls over table-manners. "Wasn't her husband a pilot?"

"Mhm," Hanna hummed. "Laverne's son ran away to the Overgrowth with a few, unsavory friends. She has been distraught ever since. Been coddling the orphans like they were her own."

Charles pitied Laverne. At least her wallowing was productive. An orphan was as good a choice as any for a mother's vagrant love.

Hanna breathed deeply, started a new sentence, and was cut off by the boisterous conversation occurring near them. Close to the Gardners were seated all of the inn's esteemed guests. Most were philanthropists and nearly all lived within the Inner Ring. The twin widows, Evelyn and Carolyn, were alight in debate. They were arguing about whether the Muhali and Redfeather had been evil for starting the war. It was only a matter of time before Degory the dockmaster had to join the conversation.

"I think we ought to just hang the Muhali we got in town. Redfeather, too."

The comment was like kindling for the conversation. Voices erupted in fiery argument. Evelyn accused her twin sister of bigotry; Carolyn accused Evelyn of naivety. Degory spat at constable Goodwind. Laverne covered an orphan's ears.

A woman clanged her glass. The table immediately deferred to the finely dressed patron. "Friends, this is an evening to celebrate. Degory, do not be so generous in sharing your stupidity. We are trying to eat."

Most patrons laughed. Degory's face crushed in upon itself and his nose twitched with anger. Charles leaned over to Hanna, asking, "Who is she?"

"Lilian Vellencourt. Her husband was a politician in Castle Rock. When he was slain, she retired to the old promontory fort."

"Ah... I thought Buchanan Bavar owned that old tower?"

"Vellencourt made him a great offer. He said he would have been a fool to not accept."

"Well," Charles ceded, "he never used the property anyways. Arthur and I thought it was haunted growing up, all derelict and whatnot." He looked at Misses Vellencourt, her face made up in powdered makeup. She wore a red and pink dress, her hands covered by white gloves. *She exudes Castle Rock fashions,* Charles thought, recalling his years at the university. The natives of that metropolis believed painting their faces the highest form of civility and cultivated their faces to be like blank canvases. *Why would someone so refined move into a ruined fort?*

"Charles," Hanna's voice began in the high pitch of a question, "Should I be worried about Arthur?"

"In what way?" Charles raised his brow.

"I tried to help him unpack, but he would not let me touch his bag. Then, just now, he said he was not hungry, that he could not breathe."

Charles licked the back of his teeth. *It is rather hot in here. Humid, too.* "I wouldn't worry about his appetite. A soldier's stomach shrinks after years of rations. One bite might have filled him up."

"And the breathing?" Hanna rotated a small spoon around an empty cup.

Charles sighed. "Give him time. He's a different man, now."

"That's why I am worried," Hanna replied. A moment later, the spoon she was twirling fell with a clatter to the floor. Charles went to pick it up. Below the table, hundreds of shoes fidgeted, tapped, bounced, and bobbed. He rose and placed the spoon in front of Hanna. Her attention was diverted. She had turned around to talk to her son.

"Aeric, why did you bring Isabelle back down? This is too much excitement for her."

The hound was visiting with as many people as would pay attention to her. She would sit at a stranger's foot as if she had known them all her life. Presently, her tail was thumping madly against the wood as Constable Goodwind rubbed her chin.

"She didn't want to go to sleep. She's a party girl," Aeric insisted. "And Emilia was already asleep."

"Okay," Hanna conceded quickly. She snapped her fingers and Isabelle's ears perked up. She waddled over to the Gardner matriarch and sat, her tongue happily drooping down the side of her cheek. Hanna looked at her son, "I don't want her at the table."

Aeric nodded and ushered the hound along. He had a hard time of it when the great dog sniffed the food. Yet soon enough, he and the animal had disappeared into the tavern crowd.

Hanna laughed and rubbed her eyes, "Oh, he means well, but that dog doesn't have Castle Rock manners." She whispered, just loud enough for Charles to piece together her faint words. "She would jump on one of these rich patrons, upset them, and we'd be out of a donation."

Charles nodded in agreement with Hanna's assessment. The inn needed its philanthropy. Good impressions were vital. He stretched, "Auldwine would get into a cleaning frenzy if he knew a donor was visiting."

"He had good sense." Hanna looked over her shoulder at the door. She shivered, "Would you mind closing the door?"

Charles smiled and got up without a word. He went to the redwood door. It was heavier than he remembered, or perhaps he had grown weaker.

The roar of the tavern reminded him greatly of the times before the war. He looked around for a place to find a drink. Aside from the bar at the far end of the hall, many temporary food and drink stations had been built. Yet just as he got in line for a glass, a faint "Charles," flew into his ears. He turned around.

Aeric waved at him and pointed at the circular table he was sitting at. There were two others with him. Charles motioned at the line he was in but Aeric shook his head and yelled, "Come on. Sit with us." *Eh, the drinks will be here all night.* He went to the table and sat beside Aeric. Galahad was there, as well as his friend.

"Momed, is it?" Charles began to introduce himself. The Muhali boy nodded, his eyes darting hesitantly to meet his own.

"Charles Eastmont," he went to shake the boy's hand. However, Momed was either unaccustomed to the custom, or was incredibly shy. Either way, Galahad reprimanded him like a father to a child. "Shake his hand," he barked, irritably.

Momed finished pouring a glass into Galahad's empty cup, as if he was part of the waiting staff. Then, he begged innumerable pardons and gave Charles a firm, albeit quick, handshake. He looked expectantly at Galahad.

Charles turned to Aeric, "Where's Emilia's dog?"

"Out with my dad. She already adores him. Though, I'm not too sure if he shares her affections," Aeric laughed and looked over at the other two. Galahad was not amused.

The former soldier sat at attention, not losing any height to a bent back. He glared down the ballroom at the rest of the town. Galahad was not very old, perhaps only five years older than Momed. One eye was nearly shut and the other was obscured by thick strands of long, black hair. The veteran looked dazed. He blinked himself out of his daydream and tossed his head back, throwing his ebony hair behind his head.

Galahad's face was swollen. One eye was purple and pulsating. His face had many deformations and his bruises were mounds, making it seem like he had walked into a hornet's nest. While Aeric avoided looking directly at him, Charles eyed the Muhali's wounds. "What happened to you?" He inquired.

Galahad raised his finger. As Charles and the other three at the table waited, he slowly drank his beverage. He began to speak but quickly closed his mouth. He looked behind his shoulder and to his sides. He raised his legs up to his chair so they protected his chest. Galahad rolled his eyes and stretched. His arms had red hand marks on them. "Simple family banter." He chugged the alcohol. "I ask if he has been day drinking. He asks if I have been laying with men. Yes to both, of course."

Galahad played with Momed's cheek, pinching it. He smiled a frown as he did so, as if he both hated and loved touching the other man. Suddenly, he tore his hand from Momed, cleared his throat, and glanced at the crowd. His face filled with revulsion and he sighed. Finally, Galahad looked up at the roof, "He says I was the worst of his three sons, et cetera et cetera."

Aeric was aghast. The innkeeper's son smacked his open palm onto the table, "You should file a complaint with the law."

Galahad stifled a mocking laugh. "The man is my father. Constable Goodwind will say he is my law—and I would do well to remember that."

Charles glanced below the table. A large, overly packed duffle bag was tucked below Momed's chair and laid at his feet like a dog waiting for table scraps. Charles' lips flicked between a frown and a smile before he inquired, "Momed... Planning for a trip?"

Momed looked over at Galahad. The man bowed his head in permission. Momed then said, "His father has no need of me, now."

Charles and Galahad caught one another's eyes. His long black hair fell above his eye. Charles could not tell what thoughts swirled within that Muhali mind. He had a soldier's stoicism and a drunk's carelessness. Charles addressed Momed, "You have nowhere to go?"

Galahad stirred in his seat.

"I have friends," Momed declared, in a voice no louder than a whisper. Pity swelled in Charles' chest. He offered, "My room. It is below, fifth door on the right. Aeric's father prepared it for me as a courtesy."

"Never I impose, not you." Momed's grasp of a foreign tongue seemed to slip away. He choked on his words while his pride and gratitude argued for his voice. "Much kind. Thousand Gratitudes. But no, it is your bed."

"I insist," Charles interrupted. "I have no need of a bed. I'm leaving for my mother's home, at the foot of the east mountain. Please, you would honor me."

Momed stirred and looked at Galahad. Charles wondered what magic that man had performed to make a stranger so loyal. He glanced at Momed's feet. His shoes were rags and his skin was similarly worn. Momed's own arms and face had the same blemishes as Galahad, though his were nearly healed. As if in answer to his questions, Galahad kissed Momed's hands and all the nervousness within the young man vanished. There was a love between them, Charles guessed.

Galahad placed his hand gently on Momed's back. He nodded. "The inn is far enough from my father and close enough to me." The two exchanged a quick kiss.

Aeric's mouth sagged. Charles saw him in his periphery and almost laughed. He nudged the boy, as he had taken to staring. In turn, the young Gardner gave Charles a worried, questioning look. Charles shrugged his reply. He did not care who Galahad chose to love.

Charles saw Momed looking at him and was stirred. The young man was restraining his tears and stuttered his thanks, "N-not a thousand, b-but a million gratitudes."

Galahad cleared his throat. He did his best to look proud as he thanked Charles, but his swollen, violet eye swiveled violently. "You are a kind man." Galahad scratched the back of his neck and played with a strand of hair. "Arthur was right in wanting you to tend his grove."

Charles could not tell if his fellow soldier was mocking or praising him. He wondered if that was Galahad's reason for saying so. "Perhaps he was," Charles replied. "But my mother has her own garden. And spring water, too."

Momed found a cloth and wiped his eyes. He got to his feet and bowed to Charles. "I must ready myself. A man does not cry."

Aeric rose as well. Charles could tell he was trying to make up for staring. He conducted his small talk well, a trick he must have learned from his mother. "I can show you to your room."

As the innkeeper's son shuffled off, Charles heard Momed ask if foreigners were allowed to use the baths, or if it was reserved for the royal Gardners. Aeric's laughter echoed over the tavern ambience. A wave of nostalgia surged through him as he remembered his youth, of wondering about his own place in the town. Charles smiled. Everyone had a place at the inn. *A shame Momed had not learned that earlier.*

After the innkeeper's son and the Muhali boy had left, Galahad leaned forward. "I will probably retire soon. I only came for the food."

"Not going to stay for the music?"

Galahad shook his head and looked disdainfully at the musicians on stage. "Music is loud and oppressive. I mean, look at them," he gestured at the dancers. "Look at how people are conducted to sway and step. Ensnared like beasts." Galahad looked around for a drink. "Quite a profession, the musician. The captains of cacophony. Well, I have had enough of captains, with their one-two-three-four, one-two-three-four."

So much for the jokester on the train, Charles played with his thumbs. The growing silence was made more evident by the loud conversations around them.

Galahad brooded and stared across the tavern. Just as Charles was going to get himself a drink, Galahad pointed at a table of finely dressed men and women. "Who do you think they are?"

"Lawyers, Lobbyists... Captains." Charles had no precise knowledge of those well-to-do people. Still, he had enough of an idea. They were upper class, travelling through the rustic town of Auberdine. No doubt they would go to their beds tonight and joke about his little town. Truly, the forest of Cottonwood was not regal like the capital. The Castle Rock rose from the sea like a crown while Auberdine sank beneath the shadow of mountains.

"Look at those rings," Galahad awed. "One of those is worth more than all the Overgrowth. People and all. Why would such wealth bother with an innkeeper's feast?"

Charles shrugged.

"Oil." Galahad said. "The war had many children and they are coming of age. Every cunt with credit will want to get their share of black gold."

Charles watched as a man and wife exchanged a dessert by kissing. The two guffawed and their friends all clapped politely. Charles began to understand Galahad's disgust. Never a moment occurred where their mouths were not full. They all spoke over one another and tried to best one another with their jokes. They held high their gemstone hands so their great rings would be visible to all.

Galahad snorted. "Why do old men, who send millions to war, feign civilization at the home front?" He muttered as he rubbed the red ring around his arm. "Everyone is a soldier and the war never ends. Battle merely lulls, waiting for some powerful captain to blow the whistle."

Charles had no reply for him. He doubted Galahad really cared for one. He left the brooding soldier at his table, hoping he might find some peace from his abusive father.

Charles decided he needed fresh air. A night breeze was carrying scents from the different trees in the grove. He could smell the fruits below the boughs as well as the herbs growing between the roots. The music faded as he walked farther down the Hill, toward the old granary. The Gardners had not used the structure in several generations and owls had taken to using its upper levels as an aviary. Auldwine had let them roost, as they were quite adept rat catchers.

The owls had just begun to stir. The hooting and flapping was its own kind of music. Charles saw them as they flew. They hopped up onto the granary's crumbled heights and leapt into a glide. Then, they beat their wings and soared up toward the moon. An owl hooted and Charles responded, '*Hoot, hoot.*' The moon was full and bright, and as he called toward the animals, their shadows turned and circled back around the moon, wondering where those calls came from.

"Charles?" croaked a familiar voice.

Arthur Gardner was looking up at him. He was leaning against the dead, gnarled tree, sweat dripping from his brow. He had a shovel beside him. Charles did not ask what the morose man was doing. It was not important. He instead stared at the tree. It had been Auldwine's favorite. Now, the cottonwood's roots burst from the soil like broken nails and its bark peeled off from its trunk. Isabelle sat next to Arthur, looking into the innkeeper's eyes like an adoring fan. A reluctant hand petted the dog's back.

Charles sat beside his friend. "Hanna was asking about you. Why are you outside?"

Arthur looked up at the moon and then down at the dirt. "Same reason as you, perhaps."

Charles acquiesced to a grin. "She is worried you are starving yourself. Best go in there and make a spectacle of eating your pudding."

Arthur chuckled at his joke and dragged his fingernails through the soil. Upon taking his hand from Isabelle, the hound immediately dove her snot-filled snout under Arthur's arm. "Gah," he said, annoyedly. He wiped his hand. "Do you think he would be happy if he were here? Or would he feel like I do?"

"Auldwine?" Charles asked, though he knew the answer. Isabelle remained insistent on a petting, so Charles extended his hand. At once, the dog reoriented her body and fell onto Charles' lap, panting from the excitement. "Aren't you just the cutest?" He cooed. He continued petting Isabelle as he listened to the innkeeper.

"Part of me thinks he would be sad if I were the one to have died. But was my brother ever sad? Would he endeavor to be happy, to be joyful despite my death?"

"Not in spite," Charles thought aloud. "He would see no reason to be sad. He would think you would be remembered better with laughter than with tears."

"Love," Arthur stated simply.

"The kind your wife has for you," Charles reminded him.

The innkeeper buried his eyes behind their lids and swayed as if fighting some nausea. "Aeric adores me," he said.

"Yes. Fervently," Charles smirked.

"Emilia... I don't know how she feels about me." He wiped his sweaty brow. "We are strangers to one another."

Charles added, hopefully, "You still have many years to see her childhood unfold."

"Two, maybe three," Arthur replied despairingly. He tossed a rock down the Hill. It rolled for some time before being lost in the darkness. "Then she will hit puberty, and she will hate me regardless."

"Even if all the world hated you," Charles began. "Your wife's love would compensate." When Arthur made no inclination to reply, he added. "Hanna looks at you the same way she did when I introduced her to you. You will always have her."

The innkeeper was silent. Charles turned away, feeling embarrassed for mentioning Hanna in such intimate ways. He tried to resuscitate the conversation with lighter words, but all he could think about were old times with young friends.

Arthur's breathing was staccato. He sighed, paused, and let out puffs of air as a hundred thoughts steamed, slipped, and spilt out of him. All the while, he gazed up at the moon in silence. The ambience of the tavern was drowned out by the croaking of frogs, down near one of the many streams of Cottonwood.

Arthur finally said, never taking his eyes off the moon, "A man in my company once told me even stars die. What hope do I have when the brightest lights cannot survive?"

Charles did not immediately reply. He looked over at his friend, and it seemed the innkeeper wanted to speak. "Hope is not easy on hard nights."

Arthur grunted his approval.

Charles continued, "I promise you, though... If you go to Hanna, you will feel better." He then thought, casually, *I would.* He cleared his throat of unsaid words. *If I had a wife, of course.*

Arthur's voice broke. The innkeeper did not cry. His voice strained and like a man restraining vomit, he whispered a wavering word. "Love." His thoughts suddenly streamed from him, like they were tears themselves. From his eyes came nothing, but from his chest came quivering whispers. "How can I accept love when all I feel is self-loathing?"

Charles responded instantly. "Accept the truth and feel like shit."

Arthur stirred and looked at his friend. The silver in his hair reflected onto the decaying bark, giving the dead tree a ghostly glow. Charles directed his friend toward several mushrooms growing at the base of the tree, just beside where they were seated. He reflected, "Shit decomposes in nature. It will decompose in you."

Arthur tapped the hollow skeleton of the decaying wood. "Always finding the profound in the profane, Eastmont." He braced his thighs and his bones creaked wearily. Charles launched to his feet and offered a hand to the innkeeper. He lifted Arthur upright and pulled the man toward him, turning a handshake into a hug. Arthur patted his back and they began toward the music.

"Are you good and properly drunk?" Arthur asked.

"In truth, I planned to be an entirely different blood type by this time. Seems I have been distracted."

Arthur slapped his shoulder, "We'll change that." With Isabelle beside them, the two walked up the Hill and into the redwood inn. Drunken cheers greeted the innkeeper when he returned. So heavily had the town imbibed, Charles was confident they would all be hungover for some time.

In the end, Charles only drank one glass of wine. It upset his stomach.

4

Son of Cambyses

A walnut tree grew at the border between the Inner Ring and the Overgrowth. Its bark was the color of obsidian. No other plant nor any other tree grew close to the walnut. Any that tried were smothered by that plant's shadow. Its branches crept up like grotesque fingernails, scratching at the clouds. Its trunk was as wide as a man was tall, and it must have been as old as Auberdine itself, perhaps older. Galahad walked beneath its crooked canopy and crossed a small bridge.

The Muhali Islet had changed little while Galahad was away. The streams had deviated slightly, as they had always done. The willow trees still transformed parts of the roadside into wilting gazebos. The liquor stores were still as verdant as the nearby vegetation. The merchants and shopkeepers still operated their businesses. They still shouted at one another and bartered with customers. "That one is 25, but for you I give for 20," he could hear. Their thick accents and bushy beards still carried scents of perfume.

The islet of the Muhali was not grand. It was a trickling of wealth, just as the streams in that part of the valley were remnants of more powerful mountain falls. Like the rest of the Overgrowth, it had its charms and its revulsions. Everyone was poor, everybody knew it, and so nobody noticed. Little children skipped pebbles across the hundred streams. Young men flirted with stupid girls. Old men did much the same.

His father's liquor store was proudly placed upon a small embankment. From his spot in the middle of the islet, Cambyses distributed his drink. Many were eager to provide their patronage and Cambyses' little mercantile was one of the most maintained. Though it was impossible to keep the gutters clean in spring, when the cottonwoods released their seed—his father tried his best. Though the marble was tarnished, the man broke his back to keep his foundations looking white. Though vine weed climbed the cobble walls, Cambyses installed flower planters all the same. His father drove himself mad trying to make perfect his house of debauchery. Meanwhile, the muddy foundation was slowly sinking into the depths.

Galahad quite hated that shop. As long as he remained there, he would be a trogg, a goblin, a mudpuppy, or dead. His father's business was mildly successful, but his father was still a goblin. The Inner Ring would reject Cambyses so long as he had an accent. And in turn, his father would reject him.

Galahad looked up at the great, grey Oleander peak. He knew all the curses and bedtime horror stories which kept young fools off the western peak. *But those are just stories. How much worse could a haunted mountain be than here? They are just fables.* Nobody else cared about the stories anymore. New miners trickled up the Oleander without any fear of deluge or demons. And from what Galahad had seen at the feast, they did not come down with fear, either.

I will go there too, he resolved. *The flood was centuries ago.* Galahad imagined his life atop the western mountain. He would have servants, stocks, and stores. All the pompous Pale folk who had treated him badly would hate him even more for his successes. *And I will relish it.* Thoughts of grandeur warmed his body like wine. He felt confident. Though he knew they were only musings, his fantasy felt real. The Galahad in his mind was not so different from the one walking with a black eye. *This poverty is temporary for me. I am better than this.*

Galahad massaged his purple eyebrow and pressed down onto the bruise, relishing the pain. He had survived the Great War. He had overcome far worse. His father was nothing. This town was nothing. He waded beside a brook. The water trickled past his feet and tickled his toes. He saw his beaten reflection in the water and glared at it. His bruises looked more painful than they were. They had already started to heal.

He continued his walk. As he came nearer to the markets, he began to feel the eyes of strangers upon him. Galahad ground his teeth and glared ahead, not acknowledging any who may be mocking him. He refused to swivel his neck and see who was looking at him. Surely, people were. His head was a rainbow of violence; anyone with a brain could tell he had been beaten bloody. *Let them scoff. Let them laugh.* He had better things to do than respond to their howling. If he turned around even once, he would lose. He could not afford to let them know he cared. *True weakness is not lack of strength, but lack of image.*

Besides, he noted great amounts of wounded warriors. Surely, they were better gossip than Galahad. The one-armed cripples and the mindless wrecks were far more entertaining than a bruised face. Galahad remembered the babbling of new soldiers after they had experienced a night of bombardments. Their teeth would clatter and they would pull out their hair. Some would run and be shot for cowardice. He smiled, *At least I have my limbs and my sanity.*

Galahad crossed another bridge. The outline of his father's store emerged in the distance. His heart began to beat faster; he tried to stop sweating. Beside him, rows of crumbling cobble were bursting with life. Doors without hinges were open to visitors. Children sat on stoops, playing or talking. A small, Redfeather teenager was calling at some woman.

Galahad chuckled and kept walking. The hollering intensified and it seemed the boy was talking to him. He permitted himself to turn around briefly. When he did, the boy was looking at him and waving his hands in a variety of odd gestures.

"Yeah pretty mama, come here and give daddy a suck."

The tattooed idiot postured in the same way all boys do when trying to be men. He was no more than Aeric's age and far shorter. The child lowered his voice into a false baritone and carried his shoulders higher to evoke a broader frame.

So transparent were the boy's insecurities, a wicked smile appeared on Galahad's face. He turned and approached the boy. Several friends were sitting on a stoop and as he came closer, they 'whooped' and went 'ooooh.' Then, Galahad flipped his long hair off his face.

"Oh, man," a boy no older than twelve said to his cat-calling friend, "That ain't a bitch."

Another said to him, "You a pillow-biter now."

Galahad neared the group of boys and looked down on them. His shadow loomed over their heads. The cat-calling boy stammered, "What you lookin' at, ma'am?"

Ma'am, Galahad rolled his eyes at the insult. Galahad noted a tattoo painted across one of his cheeks. That made it easy to guess the boy's identity. He assumed his most innocent tone, one that was empathetic and sorrowful, fatherly and tender. "Latrell, is it?"

Latrell did not speak and seemed disarmed by a stranger knowing his name. Galahad leaned into the group and beamed benevolently at the boys. He frowned at them and shook his head with disappointment. "Imagine if your mother heard you using womanhood as an insult." Galahad grinned and his canines peeked out from his lips, "Would she recall the night you were conceived? Would she recall the moment you had oozed out from her legs and wish she had swallowed you instead?"

The boys around Latrell erupted in laughter. They covered their mouths and slapped their knees and punched Latrell's shoulder. Galahad did not linger for the boy's stutters. He revolved around the ball of his foot and marched along.

The slight wind caused his long, black hair to flow from his head. He looked down at his shadow. His head looked like a comet. He felt a surge of momentum, but he tried to look his humblest. His father did not like seeing pride in anyone but himself. Galahad checked himself in a glass-blower's mirror. Once he was sure he was sufficiently frail, fragile, and unassuming, he continued his stroll.

The Pale folk of the Inner Ring were already browsing the Muhali wares. While in private they feared and spited his people for aiding the Redfeather in the Great War—in public, they paraded across their markets and lived a life according to foreign craftsmanship. *My people.* The thought repulsed him. Galahad did not much care whether someone was from the Golden River, Castle Rock, Redfeather, or anywhere else. Moreover, he found 'his people' from Muhal the most revolting and foreign of them all. He had never even been to Muhal. Those faraway deserts were hardly home.

Neither is this poor attempt at a population center. Home had never been here. The Overgrowth was a better environment for sheep, boar, wolves, and cattle. *And trees.* For every stone structure, there were six trees and double as many saplings. He sped past the Muhali hovels and thought proudly, *I am a native of the self. My footprints are home.*

As Galahad neared his father's store, he overheard the day's gossip. Some Redfeather were talking about the wreckage of their country. It was old news. Galahad had been on the front and been an active component in that nation's dismemberment. Likewise, across the street from the crowd of Redfeather folk, a group of Golden River people were playing chess and having morning tea. Their conversations were unintelligible to him, and their language zoomed in and out of his ears like the buzzing of bees. Galahad glanced at the players and noted mostly old men and children. Down the street, two Pale women were arguing. Galahad loved a good argument. He listened intently.

"Damn it, Evelyn, can you hurry up?" A woman cried.

"Don't be in such a hurry, Carolyn. Look, there!" She pointed at a replica of some Golden River shrine for sale. "Isn't it beautiful? The craftsmanship!" Evelyn put a hand on the salesman's shoulder and offered her most genuine compliments. "I am so impressed by your people."

"Evelyn, for heaven's sake. You are an embarrassment." She pulled her sister back and threw several coins down onto the craftsman's table. Evelyn happily took the temple and stuck her finger between the tiny, red pillars. Her sister chided, "Next thing you know, your boy is going to think it is acceptable to marry one of them."

Evelyn's voice faded as the sisters retreated to the Inner Ring. Galahad heard her voice echoing, "I would just adore a Muhali daughter-in-law, with their business sense. Or a Golden River girl. They are the most loyal."

Her sister screamed, "Muhal murdered our husbands! Have you no memory? And why have you stopped wearing black? I cannot dream of forgetting my Siegfried."

"Carol, it is just a little ribbon. I am still in black." She stuttered, "I, uh, I still mourn Gerald. I do."

"Just because he hit you once or twice doesn't mean you can be disloyal," Carolyn barked.

"It, it wasn't once or..." Evelyn trailed off and Galahad heard no more from the twin widows.

Galahad felt dirty to agree, even partially, with Carolyn. She was as nasty as her husband was average, but she had a point. The Golden River had its rapists. Muhal had its murderers. Castle Rock had its stench. They were all the same. Galahad gave a passing regard to a craftsman's wares. They were mediocre and only meant to awe the Pale folk and sate the eclectic's fashion sense. He held his chin higher as he departed there.

The wide stone street diverged into many small alleys. Presently, no prostitutes were leaning on garbage. No breasts sagged into the trash like rats eating scraps. However, Galahad espied a man in a black and gold shawl. His hair was matted and his skin was charcoal. He leaned against a brick tower and touted a shotgun at his hip. Galahad thought it best to address the man preemptively.

"Morning, stranger," Galahad waved.

"You lost?" replied the man, tapping the barrel of his gun.

"Not physically," Galahad answered. "What might your name be?"

The frank response threw him off. He answered warily, "Terrell."

Aaah. Galahad had heard of this one. He had evaded the army recruiters when they ran out of *willing* young boys for the slaughterhouses. He hid in the caves and crags of Cottonwood, even killing a few bounty hunters who tried to arrest him for treason. Galahad quite respected his idealism. Still, Terrell was a petty flesh salesman and wore his pride like a garment.

Galahad decided to be amiable. "Will your girls be out this evening? I just returned from the war and heard yours were the best."

Instantly, Terrell's eyes lit up. His mood was as transparent as the large shotgun at his side.

Too easy, Galahad grinned.

"Best in town. Got a new one from Redfeather. Biggest ass I've ever seen. Young, too. Perky tits. Gotta spot of crazy, though. Lost her family to a shelling, but that only makes her more wild."

Galahad had no interest in a woman. He did not need to tell Terrell that, though. He smiled, "You have a pleasant day, sir. After all, you give all us men a pleasant night. You deserve it."

"And you," the man nodded. A large, dumb smile floated up his face.

Several blocks later, the alleys receded and a hundred streams wove like a spider's web through a sprawling urban center. At the intersection of the waters was a bridge, and this led up a small embankment. There was his father's liquor store, the dwelling of Cambyses. Galahad stared at his reflection, making sure his confidence could not show. *That was my mistake last night. That was what made him violent.* He practiced speaking, making sure his father heard no hint of arrogance.

"Yes, sir," he began. "A thousand gratitudes." *Too presuming.* "A thousand gratitudes," he tried again, changing his inflection. *Not genuine enough.* "A thousand gratitudes," he tried again, adding a hint of an accent. *As convincing as it can be,* he decided.

He stepped up the mound of mud, careful to stay on the fragmented path. The sinking soil reminded him of the Tanglewood, and of men drowning in the liquid dirt. He stared up at Cambyses' store. His father had installed golden, stained-glass windows. Yet after a merchant nearby was robbed, he had attached bars to the regal windows. Stone gargoyles stood in pairs, guarding the entrance to the shop. His father had bought them at a pawn broker after they were marked with graffiti. Cambyses had made him and his brothers wash them day and night until they were perfect. Galahad always toyed with the idea of breaking off a nose or one of their giant ears. Then, he thought, they would resemble the rest of the building. Galahad patted the gargoyles and continued.

Like his own father, the poor store was in a perpetual identity crisis. The door to Cambyses' was painted red. His father bragged it had been given to him by the innkeeper as a gift, and that it was pure redwood. Of course, only fools believed such things and Galahad knew for a fact that no innkeeper had given so much as a fart for the old Muhali.

The red door was one of the many falsehoods that built Cambyses' façade. Galahad could not remember all the lies his father had told him. Cambyses probably could not either. Lies simply spilled out of him like a drunkard's vomit. Once, his father had sworn they were descended from Beauregard the miner, whose mighty mining camps would turn into the town of Auberdine. Nobody believed him, of course. His skin was almost as dark as Galahad's, a fact his father never forgot. Years later, when his father heard the Pale folk laughing about his fib, he changed his story. He insisted he had not said Beauregard. Rather, he said they were descended from the natives of Cottonwood, the wandering Wanakha. While there were several claimants to that old blood, Galahad knew his father's was a poor one. His grandmother had come by ship with her only son and she had sold her body to pay for food.

There was always a grand fable to cover the grotesque.

Galahad entered the quiet shop, still asleep with the rest of the town's drunks. His father did not notice him and was preoccupied with his hair, or rather—what remained of it. Cambyses had gone bald at a young age. Before Galahad's birth, the man had worn a wig. He styled it for an hour every morning, making sure the locks were positioned just right.

Galahad took his long hair and threw it behind him. Then, he began his act. "Many pardons for tardiness, father."

Cambyses did not turn. "So... You've learned some humility? Good. I thought a night in the dirt would temper your arrogance."

Galahad had slept in trenches infested with rats and ticks. He had used mud as a blanket just to keep the mosquitos away. A night of Overgrowth stone was a featherbed to him. Even still, it had not come to that. By chance, he and Momed had acquired a room at the inn. He was *quite* comfortable last night.

"It was cold. I am sorry, please forgive me." Galahad mimicked a stutter, "I-I will never be Cyrus or Darius."

"The truest thing you have ever said," Cambyses turned to face his only living son. "Cyrus was a warrior prince and Darius... Well at least he was a proper man."

How it would infuriate him to know I am laying with the stock boy. "It was good of you to fire Momed. He was expensive."

Cambyses eyed his son suspiciously but then nodded and sniffed. He positioned his wig once more and looked out the golden window. "Good of you to live, boy."

"Thank you, sir," Galahad said through his teeth. He had known the charade would be hard. *This is temporary*, he told himself. He noticed his hands folding into fists and fought with all his strength to relax them. "Do you need me to take inventory?"

"Already done," Cambyses muttered. "Since you took your time getting back here, I did your job for you. We are low on the medium proofs, mostly whiskey. That new innkeeper has a mighty thirst." Cambyses continued looking out the window. Clearly, the oaf was waiting for someone.

More like you drank all the medium proofs. "Do you need me to prepare anything?" Galahad asked in his most servile tone.

"Some water. I am expecting Buchanan Bavar."

Buchanan was the local tax collector and just as much an idiot as Cambyses. He was an illiterate man who had inherited his estate and his position from some extended relative. He always liked to receive payment in person, so he knew he was not being shorted. He was a fat, pasty man with milky skin, blotched by blemishes. His father's back was always crooked after seeing Buchanan, his nose always browner.

"Yes, sir," Galahad shuffled off to the storerooms for a jug of water and two glasses. When he returned, his father was opening the door for the plump pimple of a man. He saw Galahad coming to serve them and covered his nose. He bellowed in a deep, exaggerated voice,

"I would prefer not bein' served by your goblin spawn, Cambyses."

His father's eyes darted to him. He did not have to say a word. Galahad knew his job was over, for now. He departed to the back of the store, to a particularly sonorous area where he could hear even the faintest crack in their voices.

"Innumerable pardons," he heard his father say. His father had tried and failed to be rid of his accent, but the Muhali phrase was ingrained in his brain. Moreover, the Pale expected such platitudes to the point of cliché.

"Infinite pardons," his father chimed. When Galahad was younger, he found his father's politeness strange. Politeness showed humility, yet his father fancied himself the god of his home. His father ruled the little shop like a king. When anyone with white skin came by, however—his father acted like a regent. During Buchanan Bavar's visits, for instance, Cambyses babbled every courtesy he could think of.

Galahad listened closely. For a time, he heard only the shuffling of papers and the clinking of coins. He heard a newspaper unfold. No doubt Buchanan was wasting some of his father's time to make a point. He liked to do that. It did not matter the man could not read and his wide spectacles were as much a farce as Cambyses' good nature. Both men were playing their game.

"All according to your specifications?" Galahad heard his father say. Of course, all was *not* according to the man's specifications. Cambyses had been shorting the collector for nigh on twenty years. But that did not matter. Buchanan Bavar could not read his own ledgers and had never bothered to have someone do it for him.

Galahad heard the newspaper fold up. Buchanan ignored the question. "Heard talk there been more oil found up in Oleander. Some rancher's boy was digging and got blasted with the stuff." Galahad's ears were attentive. Any precious mineral could be found on the western mountain. It was why the Wanakha natives loved and cursed it as Oleander. Suddenly, Galahad's knees began to bounce and he felt like his time was being wasted. He had to calm himself.

"Goin' be a rush to the peak, justs as back when my daddy's daddy's uncle came fixin' for gold."

And were killed by rockslides and flooding, Galahad mused.

"Infinite fortunes to those," Cambyses said cheerfully. Galahad could almost see his father's toothy grin.

"What does a trogg like you know 'bout infinity?" Buchanan grunted. "You's never had an education."

Galahad giggled silently to himself. His father's bravado always took a beating when the belligerent Buchanan came to claim a portion of his pride. He could see his father's canines slip back behind his cheeks. Or perhaps his father's mouth was hanging open slightly.

"Gots another one of you's looking for a plot of land," Buchanan remarked. "Some Redfeather who fancies himself a geo, uh, ge, geo... He likes rocks."

"Another goblin?" Cambyses questioned. His father used the derogative for his own people whenever Buchanan was around.

"You thick-tongued devils pay the foreigner's tax, you'd think I be rich by now. I heard it told you troggs hide coins in your beards. And the metals what make them stink. That true, boy?"

His middle-aged father paused. He hated being called boy more than any other insult. After a moment, his father answered quietly, "I have seen my father's father do such things, it is very much true."

"I hears that son of yours is a pillow-biter," Buchanan spat happily. "If it was me, I'da hanged him."

"A wise suggestion," Cambyses replied. Galahad knew it was only half a lie.

"I gots many o' those. You goblins aught ta learn from us. We been here lots longer than you." Buchanan rose and his loud swallowing was like the trickling of a fountain. He clamored noisily to his feet and departed.

All was silent while the collector walked down the embankment. Finally, his father shuffled off to his safe, though he had no money to deposit. Cambyses always got paranoid after conning someone and had to make sure he had not been the one tricked. Once reassured he had won the little game, his father started whistling.

So it begins, Galahad remarked. He took a deep breath to prepare himself for the day. His father always waited for official business to conclude before drinking. A bottle cap flew off and hit the wall. Several minutes later, his father emerged from the storeroom and pointed at him.

"Clean the floors."

Galahad nodded and when he had finished the task, his father was tending to customers. He placed a large bottle of whiskey into a haggard cripple's remaining hand. After putting a few coins in his pocket, he took a swig of the same vintage. Cambyses called to his son, "You clean the floors yet?"

"Yes, sir," Galahad answered frankly.

"Your room is a mess. Clean that, too—or I will rent it out and send you to an orphanage."

Galahad did as his father said. He had cleaned his room to a spotless shine before he left for the war. No doubt his father had destroyed it in a drunken rage, mourning his sons or himself.

The reality was far worse. Bottles had been emptied over his bed and left to skulk as glass tenants. His sheets were torn. An old rocking chair was cracked and a hammer was lodged into the back of it. Galahad could not remove it and decided he would just have to throw the furniture out. Pictures of his mother and his brothers which Galahad had hung (mostly out of obligation) now laid broken on the floor. His dresser's contents were haphazardly strewn about and the wood was splintered.

Galahad hoisted the ruined rocking chair and carried it down toward the liquor store proper, where his father was talking to a homeless Redfeather man, both laughing at one another's crude jokes. That was good. He discarded the chair without his father seeing. When he returned to the shop, his father was alone, staring at an empty bottle. He was rotating it and following his warped face in the glass.

"You," he slurred. "Is there anything you can do right?" When Galahad tried to reply, his father quieted him. "I saw that chair. You can't be here a day without breaking something?"

"I am sorry, father." Galahad felt his heartbeat quicken. "A thousand pardons," he said through his teeth.

"And a thousand more!" His father yelled. He threw a coaster, missing Galahad by several feet. "Until your pardons bring back your brothers! They were my real blood! Good boys! Not a daughter!"

A customer came into the store and Cambyses immediately quieted, sobering up like water evaporating in the heat, "What may I do for you..." He paused to belch. "Today?"

After the customer departed with her hands full of alcohol, his father resumed his hatred. His drunkenness surged back and he finished a bottle of rice wine. "I though' when I sent you to war, it would be the end of you."

"A thousand pardons," Galahad bowed, his fingers locked tightly into a fist. He took a deep breath.

"But I have to hand it to you," Cambyses said suddenly with a jolly laugh. "You did not die."

And yet your precious Cyrus did. And Darius along with him.

He laughed. "I figured, 'Put a gun to his head—he'll go off and leave me in peace.'" His sour smile became a frown. He was silent. Galahad went to grab a broom but his father started to brood, his voice rising to a boom as he spoke.

"I hate looking at you. You, with your long, girlish hair and your love of men. The blood of the desert curses me with your dark skin." He paused and reflected on his glass, "A fine vintage."

Cambyses smiled at the ceiling. He lifted his feet onto a small table and leaned back negligently. He belched and stayed quiet for a minute. Then, he peered at his son and pointed a finger. "I says hell no, Pamela! No means no." His father looked at him like a friend seeking affirmation, "Women, I tell you." He squinted, "Stole my towel, the one with the girl on it."

Good, Galahad sighed. His father had reached the threshold where his drunkenness turned him from feral to domesticated. *He got docile a lot earlier than usual,* he remarked happily. Galahad added, knowing he and his father were having two separate conversations, "Now what will you masturbate to?"

His father had not heard him. "The assassins come. They scare the shit out of me."

Galahad sat across his father, "Don't blame them. You'd shit yourself in any company."

His father seemed to care more about his youngest son when he saw double of him. He looked positively terrified. He gazed at Galahad with one, wide eye. "You promise me not to drink?"

Ah, how can one man be so lucid and so insane? Galahad frowned, "You are the perfect role model. I will never drink like you."

His father giggled, burped, hiccupped, and sneezed. "Good." He pointed out the window and said in a hushed voice, "Keep a secret?"

"Only where you are concerned," Galahad yawned.

His father licked the front of his teeth, "I hate them all. Every single one who comes through my door."

"Quaint," Galahad remarked. He leaned toward his father and clasped his hands on his knees. His father stumbled into the same pose. "Father, you know I would never degrade myself to caring for you?"

"M'yes," Cambyses smiled, ignorant of his son's words. "Owls are always looking."

"I am saying I do not love you," Galahad continued. *Oh, I love honesty without repercussion.* He glared at his father, "But you are human. Pitifully human...You make me sad because you've not grown in decades."

"Never have to buy new clothes," his father pointed out. He sounded like he had received a divine revelation.

Galahad continued, "Seeing you is like visiting someone in prison. You take your chains with you."

His father half-heard him and grumbled, "Stop busting my balls. What the devil? Take me to Aubourg." Instantly, he forgot what he was saying and Cambyses asked, "So you're a brawler? I told him to leave."

Galahad sighed, "You go take your nap."

Cambyses scoffed, "It is my *privilege* not to have sex."

Galahad got up and pushed in his chair, "Yeah? Your privilege?"

Cambyses grunted proudly, "Mhm. Felt good."

Nothing will change, Galahad decided. He left his father to his drinking.

"Let's get you a bicycle," his father's incoherent rambling continued. "Good for the snow, I hear." The voice diminished. Soon, his father stopped speaking entirely and Galahad heard loud stomps on the stairs. A bed creaked as Cambyses hurled himself into his nap. He loved to nap before the nocturnal clientele came. It helped him sober up.

Galahad went to his own bedroom and sat on his unmade bed. He had not bothered to make it. He did not plan to sleep in his old room ever again. He was done with his father and done with his store. He only needed a little while longer. He gazed out his window and stared at the setting sun. The clouds were a deep crimson and the sun was already cowering to the moon. He idled on his bed in silence, waiting for his father's snoring to start. When it did, he went quietly downstairs.

A sign had been posted on the door which read, *Store to reopen in one hour.* Galahad knew his father would be asleep for the remainder of his dinner break. So, he walked over to his father's bar and clerk counter. He noted the honey wine which was laid out for later consumption. It was half-full.

Galahad went into the storeroom. He would have liked to be done and return to Momed, but it seemed his father's disorganization would keep him late. Cambyses was a cluttered man. Rows of liquor lined the walls. Boxes of opened inventory lay scattered between the shelving.

Cambyses preferred to drink all day, and a beverage which was mostly alcohol proved too much for even his father's gluttony. Ale, whiskey, honey wine—those were his favorites and they were strewn messily across floors, shelving, and in spills throughout the storeroom. Galahad tiptoed over Cambyses' many messes. He scoured the shelves for something in particular. After fifteen minutes of searching, Galahad found what he was looking for: pure alcohol, used mostly for mixing. The vintage tasted clean as water. Yet, it was the most potent of Cambyses' stock. It came from Redfeather and was quite costly. Only those who wished to get exceedingly drunk ever bought a bottle.

Galahad took two. He poured one into the honey wine on the counter and gave the new mixture a shake. *That'll do,* Galahad decided. He then went to the sink and filled a jug of water. He placed the jug beside the honey wine, arranged clean glasses beside it, and then poured the second bottle of alcohol into the jug.

Galahad took a step back and admired his work. The bottles in his hands sloshed. There was still enough liquor in each bottle for a few swigs. Galahad decided the remainder would be for him and Momed to share. He beamed at the spiked wine, pocketed the near-empty bottles, and left his father to the night.

5

The Sunken Glade

Charles knew he had been lucky. Hanna had given him a horse. *A horse*. He had not seen much of the animal since returning from war. Luckily, the House on the Hill always had a few mounts to spare, for when a patron needed to take the reins and go about one's business. Charles wondered if Arthur would start using automobiles like people in the city.

For his part, Charles was content with a horse. The country roads of Cottonwood were far too small for an automobile. Indeed, the path Charles followed was more a dirt carpet than an actual road. It led to the far places of the forest, the farthest being home. Occasionally, he would pass an abandoned wagon or a forlorn farm, but no people. The rural folk had left their lands when the men died and the women could not pay to maintain them.

Only Cora Eastmont remained. Her cottage was an island at the end of a sea of trees.

Home. Even with a horse, he would not make the journey in a day. He had left at dawn and rode through the sweltering afternoon. Any further haste would probably be unwise. Reluctantly, Charles patted his horse's neck, "Let's take a rest." The animal had a coat as silver as the moon; it was old, but exceptional for its age.

He dismounted and led the horse from the path and toward a stream. Water was not hard to find. The valley was a book Charles had been reading since he was a child. He scanned his surroundings for a certain species. "There we are," he said to the mare. "Cattails."

Cattails grew like fields of wheat along the banks. Wherever water was found, so were cattails. They loved water and there was always a small amount of water trickling down the east mountain, mostly from daily rainstorms. Charles parted the curtain of cattails and led his horse to drink.

He was mindful of swimming snakes, but less so than if it had been summer. He prepared as comfortable a bed as he could for the dutiful mare. He hardly knew the preferred sleeping arrangements of a horse. Nevertheless, he felt the old beast deserved a pleasant rest for all her hard work. He laid a bed of sticks at his feet and began to cover it with dirt. It took many scoops with his small shovel to cover the bed completely, and many minutes for him to level the dirt into a flat layer. He had begun to collect debris such as grasses and leaves when he saw his horse asleep in the rocks. Her tail was soaking in the stream. The full moon had risen and reflected off the water. Wisps of white scattered on her silver fur.

"Perhaps you are right," Charles conceded, dropping the vegetation. A calm wind blew red and orange leaves past his head. *Even the breeze is settling in.* He curled up onto his dirt bed and stared at the stars. He had forgotten how many there were. You could see hundreds without ever moving your eye. As the far-off suns glimmered like gemstones upon the drape of heaven, Charles thought of his time at the capitol.

The Castle Rock was a wide pillar of rock jutting out like a spire from the sea. Its high rising buildings rubbed their shoulders with the stars, but a person in that city could hardly see them. The people had too many lights of their own to notice the distant stars.

Sure, Charles had tried to find some tall place to look at the night sky—but the university was always lit. The only place one could truly see the sky was the observatory. Charles had never been permitted inside, but he heard other students talk about far-off places called galaxies, where they said there were hundreds of worlds just like theirs.

Charles had his doubts about that. So much had happened to make the streams flow the way they did. So many rocks had to fall and rise to make the mountains. He had once told Hanna as much. She in turn informed him each thing was a culmination of an infinite amount of probabilistic interactions.

Charles had nothing to say to that. He watched the birds. He studied the soil. He was far more concerned with dirt than galaxies, and mathematics did not come easily to him like it did for Hanna Gardner. He had told her so, only to have her fervently declare, "Anyone can do anything anyone else can do. You just have to try, sometimes harder and sometimes not."

And how could she believe anything else?

When Charles had met Hanna, sitting on a stone bench with her pen racing across tabulated paper, she was an enigma. She was not comely, and in fact—was likely the most beautiful woman at the university, at least by Charles' reckoning. Yet she was not at school to find a husband, as the rest of the women were. Charles had asked her,

"What are you studying?"

"Mathematics," she answered frankly. She had told him afterward, when they were reminiscing of their first meeting, that she thought he was yet another hormonal boy out on the hunt. After a moment, Charles had simply asked her, "Why?"

That got her attention. Apparently, nobody had thought to ask her why she was there. Many men had looked down upon her. Even her professors had thought her unworthy of studying their vaunted mathematics. Sure, the men asked themselves why a woman chose to be among them, but nobody had ever asked why *Hanna*, the human, had wanted to learn mathematics. She answered him,

"Because it is a challenge. Everything else would bore me."

Charles thought that answer was somewhat self-aggrandizing. He probed, "Is it a challenge because of the content, or because you are a woman?"

Hanna put down her pen. "Both." She then asked him in a tone a queen might give to a subject, "What is your name?"

"Charles Eastmont," he replied. So far from Auberdine, he gave his last name freely. Nobody knew him there. Nobody knew his mother's past. Charles had loved that about the Castle Rock. The city did not care who your mother was, nor who your father was. The city was so large, it did not give a damn who anybody was.

"That's a pretty name," Hanna had stated. "Studying what?"

"Life," he had answered. In truth, he did not want to list all the disciplines ending in *-ology* which he was studying. *That* would be self-aggrandizing.

Hanna had laughed at him, "That's a broad specialization. More like a generalization. You'll need math to piece life's puzzles together."

It had been Charles' turn to laugh. "Why would I want to complete the puzzle? Life's no fun without questions."

Hanna smirked. "You intrigue me."

Charles had replied likewise, and their friendship started a second after. They had sometimes joked about pursuing a romantic relationship, but neither really cared to. At least, Charles did not want to push the subject. Besides, romance interfered with studies, and that was their true love. When Arthur came to the university a year later, the three had explored Castle Rock to the depths and the heights, swimming under the stars at nighttime and climbing the sky towers during the day.

Charles smiled and his lungs swelled with the air of memory. The gust filled his nostrils and though the memory was happy, he smelt something he did not expect. It was foul. The stench suddenly overwhelmed him and he turned on his side. The smell grew more intolerable until Charles stood upright. His mount was still asleep. The aroma of death had yet to wake it.

Charles knew that foulness. He had been witness to it when marching home across the trench line. He had realized on that return march just how lucky he was to be a sailor. He did not fight in the Tanglewood. He fought on the ocean, whose vast depths did not allow such rank smells. He had not had to bunk with smells of death and decay and he would not start now.

"This does not smell natural," he grumbled. He sniffed the rotten air. *What the hell is that?* He heard a bird screech. Frantic wings fluttered overhead. A grim feeling settled in Charles' chest. *A bird of ill omen...* Charles was not carrying a weapon, but instinct told him he should have been.

Instinct also told him not to investigate, but a captain's confidence took hold of him and he crept away from the stream. He walked through a row of angel's trumpets; the orange bulbs briefly threw him off the scent. He paused to reorient toward the stench's source. *North,* he decided. His path followed yet another little stream. Mosquitos dogged his way and sagging willow branches tickled the top of his head. Charles swatted them both away and sniffed the air. *East,* he knew. He crept away from the water and into a dense patch of cottonwoods.

Charles looked up at the forest canopy and could not see a single star. Leaf and cloud obscured all light. A gloom had washed over the tranquil night. He stepped lightly onto the underbrush, not wanting to disturb whatever predator might still be lurking. He could not see, but his hands worked well enough. He felt in front of him, grabbing at branch, bulb, flower, or frond. He was terrified he would get lost, or his outstretched hand would land on a bear's maw. It was not cold, but Charles shivered. There was a dim light ahead. His hand crept up to a wooden tree trunk, its bark was old and crumbling. He kept his hand on the trunk and used the other to get his bearings. Another trunk was to his left. He went forward.

The canopy receded; the stars shone through. He had stumbled upon a glittering glade. The moonlight shined with dazzling brightness. Fireflies danced slowly with one another to silent music. Not a single sapling, nor one small shrub was growing. There was only a thin layer of moss and grass separating the air from the dirt.

Charles squinted ahead. The fireflies were concentrated in the center of the glade, where a tiny spring was trickling water from some underground aquafer. Charles came closer and his feet smushed against damp vegetation. The green carpet at his feet sank beneath him and water started to fill his aged boots. No amount of stealth could hide the mushing sounds of his boot against that boggy glade.

The fireflies continued to dance. Pale moonlight descended onto an oddly shaped figure. As Charles approached, he thought he might wretch. This was the source of the smell: a rotting body. The fireflies did not seem to mind. They were thriving. So, Charles put his shirt over his nose and crept cautiously.

The source of the stench soon became clear. Two corpses were entwined together in the middle of the glade. The jaws of a wolf, the largest Charles had ever seen, had engulfed a man's head. His uniform was tattered and moldy, but it was clear the body belonged to a postman. Beside the pair was a rusting pistol; it pointed directly at the wolf's festering belly.

Charles bowed his head. He felt bad for the man and hoped his family was well taken care of. He then looked at the gargantuan wolf and hoped much the same. He stared at the stars and wondered if he should say a few words.

A branch cracked.

Charles eyed his sides suspiciously. He turned around rapidly and expected to find another lurking wolf. Instead, all he saw were floating fireflies. Charles swallowed. *Bad idea to linger. I need to check on the horse.* He left the sunken glade without further delay. As he departed, owls started to hoot. A bird's warning call erupted further in the forest. A deer wailed. A pack of wolves howled.

6

Dreadnaught

Tanglewood has come home, Galahad thought as the smell of sweat and liquor filled his nostrils. The smell nauseated him even more. He stumbled back to bed, fumbling in the dark. Despite being underground, the room *could* be well lit. Yet, they both found the light disturbing and painful, and so were spending their morning under the covers.

"Never do I wish to drink, ever again," Momed groaned.

"I did say it was strong," Galahad tried to smile. He stifled a vomit-coated belch. He crawled into bed and outstretched his arms. Momed crawled into them and Galahad wrapped his paramour like a blanket. *Just like before*, he recalled. One arm was holding his head, the other was slowly rubbing his back. Momed was a foolish boy and as far as Galahad could tell, had never loved anyone but from afar. It made the young thing easy to win over. His affections were nice, but Galahad did not love him.

"What part of Muhal did you come from?" He was sure Momed had told him once before, but he had forgotten the little details. When they had met, Galahad was going off to certain death. He had not cared about small talk. Now, strange as it felt, Galahad yearned for something deeper than bodily excitement.

Momed sighed and rubbed his head against Galahad's chest. "Talukir, a village in the dunes."

Galahad asked several questions, hoping to expedite the conversation toward something more interesting. "You hate it there? Love it? Had to flee, wanted to go?"

"I liked my town well enough, but the wells we had used for generations had dried up. We had to leave or die. I crossed the desert and sold all my rags to join a small trade convoy heading for Castle Rock."

Galahad let out a gravelly cough. "Bet you lost it when you saw Cottonwood. From desert to deluge."

Momed nodded sleepily. "A stream for every person. I thought everyone who came got their own little river, like they got their own bed."

"Auberdine the ideal is very different from Auberdine the reality. The inn is a nice place, but it has no real power. Even Arthur has to pay taxes to Castle Rock."

He looked at Momed. Aside from a few scars, his skin looked unworn. *My, you are young...* Galahad wove his fingers through Momed's curly, black hair. He was only several years his younger but the difference showed.

Galahad stretched and groped for a glass of water and found one. The ice cubes of the night before had melted, leaving only a thin layer of refreshment. It was enough. He pushed Momed's head out of the way while he swallowed. Then, he pulled him back and asked, "When did you make the journey?"

"I landed in the Castle Rock a week before they closed the ports to Muhal."

"Lucky thing, you are," Galahad awed. Had his ship encountered bad weather, or left port a week later—he would have been turned away. Castle Rock had ceased trading with Muhal when they came to the aid of Redfeather, the great plains nation to the North. Galahad gazed at Momed with pity. *What a piss poor time to be a foreigner.*

To Galahad's shock, Momed laughed. "I had just joined a caravan and begun journey to this town. We were in Cottonwood when a group of angry wives, young boys, and old men protested our arrival. They were throwing sticks, stones, and I swear it on the blood of the desert—their own shit."

It hurt to laugh. Galahad struggled to restrain his chest from bouncing up and down. Galahad gestured at Momed with his chin, beckoning him to continue. "How did you make it?"

"The innkeeper," Momed said, his eyes rolled up toward his forehead. Galahad thought he was wincing from his hangover. Instead, Momed reflected, "Or, the innkeeper's brother, the one who died. He came down on a silver horse and rode in front of the crowd, a black hat held across his chest. Everybody stopped and nobody dared throw another stick. I do not know what he said then, as my skill with the language was bad." Momed yawned, "It appeared to work. The crowd went away, and with us the innkeeper travelled. He spoke to one, someone who could translate. He offered us all rest."

"How much rest could you get?" Galahad mocked. The country was on the warpath. Auberdine had just declared war against a million other Momeds. Not even a thousand beds could have provided him rest.

His paramour sighed, "The innkeeper told as much. He spoke that his people, they were all soon to be wounded. And a wounded animal can be a mean thing."

Galahad twisted his lips in thought. He had to agree with Arthur's brother. In that regard, he was right. Humans were just animals, fickle and foolish. He was content, for now—to let Momed's story end. He wished to start his day with all urgency.

Momed paused such hopes. He asked, sheepishly, "What about you?"

Galahad questioned, "What about *me?*"

"Which part of Muhal did you come from?"

An innocent question. Galahad kissed the boy's forehead. "Sweet thing, I have no Muhali accent." *Though that nuance has escaped many.* "Where do you think I come from?"

Momed stayed quiet. He was an awfully shy creature and prone to long bouts of silence if he thought he had spoken out of turn. He had liked that about Momed during their brief romance. His meekness had made Galahad feel strong when he had felt his weakest. With the war over, Galahad found his frailty annoying. He knew he had to say something or the boy would hate himself for the rest of the day.

Galahad stretched a smile, "What did you do before my father?"

"I got to Auberdine and begged for a job. I could not stand the inn's generosity, then. I felt like a beggar and after a night, I fled. But I was still begging. For a job. B-but nobody would hire me. I hardly spoke the language. After I left the inn, I spent the first year in a married couple's home. They had many bedrooms, but requested I sleep in their bed. They provided for me. As long as I excited them." Momed shook his head of the memory. He cleared his throat, "Then, your father offers employment. I accept, of course."

Galahad listened to the young thing's story. He and every mud-skinned person in Auberdine had a similar tale. The Pale were prickly and prideful. They were nothing compared to his father, though. Cambyses was the kind of man to beat you if he was feeling arrogant, but he was only ever arrogant when he was drunk—and he only drank when he was insecure.

Galahad interrupted, "How long after I left before he beat you?"

"Several weeks," Momed replied. He stuttered, "F-for a while I... I thought he was a good man. T-then, one day... he smelt of liquor." Momed trailed off and shivered. Galahad held him and whispered,

"Sshh, you are safe now." A blatant lie, but the boy needed reassurance, not the truth. Cambyses was just an appetizer. How could Galahad tell him the Pale did far more? How could he tell the trembling youth his greatest accomplishment would always be tainted by his skin? He would be a mudpuppy. No more, no less. "You are a gem," he lied.

They stayed in the dark for a little while longer, each content with nursing their own hurts in silence. They played with each other's hair and rubbed against one another, pressing their bodies close and teasing each other. Eventually, Galahad tired of the morning and wished to be off. He had much to do. Still, he had one last question which had been simmering in his skull since he reunited with Momed.

"What did he say about me while I was gone?" Galahad blurted out.

"Who?"

"My father."

Momed struggled to find the strength to speak. It was not a good sign. Galahad prepared to hear all the horrible stories, to relive his past one last time. He lost his breath when Momed began.

"Just one story. Mostly, he talked about his other sons."

"Go on then," Galahad pressed, having little patience for suspense.

"He said he made you go to the war. He thought if you did not go, the town would think he was spying for Muhal. That he was not loyal to the Rock."

Galahad nodded, "Go on."

Momed swallowed, "He said he would not have a coward playing in dresses while his sons were dying for the honor of Castle Rock."

I never played in dresses. "Honor, yes," Galahad remembered. "He always wanted to prove his loyalty to the Pale. When Cyrus enlisted, it was the proudest I had ever seen my father. Then, Cyrus died, choked by strangling gas... Darius, the funny fool— he followed our older brother shortly after. He promised my father he would avenge Cyrus. He was blown to bits."

Galahad wrinkled his nose, "When Cambyses found out his trophy sons were dead, he became a caricature of a man. Every day started and ended with a bottle. He became even worse, just a dirty drunk like those he served." He paused and looked at Momed, "What else?"

"That is it."

Galahad bit his tongue and chewed on his anger. He spat, "Many people were coerced into joining the war. Whether they were shamed by a woman into proving their manhood, or their fathers wanted them to bring glory to the family... I saw it all when I arrived. My father was different. He was more direct, though the end result was the same."

Galahad got up, pushing Momed's body off him. The boy slid from his arms and back into the sheets. He crawled forward, offering a hand. Galahad shrank from it. "He emerged behind me one day, with a gun pointed at my skull. I could feel the cold steel against my scalp. He told me if I did not enlist that day, he would blow my head off and feed me to stray dogs."

Galahad smirked and turned toward Momed, "That's *daddy*, for you." His black eye was pulsating. Momed shook his head with pity. Galahad could not bear to look at him. He did not want another person's pity. He could not control the violence in his tone when he barked, "Breakfast's on the table. I will see you tonight."

Momed uttered, "I love you." Galahad only heard the echoes of the phrase, for he had slammed the door shut just as it entered his ears. He lingered on the other side, feeling he had closed it too forcefully. He contemplated going back in and saying the same phrase to his paramour. *That time has passed,* he decided. There was business to deal with.

The petrified table had pockets of people scattered along it. The smaller, round tables had been taken and stored somewhere in the deep cellars under the Hill. The innkeeper did not sit at the head of the table, but instead in the middle, alone. He had a full plate and a clean fork. Galahad sat across from him.

"What great company you keep," Galahad commented.

"It's true," Arthur looked up. "I have the best conversations with myself."

Galahad shook his head, "You shouldn't eat alone. I have seen people do what you are doing. They think isolation will be their penance. You will echo your sadness until you go mad." He plucked fruit from a nearby basket. "Peach?"

Arthur shook his head. "I much prefer eating alone," he scanned around him. "I had forgotten how much I hate the sound of other people's chewing. Give me artillery fire any day over the clicking and slurping of these slugs."

Galahad slurped some yogurt, looking directly at Arthur with malevolent eyes.

"Fuck you," Arthur grinned.

Galahad stopped his game and rubbed his stomach. The organ had not healed from the liquor and it growled when disturbed. A few bites would have to suffice, or he feared he would vomit all over Arthur. Though the image was a humorous one, Galahad thought it best if he pushed the plate away. He looked up at the rafters, where ornamental beams had been carved from the finest redwood. "I don't know, I would love to have a lot of people at my table."

"Take this one," Arthur grunted. He leaned forward and motioned toward two boys. A large toad of a boy with fire-red hair was flicking his oatmeal at a tiny, bespectacled boy. "Evelyn's and Carolyn's. I think the little, bookish one is Wilhelm. The other with the red hair is Frederick, a fiery cunt." Frederick laughed at his cousin and then ran out of the inn. Wilhelm trailed behind.

He pointed at another group of children. "I think I've memorized those ones. All orphans from the war. The two girls are Josephine and Virginia. The boys are Lorne and Quenby." He shuddered and shook his head, "Virginia does nothing but cry, Josephine will probably end up being a whore from how she tries to manipulate the boys. Lorne and Quenby are decent, but neither quite know how to wipe their asses. The one sitting alone is Dixon, his father went missing several weeks ago. A postman. They found the kid alone, talking to himself and calling his reflection, *'papa'.*"

Galahad realized he was staring overlong at Dixon. "Then we are a town in agreement," Galahad declared with gruff grogginess. "I myself have never quite learned to wipe my ass."

Arthur pointed at a man leaning by the entrance. He was one of the oldest people in town. "Degory," he knew.

Arthur nodded. "He filed a *formal* complaint because I give out bedrooms to foreigners."

"The Pale people of Auberdine," Galahad commented. "Let him slink back to his docks and shanties." Even as a Pale man, Degory was shunned from the Inner Ring. He had lost his family's home when he was young and reckless. Now old and stupid, he worked as a dockmaster in the ruins of the Drowned Anchorage.

Arthur looked at Galahad as if he had just bitten into a lemon. "This is my table. I feed them, I shelter them, I even clothe them. Hell," he gestured at the orphans, "I raise them. And in return for *indiscriminate* love—I must float a forgiving eye over all the idiots, drunks, rapists... Niwot should have set a stronger precedent."

"Niwot died," Galahad answered simply. Niwot was the last Adawakan, the leader of the Wanakhan natives. He built what would become the inn. "And martyrs are the strongest precedents."

Arthur tapped his fingers on the table and looked toward the kitchens. "Indiscriminate love is stupidity. Not everyone deserves a bed." He got up hastily and knocked over his plate. He commanded Galahad in the voice he used in the Trenches, "Eat. Weldon and I worked all night on this breakfast. Aside from Hanna and the kids, you are the only person at this table I can stomach. You damned well better eat this food."

Galahad's stomach growled a warning. He waved, "My compliments to Weldon. A fine chef."

Once the innkeeper had departed, Galahad exited the inn. He had gotten a far later start than yesterday. He accelerated down the Hill and ran through the hedge gate. The Inner Ring was as quiet as ever, and a lone man from Redfeather was trimming a tree. Sweat dripped from his head in torrents, like a rain cloud had formed above his head. Despite his fatigue, the Redfeather man did his duty and raised a large saw toward the tree's canopy. The vegetation of the Inner Ring received finer haircuts than any person in the Overgrowth.

The Inner Ring was a place one went to think, to hear one's echoes as you walked. The stone homes and walkways made for an amplification chamber like no other. It might have been a loud place if anyone ever went outside. The residents preferred to stay indoors, though. Galahad almost wished he had lived there, but then he would have to deal with the neighbors, always poking an eye out of their window.

A dog's bark interrupted the silence.

Galahad knew one day he would escape the Overgrowth. When he did, he would not come here. The Inner Ring was the playground of the pathetic. Their pleasures were dictated by what the grand figures from the Castle Rock enjoyed; their children were dressed like puppets and danced the dance of city folk. There was not a single person he respected who lived in the Inner Ring, besides perhaps doctor Yu and his nephew.

Galahad turned a corner and the sound of barking intensified. He saw three, small figures. As he neared, he recognized one to be Arthur's daughter. Emilia was cowering with her hands protecting her head. The barking came from the girl's large beast. He had forgotten the name of the dog. It was circling around Emilia and barking. It would lunge at the other two figures before retreating and whimpering.

Galahad snarled. He walked over to the commotion and caught a glimpse of the girl's antagonists. Wilhelm was looking at his cousin as the fat Frederick bent down and grabbed a stone to throw at Emilia. Wilhelm looked for a rock and threw it too, but he had little force behind the toss. He laughed when Frederick laughed. *I wonder if you cry when he does.*

"Excuse me, little masters," Galahad began malevolently.

Wilhelm stopped at once and froze in fright. Frederick rotated his round body sluggishly and squinted up at Galahad. "What do you want, mudpuppy?"

He was not surprised by the child's words. His father had been Siegfried, a man who claimed he was the blood of the first miners. Galahad quite believed that, as the first miners were notorious twats and believed the only gems in the world were in mountains and in Pale men. In reality, Siegfried had been slow of mind and lacking in strength. He eyed Frederick up and down. Like father, like son.

As if the response were self-evident, Galahad answered, "I want you to stop hurting that lovely girl, there."

"I don't take lip from mudpuppies," Frederick yelled defiantly. Wilhelm laughed, unsure who was leading the conversation.

Galahad glared at the tiny boy. He commanded, capitalizing on the child's fear, "Boy. Name."

Wilhelm's spine cracked from straightness. "Wil. Um. Wilhelm, sir."

"Good morning, Wil um." Galahad tipped an invisible hat and smiled at Frederick. That fat child looked at his cousin in shock. Galahad's stomach swirled. He hid his glee and tormented the red-headed boy further.

"Do you know, you remind me of a submarine? The Muhali had a few of those. Deadly things." He stared into the fat boy's eyes, "Your daddy knew about them, too."

Frederick's cheeks grew the same color as his hair and his neck muscles cracked from the tension. He glared at Galahad.

"The Muhali would target defenseless cargo ships, sink them, and slink off. A single submarine was the bane of ten or twenty trade vessels."

He walked up to Frederick and poked his chest. The child faltered and nearly fell. Galahad grinned, "Well eventually, the submarine wasn't the big fish anymore. Eventually, it encountered a destroyer, or a dreadnaught. Those had guns, too. Big guns."

He swiveled his gaze over to Wilhelm, "I am dreadful, am I not?"

As Wilhelm nodded fervently, it took all Galahad's strength not to burst out laughing. He stared at Wilhelm while he spoke to his cousin, "Your daddy was a sailor, wasn't he?"

"A captain," Frederick barked. With his cousin's confidence, Wilhelm quickly added, "What do you care?"

"I don't. I just find it dreadfully funny to think about your dead daddies."

Wilhelm's chest fluttered. Galahad did not know whether he was going to hug him or hit him. He realized it was not Wilhelm who needed to be spoken to. The boy was shattered, and if the stories of his father, Gerald, were true—he had seen enough of grown men's brutality. So, he faced Frederick and stared at him placidly.

The fat boy shifted nervously. He made his voice sound deep, as if he had not just begun puberty. "My daddy would have hanged you where you stand." His voice cracked at the word *you*.

"Oh, to be sure," Galahad admitted. Then again, so would many. He put his hand on Frederick's shoulder and when the boy tried to maneuver out of his grasp, he tightened his grip. Frederick froze and his legs started to quiver.

Galahad's grin grew. "Some people died because of bad luck, sheer bad odds. A run-in with a rogue round. Some people rolled the dice and lost, but not your *daddy*." He paused. "Your daddy was just a castle captain, who warred no better than a cripple. Your daddy was destined to die."

Frederick ran into a nearby house, crying. His cousin looked at Galahad with wide eyes before he hurried away.

Galahad looked at Emilia, who was stroking her hound's fur. The dog could not find a good place to sit and paced nervously around Emilia.

"A dog that big should be more than enough protection against those gnats," Galahad was quick to say.

"Izzy isn't a fighter. She can bark, but she doesn't want to hurt anyone."

Izzy would make a great innkeeper, Galahad remarked. "All the more reason to get tough. Those boys look at you and see a little girl." He knelt before Emilia. "You need to show them you are fierce. Hit them back. Throw one stone and they will stop."

Emilia shook her head and pulled her big beast of a dog closer. The animal licked her forehead and then proceeded to sit down on the road and anxiously groom her claws. "I can't," the little girl finally admitted. "I tried once, but the rock was too heavy to throw."

"Find a smaller rock. The message will be the same."

Emilia defended herself, "It was a small rock! My arms got all weak and wiggly when I tried to throw it."

Ah, Galahad nodded to himself. "You have a gentleness about you. You should go see your mother. She seems as fierce as any."

"She told me to compliment them and to smile," Emilia protested, clearly aghast at making friends with her enemies. She pouted at him in expectance.

Galahad said quietly, "I'll tell you a secret, if you promise not to tell anyone." The girl bobbed her head.

"I'm not very good at compliments and smiles, either. I would rather hit back." He got to his feet and offered his hand to Emilia. He did not know why he cared so much about the little girl. He had served her father in the war, not her. Yet here he was... *Am I doomed to love this damned family?*

When he had doubled back to the hedge gate, he gave Emilia a pat on her back and said, "Your mother has the right of it, at least in part. Disarm them with your charm, floor them with your arm."

The girl giggled at the rhyme and Galahad told her to remember it if she felt scared. He told the hound, "You just bite those boys if they touch our friend, okay?" The dog wagged its tail, oblivious to its cowardice.

Emilia hugged him and told him Isabelle couldn't bite anyone. "She's a scaredy-cat. When we found her, she was eating out of the garbage. She walked funny for a while."

"Then," Galahad put his arms to his hips, "Best not tell anyone that. Let them think she's ferocious."

Emilia hugged him once more and ran up the Hill, disappearing into Auldwine's grove. Galahad sighed. *Let's try this again.*

He had managed to retrace his steps when a woman ran from a patio and shrieked after him. *Carolyn Kinsfeld,* Galahad remembered. Her husband had been the unfortunate idiot, Siegfried.

"Aaah, Frederick's lovely young mother," Galahad stated sarcastically. "Still in mourning, I see." Her dress was black and her veil was floating in the calm breeze.

"How dare you threaten a child? Have you no honor? No decency? What do they teach you people?"

"I can't speak for *you people*," Galahad bit back, "As for threatening children, you would do well not to let them bully the innkeeper's daughter. If they continue, I can make no promises... But if you'd like, I'll give you an anecdote."

Before Carolyn could ride her angry momentum, Galahad was speaking over her. She stewed in silent contempt as he recalled, "I never saw their faces, but I shot all the same. I am sure many of the faceless soldiers I slaughtered were a lot like your proud, beautiful boy."

He paused. Carolyn's anger did not seem to have much of a foothold. A mother's fear was easily manipulated. He continued, "Oh yes. I must have killed thousands. I daresay I never once asked for a thousand pardons. I killed them in the day and in the night, do you know? I still found the time to masturbate."

He could not hear Carolyn's roars as he strolled on. He'd rather hear his own whistling, and he chose a lovely marching tune to drown out her bellowing. He did not have time to deal with the inept and inert Inner Ring. Of the choice words he cared to hear, most were variants of 'mudpuppy,' or 'trogg.'

When at last he came to Cambyses' shop, the afternoon heat had begun to make him sweat. He tied his hair in a tail. It may be Fall, but Summer weather often poked its head into Winter. He thought about the Muhali deserts. *I could not bear that heat.* He approached the red entrance.

A sign on the door read, *'Store to reopen in one hour.'*

Someone's voice came from behind him. "That has been up since I have."

Galahad turned. The voice was Terrell's, the flesh salesman he had encountered the day before. Acting ignorant, Galahad asked, "I have no idea why my father put that sign up. Do you need something?"

Terrell let out a surprised grunt of laughter. "Cambyses is your father? I pity you."

"I pity me, too," Galahad changed the subject. He unlocked the door and led Terrell into the dark store. He pulled a string and a few lights flickered. "What can I get for you?"

Terrell struggled to remember. "Ah, some Redfeather piss. One of my new girls is from there. Firm ass and good for a ride, but damn her accent is thick. I'd rather have her use those lips for something productive, but when she's drunk she performs better."

"How about this?" Galahad suggested. "I'll give you one of every bottle I know from Redfeather. With the war over, they won't be nearly as expensive." He didn't care if they were expensive or not. The inventory was nothing to him.

"Fuck me, you're joking," the flesh salesman gasped. When Galahad did not blink, he inquired, "How many bottles is that?"

"Let's see," Galahad said. He began weaving through the aisles and picking up choice bottles. He had to double back multiple times when he remembered another variety. He pulled out two bags and began loading alcohol into them. He came back to Terrell, who was leaning against the clerk's counter as if he owned it. Galahad handed him the heavy bag and said, "Nineteen."

The smile on his face made Galahad grin. He looked at him and said, "What is it you Muhali say—A thousand gratitudes?"

"Nineteen will do," Galahad smiled.

"You just come by whenever you need a lay, no charge."

Galahad thanked him for the offer. He would much rather take the flesh salesman for a ride, but he did not need to know that. Friends who carry shotguns at their hip were good to have.

As soon as Terrell was out of sight, he closed the door and reinstated the sign to its post. Galahad turned the lights off and for a minute, he contemplated in the darkness. After that, he went back to the clerk's counter to find two *quite* empty bottles of liquor—the very same he had filled the day before. The sight made Galahad giddy with anticipation. *Now where is my lovely father?*

He had been waiting all day to see him. He knew he was sprawled out in bed. If a single small taste of that alcohol had incapacitated Momed and intoxicated him... His father's tolerance could only take him so far. He crept up the stairs. He had only managed two steps when he heard a knock.

Son of a bitch, he winced. Galahad went to the door and found two men standing there: Yu, with a bag of medical equipment in his hand, and his nephew.

"You-a father called. Up, let's go." Without so much as a word, Yu raced past him and charged up the stairs. Yang gave him a cursory frown, as if saying he did not want to be there.

"My father request you?" Galahad inquired, already suspicious. He wondered if that damned doctor was already upstairs, figuring out what had happened. *Of course not*, Galahad assured himself. *He was a degenerate and a known drunk.* Yu would know as much and nothing more.

"He vomited on one of his customers," Yang said without the slightest hint of emotion. "She decided the man might need a doctor."

"He may," Galahad confessed. "He's been day drinking for half a decade."

"Don't worry," Yang reassured. "My uncle is the most talented doctor around."

Let us hope not. Galahad replied, not seeing any need to hide his grim demeanor, "He is the only doctor around."

He saw Yang's eyes twitch before the student replied, "For now."

"Do you always join him on his calls?" Galahad asked, growing irritable. *Or do you just wait outside and light his cigarette?*

"Now that he is back," Yang answered. "Shall we go up?"

Galahad went to his father's resting place. He was sprawled out on his bed and his legs twitched occasionally. He was reeling in pain and several buckets full of foul liquid were ruminating in the corner. His sheets were thrown off the bed and he was groaning like a dying animal. His wig was stuck to his damp head. The sight almost made Galahad turn away. *I have seen worse than this*, he reminded himself.

"You do not-a have to be here," Yu said to him, not taking his eyes from his father's throat. He placed an instrument against the man's chest and asked. "How much drink?"

"A glass," Cambyses breathed. The words barely came out of his gritted teeth.

"You-a lie," Yu replied briskly. "I never see one so sick from drink."

"I drank as much as I always do," Cambyses groaned. He curled up in a fetal position which seemed to give him some relief. Then, he shrieked and vomited. He laid back down. A second later, his stomach surged like it was attached to a fisherman's line and his body was being pulled upwards. Then, he fell and began to weep feebly.

Galahad shivered at the sight. He forced himself to remain.

Yang opened his satchel and pulled out a bag of crushed leaves. Yu told Cambyses to chew on them and his discomfort would go away. Cambyses thanked him with a brief, "Go to hell," and Yu beckoned Galahad over.

"Outside, if-a-you please."

He and Yang followed the old doctor into the corridor and down toward the dark store. He asked, "You father. He a drunk."

"Yes," Galahad replied. No thought needed to be given. He would answer the questions simply.

"How-a much drink?"

"At least several bottles a day." He saw the opportunity to weave a lie. "Yesterday he was quite sad. I saw him take several bottles of the highest proof alcohol. I left the shop early when he did that."

"I-a not lie. You father may not live. If he vomit, and not on his side, he die."

If there is a god, at any rate. He closed his eyes and staggered his breathing. He stuttered, "N-no. You are sure?"

Yu shook his head disdainfully, "Of course I am sure. I am doctor." He looked at his nephew and declared, "You console family. I-a too old for crying." So, the doctor stepped outside and lit a cigarette.

The boy was frank, just as his uncle was. "Keep him away from alcohol. He may try to drink, as it does have a nullifying effect. It will not help, and it will actually hurt him more. Make sure he sleeps on his side and give him some water. Some food would do, as well. Have him chew on those leaves if the pain gets to him, but do not let him replace one addiction with another."

"Thank you," Galahad said, holding his brow low with sadness.

"You are most welcome," Yang smiled. "I am sure you know where our house is. Call on us if you need, even at night. My uncle will probably just send me and scold you, but that's not a problem."

"Will do," Galahad lied. After Yang had left, he heard his uncle say, "You-a did good. Not great. All the same. You-a did good. You may grow into good man, yet."

Further in the distance, he then heard Yang's uncle scold him, saying in a pitch high with admonishment, "Do-a not be arrogant. You is *second* in class, remember? You win that chess game, hmm? What man cannot win against himself? Shows a lack of-a discipline."

Galahad grunted and sat down, now extremely exhausted. *I suppose everyone has their issues.* Even Yang, who had the *privilege* to live in the Inner Ring... Even he had his own Overgrowth to weed through. He listened to his father's whimpers, now louder than before. He wondered if the man would live and if the experience would change him. Would the fool stop his drinking? Galahad thought not. No... *He would only grow meaner.*

Galahad entered the storehouse and went upstairs with a clear bottle in his hand. He entered his father's room and sat beside him. Cambyses looked at him like a stranger. When Galahad spoke, his father sighed a sour frown. "You have been taking your skin whitener? You look like your brothers."

He had done no such thing. He did not respond to the question and asked his own. "Father, are you well?" Galahad began.

"Eat shit," Cambyses grunted meekly. "That doctor did not do a damn thing. He leave any more of those leaf things? I want some." Galahad eyed the container on his father's desk. His father coughed and his eyes swiveled up at the ceiling like a frightful doe.

"He did not. He told me it would be good if we staggered your alcohol use. Just a few glasses every hour. It'll flush out whatever is in you and get you performing normal."

"More?" His father grunted.

"I am surprised, too," Galahad formed his lie. "But doctor Yu had his reasons. He said a body like yours is too dependent on your beverage. We cannot let you go without. It will kill you."

Cambyses vomited and bleak laughter followed. "Smart man. Well then, boy?"

Galahad leaned over his father and pocketed the container of leaves. He poured his father a glass and lifted his head gently, allowing him to consume.

"You know," Cambyses grunted. "You are a decent boy." He added swiftly, "Not your brothers, but you aren't a villain."

Galahad raised his brow and looked to his side. *He only says it because he needs someone to take care of him.* "Many gratitudes, father. I am glad you think so. I will check on you in an hour and give you your medicine."

His father drifted into a restless sleep for the next hour. Galahad listened in the corridor as he murmured, "Cyrus, Darius, Yasmin." He was recounting all the people in his life, as if in a haunted dream... Galahad was never mentioned. He walked the hollow halls of the storeroom, waiting for the hour to come. After forty-five minutes, he went into his father's room and gently lifted his head.

Galahad looked down on his father. He was like an infant, and he was the mother—nursing him at the breast. *Don't think about it, just do what needs to be done and leave.* He poured a glass for his father's consumption and Cambyses took it eagerly. Galahad lifted his father's head higher so he could drink comfortably. His words grew less and less coherent, but as Galahad left for another hour, his father whispered,

"Good boy. I love you."

"I cannot say the same," Galahad replied as he gently closed his father's door.

"Good night, Cyrus," his father said.

Galahad stood there, his eyelids narrow and his eyeballs roving in thought. He would not be seeing Momed that evening. He had a long night ahead of him.

7

The House on the Hill

At least he is laughing again, Hanna smiled. Last night had been especially hard for them both. Apparently, Arthur had been having a nightmare when he suddenly shot to his feet and rushed to the window. Hanna had woken up and thought a robber was in the room. She asked him what was wrong, but he would not tell her. Arthur simply stared out the window and, after an unbearable minute, told Hanna he was sorry and to go back to bed. She had tried her best, of course—but it was hard to sleep after that. Especially because Arthur spent the next few hours in the restroom, staring into the mirror and muttering to himself.

Now in daylight, Hanna felt much better about things. *He was just having war dreams. Other wives talked about that. Nothing abnormal.*

Even with the sun shining on their feasting table, Arthur seemed preoccupied with shadowy thoughts. He had skulked all morning, staring suspiciously at his uneaten breakfast. He had not spoken at all until that Galahad sat with him. He had laughed then, but it was not the laugh she remembered. He was no longer the booming man who lit up the room. *That's okay.* She would not complain about it, especially not to him. Her husband had a right to be sad. Everyone did. It was not the worst thing, either. He still kissed her before bed. *His good humor will return in good time.*

When Hanna went to check on him, Arthur had left the table and Galahad was nowhere to be seen. She cleared the untouched plates, went to the kitchen, and left them in a dish bin. She noted her husband had tidied many cabinets and spice racks. The grills and stove tops were all scrubbed and the scent of cleaners was in the air.

Hanna did not know where her husband was in that charred and smoked room, but she knew he was cooking. He always worked more when he was stressed. She did not know whether to go find him or leave him be. He had not been able to go back to sleep last night. He had sworn and slammed the door in frustration, leaving Hanna to sleep alone.

Regardless of his mood, Hanna wanted to say good morning to her husband. If she did not, it would be hours before she spoke to him. Besides, if she let him be, there might be some uncomfortableness between them. Perhaps he felt bad about slamming the door, perhaps she felt bad about not kissing him in the morning? Hanna was resolute. "Where are you, you little curmudgeon?"

She passed an open fire grill, its flames had painted the red brick black. Ingredients were strewn haphazardly along the counters. At the grill was a man. He poked at a pan of peppers and mushrooms.

"Good morning, Wenton," Hanna smiled.

"An' you, ma'am," the bald chef tipped his chin. The man was not what Hanna might call attractive, nor were his table manners particularly refined. His food was excellent, though. He made up for his drooping eye and vulgar humor by loving his work. He cooked like a scientist measures, always attending to small and large details. Wenton was also the kind of man to make a mistake for the hell of it. He licked his fingers and tutted his tongue against the roof of his mouth, "More." He tossed shredded cheese into a pasta he was crafting.

"Is my husband working back here?" Hanna asked.

"He is, ma'am," the cook replied.

Wenton sniffed his pasta, wafting the scent into his nostrils. His loose eyeball rolled to the side. He nodded rapidly. "Good. Any more w'be a risk." After deciding the amount of cheese was sufficient, he grated up several more cubes and tossed them in without a care. He pointed toward the freezer, "Yo' husband. Saw'm with ya boy."

Hanna clicked her pen. She departed with a brief, "Thank you." She added, hastily, "Don't make that food too cheesy or when Emilia gives her puppy half of it... Well, the flatulence is frightening."

Wenton laughed. "This 'bout to be the cheesiest pasta, y'all don' even know."

As she entered the lower freezers, the temperature changed dramatically. Hanna went from sweating to shivering. She could see her breath in that subterranean glacier. Icicles with sapphire hues hung from the frozen stock. Some of the store was the innkeeper's own bounty. Other portions had been gifted by townsfolk and thankful merchants. The freezer was one of the newer additions to the inn, and one Hanna still appreciated for its novelty. It was powered by oil and gas, a most useful type of chemical. It fueled a lot of modern technologies Hanna did not have the patience to understand. Aeric told her it was like water for machines—that all the newest things at the Castle Rock used it.

She heard her son's voice echoing further down the frozen storage room. It reverberated against the ice and deepened her boy's voice. He sounded like a man.

"Let me help you with that," she heard Aeric say.

"No, I am fine," her husband replied.

"Give it here. Come on," the boy insisted.

"Get out of here," her husband went. She could see him waving his hand like a traffic conductor.

Hanna chuckled. When she had met Arthur, she was surprised by how he seemed to fight for the right to do everything. Once, she and Arthur had gone to a theatre. They had recently started dating and she was not aware of his ethic. Just as she was pulling out her purse, Arthur pushed her out of the way. Hanna had fallen into the grass as he had surged to the ticket booth, coins proudly in hand. They had laughed about it later, but Hanna was furious at the time.

Her son had acquired a similar propensity for fighting over menial labor. Hanna knew he did it out of love, as did her husband. She thought it was a good way to show affection, even if she occasionally missed the boy who would lie in her lap and laugh with her. He was almost a man, she had to remind herself. Hanna sighed and thought of all the long years her boy would work. *I wish he would relax sometimes. He is going to miss his childhood one day.*

"What are my boys doing down here?" she called out to the icicles. Frostbitten words echoed back to her,

"It's mom!" Her boy yelled, clearly caught in some machination. "Take it," her husband tried to whisper.

Her husband's hushed voice came unintelligibly back to her. A second later, they both appeared from behind a large stack of frozen pie crusts and shelves of dough. Her son was hiding something under his arms and she could tell it was hidden for her eyes only. She raised her brow interrogatingly at her husband.

"Are you plotting, Arthur Gardner?"

Her husband loosed a wicked smile. "Only a little."

She narrowed her eyes and tutted her tongue She pointed a thumb behind her and told Aeric, "Go on, honey. Your father's scheme awaits."

When their son had left, they lingered in the freezer a while longer. Hanna came close, so their rising chests touched one another and their frozen breath merged into one cloud. She spoke and the wisps of her breath obscured her husband's face. "Are you alright?"

Arthur sniffled and contemplated an answer. "No, but I'll get there. No need to worry about me." Hanna thought he believed his answer at the beginning of it, but by the end his words were riddled with disbelief and even indignation. Had she offended him?

She did not have time to question herself. Arthur drew air into his lungs. He relaxed with a long sigh, like a bow's string returning to rest. Her husband smiled at her and pinched her cheeks, the very same chubby cheeks her daughter hated having. "I'm making you muffins, special."

Hanna let out an involuntary, "Oooh," as she hugged him. Then, a joke came to her which she could not help but tell. "You're a muffin."

Arthur laughed and led her up the stairs, toward the grills, "A muffin!?" He played, his voice rising higher in pitch than it ever would for another person.

"A stale muffin," Hanna corrected herself. "Hard on the outside, complete mush on the inside."

"Don't tell anybody?" Arthur pleaded. "My mush is a closely kept secret."

She suggested, "Perhaps for a foot rub, my silence can be bought?"

Arthur shook his head. "To think, I was worried about criminals in the Overgrowth." He kissed her on the forehead. "And there were extortionists under my very roof." He pulled out a large cooking sheet and began putting the necessary ingredients for his recipe in a tidy corner, just beside the oven.

He's doing better, Hanna thought when she left the kitchens.

A winding staircase in the far corner of the main hall led to the Gardner residence. The woodworkers who had built the inn did an exceptional job, as Hanna could never hear the tavern below, even on the most raucous nights.

Her bedroom had been far too large while Arthur was away. With him back, she thought it was comfortable enough. It had soft sheets, safe walls, and silence. It was not splendidly decorated. Neither she nor her husband were ornamental people. Across her bedroom was Aeric's and beside that—Emilia's. Aeric's room was by far the biggest, as it had been Auldwine's before him.

Hanna was quick to turn Aeric's old room into the study she had always needed. The inn had a library, but it was deep underground and quite inconvenient.

Her study had shelving space for papers and notebooks, a small bookshelf for the texts she had an immediate need of, and a large desk for all the clutter she created in a day's work. A large encyclopedia mathematica was at the corner of her desk and never moved unless to be referenced. It had all the integral tables, logarithm rules, and trigonometric shortcuts if she ever forgot them. A large layer of dust had accumulated on the cover.

On the other corner of her desk, a block of wood carved into the shape of a book housed her pens, rulers, and different-sized compasses. Charles' mother gifted it to her the day they had met. Cora was the smartest person Hanna had ever known. She was stronger than Hanna and wiser than her, too. It had taken Cora only one day to show Hanna the humility no man had ever been able to.

Hanna's guilt swelled within her and she swatted it away with a fierce closing of her eyes. She had not been to see Cora in ages. *I hope Charles tells her how busy I have been.* She probably knew, already. She wrote on a piece of paper, 'See Cora,' next to several other duties. Most notes had been crossed out, though there were always more to be added.

Hanna stared at her desk and contemplated doing nothing. Once the overwhelming feeling of complacency boiled over in her, she swiped a blank piece of paper and began several calculations. The task was mostly brute multiplication as she had already created the relevant equations. Arthur had bought her a fancy calculating device which used electricity. It remained unused, resting in a box, deep in the cellar. Hanna did not believe in using a calculator when hers worked perfectly fine. After half an hour of tabulation, she had calculated and graphed the inn's expenses and meager profits up to the Autumn harvest. Nothing out of the ordinary, and a slight increase in the profit's slope after the war's end. All was in order. The taxes due to the Castle Rock would not affect them terribly.

Hanna placed down her pen and smiled at her study. She took a minute and played with several theorems. She had started reading about cosmological mathematics. She did not really like the perverse way the scientists used equations, but she could not deny the theorems were quite fun. They were full of nasty derivatives and riddled with little shortcuts one had to know. Hanna loved the challenge and it kept her busy between financial tabulations. The harder the math, the better. She opened the book on cosmology and began reading about curvatures.

Just as she reached a rather fun topic on metrics, her head began to thump.

Hanna knew what it meant. She looked at the pen longingly, inhaled, and calmly got up. She left her study and crawled dutifully into bed. Within a minute, her head was a beating of drums. The headaches occurred in the same way every time and were increasing in regularity. She would feel the thumping and heed it as a warning. Lie down or fall down.

Hanna tried to sleep, but the faintest sunlight coming through her shades made her head surge with pain. She groaned and tore at her covers. She buried her head under a pillow and pressed it down to her ears. Though the pillow was a brief respite, the headache always surged back with more strength than she could counter. *Please, Yu. Hurry up.*

He had promised to see her in the late afternoon. She turned restlessly, waiting for the doctor to arrive. She debated asking for his nephew, but Yang would be trailing after his uncle, now. Yu wanted to train him. She swiveled her eyes back and forth. The pain had travelled to her stomach and she felt the urge to vomit. Indeed, Hanna wanted to. Vomiting seemed to help. She tried to wretch. Nothing.

She wanted Arthur. *He would make it better, even if just mentally. I don't want to be alone.* She placed her sweaty hand on the nightstand beside the bed and hoisted her body upright. Her hair was a tangled mess. She grimaced and made for the door.

Just then, it opened and Emilia came running in. She leapt onto the bed and started shouting joyfully. The sound bit Hanna's ears. "Child, sugarbear," she tried. Emilia tugged at her mother's arm and stuttered, trying to catch her breath as she told her story. The girl's excitement was too much. Hanna shouted,

"Emilia!"

The girl froze. Her eyes wiggled in their sockets as they hid. Her lip quivered and she turned away in tears. Isabelle had been waiting in the corridor and followed the girl's heels.

Damn it, she cursed. Hanna forgot her pain and hurled herself to her daughter's door. It was not closed, and Emilia was holding Isabelle. The dog was licking her face while she clung to her shining black coat, petting it like a razor shaves.

"Baby," Hanna said wearily. "I'm sorry."

"It's okay," Emilia said in a rehearsed tone which told her it was *not* okay.

"No, it is not. I am sorry, sugarbear. Mama was having another headache, but she shouldn't have snapped at you."

Emilia nodded and began petting Isabelle more softly. The hound laid down and closed its eyes.

"Now," Hanna said, ignoring the sword plunging through her head. "What were you so excited about?"

Emilia's face lit up. Her smile was always a nice thing. Hanna was glad she was feeling good. It made her feel a little better, too. "Frederick was throwing stones at me again. He even convinced Wilhelm to throw one."

Her pain surged back with the tide of anger. Wilhelm was an impressionable boy. She was not surprised his demon of a cousin convinced him to do such things.

"If that fat turd laid a finger on you, I will rip it off," Hanna promised. She had choicer words for the boy's mother, that harpy. She knew fully well Frederick had been affected by his father's death, and his mother took to being a widow more than a spider on a wall. Still, Hanna had her own pain and her own family. Being an innkeeper did not mean she would stand idly by as her baby was bullied.

"He tried," Emilia confessed. She put her hands on Hanna's chest like a wave, "But then Mister Galahad showed up."

"Did he now?" Hanna was struck. Her first impression of the man was not of a protective, fatherly type.

"He said submarines blow up cargo ships, but sometimes the submarines meet a dreadnought." She roared happily at Izzy, who barked back at her.

Hanna chuckled. No doubt the Muhali had given the boys a fright. She hoped the terror stuck. "That's great, sugarbear. Where was Izzy when the boys threw their rocks?"

"Barking at them to stop," Emilia replied in a defensive tone.

This dog. Were she not seething in pain, she might have giggled. *The biggest beast in town and it thinks it is the smallest.* They had found Isabelle cowering in a garbage can. She had been no more than a month old, had a fancy collar, and was well-groomed. Aeric thought someone from the Inner Ring was unhappy with her, that she had bitten someone. Hanna told him no puppy was born vicious. *Especially not this one,* Hanna remarked as she looked at the hound, anxiously grooming her claws. Her paws were orange from how wet they always were. Emilia had seen the dog and immediately bonded with it. She played piano for Isabelle that very night. Though the girl was not very talented, Izzy loved it.

"Good girl," Hanna encouraged. Isabelle did not need to be vicious. She looked her daughter in the eye and said, "Emilia, listen to me."

The child played with her thumbs and looked away.

"Look at me, sugarbear," she smiled. Emilia looked at her.

"Bullies hurt a lot of people in their lives. But they never hurt anyone as much as themselves. Now, you go and play."

Emilia hugged her mother and beckoned for her dog, "Come on, stinkbug— let's find some sticks." They ran down the stairs far too fast to be considered safe. Hanna did not call after them. She was glad to return to her bed and to the silence. Her headache had not gotten worse or better; it simply remained.

Hanna became intimately familiar with the passage of time. She listened to the quiet ticking of the clocks, agonizing over the seconds and cheering for every new minute. Twenty minutes had elapsed when her husband came in with a smile. There was immense care in his voice.

"Darling," he said, sitting beside her. He put his hand on her leg and asked, "Headaches again?"

"Mhm," Hanna hummed. She was suddenly very tired.

"Poor baby," he said. He offered her a smile, "I brought you something." He held up a muffin in the shape of a heart, "Want to share it with me?"

"Another time," she said weakly. "What time is it?"

"An hour and a half after lunch," he replied. He stroked her eyebrow softly and his finger travelled up to her hair. He played with it and anticipated her question, "I've not seen Yu, but he should be here any moment." He added, "I'll go tell Aeric to be on the lookout and send him up."

"Thank you," Hanna said breathily. She meant it. Even the slightest love made her feel she did not suffer alone. Her pain remained. The fear did not.

He left the muffin on her nightstand, kissed her, and made sure all her sheets were properly laid on top of her. Then, noticing the light from the window—covered the drapes with his blackest clothes. After getting her a glass of water and an extra pillow, he left her with a kiss and a promise to bring the doctor. She fell asleep shortly after. When she awoke, the room was even darker.

How much time has elapsed?

Her headache had gone away for the most part. Only a slight tingle remained. There was a knock on her door and her heart fluttered with hope. *Finally.*

"Alright, let's see what we can do," Yang smiled.

She yawned and asked, "Where is your uncle?"

"Still trudging up the stairs. His lungs aren't what they used to be."

His uncle entered the room as Yang was asking her some preliminary questions. He had found a seat and pulled it toward her bed. He leaned toward her and was listening to her heartbeat with an odd utensil. "Are the headaches more localized to your forehead, or your ears?"

"Forehead," she answered.

She could sense Yu standing over his nephew. Had there been enough light, his shadow would have surely covered them both. Yang continued, "Any vomiting or nausea?"

She nodded and hummed, "Mhm." Yu was quick to ask another question,

"When you vomit, what-a color is?"

Hanna giggled with embarrassment. *These are professionals, after all.* "Uhm. Whatever color my meal was, I suppose."

Yang looked up at his uncle and they both shared a nod. Yu declared, "That is good." He clicked his tongue and said something in his own language. Yang rose obediently and let his uncle sit beside her.

Yu put his hand on her forehead and pressed. "Pain?" He asked.

Hanna was unsure how to respond. Of course it hurt. He was pressing down on her skull. "Yes," she said.

He moved his hand. "Pain?"

She nodded.

After several of the same exercises, he put his hands on his lap and said to Yang. "Always check that. If pain is local, remedy must-a be spearpoint. If general, must-a be bomb." He placed his hand on a different place.

Hanna squirmed. *That* hurt.

"Pain?" Yu asked, suspiciously.

"More than the others."

"I press again," he warned. It hurt again.

The doctor grunted and put a finger on the tip of his nose. He contemplated a few things and muttered in his own language. Finally, he asked her, "When you vomit, you feel better?"

"Every time," Hanna replied without needing to think. Vomiting was the only thing that ended her headaches prematurely. "Sometimes, I try to force myself to vomit, just to be rid of them."

Yang's eyes swiveled back and forth; he clasped his chin with his fist. When Hanna looked at Yu, the old medic was staring right through her and grasping at some thought. They both made Hanna uncomfortable. *They suspect something.* Yu slid his bottom lip under his teeth. She watched as his jaw went from left to right. *Am I dying?* She thought to ask.

"I take blood test. It take-a time. We will know after test," the doctor declared. Yu faced his nephew and began speaking as if Hanna were not there.

"I administer test. Go downstair, tell innkeeper no charge."

"Can we afford that?" Yang said quietly through his teeth.

Yu reprimanded his nephew like a man swats a fly, "We can afford to talk about-a later. In private. Go."

Yang nodded obediently. He looked at Hanna and gave his widest smile. He sighed and left expediently, as if her bedroom had been suffocating him. She looked around her at all the clutter, the mess, the darkness. Was it suffocating her? *Let's get this appointment over with. I have derivations to complete.*

Yu lit a cigarette and offered it to her. Clearly, he thought his burning plant wrapped in cheap paper would somehow make her feel relaxed. She shook her head and he nodded. Yu cleared his throat loudly and placed his hand on her shoulder. She could tell he was trying very hard to appear comforting. "Misses Cora, there are several options on the table."

"My name is not Cora and she is not married," Hanna interrupted. It took all her strength not to hit the man where he sat. As Yu apologized for forgetting her name, she spoke over him and asked, her patience wearing on her politeness, "What is wrong with me? Do you know?"

Yu looked down and avoided eye-contact with her. "I don't know."

Hanna forewent her courtesies. "It is okay not to know." Yu looked up at her and she added, "All the same, do look me in the eye when giving bad news."

"Okay," Yu acquiesced. "There are several possibilities. Few treatable, others..." Yu shook his head. "We know more soon."

8

Cora's Cottage

An ash tree's dead branches rose to greet a neighboring spruce, forming an arch. Charles' mother lived just beyond the embracing trees. He patted his mount's head.

"Good job," he encouraged. The old mare was steadfast and did just as well as any young horse. He looked past the lover's downfall. The setting sun had created a rainbow above his mother's cottage. The surging stream had dwindled after the morning rains and now only peaceful rivulets trickled beside the cabin. The aspen leaves were turning a beautiful yellow and rustled against the wind. He urged his steed along.

The bristlecone pines greeted him with their bushy bristles. Their branches looked like little green men, their arms open and welcoming. The sandstone outcrops sloped toward him. Cascading pines reached with their green hands to touch him. Charles reached out and brushed his fingertips along the foliage. He had missed the wood almost as much as his mother. Now, after years on the warfront, Cora's cottage was back in the forefront.

And in the background stood the east mountain, a wall of lichen, moss, and stone. The Wanakha called it the mountain of riddles. Charles stared up at the peak, or rather—one of many mirages. Nobody had ever summited the east. The old settlers had tried, but every time they approached a peak, another pathway opened. Every summit was illusory, every mountaintop a mirage. The mountaineers only ever found water up there. There was not a flake of gold anywhere in that riddlesome rock. The Oleander had seemed a far greater opportunity and the Pale abandoned the foggy east.

Charles averted his gaze from the mighty stone pillar. Looking at the cottage hurt his neck far less.

He thanked his horse again and dismounted. He walked along the path his mother constructed from polished river stones. The wildflowers which grew between the rocks were in their final Fall bloom. He passed the old hammock, creaking peacefully in the breeze. The aspens above shivered and donated a few leaves to the growing pile on his mother's patio. Charles jogged up the mossy steps. Despite the paint peeling off the old door, Charles noted the new shining silver shingles. *The nails aren't nudging from the gutters anymore,* Charles remarked. His mother must have been terribly bored to care about fixing those.

He took off his boots, careful not to track in dirt from outside. Many greetings flew through his head as he wondered what he would say to his mother. A nervous giddiness welled up within him. He raised his fist and knocked once. Then, he grinned and knocked in rapid succession. *She'll know it is me.*

Yet seconds became minutes and Charles began to worry. He let out a hesitant, "Mama?" Adding later, "It's Charles, I'm home."

He put his ear to the door. He listened. The hammock creaked. The rustling of the leaves became deafening and he could not home in on the silence inside. He pressed his body against the door and cupped his ear. Cicadas began to buzz. "Mama!" He shouted, starting to worry.

The door opened. A shrunken figure looked up at him.

"Ma?" Charles recoiled slightly.

His mother was not as he remembered her. Cora Eastmont's perfect black skin had wrinkled. A terrible weariness had sunken her gaze. Her pupils were dilated, her cheeks were wilted, and her lips were a faint white. Her hair was grey. Her arms were frail and boney.

"Is that...?" his mother could not finish her sentence. She fell onto her son, crying. Her sobs were like laughter, her tears flowed down onto smiling lips.

Charles was surprised by how little his mother weighed. "It's me, mama. I told you I would be back."

Some color came back to his mother and Cora gave a hoarse giggle, "So did Auldwine." She coughed and ushered her boy inside.

"You did not get my letter, then?" Charles had sent her notice of his coming.

"The postman will not come. Says it is too dangerous, now."

He was probably right about that. Charles did not tell her of his encounter in the sunken glade. He touched his mother's hand, "You're sick."

"Dying," his mother replied simply. She walked to the back of the living room, where a dining table had once sat the tiny family and their few guests. Now, the table was empty of all but reading materials and dirty dishes. She went behind the table toward the right end of the room, where wall dividers separated the kitchen from the rest of the room.

He could hear her moving wood from the log-holder. Embers crackled in the fireplace. She shuffled back into view, took the dirty dishes on the table, and disappeared once more. He heard the pots and plates land in the wash bin beside the fireplace. His mother waddled back into view and walked around the dining table. She rejoined him at the front of the cottage. A semi-circle of crimson bookcases wrapped around the first half of the living room, forming a comfortable nook. Together with a couch against one wall and a long chair against the other, the bookshelves created a room within a room. The little library was one of two in the cottage and housed all of Cora's books.

His mother cleared a mountain of blankets from the couch. A bucket had been laid beside the sofa. Cora strained to lift it.

"Let me carry that," he offered. *She can't be that sick.* Charles decided she must be getting an autumnal cold.

"I will not make you carry your mother's vomit."

Vomit, the word echoed in his ears. He swallowed. Charles watched as she moved. Her hand slipped on the door handle. She set down the bucket and used her shirt to grip the metal. She got the door ajar and used her foot to cumbersomely open the way. Then, she hobbled with her heavy bucket toward the end of the patio. Finally, his mother tossed out the bucket's contents and lumbered back to the couch.

She pulled the long chair toward the couch and hoisted her legs onto it. Cora Eastmont let out a rasping sigh. Her chest rose slowly and mechanically, each breath louder and more laborious than the last. Charles struggled with the sight, unsure of what to do. *You can't be dying*, he kept thinking. The war was over. *Mama can't be dying.* He looked out the dirty window beyond Cora, where the cicadas seemed to mock him with their chatter.

"Awfully quiet for someone who has years of catching up to do," Came Cora's wispy voice.

"I can't be bothered with small talk when you are like this." Charles turned and walked into his mother's bedroom. A chest of letters was open and many papers were scattered throughout the room. Old newspapers were underlined and ripped up, jars of paste were messily thrown atop fallen waste bins. His old books and Auldwine's journals were heaped in a prominent stack. Her red bed was as wilted as the Fall flowers, its canopy sinking low like a valley. He asked from her room, "What medications are you taking?"

"No medication for this," she yawned. "Baby, come keep your mother company. It is not small talk I want."

Charles went around the dining table, passing the ornamental divider and into a small, neatly organized kitchen. He opened the myriad cupboards, darting to every crevice in the cottage for some salve. "Mama, you need help. Do you need pain medication?"

His mother's voice was a whisper. Charles heard the strain in her voice and the quavering weakness in her chest. "I haven't heard… your voice in five years. That is… all the pain medication I want. You."

Charles nodded solemnly. He closed the cupboards and poured her a glass of water. He set the glass close to her and looked around, unsure of what to say in such a foreign place. He glanced at the grand violet rug below him. It was smudged with dirt. He looked up and through the window which was similarly stained. He could hardly see through the glass.

"How is Hanna?" His mother let out a sigh, "I have not been to see her." She motioned for the water. It was just out of reach, on the edge of the coffee table. She winced and pulled back to the couch.

Charles rushed to give her the glass. His mother opened her mouth slightly and a trickle of water made it into her mouth. The rest pooled onto her lap. He took the glass from her shaking hands and gently set it aside.

He tried to brighten his tone, "She feels bad about not seeing you." He felt like he was talking to a child, not the strongest woman he had known, the mother who had raised him from an unwanted pregnancy. *She should have come.* He looked at his mother's old, drooping face. *Hanna should have come.*

"She was busy taking care of the war's wounded," Cora coughed. "What else? How is Isabelle?"

You are just as wounded. "A perfect complement to Emilia I think."

His mother hummed her approval. "That dog can read emotions better than I can read books." She turned over. Charles could tell she was hiding a spasm of pain from him. A horrible shiver came and shook her body from foot to head. She fell forward and vomited into the bucket. She wiped her mouth. "Oh, this is not how I wished to see you home. I must prepare you a roast."

How can she be thinking of me? Charles shook his head, "No, mama. I'll be taking care of you now."

"I suppose," she breathed deeply, smirking, "I cannot contest you."

Her smile was as hard to bear as her cough. *She can hardly raise her cheeks.* "That's right," Charles smirked back.

"What of the Gardner men? I worry about Aeric."

Charles stared at his mother, the outline of her skull was far too prominent for his liking. There was hardly any skin surrounding it. Her entire body was more skeleton than flesh. *She looks dead already,* he could not stop himself from thinking. A chill went through his spine. He grimaced like he had stubbed his toe and bit down on his lip. He shook off the chill and wrapped his mother in yet another blanket. "Takes after his father. I hear he is quick to fight. More than his uncle ever was."

"Auldwine was one in a million," his mother said. She laughed mockingly, hacking a glob of phlegm into her waste bucket. "That bumbling idiot." She looked at him and raised her brow knowingly. For a moment, Charles saw the same roving wisdom he had grown up with. With few words, she always said a hundred. "And the innkeeper?" Arthur's new title did not slip easily off her dry tongue.

Charles tried to answer with humor, "I don't think he likes his promotion." His smirk was short-lived. "I think he wishes he were the one to have died."

"So do we all," his mother said nostalgically. She sounded almost happy.

Charles hated hearing his mother say such things. He hated himself for being away. "I should never have gone to war."

"Stop that," his mother swatted his arm. "You cannot solve suffering with hypotheticals. That is only self-hatred I hear. I need you to be happy."

"How?" Charles asked. A knot was forming around his chest but try as he might to untie it, the feeling in his gut was pure emptiness.

"You can start by eating," his mother encouraged. She pointed a wrinkled finger toward the kitchen. A stove-pot waited above the fireplace.

If she can smile, I can. Charles nodded and went to the pot. *She needs me to be happy. Be happy, then.* He blinked at his mother as he tried to appear joyful.

"Are you still struggling to defecate?" his mother asked. "Plenty of fiber in that soup. Eat up."

"Mama," he rolled his eyes. "Only dictionaries defecate in normal conversations. My poops are fine."

"I hate normal conversations," his mother folded her arms.

Charles was happy to hear it. *Still herself.* He noticed a dripping noise and investigated the wash basin. He opened the cabinet door beneath it and saw the problem. The grey-water pipes had corroded. A small leak had created a larger puddle. *Certainly no deluge,* Charles nodded positively. *Nothing I cannot fix.* Charles tried to pinpoint the puncture in the metal. He probed his finger along the pipe. "How long has this leak been here, mama?"

"There's is always something leaking here, baby. Don't lose sleep over it."

Charles made a note to fix the leak before going to bed. "Who replaced the roof?"

"I did," his mother admitted proudly.

"Had you ever replaced rotten wood before?"

Not a second passed. "My whole life has been a changing of rotten wood... I can learn from Auldwine's books, same as he could."

"Well," Charles clapped his hands. "You impressed me." He took out a small wooden bowl and a copper spoon. He filled a meager ration into his bowl. He ate standing while his mother continued.

"All is well at the inn, then?"

Charles understood why she was asking. "Hanna did a fine job managing it. Arthur has a solid foundation." He slurped a spoonful, "Wants me to tend to Auldwine's grove."

"Ah," his mother seemed happy at the suggestion. "Innkeeper of the forests." She eyed her son and hummed, "Mhm." She wiggled her pointer finger toward the ceiling, "A fine choice, too. Arthur was never the kind of boy to play in the dirt. He was happier laughing and fighting. When do you plan to start?"

"Start?" Charles reiterated. The question startled him.

"Proceed to begin," Cora's eyes met his own, "Go, shove off, commence." All sickness left her as she stared with one brow raised. "Antonymous with end."

His eye twitched, "I didn't accept. And now... Of course I am not starting." He stopped eating and paced over to her. He approached with a smile and she waved him off. She sat up and looked at him as if he had just offended her. She stared at her boy in disbelief before humming a brief *uh-uh*.

"You have to live your own life."

Charles gulped. He went to the fireplace and rotated a burning log, briefly rekindling the fire. "You gave me life. I don't want to abandon you."

Cora scoffed. "Auldwine abandoned me." She wheezed, struggling to make her point. She slammed her fist down onto the arm of the couch with as much strength as her feebleness allowed. "A son living his life is not abandonment. That is natural."

Charles stuttered, unsure if he was angry or sad. He got up from the charcoal fire, casting his shadow on his mother in the process. "But I cannot... You're sick!"

"For now," she smiled.

"Exactly," her son said confidently, pacing back and forth with his hand upon his chin. *I can fix this.*

Cora patted the seat beside her. "Sit with me, baby." Charles obeyed. She welcomed him into her arms and hugged him. Kissing his forehead, she then stretched and cracked her knuckles. His mother gestured toward her bedroom. "You saw my mess in there?"

Charles nodded.

"I got sick a few months ago. Around the time the mailman started saying things were dangerous." She trailed off, seeming to forget what she was saying. A minute passed before she looked back at her son with a frown. "It started with a headache here or there. Before I knew it, I was too weak to walk."

Charles nodded, taking in the story.

"I did what Auldwine would do. Or you," her voice was faint but proud. "I researched all the viruses native to the region, all the diseases." His mother let out a gravelly cough. "Too fast," she reprimanded herself. She raised a finger to her son and stared at the ceiling. Then, she dry-heaved. Cora wiped her mouth and giggled at her dirty reflection in the window.

Charles shook his head, denying his mother's sickness. Cora had never shown pain. She had never even cried, not in all his years. His mother was the antithesis of pain, the opposite of suffering. And yet, when his mother spoke, Charles heard agony.

"Despite all my research, nothing fit. By the time I realized I needed a professional, the tremors began."

"Well," Charles began, "Cottonwood's riverways contain numerous bacteriophages. They specialize in attacking diseases. Your illness cannot be bacterial."

A light twinkled in his mother's eyes. "A well-made word," she declared. His mother loved words and their meanings. "An assassin of bacteria."

A hundred hypotheses swirled. Charles posited, "Have you checked my textbooks?"

"Every one of them," his mother's feigned positivity cracked under a tone of woe. "The descriptions do not fit. They say aspen cannot grow tall at this altitude, yet here they are. They say bacteriophages inhabit the rivulets, but I recall blue algal blooms last spring." His mother sighed, "So, I gave up."

"What are you saying?" Charles turned.

"I lived a good life."

"And you will continue to live one," Charles' voice rose. He could hear the selfishness in his voice. He did not care. *She just needs some care. Some good herbal teas.*

"Baby, I have tried to fight. Now, I want to rest, to see old friends."

"But—" Charles stopped himself. He recalled the years of playing with Auldwine in the garden, of Arthur fighting anyone who dared make fun of him. *He was always so much smaller than me, too.* His mother was in every memory. He looked at her now, without her youth, her Auldwine, nor even the will to live. Had she become a shell where once Cora Eastmont resided? "Mama," his voice cracked.

"Quiet, my sweet son." She smiled and felt the stubble on his chin.

Charles faced away.

His mother made him look at her, "The day is not today." Her eyes sockets were hollowed, her eyes were bloodshot. The color had not faded from her pupils, though. Her beautiful blue eyes still shined as they always had.

I have her eyes, Charles remembered. The thought made him happier, albeit briefly.

Cora went on, "Let's relax. I have enough life in me for that. Get a blanket and some old newspapers... We'll laugh at the stupidity of the common word."

Charles wiped his tears and chuckled. "Okay, mama. Whatever you want."

Hours passed as the Eastmonts talked. Charles learned his mother had quit smoking recently. With the post halted and her condition worsening, it was just too inconvenient. He learned also that most crofters had moved away following the war. That saddened him, as the crofters were the closest things to neighbors the Eastmonts had.

"And the rains have not been as regular," his mother continued.

"As in they are not coming at the same times, or—"

Cora interrupted him excitedly. "Some days, it doesn't rain at all!"

In any other part of the world, that would not have been news. In Cottonwood, specifically at the base of the mountain of riddles, it was quite strange. "We always get an afternoon shower," he remarked.

Cora pressed her lips together and looked at him knowingly. "Mmm," she hummed, shaking her head. Before silence had a chance to voice its opinion, his mother was already onto another topic. She seemed rejuvenated by simply talking to someone.

"Oh, I miss Hanna."

Charles shuffled in his seat, "Me too."

Cora turned and smiled at him sadly. Then, she rubbed her hands together as if beside the fire. "I remember the letter you wrote after you first met her."

Charles pretended he did not. "Oh yeah?"

Cora saw past his façade. "Said she was stubborn, arrogant, and too smart for her own good."

"I did not," Charles rebuked.

His mother smirked at him. "No, you did not." Like Yang playing a game of chess, she asked a question and put him in check. "And what *did* you say in your first letter? Do you remember?"

Charles knew perfectly well. Still, he did not see the point in bringing it up. He had only just met the woman and was positively stupid with youth. "Not very well," he lied. "I remember saying I liked her."

"*She is wildly smart,*" his mother quoted from memory. "*Somewhat arrogant and not really a family type—but she is so much like you. Nothing gets past her. She can turn your words against you or make a casual slip a hilarious joke.*" Cora continued, "*I am so immobilized when I am—*"

Charles could not bear to hear anymore. "Mama, please—that was a long time ago. And Arthur would not appreciate us talking about his wife like that. Nor would Hanna, I'd wager." His heart pounded with embarrassment. He stared at his feet and awaited something less improper and childish to talk about.

"Well," Cora folded her arms, "You have always been a bad gambler." Before her son could get offended, she raised her arms in surrender, "Alright, Alright. I just love the girl, that is all."

Charles smiled. "I know you do." He took a deep breath and relaxed his posture. He leaned back on the couch, closed his eyes, and thought about the leak he would have to fix tonight. *I must do it tonight. A little problem can be a big one if left unrepaired.*

"But do you know that *you* do?" Cora asked. Knowing she had disarmed her son by waiting just the right amount of time before pursuing the topic, she continued, "Charles, a lie is the most vulgar when to oneself."

Charles wished she would just stop. Even after Arthur's wedding, Cora would pester Charles with little questions of this sort. Not even the birth of Aeric had deterred her. For some idiotic reason, she assumed her son had latent feelings for Hanna. *Entirely detestable, improper, and vulgar. To even suggest it.* He began to form his argument, thinking, *Come on, mama, you of all people should know—*

Cora saw where the conversation was going. She let the topic fade and put her feet on the coffee table. "Forget I said anything. Did you hear Buchanan Bavar sold the old fort?"

Charles abandoned his argument and said, after a sigh of relief, "I did. To some Castle Rocker."

They began to talk about all the folk they hardly knew. His mother filled him in on the happenings of town; Charles filled her in on the happenings of the nation. As the night wore on, they each took to reading. Charles glanced at his mother and smiled. They had each leaned back onto the sofa, lifted their feet onto the long chair, and crossed the right foot over their left. When they turned a page, they licked their fingertips. It was quite easy to tell when the other read something which resonated with them, as they would grunt an approving 'hm.'

"Oooh," his mother pointed at the paper.

Charles looked up from his book, a dissertation on transalpine diseases. He squinted toward his mother's finger. He was too far to observe the fine print.

"They capitalize 'Western Mountain' in the first paragraph. Then, look here. They don't capitalize 'eastern mountain.'"

Charles shrugged, underlining a stopping point. "Maybe the writer forgot the standardization of capitalization?"

His mother yawned, "Oh sure." Her throat closed and made a sound like the creaking of a door. She spat into her bucket and wiped her lips. "It is why no one else has bothered with the east. No profit in it."

She pointed at Charles' journal. "That research is old. I read it, too."

"The scientists conducted the experiments only a decade ago," Charles reminded his mother.

"They cite forests that do not exist anymore." His mother yawned again, "The ash groves of southern Cottonwood were decimated by emerald beetles eight years ago. I remember Auldwine going on about it quite well."

Likewise. Charles eyed the paper in his hand. *Curious.* He closed the book and stretched. "Do you need anything before I go to bed, mama?"

His mother yawned again. "You are home," her voice was an empty gust of wind, hardly audible. "That should suffice." She tried to get up and hug her son, but Charles rushed over and urged her down. He fluffed her pillows and made sure her blankets were just the way she liked them—piled in a multitude of layers.

"Good night," Charles smiled at his mother, wrapped up like a caterpillar in a cocoon. He turned toward his old bedroom, parallel to his mother's.

"Charles," his mother stopped him.

"What is it, mama? Water?"

"Sure," his mother agreed. "But... I just want to say you were the greatest joy of my life."

Charles' mouth opened and closed. He felt sad, but mostly he felt grateful. He briefly squinted at the wall, as if blinded by a light. Then, he scratched the back of his neck and said with a tremble in his voice. "You did not have to raise me. You could have abandoned me and nobody would have spited you."

Cora waved her hand in dismissal. "The vulgar euphemize rape with *malchance...*" She smiled up at her son with pride. "But no mother could have had as fine of luck as I did with you. You were worth everything."

"I hope my own children can say the same things about me," Charles admitted. Lately, he had questioned whether he would have any children. *Or for that matter, a wife.*

"They will," Cora said with surety. "And more."

Charles went to bed that night and dreamt of nothing horrible. It was a nice change. Instead, his dreams were as ordinary as life. In them, the Gardners were playing. Arthur was dancing with Hanna and Auldwine was helping his mother recover. Spring was in full bloom and all were running freely amongst the growth. No clouds were in the sky, no shadows formed. All his friends, all he had loved—all were content and happy. Yet Charles was not among them. He thought perhaps Auldwine was searching for him, or he was searching for Auldwine. Yet, he was not worried. He watched over them all, happily.

9
Toppled Stones

"Are you sure you can handle things?" Arthur asked her yet again. *He did not think she could handle things.*

"Quite sure, love." *I saw a doctor, not a mortician.* Ever since Yu ordered more tests, her husband had been treating her differently. In some ways, it was quite nice. Arthur came in every morning with breakfast, tea, coffee, or anything else she wanted. He massaged her feet at night and if her back was sore, that too. He always had soothing words to say.

"Okay," Arthur frowned. "Promise me you won't leave today? You should stay by your bed until we know what the headaches are."

Hanna's mouth moved left and right, up and down. She did not want to be treated like a child. Still, all her protests seemed childish. Arthur was right and Hanna knew if she argued it would only be for argument's sake. Finally, she had to admit he was right and promised, "You don't have to worry."

He did not seem to hear her. Her husband had not slept last night, nor the night before. He was always so tired, now. Hanna wanted him to at least *try* to sleep, even if it meant tossing and turning for a few hours. She looked at the bandage around his hand and then kissed his cheek. "It is you who had better worry, taking walks in the middle of the night."

"I'd rather have a scrape than a nightmare," Arthur grunted in his I-am-done-talking voice.

"Well it was a mighty large scrape," Hanna reminded him.

"Yes," Arthur agreed, investigating the hand. "I would tell you how it happened, but I cannot remember."

"Because you've not slept in two days."

"Because it was dark." He was fixated on his hand now. "Couldn't see a thing." He whispered, "Not a damn thing." Arthur raised his brow, "Have you noted any wild animals in the Inner Ring of late?"

Hanna smirked, "Do drunks count?" She thought his question odd, "Why?"

"Nothing, nothing." Arthur hiccupped. "Galahad wanted to know."

"He should worry more about his father than wild animals," Hanna yawned.

"One and the same," Arthur yawned in reply.

The innkeeper was dressed in all black. Her husband assumed it was respectful to dress in mourning colors preemptively. Hanna thought it more disrespectful to assume someone was already dead, although she kept her comments to herself. Besides, she did not very much care about Cambyses. Sure, he was a citizen of the town and by rights deserved a bed and food at her inn. That did not mean she had to weep at his passing, though. In the end, she thought Cambyses had earned a fitting comeuppance. *He is succumbing to the same disease he profited off for years.*

"Galahad has been trapped there for a week, like a fly in a web," Arthur cleared his throat and went to the closet. He began scouring the mess he had created. His eyes had grown worse with age, and a far-off lamp was little help for him.

"Take him a biscuit," Hanna replied.

"You sound like his mother," Arthur grunted a laugh.

"I am everyone's mother depending on the day," Hanna frowned. She had not always been so maternal and remembered the days when all she cared about was herself. Those were easier days, but lonely, too.

Arthur's boot thudded onto the wood. He strapped a leather binding across it and tied them tightly. He lingered with his back bent, sighing, "I told Emilia where I am going."

Hanna lied, "I think that's for the best." *She is already worrying about me, you bumbling...* Hanna laid down, conscious of her headaches and wary one might come at any moment. She figured stress was the last thing her head needed.

"I think so, too," he stood up. "She can't hide from death all her life."

Hanna did not feel like arguing with him. Emilia grew up in the Great War's shadow. Many soldiers had been saved under her roof. Many more had died. Shivering last breaths and shrieking soldiers were her nursery rhymes. "She grew up in a war hospital. She could not hide if she wanted to."

"All the same," Arthur persisted in his I-am-the-man voice, "The war is over. The inn is back to normal."

Her daughter's idea of a normal inn *was* as a house of death. Her childhood was stolen from her the moment the first stretchers came through the door. Tranquil evenings were as foreign to her as Muhal to Auberdine. Her youthful imagination was tainted by all the horrific things she had lived through. *She is just a little girl,* she mourned. *That poor, poor baby.* Hanna scratched her eyebrow, "How is she?"

"Last I checked, she was asleep with her arm around the dog."

If Arthur shared her worry, he was hiding the emotion well. He was unperturbed by Emilia's anxiety. *He thinks this is normal.* The thought saddened her even more. Her husband could not remember a time when their daughter was not tormented. How could he? *She was only two when he went away. Not even she remembers, so young as she was.*

"Alright, I'm going to go," he declared, hastily going toward the door.

Hanna's back cracked as she rose, reluctant to start her day. She would rather lay in bed with him and not attend to anyone or anything. That was not her fate. She called after her scrambling husband, "You come back here, Arthur Gardner." She pointed a finger down at the bed demandingly. He smiled and bowed his head. He waddled over and leaned into her arms.

She kissed him on the forehead, both cheeks, and on the lips. Then, she sent him off, "Bring some breakfast for Galahad."

"He won't eat it," his voice carried from the corridor.

"You better make him eat," she called after him. *His father has been dying for over a week now. I bet he is exhausted.* Yang had seen Cambyses twice, once with his uncle and once without. Both times, he had told Galahad his father needed rest and water. Still, the old drunkard refused to live. Yang thought it might be liver failure.

But Yang thinks a great many things, she frowned. Yu had assumed a 'dignified' silence on the matter of her headaches, insisting it was not proper to theorize before knowing more from her blood test. She had no patience for proper and sought out Yang. He had stuttered his rebuttals to no avail. After five minutes of harassment, begging, and cajoling, the young doctor had bowed to her wishes. He told her all his theories.

Hanna sat on her bed, contemplating. Breakfast was already on the table. Wenton had the orphans helping him in the kitchens now and by all his accounts— Dixon was a fantastic baker. The others were relatively useless, as Wenton put so delicately. "Bu' they wash dishes nice," he had smiled.

Food is prepared, taxes are calculated... Hanna had several hours to spare. Though she wanted to put pen to paper and solve a few problems, she was afraid the strain would send her into another fit. So, she left the bedroom and descended the winding staircase. The tavern was quiet and only a murmur of ambient talk could be heard. Most had already eaten. She scoured the table for her children. She found Aeric wiping up the guests' leavings. He was sweating profusely.

"Aeric, have you taken a break?"

"I was going to take one, but then I realized this part of the table needed cleaning, so I'm going to finish this before."

"My sweet boy," Hanna shook her head. "You have been working since before dawn. Look at you, all you clean is wet with sweat. Sit down."

Aeric argued, irritation mixing with a child's pleading. "Not yet, mom."

Other children beg to play with friends and stay out into the morning. Not Aeric. He did not play and he seemed to scorn children who did. She had thought perhaps he would take to being an older brother for the orphans. Instead, he was their sergeant.

"You are just like your father," Hanna told him. Aeric smiled at that. She added, "How badly do you want bags under your eyes?"

Aeric frowned, "They mean he is a hard worker. They are an admirable blemish."

Hanna used his own words against him, "If you faint onto my feasting table, *you* will be an admirable blemish."

Aeric chuckled, took out one of many rags stored in his back pocket, and wiped his brow. Her son continued the conversation. "Josephine tried to stuff Virginia's head in the oven this morning."

"I am glad she only tried," Hanna shrugged. "Have you been talking with Lorne?"

"No, he is boring. All he likes are automobiles and machines."

And all you like is work. "What about Quenby?"

"He is a stupid child. I caught him in the kitchens with his hands in his pants. Wenton roasted him like a pig for that." Aeric finished scrubbing the table cand put the dirty rag in his back pocket. "Dixon is nice. Quiet, but a hard worker."

"That's good," Hanna smiled. *It is like I am staring at Arthur in his youth.* Aeric, like his father, worked as a shark swims. If he ever stopped moving, Hanna was sure the boy would die. Curtly, she commanded, "Take your break or I will disown you."

"It doesn't make sense to take it *now*," he began. "I am already down here. I should give the chairs some varnish, perhaps a good dusting." He interrupted her before she could say no. He blurted, "Miss Vellencourt is coming. Can't risk offending her, right? Not one as wealthy as her?"

Damn, he is clever. Lilian Vellencourt was a widow of a Castle Rock aristocrat and a philanthropist of high regard. By common reckoning, she was the wealthiest person in the town. She had requested a meeting to discuss important matters. Hanna acquiesced, "Alright, take your break at the table. Then you won't have to walk back." She left her son to his work. If he enjoyed labor, then more power to him. *A strange hobby for a child, but it is better than what other boys his age are doing. At least he is not committing crime.*

Hanna Gardner left the inn and walked the groves. The trees had grown tall since Arthur's brother planted them. So many years untended, branches were beginning to creep above the house. Should a winter snow come, the branches might crack and crash onto the roof. Hanna had tried her best to maintain the grove, but there was always something new growing. She was nowhere near as skilled as Auldwine, nor as knowledgeable as Charles. She frowned at a growth of saplings encircling a larger forebear. They were like grasping hands and no matter how much Hanna worked through spring and summer, they kept coming. *I wish Charles had taken over here. This place needs a pruning.* Her attention turned toward a dead cottonwood with white, skeletal bark. Nothing had grown on the tree in several years. Hanna often saw her husband standing pensively under its bones.

The grove rustled and leaves flew in front of her face.

Since Yang had told Hanna of all his theories, she had made it her priority to understand each and every one of them. She went to the cellars and combed the deep libraries under the Hill, finding anything relevant to the possible afflictions. She brought them to her study and had devoured their knowledge. Still, she wanted to know more. It felt good to study. Knowing about her potential ailments made her feel like she was actively fighting them. It was all she could do to stay sane. Yu had given her an estimate of a few weeks before he knew conclusively. The days of waiting were becoming the longest of her life.

There were some diseases and afflictions Hanna worried about more and had thus studied more rigorously. Trench Rot scared her at first, but Yu had quickly ruled it out as the likely candidate. The disease had recently been discovered and only seemed to spread to soldiers in the Tanglewood.

Hanna was not worried about *that* sickness. Dehydration did not seem to be a likely candidate, as she had tested the theory by drinking as much water as her stomach would tolerate. The headaches persisted. Yang had also told her of a certain parasitic fungus which had a penchant for attaching to the head. It would wriggle into the parts of the brain controlling memory and make you lose your head! Hanna shivered. The idea of a parasite draining her body caused her skin to crawl. *Most unpleasant,* she told herself.

She looked off at the Inner Ring. The neighborhood of the wealthy was prettiest when the Overgrowth was its backdrop. Up close, she found the beauty diminished. Hanna felt a tickle of wind against her scalp and immediately thought a headache was budding. She began to sweat in anticipation. A minute passed and nothing came of the tingle. *Just the winds,* she smiled with relief.

Yang's fear was her heart had a defect. When she asked him how the heart could give the head an ache, he replied the body was not a sum of disconnected parts. Apparently, she might have a rare condition of circulatory failure in which one of the heart's pumps has only two valves instead of three.

Yu had added to his nephew's hypothesizing, begrudgingly, "It-a goes unnoticed by most who have. When it fail, usually fatal."

Of all the possible afflictions, a terminal heart condition scared her the most.

Yang was quick to point out such cases were rare. He added, "I know someone at the university who has the condition. He was fixed by a new procedure the surgeons are pioneering."

That had made Hanna feel better. Then, his uncle reminded them both, "Most pioneer die."

That had made her feel worse. Yang insisted defiantly, "Still, the man is a modern invention."

"Probably has some modern side effect." His gravelly voice came to a crescendo. "He'll be dead at twenty-five."

"Fifty," Yang asserted.

At that, Hanna had stopped them. She would like to live to see her grandchildren, thank you very much. They had both promised she would, yet their bickering had only annoyed her.

Hanna looked at the grove and admired the autumn beauty. The trees knew Fall was upon them. The leaves were various shades of red and orange. The House on the Hill was awash in the colors of the setting sun. Time escaped Hanna. Trees, hills, mountains, and towns—she stared at them all and thought about her headaches. Everything seemed to take on new meaning now that she had a health condition.

Before long, she found herself sitting alone at the petrified table. Arthur was not present. She caught herself repeatedly playing with loose skin around her fingernails. She swatted away the nervous tendency and tried to remain calm and dignified. Her husband was the one Lilian Vellencourt requested. Hanna hoped her presence would suffice.

"Mama," a groggy voice came from behind her.

She's slept all day, Hanna realized. She patted the seat beside her, reserved for Arthur. Her daughter climbed onto the tall seat, her feet swaying from the heights of the chair. The edge of her lips was red from how often she had been licking them.

"Sugarbear," she frowned, "What did I say about licking your lips?"

Emilia bowed her head. She whispered, "I don't even realize I am doing it."

Hanna felt her peeled cuticles. She scooted closer to Emilia, wrapping her arms around the girl. "What is it, sugarbear?"

Emilia looked at her without saying a word. Hanna could tell she wanted to talk. Emilia would come to her often to ask her about a fear she was having, only to be unable to speak of the terror. Emilia opened up her arms. Hanna smiled. "Oh, come here," she said, setting her daughter on her lap. *She is getting big.*

She knew soon Emilia would be too old to sit on her lap and made a deliberate note to relish the affection. Aeric had taught her a mother's love could be ignored or even spited, that a child's love changes form as they age. She knew it was foolish to think Emilia would turn out any different. Nevertheless, she kissed her daughter's forehead, ran her fingers through her hair, and hoped Emilia would seek her advice for many years to come.

"Mama," she squeaked, her voice muted as she buried it in Hanna's shirt. "Are you going to die?"

"Of course not," Hanna replied immediately.

"Galahad's daddy is dying," Emilia pointed out.

Hanna could not simply say everyone would die. Emilia knew as much. Hanna held Emilia closer, unsure of what to say to her child. *I wish you were ignorant of all these nasty things...* For a time, they just sat in silence. The only noise was Aeric ordering the orphans around. Occasionally, Isabelle would lick herself and rearrange, letting out a staccato sigh.

"I don't want to lose you," Emilia's voice cracked. Hanna had heard that crack hundreds of times. Her baby was going to cry now.

"You won't lose me," Hanna fought her own emotions. She had to be strong. "Everybody gets headaches, right?"

"But... You saw a doctor for yours," Emilia looked up at her. The whites of her eyes were reddening and her cheeks had left a wet spot on Hanna's clothes.

"Sometimes, daddy and I will need to see doctors. We have to see if our bodies are working well. That's all."

"I don't believe you," Emilia declared. "The men who came here saw lots of doctors and they died."

"Those were soldiers, sugarbear," Hanna reminded her daughter.

Emilia gestured to be put down and Hanna helped the girl to her seat. She sat down and looked at Isabelle while she cycled through her mind. She put a hand on Isabelle and the hound looked up at her, coughing slightly. Her daughter always felt better when she sat with her dog for a moment. Emilia rubbed a finger across Isabelle's snout.

Meanwhile, Hanna listened to Aeric ordering the other orphans about the kitchens. He roared, "Quenby, I swear I will serve you to the guests if I find—"

Emilia interrupted the echoes of her brother. The work in the kitchen was muted the moment her daughter decided to speak again. "They say there is not enough food. That the war took our harvest."

"Who said that?" Hanna asked, already accusing several gossipers in her mind. There were always a few doomsayers at wintertime. Emilia ignored her for another question,

"Are they right?"

Hanna had to be tactful. Emilia's mind was a nasty web of fears.

"Is that why daddy is gone again?" Emilia persisted, "So we have enough food?"

Hanna wanted to squeeze her daughter until all her shadows oozed out of her like puss from a pimple. "No," she replied. "Your father is helping Galahad. You know that. He is not going away again." Before she could console her further, her daughter cried,

"Promise?"

"Promise." Hanna knew what made *her* anxieties go away, though her logic and emotions were not her daughter's, nor were they the town's views. She could not just talk about probabilities, infinitesimals, and other mathematical truths. Nevertheless, Hanna would not leave her daughter with idle comforts. She tried to explain what she knew to the child of eight, careful not to use any jargon she would have to explain.

"Do you remember the stories of the last Adawakan?"

"Niwot," Emilia half-smiled. She loved being right, as all children do.

"That's right," Hanna beamed. She swept out her arms like she was swimming and declared, "His wife and his child built the first inn on this hill. And why this hill? Because it is the precise point where the Oleander's snowmelt and the east mountain's rainwater meet. We have the richest soil for hundreds of miles. Too rich, I'd say. Perhaps only the Golden River is more suited for growing food."

Emilia was unconvinced. "What about floods? The Overgrowth was like the Inner Ring until a flood."

I wish Aeric had spared you the gruesome aspects of our history. She was not wrong and Hanna dared not lie to her. Emilia knew when she was right. The Overgrowth had been as palatial as the Inner Ring. When the miner's deluge swept down from the Oleander, the lowlands were destroyed and never rebuilt. Hanna tried to explain, "The Oleander floods and every time it does, the Hill grows in size. The first inn was small. After the deluge, all the dirt and debris made the Hill huge, and the inn with it."

Emilia licked the circumference of her lips. She stared at the empty table and glanced nervously at the door. "What if another flood comes and everyone has to live with us? What about goblins? People say they will rob us if they get the chance."

Hanna had to be stern. She shook her head, lovingly, "Oh, sweet sugarbear. Don't use that word."

"Why?"

"Because it is not the proper name to give a neighbor. You wouldn't call Miss Cora a goblin, would you? Or Charles, malchance?"

Emilia fidgeted, her eyes roving up and down. She stated curiously, plucking a memory from her mind, "Miss Cora told me words have too many definitions to be truthful... That if she struggled over every word as she should, she would never write down her name."

Hanna chuckled silently. *She remembers everything.* "Fair enough," Hanna forfeited. *I'll have to tell Cora she's making a linguist out of Emilia. She will love that.* She redirected her line of questioning. "Aren't people scared of your Izzy?"

"No," Emilia answered, shocked at the suggestion. The large hound drank from her water bowl, soaking the wood with droplets. Ever too quick to swallow, the hound began to cough. She walked over to the two Gardner girls and sat between them. She coughed once and looked up at Hanna with amber eyes. After a moment, the hound dove her head under Hanna's hand, forcing a pet.

"You drink too fast," Emilia scowled and smiled.

"Well," Hanna continued telling her daughter, "I know a few people who are scared of Izzy."

"She's *just* big," Emilia argued emphatically.

"She isn't mean, is she?" Hanna asked.

Emilia shook her head vehemently, "They think she is. But she only eats, poops, and kisses." Isabelle gave the girl a lick on the hand, demanding a pet. Emilia ignored Isabelle's wet nose when the hound begged for another cuddle.

Hanna placed her hand on the hound's neck and stroked her fur. She leaned toward Emilia and smiled. "Most people are like Izzy."

Emilia shrugged. Like a stone, she sat in thought. Then, finally—she frowned and nodded. "You're right... I'm still scared."

Hanna nodded solemnly. Emilia was a young child and as strong as any her age could be. "When I was your age, I did not fear death." She remembered, "I did not fear anything. I was arrogant. Your mother," She had to laugh at herself. "Thought she was invincible."

"Nobody is invincible, though," Hanna continued. She forced a laugh, hoping her humor would bring a smile to Emilia's face. "I feared nothing and you fear..."

She wanted to say *everything* but thought that might sound accusatory. She substituted, "What is rightfully feared."

"You don't think I am crazy?" Emilia's eyes were like Isabelle's, wide and wanting.

"Everybody has their own crazy to deal with, sugarbear. You are as normal as the next person."

Some self-confidence seemed to be restored because she looked down at Isabelle and said determinedly, "Izzy, let's go outside." She went to run and crossed the kitchen doors just as Josephine and Virginia were running into the tavern. Virginia was shrieking wildly as Josephine chased her, both giggling fiercely. Virginia circled the tavern's mighty pillars, hoping to lose her pursuer. Josephine taunted her, close behind. Virginia broke from the pillars and darted across the open tavern. The two girls nearly collided with Isabelle. They stared at Emilia.

Her daughter stared at the girls, both younger than her.

"Do you want to chase with us?" Josephine asked, swaying unsteadily.

Emilia froze and looked at her mother and then at the hound. She shook her head wildly and ran away from the girls, uttering "No, thank you." She cast her head to the floor and as she fled the inn, echoed another, "No, thank you."

Hanna frowned. *She might need some help with making friends.* She waved at Josephine, "You and Virginia having fun?"

They were panting wildly. "Quenby chased us with his booger finger. We were too fast."

Hanna smiled. *I am sure Aeric has thrown him into a stew for that.* "You girls are too cute. How about you play outside?"

They shouted breathy 'okays' and Josephine turned toward Virginia. The two girls froze. Virginia took off squealing with glee. Josephine was closing in on her when they darted through the door. A shout came from outside. A woman's shout.

Hanna sat straight in her chair and began picking at her cuticles.

Carolyn entered the tavern, garbed in all black—her head obscured by a veil. Behind her came a woman in bright pink and yellow. She wore a hat with the feathers of many different birds. Her shoes were lined with felt and furs, and her skin was powdered moonlight white.

"Miss Vellencourt," Hanna smiled politely. "And Carolyn," Hanna noted. *I wasn't aware I would have two meetings.* "Pleasure to see you both."

"Where is Mister Gardner?" Lilian Vellencourt asked in an inquisitive tone.

Carolyn stumbled to Hanna's side. She pulled out a chair, loudly fumbling over the furniture. She sniffed and Hanna looked over at her, distracted from the previous question. Hanna noted the crimson eyes behind Carolyn's veil. *She has been crying.*

"Gone, sick, dead, predisposed?" Vellencourt asked again, her voice carrying far.

"Ah," Hanna smiled. "He is taking care of a matter in the Overgrowth."

"I do not envy him," Vellencourt said in a grim monotone. After a second's silence she said, excitedly, "Well, I suppose we women will have to rule the roost."

"I suppose so," Hanna could not take her eyes away from Carolyn. Despite the woman's flaws, Hanna pitied her. "Carolyn, dear, what has happened?"

"I'll just wait my turn then," Vellencourt rubbed her hands. She put a powdered hand on Carolyn's shoulder, leaving a white stain on the black garment. "Carolyn—be strong, dear." She made her way toward the far end of the table. Her steps were deliberate and full of pomp, her heels popping with every movement.

Hanna wondered what kind of insecurity might be responsible for such bravado. Lilian then sat, crossed her legs, folded her hands, and waited.

Hanna turned her attention back to Carolyn.

Bloodshot eyes looked at her. They twitched. Carolyn lifted her veil with dignity, puffing air upon her wettened cheeks. She wiped her eyes and squirmed in her chair to get comfortable. She looked at Vellencourt and then at Hanna, more spite than sorrow in her voice. "Frederick is missing. Wilhelm says he heard a scream."

"What were they doing when he heard the scream?" Hanna asked, immediately horrified a child could go missing so close to her own home. She tapped her foot, wanting to bring Emilia inside immediately.

"He and Wilhelm were playing in an abandoned building. They were building cairns. Wilhelm said he went out to look for stones and while he was out, he heard a scream. Frederick was gone when he came back."

"The scream?" Hanna asked, hesitantly. "It was your son's?"

Carolyn shook her head and said breathily. "No... Wilhelm said it was a man's voice."

Hanna was in disbelief. Had the moonshiners and flesh salesman gotten worse? She tapped her armrest and looked at Arthur's empty seat longingly. "I will bring a search party together at once. We will find your boy."

Carolyn nodded appreciatively, fighting her tears with typical Inner Ring stoicism. She shivered and wiped her eyes again. Carolyn rolled her upper lip. It flattened just below her nose and fell slowly back to rest. Her eyes fidgeted with her surroundings, darting to Hanna and beside her. "The day before Frederick went missing, he was threatened by a returning soldier, a Muhali."

"Galahad?" Hanna inquired. *He was defending my girl,* her motherly instinct was quick to point out. She could feel herself getting defensive and tried to repress the unhelpful urge to scold Carolyn and call Galahad a pure and honest man. "Before you tell me everything," she paused to look at Vellencourt. The wealthy woman was staring intently at the exchange. She caught Hanna's eye, smiled, and proceeded to drift off and look at the tavern's pillars.

Hanna blinked and asked, loudly, "Do either of you need water? Food?"

The two shook their heads adamantly and simultaneously said, 'Thank you, kindly—but no.' Hanna expected as much, but cordialities could never be forgotten in conflict. Hanna glanced again at Vellencourt.

Like most women in Auberdine, Lilian was a widow. Though unlike Carolyn, who refused to wear anything other than funeral black—Miss Vellencourt was quite open about her joy. It was said she mourned for twelve hours upon hearing about the late Mister Vellencourt's passing. Then, she put his estate up for sale and moved to Cottonwood. She bought the derelict old fort on the edge of town. The decrepit ruin had been in a perpetual state of decay. Lilian did not mind and bought the property right up. Buchanan Bavar, the previous owner, had bragged about the sale for months. He thought the deal the greatest bargain of his career.

Vellencourt had quickly become an esteemed philanthropist. Hanna did not like her. She always got the suspicion the widow was weaving some web. She reminded Hanna of herself, though younger and more ambitious.

Carolyn wiped her dried eyes. Her minimal makeup was already ruined. Black streaks like blood flowed as arteries down her face. Unlike Lilian, she did not adorn her face with white powder.

Hanna liked that about Carolyn, as she had always found that fashion rather stupid. She also thought the city's prejudices were rather stupid. However, Carolyn had not escaped *that* fad. The woman in black tried to control her quivering voice, "That *goblin* threatened my boy. I witnessed it."

Hanna restrained her response. She asked ignorantly, "What was Frederick doing at the time?"

A light seemed to turn on within the woman's pupils. Lilian shifted her weight and watched Hanna. Carolyn sniffled and with a resolute voice declared, "My boy was skipping stones."

The bitch was testing her patience. Hanna put aside the truth and asked, "I will tell everyone who walks through my doors your boy is missing and to keep open a keen eye. You have my word."

"I hear his daddy died," Carolyn fumed, playing with a dangling clump of tangled hair. Her eyes swiveled to the side as if acknowledging something which was not there.

Hanna had no patience for the accusation. "You are free to speak with Constable Goodwind and inquire into a possible abduction, but if you presume to frame a poor Muhali, I hope the frame fits the picture."

Carolyn bit down on her lip. "You don't believe me."

"I believe your son is gone. A mother would never tell such a heart-wrenching lie." Hanna stared at the woman, adrenaline pumping through her heart. It energized her. "Your son was skipping stones, alright. He was throwing them at my daughter, as was his cousin."

Carolyn recoiled. "My family has the honor of the Castle Rock," Carolyn stated, "Just like you. You would defend a Muhali?"

"Only the truth," Hanna replied.

Carolyn's cheeks puffed out in offense. She rose from her chair and looked over at Lilian. The other woman's facial features were obscured by the coat of white powder on her skin. The woman was placid.

Carolyn took in a loud breath, puffed her chest, and stormed out of the tavern. As she went, Vellencourt bowed her head. Immediately, she left her spot and took Carolyn's empty seat. She apologized. "She is addled by pain. No doubt this Muhali man is innocent."

"No doubt," Hanna echoed, analyzing the woman. "But you did not come here as an emotional support for an addled mind." She left her question unasked.

Lilian sighed and made her face into a frown. The woman oozed the pompous sincerity of the Inner Ring Hanna had grown to dislike. *And that awful whitening powder*, Hanna remarked. *What an atrocious fashion.* Lilian interrupted Hanna's judgment, "I have a sympathetic heart for my neighbors."

"How good of you," Hanna smiled. *You are lucky Arthur is not here to scold you.*

Lilian looked around. Aeric was showing Dixon the best way to carry large amounts of dirty dishes. Wenton's curses echoed inside the kitchen as he decided some meal was not to his liking. Laverne like a shadow was sweeping the far end of the tavern. "I have heard news from the Oleander."

Hanna hummed her response, begging the woman to continue.

"I have a little company up that way."

Hanna smiled. "As many do, I am sure."

"Oh sure," Lilian agreed before rapidly continuing her point. "A month ago, at least. But black gold requires a lot of resources to manage properly. Most of the smaller companies have been absorbed." Lilian scooted her chair closer to Hanna's and brushed a hand against her shoulder. Hanna did not approve of the touch, though she felt obliged to reflect Lilian's smile. She asked, "Did you live in a sky tower?"

"I did," Hanna replied. She had thought Auberdine very claustrophobic when she first arrived. All the buildings were so close to the ground and even the House on the Hill was a small thing compared to the sky towers of Castle Rock. "You did, as well?"

"Not originally," Miss Vellencourt frowned. "I was born to a poor family. We lived cliffside in a sea shack."

"Until you met your husband," Hanna said positively.

"Correct." Lilian feigned a sad expression so poorly, Hanna thought perhaps the woman relished the game of mourning. "Cliffside neighborhoods are precarious things. With one wave, the entire structure could collapse. Still, we had nowhere else to go. Our landlords knew this and charged us double what the properties were worth."

Hanna caught herself glaring at the woman. She rectified her face and flinched a faint smile. "Yours is a story of perseverance then. An admirable tale."

Lilian might have blushed were it not for the pale powder upon her cheeks. "You are too sweet." She touched Hanna's shoulder again.

She reminds me of the university girls. Will you giggle behind my back and insult me when I cannot hear? Hanna had always hated the mannerisms of women, their way of talking which was never direct. Suddenly, Hanna felt like a child again. She could feel her own cheeks reddening and felt naked because of it. She crossed her legs and scrunched her lips, quite unable to seem happy. Hanna looked down at her hands. She had been picking at her cuticles again.

"Anywho," Lilian whisked around and stood up. Her eyes fluttered. "I was wondering if you might be interested in a proposition."

Hanna blinked in anticipation. *Not without details.*

Vellencourt giggled and put a hand on Hanna's back. "That was rather vague. Sorry." She removed her hand and gazed at her surroundings. "I would like to increase my monthly donation to your establishment tenfold."

Hanna let loose a surprised chuckle. "That's more than all the other donors' contributions combined."

Vellencourt beamed and nodded. "What use is my company's wealth if I cannot share it?"

Hanna smiled back. "Well, I am sure my husband will agree to the increase. We have a terribly neglected gr-"

"Of course," Lilian stopped her. "As your premier financier, I would expect a certain level of exclusivity."

"Exclusivity?" Hanna tilted her head.

"What exactly is the name of your establishment? Gardner Inn?"

"Whatever people want to call it," Hanna lifted her shoulders. She acted as if she did not know what Vellencourt was proposing. "Some call it Auberdine Inn or the Redwood Refuge. Others call it the House on the Hill. The Muhali call it Castle Gardner occasionally."

"So many names for one place." Lilian pulled out a piece of paper and slid it toward Hanna, "I have a few suggestions. Names to suit the inn better. Proper names."

Hanna read the list aloud, "Vellencourt hostel, Best Oil and Gas Inn?" *How pretentious can you be?* She pushed the list back to Lilian.

"Ah," Vellencourt's face twitched with feeling. She swiped the sheet of names and hid it from view. "Of course, I am open to suggest—"

"And we would have to be as well," Hanna asserted. She had made up her mind.

"Pardon?" Vellencourt paused.

Hanna stood up, pushed in her chair, and stated, "We would not be an independent association if we got used to a single person's donation. The hand that feeds chooses the food, and how long would it be until our kitchens were stamped with a 'V'?"

"Well," Vellencourt laughed, "Your inn is already a success, I would n-"

Hanna walked toward the exit. "We are honored to be in such high regard with you and hope our present arrangement will continue to benefit us all."

Miss Vellencourt frowned. She lifted her finger into the air and rubbed her hand gently. "I will see—for now—that my current contribution is maintained."

"Thank you," Hanna smiled a glare. *Have I been careless?* She hoped Arthur would not be angry with her. As Lilian motioned to get up, Hanna could not help feeling dumb. *Have I let a past insecurity ruin a good idea?* She had to admit, at least to herself, that she had not entirely heard out the woman's offer. *I just don't like her.* There was too much of the capitol in Vellencourt.

The woman rose slowly, pushed in her chair, and walked over to Hanna. She caressed the air in front of her with a wave. She sighed and smiled optimistically, holding her hips like a conqueror. "Such is business."

Hanna opened the door. "You are free to a bed and a meal at any time."

Lilian's resplendent dress flew in the wind and she brushed her hair to one side. The woman began to walk away. As if the topic no longer concerned her, she yawned and turned to leave. "I do hope your head gets better." She waved happily and walked down the Hill.

The woman's arrogance astounded her. Hanna could not think of anything adequate to say before Lilian was already passing under the hedge gate. *What does she mean by that?* Had she insulted her intelligence, or had Lilian heard of her headaches? Either way, the comment kept Hanna scowling long after Vellencourt had gone.

Suddenly, a fly flew in front of Hanna's eyes. She spouted a gust of air at the bug, but it continued its buzzing. She swatted in vain. The bug was persistent. She had quite forgotten how unpleasant the sound was. She fled the irritating insect and opened the redwood door. She slammed it shut.

Emilia had snuck up behind her mother. She whispered, "Mama, who was that?"

Hanna smiled and massaged her forehead. She yawned, "A mean woman. That's all." She could still hear the buzzing of the fly outside.

10

Gluttony Got Him

Galahad washed his hands of his father's coagulated blood. The sink was filthy with his fluids. The old man had shit himself and sullied the entire store with the stink of half-digested drink. He sweat liquor, he shat liquor, Cambyses even started to bleed liquor. His corpse befouled any room it was in.

"It has been one hour and he is already rotten," Arthur said, taking off a pair of rancid gloves. It was well into the night. "How could a man vomit so much? It was like he was being engorged. Gluttony got him, I am sure of it."

Galahad sat down, crossed his legs, and bounced his foot. *One murder among a thousand, but it is the thousandth that will torture me.* Galahad was disgusted with himself. Why did Cambyses deserve to haunt him and not the faceless boys he had gunned down? They *had* to be better than his father.

It is because I have to look at him. Say what the poets might about the Great War, Galahad was happy he rarely had to look his enemy in the eye. *I will not have to look for long,* he sighed. "I scheduled a funeral two days ago. I will have his rot away soon enough."

"It is almost like you planned it," his friend let out a weak cackle.

Galahad uncrossed his legs and leaned back. He laughed, "No harm in being prepared. Just in case." He chuckled again, trying to act normal. They had chatted beside corpses before. Galahad needed only to act natural. He tried to ignore the fly buzzing in and out of the corpse's nostril. He searched his mind for a joke.

Galahad had learned to laugh at death early in the war. He found it harder to laugh at his father, though. The corpse felt like a morbid reminder of Galahad's childhood. He looked at its sunken eyes and saw him and his brothers playing, his mother before she died. The corpse had been a man once. It was hard to look at the body for any length of time and not come to the conclusion that Cambyses was a good man, after all—that he had once been a good father.

Arthur cackled again, like far-off thunder, "Do you remember Phillip?"

"Aubourg's connoisseur of the finest tobacco?" He remembered the skull well. They had been sent to occupy a portion of the western trenches. Upon arriving, they met a company which was retiring down the line. They told them to give their regards to the admiral. When they arrived, they saw a corpse entombed in mud. He had fallen during a rainstorm and drowned in the mud. When the mud washed away, only his skull remained. The vermin had picked him clean in his earthen tomb and some unknown soldier had put a pipe in the skull's jaw.

"The very finest," Arthur washed his hands. "I wonder if he is still smoking his pipe?"

"I still cannot believe someone wasted a perfectly good pipe on a skull, just for a laugh."

Arthur giggled, "They probably figured old Phillip needed a smoke more than they did."

Galahad forced himself to laugh as he would have if his father were not rotting in the adjacent room. "I could use a smoke," he admitted. He pulled out one of the leaves Yang had given to his father. They had a pleasant taste. Moreover, they provided immense energy while also relaxing him.

"Yu will be here eventually. I am sure he would spare one of his cigarettes."

"Yu is not the most sympathetic of doctors," Galahad pointed out. He quite liked that. The man was a professional and could not be said to be emotional. Galahad respected the doctor, though he did not envy Yang.

"You are sure you don't want to move him?" Arthur's voice rattled, unsure.

"I will not keep you from your wife," Galahad reminded him. He would rather not parade his father's corpse through town.

"You already have." Arthur sniffed the air and recoiled. "I have no idea what I'll say to her."

"Tell her the truth. That Galahad's father writhed and tried to run madly outside. That it took both of us to restrain him. Tell her he tried to wring both our necks as he choked on his last chunk of vomit. She will understand." Galahad had not anticipated the fight his father gave death when it came for him at last. Cambyses had reached for Arthur and shouted at him in an unintelligible, drunken babble.

The last moments of Cambyses' life were the most wretched. Despite knowing better, it seemed as if Cambyses knew in the end. *He knew what his son had done to him...* Galahad tried to remember that Cambyses had been a drunkard before the spiking. *Alcohol coursed through his veins before this week.* Galahad looked at all the stains beside his reflection. He would have to clean this mirror.

Alcohol. He was never more repulsed by the substance. It revolted him and he reviled it. He took solace with a bite of Yang's leaf and tried to forget the terrible, addictive substance.

After chewing on the leaf, his mind drifted away from unhappy thoughts. He felt strong again. More a man. He felt happy while he chewed the medicine. He peeked a wary eye at his father's corpse. One of its arms was hanging off the bed, still reaching for Arthur. *Or a drink,* Galahad snarled. After a second, the snarl became a frown. He turned to the innkeeper and declared, "I will never drink again. I am sure of it."

"The liquid is in the walls, it might be in my bones," Arthur sent a gust of air rolling about his lips, lazily.

Galahad thought it best not to speak, though he could not restrain himself. "It is as if I am a part of his death. I am practically drunk off of it." Telling even a veiled version of the truth eased Galahad's mind.

"I wouldn't be surprised. Let's head downstairs. The store won't smell nearly as bad."

Galahad followed his friend and they stood in the dimly lit shop. The dusken sun reflected upon the glass bottles of alcohol, giving all the store a chromatic hue.

Reds and blues were intertwined as purples. Galahad could not make out any single color amongst the many shades and combinations. The glare from the light hurt his eyes and he looked away. Galahad pondered with one eye closed. "Did war make us into killers?"

"I am not sure I ever killed anyone," Arthur shrugged. He motioned toward the door. "I just shot toward the horizon."

"You may have killed. It's a big war." Galahad felt a cool tingle wash over him and relax his mind from all worry, "I am certain we are all accessories."

Arthur gave him a queer look. His eyes roved left and right with words that did not come out. He tapped his thigh.

Galahad winced slightly, "Bad joke."

"Witty," his friend raised one cheek to smile. "Well," he frowned. "I am going to get home. Hanna will be waiting up, wondering where I am. Are you going to stay here, or?"

Galahad completed the question, answering, "I'll journey up soon, I just have to clean what I can." He closed the door behind him, "Tell Momed he can stop asking about me."

"Gladly," Arthur waved goodbye.

Only silence could shut a door more quietly. Galahad waited for the footsteps to dissipate before bolting the lock. He sank to the floor and sat, his back barring the door. His father was dead and he had killed him.

He stretched his cheek, thinking. *Am I the shooter or the bullet?* If he were the shooter, then it was the liquor that killed him. *Or am I the bullet?* Galahad's thoughts drifted to the ways in which a bullet caused death, to the complications the bullet created, and finally—he spat. "Just a metaphor." He rose and stood tall.

He went to his father's bedside and loomed over his corpse. "You would have done the same to me," Galahad whispered.

The romantics always claimed the dead looked peaceful. Cambyses looked like a battlefield. His stomach had shriveled. His ribs were showing through the thin, stained fabric collecting like a wet rag at his waist. The sight abhorred him. Galahad stared. A fly had landed in the corpse's mouth and was wetting its legs with drool. "Many pardons," Galahad walked away.

The smell of his dead father was only growing. Galahad poured himself a cup of tea and sipped it, trying to ignore or grow accustomed to the stench. He went to his father one last time. The fly on the mouth was exploring the caverns of its throat. Galahad found the sight oddly gratifying. Something else would benefit from the death. *A comrade.* The fly buzzed out of Cambyses' mouth and circled the body. It landed on the corpse's belly and licked at the rancid fluid. Then, it took off once more and circled wildly. Suddenly, it changed its path and flew straight into Galahad's cup.

He looked down at his tea. The fly was drowning. Overcome with fear and disgust, he threw his cup at the wall and tore out of the room. He wiped himself clean like he had fallen into the mud. He hopped upon one leg while he checked his other. A shiver went through his spine and he swore. He threw open the door, slamming it against the wall like a cannon.

Galahad took another bite of Yang's leaf and stared into the blackness.

The Cottonwood had settled into the night. The crickets were in chorus. It was an odd night when the Overgrowth was quiet for long. Galahad found the peace disturbing. He had no idea what to say to this silence. He stared at it like a once familiar friend, now become a stranger. He could see lights further down the embankment. A parade of lamps floated through the water. Elsewhere, brightly lit windows burned with candles.

The air is fresh out here, Galahad remarked with a smile. He felt a tinge of soothing feelings ripple down his spine.

A flute played music in the golden scale. Across the Oleander Wash, the Golden River people were living as if they had never left their great, carven gorges. The flute reached for a high note and rolled down its scale. Galahad looked toward the Wash and at their illuminated square. *Auberdine is a quaint town.* The squalor of his neighbors never deterred them. They were almost monastic in their poverty, devoted to it like a god. They did not seem to mind that their life teetered on the edge of peril every day.

Galahad quite thought his neighbors and he shared the peril of an undeath, forced to lumber about in a state between life and death. *And I am the only one to notice.* His neighbors seemed ready to remain poor, losing their wealth every night to their own demons. *These poor devils worship with their own twisted form of piety.*

The flute played its contemplative song, going up and down the scale with no clear end. Galahad glanced down the Muhali Islet. The nocturnal population was awakening. Some were wives and daughters, the overnight cleaners, cooks, and servants of the Inner Ring. A few were men, taking a midnight route to Aubourg where work was easy to find. Yet these were the early risers. More would rise with the moon.

Galahad stared hopelessly at the Oleander. *It will not be long before there are no shares to claim.* Soon, he would be late. There would be no wealth left. The black gold would feed the Pale and adorn their fingers with gems. His frail, mudpuppy skin would be left naked.

Damn this self-pity, he scolded himself. Rage boiled from within him until all he could think about was releasing his anger. He walked quickly through the Muhali market and toward the Inner Ring. He stopped at the huge walnut tree where nothing else grew. He spat on its obsidian bark and punched the mighty tree.

Galahad cursed as tears simmered in his eyes. *Damn me.* He had to control his anger and yet, everything infuriated him. The whole world seemed an oven and he was baking within it. The lamenting flute irritated him. He put his fingers to his ears. He tuned out the flute but silence eluded him. He heard faint laughter from the Drowned Anchorage, where poor Pale squatters lived in squalor. *Do they not understand their lot?* He fumed. *They are the shattered cannon fodder of a crumbled country.* Galahad hated their laughter. *So ignorant,* he snarled.

The walnut was an uncomfortable tree. Galahad saw nowhere he could sit. He looked ahead toward the House on the Hill, and behind him at the western mountain. *Laughter in the Drowned Anchorage, music from the Wash...* A shiver crept up his arms. The air grew cold. Under the wicked tree with its fingers of obsidian, Galahad ground his teeth. *Where to go?* The army had given him his direction and before that, his family. Now, he was finally free.

Galahad resolved to go toward the inn. His feet were heavy and his eyes struggled to stay open. His fingers moved with soreness, as if he had been lifting a heavy object. His body was stiff, his head was swelling. *I could go anywhere.* The realization was a daunting one. *Anywhere,* he repeated. He glanced nervously behind him. The walnut waved, a crooked bark branch creaked with the breeze. He lingered on the border of the Overgrowth, one foot wallowing in the mud. His other foot was firmly placed upon the stone path of the Inner Ring. *Anywhere.* Galahad's heart began to beat. Many dark things appeared from the shadows, boogeymen and haunts, ghosts and devils. The possibilities were infinite.

He tried to move. He could go anywhere, but his foot was stuck in the mud. He pulled it, but his other foot only slipped and sank further. Swearing, he grabbed a lamp post and hoisted himself up from his bondage. He barreled forward clumsily. Galahad blinked at his surroundings. He was lost. *I've walked this road a hundred times,* he tried to recall. Everything looked foreign. Even his own hands were not his own, but instead were grotesque claws. He grimaced, seeing every blemish and scar with renewed disgust.

Galahad placed his hands in his pockets. If he could not see them, the blemishes would go away. The Inner Ring was oddly loud and he thought perhaps he should whistle. He did not want to appear a villain in the night. He tried to make a tune, but it was drowned out immediately. A great commotion was coming his way. Galahad quieted his breath, fearing it unwise to attract attention. *Best not attract the rich to a poor man's murder. They would adore to hate me.*

He clung to the shadows and watched as wheels rolled and metal clanked into view. A horse-drawn wagon wheeled forward. Galahad squinted and walked closer. Another wagon succeeded the first, then another, and another. Little lights flickered within the wagons, accompanied by voices. Galahad could not understand them, though he had lived long enough to know the languages were varied. He could pinpoint a Redfeather tongue there, a Golden man's accent here. Inside some wagons, Muhali men prayed to their desert gods. In others, Pale folk played cards. On the wagon train went. They were heading west.

Galahad's leg twitched. The last of the wagons came and went and the quiet cricket chatter came back with a crescendo. *They are all heading to Oleander,* Galahad watched wistfully. *All those people. There will be no black gold by the time I get affairs in order here.* Just as he began to think all was hopeless, one last wagon followed the rest. Only, as it neared, Galahad found it was not a wagon. Rather, the carriage was an automobile, powered by gasoline. Galahad could understand the voices within. He recognized the posh accent of Castle Rockers.

"Nanny, is there an inn on the mountain?"

Galahad's ears perked up. Many hundreds of unintelligible thoughts flew through his mind. He looked at the people in the automobile. Their powdered faces glinted in the moonlight.

"There is an inn down here," a woman with a stuffy voice declared as she fanned her face. The child's response was faint as the two receded into darkness.

"But is there one on the mountain? What about shops? I don't want to look like these people."

"It would take a lifetime of mediocrity to look like these people, darling. If there aren't shops, your mother will make some."

Galahad smiled. He might not have the knowledge to extract black gold from the dirt and process it into fuel for automobiles, lamps, and other technologies—but that did not matter. Most of the old miners had remained poor; it was the shopkeepers, blacksmiths, and tavern owners that became wealthy. He gazed at the Overgrowth, the remnants of the old outer ring. *Yes, let them mine minerals. I will mine people.*

Galahad felt a surge of excitement. He did not want to waste a second more. He jumped from his concrete stoop and followed the newcomers toward the inn. He wondered whether Momed was up. As he neared the Hill, he found his pace quickening. He could feel his leg muscles strain atop the earthen slope. He gasped, *When had this hill become a mountain?*

The sight of the inn gave him visions of home and memories of his family. He thought of his dead mother and the father joining her in non-existence. He thought of his two brothers, rotting in the bellies of rats and other vermin. The disquiet of his mind put his feet in disarray. His sole did not heed the path. As the hedge gate came into view, his balance left him. Galahad tumbled into the dirt and his face plummeted.

He laid there, fuming. Dirt sank into his teeth as he screamed. He pushed his weight from the dirt and spat upon the hill. Galahad put his hand to his head and felt the stinging of a shallow wound. He sat there, looking around to see if anyone had noticed him. *Of course someone has,* he scowled. Everyone was being watched in the small town.

The House on the Hill seemed higher than Galahad remembered. He would pass a portion of the grove and think he must be at the redwood door, but only more trees greeted him. His legs shook from fatigue and his feet chafed in his worn footwear. By the time he reached the inn, he was completely out of breath. He fell into the door with all his weight, stumbling like a drunk into the tavern.

Only candlelight greeted him. He peered along the petrified table. At the head of the table, Arthur sat with his hand resting upon his chin. The innkeeper looked exhausted. He was listening to Laverne recount the orphan children's accomplishments like a proud parent. Every time she spoke, Arthur's eyes rolled to attention and he would stare for a time, punctuating his boredom with a brief. "Mhm."

Nobody was watching him. *Nobody I can see,* he reminded himself. Every shadow's flicker made Galahad think he was being ambushed, that Constable Goodwind had come to take him to the firing squads. Galahad squirmed at the thought of a dozen bullets tearing through his body.

"Galahad," a voice muttered from the shadows.

His heart skipped a beat and he dared not turn to greet the mysterious person. Was it Momed? He could not look. He closed his eyes and accepted his fate. He could feel his arms rising to meet his chains. Instead, a hand landed on his shoulder. He opened a single eye and saw Hanna. The candlelight bathed her in orange and yellows, her head was dripping wet. Her hand retreated from him and he saw that she was holding a washcloth to her brow.

"Are you well, ma'am?" He asked, quite preferring to focus on someone else's problems. The woman was shivering. *She looks worse than me,* he realized. He felt ashamed of his self-loathing. *Other people are more deserving of your pity,* he reprimanded himself. She cleared her throat to speak and Galahad's muscles stiffened. He felt the sudden urge to be of service. The only thing that mattered was a good deed. She spoke in a tone meant for him.

"Just headaches," she said, her bravery seeming like admirable bravado to Galahad. "You'll find Momed in his bedroom. He tried to wait up for you, but his watch finally wore on him."

"Watch?"

Hanna raised a heavy head in a nod. "He has hardly slept since you went to see to your father."

Galahad's bottom lip slid across the top. *Fool.* "Why would he do that?" He flinched from his irritable tone. He wrapped his arms around his chest, "Never mind."

"Do you need anything?" Hanna asked.

Her eyes reminded him of his mother, so long gone from the world. *Is that how a mother speaks to a child?* Galahad shifted his stance awkwardly. "No thank you, ma'am. Thank you for caring..." He added hastily, his cheeks turning red, "For Momed. I'll go see him now."

As he left the Tavern, Galahad shook his head. *If only she knew whom she was helping.* He descended in disgust. Galahad blinked and when his eyes opened, he was at the bedroom. Momed would be just behind the door, waiting for him. He sighed, dreading the love he was soon to receive. He took the doorknob and it squeaked to the right. The door slid open.

A pair of arms surrounded him. Galahad squirmed away from them and shouted. "Off of me, Goodwind."

"G-Goodwind?" The familiar voice chirped.

You paranoid cunt. No other voice could it be. Momed's feeble arms fell and he stepped away.

Galahad stretched one side of his face and his lips caved in on themselves. He sniffed and tried to change the subject, "I hear you have been waiting for me." He cleared his throat and looked around at the furniture as if he cared about décor.

"I've been so worried," Momed's head sank into Galahad's chest.

Galahad's nose shriveled with repulsion. He patted the teenager's head out of obligation and then moved to the bed. The meek Muhali followed him toward the bed and when he sat, so did the boy.

"Imagine that," Galahad grinned hatefully. He laid down and so did his paramour. He was a follower. Galahad thought he had liked that about Momed, but now he was not so sure. *His love is servitude. He has no right to love me.* He turned from his thoughts and rolled onto his side. Momed smiled at him.

Galahad cleared his throat uncomfortably. The Muhali was waiting for him to say something, to make his desires known. He admired his patience, though he felt his nose curling up again. He rubbed his teeth against his lip and caressed his own arm.

"I am s-sorry for not visiting. I was afr-"

"It was good you did not. The terror might have killed you," Galahad laughed and rose. He towered over the boy and for a second, his old sensations returned to him. He reveled in the height, engrossed in the discrepancy between the small Muhali and himself. His long black hair fell forward in front of his eyes and when he brushed it away, disdain filled him again.

The shy boy smiled and dutifully undressed. His caramel skin was unstained excepting the odd bruise or scar. He was a pristine thing. *What son fucks the day his father dies?* The idea made him grimace and yet, his old hatreds had not died. A part of him wished to lay the boy on his back and spite his decaying father.

The young man's cock dangled, waiting for him to act. Galahad cursed his own name and undressed. He looked at the boy and felt only hatred. He readied Momed, his paramour's moans of pleasure revolting him with every utterance. He groped and felt, trying to enjoy the carnal pleasures he had taken only days earlier. He looked down at himself. *Soft,* he seethed.

Ignoring the fact, he thrust limply into the boy, trying to take some solace in the sex. He tried biting the boy, slapping him, and brutally penetrating him. Nothing excited him. He glared at the boy, now wincing. *You are in pain and you say nothing to me.* Galahad could not stand the sight of the naked Muhali. He retreated from the boy and laid naked beside him.

Momed put his legs to his chest like a helpless child. "Have I-I done something wrong? Am I offensive?" He gazed, longingly.

"Not now," Galahad quaked with rage. He felt his tears finally release themselves. He rolled back on his side, away from Momed. He looked down at his wrinkled clothes and groped the pockets. *I just need some help relaxing.* He took out another of Yang's leaves and began chewing it, hoping he would fall into a dreamless sleep.

11

The Callousing of Life

Cora Eastmont stared at the glass of water in front of her with a raised nostril. His mother looked like she was going to vomit. She swallowed, pushed the glass away, and folded her hands on her lap. "Children can be such awful bullies."

He did not bother trying to reply while in the kitchen. The ornamental room dividers made even a fox hard of hearing. Charles carried the carrots to the wash basin. He soaked them and placed them in the pot beside him. *Salmon, carrots, potatoes... Onion!* He peered into the cupboard above him. No onions. Charles shrugged, closed the cabinet, and ground the remainder of his mother's salt and pepper into the pot. He took the handles and placed it into the fireplace to his left. He exited the kitchen and walked over to the dining table.

His mother looked up at him, "It's why I wanted us to live far away from that. No child should grow up thinking they are just some bully's name."

Cora was clearly reminiscing. She was staring at the front door like it led to some part of her own brain. Charles sat beside her. "What's on your mind, mama?"

She smiled at the door. "Thinking about Hanna and her children." She winced and her voice grew weak, though she tried to hide her reaction to the pain. "Emilia stayed with me for a week last year," she croaked.

"Water," Charles insisted.

His mother took a slow sip. She then pushed the glass even farther away from her.

"Why did she stay with you?" He asked.

"Hanna thought it would help her anxiety."

Charles had his own dealings with anxiety. Nothing helped. There was always something stupid to fear, something odd and obscure that needed his panic. "How did that go?"

"Apparently," Cora grinned. "A nasty little boy had been tormenting her. Calling her names and insulting her whenever he saw her."

Charles twitched a smile, "Sounds familiar."

"Yes, I thought it might," his mother went on. "Well, I told her that she should not care what Frederick calls her. That if—" she held in a cough. Her chest tensed. She shook her head and continued, "If I wanted every word said about me to be true, I wouldn't even write my own name." She zipped her hand past her hair, "Went right over her, I fear."

93

"You tend to have that effect," Charles joked.

Cora pointed toward the kitchen, "Better go stir that pot."

He went to the fireplace and knelt before it. Charles poked at the logs, turning them over. Then, he grabbed a long, metal ladle.

"It was hard to have the girl here, if I am honest."

"Emilia?" Charles stirred. "Why was that?"

Cora did not answer for a second. When she did, her voice tremored. "I always wished *you* had married her."

"Emilia?" Charles played dumb. He knew perfectly well who his mother meant.

"Hanna," his mother rasped.

He could hear the nostalgia in his mother's voice. Charles continued stirring the pot, "She wasn't interested. Neither was I." He got up and walked back into the living room. He paced around the table.

"Not true," his mother pointed. "You were ignorant of the game, not of its existence."

Charles walked toward the nook at the front of the room. *So much dust*, he remarked. "The game being?"

His mother was quick to answer. "Love. You both played it like a game of duck, duck goose. Where both of you were the goose."

Cora Eastmont had her theories. He had given up trying to convince his mother otherwise. Charles returned to the kitchen and filled a bowl, portioning as many vegetables as he could. He placed a cut of salmon on top and delivered it to his mother.

She looked at it with trepidation.

Charles took his seat beside her. "The more you eat, the better you will feel."

Cora took her fork and stabbed a potato. She nibbled on it and placed the silverware and the vegetable back into the bowl. She frowned at him, defeatedly.

She needs to eat. This cannot go on or she'll have nothing left on her. Charles bowed his head and took the bowl from his mother. "There is more in the pot when you get hungry." *When.* The word stayed in his mind; with every echo, it felt like a lie.

"And then," his mother interrupted. "Arthur follows you to university and steals her away."

Charles rolled his eyes. "He didn't rob a bank, mama. More like he walked in and the money walked out with him. Besides, it is better this way. What if Hanna and I had married? Our children would be mixed. Mixed! Imagine the strain that would put on Hanna, to see her children tormented."

Cora stared at her glass of water, shaking her head. She stretched for it, took a deep breath, and slurped as many tiny sips as she could. Water trickled down her neck and her hands shook.

Charles bit his lip and bared his teeth. His mother's dexterity was failing. *Not failing. This happens with old age.*

Cora's hands continued shaking. The water in her cup started vibrating and little droplets flew from the glass. "A good friend would not have done what Arthur did."

Charles saw her hands trembling. "Don't do this, mama." He relieved her of the glass and set it beside her. "Don't be bitter."

Cora Eastmont frowned and rested her hands on the table. "I just love that girl... And you do, too." She anticipated her son's response, interrupting him before he began. "It would have taken half a lifetime, but you would have married her." She scowled, "If you had come from a different, uh, family—you would have wasted no time!"

Charles fidgeted with a fork. "Different family? You were the best mother I could have—"

"But not the best father."

Charles placed the fork gently back on the table. He nodded, "That's true." Charles knew nothing about the man who fathered him. Cora never described him, never even told him the rapist's name. She might not have known. Regardless, Charles did not care. He shivered as a spasm of stress swept up his spine. "But it is not his fault I am not married. To Hanna or any other woman."

Cora wiped her mouth. "It is precisely his fault. You are obsessed with being the perfect gentleman. It has made you entirely incapable of pursuing your own emotions." She quickly pointed a spoon at her son, "Do not deny it. You are the epitome of respectful."

"Hard to argue with a compliment," he joked, hoping to dilute the topic with a non-response. He had loved Hanna, once. But the pubescent curiosity of a young boy was nothing to fixate on. Nor was an idle fancy for his best friend's wife something Charles wanted to speak openly about. The entire affair was wanton, reckless, and vulgar. Arthur was married to Hanna.

"I am not complimenting you," his mother chided. "You tiptoe on issues of love and have all your life."

Charles made his argument with a blink at the soup he had cooked, the rug he had cleaned, and the water he had placed in front of his mother. He smiled slightly and waited for her to take his meaning.

She rolled her eyes and scoffed with impatience, "Oh Charles, stop trying to outwit me. You know perfectly well that I am referring to romance, not familial duty."

"You are not a duty," Charles corrected. He enjoyed taking care of things, his family most of all.

Cora stopped just before continuing her point. She stared at the ceiling for a time and rubbed the bottom of her chin. Then, she took a deep breath. She spoke calmly. "There will be a time when I am gone." She raised her finger and stopped her son's ruminating reply. "Stop. Whether or not I die tomorrow or in ten years—I will be gone."

"I know," Charles whispered. Death was an easier topic to discuss when it was just an abstract actor in one of his books.

"And when I am gone, you will still have that admirable love of yours." She gave her son a pitiful frown, "You need to learn to be okay with loving others. Or at the very least, yourself."

What an odd thing to say, Charles wanted to reply. He sang to children, he sang to farm animals. He had perfectly quaint conversations with the quietest of trees. *I quite love others, thank you.* Charles' lips twitched, but instead of arguing—he just bowed his head. He acquiesced, "Okay, mama." Whether from reason or sheer persistence, Cora Eastmont always won.

His mother studied him for a second. Then, she smiled and started to leave the table.

Her sickness bid her stay. Cora lurched forward, put a fist to her mouth, and winced. Her spoon fell. She froze, stooping over the table with engorged eyes. They swelled and her body shivered. Her head twitched. She made a gurgling sound. It was silent for a second, until she squinted and swallowed. She shook her head madly like she had bitten into a lemon. Cora Eastmont rolled her eyes and grumbled. She looked at her son with a smirk and a frown.

She put up her hand like a white flag. "It is just... I admit I am projecting." Cora coughed madly and when his mother spoke next, her speech was faint and airy. "It took Auldwine years to say he loved me."

Charles leapt to his feet and got her a fresh glass of water. His mother took it thankfully, though she hardly drank.

"So," she set the water down. "Arthur wants you to tend his trees, hm?" Cora eyed him with a knowing grin.

He cleared his throat. The image of his mother alone and dying stole his words from him. He tried to rid himself of the thoughts, but they pursued his speech. "Mhm," he managed. *You need to drink more water.* "I imagine I will be lost, er... He will be lost..." He added when his mother simply stared at him, "Where that part of inn-keeping is concerned."

His mother nodded her whole body in agreement. She put her hand on Charles' and asked, "Why don't we go to the library?"

Charles stood up and guided her toward the red bookcases. Auldwine had built them for his mother when the family began to acquire too many books.

"No," his mother rasped. "Yours."

Charles obliged. They entered a room unlike the other two. Most furniture in the house was red, excepting the occasional piece of wall décor. Yet, the colors in his room, from the massive armoire in the middle of the room, to the bookshelves surrounding it, to his own bed—those were all black and gold.

Cora hobbled past his bed and sat down on the book bench. Instead of armrests, two columns rose up on the sides of the bench. Inside the columns were the books Charles read most. His mother shook her head as her son sat on his childhood bed. "Always too small for you."

It was true. He had outgrown the bed early in his teens. If Charles stretched out, his feet dangled off the edge. "I usually sleep curled up anyways."

His mother bent forward and scanned the different books which filled the bench. She looked at the shelf to her left. "*Hydrology in the Modern Era. Electricity in Nature. The Geology of Cottonwood Valley. Chemistry of the Protist. An Introduction to Cosmology...*" Cora lifted her head and stood straight. She eyed her son with the look she gave right before sharing a novel thought. "Funny. Humans have so mastered the different parts of nature, we have ceased to know much about it at all." She grinned and started another comment. She had hardly begun when she winced and grabbed her brow.

Charles wanted to dote on her, to make her drink and eat, and to get her everything she needed. *But,* he reasoned, *that's not what she wants.* Her pain was so obvious and yet, Cora Eastmont refused to look frail. Only a second went by before his mother reassumed a dignified placidity. She folded her hands and looked around the room. "Auberdine is beautiful, people aside. You'll like it."

"You talk like I'm a foreigner," Charles chuckled.

Cora's face grew serious. "You are." She stared at the black and gold dresser standing like a pillar in the middle of the room. Within were clothes which were too big or too small. His mother had never been a talented seamstress. Charles, however, had never been a talented complainer. She continued, "You never lived in town. Not since you were an infant."

Charles pointed out, "I've stayed at the inn for weeks at a time."

Cora's eyes darted to the ground. "And during those visits, how many little boys picked on you? How many Pale called you a mudpuppy?" She looked at him, narrowing her gaze. "Malchance?"

Charles took to sarcasm, hoping to lighten his mother's grim tone. "You're making a great case for going."

Cora closed her eyes. An intangible sound escaped her. She shut her mouth and rested her chin on her hand. She rasped, "Places like that are bad for children." Clearing her throat, she continued in a whisper. "Now you are a man."

Charles had her. "What if I want to stay here?" He used her own words for his argument. "Shouldn't a man choose his own path?"

Her voice trembled. Her mind did not. "You are afraid of leaving me, of being disloyal."

Charles shook his head. His mother interrupted him before he could even think of a rebuttal.

"Do not argue," she pointed her finger. "I have been around long enough to feel what you are feeling." She let out a hoarse laugh. "When Auldwine..." She bowed her head and a shadow lined her wrinkled face. A bead of sweat glimmered against her black skin. "Hanna thought I had lost to will to live."

"But you haven't," Charles smiled hopefully.

Cora rubbed her eyes. "No more of this. It hurts my head." She folded her hands and dragged them over her hair. "Promise me," she paused, out of breath. "That you will go. If not for yourself. Then for me."

Charles gulped. He could not say no to that. "I promise."

Cora nodded. "Good." She laid across the book bench. "Just remember, baby. People are quite like you, but not quite. And it is the 'not quite' part that they fixate on."

Charles did not fully understand. "I'll remember."

Cora smiled wide, her wrinkles shriveling out of view. "Very good. Because no matter what happens..." She looked up at the ceiling and asked her son, "What was it I used to say?"

His mother knew what the phrase was. She only wanted her son to say it. He repeated. "Suffering is the callousing of life."

Cora exhaled for several seconds and quiet contentment took hold of her. She nodded to herself, as if hearing some song. Charles waited for his mother to say something else but suspected she had fallen asleep. He laid on his own bed and tried to nap. It was still early in the afternoon and he was not tired.

After a futile five minutes of tossing and turning, he decided the trouble was not worth it and sat up. *Besides,* Charles remembered, *mama's snoring will just keep me up.* His mother was an awful snorer, the loudest he had ever heard. Auldwine had always joked that she sounded like a mix of a pig snorting and a raccoon rummaging. Charles looked around the room. Birds were chirping outside and the wind was rolling along the roof. It was quiet and peaceful.

Charles blinked. It was quiet. He turned his head slowly toward where his mother was laying. She was not snoring. It had only been a few minutes. Was she already in a deep sleep? He squinted. Her chest was not rising. Charles leapt up and walked toward her hesitantly.

Charles put a hand on her shoulder. Cora Eastmont did not stir. He knelt and nudged her. Her body moved, but quickly returned to its original position. He grabbed his mother's hand and rubbed her palm. Charles pulled his hand away, unwilling to read a pulse. He rested his head on her knees and hugged her legs. He mouthed the word, "Mama," but no sound came out. He looked up at her face. No one looked back.

"Mama?"

12

A Woman's World

Hanna thought the funeral a grotesque circus. The body looked like it had never been lived in, that Cambyses was a quilt of flesh and nothing more. *I would never want an open casket, especially if I looked like this.* She retained her revulsion in silence, trying not to appear like she was avoiding looking at Galahad's father. *Or what remains.* Her nose wrinkled. Every feature of his body was distorted. His nose was red and green. A thin film of flesh had shriveled around his stomach, rippling like waves whenever the casket rocked into position.

The plot of land Galahad had chosen for Cambyses was at the base of his father's store. *Galahad's store,* she corrected herself. A hole had been excavated just above the passing streams. *Come the wet season, the casket will be drowned and rotten.* Hanna looked at a perimeter of steel protrusions, meant to stop the casket from rising after a monsoon and floating down the market road. A shimmering scale web would then be laid above the casket, so it would not move with the mud.

Galahad was grinding his teeth. Everyone could hear it. Hanna saw the others casually glance at him. She feigned deafness. *I would be clenching my jaw, too.*

"Look at all these cunts," he whispered to her. "If they were truly my friends, they would have stayed home like Arthur."

"It'll be over soon," Hanna said.

"I doubt it," Galahad seethed, chewing on his cheek.

Hanna looked around her. Terrell, an infamous flesh salesman, was bowing his head. Hanna did not know why he was there. Galahad had seemed friendly enough toward him. The two exchanged a handshake and Terrell offered him a complimentary night with any of his girls. Galahad had politely declined.

Many of Cambyses' clientele surrounded his corpse. Hanna had never seen them at the inn. Most looked dreadfully tired, emaciated, and unkempt. Their hair was knotted, their skin was dirty, and their clothes were rags. Their breath stunk so heavily of liquor, Hanna forgot their names when they introduced themselves. She counted nine such attendees in total.

Carolyn was present as well. Hanna thought it exceedingly rude for her to be at the funeral. The constable had taken search parties in and around Cottonwood, searching every hovel, home, and dilapidated ruin. Despite their thoroughness, Frederick remained missing. *I wonder if Galahad knows about her accusation.* For Hanna's part, she felt Carolyn was brewing some mischief.

Lilian Vellencourt stood next to Carolyn, frowning over the corpse as if she had known Cambyses all her life, as if she and the shop-keep were the dearest of friends. Galahad was clearly irritated with her. *But what can he do?* Vellencourt had enough clout to walk up and kiss Cambyses if she wanted.

Beside the two widows were the doctors Yu and Yang. Yu looked resolutely at the corpse as if it were his duty. Yang avoided looking at Hanna as if *that* were his duty. She had walked up to them eagerly, only for Yu to say he needed to stop by the post office for the results. *I can wait until tonight,* she calmed her nerves. Still, as the casket swayed upon its lever and pulley system, she wished the old corpse would be gone and buried. The anticipation was gnawing at her. *This is not about you,* she reminded herself. She forced herself to look at Cambyses as penance for her wandering, disrespectful mind.

"Kind words from unkind lepers." Galahad coughed. He sank his teeth onto his bottom lip. His canines tilted ever so slightly toward Carolyn. "It is all recitation. Sheepish condolences. Nobody knows what to say. They ought to stay quiet and let the man rot."

Hanna sucked in her lip. *Let him mourn, even if that is in anger.* She thought it was awfully bad manners to scorn people who took time out of their day to see a bad man buried. *Unless he knows about Carolyn's accusation.* Presently, the widow was clenching her nephew's hand. Wilhelm pulled away only to be more tightly restrained.

Galahad sighed as the casket was shut. It clanged against the steel posts before landing clumsily into the mud.

"You shouldn't be alone," Hanna risked. *He can't soak in this sour attitude. Arthur will cheer him up, or the kids.*

At that comment, Momed rested his head on Galahad's shoulder. Hanna watched the scene from her periphery, trying not to be an eavesdropper. Galahad shrugged him off and scolded, "Not here." Then, he glanced at the other attendees, wiped his brow of sweat, and put a single leaf into his mouth. Hanna caught Momed's eye. The Muhali tugged at his collar and faced the grave with dignity.

She turned from her right to her left, where Aeric stood stoically. Beside him, Emilia fidgeted. Her hands did not know what to do without Isabelle to pet. *The crowd, the body. It has all unnerved her... I should not have let her go.* Hanna sighed and stopped staring at her. *She wanted to go, well here she is.* At first, she had been proud her daughter wanted to support Galahad. She had thought that perhaps the girl was getting better. Now, as Emilia nervously scratched at her little arms, Hanna felt she had made the wrong decision.

"I know I'm being a bit of a shit," Galahad admitted. "I am glad *you* three came." Momed swallowed. Galahad sniffled and turned toward Momed. He patted his back several times and then turned away.

"Of course," Aeric replied, his smile not as genuine as Hanna would have liked.

"Are you going to live with us now?" Emilia asked, holding herself with scratched, red arms.

"Oh," Galahad began, not sure how to respond. Mud was being mechanically placed on top of the casket. The funerary company was indifferent to the solemn nature of the sepulcher. Burying corpses was just a job to them.

Hanna helped answer, "For a time, I am sure. Galahad has inherited his father's house, along with all his stuff."

The grinding of Galahad's teeth spoke first. Then, he answered Emilia. "I'm sure I'll stay at the inn for a little while." He smiled with sad eyes at his store. "But as for this place," he put his hands in his pockets and took out another little, green leaf. He eyed it, lost in thought. He seemed to forget what he was saying for a moment. Then, he shook his head and put the leaf back in his pocket. Momed smiled as the leaf went away. "I can't take it. Not now."

"All the inventory, Galahad," Hanna remembered to keep her voice low. Galahad's had been rising steadily over the conversation. Once the corpse had a layer of mud atop it, he seemed to forget he was attending his father's funeral. "At least sell it off."

"I don't own any of this," Galahad's jaw cracked and he winced. "It is not mine to sell."

How peculiarly we all grieve. He will regret it all. "Where will you go?" Hanna asked. "The mountain seems a wise choice, eventually."

The mountain has never been a wise choice, Hanna wanted to say. It was hard not to be nervous about the oil boom to the west. Auberdine's youth grew up on stories of flooding mountains, Wanakhan curses, and greedy miners getting their due. She stifled her superstition, "Will you be joining the pandemonium over this black gold?"

Galahad chuckled. "I haven't the faintest idea." His tone made Hanna think that he did.

The pleasantries of the funeral were quickly dispensed with once the last layer of mud was thrown atop the grave. As per Galahad's instruction, a walnut seed was planted as a gravestone. Yu thought the choice a misguided one, as his people used walnuts to denote the graves of evil rulers and corrupt emperors.

Galahad smiled politely at Yu, "We are all corrupt emperors in our own little lives." The old doctor lit a cigarette and bowed. He walked away from the funeral, glancing at Hanna as he left. He afforded her only one eye and he quickly revoked even that. He towed Yang behind him, though his nephew at least smiled at her.

A horrible dread was festering in her heart. She expected bad news.

It was time. "Alright. Emilia, Aeric. Say goodbye to Galahad."

Emilia hugged Galahad so tightly, Hanna was embarrassed. She went to apologize for her daughter's affection but stopped herself when she saw Galahad was choked up, unable to speak. At that, she smiled at her daughter. Pride welled within her. Then, Aeric shook Galahad's hand once, pulled him close, and exchanged a pat on the back. *The way men show affection is crude,* Hanna remarked.

"We will see you at the inn," she hugged Galahad.

"Hm?" he asked, unaware of his surroundings.

"See you at the inn," Hanna said, louder.

"Ah, yes," Galahad looked up at the sky. He licked the circumference of his lips and cleared his throat.

"Okay," she concluded.

She walked away from the funeral, her children beside her. As she did, Carolyn walked rigidly over to Cambyses' son. She handed him a letter and departed, allowing Lilian to loudly introduce herself.

"I do hope we might talk about your father some more," she started.

She never misses an opportunity to make an impression. Hanna squinted, not liking the scene in the least. *One worry at a time,* she frowned. The doctors Yu and Yang had already gone to the post office. She made haste to meet them back at the inn.

The Muhali Islet was filled with the chirping of birds and the clattering of merchants. Hanna knew the neighborhood was safe enough in daylight. Nonetheless, she watched her sides suspiciously. If Carolyn's boy could go missing, so could her children. She pulled Aeric closer and held Emilia's hand tightly.

Across the market, fishers were crying out their catches from canoes. The river wharf echoed with, "Trout and bass!" Hanna could smell the fish. It smelled rotten. *And yet, the lines still form.* Some people would rather pay to eat poorly than eat for free at the inn. *Well,* Hanna covered her nose, *their pride comes with an awful smell.* She led her children over a narrow rope bridge, careful to keep Emilia upright. Below the swaying bridge, a pool of bubbling blue algae was burping fumes. Downstream, a dead ash tree was awash in beetle larva. Hanna hurried her children along.

There was space enough in the outer ring for many thousands. The old settlers were more numerous than the people of Auberdine today. Between the wild growth of trees, weeds, and vines, there were the remnants of ancient homes. Hanna saw many humble abodes made among the ruins of the Overgrowth. The stairs leading to old mansions were the stoops of children. Women flirted atop the mossy rooftops with men of ill repute. Flesh salesmen and the many moonshiners did business in the parlors of old. Games of dice were played in the shaded alleys. Empty bottles and laughter filled the streets.

Across the road, a group of young boys sat on their stoop. They talked without care. They swore loudly and said anything. Hanna surveyed her surroundings without moving her neck. She saw a Redfeather boy with the same onyx skin as Charles. He spoke about breaking into 'the business' and how they all could easily do it.

"If you know someone, that is," he said.

She turned to get a better look at the child. She knew his face right away, as he had once lived at the inn. *Latrell.* He and his mother had left the family croft when their father was slain in service. The boy had been quite sweet before the world turned him astray. He ran away to the Overgrowth a few months ago, intent on becoming his own man.

Hanna pitied the boy's mother, Laverne. *First, she loses her husband, then her son abandons her.* The runaway's mother still lived at the inn, doting upon any orphaned child as if it were her life's calling. Hanna could not imagine Laverne's sorrow. She had invested so much love and time into the boy, only for Latrell to leave her all alone. Without thinking, Hanna shook her head. The motion attracted the boy's attention and Latrell yelled,

"Ey, inn woman. How 'bout you come here an' suck this." He thrusted his hips into the air.

Hanna said nothing and squeezed Aeric's arm as tightly as she could. Her son tried to break away, goading the group, "Come a little closer, cowards."

"You a good dog on mama's leash, ain't ya?" Latrell laughed.

Aeric tried to pull away from his mother, but Hanna clenched tightly. Her son looked at her angrily, "He cannot be allowed to say that to you. You fed him, you gave him a bed."

She whispered, "Do not disobey your mother. Do not pay them any mind. Emilia, dear, stop staring." She marched her litter away from the neighborhood. Meanwhile, Latrell and his group of boys called after her.

"Look at how that mama ass jiggles, give me some o' that!"

"Save some for me, Latrell. I like 'em old!"

"I wonder if that little girl want a sister?"

Once they had turned a corner and were well within the confines of the Inner Ring, Hanna paused. Aeric was fuming. Emilia was looking left and right, expecting something to happen. She had tried to get as close as she could to her mother, almost tripping Hanna.

"Mother," Aeric scolded her.

"Don't you 'mother' me," she chided.

"You cannot let them say that to you. You are an innkeeper."

Hanna smiled and brushed her hand through Aeric's hair. "Innkeeper's wife."

He flinched back. "It doesn't matter!" Her boy shouted.

Hanna sighed and shook her head. "Oh, sweet child." She wanted to spare them both from the realities of the world, to tuck them away someplace safe. *They are not jewelry,* Hanna frowned. She walked several paces to a nearby bench. A maple tree provided them enough shade from the light. "Sit with me, you two."

Emilia was more than happy to snuggle up next to her. Aeric took some convincing. He approached the bench and stood, looking around for something to glare at. He averted his attention from her. Hanna began anyways, saying, "When a man insults me, I cannot seek retribution."

Aeric scoffed.

"That's a man's instinct," Hanna said, sympathetically. *Now don't get offended,* she watched her boy intently. He relaxed his posture and leaned on one leg. She continued, softly. "I have you two with me. If they have the audacity to speak to a stranger like that, what other things might they do?"

Emilia shivered and scooted even closer to her mother. Hanna held her head. "Aeric, you have to understand that a woman's world is not a man's world. You have to understand, for your sister's sake. For my sake."

Aeric pointed back toward the Overgrowth, "But if people can say stuff like that, they will walk over you. Dad always says that."

"Your father is quick to anger," Hanna could not stop a chuckle from escaping her. "It is his worst quality." The maple tree was a cacophony of little birds. They jumped from one branch to another, singing as they leapt. Hanna wiped her brow. She yawned and placed her hands on her lap. Emilia rested on her shoulder.

"Neither of you know what happened to Cora."

"I do," Aeric protested, sitting down beside his mother.

Hanna and Aeric stared ahead at a beautiful mansion. It would be the envy of many in the Overgrowth, with its vaunted tapestries and gilded rugs. A mighty stone fence obstructed any from getting a proper view of the place. Hanna told her son, "You think you do because you have heard the vulgar say *rape,* and they say it happened to her. Rape is just a verb, as Cora says herself."

Aeric looked at her, as if in understanding. "They wouldn't have... You know, done that. Not with me around."

"You are young, even if you don't feel like it. You cannot know all the problems of your own world, let alone the problems of others." Hanna shook her head, "Being a woman is a mix of wanting to feel safe and not wanting to be afraid. You'll need to know that when you have a wife."

They sat there in silence. Aeric's glare had withered into vain contempt. *He's processing.* Hanna had met many good-hearted men like her son, who thought a woman walked a street the same way as a man. She looked lovingly at her son. *You will not be one of them,* Hanna promised. The words echoed in her mind. The doom of Yu's results loomed over them. She motioned to move, but just then Emilia uttered,

"Mama."

Hanna remained in her seat. "Yes, sugarbear?"

"Am I weak because I am a girl?" She looked at her brother and then down at her feet. "Aeric isn't ever scared."

Before Hanna had a chance to respond, her son did so. "Mama told me once that a woman's power is in her love."

Hanna could not help smiling. Like a beach ball in water, she tried to keep the smile from rising. *You've got your father's fighting spirit, but at least you listen.* "That's right," she echoed, breathily.

"How?" Emilia asked.

Hanna paraphrased what she had once told her son. "A man fights like a snake strikes, but we are the power behind the strike. We are the snake charmers. Our flutes are our nods, our caresses."

Her daughter's cheeks puffed out, "That's stupid. You don't really think that is power? Do you, mama?"

Hanna curled her upper lip toward her nose. Her mother had told her the same story once. She recalled not thinking very highly of such a feminine ideal. It had seemed like subservience, not strength. She quietly admitted, ashamed that she had let some of her mother's bad teachings influence her. "Not really, no."

Emilia declared obstinately, "Good. Because I don't like snakes. I don't want to be a snake charmer."

Hanna stood up and took her daughter's hand. Aeric rose beside her. She said to her daughter, as the shadow of the maple moved on with the passing of the sun, "Then you better take your studies seriously."

They walked home. Leaves fell from the hedge gate onto their heads. A ring of yellow leaves fell onto Emilia's hair. Hanna giggled and wiped off her daughter's crown. Then, she leapt into the moat of fallen leaves which had accumulated at the base of the Hill. Aeric watched stoically as Hanna and his sister spent the next few minutes stomping and crunching.

When they continued up, the Hill was full of children's laughter. Laverne had taken the orphans to play. Even Dixon had come out, though he only stood beside the woman, watching the younger children like he was charged with their safety. Josephine and Virginia ran among the grove, climbing the dead tree's branches and jumping from them. Meanwhile, Lorne and Quenby were busy digging for bugs to place in glass tubes.

"We are making a zoo," they exclaimed to Hanna.

"We would love to see it when you are finished," Hanna encouraged. She could feel Emilia drift toward the children, wanting to join them. She whispered to her daughter, asking if she would like to play. Emilia nodded sheepishly and wandered hesitantly over.

Hanna hoped her daughter would have some fun. Aeric, however, was not interested in fun. He followed his mother and helped her up the patio, where the stairs greeted her weary knees. Hanna climbed those anxiously. "Do you want me to go with you?" Aeric asked her.

"Only if you want to," Hanna did not want to force him somewhere he did not want to be.

"Do you want me to, though?" Aeric persisted for a clear answer.

Hanna was quick to decide. "No."

Her son nodded and hugged her. Then, he joined his sister. She could hear him admonish Josephine for jumping from too tall a branch. *He will be a good father,* Hanna smiled.

She climbed toward her family's quarters. Every step wearied her and silly thoughts crept into her head. *If I do not hear the results,* her musings protested, *I will not be sick.* She waited at the top of the stairs, staring at the corridor. She could not seem to move, though she heard muted voices from her office. Her husband was in there, his voice was deeper than it usually was. *He has company,* she knew. Her toes twitched, but she could not move.

Then, like a dream, Arthur came out of her study and guided her forward. His words were calm and soothing, but she did not hear them. She saw Yu and his nephew sitting. They rose to shake her hand and she could not feel their grip. Arthur placed her in the chair and knelt beside her, petting her hand. Yu had the letter, the results from the city. When he spoke, it was like Hanna was underwater. She blinked.

"Sorry," she began to sweat. "Could you repeat that?"

Yu sighed and nodded. "It took-a so long because I did-a not believe the results."

"Which are?" Arthur glared, his tone already angry.

Hanna looked at her husband and shook her head. She kissed his hand and smiled. He frowned and looked solemnly at his feet. *He acts as if this is his diagnosis.* The doctors did not speak for a time. Hanna did not mind. She was still processing what Yu meant by 'not believing' the results. When he continued his conclusion, Hanna's head was light and she stared blankly at him.

"But after-a consulting many specialist, the results are verified." He made a deliberate effort to look into Hanna's eyes. She was not sure whether she hated him or loved him for that. He cleared his throat, coughed, and cleared it again. "Trench Rot."

Hanna laughed. She knew it was an inappropriate response, but she could not help herself. *Nonsense.* She looked around at her husband, at Yang, and then at the grim doctor. *Why am I smiling?* She bit her lip and tilted her head. "I thought you said there were no confirmed cases in Auberdine?"

"That was true," Yu replied. "Until today."

She appreciated his frankness. She breathed in and looked at Arthur. The innkeeper's eyes darted away from his wife. He jumped to his feet and stared at the doctors. "What is to be done?"

Yu replied, "There is no cure."

Yang shifted uneasily and nodded profusely.

Hanna stared at Yang. *He knows it is a lie.* She realized he could not look at her. *I am his first death sentence, then.* She shivered at the thought and shook her head. *No, no. No. There is a surgery, I read about it.* She had given Trench Rot a cursory study. Soldiers started getting it in the War. Nobody knew how it spread.

"Liars!" Her husband growled. "What kind of doctors are you to not have a cure?"

Yu answered as sadly as his lie allowed. Hanna hated him. She was sure of it. "Some disease have-a no cure. I am sorry."

"Damn your apologies, you..." Arthur looked around the room. He found a small garbage bin and toppled it over, scattering the contents.

"Arthur," Hanna tried to stop him.

He did not hear her and glowered at the old doctor. "You probably let hundreds die on the front. Is it from laziness or pride that you won't help us?"

Yu stood up and bowed. He left the room with a hoard of unheard apologies, leaving his nephew idling in his seat. Hanna would have felt sorry for him.

"Arthur," Hanna said again. Finally, he looked at her. His chest was heaving up and down and his eyes were menacing. *He hates this more than me.* "Control yourself." Before he could respond, she addressed Yang. "I know why you are silent."

The doctor looked up in horror. "It is too dangerous. My uncle forbade me from mentioning it."

Arthur sat down next to Yang, trying to intimidate the boy. "Mentioning *what?*"

"Arthur, please. Let the man speak."

"He's not the sick one," Arthur looked into Yang's fearful eyes.

Taunting him won't save my life. Hanna took her hand to her forehead. "My head, darling. I feel another bout coming on. Can you please get me a glass of water and some fresh fruit from the grove?"

Arthur gazed at her in confusion. She did not allow him time to think. Wincing, she pleaded with him. "Please, water!"

"Don't worry, baby." He sprang toward the door, glared at Yang, and departed.

When Arthur had at last hurried away, Hanna yawned and rubbed her eyes. Yang's healing instincts seemed to return and he asked, "How bad are they?"

"Hmm? Oh, no headaches this time. I just thought you might prefer to speak with me alone."

"You are right," Yang nodded.

Hanna wasted no time. "I know about the surgery."

Yang shook his head. "My uncle will not perform it. Even if successful, the intrusion into the brain will leave you in a state of infancy. Retardation, the term is. You would have to relearn speech, you might never be able to do mathematics again."

Hanna swallowed. "Better than dead."

"Perhaps, but I cannot do the surgery." He began to vomit a string of excuses, each one more hastily said than the last. "I am hardly out of school. I do not have the proper credentials. It is illegal. My uncle would disown me."

Hanna could not look at him. She closed her eyes and tried not to think of Aeric and Emilia standing over her gravestone. She thought of Galahad. "Would you bury another parent today?"

"You don't understand. If I disobey him, he will disown me. I-I..." Yang quieted and looked at his feet.

"I will be interred." Hanna finished. "Your uncle's pride is more important to you than a patient's life?" She asked. It took all her power not to shout as Arthur had. *What a weak, pathetic, piece of absolute...* She had to remind herself, *He is just a child.*

Yang's voice quivered. "Should I be successful, I will be mocked as a failure. Should I be unsuccessful, I will be hated as a failure."

Hanna had him. At least, she hoped she did. "This is not a game between oneself, but a very real dilemma." *Come now, you're smart.* "Don't make me into one of your chess matches. Is my life a game to you?"

"Of course not!" Yang shouted. He leapt to his feet and before Hanna could try again, he stormed from her study and descended loudly down the stairs.

The room buzzed in silence. Hanna looked around her, wondering whether Arthur would remodel the room when she had died. She looked at her desk, at her calculations, at her years of study. *All for nothing,* she pressed a finger to the page. She looked at the corner of her desk, at the encyclopedia mathematica looming like a tower. *Useless.* She swept her arm across the desk and the contents flew off. Hanna stared at the cluttered pages and books. She could not stand the room any longer. She ran into the corridor, looking for escape.

Those seconds in that hallway were both the longest and shortest in Hanna's life. She remembered them exactly as they were and distorted them until she could no longer remember the facts. Her knees trembled. She saw her husband standing in front of her, sweat on his brow. When he hugged her, it was as if she was watching some other woman embrace her husband. She watched as Hanna Gardner wrapped her arms mechanically around the man. He held the woman tightly, squeezing her and refusing to let go. All the tears Arthur could not shed himself became the woman's and they slipped from her like a leaky faucet.

"Ssshh," he put his hand around her head. Her tears were already soaking his chest. "Ssshh, baby girl. I won't let you die."

"They won't," she sniffed. She tried to calm herself. Her voice only grew higher in pitch and volume. "They won't fix it. T-the surgery."

She felt his knuckles crack and hated herself the more for it. "D-don't blame yourself when I'm gone. You have, have... Oh my sweet Aeric...Emilia needs h-her." She broke down, unable to say the word. *Mother.*

"Shh," Arthur soothed, sweetness in his voice. "Come here," he outstretched his hand. "I put your water on the bedside table. I've got a bowl of your favorite fruits as well."

She burst into tears again. "You're so sweet to me."

He kissed her forehead, "I don't mind. I like caring for you."

Hanna nodded. She tried to joke, but the humor did not come out. "That's good. I'm just going to be a burden."

Arthur pulled her into the bedroom. He fluffed her pillows and piled them against the wall. When she had gotten comfortable he sat next to her and put his hand on her lap. They both stared ahead. Neither spoke for a time, though Arthur occasionally turned to his wife and looked as if he wanted to speak. Then, his gaze returned to the wall. After several minutes had passed, Hanna started feeling insecure. "I don't want to ruin your days with my... With this."

Arthur sniffed. Just when Hanna was sure he was going to leave her alone, he turned back toward her. This time, he spoke. "I like it when you're sick."

She was thrown off guard. "What?" She snorted.

Her husband bowed his head and rubbed his hands. "I, uh. Well, it just makes me feel wanted." He smirked at her. "I'm not exactly a catch. I'm half-mad and zero fun."

Hanna caressed Arthur's shoulder gently. "I'll always want you, Arthur. You're my husband."

"I know, I know," the innkeeper quickly replied. "But it just gives me purpose. Makes me feel," he sighed and licked the inside of his cheek. He bit his lower lip. "Safe?"

"Arthur," Hanna said sternly. "I don't care if you have nightmares."

He swallowed. "No?"

"No," she reiterated. "Besides," she smirked. "You're only half-mad." Hanna looked up at the ceiling. "The other half is pure mush."

Arthur grinned and groaned, "Enough about my mush!" Then, he fell onto his wife and started tickling her neck.

"Arthur," she giggled frantically. "Stop! Get off!"

"Not until you swear to hold my secrets!" He growled playfully.

"Fine," Hanna squirmed. "Your mush is my secret!"

Arthur stopped his assault and gave her a coy look.

Hanna tilted her head and informed her husband, "This is the part where you get off your ill wife and comfort her."

A second elapsed where Arthur did not seem to hear her. Then, his eyes darted to hers and he said softly, "You're right. Let's get you some cuddles."

13

Letters to the Dead

Grief followed him everywhere. Every stream, hill, rock, and glade was filled with specters. Whenever the wind picked up, Charles swore it was his mother putting her hand on his shoulder. Whenever the leaves rustled, he heard his mother shuffle toward him. The thunder atop the east mountain was Cora's word. The songbirds were his little family's laughter.

Thunder crashed upon the slopes. The storm was mustering for another midday shower. Charles jolted upward out of instinct, thrust from his mind. It had been impossible to escape his unhappy thoughts. Even when he tried, he did so halfheartedly. He wanted to feel worse, like an addict chasing a euphoria.

Charles recalled his conversation with Arthur at the harvest feast. *Shit decomposes in nature, it will decompose in you.*

"Bah," Charles hated how easily consolation came when it was another's suffering. He felt like an idiot for moping, for chasing sorrow like a wide-eyed admirer. *You're useless like this. You have been idle. Selfishly idle.* He felt worse.

Becoming conscious of how he now felt, he rolled his eyes and groaned. "This cycle is exhausting." His grief was an intolerable burden and a necessary reminder, depending on how he felt in that moment.

If you leave, you abandon her.

If I don't leave, I lie to her. That's abandonment, right?

She was sick and not in her right mind. She did not mean for me to go. This was our home. Now you say she is senile? You are an awful son. Disloyal.

Charles slammed his fist onto the dining table. Glasses clanged. A book fell off a shelf. The wind picked up. Sunlight stopped shining through the window as clouds coalesced.

He needed an escape from his thoughts. He could not be idle in his grief. *It will kill me.*

It had been easy to grieve when work was to be done. He had wept at first, but soon it was clear he had to do right by his mother. That first day had been the easiest. Charles took a spade and dug his mother's grave, breaking himself upon the task. Afterward, he fashioned his mother's headstone and engraved her initials upon it. Just before the day concluded, he took her body in his arms and laid Cora Eastmont to rest. He filled her grave as night came. Then, in the darkness, he fashioned his own headstone. Charles knew it was profane, even silly—but he felt he fulfilled a promise by putting his future grave beside Cora's. He knew it was morbid, but he felt nearer to his mother when he looked at those identical initials carved on identical stones.

That first day was so straightforward. He knew what he had to do and he had done it. *Now how do I honor her?* He felt like a dog chasing its tail. Of course, there were other things that needed doing. For one, his mother's bedroom was still in disarray.

Charles sighed and approached the entrance to her room. He had passed under that doorway so many times without a thought. Now every time he stepped foot into that chamber, it felt as if he crossed death's ferry. Even the smallest items were keys into Cora's life. He entered the room and gazed at the untidy mess. To him, the room was more than a collection of clothes, papers, trash, and furniture; For Charles, they were a looking glass. The trash in the bins replayed the stories of autumn sneezes. The ruffled sheets like a swell portrayed a woman sitting upright, with all the blankets surrounding her.

Charles sat on the edge of the bed, careful not to disturb even the blankets. Cleaning and repairing Cora's cottage gave him some purpose—but not that room. He could not bring himself to clean it.

Charles sniffled and looked around. He twitched a smile at a pile of books. They reflected his mother's interests. Poetry collections were on top, their pages worn. Mystery novels were below that, and then a few of the classics. At the bottom of the stack were several scientific journals. Charles reasoned, *This room is her. Once I start picking and choosing what stays and what goes—it will be over.*

Oh, come off it, he thought in his mother's own voice. *Do you forget when I would call you into your bedroom, throw your clothes onto the ground, and make you refold them?*

Charles did remember that. He chuckled. *Mama would want me to clean this up,* he finally admitted. Reluctantly, he turned toward the many letters strewn across his mother's sheets. Pages and pens littered the bed like a quilt. *These are not ordered. I will have to sort them.*

Charles treated each page like a divine relic, only glancing at the date. The first few words were casualties to his sight and Charles felt horrible for having read them. It felt like proper evil to read his mother's intimate writings. Charles allowed himself some leniency where he was concerned, picking up letters addressed to him and placing them aside for himself. However, most of the letters were between Cora and Auldwine.

Once the correspondences had been assembled, Charles brought them to his mother's storage chest. He did not want to place them haphazardly, with no regard for categorization. *This needs to be ordered, too.* Charles dumped the entirety of the chest onto the bed. He would sort each envelope by age. The oldest of the letters were easy to discern due to the frayed edges and torn pages. Charles placed them in the chest first, hoping the weight of newer letters might protect the older.

Darkness sheared through the curtains as Charles continued.

Over thirty years of love were stored within Cora's mighty chest. Charles awed at the sheer wealth of writings Auldwine and his mother created. From early in Charles' life until the wartime years, Auldwine never stopped writing. Despite his best efforts, Charles started to read more than he would have liked.

His curiosity increased. He peeked out from his mother's bedroom at the dining table. *Oh, this is wrong,* he scolded. Yet like a puppet on a string, he floated to the bedroom door and shut it as quiet as a mouse, careful not to disturb the dead. He raced back to the bed and took a letter in hand. The date was six years prior.

The start of the war, Charles noted. He began to read a letter from Auldwine to his mother. As he did so, it was like they had never died.

Cora,

I went south to stop a mob today. A few townspeople were harassing Muhali coming from the Rock. They shouted 'mudpuppy' and told them to go back to their own homes. The war notwithstanding, I find their actions ill-informed. My ancestors came from the Rock. We were not natives. The Wanakha came from the floodplains. Not even they were natives of this valley. We are all foreigners if we remember the depth of our roots. If the universities are right (And Charles, by extension), even continents move. I should think the words "native" and "foreign" have no truth where time is concerned. "Here" is not even a native here.

I hope this brief letter is sufficient while I am away at the inn. There are so many preparations to make. I have talked with Hanna about daily duties. I do not plan to die, but best be prepared, no? I worry for my brother and the rest of the men. They will march to war as if this is a sport. Perhaps the war will indeed be over by winter's coming. I doubt it.

You cannot stop Charles from joining. You may succeed for a year, perhaps two—but eventually he will go. The only variable is whether he will be forced by the authorities or be allowed to join of his own volition. Love your time with him, but remember he is a man who must make his own decisions.

I do not mean to hurt you, dear. I know a mother's love goes beyond one's sense of patriotism. I will be up to visit as soon as I can. This town is bewitched by the war. I need a break. I cannot wait to be with you and Charles again.

Yours,
Auldwine Gardner

Charles set aside the letter and wiped his eyes. He chastised his actions. *This feels like gluttony.* Still, he did feel better for reading the letters, like not all was lost forever. He wished now he had listened to them both and never joined the war. He apologized to his mother and to Auldwine. Then, he searched for his mother's reply.

Auldwine,

The Inner Ring can be so negligent where human decency is concerned. I do hope the Muhali are treated fairly.

My dear, I quite agree with you as to the matter of 'hereness.' Here and there is neither here nor there, but somewhere else entirely!

I read the papers, add up the combined intellect of the nation, and am positive I am in the negative. I am certain that if there were a competition of wits, you and I would win by infinite margins. Maybe Charles could give us some competition, but not the common person. Pride! Bah, I will show them pride. Those lickspittle's wits are so little, they cannot be whittled. Do not be angry at those poor folk! You cannot hold them to the same standards as you hold yourself. If you compete with them in virtue, it will be like challenging Buchanan Bavar to a spelling bee!

Oh, I am only cynical. Charles cannot stop talking about the war. I told him the front was no place for his nature. He said his nature was no place for a war, and he'd not stand for it. Just as much an idealist as us, I am afraid. I did not show it, but I was proud of him. I hope he does not go.

But if he does, promise you will protect him?

I just hate all of this. The Golden Empire is in ruins and the Rock presumes to fight a two-front war? Our leaders have run afoul of wisdom. Why must a million die for the handful's ambition? When the arrogant collide, innocents are caught in the collision. Disgusting.

This letter will find you before your trip to the mountain. Therefore, I wish you a quick journey and send this letter bearing many kisses. That should hold you over.

Love,
Cora Eastmont

Charles looked for the next letter. Two months had passed. Moreover, the letter was written on army-issued paper. Scribbles were littering the letter and scratched out words were almost as numerous as those Charles could read.

My dearest baby, my love, and my sole hope in this wasteland,

I am sorry for leaving Auberdine without a word. We were dispatched earlier than I had thought. I hope Hanna delivered my sorrows to you in good fashion. I weep that I could not see your face one last time. The war is worse than the papers are allowed to write. I have sent this letter through courier to avoid censorship. I just must tell someone.

The Redfeather use a type of gas. They send it over to our side in huge clouds. The first few times they used such devilry, it nearly won the war. They didn't seem to realize the effectiveness then, and now we are prepared. Everyone is issued a mask to put on in case of gas attack.

But of course, things get lost in the commotion of war.

I was tending to a man, I forget his name. He had been shot in the arm and I was bandaging the wound. He was a logger from Cotswald. I told him I had a tavern south that way. We got to talking and I told him about you and Charles, about how we used to garden. He liked that. Said he'd love to have a garden one day.

Then someone cried, "Gas!" and we looked at one another. I do not know how it happened, but I had misplaced my mask. The man I was tending to had his mask beside him and both our gazes turned toward it. We glanced at one another. Then, I lunged for the mask. Due to his wound, I proved the stronger. I buried his head in the dirt and secured the mask to my face. Then, as the clouds wafted over— I watched as the man I had healed die by my actions.

Was it self-preservation? Was it selfishness? Are they one and the same? I see that man's face in my dreams. Only, the man's face is you. I cannot stand this place, this Tanglewood. At night, there are no stars but the lights of artillery. Strange wolves howl at...

Charles had enough. He would rather be ignorant of Auldwine's last years. He knew enough of Tanglewood to last a lifetime and that was very little. He put less care into sorting the wartime letters, not reading anything more. He finished his business and shut the chest, securing it tightly and placing it beside the red library. He felt grateful he did not fight on the Tanglewood front.

Charles felt the need to eat as he never had before. He charged into his room and changed into a fresh pair of clothes. They were too big for him, but they were warm enough. He lit several sconces, not bothering with illuminating anything but the dinner table. Then, he opened a can of beans and poured them into the pot. The fire had not been rekindled since his mother's passing and it took quite a while for a flame to spark. After a minute, Charles' stomach decided he was fine with cold beans. The cicadas chirped on, but Charles did not bother with hearing them.

Only as he finished eating was the flame rekindled. Charles grunted. He put his plate in the wash bin and began scrubbing the grime away. There were many messes that needed cleaning and Charles felt he had wasted valuable time. The silverware was the least of his concern. The couch his mother had been confined to needed cleaning. The entire nook needed a proper dusting. The library was scattered, the windows clouded, and the rug ragged. Charles felt rejuvenated. *Alright, mama, time to get to work.*

"I won't dwell on hypotheticals," he told the empty room. "Promise."

He walked toward the nook and began folding the heaps of blankets on the couch. They were the heaviest things he had ever lifted. Charles felt his doubts resurge and he wondered if it was wrong to clean the nook, his mother's favorite spot. *This is how she left it... So leave it.*

Charles shook his head violently and continued cleaning. He ripped the rug up from the ground and took it outside. Like a priest baptizes an infant, he plunged it into the rushing river. Fresh rainwater washed the dirt from the rug as the swollen stream surged past. He pulled it up and hoisted it onto his back, soaking him in the process. Then, he heaved it onto the hammock to dry.

Next, he began dusting the ornate bookshelves. Auldwine had crafted them for his mother long ago. They were well-made and showed no signs of rot. *Even the most well-made wood needs a dusting...* With a rag in hand, he began to clean the bookshelves. Designs and engravings began to reemerge from under the layer of dust.

The next day, Charles went outside and stared up at the storm clouds. It had yet to rain and the temperature had dropped considerably. Charles bowed his head and paid respect to his mother. He then went out to the edge of his mother's land and picked several wildflowers which had not yet wilted from the night's frost. He placed them on his mother's grave and went to fetch the violet rug atop the hammock. Now dry, Charles moved the coffee table and rolled the rug onto the floor.

It took all Charles' strength to scrub clean the windows but when he had, the afternoon sun shone into the cottage, brightening it. The nook took on an entirely different color. He stared at the bookshelves and the vibrant patterns which had been reclaimed from the dust. The violet rug gleamed.

Charles breathed deeply and sat on the sofa. He did not feel happy, not even close. *I wish mama could see how good it looks now.* He sighed, not quite sad, either. He leaned back and shut his eyes. For the first time in many days, the silence did not disturb him. His idle mind did not immediately begin to torment him with worry and doubt. Charles did not care to smile, but he had no urge to frown.

The quiet repose lasted all of two seconds before Charles noted the dripping sound coming from the wash bin.

Charles went to his bedroom and emerged with a toolbox. The grey-water pipes were rusted and prickly. Metal peeled off in a thousand miniscule spots, poking at Charles as he tried to mend the leak.

"Ah," he winced, trying to ignore the little pricking sensations. He glared at the pipes and then, he remembered a phrase his mother liked to say when life got hard. He smirked at the puddle below the leaking pipe and said, in the tone his mother might have used when he was little,

"Suffering is the callousing of life, baby."

14

Gluttony and Guile

What was the matter with him? *Am I diseased?* Galahad's skin crawled. Momed thrust deeper into him.

"Harder," Galahad snarled. His wrists were starting to ache from holding up his body. The view of the ground was getting harder to bear; he wanted Momed to push his head down onto it. His legs quaked and yet not enough.

Momed's hips rocked more and more quickly, slowing after just a minute.

Galahad sighed while the boy's moans continued. *What a theater I am running.* He looked at his clothes folded on the chair across from him. They were neatly put out, ready for him and his day of freedom. His wrists chafed as the bed clanged. Sex had become an obligation, an appeasement. He could feel Momed strain to sustain but wished he would finish. "Go on," he said coolly. The boy needed no persuading.

Once finished, Momed immediately came out of his trance. "Why do I repulse you?" He asked, some strength in his voice.

Galahad had no answer. *You don't,* he wanted to say. *I just feel judgement from you whenever I need to relax.* He got up and went toward his clothes. He watched as Momed backed against the wall and covered himself to the head with blankets. He smiled at him, "You do nothing wrong, I only have a lot on my mind."

"Your father?"

"Mm," he answered with neither a yes nor a no.

"Talk to me about it?"

Galahad put a hand on Momed's shoulder. "Not today."

Momed whispered, trying so desperately to sound loving that Galahad thought he might punch him. "Maybe tonight?"

"Yeah," Galahad smiled for a second. *I cannot ease his mind. He must do that himself. Men do not have crutches.* Galahad could smell the sweets baking. *Oh, I am famished.* He stopped himself as he was putting on his boots. *I ought to bathe. I smell awful.*

"I am worried of that leaf you chew." Momed had to clear his throat of phlegm before continuing. His voice cracked, "It has changed you."

"Momed," Galahad remained as calm as he could, though hearing Momed's slight Muhali accent infuriated him. "My father's rotting has changed me. Don't shame me. Not you."

Momed looked down with guilt. "I am sorry. I just miss our nights. You don't speak to me anymore."

Galahad fought the urge to insult him. *So selfish,* he seethed. Finally, he settled his spite long enough to reply, "You are right. Now that my father is... Things will return to normal."

"And the leaf?" Momed rolled over on his side.

Look at me, Galahad almost snapped. "Yang gave it to me to help with the grief. Once it is gone, it is gone." Galahad blinked and debated kissing the boy on his forehead.

"Okay," Momed said in a monotone.

Galahad's eyes rolled over in wrath. *Fine, suffer. I tried.*

He left the room and went down a spiral delving of stone steps. After a minute, he reached a metal door. With a push and a groan, the door opened. Humid water vapor brushed past his head, frizzling his hair. Galahad stepped into the bathhouse, which was unfortunately occupied. *Alas.* He frowned and undressed. He took a bite of Yang's leaf, knowing the herb would help tune out the unwanted guests.

Laverne was present, bathing all the orphans as if she were their mother. *An odd reaction to losing her son, but we are all odd reactions to loss.* The woman had an annoying charm about her. At the very least, she was hard to hate. He entered the bath on the other side of the water, not wanting to be bothered by rampaging children.

Galahad was not allowed to relax. The woman told her litter to stay put and then swam over. She greeted him with such a bright smile, Galahad was sure she wanted something from him. Her massive breasts were like driftwood in the water. Her skin had not a wrinkle on it, yet motherhood had left its mark. She was not particularly old, but not quite young, either.

"Dear, I am so sorry to hear about your father."

"He did it to himself," Galahad had no patience to play the part of a mourner today. Besides, Laverne's orphans were giggling at him. *Do they think I am a child?* He determined that if Laverne was to be a surrogate mother to those vermin, she had best teach them manners.

"All the same, you must be terribly lonely," Laverne smiled. "Ah, well. I can see you want to be alone. If you ever want to talk?" She stopped, clearly wanting Galahad to finish the agreement.

"I will come to you," he nodded, hiding his irritation. *She presupposes too much.*

Despite the unwanted company, his bath was much needed. He had not washed since Cambyses' death and filth had started to coat his skin. Galahad took in a breath, filled his lungs, and pushed off against the bottom of the bath. Yang's leaf was beginning to take effect. He outstretched his arms and floated, not bothering with the world. His head was a blissful buzz. His ears were clogged with beating serenity. The light shone onto his closed eyes and he basked in the heat. He might have laid there all day, had a shadow not formed above him.

Galahad opened his eyes. Water and panic filled his pupils as he felt his body sinking. He kicked and swatted. He shot up from the water, coughing. Water dripped down his eyes. He heard the orphans giggling at him. Laverne's sympathetic look filled him with rage. There was nothing else though, no shadowy figures or looming men. *Just the misfits,* he scowled. Galahad stormed out of the water, slowly. He was sure everyone was staring. The bathers made him feel the most insignificant and most watched person in all the world. He looked at his feet as he dressed, ignoring Laverne and her orphans.

Galahad climbed toward the tavern. The rooftop windows were letting in beams of bright light. The petrified table had a scant breakfast prepared, only the pastries he had smelt earlier. He looked around, betrayed by the lack of bounty. Aeric was sitting at the head of the table with Emilia and that beast of a dog.

"Oye, Aeric—what has happened here?"

As if sharing in the same tragedy, Aeric looked at the table sadly. "My father will not come inside. He tried to cook this morning, but I found him skulking in the freezer."

That depressed lunatic, Galahad fumed. He took a handful of croissants and stuffed them in his pockets.

"Mister Galahad?" Emilia said as he went to leave. His feet stopped at once. *Mister?* The title was like tar to his drifting thoughts. He felt like an observer of his surroundings, not a participant. He looked at the girl, aware he was not as attentive as he should be. His head fluttered in high.

"Will you protect us?"

The question was so innocently asked, the vulnerability shown so shocking, Galahad's haze briefly cleared. *Children are the best of us*, he declared to himself. "Consider me an uncle," he promised to the girl. Emilia's smile warmed him and left smiling, too.

Once he stepped into the cold autumn air, his high surged back. Galahad turned toward the derelict granary. His arms felt like they were being massaged. His legs were being tickled. His brain drifted leisurely, like his head still floated in the bathhouse. *I would like to feel this way forever.* Yet, he could tell his peak had come and gone. *I cannot chew another, not yet.* Worry and sadness were knocking on his skull. *I need to feel better.*

"God, I am bored," Galahad complained aloud. He contemplated half a dozen activities, decided each one was the pinnacle of excitement, and a second later found them irredeemably dull. Nothing seemed fun; everything seemed too difficult. He skulked in the autumn air. The tingles of Yang's leaf surged up and down his body in a hypnotic rhythm.

A devious thought then came to him. Galahad did not give the idea any further consideration. *Too risky, too condemnable...* The deviousness only made the thought more exciting. He widened his eyes and peered to his side. Without further delay, he sped into the abandoned granary. It smelt like something had died in there, but Galahad did care. He threw down his pants. The owls on the top floor were creating a grinding sound; Galahad grabbed his penis anyways. The disturbing, public act became a feedback loop for his senses. He did what Momed could not and finished himself. As his body surged, he bowed low to his ecstasy.

His reason came back to him. His high twisted and morphed. Galahad's stomach shook and he looked around anxiously. A thousand peering eyes seemed everywhere at once. He pulled his pants up. Sudden shame filled his heart. *Oh god*, he panicked. That he had just spoken so chivalrously to a child and then done this… He was positive he could never look into a mirror the same way. He wiped his hands in disgust.

"Galahad?"

The noise came from on high like some sort of god. The call came and smacked Galahad into a fright. *I am caught.* He would go to the gallows, and Constable Goodwind would break his neck upon the rope. He said nothing.

"Galahad." The voice was Arthur's. The innkeeper came down from the stairs, "I had thought you might have been another owl."

He seems oddly content. Galahad glanced up. To his horror, he had a knife and blood-soaked hands.

Lord, lord, lord, lord, Galahad's mind repeated in alarm. He knew he was doomed.

Arthur looked down at his chest, a grim fascination coated his face. "The owls. Between them and that damned grove, we're halfway to living in the Overgrowth." He looked at the crumbling stone roof, "They were making an awful mess of things."

As am I, Galahad might have laughed.

Arthur shrugged, "Just gutting them for supper. We've had frozen meat far too often. I am the innkeeper, not some beggar beholden to the tastes of others."

I would toast to that. "The tastes of others are vulgar," Galahad agreed.

"I'm sorry about the breakfast," Arthur walked to the top of the granary, where the owls had made their roost. Galahad followed him up. He noticed his high was quickly fading and lamented the fact. *Though perhaps it is for the best.*

"No problem," Galahad decided reluctantly.

"I just could not stand the inn." Arthur sat on an old wooden crate and took his knife. He had a bucket of bloody plumage on one side of him and a sack of flesh on the other. He grabbed a half-flayed owl and severed the legs. "I received a letter from Goodwind."

Galahad's heart stopped. *Oh great, a trial.* Galahad knew Carolyn was to blame. The bitch had delivered a letter of pomp accusing him of slaughtering her fat shit of a kid. *At my father's funeral, no less.* She must have thought she was terribly clever to deduce it. *But you are not clever, just destructive.* Galahad glared behind his friend. He pictured Carolyn and the lies she would spread. *As long as she continues spreading rumors, this ravenous town will continue to hear them.*

Arthur continued, "He wanted help searching for Carolyn's toad. I told him Frederick was a little cunt and for my daughter's sake, I hope they never find him."

"You said that?" Galahad said with disbelief.

"No. But I thought it." Arthur scratched his scalp, "Thank you for protecting Emilia, by the way. If I had been there—" He brought the small owl closer. The innkeeper froze for half a second and then plunged his knife deep into the carcass. "So, this snooty Castle Rocker sends me a letter...

What if someone figures me out? Carolyn's accusations are a problem. Cambyses might be an appealing mystery for the Pale to solve and I would be a quaint monster for their idle fancies.

"... Says he works for a local mining company... Maybe it's a good idea."

"Yes, perhaps," Galahad agreed without thinking.

Arthur sliced the last feather off the owl's back. Only a red carcass remained. He carved the body at the base of its ribs and took out the intestines, throwing them into the red bucket with the rest of the undesirable bits.

"Aeric came to me today."

Sexual innuendos flooded Galahad's mind. *How disturbing,* Galahad allowed himself an inner joke.

"Said some cunt kid insulted my wife. Latrell." He stuck his knife through the owl's head, pinning it to the crate. He rose and spat into the bucket, "The same kid my inn provided for... We should have starved that little cretin. Or at least charged him for the food. That's another tradition I wish we did not inherit. Generosity worked for the Wanakha. Well, for a time at least. Now, we live in a Pale world. Everyone else charges fees, why not an inn? Why must I look the other way?"

Is this a veiled metaphor? Galahad's paranoia chimed in. He looked down at his legs, thinking to see a stain which had given him away. No clues to his terrible deeds—recent or past—were on him. He continued his charade, "That vile child."

"I'd kill him." He added after a belch, "If I weren't a glorified public servant."

Galahad risked a little truth. "Sometimes, it might be necessary to kill, uh, under certain circumstances. To be a public servant, that is."

Arthur stared blankly and then, to Galahad's shock, he chuckled. To show comradery, Galahad giggled quietly. Arthur beamed at the bucket of flesh. "I needed to hear that."

Galahad's knees were shaking. "I had better go. I was only in here for the quiet."

"That so?" Arthur asked with a voice that did not care.

"Just so." Galahad did not elaborate. He exited the granary and gasped for air. It was as if he had not breathed all his life, like he was an infant just taking his first lungful.

Galahad observed his surroundings, his eyes slow to move. Hanna was hugging Aeric and giving him a list of things to accomplish. Her speech was slow and raspy, her cheeks ghostly. She strung a satchel around her son's chest.

"Give those lemony ones to Yang. Those are his favorite. If he seems troubled, do not fret. He is having a hard day."

"I don't understand. If you want him to come over, you should ask."

"No," Hanna said to her son. She seemed incredibly tired and her eyes reflected a sleepless night.

"He's being an idiot."

"Name-calling is not in your best interest, you stubborn little boy. Deliver those pastries and then come straight home."

Aeric whispered into his mother's ear. Hanna leaned in, listened, and then rose, putting her hands to her waist. She yawned and begged her son, "I know, dear. I know. Ignore them should it happen. They are just children." Her son swore, though Galahad could not pick out any particulars.

Aeric looked at his feet. Then, he turned toward town. "A doctor should do his duty. Dad should force him."

Hanna hugged Aeric and gestured at the pastries, "Yes. Though, sometimes it is best to fatten someone up before rolling them over." She kissed his brow and went inside, holding her head.

Such a sick woman does not deserve the stress of innkeeping. Galahad felt sad for Hanna, that Arthur seemed so disinterested in managing affairs. He wondered what business concerned the boy doctor, Yang. Galahad shrugged. *Hopefully Yu will sort out those headaches.*

Galahad left the inn and hurried down the Hill, catching up with the Gardner boy. Aeric glanced behind warily, a look of distrust on his face. When he realized who it was, Aeric politely said, "Hello."

Galahad looked up at the storm clouds gathering to the east, "Looks like we might get an early snow this year."

"Mhm," Aeric agreed.

Not very talkative, are we? "Your mother seemed concerned for you," Galahad commented.

"She thinks I can't handle myself," Aeric said, sounding awfully his age.

"This about that Latrell kid?"

"I'm not going to seek out a fight," Aeric said defensively, passing beyond the sight of the Hill and entering the Inner Ring. "If he says something again, though, I won't be a coward."

"I believe you," Galahad smiled. "What did he say?"

Aeric's anger grew as he remembered, "He talked to my mother like she was meat. After all she did for his mother and him. Even now, Laverne lives at the inn... I don't even know why we take care of all these degenerates."

"Tradition," Galahad said, bluntly.

"Well, I won't be so foolish when I am innkeeper," Aeric declared proudly. He pointed at the Yao household, "This is my stop. Where are you heading?"

"I've not the slightest idea," Galahad admitted.

"Well, I am okay. Tell my mother not to worry about me, okay?"

Galahad smirked and shook his head. "You do not have to convince me. This is a Pale town and you are a Pale boy. You are as safe as can be."

Aeric stepped back and said, with slight hostility, "I am more than just a Pale person."

Galahad's eye twitched. *Of course you are.* He nodded, "And all the world believes you." He stared blankly, unable to articulate what he wanted to say. He wanted Aeric to understand what he himself did not, either.

Aeric laughed, unsure how to end the conversation. "Right, well... I should deliver these to Yang."

Galahad nodded. He watched the boy hasten away and scolded himself, *What a prick thing to say to a kid.*

He continued to the Overgrowth. The Muhali Islet was already crowded with the day's traders. A hundred voices bartered like dogs barking over bones. *Why should the inn provide for these people?* Galahad thought of Hanna being disrespected and found himself agreeing with Aeric. If he were innkeeper, he would only lodge decent people. He wondered how many despicable youths took shelter in the overgrown ruins of Auberdine, of all the vile people who had benefitted from the good-hearted Gardners. *How many Latrells are there in this town? How many Fredericks?*

Galahad veered into the alleyways between the wild ruins. His feet sank under layers of moss. The market faded and the steady dripping of broken gutters replaced it. A willow branch was growing out from the middle of a nearby ruin. The wood twisted out of the rubble and wrapped itself around the neighboring masonry. The weeping vegetation created a thick curtain. Galahad parted the willow's veil and continued walking, growing angrier and angrier as he thought about Latrell's disrespect.

I must do something. The prospect of doing a good deed gnawed at his mind. *What can I do? Kids are vulgar. They make mistakes.* He shook his head, laughing at himself. *Hanna has been disrespected before and she will be again.*

The weeping willows grew like weeds, their veils obscuring the way. As he parted the branches, trying to continue as best he could—all he could think of was Cambyses. He kicked in frustration, stomping away the terrible thoughts. They persisted, the ghost of his father manifesting in his disheveled mind. *I am an awful person. No point denying it.*

Galahad closed his fists and despised himself. He looked for solace and instantly thought of Latrell, someone he could despise more. *I must do something, for Hanna.* He swallowed, nodding rapidly. Like a sailor baling water, he quelled his anxieties. *But what? Latrell is a boy. Just a boy.* Galahad stopped and wondered what someone *truly* respectable might do.

They would try to help him. Latrell was his good deed. *He cannot go on speaking like that, or he will get killed. He must learn the rules of the Rock.* His feet sank in the mud. Galahad stepped forward, contemplating the best way to teach Latrell his place in society. His feet were stuck. He pulled and pulled with all his strength and when at last the mud relinquished him, Galahad smiled. *Mudpuppy...*

Terrell the flesh salesman was finishing with a customer, his metallic shotgun gleaming. As the happy customer shuffled off, Galahad approached.

"That glare for me?" Terrell laughed.

Galahad shook his head. "No, I am just annoyed." He acted as if he was lost in thought and pouted for a moment. He watched Terrell, ever posturing with pride. The whoremonger was overfilling with bravado.

"'Bout what?" Terrell raised his brow, "Something a lay can fix?"

"I doubt it," Galahad went on. *Yes, this will do.* "It is only..." He waited for the criminal to inquire further.

"Come on, we're friends," Terrell smiled.

Galahad nodded solemnly. He let the silence speak while he formed his quaint little lie. He looked up at Terrell and stuttered, "Many p-pardons, but as you said, we are friends." He let his glare return to his face. "Just, I overheard a gang of children mocking you." Galahad stared at his open palms, "I'm a simple man. Weak. I couldn't say anything."

Terrell rolled his shoulders and breathed deeply. His nose wrinkled in rage. "You're a good friend." He rolled his lips and tensed the muscles in his face. "What they say?"

"The young one of the company... Latrell, I think. He said you were a pillow-biter." Galahad quivered, "I am sorry I did not defend you, friend."

"No need," Terrell said, apathetically. A vein on his forehead began to pulsate. He pushed past Galahad and marched beyond the willow veil.

Galahad went along with his business. It felt good to be helping Hanna and Latrell. He held his head high as he emerged from the dark alleyway. Cambyses' store stood upon its embankment. The stained glass glimmered behind metal bars. *What good they did.* As Galahad walked up the little hill, storm clouds shadowed the market.

He reached for his keys. Galahad fumbled over them and they fell into the mud. He leaned down to pick them up, pressing his hand upon the door. It moved slightly, already ajar. *Unlocked.* Galahad blinked suspiciously, silencing his breathing. He picked up his keys, as silently as he could. He peeked into the store. A light was on.

"Do come in," came a woman's voice.

Galahad obliged. He entered his father's store and found Lilian Vellencourt, smugly sitting atop the clerk's counter, kicking her feet like a girl on a swing. She got up to greet him with a hug. Galahad halted her, raising his hand and his voice. "I was not aware I had left the door unlocked."

"But you didn't," Vellencourt giggled. She added, as if it were not substantial information, "Old Buchanan forgot a trove of spare keys when I took over the promontory tower." She crossed her legs and continued, "I cannot believe you all trust such a buffoon with tax collection."

"I don't trust any buffoon," Galahad replied.

"You must mistrust your every decision," Vellencourt smiled.

"Do you mean to insult me?" *What are you playing at, woman?* Galahad burped.

"Do sit with me, sweetie," Vellencourt said in a pleading, patronizing voice.

"Shall I get you a drink?" Galahad smiled at her.

"Oh, no thank you. Your father's fate turned me off to such things," Lilian Vellencourt's smile dissipated. No emotion came from her eyes and then, she erupted in girlish laughter. "I've not had a man sit with me since my husband."

"I am a lucky man," Galahad sighed. He put a fist to his mouth and stifled a burp.

"Luckier than you know," Vellencourt leaned forward. "I used to come here, you know? When I needed a refreshment." Her flowery, purple dress gleamed in the morning sun. "I know your father never cared for the highest proofs. Though neither does the constable, I am told. He'll take the lowest proof and accept it."

As if from forgetfulness, she added, "Few take kindly to the burning taste of pure proof." She looked around the shop and asked, "What will you do with all of it? The inventory, the store?"

"Burn it," Galahad said at once, hardly joking. *How could some recluse, some woman... No*, he decided—*She cannot know.*

Lilian Vellencourt laughed. "Oh, you are a silly one." She looked down at her chest and readjusted her cleavage. "Are the rumors true, then?"

"In this town," Galahad began, "such a question has many different answers." He feigned a yawn, "Which rumors are those?"

"That you enjoy the company of men," Vellencourt said, pitifully. She uncrossed her legs and let out an exaggerated yawn.

She's mocking me. Galahad left the table. He went behind Vellencourt and put his hands on her shoulders. "I would not trust rumors." The smell of her perfume nauseated him. He put a finger through the widow's flowing strands. "Now," he let her hair fall, "Enough of this game. Why are you here?"

Vellencourt shook off his hands, stood, and looked at him with sad eyes, "I should know better than to test the patience of a murderer."

Galahad dared not think she knew the *actual* truth, but it was freeing to hear another person say the word. "So you come on Carolyn's behalf?"

"Carolyn?" Vellencourt feigned shock, covered her mouth, and giggled. "I come and go as I please, not on anyone's behalf."

Galahad tried to seem ignorant, staying silent. *She knew he did not drink the highest proofs. She knew him.* He gulped, wondering if Vellencourt saw his legs shaking. He stifled another burp.

"Awfully flatulent you are." Lilian pointed at his shaking knees, "Sit."

Galahad took his seat once more. Once he had done so, Lilian Vellencourt lost all will to speak and basked in the quiet. Galahad looked away, hating the eye contact she was making with him. He noticed his leg bouncing up and down. He slowed the motion, not wanting to draw attention to his nervous tick. After a minute, his legs stilled and Vellencourt ended her silence.

"I would have killed Frederick, too. Had I such loyalties to the Gardners..."

Galahad opened his mouth, ready to defend himself. *Frederick.* The name stopped him before he could speak. He shut his mouth. Was she only using Carolyn's rumor to manipulate him?

"Care for a drink?" Vellencourt asked, politely.

Does she know about Cambyses, too? Is Frederick just a piece of her game? Galahad ignored her, "Shall we go to the constable with your accusations?"

"Oh, nonsense. I would never turn an innocent man in. Frederick was a nasty little bully."

"But you just said-"

Lilian Vellencourt put a finger to her lips, "Ssh shh. None of that now." She looked around, happily. "Would you like to know how I became a widow?"

Not particularly, would have been Galahad's answer. He nodded for her to continue.

"My husband was an officer in the war. Not a very dangerous assignment. Most politicians received such placements." She rubbed her exposed arm, dancing fingers over her skin as she tickled herself. "Well, the war dragged on and I found I liked being alone." She frowned at Galahad, "You understand, don't you? Men just take and take. They never give. Mister Vellencourt cared only to breed me, to use me."

"That's what women are to men," Lilian sighed. "Mister Vellencourt touted me amongst his friends as a prize for his pride. He loved that I was beautiful. Not for my own sake, but because it made others wish they were him. I was only ever an ornament to his power." She tapped her fingers on the table. "So, one day, I went to see the magistrates. I told them that my husband was bored with his position. I had come prepared with a forged letter. My husband begged for a combat role."

She laughed, "Mention honor once and all men froth like beasts." She tutted her tongue and frowned again, "He was dead soon after."

If she had meant for Galahad to be more relaxed, she had not succeeded. He had an odd suspicion that Vellencourt would never leave him be so long as she saw something to gain. He started to speak but had to clear his throat when no words came out. "W-Why tell me this? Are we... fellows?" He looked toward the west, "Martyrs against a cruel world?"

"Oh, no. We are the cruel world. Some of us pawns, some of us queens..." Vellencourt stood up, "I would like to buy your store."

"It is not mine," Galahad growled.

She frowned. "Sure it is. That is how property is inherited, silly boy. From dead to closest kin."

You spiteful, little bitch. "I-" Galahad stopped. *This is useless.* He could not afford any more attention being drawn to him. He may not have killed Carolyn's boy, but he was not innocent. *She may still know about Cambyses.*

"The truth flies easily in this drunken little town, from cup to cup. So do lies, actually." Lilian did not elaborate any further.

Galahad tried to appear indifferent. Her pride was hard for him to stomach. *Being blackmailed could be worse.* He stretched and looked laxly at the shelving. "What is your price?"

"Fair," Lilian's voice lost all its seductiveness. She towered over him and put her hands on his shoulders. "Two hundred."

"That is half of what the place is worth," Galahad shoved off her hands.

"But double what your freedom is worth, I would think," Lilian said behind him.

Galahad rose. She was tall for a woman and matched him in height. *I have no choice.* Galahad licked the inside of his lips and spat. He looked around at the awful store, his father's doom. *Even if nobody uncovers the truth, innocent men have gone to the gallows before.* He was a mudpuppy to them, forever and always. He looked into

Vellencourt's hazel eyes, "Draw up the documents." He did not bother seeing Lilian out, leaving her to the empty plot.

Vellencourt's automobile was on the other side of the embankment. The exhaust pipe was leaking black sludge into the water. The afternoon sun had entirely departed behind the clouds. The air was humid and cold. Galahad marched past the happy traders and loving families. He saw his breath. Seeing it, he wondered if he deserved to be manipulated. Galahad wanted nothing more than to forget the whole affair, take her meager money, and sink into a perpetual high. *I hope Momed is not in the room. I don't want him judging me.*

Galahad fled the Overgrowth with all haste, unaware of his place. His feet fell heedlessly onto the walnut tree. It was black as void. He collided with one of the roots, nearly losing his balance. He swore, violently turning to kick the root for interrupting his stride. As he did so, he saw not the walnut's root—but Aeric Gardner, slumped against the trunk. He was cradling his stomach.

"An odd place for a nap," Galahad grumbled.

Aeric groaned and looked up at him. He removed his hands from his stomach; they were wet with blood.

"Oh dear," Galahad's eyes widened. All his thought shifted to helping the child. His soldier's training returned instantly. He lifted the wounded boy onto his shoulders. "Lucky place to be hurt. I'll get you to the doctors, just keep your hand over the wound." Galahad's legs shook under the weight but he paid no regard to the pain. He climbed the stairs toward the Yao residence and gently laid Aeric down. Then, he banged his fist against the door. He did not relent until it opened.

"What, What? We cannot help," Yang grumbled, irritably. His face turned to horror when he looked down.

"The hell you can't," Galahad snarled, bringing the bloody boy inside.

15

An End to the Game

Yang's chess pieces were scattered throughout the room. The game he had played against himself ended the moment Aeric was carried inside. *No winner, no loser—* Hanna cared little for his longstanding match. Nor did it seem that Yang cared. The young doctor was tending to her boy like water to a shoreline. He had done so through the night. Long after Yu had declared the boy healed and the bullet taken out, Yang remained beside Aeric.

Only, there was not much left to do. Even Hanna could see that. Her son was no longer in pain, his groans stopping once Yang gave him an herb. Still, the young doctor continued his vigil by making sure Aeric was always comfortable. He would place a heated rice-pillow below her son's head. When it cooled, he took it and heated it over the stove.

Outside, the world carried on. The Inner Ring was as tranquil as ever. Some of the Muhali tradesmen had left their market stalls and were bartering at the base of the Hill. They shouted over one another at a hundred words per second, each professing to have the lowest prices. "I am sorry for the noise," Yang said to the unconscious boy.

He would cure loudness if he could. Hanna was glad her son was alright, but... She sighed and took her leave. It was too hard to watch the doctor care for Aeric. *He will be fine,* Hanna assured herself. She went to go, but Yu entered from the streets. Yang's uncle took little care to be quiet.

"Streets is-a congested, like-a snot." He walked past Hanna and placed a carton of cigarettes beside Aeric. "Damn automobiles. Street not-a made for machine." He zoomed back to her, turned toward the window, and spoke with his head bowed. "If he wake-a up, let him-a smoke. Good for health."

"Thank you," Hanna glared at him. He did not notice. *How could he?* The old doctor looked at anything but her, now.

"Yes," the doctor replied, marching back into the street on his endless errands.

Hanna was glad Aeric had proper care. *Though I wish Yang would go. I would like some time with my son.* She tried to remind herself that it was Yang's house and not hers. He and his uncle had been kind enough to allow Aeric to recover under their roof. *Besides, it is a good doctor who keeps a watchful eye on a patient...* Hanna wrapped her arms around her chest, feeling uncomfortable in the silence of the room. The crackling of wood in the fireplace only reminded her of the silence between them. Yang shifted in his seat, tapping his feet against the hardwood. He tried to whistle, but his lips were too dry and only a breathy breeze escaped his lips.

"Arthur thinks a storm is coming. Early snow, he says," Hanna remarked. Yang said nothing, nodding quietly. *You made this situation uncomfortable, boy.* Hanna had to close her eyes and compose herself. Her annoyance with Yang would have to wait for when Aeric was healthy.

"Cold," Yang's voice cracked.

"Mhm," Hanna tried to keep the conversation going. Embers flew from the fire as it, too, struggled to burn on.

Yang words coalesced into an unsure stammer, "I-uh ..." The boy cleared his throat. He looked over at the chess pieces on the floor and began to pick them up. One by one, he placed them into a bin and folded up his board. "My uncle once told me I was his proudest failure."

A terrible thing to say to a boy. No wonder he is obsessed with success. "Few little boys from a small town in the Golden Empire could have done what you have."

"To do what? Watch my uncle? I have all this knowledge and it is useless," Yang put away the bin and board. He wiped his brow. Purple circles had formed around his eyes like he had been beaten. He grinned, imitating his uncle, "Self-a pity is ugly trait."

Hanna returned his smile.

"The surgery," Yang swallowed, "My uncle won't stop talking to me about it."

"Oh?" *A change in the wind,* Hanna raised her brow. Aeric shivered and pulled the covers over his body.

Yang looked at her son. He closed his eyes. "He says a procedure that takes someone's mind is not medicine. It is sickness, too." Yang shivered, "My uncle will never admit it, but he is ashamed."

Hanna frowned. *As are you,* she hoped. "What do you think?"

Yang was not quick to respond. He frowned at Aeric and took a metal rod to the fire, rotating a log and rekindling the flame. Hanna could feel the room warming. Her son did as well. Aeric murmured happily, turning over and unwrapping the heaviest blanket from his snug cocoon.

Finally, Yang pulled up a chair beside her and gestured at Aeric, "A blanket provides warmth but can overheat you, too."

Hanna looked at her hands, unable to stop picking at her cuticles. Her fingertips were bloody. *Oh this is uncomely.* She hid her hands behind her back. "Does this mean-"

"No. Not now," Yang interrupted with irritation.

Aeric was stirring. Her son yawned and kicked off the blanket. He groaned, grabbed his stomach, and looked over at them.

"Drink," Yang offered him a cup.

Aeric shook his head, "The gang. Latrell. What time is it?"

Yang pulled at his collar. He deferred to Hanna.

Hanna bowed her head, "You slept the day and night away." She smiled weakly at her boy, whose hands were fists, "As for Latrell. Relax. He was found dead hours after he assaulted you. Several of his gang, as well."

"Dead?" Aeric looked at Yang. The doctor nodded. Her son went to speak; a small squeak came out his mouth. Then, he let out a ferocious spate of giggles. He went to wipe the tears from his eyes, but the pain in his stomach surged back and he grabbed his belly instead.

"Water," Yang offered again, wiping the boy's tears with a tissue.

Aeric took it, eagerly. More water dripped onto him than made its way down his throat. Nonetheless, Aeric drank the glass and another before wiping his mouth.

Hanna went to him and fluffed his pillow. Aeric raised a hand at that. "Please, mama." He looked at Yang and smirked, "No offense, but I am tired of sleeping."

"You got shot," Yang reminded him.

"I remember," Aeric grunted. "They left me for dead..." Aeric eyed the young doctor curiously, "I am surprised you didn't, either."

"That is an odd sort of thank you," Hanna shot back. *Though I quite agree.*

Aeric ignored her, "Where is Galahad?"

Hanna felt his forehead. *No fever.* "The inn, with your father."

He tried to stand up, saying, "I want to thank him." His legs wavered and he groaned. He clenched his stomach and fell back to the bed. "Has breakfast been prepared?"

"There is time enough for that," Hanna said. "You stop worrying about work or you will finish what Latrell started."

"At least..." Aeric looked out the window at the passersby. "Give my thanks to Galahad."

Yang quickly agreed, with Hanna adding, "So long as you get some rest."

Aeric licked his lips, frustrated but compliant. "Fine. For one day."

"We will see," Hanna stared at Yang.

"Uh, yes," Yang rubbed the back of his head, "We will see. Misses Gardner, if you would be so kind... I, um, need to..." His eyes darted from her toward her son, and then to his medical tools.

Hanna scoffed, "I am the boy's mother, I have seen it all before."

Aeric's protests interrupted them, "Mom! Please, leave a man with his dignity intact."

Fine, fine, a boy doesn't want to be naked in front of his mother. Hanna opened the door. It was quite cold outside. The sun was nowhere to be seen behind a grey curtain of clouds. "Yang, see he has what he needs and then come with me up the Hill?"

"Yes, ma'am," Yang replied.

Soon, they were walking wordlessly toward the redwood refuge. The silence was not as uncomfortable. For Yang's part, he seemed restored by Aeric's awakening. *As if it were his own...* No, Hanna stopped herself from hoping. Besides, there was ample distraction to be had. A throng of workers was busy building a wooden scaffold near the hedge gate. Her husband was leading them.

Arthur glanced their way and marched over, scowling. "Hanna, go inside. This is no place for a woman in your condition."

"In my condition?" Hanna said through her teeth. "I managed the inn when it was a wartime hospital, or is there a bullet in that stubborn head of yours?"

Her husband sighed. "You know what I mean."

Hanna did not want to make a scene and so whispered her annoyance. She would have much preferred to scream at him. "Fine," Hanna glared. "Where is Galahad?"

"How should I know?" Arthur brushed his hand over his hair and looked at the scaffolding, "This doesn't seem like justice."

Hanna asked with surprise, "Have they found him yet?" The latest news from the constable was Latrell's murderer had fled into the sewers.

"No, and that fat fucking constable couldn't well follow him. Goodwind had to send volunteers to do his job." Arthur frowned, the veins in his clenched fists pulsating with blue blood. "I wish I could let him go."

Yang stumbled over his words, "Got to set an example, though... Right?"

Arthur peered down at the smaller man. "You have a lot of nerve speaking to me and my wife with such hollow platitudes."

"Arthur," Hanna groaned. "Let it rest."

"Until they let you rest?" Arthur's anger mounted. Suddenly, her husband diverted his gaze from the young doctor. He grunted in disgust. "Ask your uncle how cowards were treated in the war. That is how we soldiers set examples."

Hanna shook her head and pointed a finger at him admonishingly, "This man's uncle removed the bullet from our son's chest."

Arthur turned around and kicked a stone toward the gallows, "And what did *he* do?"

Hanna saw no point in arguing with him. *Not when we are on the same side.* She eyed Yang, whose face was buried in his chest. The boy was clearly ashamed. *Good.* She frowned at Arthur and motioned for the doctor to follow her up the Hill. They entered the tavern and just as the door was closing, a man called after her.

"Misses Gardner."

Constable Goodwind was perpetually out of breath. He sniffled up a wad of snot, swallowing it. "Dreadful cold."

You always have a cold. His white mustache was coated with a thin film of mucus. From the sagging gut he touted about, Hanna was quite sure the constable had never run a day in his life. "Yes, sir?" She beamed.

"We have found the murderer."

"Oh?" Hanna wondered who would have wanted Latrell and his gang dead. She remarked, *A rudeness such as his was bound to catch up with him.*

"Some whoremonger," the fat lawman gasped for a breath.

"Lord, man, compose yourself," Yang grumbled.

Edric Goodwind raised a finger and hacked up a cough, "When you get to my age, master Yao, you will eat yo' words."

"Not in such copious quantities as you eat yours," Yang uttered under his breath.

The constable was predisposed to sucking up his snot and did not hear him. "What's that? Quite so," he turned to address Hanna. "Your husband has the right of it. A heavy hand will keep these foreign types from takin' advantage of us. With the Oleander attracting them ruffians, can't be too careful." The constable hoisted his belly like a flag. He bowed as much as his girth allowed. Edric Goodwind left singing, *"One little goblin hanging from the gallows, don't commit no crime for this place is hallowed!"* The old lawman was poor with melody and dreadfully off key. His inability to follow a time signature was an embarrassment to all that heard him.

Yang looked at his wrist, where no watch could be found. "If I may find my uncle, misses Gardner? There is a dreadful cough going around the Drowned Anchorage."

Hanna rubbed her fingers against her crimson cuticles, feeling for more loose skin. She did not want to let the young man out of her sight. *He will save me, I know it. I know it.*

The young man did not wait for permission. He trotted out the tavern, waving behind him, "I will check on Aeric soon."

He was gone before Hanna could call after him. *Aeric will be fine, but...* She rubbed the hairs on her arms, unsure if she felt lonely, scared, or just tired.

"What did he want?"

Hanna shivered and swirled around, putting her hand to her heart when she saw who had spoken. "My word, Galahad, don't scare me like that." She allowed herself a giggle, "Which one?"

Galahad eyed the constable, "Both, I suppose."

"Well, what Yang is doing is anybody's guess," Hanna said. She frowned, "As to the constable... They found the murderer of that boy."

"Indeed?" Galahad did not seem very interested.

"Yes, a flesh salesman, of course."

Galahad gasped, "Terrell? What will they do to him?" He asked, almost yelling, "Did he say anything?"

"I don't much care." She remembered her son's request. "Aeric wanted me to thank you. Words can only express my family's gratitude so much... No, no." Hanna felt it was her duty to say, "Our family. You have been a guardian to the children. No thanks are sufficient."

Galahad coughed a laugh, closed his mouth, and scratched the back of his head. He looked behind him and around Hanna. "You are too sweet."

Oh, I have made him uncomfortable. "I'm sorry. That's a lot to take in." She gazed sternly at him, "True, though."

"No, no. It is not that." Galahad blinked several times and burped, "Have you seen, uhm," he took a slimy object from his mouth and deposited it in a nearby waste bin. "Thousand pardons, chewing gum is just awful after a while. Have you seen Momed by chance?"

Hanna shook her head and out of instinct felt the man's forehead. "You need to get some rest, Galahad. My, you are burning up. Have you slept at all since yesterday?"

Galahad coughed, "I slept somewhat. But my father has been on my mind. That's all."

Hanna replied with a supportive tone, "I bet he has. What to do next, right?"

Galahad's head teetered left and right, "That's about it. I am selling the store."

"Oh good," Hanna exclaimed. "What made you change your mind?"

"Lilian Vellencourt," Galahad coughed violently. "Made me an offer too good to pass on."

"How exciting." Hanna beamed. She kept her surprise to herself. *Vellencourt? What is that prowling woman up to?*

"Yes," Galahad nodded, happily. "I will be heading west."

Oh, Galahad. You are smarter than that. The west was the temptress of wayward ambition and the doom of the disadvantaged. Miners had gone up to the Oleander once before. Everyone seemed to be forgetting what happened to them. *I hope there isn't another flood...* She shrugged and smiled at the Muhali. *We must all be allowed to fail.* "Do be careful of Lilian," Hanna warned him. "I hear she has a little company up that way."

Galahad had already turned around. Thinking the conversation quite concluded, he departed. Hanna sucked in her lips and popped them. *Am I everyone's toy to chew and discard?* Hanna decided she deserved better that evening and climbed wearily to her bedroom. The bed was disheveled but she hardly cared. *I am so tired.* First her diagnosis, then Aeric... She laid down and her back cracked loudly.

Something made a thumping sound below the bed.

"Someone there?" Hanna asked. She clenched her sheets as if they would protect her. She feared someone had slipped into her room. She could feel her heartbeat in her head.

"Mama?" Emilia crawled from underneath the bed. Hanna hung her head down and looked. Isabelle's tongue met her squarely on the nose. Hanna snorted, bemused.

"What are you two doing underneath mama's bed?" She took Emilia's arms and helped her up. Isabelle jumped up and circled around the foot of the bed until she had patted the sheets thoroughly. Then, she sat with dignity, crossed her paws, and chewed her nails. Hanna spoke to the sound of the hound's anxious grooming.

Emilia could not take her eyes off the door, "It felt safer."

"Nobody is going to hurt you." Hanna did not quite believe it herself.

"I don't care about me," Emilia said defiantly. "Aeric-" she wavered, unable to continue her thought. She moved on, "And daddy is outside working. I have to, mama. I have to make sure nobody hurts you."

"Oh sweetie," Hanna pulled Emilia to her chest and kissed her hair, holding the back of her head like she was still a baby. "Mama is alright."

"You are a bad liar," Emilia muttered.

She continued kissing her daughter's head, unable to respond for a time. *It is no use lying to her, she may be anxious but she is not stupid.* "Yeah," she snorted. "I am."

"Don't worry, mama. Izzy will protect you."

Hanna peeked over at the hound. Isabelle was on her back, kicking into the air as she scratched herself. She looked like she was riding an upside-down bicycle. Hanna looked at Emilia and giggled, "Ferocious."

"I don't get it, mama." Emilia may not be stupid, but she was still just a child. "If you have a small bug hurting you, why can't Isabelle squash it?"

"Sometimes the little things are the most powerful, and the biggest things the most vulnerable."

That cheered her. Emilia's cheeks puffed out and she pushed her mother, "That means I am strong because I am little."

"That's right," Hanna assured her. "You and Izzy are the best guards I could ask for." She bent her head as if to tell a secret, "Think you could guard mama from the other room? She's feeling real sleepy."

Emilia darted to the door, excitedly, "If anyone comes up, I'll kick them down the stairs."

Hanna laughed, "Maybe don't do that. A stern warning and a bark from Izzy should do the trick."

"Okay," Emilia sounded disappointed. "If they don't listen," she bent down and kissed Isabelle's head, "We bite." The hound licked the girl's head while her tail spun in a spasmic circle. Emilia reached for the bedroom door, "We'll keep you safe, mama."

Oh how am I going to go to sleep now? Hanna rolled onto her side. *I have the sweetest children in the world. They will be the kindest, the ablest innkeepers.* Hanna was filled with happy thoughts. She wondered what kind of woman Aeric would bring home. She daydreamed of all the things Emilia might do. *She could be a doctor...*

The thought quelled her happiness instantly. *Why must these doctors insist they know what is best? I do not care about the side-effects.* Hanna was convinced the pride of a few was the doom of many. Gloom came into her room and Hanna put the covers over her head. Suddenly, it was too painful to think of her children growing up. *They will grow up without mama.* Though the process took an hour or more, Hanna forced herself to rest.

Arthur woke her later. He was massaging her feet and smiling like there was nothing wrong in the world. Hanna disliked his smile. She did not appreciate his patronizing baby-talking either.

"There she is, finally awake. You slept for hours, baby girl."

Hanna's feet recoiled. She sat up. "What time is it?"

"Five." He opened his eyes, continuing to spew out affection, "Need anything?"

"No, that's okay," Hanna replied.

Arthur loomed over her, "Then why do you speak to me like it is not okay?"

"Because you treat me like a child. I'm dying, not inept."

Arthur did not speak. He nodded sadly. His towering shadow dissipated and he sat down next to her. "Come here," he beckoned.

"I don't want to." *He cannot simply say nice things when it suits him.*

"I take my stress out on you," Arthur said, much to her surprise.

"Yes you do," she admitted. She was careful not to sound too forgiving.

Arthur put a hand on her lap, "I will work on it. You aren't a child. You are far smarter than any adult. You're stronger than many men." He leaned in, "When I first met you, I was afraid of you."

"Men are easily frightened," Hanna glared. She wanted to laugh, but it seemed easier to be hateful. *Why am I so angry?* She shook her head and smiled weakly at Arthur. She wanted to kiss him, but she could only express unhappy thoughts. "I do so much for everyone. I feel like you take me for granted."

Arthur gulped. "I do," he admitted. "It's just this business with Frederick. And now Aeric…"

His honesty always stunned her. *He never lets me stay mad at him, that bastard.* She laid down onto his lap. Arthur put a hand on her back and used another to stroke her head, weaving his fingers through her hair.

Hanna muttered, "I get so sad when I think about you." Her windpipe narrowed and only the ghost of a voice emerged, "You are going to be so lost."

Arthur tightened his hold around her, letting her tears soak his clothes. Hanna could tell he was trying to sound happy, for her sake. "You're right. I will be."

His attempts only made her sadder. "I would never remarry if it was you," Hanna said. She quickly added, "But I want you to, if it will make you happy."

"I won't," Arthur said immediately. "It will take some time and I will be incredibly sad, but I will find a way to cope." He kissed her head, "I'll just say your name to hear it. I will go to our favorite places and reminisce."

The image was too real, too imminent. She could picture him sitting on the park benches of Castle Rock, his arm over an empty seat. Hanna buried herself in his clothes, hoping to stifle her crying so Emilia would not hear.

"I will go to our favorite parks and point at the muskrats and the waterfowl," he went on.

Hanna latched her arms around him.

"And I'll say, look there darling, the baby geese are swimming."

Hanna did not so much care that she was dying, not truly. She rolled over and looked up at Arthur. All the wounds from the Great War suddenly went away. Hanna saw the young man who had taken her into a vibrant world, the man who made her a woman, a mother. The man wiped away her tears. When he continued, more took their place. He wiped those away, too.

"I first said I would marry you there, at the park."

Hanna choked, laughing and crying all at once. "You did." She wiped her own tears, "You were wearing those ugly white socks."

"Where did those go?" Arthur inquired.

"I do the laundry. I can throw out whatever I want."

Arthur puffed out his lips and admonished her lovingly, "Those socks were good to me, not a hole in them."

"Well I am better to you."

"Yes, but you have a few holes," Arthur joked.

Any comic meaning was drowned by another meaning, one of doom. Arthur frowned. Hanna began to search for something to say. She liked it when they both were happy. *Let's not skulk, come on.*

Arthur swatted a fly away from his eye, "We should invite Charles and Cora to stay. I miss them."

"Good luck without the post operating."

Arthur shooed away the dilemma, "Bah, I can send someone." He shifted his weight onto her hair, pulling her head down.

Hanna gasped in pain, "Ah, ah, ah."

"Oh, sorry, sorry," her husband quickly repositioned.

Emilia burst into the room, "Mama?"

Hanna felt a tinge of pain in her head. Immediately, she got up from Arthur's lap and laid flat across the bed. "It is nothing, sugarbear. Daddy and I are getting excited is all."

Emilia turned her child's face into a stern scowl. She spoke like a parent, "Not too excited."

Arthur reached down from under the bed, pulled one of Hanna's slippers, and tossed it lightly at his daughter. "Stop reading your mother's books."

"No!" Emilia laughed, fleeing her parent's room.

Arthur raised his brow at Hanna and smirked. "We could, you know?"

Hanna was in no mood for sex. Her head was spiraling into another painful session. She could feel the dance of tiny needles poking at her skull, the spasms of nausea coursing up her throat.

"Are you okay?" Arthur inquired.

"As good as can be," Hanna lied.

Arthur took off his boots and crawled over to her. "In that case..." He let out a loud, repugnant fart which vibrated the entire bed. He grinned at her devilishly. He flopped onto his side, holding his head with one arm while the other laid flat across his body like a model.

Hanna blinked. She raised her head slightly and looked at him with a half-smirk and stern eyes. "Gross." She did not look away from him until he spoke, which took some time. Arthur scratched his neck.

"Sorry, darling." He smirked, "War humor is hard to shake off."

Hanna stopped him right there. "You were always gross. Don't blame the war."

He flicked her shoulder with a finger, saying, "My first day in Tanglewood, I had to shit..."

"Arthur, I do not want to hear about your shits."

He ignored her, "So I ask Auldwine, 'Oye, where is the latrine?' He points it out to me."

Hanna smirked. She tried to chuckle, but her muscles would not allow it. She cringed and her pupils pulsated. She let out an exacerbated sigh. "Oh baby, I am so tired of these headaches."

Arthur immediately got up, "What do you need, darling? Water, fruit? I heard Yang gave Aeric an Oleander leaf. I could snatch some? OH! I'll get the Yao."

"No, no," Hanna raised her hand, calmly. "It will pass." *Or I will,* she frowned. *The Yao men are useless.*

"Are you sure?" Arthur looked at the door and reached for his jacket, "Yang wanted to come see you once you woke, anyways. He is probably downstairs."

Hanna cleared her throat violently, "No. I want to rest. I don't want any visitors."

Her husband looked as if he had just been shot, like a deer stunned by the sight of a predator. He froze, his lips hardly moving, "Even me?"

Hanna's heart melted. "No. You cannot leave." She opened her arms, making the inaudible sounds which begged him to hold her.

16

Mudpuppy, Whatever the Case

Lilian lived in the military fort of old Auberdine, on the outskirts of town just beyond the outer ring. The towering fort stood upon a natural promontory, overlooking the town. What the bleak, black building lacked in beauty, it made up for in practicality. The Oleander's waterways coalesced behind the structure, making a western attack impossible. Moreover, two waterfalls fell from the promontory, guarding the northern and southern flanks. The only entrance was a small door at the base of the promontory. One had to traverse the Oleander Wash, walk a narrow, slippery bridge, and then hope the door at the base of the rock was unlocked. If not, soldiers at the heights could easily bombard the unlucky.

The Pale knew a defensible location when they saw one. The waterfalls were deafening. His shoes were soaked. *How does Vellencourt stay dry in this place?* He approached a stone entrance. The door was dwarfed by the steep escarpment above. Galahad knocked. The noise was muted by the falls.

Galahad never understood why the richest person in town would choose to live in the Overgrowth. Even Buchanan, whose family had owned the tower for generations, had preferred to live in the Inner Ring. The Overgrowth was the place people wanted to escape, not the place to retire. Vellencourt was an aristocrat of Castle Rock and had lived life in reverse, retiring to a decrepit old tower on the edge of an impoverished ruin.

Galahad knocked again. *How can she even hear the knock?* He peered up the rockface. The base of the tower was not visible.

The door opened. A woman with a bent back opened the door. Galahad could tell immediately that she was Redfeather. Despite this, her skin was covered by whitening powder. She smiled. A metal brace lined her crooked teeth. "This way. Miss Vellencourt has been quite excited for your arrival."

"I am sure the misses is quite excited," Galahad grunted.

"Miss, if you please," the crone grabbed the side of the door and began to close it on him.

"Miss," Galahad acquiesced. The woman nodded and turned around, allowing him to roll his eyes.

Galahad had never been inside the ancient fort. He knew the miners had delved a stone fortification within the rocks itself but could only ever imagine what the place looked like. Buchanan had never been keen on visitors, nor did he care much to maintain the structure. Children used to say the fort was haunted, and that Buchanan Bavar fed those who did not pay their taxes to Wanakhan cannibals.

Galahad eyed crumbled passageways. Barred iron gates led to abyssal blackness. Palisade walls guarded abandoned corridors. Cobwebs defended bulwarks. "Quite a renovation the queen is ordering."

"She said you had a penchant for arrogance," the crone replied.

"*I* do not live in a castle."

"No, you do not. Show some respect or you will have a back like mine."

Galahad poked her shoulder. "What is your name?"

The woman swatted and let out a sheer shriek. "DO NOT TOUCH." She shuddered, wiped the spot clean, and grumbled, "Filthy men."

She led him to a winding stone staircase. It reminded him of the one under the Hill that led to the baths. *Except this one can fit several men abreast.* All along the stairwell hung glimmering weapons of a bygone age, muskets and scimitars, halberds and bows. The fort had not seen combat since the deluge, but its wartime past was unmistakable. Galahad dared not show his awe. The crone would not get to revel in his adoration. "Quite rustic masonry," he scoffed.

"You would do much better, I am sure." The crone left him at the bottom of the stairs. She waddled over to an iron gate and lifted a lever. The gates opened and she stepped inside. "Please," she said as machinery began to groan, "Start walking. It will be the first hall." The woman disappeared as the carriage carried her up. Galahad went toward the mysterious device and watched it levitate. *The rich cannot afford to walk?* He waited for the carriage to return to the bottom level, but after several minutes— he knew it was not returning. Galahad looked at the stairs. *She wants me to walk. It's all a game to her.* He felt the deed to his father's store. Despite his spite, he started scaling the stairs.

He climbed at least a thousand steps. Galahad found himself rounding every bend, expecting to reach the tower proper. "First hall," he spat. After several disappointing glances, Galahad looked mostly at his feet. He kicked any loose stones or pebbles down the stairs, their echoes seeming to carry forever. *A fall from these heights would surely kill someone.* Galahad imagined Lilian in her finest dress, slipping on the fabric, and tumbling to the depths. That put a smile on his face.

Galahad's legs were burning when he finally came upon a vast room. He hid his exhaustion and stepped into a spherical hall.

Lilian Vellencourt had a house like emperors have nations. The floor was made of polished black marble. Galahad conceded to his curiosity and looked at the walls. Ancient tapestries draped down, depicting past worlds. He recognized them as Pale crafts. *Curious,* he remarked. Though made by Pale tailors, the scenes on the tapestries were of Wanakhan tales. The images were easily discerned. In one, Galahad noted the hungry fisher. The story was woven onto the wall. A man sat beside huge, uneaten catches while he fished with a lure made of his own tongue. On another tapestry, there was a woman with a lazy eye lying on a feasting table. Men gathered around her, devouring her flesh. All the while, she smiled and petted their heads.

Windows around the perimeter illuminated the circular room, though the black marble kept things dim. The rays of light met in the center of the room, where came Lilian's voice.

"Is everything prepared for our arrival? My daughter, she—she needs silk sheets or she cannot sleep."

Daughter, Galahad smirked. He heard in Lilian's voice something he had never before. There was a hint of vulnerability, a slight vibrato in her words.

"All preparations are made," came the crone's voice.

"Good," Vellencourt replied in a worrying tone. Lilian's voice immediately returned to its old state. She sounded to Galahad like a woman impersonating a man. "Good, good. Greta, does she need anything? Money, toys?"

The old crone whispered, "I can schedule a visit tonight and you can see if she needs anything more?"

"Quite," Vellencourt agreed. "We do need to have our weekly dinner together."

Schedule a visit? Galahad could hardly believe it. *I always thought business was her baby, but I suppose her baby is just a business.*

"Ah," Lilian smiled at him. She shooed Greta the crone away. "Go upstairs. Tell Elizabeth she can play if she is quiet." She snapped her fingers, "Galahad. Do sit down."

Galahad approached. Lilian was lying across a dark grey sectional sofa, sprawled out in a transparent nightgown. A bowl of nuts and fruits laid on an adjoining table. Lilian leaned over to a fruit basket, got up, and repositioned her gown. Her entire body was visible under the thin garment. She tossed several grapes in her mouth.

Galahad was confident if he was like other men, he would have been disarmed by the woman's flesh. *Lucky for me that I fancy other rounded features and protruding extremities.* Galahad found the air in the room quite too stuffy for his liking.

Vellencourt did not seem to mind. "Come, let's walk. You found things well enough?"

"Well enough," Galahad agreed. As the woman walked, a trail of servants followed her.

"I beg you not to be distracted by my companions," she began.

"Servants," Galahad corrected.

"Please," Lilian urged him, "These are disenfranchised women from your disgusting little Overgrowth. I employ them as a service more to the community than to myself."

Galahad saw through the charade, "If you find the Overgrowth so disgusting, why live here?"

She replied as if the answer was self-evident. "Because I am connected to the people."

Galahad narrowed his gaze. "I have the deed."

"Now to *do* the deed," Lilian walked toward a desk as black as the floor. Galahad looked behind at Vellencourt's serving women. They scrubbed her footprints clean from the surface, leaving no impression that she had walked over it at all. Lilian caught him staring and said casually, "I hire only women as a general practice. I find a man's company... intimidating."

I seriously doubt you find anyone intimidating. "I will be sure not to linger," he promised.

"Here you are," she handed him the envelope. Galahad tossed her the deed and counted the money. "This is a hundred," he saw at once. "We agreed on two hundred."

"We can agree on fifty, if you would like?" Vellencourt let out a feminine cough. "I wonder how a dead father will play into Carolyn's accusations?"

She will never admit she knows. Galahad could not assume his secret was safe, not with someone like her. He tried to be positive. *This is a hundred more than you had yesterday. You were not even going to sell the store before all of this.* Galahad pressed his tongue against his top teeth, pushing his loose incisors toward Lilian. He agreed with his mouth closed, "A hundred will do."

Lilian slammed her fists onto her desks and stood up excitedly. "Fantastic. It seems your father's death had a few positives. What was his name, again?"

Galahad had no wish to play her game any further. "Mudpuppy, whatever the case."

Lilian looked at him like he was a toddler who had just said his first word, pointing her finger at him. "Do not think me prejudiced for this. I do not partake in such pretensions."

Galahad half-smiled and said, "I do." He looked over at the women scrubbing Lilian's footprints. They were Muhali and Redfeather, but they coated their faces in customary white powder, just as if they were from the Rock.

"A word of advice from a friend," Lilian walked toward him and put her arm around his shoulder.

It took all his might not to insult, beat, or otherwise maim her. *Of all the days to run out of Yang's leaf, too.* He had chewed the last of it the evening before to calm his anxious nerves. Now, he had nothing to relax him.

Lilian guided him to the elevator, "Everyone is a trogg, everyone is a goblin." She guided her hand like a rainbow, "Everyone is a mudpuppy. You just have to paint them one."

Galahad seethed and stepped inside the elevator. Lilian waved him goodbye and pulled a lever. A servant wiped the mark her hand had made. The machine jolted down and steel echoed in the vast depths. *Yes,* Galahad mocked her, *give money a pen and the weaker will always be painted black.*

Galahad's eyes had adjusted to the darkness of Vellencourt Tower. When he emerged from the cavern door, the bright light blinded him. The air was dry and cold. Galahad could feel his skin cracking against the wind. *The Fall has been quick, the Winter will be long.* The Oleander Wash had sensed the sudden change in seasons, too. Few were outside. Smoke rose from chimneys. The only noise was muted laughter from inside homes. Everyone was spending the chilly day with their family.

Galahad stood in the middle of the square, analyzing the homes with disgust and envy. He had more money in his back pocket now than any of these wretches would have for an entire year. Galahad's stomach growled. He yearned to have more of Yang's leaf. *No, no.* He had to constantly remind himself that the medicine could have a corrupting influence, that it was wrong to have to schedule one's day around the leaf.

Gah, Momed... He did not know why he dreaded his company so much, only that he went to bed to be rid of him and awoke to avoid him. Galahad remembered their time before he went to war with great fondness. A part of him wished to rekindle those old feelings. *We had a lot of fun...* The empty square was too lonely. Galahad looked behind him, certain he was being watched. Then, he pocketed his hands and hastened to the inn.

When Galahad reached the hedge gate, Arthur was standing before makeshift gallows, staring up at the empty noose. He waved at him and at first, Arthur did not notice. Galahad coughed and the innkeeper turned.

"Ah," Arthur sniffed. He put his reddening hands in his pockets. "Come to enjoy the cold, too?"

"Not particularly. Just finished selling my father's store."

"Good, good," Arthur nodded, absorbed with the gallows. A half-second passed and the innkeeper changed the conversation. "What do you think about this hanging business? Is it wrong to murder a man who, whether indirectly or not, righted a wrong?"

Galahad scratched his chest, unsure how to respond. He cleared his throat but a rasp remained, "Uh, hmm… That's a difficult question to answer." Arthur waited nonetheless for his friend to answer it. Galahad scratched his throat and looked up at the gallows, wondering what it felt like to hang. *Better Terrell finds out than me.* "I think killing begets killing," Galahad replied. "Gotta nip the behavior in the bud, or it will spread like rabbits."

"Mmm," Arthur half-frowned. "That is what everyone is saying." He turned toward his friend and chuckled, "I could not care less about a whoremonger, if truth be told. Just makes me wonder about the, uh, the war. That's all." The innkeeper's voice wavered and he kicked the foundations of the gallows, "Aeric was just a boy, never went to war—and he still got shot?" He shook his head, "I don't know how Auldwine did it all those years. I cannot love this town."

"He loved an ideal," Galahad posited. "Or maybe he was blind to badness."

Arthur shivered, "Let's go up."

Galahad smiled and the two went up the Hill. The innkeeper held the door as he asked, "Where you been all morning? Laverne asked for you. I said you were probably out fishing."

"I hate fishing," Galahad tilted his head. He grinned, "You knew that."

"I am an agent of discord," Arthur smirked. Then, he began to whistle. He went off to the granary, where wooden planks waited beside a box of tools.

"Ah, my love," Momed appeared.

Galahad's face flickered with happiness. "Hello, hello."

Momed hugged him and slowly, Galahad returned his embrace. After a moment, though, Galahad felt the urge to leave the public eye of the tavern. He patted Momed's back and the boy released him.

"How did it go?" he asked.

"Not too awful," Galahad said with a peck of annoyance.

Momed could hear the slight irritation in Galahad's voice like a bloodhound. He saw the boy's demeanor change.

"Oh."

God damn it. Why must you be so sensitive? A thought bit back in response. *Why must you be so transparent?* Galahad endeavored to put on a positive face. He would prefer to have a tranquil evening without any passive enmity. Hoping to remedy Momed's mood, he smiled and kissed the boy's cheek, "I am doing fine."

"Okay," Momed nodded, not convinced. "You seem happier, more alert."

Galahad felt his eye twitch. *He knows I ran out of Yang's leaf.* He fought the urge to quip back at him and smiled as happily as he could. "I really am…" *Maybe a little bit of alcohol will make me more relaxed.* The idea caused him to gag and Momed tilted his head.

"Are you alright?"

"It was just so cold outside," he beamed. Momed nodded and enthusiastically recounted the day's weather. *Yes, just make small talk and it will be okay.* "I know," he replied to Momed, though he did not hear a word the boy was saying. "Definitely," he said with a frown. "I think so," Galahad put a finger to his chin and smiled, adding a deviousness to his face when it seemed Momed might respond well to it. He did.

"Give me five minutes?" Momed said, leaning his head on his shoulder and swaying his hips.

"Uh, yes, definitely," Galahad tried to seem enthusiastic. He was sure an orgasm without Yang's leaf would feel mediocre. Nevertheless, he would do his duty. He grabbed Momed's hands and kissed them. The boy skipped downstairs and left Galahad sweating with nervousness. *This has to be good sex or the next week will be agony. For both of us.* Galahad wrapped his arms around his chest and swayed like a flag in the breeze. He closed his eyes and took a deep breath. *Why can't things be easy anymore?* Suddenly, the tavern erupted.

Galahad's eyes jolted open. He thought he was imagining the cheering. He blinked and looked around. *Are they cheering for me?* He looked down the petrified table. The clapping was not for him.

Hanna was escorting her son into the tavern. Everyone was clapping for Aeric and cheering at his recovery. Galahad stared at the boy, perplexed. Latrell had tried to murder him. *And I murdered Latrell. Perhaps Terrell, too.*

Galahad was not sure if he had done his good deed. He had only meant to scare Latrell straight. *The cunt wasn't supposed to kill him, just rough him up.*

He did not know what to think. Aeric was alive in part because of him. Latrell was dead in part because of him. Did the two deeds cancel each other out? Did one weigh more than the other? Was the murder some twisted form of retribution because Latrell had acted first, shooting an innocent child? If it was retribution, he had done his good deed after all. *But I didn't even know about Aeric. If Latrell had done nothing, the same result would have occurred.* The thinking hurt his head and his chest ached.

Galahad decided he did not much care about Latrell. The boy was an oozing pustule on an already blemished society. That the boy harmed Aeric was neither prophetic nor exonerating. Galahad waved at Aeric.

The boy struggled to look at him without crying. He had his father's reluctance toward showing emotions. He stopped himself before saying anything else, "I uhm... If you ever..."

"You are welcome," Galahad smiled.

Aeric nodded. He held onto his mother's shoulder with one arm and held his stomach with another.

Hanna ushered him along, "I wish we could stay. He needs to rest up. Evelyn let us use her automobile, but we still had to climb the Hill." She moved her son along, "Do you want that herb Yang gave you?"

"Nuh-uh," Aeric answered. "I don't like how it makes me feel. Honestly," the boy paused and tossed the pouch into a nearby garbage bin. Galahad watched it fly.

He waited for the two to disappear. Then, he looked behind him at the patrons. He tried to appear like a lowly worker and went toward a cupboard, took a bag, and replaced the bag in the bin with a new one. He then walked outside and felt for the herb pouch. *What are you doing?* He caught himself thinking. He paused. *You are just becoming your father.*

"I saved a boy's life," Galahad said aloud. He took Yang's leaf and threw the remaining bag at the Hill. The wind lofted it away. *No more of those nasty thoughts,* Galahad grinned. He could feel his heart pounding, anticipating the lovely night to come. *You are not your father,* Galahad told himself, *you never drink. Besides, I only do this at night.* He glanced over at the abandoned granary.

Galahad said to a random Redfeather man, "Chilly." *That's good. Small talk is important for appearances.*

When he went to check on Momed, he felt extremely hopeful for the night ahead. He took the Muhali by his arms and swung him around. Momed seemed slightly taken aback by the change but was swept away by Galahad's infectious happiness.

"We are sure to sully ourselves," Galahad's face sank with sarcasm. He skipped toward the door, "We should eat before we begin, so we can hide under the covers all night." The prospect of lying in bed all night did not *really* appeal to him, but he felt giddy seeing Momed happy. The boy readily agreed. That was good, as Galahad was hungry.

Galahad ate little that evening. He had taken to a smoked salmon with ravenous appetite, but after one bite, he was no longer hungry. *Perhaps I need to wait for the leaf's effects to heighten.* Galahad knew the herb amplified his taste buds. So engrossed with trying to enjoy dinner, to make Momed feel like he was happy, Galahad spoke very little to the boy. Momed did not seem to mind and they retired to the room quickly.

They immediately began undressing. It was like they had just met for the first time again. Galahad stared at Momed with newfound appreciation. The young Muhali suited him nicely. He dragged his nails down Momed's back, staring into his eyes. Galahad felt good but he was ready to feel even better. Ever willing to please him, Momed went to his knees and pulled his pants down. "Lift your foot," he looked up.

Galahad did so.

"Other one, now," he commanded in a teacher's tone. Galahad liked that. He kicked the pant leg off his foot. The clothing fell toward the bed and Galahad put his hands on Momed's head.

"Let's go to the bed," he took Galahad by the hand. "The floor, it hurts my knees."

"Whatever you want," Galahad followed. He grabbed the young man's ass, squeezing it in anticipation. Momed bent over slowly. His arms rested on the bedside; they then dropped toward the floor. Momed tilted his head toward something. He sifted through Galahad's pants. *Come on, you tease.* Galahad rubbed against him, longing to continue. He put his other hand on Momed's hip.

Momed swatted it away. He rose slowly.

"Feisty, tonight," Galahad smirked. He went to kiss him.

Momed raised the herb pouch. Immediately, Galahad felt a coldness enter the room. They stared at each other for a moment while Galahad debated lying. Meanwhile, Momed judged him with unblinking indifference.

"Yang thought I needed more."

"Mm," Momed said, not convinced. As Galahad reached for the pouch, Momed pulled it away.

"Give it to me," Galahad ordered. He approached Momed, who now leaned onto the bed while his arms remained adamantly at his side. Galahad stepped ever closer, staring at him. "Come on, let's have some fun." He smiled at the boy and tried to rub his cheek. Momed shied away, tossing the herb pouch.

"No. Not like this," Momed said, morosely. He walked toward the door, sighed, and then stared at Galahad. His sad eyes were accusatory and infuriating.

Galahad met them with a glare. He grabbed the pouch and placed it on the chair, in clear view.

Here we go. Galahad gave up. He shrugged, put on his clothes, and crawled into bed. *We will both feel different in the morning. He needs to calm down and think about things.*

"Sleep already?" Momed asked. He made no effort to hide his irritation.

Annoyed, Galahad rolled over and said, "I am tired."

"Why do we bother with this charade," Momed stated.

"Are you asking rhetorically?"

"I'm asking literally."

Don't burn your bridges, Galahad told himself. He closed his eyes and hoped Momed would take the hint. *In five minutes, he will assume I've drifted to sleep.* Five minutes elapsed and Galahad opened his eyes. Momed was glaring at him. He was holding the herb pouch.

Galahad did not think. He bolted upright and snatched the pouch from Momed's hands. "Do not touch my things."

"There was a time when you liked me to touch your things." Momed's eyes welled.

"I would have liked you to this evening, but you had to go... Oh don't cry, damn it." *He is going to ruin my night.* "I can't go to sleep early?"

"It is not that. You-you do not care anymore." Momed put his elbows on his thighs and covered his head with his hands. "You would rather be with that leaf than me."

"I am grieving. It helps me."

"Is that what you call it? Grieving?" Momed wiped his tears. Galahad had never seen him so angry before. His eyes were twitching wildly. "I am no fool."

Galahad swallowed. "You're right. You are not a fool. I am sorry."

"Good," Momed shouted.

Galahad went to embrace Momed. "I think we should sleep on this and get clear heads. The both of us."

Momed pushed him away, "You never have a clear head anymore."

Galahad's nostrils twitched. *I don't need this.* He would rather be alone than have to make amends for a crime he never committed. "I think a night apart would suit us."

"Yes," Momed muttered.

Galahad looked down at his pouch. *I will be happier without him.* He gathered his things in silence, his trinkets and a few pairs of clothes. He could feel Momed's glare wherever he moved, though Galahad did not give him the satisfaction of looking into his eyes. They did not say goodbye. They said nothing to one another at all. Galahad closed the door and looked around with spiteful happiness. "What a quaint day it is today, good for a walk."

The quiet corridor left him feeling like a child. *What an idiotic thing to say.* Galahad's head jolted down in shameful rage and he stormed up the stairs. He managed to avoid any prying patrons, weaving unseen around the wooden pillars. He escaped into the cold night and immediately chewed another leaf.

It was taking longer for the effects to hit him. *Best chew another,* Galahad decided. *Arthur will let me sleep in the kitchens if I tell him what has happened. If I tell him what has happened...* The mere thought of admitting what had occurred embarrassed him. Galahad glanced at the granary. *That room is vacant.* Galahad shook his head fiercely.

His deviant act was too haunting for him to go back there. He sighed and laid out his clothes, creating a makeshift quilt of his meager outfits.

"Mind if I sit with you?"

Not this woman. "Will you go even if I say no?"

Laverne smiled and shook her head. "I know a boy who needs to talk when I see one."

I am a man, he glared at her. "Latrell, too?" Galahad's anger turned to shame and he shook his head. *She was his mother, you cunt.* "That was wrong of me to do." Galahad burped, "Uh, say, I mean."

"Latrell wanted to be his daddy, a crofter, a hunter, a man's man." Laverne looked into Galahad's eyes, "You don't strike me as someone who wants to be their daddy."

Why does everyone seek to shame me? Galahad made sure his herb pouch was deep in his pocket. "Not at all," he admitted.

Laverne looked at his clothes sprawled out on the grass. "Honey, why you out here by your lonesome?"

Galahad contemplated scorning her affections. He was not Latrell. "Why do you seek to adopt every orphan you come across?"

"Guess I'm payin' for some crime," Laverne looked up at the clouds. "Such gloomy weather. I suppose it's poetic."

"How so?" Galahad grunted.

"Apt weather for a gloomy occasion."

"We had a poet in the war," Galahad found himself saying. "Liked to scribble down notes. Everything about Tanglewood seemed to relate to his own philosophy. One day, the poor bastard was blasted by artillery. We found him dead, his pen lodged in his throat."

"Bad case of writer's block," Laverne joked. A snowflake hit her cheek.

Galahad could feel the leaf's effects. He laughed deeply and when he opened his eyes, he found Laverne less repulsing than before. "Funny," he admitted. He scanned around him. *Is it snowing?*

"Son," she said, sternly. "How's about you stay in my room?"

Galahad looked down at his clothes and before he could decline, Laverne said, "Less you wanna freeze. Everybody talkin' 'bout a blizzard comin' down from the east mountain."

"Ah," Galahad nodded. "Fine." Laverne helped him to his feet and gave him a hug. She tapped his back and tutted her tongue, "This will not do. We gon' have ta get you some proper winter clothes."

"We'll see," Galahad hesitated. *Generosity always comes at a price.* Surely, Laverne had hers.

"You god damn right," Laverne nodded. "We gon' see you lookin' sharp."

Laverne guided him back toward her room. Unlike the other guest rooms, Laverne's lodgings were located past the kitchens. "Ole' Gardner said she had no use for the space. Me and 'Trell came here after his daddy passed."

She said hello to Wenton. The chef grumbled and waved. He was experimenting with a form of hot sauce which required his full attention. They veered to the left and she unlocked a storage closet.

"Hanna had the storeroom replaced, even had it painted purple for Latrell." She looked back at Galahad, "That was his favorite color."

She doesn't seem bothered by his murder in the least. Galahad nodded, "That's good." The layout resembled most other guest rooms. A large bed, a dresser, and a rocking chair were the only pieces of furniture. However, Laverne had taken some of her belongings from her past house with her. A white and blue crib rested next to the rocking chair. She saw Galahad staring at it and commented, "I just could not be parted with it." She sat down in the chair and caressed the wooden posts, "So many memories... Besides, lots o' babies without proper care these days."

"Probably," Galahad frowned. "Where, uhm, should I sleep?"

"The bed, o' course."

Galahad sniffed, "With... uh... you?"

"I like sleepin' in the chair in my older age," Laverne smiled. She was in her thirties but acted as if she were fifty. "And I'm sure you be needin' to stretch out. Go on, you take the bed. I won't mind."

"Thank you," Galahad beamed. He felt the need to ask permission, "Mind if I go down to the library?"

"Go 'head," Laverne began to knit. "You see Dixon, you tell him to come see me? I gots his hat almost done."

17

A Stranger in the Den

Charles feared the growing storm clouds. Usually, they rolled in every afternoon and disappeared by the evening. Yet, these clouds only kept expanding, swallowing the sky. He eyed the clouds suspiciously; Charles did not know how to prepare for weather he had never seen before.

Charles remarked, hoping to quiet his anxiety, *The essentials will suffice. I have enough for a detour.* He had brought a handful of outfits, several books, and enough food for four days. His mare was not overburdened, but she was carrying a heavier load than she was used to.

As am I, he remarked. He glanced up at the sky with trepidation. The storm was moving with him.

Charles feared those clouds and their green tint. He sighed and felt his back pocket. He had taken some letters he had once written to his mother. He had already reread them all, laughing at old jokes, crying at gone joy, and agonizing over misspelled words. His mother had noticed the misspellings too, marking them like a teacher does a student's paper. Charles tried to smile. *She's not entirely gone,* he wanted to believe. *I've got her words.*

Still, Charles had taken perhaps more than he should have. A travel chest was fastened to the mare's side. Deep within, past his books, clothes, and food, were several letters between his mother and Auldwine. He did not know whether he would read them, but he wanted to have them nonetheless. He hoped they would not be too angry, if ever the dead could see the deeds of the living.

He sniffled. His mare snorted.

"You're the most talkative horse I've ever met."

The mare stopped, stomped, flicked her eyes, and then took him away from his mother's cottage.

"Off to new purpose," he declared. Charles tried not to look back at his mother's home, but turned nonetheless. Intertwined branches of spruce and ash swayed in the breeze, waving him off.

Charles patted the horse's head. "You need a name." He recalled the figures of old he had revered, the ancient names of past heroes, and names he thought simply sounded nice. He happened upon the story of the last Adawakan.

Charles patted the mare's mane. "You're an innkeeper's horse." The animal snorted a response. "Opinionated, too," Charles nodded. "Well, the innkeepers are

145

descended from Niwot, the last Adawakan of the Wanakha. They were the first people to live in this valley, and he was their final leader." The horse snorted, this time more aggressively.

"No, no. I won't name you after a man. Besides, Niwot may have been a great leader and may have founded the site where the inn stands—but he was not the first innkeeper." Charles cleared his throat. The cold air was giving him a runny nose. "Now, some claim the first innkeeper was Niwot's son, but I disagree."

"After the deluge killed the miners on the Oleander and drowned the outer ring, Niwot's wife gathered the survivors. She was Pale by birth but had taken a Wanakhan name. Were it not for her—nobody would inhabit Auberdine today."

"I think I will name you after her. Here's to you, Atlani." Charles looked back again. The forest had swallowed the cottage and he could no longer see it. *Auldwine's favorite stories were about the Wanakha...*

"Are we related to Wanakha people?" Charles had once asked while on his mother's lap.

Cora Eastmont had no easy answer for such a question. "Some people claim they are, but most are fibbers trying to add something grand to their own little stories."

Charles bounced along the rocky road, reminiscing. His mother had told him that they were descendants of the Redfeather, a nation far to the north of the Castle Rock. As a boy, he had been disappointed by that answer. The Redfeather were hardly mythical. They were just an ordinary people who sometimes fought the Castle Rock. His mother had read the dissatisfaction in her son's face.

"You might have some Wanakha blood on your father's side," Cora posited.

"No," Charles shook his head. "The Wanakha were not evil."

His mother had not allowed him such thoughts. Nor had Auldwine. They curtailed youthful ignorance wherever they found it. "Nobody is evil, nobody is good," they had told him. "Not entirely."

Charles had never believed them, not entirely. Charles felt a drop of water on his cheek. He wiped it off and said to Atlani, "They were." Another drop hit him, this time on the arm.

"Ah, a little downpour. It is about time," he declared. Charles looked at his arm as the drops fell, but when he saw the spot where the rain had fallen—the drop was solid, not liquid. His next thought, a single word, echoed long in his mind. *Snow.* A dozen little flakes were gently falling. Charles cursed his bad luck.

"Atlani, dear," Charles frowned, "We will need to hasten." He urged the old mare along at a quicker pace.

In the back of his mind, Charles knew continuing was a bad idea. Snow was no trifle. Nonetheless, he persevered. He was not going to be waylaid, not by a little precipitation. *Fall snows melt before they begin.* He would not go back. He was afraid if he did, he might never leave the comfort of his mother's hollow. *I must go forward. Mama would not want me to turn back.* But how dearly Charles wanted to turn around. *It is a sign,* a quiet voice told him, as pervasive as a woodpecker's drilling. *A bad omen.*

He heard his mother's voice. *It could be a good sign,* she said to him. *Omens are just probabilities personified.* He tried to think of a benefit the snow would provide him. *Fewer predators will be out. I won't make as much noise.* Charles smiled. He could see his breath. *Yes, this is a good sign.*

As he continued down the valley, the snowflakes became a gentle blanketing. *Strange,* Charles pondered, *the rain is always strongest near the peak. Though I suppose this is snow.* Charles narrowed his eyes and tried to recall the last time it had snowed on the east mountain. *Surely, when I was younger... No, no that was just cold rain...* It always rained, but Charles could not remember the last time it had snowed. Despite the heights of the two Cottonwood giants, only the Oleander mountain ever had winter storms. Snow was a foreigner on the eastern mountain.

Charles looked around at the forest, wondering what strange change was in the air. *Even the storms are different since the war.* He felt uncomfortable with the change, mistrusting the curious calls of birds he had never heard before. He looked down at the frosted ant hills and espied species he knew were found farther south, at lower elevations. A creature howled and at first, Charles thought it was a wolf. *That's not a howl I've ever heard.* he analyzed Atlani, wondering if the howl had startled her. The mare's ears fluttered. Another howl echoed across the high hills.

Charles shivered but not from the cold. He peeked behind him but not from wistfulness. Where snow did not reflect a blinding light, dark crevices casted looming shadows. Gnarled roots and twisted branches reached up like monstrous claws. The forest grew more and more tangled the further they travelled. Even his mare noticed the change as they crept west down the mountain. Atlani whinnied, pausing every few minutes, her ears flicking back and forth. She would stomp, clearly disturbed by something Charles did not have the sense to see. Then, with his encouragement, Atlani would continue. The mare's ears never stopped moving, though.

Plenty of bears and mountain lions in the forest. Charles shook off the thought. *The birds would let me know if there was a predator.* Charles scoffed, telling his wayward worry to find somewhere else to loiter. "Nothing to fear," he smiled.

Nature responded with cold silence. Not even the wind made a noise. All was still, like the world was a picture Charles found himself wandering through. Insects that had not found shelter before the snows laid motionless on the dirt while snowflakes covered them in white caskets. A spider's web glistened with frost. The spider hung from its silk, suspended in death. Its egg pouch was still attached to its body.

"Waking corpses," he licked his cracked lips. Charles put his hands in his overcoat. *Winter did not wait for Fall, it seems.*

Atlani snorted her displeasure, stopped, and glanced to her right. Charles followed her lead. Through a thicket of brambles, he saw the remains of an old crofter's home. Built on a stone foundation, the wooden walls were thick with dead vine weed. The roof already had a layer of snow from the ongoing dusting.

"Smart girl," Charles patted her side. "I agree." He dismounted and followed Atlani into the thorny thicket. What once was a passable path was now nothing more than a thin, winding trail, enclosed between wooden jaws. Weeds had grown in every hole. Prickling thorns poked from every angle. Atlani did not seem to mind the goat heads, but Charles was less calloused. The barbs embedded themselves in his ankles, forcing him to stop. He plucked sharp seedlings from his socks, though there were simply too many on his soles to be entirely rid of them. By the time he had finished, his boots had accumulated dozens more barbs and Atlani was far ahead of him.

"Oye," he called after the mare. He did not like being left alone in the cold, with nothing but an abandoned croft for company. He tried to ignore the pain of the barbs and ran after his horse. Atlani was far ahead, blazing through the brambles in search of someplace warm, somewhere dry.

The storm was gaining momentum. Storm clouds were heading west with Charles and showed no signs of dissipating. Charles looked up at the trees. Some had yet to lose their leaves and pockets of orange sagged under the growing weight of the storm. *Those branches will be broken come tomorrow*, he knew. The wind started to surge, whistling through the forest. Flying leaves battered his face. Charles squinted. He could hardly see Atlani. Her tail was tucked against her body. She stomped her hooves.

"Now let me catch up, you rascal," he called after her. He was starting to get annoyed with the stubborn beast. "Not all of us have four legs."

A branch cracked and the mare whinnied. Atlani sent a gust of air fluttering through her nose. A dozen sticks broke at once. The horse was suddenly nowhere to be seen. A jolt of fear shot through him. "Atlani," Charles whispered. A wretched sound echoed in far-off reply. *That sounded awfully like a shriek*. He froze. Then came another, fainter shriek. Then, nothing. The lull of the forest resumed. Charles looked around and put his back to a large aspen trunk.

Fuck me, she had my tools. My weapons. Charles reached into his pocket for a small knife. He glared down at it. *Little good this will do against a cougar or a bear*. He peered ahead. The abandoned building was not far now. He need only pass over the crofter's fence and he would have shelter. After the storm, he could find Atlani. Yes, that would do. He moved toward the house.

Charles scanned the horizon as he went, hoping to find the horse. The wind beat against his eyelids and his eyes filled with water. He lingered on every dark shape. Nothing moved. His lips were starting to bleed from the winds. Charles spat and lifted his legs gingerly over the weeds, hoping to avoid the wooden daggers growing out of the rocks. He grunted, sliding his body through the burned remains of two fallen pines. Charles caught his breath and looked up at the homestead. A broken window served as a sufficient doorway.

The derelict structure was much like the trail leading to it. Furniture was overturned, curtains and blankets had been ripped. The pantry had long ago been raided. The pillars holding up the house were filled with webs, but those hovels too were emptied. Charles heard a raccoon family in the chimney above. Mouse droppings clung to the walls. A wild foulness permeated the air. *But at least it is warm*.

Charles fell onto an old rocking chair. The wood creaked under his weight. An arm of the chair collapsed. Charles winced as a splinter shot through his hand. *The floor would be better*. The rest of the furniture was in a similar state of disrepair. The fabric of the couch was ripped in many places. The bedroom smelled the foulest and the bed was wet. The sheets were torn.

Charles walked around the home, hoping to find some scrap of food the animals had not picked clean. All he could find were the remains of small critters. The house was barren. The only items left to him were small, shattered bones scattered in grim piles throughout the home. Layers of bone dust accumulated around the heaps. Charles bent over to examine one of the bones. Tooth marks had gnawed the marrow clean.

Charles rubbed the handle of his knife. He suddenly preferred the snow to the house. He started for the exit. He put his hands on the broken window frame, about to hoist his body up. Then, he stopped.

A quiet whimper came directly behind him. Charles closed his eyes, not sure whether to turn around and barrel out the window. The creature made another sound, like a high-pitched yawn. Charles grimaced and reluctantly glanced behind him.

A small canine was curled up on the same rocking chair Charles had just sat on. *Wolf pup,* Charles gulped. The pup tilted its head at him and licked its leg. Charles looked to his left and right. *No adults...* "Are you on your own, little guy?"

Damn it, Charles, go. Not everything needs your love. Charles continued approaching, careful not to startle the creature. The pup did not seem to mind the company, either. It was more preoccupied with licking its leg. As he neared, he saw why. The little thing had a terrible cut across its leg, probably from the infestation of weeds outside.

Charles knelt. "Okay, fella. Don't worry, Mister Eastmont is here."

The wolf pup skittered back toward the chair.

"That means I am a friend," Charles smiled. *It doesn't want your help.* The wolf let out a weak snarl, showing him its teeth. *Leave it.*

Charles nodded. Not everything needed to be saved. Most things did not want to be saved, or if they did—they wanted to be saved by something in particular. He was not the wolf's mother. He was not a wolf. *For all I know, a human killed its mother.*

His knees cracked as Charles lifted himself up. He left the wolf pup and went toward the window. He sighed and wiped his eyes. He snorted up an accumulation of snot. The snow was accumulating fast. The ground had disappeared. The forest floor which had before been a quilt of many colors was replaced by a blanket of white. *Onward,* Charles decided. He hesitated as he placed his hands on the windowsill. Out of the periphery, a low shadow crept closer to him.

Charles blinked a hundred times, froze, and turned his head an inch. A massive wolf had prowled up to him. Now, it was only an arm's length away. Charles made no indication that he saw the beast. Meanwhile, it positioned its hind legs. Behind him, the cluttered carpet sifted noisily. He was encircled. Beside him and behind him, the pack was ready to pounce. In that moment, he regretted ever showing affection to that accursed pup.

Charles thought of a wolf's hunting habits. *They will not attack until I flee.* A wolf behind him began to growl, those beside him threatened him with swipes of their paws. *They will try to intimidate me.* A hundred ideas came to him and ninety-nine went unheeded. A surge of adrenaline surged through his body. His mind went blank.

18

A Horse and a Hanging

The snow's beauty was not lost on her. Each snowflake was like a diamond. The glittering grove gleamed like a shawl of gems. Hanna rocked in her chair, watching the children play from the patio. Laverne sat beside her, though neither of them had said one word to each other that morning. The woman was quite content to knit and chuckle gaily at the playful children. Hanna was glad she did not make an effort to speak to her. Her upbringing told her to be polite and strike up a conversation; despair and worry told her small talk was moot. So, while Laverne grunted with amusement at the orphans, Hanna watched her own family.

Arthur was shoveling a pathway toward the inn. *You said Yang wanted to see me. Well?* She thought surely the young doctor had changed his mind, that he was ready to heal her. Instead, two days had passed, a snowstorm had come, and Yang had not. *My door is open and still he stays away? Does he toy with me?* He had been one word away from agreeing to the procedure. *Until Aeric woke up...*

Her boy was working as tirelessly as his father. They both had shovels in hand, their pale cheeks red with cold. While Arthur worked from the top, Aeric was shoveling at the hedge gate. Only when his father took a break would Aeric as well. She could see him wince and grab his wound, but nothing she said deterred him from helping. No amount of pain would stop him from doing less than anyone else.

Stupid boy, Hanna found herself thinking. As much as she loved her son, she was in a foul mood. *He should be resting, not working in the cold. He is going to get sick.* Hanna stopped herself just as a hundred hateful thoughts began harassing her for attention. It was becoming harder for Hanna to smile, to not take things personally. Even the wind upset her. *I don't want to die in a snowstorm.*

Hanna put a hand over her eyes and tried to act as if there was not a rot in her head. She watched the orphans play and wondered how she might feel if she were whole. Hanna was sure she would be happy or at the least bemused. Josephine and Quenby were climbing on the hedge, leaping onto the deep snow piles which had accumulated at the base of the Hill. Virginia, meanwhile, was teasing Lorne. As the boy bent down to take a handful of snow, Virginia pelted him directly in the face. Hanna grunted a laugh.

Meanwhile, Dixon watched them like a warden. "You two shouldn't be jumping from the hedge like that. You are going to break something." Josephine and

Quenby looked at him and then at each other. They taunted him and continued jumping.

"Fine, break your bones. I don't care." Dixon then turned his attention toward the other two orphans, who were running out the hedge gate. As they left, he bellowed in a prepubescent roar, "You can't go past the hedge! It is not safe!" He raced after them and the wind muted the sounds of their confrontation.

Hanna looked through a corridor of snow-covered trees, eyeing the hedge gate. A minute passed before Dixon, who was a head shorter than both Virginia and Lorne, reappeared dragging both by the arm. Virginia was furious, and the wind did not mute her,

"You are just as old as us. You aren't a grown-up. Let go."

Dixon threw her onto the snow and yelled, "You cannot go that way! It is not safe."

Laverne placed her knitting on the arm of her rocking chair and stood up. "Dixon, baby. Come here."

The postman's child looked at the other two orphans and then at Laverne. He pointed at them.

"Just you," Laverne commanded.

Hanna sat back to watch the events. The distraction was a welcome change, especially because the conflict did not concern her.

"What?" Dixon asked indignantly.

Laverne placed her hands at her hips. "What ya doin' pushing Virginia for?"

"They were running away," Dixon barked.

"They was playin'."

"They were going East," Dixon complained in a leading tone, clearly expecting Laverne to see his point of view.

Laverne pointed down the Hill, where the four other orphans were watching the scene intently. "So you pushed her?"

"Well..." Dixon scratched his ear and looked at his feet. The postman's son stuttered, "T-t... My daddy, he went that way and he never came back."

Laverne nodded. Hanna frowned and was glad, at the very least, that the boy had someone to hug. Latrell's mother embraced the orphan and kissed his head. She replied, "That don't mean the others can't go that way, 'specially not if it's just down the road."

"They call it the mountain of riddles," Dixon protested.

"I don't care if they call it the monster's maw," Laverne raised her voice. "You think you's the only one can protect them, soon you just a jailor. Ain't no child want a jailor for a daddy. 'Specially not one their own age." She sniffed, "Now get on inside and take a bath. Ya smell obnoxious."

Dixon licked his lips. Hanna could tell he had several choice words for Laverne. The muscles in the boy's face tensed and stretched. His nose flared. Then, he flailed his arms, let out an incoherent shriek, kicked the patio wood, and stomped into the tavern. He slammed the door behind him. The orphans were pointing and laughing. Laverne pointed back, "Y'all get on before I lose my religion." They dispersed like mice.

Laverne looked at Hanna and giggled. She went to sit back down, but just then Galahad came outside.

"Dixon seemed disheveled," Galahad commented, rubbing his hands together. "Oh, I can see my breath."

Laverne marched over to him and pulled the fabric of his shirt. "So why ain't you wearin' yo' winter coat? You gonna freeze."

Galahad shared a brief frown with Hanna before scratching the back of his head. "It's heavy, is all."

"Six feet a' dirt heavy, too," Laverne glared.

Galahad raised his shoulders and pocketed his hands. He asked Hanna, "Arthur ready to go, yet?"

Hanna frowned, "The snow just keeps coming down. They probably have another half hour of shoveling."

Galahad nodded. He took a step to join the workers, but Laverne stopped him. "We ain't done talking."

"I am," Galahad muttered.

Laverne recoiled like a snorting bull. "You got some fool ideas if you thinks to go shovel without a winter coat. You gon' go up Oleander without a coat, too?"

"If it suits me," Galahad bit his lip. He was trying to restrain himself.

When Hanna had learned he and Momed had a falling out, she was sure he would want a room. Then, upon hearing he was lodging with Laverne, went and offered one to him. Galahad had declined, saying he would not be staying in town long. If Hanna did not know better, she would have assumed he was sleeping with the woman. It felt awkward standing between the two of them, whose relationship Hanna could not quite discern. She distanced herself from them and leaned on the railing. She decided she would look at the snow and appear fixated on the storm. *Don't mind me...* She tapped her fingers against the wood while the two continued bickering.

"Is a fool thing, climbin' mountains in a storm."

"I will wait for the storm to subside," Galahad said, coolly.

"You see any end to this storm?" Laverne asked. She answered her own question, "Nah. It ain't stopping. And ain't no riches up there any damn way."

"I respectfully disagree."

"Misses Gardner," Laverne blurted out. Hanna turned and saw her pointing toward the Oleander. "You know the story of the hungry fisher?"

"Mhm," Hanna admitted, somewhat reluctantly. She shrugged at Galahad.

"Course you do. I bets Galahad does, too. But I think he needs a refresher." Laverne pointed at the chair and Hanna almost laughed. Then, to her surprise, Galahad obeyed. He sat down and looked up at the woman. Laverne began the old Wanakhan tale:

"They said a fisher lived up the Oleander, where the Crimson Gorge is today. Well, he put a worm on his hook and caught a small fish. When he returned home and ate the fish, his belly was still full. So, he returned the next day, caught a small fish same as last. Only, this time, he uses the little fish as bait. He catches a bigger fish, goes home, eats it. His belly still grumbled. Next day, he catches the bigger fish, uses that as bait, and know what?"

Laverne paused, waiting for Galahad to ask. Hanna thought the man may have rolled his eyes, but he played along. "What?"

"He was still hungry. Eventually, he realizes he can't catch no bigger fish. He knows there always a bigger fish, though. If he ain't catching, it's cause his bait ain't cuttin' it. So, he takes to thinkin'. What he think?"

Galahad sighed, "He came to the conclusion that he was the biggest fish."

"Mhmm," Laverne nodded. "That's what them old miners thought, too. Then the mountain shed them like a damn winter coat and they all died. These new miners the same sorta prideful." She glanced at Hanna, "What the fisher do after comin' to his conclusion? I think Galahad needs ta remember."

Hanna cleared her throat, uncomfortably continuing the story, "Um, well. He, uh, cut off his tongue."

"Snip," Galahad added.

"And attached it to the lure," Hanna said.

Laverne took over. "That's exactly right. He put his own tongue on the lure, and you know what happened? Instead of catchin' fish, his tongue got to tastin'. Let from the body, the tongue started rovin'. The fisher no longer had control over his pole, and the tongue dragged him into the water. It looked and looked for the prized fish, the biggest of them all. He swam in circles, not knowing why no fish was appearing. But ain't no fish was big enough 'cept the fisher himself. He swam and swam, exhausted. Eventually, he drowned and the little fishes ate his bones."

"And that is why we call it the Crimson Gorge," Galahad smiled, clapped his hands, and raised his brow sarcastically at Hanna. "The hungry fisher is just a story."

Laverne shrugged. "Oh boy... If you believe that, you already lost."

Galahad scratched his ear and burped. He stood up and declared, "Well, I do know that there is a shovel with my name on it." He marched confidently toward the storm.

Laverne sat back down, took up her knitting, and muttered, "Boy gonna get himself killed or worse." She scoffed, "Just a story. Can you believe it?"

Hanna cleared her throat again. "Uh-"

Laverne continued, "Next thing he's gonna say Beauregard's Palisade is a myth. Yeah, there *probably* ain't no ravenous ghosts up Oleander, but there is truth to story."

"Sure is," Hanna acquiesced. She liked Laverne better when she was silent and knitting. Thankfully, Laverne did not linger much longer on the patio and went to check on Dixon.

The storm was only getting worse. *Galahad really should have worn something warmer...* Hanna stopped herself. *I am not his mother.* She stared down the Hill, where the outlines of three people were shoveling snow. The pale veil surrounded them all like fog. The glade groaned as many branches still with leaves held heavy clumps of snow. A few branches had already broken, the leaves falling at last under winter's heavy burden. The only tree which seemed unaffected by the sudden storm was the dead one. Its white skeleton had lost its leaves years ago. It always looked like it was in the depths of winter.

Hanna sighed, wishing the men would be done and they could get on with the day's event. She did not even want to go, but Arthur convinced her it was her duty. *I don't have to enjoy it,* Hanna told herself. Indeed, she doubted she would enjoy any hanging, no matter who it was for. *Even if it were for Latrell.* The sooner they finished the nasty business, the sooner Hanna could get on with her own dying.

She looked down the Hill, toward gallows obscured by snowfall. A faint figure outlined in frost was coming up the Hill. Hanna squinted and put a hand over her eyes. She could not discern who it was, for the figure was faraway and hooded. They were dragging a large chest behind them which must have weighed as much as the person. She saw her son point at the person. The wind knocked back the figure's hood and, fighting against their own gravity and the slippery slope of the Hill, they fell onto their back. Galahad and Arthur paused and leaned on their tools while her son ran toward the person. Aeric helped the figure up. They brushed the snow off their face and Hanna saw that the person was Yang.

The young doctor was struggling not to slip. Aeric gave him a hand. The chest was as big as the boy, and even with Aeric's help, it took Yao Yang a long while to bring it and himself up to the Inn. The storm intensified as he did so, but the doctor continued trudging up. He passed Arthur, bowed his head, and continued while her husband glared. When he at last made it to the top of the Hill, he breathed deeply. Then, he stood tall and declared in an I-am-a-man voice, "My uncle has kicked me out of his house."

"A shame," Hanna frowned. She let him stand with his feet in the snow for a few seconds. Arthur and Galahad approached, watching the young doctor intently. Finally, Hanna asked, "Why?"

Yang swallowed. Hanna could tell he had been crying. His tears had frozen onto his cheeks. He bowed his head in shame before shaking his head, "I told him he was wrong."

"About?" Hanna let a fleeting smile escape her lips.

"I said I would rather fail than never try, that I don't care about his pride or my own." He turned toward Arthur, "Even if I am successful... Are you willing to care for your wife, no matter how she is affected?"

Arthur laughed mockingly. Yang stepped back and looked at everyone present like a frightful child. Then, Arthur raised his arm. "When you love someone like I love that woman," he glanced at her, "you will understand how stupid a question that is." He glanced down at his hand. Hesitantly, Yang extended his own arm. The two men shook hands and Yang's face flickered with sadness and joy.

"Then," he approached Hanna, "I will try my best to cure you."

Aeric laughed and went to pick up Yang's chest of belongings. The doctor stopped him, "Please." Aeric looked at him strangely, tilting his head. Yang stared up at the towering redwood inn. The wind beat down upon his face. Then, he nodded to himself and got his things. "This burden is mine."

He heaved the chest up the steps. Once up the stairs, he paused to rest. "I, uh, will set up in your room?" He leaned against the door, awaiting permission. Hanna nodded at him and Yang disappeared into the redwood refuge. Somewhere in the Oleander Wash, a flute was playing in the golden scale, never dwelling long on a happy or sad melody, always ascending and descending to some other note.

Hanna blinked at her husband. Then, she burst into happy tears. She felt Arthur embrace her. He lifted her up and joined her in laughter. They kissed, hugged, and stared into one another's eyes. Arthur held her with newfound strength, sweeping Hanna up as if she weighed nothing to him. *My protector,* she smiled at him. He held her so tightly, she felt nothing but his warmth. It did not seem so cold outside anymore.

Galahad burped and motioned toward the hedge gate, "I hate to ruin a happy occasion... But, uh, there is a hanging to get to."

Arthur giggled and brushed his hand across Hanna's head, sweeping her hair from her eyes. "Yes, cannot leave the Inner Ring waiting too long. They'll be wanting their show."

Hanna held out her hand for her husband and he took it happily. *This won't be too bad.* Hanna would do her civic duty and then they could celebrate. *I don't even have to watch.* They began to depart, but Aeric called after them. "Uh, dad?"

The three turned. Her son's stalwart strength had withered. Instead, his legs shook. He stared down at the Inner Ring, where the gallows were waiting. "Do I have to go?"

Arthur looked at her and bowed his head. Hanna shook her own, "No. You get on inside."

"I could help Wenton in the kitchen?" he asked, scratching his forearm.

"Why don't you get some hot chocolate for you and your sister," Hanna smiled, glad Emilia would have some human company while they all were gone.

Aeric nodded, relieved. "Thank you."

The three left for the gallows. Only the wind spoke for some time. Then, as the outline of the hangman's noose became more and more of a reality, Galahad said, "I would not want to come, either. If I were him, that is."

"Yeah," Hanna and her husband said at once.

The murmurs of the crowd like cicadas in spring gradually grew louder. Their heads bounced like a wave in a storm, their bodies drifted wherever small talk led them. Hanna saw townspeople she had forgotten about, mostly Inner Ringers who kept to themselves. Indeed, as the three found a position amongst the mob, Hanna saw mostly Pale faces.

Terrell's face, meanwhile, was swollen up like a fruit. The whoremonger was more purple than black and dry blood stained his cheeks. His hands were knotted behind his back. Hanna heard behind her, "Look! They really did step on his fingers!"

"Good," snarled a man. His voice was hot with anger. "A goblin's a primal thing. Best hang him quick."

Hanna was uncomfortable with the notion that she was watching a human life being extinguished. *How can these folk be so...* Hanna stopped herself short of insults. She held her mind's tongue. They had the *privilege* to watch the sum of a mother's work and a child's ambitions. Millions of generations, uncounted children and innumerable parents—all to culminate in a hanging. *What a waste.*

Constable Goodwind was reading him his last rites, pausing every few seconds to take a breath or wipe his nose. He asked the flesh salesman if he had any final words. The condemned said nothing for a time and despite the whispers of the crowd, Hanna could hear Galahad grinding his teeth.

They were acquaintances, Hanna remembered. *I wonder how well they knew each other.* She smiled at Galahad, though he did not see. He was watching the gallows intently.

"No," the whoremonger finally said, defiantly. "Nobody wants to hear a mudpuppy's defense."

"Hear, hear!" Cried several men, drunk off the event.

Galahad burped. His eyes met Hanna's and he started to cough. He pounded his chest once, stifled another cough, and looked diligently at the noose.

"Alright," Goodwind declared. He placed a black mask over the condemned and moved his body toward the rope. It took several minutes for the constable to maneuver the noose with his fat fingers, giving the town ample time to converse. Hanna tried to ignore their callous small talk, but it proved difficult. Lilian Vellencourt and the twin widows, Carolyn and Evelyn, were speaking in loud whispers. Vellencourt was giggling madly with Evelyn about some joke. Meanwhile, Carolyn was arguing with Wilhelm.

"You watch, ya hear?"

"I don't want to," Wilhelm protested, wriggling away from his aunt's grasp.

"This man..." She paused to glare at Galahad. "Is a bad man. You watch."

Hanna peeked at Galahad. If he was aware of Carolyn's stare, he did not show it.

Finally, Goodwind managed to wrap the rope around Terrell's neck. He tightened it and walked toward the lever. The crowd hushed. The constable cleared his throat as the gales intensified.

"This man has been accused of murder and is sentenced to die. Do any present object to his fate?"

None spoke but the wind. The gusts roared and the gallows creaked. Galahad continued grinding his teeth. Hanna rolled her eyes at the theatrics. Of course no one would object. Objections were for weddings and trials, neither of which the poor criminal could ever hope to have. There had been so many witnesses to Latrell's murder, it was claimed no trial was needed.

The crowd grew restless. Impatient groans coursed through the convocation.

Goodwind waited for a minute before declaring, "Then let death weigh this man's soul fo' its worth."

The lever fell. The rope tightened. Bones cracked. The wind pushed the writhing body. A few cheers erupted from the crowd as the whoremonger kicked. Hanna looked away. It seemed the whole town was enamored with the display. Carolyn watched with white knuckles. Despite his initial revulsion, her nephew was equally captivated. Even after his glasses fogged, little Wilhelm watched as life left the condemned. The sporadic struggle continued for minutes which felt like days. Hanna could not escape the grunting and choking from the gallows. Arthur was steadfast in his watch, though his eyes were twitching. Everyone was watching the affair like they were bound by a spell. All but Galahad, who stared down at his feet.

At least you know something is wrong here. She offered Galahad her hand, but he shook his head. *He was his acquaintance...* Hanna put her hands in her pockets, closed her eyes, and waited for the man to die. She could hear a woman crying, or perhaps two. She could not bear to look up and see who would shed a tear for a murderer.

Eventually, the body stopped moving, its clawing hands rested at its side, and the crying stopped. The corpse's toes, which had been erect, fell limply toward the ground. The corpse swayed with the wind. Goodwind waddled over to the body and checked for signs of life. A minute passed and the crowd held their breath.

"May death treat him better than life."

The crowd erupted in cheering. Hanna thought she might vomit.

"We are an odd sort of creature," Galahad grunted. He burped and turned toward the inn.

"Arthur," Hanna put her hand on his arm, "Let's go."

"Alright," her husband nodded. "Yeah," he agreed again.

Hanna sighed. "I hope Aeric is okay."

"He'll be fine," he replied. "Come on," he led her up. They had passed under the hedge gate when they heard some onlookers shouting. Hanna turned, expecting them to be poking the hanging body with sticks, but instead the crowd had split in two. The onlookers were pointing at a horse. It limped toward the inn.

"Hanna," Arthur said, knowingly. "Is that one of ours?"

The horse came nearer and stopped beside the hedge gate. It whinnied at Hanna and bowed its head. She blinked at the creature. The horse looked into her eyes. Hanna's arm shook as she raised it up, resting it below the horse's bloody mane. It stomped and pointed its head east.

She swallowed, "I loaned her to Charles."

19

Smothering Embrace

Hanna smiled back, shaking her head. "No... You've got to find our friend." Arthur stammered, "I cannot leave you. For all we know, Charles is sipping hot chocolate with Cora beside a roaring fire."

Galahad blinked a hundred times and put his hands behind his back. *I hope he does not ask me to go. I'd rather not freeze to death.*

"He is not. We both know it."

Yang interjected, quietly adding, "Mister Gardner... There will be very little for you to do here."

"I want to be here when she wakes up," The innkeeper's voice rose. Hanna opened her arms and beckoned the man to embrace her. He did so like a fish caught on a line.

Galahad looked at Yang and gave him an uncomfortable smile, hoping to find a comrade. Yang noticed nothing. He was fixated on his tools.

Hanna patted his back, "Send the constable."

"He is too fat," Arthur chuckled, grimly. "Besides, Yang told me you would need my support."

"Eventually, yes," Yang nodded. "But for the first few days, the only utility you would have would be fluffing her pillows."

"Then I will do a damn good job," Arthur declared.

Hanna started, "Oh, Ar-"

A thud came from downstairs. Galahad turned toward the sound. Another louder thud reverberated. The chandelier above them shook. The glass jingled. Something heavy was coming up, slamming onto the stairs with great force. Arthur swiveled his neck and Hanna lifted her head slightly. She complained, "Someone tell Emilia to stop stomping."

Before she had finished, Arthur was at the door to fulfill her request. It opened without his doing. The constable heaved a huge chest onto the floor. Then, he hacked a horrible cough. Mucus sprayed forth. Yang barreled over to him and yelled,

"Cover your mouth, you imbecile! This is a sanitary station, go!"

Goodwind's eyes met Galahad's. Terrell had not said any last words, not in public at least. Still, Galahad was suspicious that someone had found him out. He smiled at the lawman; he took a step back when he saw the constable raising his arm.

159

Goodwind put his hand to his mouth and coughed. He ignored the young doctor and said to Arthur, "Found this washed up on an embankment, little east of the Muhali Islet. Luggage."

"Charles'?" Hanna was quick to ask.

"Or his mother's," Goodwind added. "There were some letters 'tween the innkeeper and Cora."

Arthur raised his brow and looked at Hanna with a shrug.

"Pardon," Goodwind giggled. "Your brother, Auldwine."

"Ah," Arthur nodded hastily. "Yes, well..." He faced his wife.

Galahad watched their silent exchange. Hanna bent her head toward the luggage and widened her eyes. Arthur frowned and looked down at the frozen container. He stared at it and rolled his lips. He thought for a moment and then blinked at his wife. Hanna shook her head and pointed her head again at the chest. Arthur kneeled, his joints cracking loudly. "Help me with this, Galahad."

The chest was frigid and soaked. A layer of ice had glued the locks together. Galahad and Arthur each took a lock and pried it from its icy prison. The locks unlatched. They slowly opened the container. Galahad peered inside. The latches did their job well, as the contents were quite dry.

Arthur began taking out items, narrating for his wife as he did so. "Clothes. Several outfits. Definitely belongs to Charles, unless Cora had a growth spurt. Some books. Food. More food. And just as the constable said, letters."

Galahad had the urge to read them and glimpsed at the paper. He could hardly read the handwriting on one letter. The other was easier to read, but he only caught the name 'Cora Eastmont,' before Arthur took all the letters and deposited them in his nightstand.

"I will file a report immediately," the constable asserted.

Arthur turned toward his wife with a frown. Then, he glanced at Yang with a glare. "You heal her, you hear?"

"Deafeningly," Yang rotated back to his workstation and began to scrub the entire place with pungent disinfectant.

Arthur went to his wife. He leaned down and kissed her damp forehead. He asked her forgiveness with wide eyes and a trembling smile. Before he had even opened his mouth, she replied, "I know. No apology needed." She bowed her head and put a hand to her heart. The innkeeper took the hand and kissed it.

"I need to go prepare. I'll be back to say a proper goodbye."

"I love you," Hanna whispered.

Arthur nodded. "I love you, too." He stepped toward his wife, intent on saying something else. His lips moved but his mouth remained shut. The innkeeper tapped his foot. The tapping intensified until finally, he turned around and ordered everyone but Yang out.

Galahad waited beside the constable, not daring to look at anything but the floor. Goodwind tried to whistle. If the lawman knew about Galahad's part in Terrell's deed, the oaf was making a surprisingly good show of ignorance. He briefly let his guard down and listened to the sounds coming from the Gardner bedroom. He heard rummaging, shuffling, and a few curses. He heard an, "Ah, there we go," followed by another, "Okay, I love you."

Arthur emerged with two items: a rifle and a map. He said nothing to Galahad or Goodwind. Galahad followed the innkeeper. Goodwind trailed Galahad. As the three men trotted down the corridor, Constable Goodwind asked what the innkeeper meant by 'preparing.'

"I assumed, because of your girth, that you would not lead the search for Eastmont," Arthur responded, taking no precautions as he walked over the constable's pride. Galahad stifled a chuckle. It seemed imprudent to laugh while the lawman was at his back.

"Well with this weather," Edric began to defend himself. "Sir, I don't think it's wise fo' *anyone* to go out."

Arthur hoisted the rifle's strap around his shoulder. He marched toward the petrified table and ordered all patrons to their rooms. "Everyone out. Guests, patrons, all of you. Now."

The tavern quickly dispersed, leaving the three men alone. The innkeeper unfurled the map and pointed, "The Muhali Islet is a product of several streams, all coming from the eastern crofts."

"Mister Gardner," the constable insisted.

"Mister Goodwind," Arthur mimed. He stared into the constable's eyes.

Galahad felt the urge to break the uncomfortable standoff but dared not speak. Every time the fat man looked at him, Galahad wondered if he was waiting for the opportune moment to apprehend him. *I could outrun him if I needed to.* He burped.

Both men glanced at him. Arthur was quick to resume his glare, but the constable fidgeted nervously. He cleared his throat, "W-who is goin' to run the inn if something happens to you, yo' wife?"

"Aeric," Arthur declared immediately.

"Uh," Galahad sniffed. He laughed at the constable, who was now looking at him accusingly. He glanced behind his back. "Hey, hey, look who it is." Aeric was rushing toward the convocation as fast as his wound allowed.

The innkeeper's son declared in disbelief, "What about Galahad? He knows how to run a business."

Into the ground, Galahad thought. What was the boy doing trying to make him an innkeeper? *How presumptive.* He did not want the burden of a hundred degenerate mouths.

"As do you," his father eyed him in a monotone. "You will do a fine job while I am away."

The boy looked like he had just been shot again. He shook his head and pointed down at the map, "No, I am going with you. I am a good shot."

Arthur would not hear it. "You got shot good." He did not let his son speak another word. "Your mother needs you here. Your sister needs you."

Aeric's cheek twitched. He began to speak.

"It is settled then," Arthur started.

The constable spoke with a quivering voice that grew stronger as he went. "W-who will look for you... When the b-blizzard takes you?"

Arthur rolled his tongue toward his bottom lip like a snake. "Certainly not you."

"Sir," the constable adjusted his weight to one side as he begged.

Arthur put up his hand like an officer directing traffic, "Something bad has happened. I know it."

"With all due respect—" The constable started.

He is going to insult someone, Galahad knew.

"—Charles Eastmont was born a bad happening."

Arthur licked his lip again like a viper. He took one step toward the constable. "My brother had to restrain me when boys said things like that to Charles." He narrowed his gaze and repositioned the rifle on his back. The innkeeper sniffed, adding casually, "But Auldwine is dead. And you just insulted my friend."

The constable took a step back.

Arthur exchanged a period of silence with Goodwind. Finally, he spoke. "You should get some sleep."

Goodwind responded with a mix of fear and frustration, stuttering a hundred responses and finishing none of them. Finally, he waddled away, grumbling incoherent phrases under his breath.

Once the lawman had left, Galahad felt his strength come back to him. He cleared his throat and told his friend, plainly, "You cannot go out into this weather alone."

"I do not plan to," Arthur answered. He leaned over the table and gazed at his map. Aeric and Galahad looked at each other, unsure of what to do. Finally, Arthur barked a command at his son.

"Aeric, find Laverne and bring her to me. She lived in the eastern crofts for many years. Then, check the guest registry and bring me every man young enough to march and old enough to carry a rifle."

Aeric hastened away.

Galahad stared at the innkeeper. In the span of a few hours, he had reverted to a wartime officer. Nothing remained of the morose tavern-keep who had drifted from task to task the past month. Galahad smirked at the stoic soldier.

"What are you grinning at?" The man asked.

Galahad raised his brow, "Shame old Phillip can't join you."

Aeric darted out of the kitchens and headed for the residential quarters. Both men turned their ears toward the sounds of knocking. Grumbles and faint questions echoed from the guest rooms. Then came footsteps. His father's troops were mustered.

Arthur watched as timid men walked toward them. "We may have a few Phillips before this is over."

Galahad laughed, "Make sure everyone has their tobacco ration." His chuckling soured in his mouth when he saw Momed. Their eyes darted to one another and quickly drifted elsewhere.

Along with the Muhali, several other patrons had been called to action. Aeric had found an exile from the Golden Empire and two loggers from Cotswald. Galahad eyed them with quaint surprise. *They must have been too lucky or too young to die in the war.*

Arthur had the men line up. He inspected them like the captains had done before deployment, so many years ago. The innkeeper eyed each one, head to foot. Arthur grunted at Momed, "I know you. Ever fire a rifle?"

"Never," Momed replied sheepishly. The boy's voice irritated Galahad to no end, and he joked,

"Practice aplenty in the forest."

Momed glared at him. Then, he saluted Arthur. "Eastmont gave to me his room. I will help find him and clear that debt."

Seeing the weak little thing saluting Arthur tickled him with annoyance and embarrassment. He almost wanted to pull the boy by his ear and chastise him for making a fool of them both. Galahad laughed at the Momed's absurdity.

Arthur turned toward Galahad. With eyes of stone, he asked, "What *exactly* is funny?"

Galahad blinked and chuckled, "Nothing, commander." He gave the innkeeper an exaggerated salute.

"If you are going to make jokes, get the fuck out." Arthur barked.

Galahad looked at the innkeeper, then at Momed. The boy was grinning at him. *You are going to defend him? This wretch?* He scoffed and pushed past them all. *Good. Get him out of my sight.* His rage turned him around and he put his hand on Momed's shoulder. "Remember your tobacco ration." He did not hear the Muhali boy's stutters as he stormed down the steps. He passed the residential quarter and debated punching Momed's door. His malice was checked when an orphan horde charged past him. They knocked him against the wall without so much as a look in his direction.

This should have been a happy day. Galahad shook with rage. His own friend had told him to go, choosing a pathetic boy over their friendship. *Damn them all.* Galahad looked around the empty corridor. He was sure if someone were present, he would punch them. *Breathe,* Galahad tried to calm himself. *Breathe.* A few deep breaths did absolutely nothing and Galahad felt even more upset. *I just need to get out of here.*

He went toward the stairs but paused when he realized he would have to make an appearance before Arthur's silly band. *They were laughing at me, I know it.* Galahad waited, counting the faint ticking of clocks in other rooms. He lost count of the ticks and his patience evaporated. He tiptoed toward the tavern and remained at the perimeter of the room, weaving around pillars and furniture to avoid being seen.

Yet, nobody was in the tavern save one person. Laverne was shaking her head and looking at the map with a tear in her eye. Galahad tried to make for the exit. Laverne's quiet crying stopped him. He felt indebted to her. Whenever he was around the woman, he felt the need to show her he was a good person, one who deserved her compassion.

"You," his voice echoed in the empty tavern, "Uh... Okay?"

Laverne wiped her eyes and smiled at him. "Oh, I'm just rememberin' is all."

"Remembering what?" Galahad went to her.

"My husband," she frowned. "My boy." She shook her head and started weeping, "I tried ta be strong today, but seeing that man hang just made me feel all flavors of wrong."

Galahad's lip twitched. *Me too.* "He's gone now." Galahad's airway tightened. It felt as if a claw was wrapped around his throat. He squeaked, "Latrell is avenged."

"Latrell was a nasty boy," his mother declared. She smiled at him with a memory in her mind, "Wasn't always, though. He was sweet, once. Always making his papa and me laugh." Laverne closed her eyes and wiped the tears away.

Galahad had nothing to say to her. He could lie to anyone about anything, but not to her. Something about the woman made Galahad want to be a better person. "You can still laugh," he smiled. "Dixon and the others, me. We can help with that."

"Oh," Laverne beamed. "That's a good thing to say."

Galahad made sure the tavern was empty before he shooed away his embarrassment. He hid his smile from sight. He titled his chin and shielded his neck. It felt good to be praised, for once. The day had been one hardship after another. After a moment, he looked at Laverne and felt the overwhelming urge to hug her. Then urge was short-lived.

"I did a bit of pokin' around," Laverne frowned. She pulled out the pouch containing Yang's leaf.

Galahad turned around and said nothing. *Not you, too.* He muttered, "It's for my pain." He did not expect *her* to understand. Nobody else did. Her hand rested on his shoulder and she spoke in a tone he did not expect.

"You been havin' pain?"

Galahad blinked, meeting her gaze with a downcast brow. She put the back of her hand to his forehead. "Well you's pretty warm, no denying that."

Galahad smiled. *She... She isn't scolding me?* He found himself asking, entirely naked of his pride, "You aren't mad?"

Laverne was taken aback, "Now why would I be mad a boy has a hurt?" She shook her head and let out a deep, resonant hum. "You in pain now?"

Galahad thought of Arthur yelling at him, of the faceless man hanging from the gallows, of Carolyn's spite and Vellencourt's girlish smile. He thought of his father's hatred. He thought of his own hatred and the awful deeds which had come from the hate. "Yes," he admitted.

"Come on," Laverne ushered him along. He followed her into the kitchens. His body tingled like it had fallen asleep.

"Wenton!" Laverne shrieked.

The chef poked his head out from one of the stoves, "What you want?"

"Where you keep the mortar and pestle?"

Wenton yelled back, "What you need mortar and pestle for?"

"To grind that dumb head of yours into jelly. Now where ya keep it?"

"The six-by-eights," Wenton answered.

"Come on," Laverne said to Galahad. She led him to a shelf with stacks of pans, plates, and other cookware. She scanned the shelf for some time before yelling, "Ain't no mortar and pestle here, Wenton."

"Your eyes as bad as your tits is big," Wenton shouted. "Look again."

Laverne tilted her head up toward the ceiling, "I am lookin', you joker."

A moment of silence passed. Galahad started to say it was alright, that he did not need anything special. Just then, Wenton laughed and exclaimed, "Oh, damn me." He walked with mortar and pestle in hand,

"It was right next to me."

Laverne grinned at Galahad and hummed an "Mhm." She snatched the tool from Wenton and they departed toward the bedroom.

Galahad still found it strange to sleep in the woman's room. Though with every passing night his embarrassment decreased. Besides, Laverne never slept in the bed. Galahad was not sure she ever slept, as she was always awake when he was. He liked that someone was always around, watching over the room. The woman dumped Galahad's leaves onto the bed and placed a handful in the stone bowl.

"What are you doing?" He inquired.

"Ole' crofter's trick. This'll help you with your pain more than chewin' ever could."

Galahad gulped, half-excited and half-afraid. "Thank you."

"Nonsense, baby." She crushed the leaves with the pestle, swirling it around the bowl. In a minute, a fine powder was all that remained. She offered the bowl to Galahad.

"Um," he smiled. *It's too early. Too early.* "I don't know if I should, right now."

"You in pain?" Laverne interrogated.

"I mean," Galahad began, "Yes-"

"Not another word then, go on."

He eyed the bowl, wondering how best to consume the powder. He blinked at it, afraid of the effects such a concentrated dosage might have on him. *It's not nighttime yet. Arthur wants me to watch over Hanna.* He recalled their brief altercation. *Fuck Arthur.*

Laverne was holding a glass of water in front of him. "This'll dissolve the powder. It'll take a while, so you could also sniff some if you's in pain now.

"Sniff it? You mean... Snort it?"

Laverne gestured, "Go on, baby. You'll feel better."

Galahad needed no more convincing. He poured the powder into his palm. With one last thought given to his worries, he snorted the powder. It singed his nostrils and bit his brain. Galahad wretched. He forced his innards to remain, not willing to lose a potential high. After the initial revulsion subsided, he blinked and looked around.

"I feel better already," he said, dumbstruck by how effective the method was. *I was doing things all wrong...* He stared at Laverne and hugged her. She held him tightly, patting his back.

"Good," she said. "Ain't no sickness mama 'Verne can't fix."

Mama 'Verne. The phrase echoed in Galahad's mind. He pulled away from the hug. Laverne held him tighter.

"You just tell me what you need. I'll make your medicine special for you every morning."

Every morning, Galahad smiled with distress. Pleasant sensations were coursing through his brain and body, nulling his anxieties. His heart was beating so hard and fast, he thought he might be dying. "Maybe," was all he could say.

Laverne let him go and looked down at her shoulder. There was drool on it.

"Oh my," she smiled, wiping away the drool and pinching Galahad's cheek.

He giggled at the touch. Deep in his mind, he felt absurd for drooling on the woman, for being so coddled and cared for. Murmurs went unheeded in his blissful mind. Thoughts like, *"this is too much, you are breaking the rules you've set for yourself,* and *you are not a child,"* trickled about his surging, euphoric mind. He noted the worry in his mind but smiled heedlessly. Freed of his horrible day, he said without thinking, "I love you."

Galahad's mind and body were split into two separate components. His senses and his thoughts interacted slightly but worked independently. He did not hear what Laverne said to him. He was being smothered in the woman's embrace.

20

A Candlelit Dinner

At least the storm had subsided. The cold made his bones feel broken. Perhaps they were. The gash across his legs added to the feeling. He had wrapped a sock around his thigh to stop the bleeding and there the bloody cloth remained. It was not a deep wound, but the shallowest cuts hurt the most. He winced with every step, lifting his injured leg over the thick layer of snow. The wolves had pursued him into the blizzard only for the winds to scatter his scent. Whether they were only defending their pup and their den, or whether they were hungry—Charles did not know. He knew only that the storm hindered them as much as it did him.

Nature giveth and nature taketh away, Charles chuckled. If he did not laugh, he was sure he would die.

He was hopelessly lost in Cottonwood. The forest he had known was broken by the storm. The beautiful boughs bowed low to the heavy snow. The many-colored autumn trees snapped under the weight of smothering white. For some trees, the burden was so great that the entire tree fell. First, the trunk would snap like a cracked bone. Then, it would tumble as a thousand frozen leaves shivered and rolled back like the tide.

Dusk was approaching. Charles might have persevered before the storm, but his zeal had been tempered by the frost. He needed shelter. The snap of another tree trunk, the withering shiver of leaves, and the crash of the timber urged him along. He scanned for anything that might be warm. There were many such respites, hovels and holes—but these he knew were already taken. He dared not enter any abandoned croft, nor any cave. Those, he surmised, were vaunted properties in the wild. He had learned that from the wolves. His dwelling had to be unattractive, at least to wolves, bears, and other beasts. The horizon gave a crimson glint to the frozen forest.

Miles away, a herd of elk bugled. The males had been competing all day, and all the forest knew it. Charles hoped the forest's predators would be attracted to the noises, leaving him be. *I cannot outrun a turtle in this state, let alone a cougar.* He glowered at his thigh and his blood-stained sock. His stomach growled. He had not eaten since Atlani deserted him.

"I've gone without before," Charles told the forest. He rubbed the bark of an old ash tree.

He continued his search for shelter, staying near the banks of a frozen rivulet. Charles passed under a large willow. Its weeping branches had grown sharp icicles

167

that refracted the setting sun. Greens, blues, and purples all danced aside reds atop the white canopy.

Charles smiled at the illusory gems, spiting the throbbing pain in his leg. He would not despair, even if he was to die. His mother's last requests were for her only son to be happy. When all other roads disappeared, that was the one he traveled. Happy he would remain, to the very last.

He would not wallow under the willow. He bit his cheeks to distract from his hunger. The march continued. Yet, as he passed under the frozen willow, with its icicles like daggers plunging toward the frozen rivulet—Charles felt he was walking into the maw of a beast—tooth, tongue, and all. Darkness settled in for the night.

Charles continued along the frozen waterway, looking up occasionally at the stars for hope. His foot ached. His big toe pulsated with pain whenever he put pressure on it. So, he looked at the bejeweled sky. He tried to smile and accept whatever fate would befall him. *Too many clouds,* Charles frowned. *No stars tonight.*

He continued, trying his best not to spite his horse for leaving him to die. *She may well have been attacked by a mountain lion.* The beast's flight had been quite sudden. He might have run, too, if a prowling cat had pounced upon him. *I should never have dismounted. We should have stayed on our course.* He slipped along the black ice.

"God damn it," he cursed, trying to regain his balance. He grabbed a bush; the barbed bark caused a thousand unseen cuts.

We could have fought off a mountain lion, or the wolves. A horse was a huge animal, more than capable of defending itself alongside a human. If he had just stayed mounted. If he had only carried a rifle... *I cannot dwell on hypotheticals.* The words were easy to remember but harder to live by. *Living is a hypothetical,* he glared. *Mama is dead, I will be dead...*

He could not see a damn thing. Without moon or stars, all was black.

"I can't even see where I am going," he muttered. The frost was working its way through his body. He had long ago lost feeling in his face. Now, his chest was chilled. His heartbeat was slowing.

There is no point in continuing. Charles looked around for anything remotely hospitable. The black night revealed nothing to him. He saw what was directly before him and that was darkness. His stomach growled. The bile in his body vaulted upwards. He wretched, tasting the revolting acid of his own self. He bit his lip. All he had to eat was his own blood.

"Ach," he spat. His blood had mingled with the bile in his throat. He bent down and dry-heaved. The more he gagged, the tighter his throat became and the less he could breathe. He tried to stop, but he only heaved more. He clenched his fists and shut his eyes, straining to hold down whatever was left in his stomach.

Eventually his body came to the same conclusion as his mind—there was nothing left. Charles wiped his mouth and looked around him, gasping. Liquid leaked out of his eyes. There were tiny, glimmering patches in his eyesight. *What are these lights?* Charles wiped his eyes, wondering if his vision was beginning to frost over. The glimmer remained. He looked up at the stars, expecting the clouds to have gone. Perhaps they had departed and stars now shone, but he could not tell. They were obscured by a brighter light. He saw an ocean of color. An aurora.

Waves of green and purple rippled through the sky. Charles forgot his pain and his jaw dropped. It was as if an artist was dragging his brush across the sky, painting the night anew. Colors Charles had never seen dominated the black background. *This is once in a lifetime...* As far as he knew, there had never been an aurora in Auberdine. The light danced across the sky, illuminating what the stars and moon could not.

The aurora gave the Cottonwood a chromatic color. Though not a religious man, Charles could not help but follow the aurora's course. If anything was a sign, it was this. He trailed below, deviating from the rivulet when the lights danced a new direction. An owl hooted at him as he walked by. Charles tried his best to smile. *Nature giveth and nature taketh away.*

"Hoot," Charles croaked in reply. The owl flew into view, perching on a branch in front of Charles. It hooted again, looking into Charles' eyes.

"Charming," Charles whispered. The owl flew off. It too was following the aurora.

If I could fly, he frowned. He groaned, lifting his leg above a mighty tree root. His leg was growing weaker the more he walked. *I need to rest.* He looked around. The light helped him see, but it did not provide shelter. There was nothing but brambles, branches, and barn owls. He could see them circling in the sky—their silhouettes soaring under the shimmering sky.

He continued along the aurora's path. The emerald and amethyst dance was tinged with orange. Yet, the orange was not bound to the sky. It was faint, not like the rays rippling through the roof of the world. It glimmered ahead, sheltered under the forest canopy. As Charles approached, he suspected he found Auberdine at last.

The light grows brighter. That's a lantern.

"Here," he tried to shout. He choked on his gravelly throat. He yelled over his discomfort, "Here!" The lantern was getting larger.

Not a lantern, but a town. That's a home.

He called out to the townspeople, "Help me. Please."

The owls hooted in response. The people in the home answered with indifference. Charles would have to knock. He started to run, not abiding by the searing agony of his inflamed thigh. He grabbed the wound and hobbled forward. He passed through a thick growth of ash and cottonwood, pushing aside bush and bramble. The orange light fractured. Charles stopped.

A million little fireflies fluttered. Charles' eyelids fluttered in disbelief. He had been here before. His feet sank and yet not in snow. He felt warm, not cold. *The sunken glade.* The aurora faded, leaving the fireflies as the forest's sole illumination. Hot vapor steamed through tiny fissures like smoke from a dozen campfires. Charles grinned in disbelief.

Suddenly, he remembered the gargantuan wolf. Man and beast were entombed in that glade. He grew fearful and began to flee. He stepped back into the forest. A wall of cold awaited him. Charles paused, unable to walk. He could feel his frostbitten foot returning to life. His face tingled with feeling. It hurt less to breathe in the glade. *I've not been warm since leaving home.* He weighed his worries and found one of them wanting. *Dead beasts versus living... Hot spring versus frozen forest...* Charles stared out into the forest of shadows and shrugged at his fear. *If something is lurking, at least I will die warm.*

He turned back toward the fireflies. In the middle of the glade, bubbling water steamed to the surface. He approached the water, his feet sinking slightly. The fireflies danced around him, curious of the newcomer. Above flew the owls, who swooped down toward the center. When they glided back toward the clouds, they carried rodents with them.

Charles paid little attention to the fireflies, the owls, and the spring. His eyes were fixed upon the monster he had seen before. The two entangled bodies had been stripped of their flesh by rats and other scavengers. Only bones and scraps remained. The disarticulated vertebrae were all that remained of the mighty wolf. The bone-crushing maw was no more than bones itself, and the cluttered remains were laid around the human's like funeral offerings. The skeleton of that unlucky fellow was less disarticulated. Spring water bubbled through its open, unhinged jaw. Charles frowned at the poor postman.

"Deepest apologies," he said to the skeleton, moving the skull away from the source of fresh water. He was no longer afraid of the scene. He was too hungry, too cold, and too pained to be afraid. He knelt and drank his fill. When he looked up from the fountain, the skull of the wolf was staring at him.

"And to you," he apologized to the fallen creature.

Charles looked at what remained of the massive canine and the tiny primate. Only scraps of flesh forgotten by rats remained. It was not much, even for the few maggots making their way through the flesh. Charles Eastmont licked his lips. The spoiled bits of rancid meat made his mouth water. The maggots seemed the juiciest snack. His stomach rolled and roared. He turned back toward the human skull. "If it is any consolation," Charles plucked a maggot from the wolf's carcass, "Nature giveth, now."

Above him, owls hooted happily in firefly light.

21

Skipping in Quicksand

Laverne finished grinding the herb. "I know you ain't telling me something." Galahad did not want to burn any bridges. He did not want to tell her *exactly* what was on his mind, fearing what might happen. He wanted to wait a little while, enjoy a few hours of sobriety—but he could not tell Laverne that. If he did, she might stop asking the good doctor for herb. He looked at Yang's powder, salivating. He turned away and replied, "My father is on my mind. That's all."

"You 'fraid you gon' turn out like him, huh," Laverne stated with a loving smile.

A surge of worrisome thoughts caused his chest to convulse. Galahad wrapped his arms around himself. "No, not really."

"Good," Laverne gave him the powder and felt his forehead. "You ain't Cambyses."

"I know," Galahad said, his voice cracking.

"What you say the pain was?" Laverne inquired.

"Anxiety," he answered immediately.

Laverne stared at him.

"And headaches," he added. It felt wrong to lie about the symptom. Especially when Hanna Gardner rested upstairs, recovering from *very* real headaches.

"Well," Laverne patted his back, "Go on, then."

Galahad acknowledged that he was breaking his rule of only using at night. He noted, however, that with the recent snows—he was practically on holiday. *There will be nothing to do until the snow melts. The west will wait.* Galahad glanced at the powder in his palm. He swallowed the saliva flooding his mouth. *I can have a little fun. I have no business to attend to, no dead fathers to bury.* He snorted the powder.

"From what you tells me," Laverne went to her rocking chair and took out a crocheting needle, "Your papa was a mean man. You's is kind. Always helpin' look after them Gardner kids and the other children."

His head swelled with happiness. Despite Laverne's tendency to be overbearing—he quite liked her encouraging words.

"Shame your mama died so young. A woman always tempers a man's madness."

171

"Yeah," Galahad looked at her, wondering if she was making him another winter coat. The first was far too warm for even the coldest days. *I hope it is just a sweater, if it's for me.*

"-If I am honest. You know?" Laverne asked.

Galahad had not heard her. He responded vaguely, "Mhm."

Laverne looked at him knowingly, "Your daddy had tragic flaws. We all have 'em. 'Cept some gots flaws that hurt them later in life. See, you ain't your daddy 'cause-"

Her words warmed him. Galahad allowed himself a giggle and a gleeful look at Laverne. She always knew how to cheer him up. His mind raced to all the things he wanted to enjoy that day. He wanted to float and feel all the tiny sensations of water rippling around him. He wanted to think deeply on random subjects and seek new perspectives.

"He was consumed," Laverne paused, thinking to herself. She nodded at her thoughts, "Consumed with consumption. He could never succeed. You gets a low self-image-"

I hope she finishes soon. I would like to take a bath, just float and relax. The leaf had made the baths exceptional. Powder will be even better. That was, if Laverne ever stopped talking. He waited patiently for her to finish complimenting him.

"Take my boy, 'Trell. He lost his daddy and tried too hard to be a big man. Well, that killed him." She shook her head admonishingly.

No, I did, Galahad commented to himself, frankly. A second passed and a coldness swept through him. He shivered.

"Y'all right?" Laverne stopped.

"Mhm," Galahad smiled.

"Your daddy the same."

"How so?" Galahad asked, not following the point. Her words entered his mind slowly, and by the time he registered their meaning—she had said a dozen more.

"Why he drink?" She questioned.

"Probably because he hated who he was," Galahad said, wary of every word. He found Laverne staring at him, and glanced down, suddenly fearing he was naked. *I am too high for this. I need to be alone.*

"'He looked for somethin' in his bottle, but it wa'dn't drunkenness. At the bottom of e'ry bottle was hope." Laverne began crocheting a new garment. It was shaping up to be quite warm. Galahad hoped he would not have to wear it. "He got one good feeling and never let it go 'cause he thoughts he was fixin' a flaw. But he was just creatin' another."

"But happiness in the heart," Laverne stared at him. "When you look elseways, you's just skippin' in quicksand."

Is she talking about me? How could she not be? Her words are made for me. Galahad scratched his arms and turned toward the door. He flinched when she spoke next.

"But I bored you 'nough. I'm sure you's wantin' to check on Misses Gardner. I hears the surgery was a success."

"Mhm," Galahad said, feeling guilty for not thinking about Hanna. "She hasn't woken yet, though." *I should have waited to use until the evening.*

"Some of us gots tragic flaws. If you don't master 'em, they inoculate you against success." Laverne put down her craft and stood up. She went over to him and looked at his eyes. "Goodness, you feel cold as the dead."

"Sorry," Galahad answered, angry at her for subjecting him to this. He did not feel in control. He could feel his heart escaping his chest. "I need to go to the baths. I'm freezing." *A good wash will sober me up.*

She said something about the orphans to him, but he did not hear her. *I have to be more disciplined. I cannot keep bending the rules.* He walked through the kitchen as Wenton argued with himself about which two steaks tasted the best. The chef decided, "If I'm hungry, this one. If I'm not, then that one."

Galahad hated how applicable everyone's words were to his dilemmas. *Is this some god's retribution? Everything has a double meaning.* Galahad dared not think too hard about deities. If there was a higher power, he would not be looked upon favorably. *No, there is nothing.* There was no god except the idealized self, the perfect Galahad which existed only in his dreams. *That is what people pray to. Nothing more. Nothing less.* Galahad marched through the tavern. People were waiting in line to see Aeric and give the family their support. Galahad pushed past them.

All their faces watched him. He could feel their stares upon his back as he went downstairs. *I must look so intoxicated. My eyes, my mannerisms. They know.* Galahad looked down at his feet so others would not see his swollen eyes. His head swirled. *Once I get a bath, I will be able to relax.*

Yes, he beamed at the heavy, metal doorway leading to the steaming room. He gripped the handle and peaked in. Nobody else was bathing. He could sprawl out and drift atop the water, not needing to worry about bumping into someone. *This will be great.* Galahad tiptoed into the baths. He reminded himself, *You've never bathed so high before.* Galahad hoped he would get lost in sensation and undressed hastily.

Galahad dipped his foot into the water. Vapor floated up to him like wisps. "Oh that's nice," Galahad moaned, submerging the rest of his lower body. "Guh," his body tingled. *This is what I needed.* He lifted off from the bottom and floated on his back.

Galahad felt each individual wave dip below him, like the most delicate of massages. He breathed the serene, hot air. His ears were more attuned to his surroundings. He could hear a mouse moving. He could smell everything, even Wenton's faraway steaks. He knew not how long he drifted through the water. Galahad watched the ceiling move and when that bored him, he submerged his eyes. He swam as deep as he could, imagining he was a whale scraping the seafloor. He surfaced to breathe and then dove back down. He listened to the distortions of the water and imagined he was in the middle of a wide sea, that he was the largest swimmer in that mighty pool.

Galahad opened his eyes. The water was cloudy with salt. With only the slightest suspension of his senses, he imagined he was far from Auberdine. He turned in every direction, unable to see the edge of the baths. *I am the whale of this ocean,* he thought, assuming it must be the most profound thing he had ever thought. He imitated the breaching of a whale. He fell back into the water and swam to the bottom. He revolved onto his back and looked up at the water. *Do whales think they are falling when they surface?*

Galahad giggled and water filled his mouth. He fled toward the air, choking on his laughter. After coughing wildly, he looked around happily. The water continued to massage him. "Whales are the biggest creatures but they eat the smallest..." Galahad cackled with laughter as he thought, *Now that is humble pie.*

A noise interrupted his laughter. He thought someone had come to the baths and waited for their entry. He sobered himself up. He cleaned his armpits, acting as if he was only washing and not playing like a child. No one came and Galahad attempted to lower his guard. He continued hearing various, strange sounds. He could not determine where they were coming from and he dipped his head into the water, leaving his eyes at the surface like a lurking crocodile.

After ten minutes of turning toward ominous sounds, he decided his mind was playing tricks on him. He resumed floating. After a minute of doing so, he grew impatient. He did not feel the waves as acutely as he had a moment before. Nor did the water feel very exceptional on his skin. He started fearing that something was lurking below him.

The thought ended any attempt at relaxation. Galahad bolted out of the water, hoping no beast was pursuing him. Once out of the water, he peered into the pool. He saw nothing.

"These baths are too hot," he said, making small talk with the empty room. He dressed, wondering if he was still high.

I think so... He looked back toward the tavern door. He did not want to face a crowd of people while he was still intoxicated. *But am I still?* He was not sure. He no longer felt euphoric, but he did not feel sober, either.

I would rather be alone, anyway. He decided to go lower, toward the inn's library at the bottom of the Hill. There, he could enjoy silence and revel in his thoughts. He left the bathhouse and descended a dark, dim passageway to the Hill's deepest delving. He had never learned to read very well, at least not well enough to enjoy it as a hobby, but he had always liked how quiet the library was.

Only faint, electric lights eyed him when he peeked his head inside. Their flickering was the only noise he could hear. *That is good.* The untraceable thuds and booms were unnerving him. *The quiet will be good.* Galahad decided he would simply allot some time for doing nothing. He found a comfy chair with sinking cushions and fell into it. *Oh yes*, he smiled, *this will do.* The dim light was perfect for his head, as the brightness of the baths had begun to nauseate him.

What to think about today? He looked around for stimulus. The endless rows of bookshelves stood unused. All the years of Auberdine's history laid in that room. Even the wide world's history was down there, or so people told him. *Will Hanna be able to read when she wakes up?* If she could not, he did not know who else would use the library. Arthur did not read. Nor did most townspeople. Apparently, Eastmont had been an educated man—but he was with his mother. *Or dead,* he acknowledged. He thought about the odd case of Cora Eastmont.

Would I flee town like his mother if something similar happened to me? Galahad could not think of a scenario where *he* would be raped. That was the realm of woman's worries, not his. *But what of a metaphorical rape? Does my skin subject me to a similar experience?*

Galahad sighed and made sure he was still alone. He was bored with philosophy. *I can twist words all I want.* He did not feel like his ideas were very profound, not like he did when he first chewed on Yang's leaf. *Fairly average, I would say.*

Galahad caught himself thinking, *I should have taken more,* and immediately recoiled. Laverne's lecture from earlier crept back into his conscience. He felt guilty for taking advantage of her. The woman had gone to doctor Yang and complained of pain, sparing Galahad the shame of asking himself. She had done all she could, selflessly, because he had lied. *I am using her, just like I used Terrell, my father.*

God, why do I do this to myself? Galahad groaned. Thinking he had accidentally said something aloud, he peeked out from his spot in the library. Peering down the rows of bookshelves, he waited a moment to assure himself he was alone. Galahad stared up at the ceiling, wary of what was above him. Eventually, he leaned back in his cushion. *I need to quit.*

The resolution calmed his anxieties. Galahad suddenly felt awfully bored of just sitting around. *I still have this last high to enjoy.* Everything he wanted to do was done. No activity grabbed his attention for more than a second. Everything was boring. *I am still too high to enjoy others. I should stay down here.* He wanted to make the most out of his last high.

What to do?

There seemed only one option which would not immediately bore him.

He paced around the library, investigating each row. He was alone. Enticed, he returned to his sinking seat and pulled down his pants. He took out his penis and began to pleasure himself. The thrill of publicly masturbating soon wore off, though. *Think of someone. Oh, yeah. Momed—that little gnat.* He pictured his old paramour, bent down and in pain. A quick sensation surged through him before decaying away. *Fuck Momed. He is nothing.* He thought of other men, faceless attractions he had seen throughout his life. He imagined grotesque acts and wild orgies, hardening at the initial shock of the images. He began sculpting the best scene, making sure every detail was perfect. He worked toward the perfect orgasm. *What would be the color of the room? What would be his girth? I think I would like him bent over at first, and then we switch to oral. No, no. Oral first. How would I get both of them to do that? I would have to spend some time wooing them. What would I say? Should I dine them somewhere? I bet one of them would be a vegetarian. That would make things difficult. Perhaps food is not the best idea. I think one would be a soldier, but the other would be a farmer. Perhaps one could be a clothier. Yes, more of a feminine type to counter the masculine.*

He was completely soft.

God damn it. He persisted, hoping sheer determination would eventually bring him to climax. His inability made him more fixated on finishing. Yet, no matter the speed of his stroke, the strength of his grip, nor shock of his fantasies—he remained incapable of getting an erection.

After tireless minutes, he gave up and put his pants back on. *I should have done it earlier, before the lethargy of the leaf took hold.* He would have to take more next time, to compensate.

He winced. *There can't be a next time.*

Galahad sensed he was not alone. He walked casually through the library, seeking the eavesdropper. The only person he saw was himself in a dusty, discarded mirror. *There is someone here, I know it.* Galahad crept again down the line of bookshelves. *There was someone...* The person's identity remained a mystery.

Galahad was done with his solitude. He fled upwards, seeking someone to talk to. There were several men in the baths. They looked at him with judgement. Galahad fled from them and ran toward the residential quarters. A Redfeather child held the hand of his mother. They both looked at Galahad fearfully. He grimaced and fled them, too.

People in the tavern seemed less interested in looking at him than discussing with each other. Everyone was speaking about the 'wonderful talent' of Yao Yang. Everyone was chatting. All except Aeric Gardner. He was sitting alone at the head of the petrified table, petting the family hound. He looked almost as exhausted as Galahad and as dour as his father.

He went to talk to the boy but decided he should wash up first. He went into the kitchen and applied a generous amount of soap to his hands, cleaning them twice before going back to the tavern. He sat on the right side of the Aeric, who made no effort to speak to him.

Galahad cleared his throat, "Lots of visitors, huh?"

Aeric ceased petting the dog. He folded his hands and raised his brow in mock-enthusiasm. "All here to show support."

The dog looked up at Aeric and started quietly coughing, never breaking eye contact with the boy.

Aeric shook his head, "Oh stop it." He continued petting the dog and rolled his eyes, saying to Galahad, "She always coughs when she wants something. Acts sick to get affection. Little manipulator."

"Smart girl," Galahad smirked for a half-second before blinking at the dog. How was it he and a dog shared the same mannerisms? *How is my day playing out as if it were already written, morals and all?* Galahad swallowed. "How's Emilia? Isn't she always with the dog?"

Aeric complained, "I had to pry Isabelle from the bed. She wasn't leaving my mother's side."

"A loyal beast," Galahad commented.

"If you don't mind," Aeric looked away, "I would enjoy being left alone."

"I understand," Galahad said, feeling similarly. He looked warily at the people mingling in the tavern. *A walk might clear my head.* He left the inn. The snow was beginning to melt, but only in specific places. The eastern side of the Hill had melted; the western side was packed with snow. The hedge gate was entirely dry, except for a muddy puddle at its base. Galahad leapt over the puddle, landing with one foot in the mud.

The splash coated his legs in muck. Galahad snarled and shook what he could from his clothing. *What a dreadful day,* he decided. Nothing had gone right. He would *certainly* be needing another bit of Yang's powder tonight.

He winced. *I should have left weeks ago, before the herb was such a prob-*

Another thought interjected, *There is no problem. Once I am on the Oleander, I will have no choice but to give it up... Yes, any problems I have in town would be solved once-*

"Goblin!"

Galahad heard the word and immediately sobered up. He exhaled deeply and then turned around. Carolyn was leaning on her fence, no mourning garb to be found. Instead, she wore tattered linens stained yellow and red. It was evident that Carolyn had been drinking. Galahad approached, standing several feet from her fence. The vindictive widow's eyes could not focus on him, nor his on her.

Carolyn's lips twitched up and down. Galahad could not tell whether she was laughing or crying, smiling or frowning. She tried to point her finger at him, but her drunken eyes deceived her. She pointed at the walnut tree, seething. "Maybe you did not kill my son..." She squinted, stifled an odorous burp, and continued, "But you are still a vile goblin. Who, who knows what your words did to my boy? He was playing in some r-ruin because he was afraid of you."

Galahad had hoped to meet with Carolyn after Terrell's hanging. That the woman was drunk was only an added benefit. Galahad posited, "That whoremonger killed one arrogant boy." He blinked at her, letting her drunken mind catch up. "Maybe he killed yours, too?"

Carolyn's smug face had a prepared response. She opened her mouth before Galahad had even finished speaking. But by the end, it hanged open. Her lips quivered and he assumed she was crying. Finally, she declared, "You are a mean man with hate in your heart."

Galahad smiled, "And you are a barren woman with absolutely nothing in yours."

"You did something." Carolyn spat. "And whatever it is, you need God." She turned around and stumbled up her stairs. She gave him a wicked glare and slammed her door shut.

"Mm," Galahad grunted. *I need a lawyer, not a god.* He smirked at the sky. *If there is a judge in the sky, let him strike me down.* He scanned the sky, waiting for a bolt of lightning to pierce the cloudless horizon. The whole heavens were blue, save a tiny grey cloud directly overhead. Galahad walked back to the inn. He approached the hedge gate and looked up again. The grey wisp was still overhead. It had followed him against the wind. The sight perturbed him.

Suddenly, Galahad felt his throat tighten. An obstruction had lodged itself in his throat. He inhaled, but there was an anvil's weight on his chest. His mind grew hot as his heart started to hammer. His lungs stalled. He was choking. Galahad garbled and fell to his knees. A pressure was building in his eyes, like they were about to pop out of their sockets. His head became light.

Galahad hacked up a black pebble. He gasped for air, licked his lips, and looked around. Nobody had seen him, hopefully. Galahad blinked, fascinated by the little stone. *How had I swallowed it?* He got to his feet, hastily brushed the dirt off his knees, and rubbed his eyes. He looked up at the cloud. It had dissipated, leaving only a few white strands in its wake.

Must have been the leaf, Galahad decided. That his day had been a series of odd coincidences was only because his mind was turned inward. His introspectiveness had made it easier to interpret the world with metaphors in mind. That the metaphors related to him was only because he had been concerned with his own relations. *Simply the power of interpretation.* Galahad wiped his eyes and climbed up the Hill. When he saw the redwood door and heard laughter coming from the tavern, he reiterated, "Must have been the leaf."

"What?" asked a familiar voice.

"God damn it," Galahad flinched. Doctor Yao Yang was standing there, eyes fixed upon him.

"Leaf?" Yang averted his gaze. His eyes darted across the town of Auberdine.

Galahad's surveyed the horizon. He espied no grey clouds, nor any black pebbles at his feet. He giggled, "I think I may have brushed up against some poison ivy."

The doctor replied, apathetically, "Talk to my uncle about getting some salve for that." He lit a cigarette, inhaled, and began to choke. He pounded a fist against his chest while his cheeks flushed red.

"Not much of a smoker, eh?" Galahad tried not to laugh.

"Fuck you," Yang replied, taking another drag from the cigarette.

Galahad raised his brow, "Not very happy for someone who has just saved a life."

Yang shook his head. "I extended her life, but it was not saved." He flicked the ash from his cigarette and stared at it with disgust. "Want a drag?"

"No, thank you," Galahad declined. *I've had enough of your medicines.*

"Fair enough," Yang shrugged. "It's a nasty habit. One my uncle has never overcome."

Galahad burped, "I bet he is furious that *you* were the one to do the surgery."

"Understatement."

Galahad rolled his eyes as he tried to think of how to resuscitate the dying conversation. He scratched his cheek. Yang seemed indifferent to his presence and continued staring down at Cottonwood. He finally asked, "What are you doing out here?"

"Listening."

Galahad was growing impatient. He had better things to do than skulk. "To whom?" he questioned, quite aware that it was not him.

Yang snorted. He stared out at the valley below like a captain of a ship. "You haven't heard it?"

When Galahad remained silent, Yang simply waited. Several minutes passed before Galahad got his answer. A howl. It was answered by another howl, and another. Yang pointed toward the base of the east mountain, "There's a hunt. Been going since last night."

Galahad thought of Arthur and his band of boys. "The innkeeper had best be careful. They seem close."

Yang commented, "The packs usually don't come this close to town."

"They do in the Overgrowth," Galahad told him.

The sun was setting. The Inner Ring was as calm as ever. Only one person was about. *An exceptionally fat person*, Galahad noted. The figure had a hat as inflated as their belly. Garbed in black and blue, it was obvious the person was Constable Goodwind.

"As wide as he is tall," Yang mocked.

Galahad smiled. The lawman approached the inn. Galahad felt his throat tightening. His hands began to sweat. He had a clever reply but dared not mock the man whose power it was to sentence murderers to death. The man stopped. Galahad held his breath. Then, Goodwind turned. Galahad exhaled and chuckled. The constable was not after him.

"Why we entrust the law with a glorified blueberry, I'll never know."

Galahad wiped the sweat off his brow. "He's not the most threatening man," he joked. "He must see some treats to be walking at this hour."

"Oh no doubt," Yang quipped.

Galahad squinted. Constable Goodwind was approaching a home, pausing every few steps to catch his breath.

"Pathetic," Yang spat, lighting another cigarette. "I suppose a man will do anything for sex."

"What do you mean?" Galahad questioned. Goodwind was not known to indulge in much else but food.

Yang laughed, "Why else would he be knocking on the door of a widow?"

Widow. Galahad's heart stopped. The lawman was greeted at the door by a petite woman.

The young doctor made another joke that Galahad did not hear. The unfolding scene had captured his attention. Carolyn shook the constable's hand and welcomed him inside. The door closed, but he knew well what was happening within those walls. He could not hear the conversation, yet he knew what words were being said. Galahad's accuser was finally making her move.

22

First Words

It was getting harder to breathe. Every time she tried, the hands wrapped tighter around her windpipe. Hanna did not know who was choking her, only that they had a bloody face. She feared those hands, but when they loosened—she felt cold and even more afraid.

"It is for your own good," the face smiled, blood dripping into its mouth.

Hanna believed it. The choking resumed.

"You need this," it encouraged. Hanna's lungs struggled. She gasped as quietly as she could, not wanting the face to take offense. She let the last hints of life leave her.

"That's good," whispered the face. An invisible hand brushed back her hair. She felt it reach into her head, probing within her. The bloody face took her brain from her cold body. It kissed her forehead and frowned. Then, it swallowed her brain.

"Just for safe-keeping," he heard it say in a soothing voice.

Suddenly, Hanna was lying on the rocks. Thunder crashed and lightning pierced her eyes. Several rocks fell from a waterfall, scattering into a golden stream. Her husband leapt from the cliffs, pursuing the rockslide. She heard him yell, "No more visitors!"

His brother's shadow descended from beyond a veil of storm clouds. Auldwine answered her husband, "Does that mean me, too?"

The two brothers paused. Then, the storm clouds departed and Auldwine's shadow flew toward her. She was in quicksand now, her body falling back toward the bloody face. She could feel it lurking beneath her.

"Your uncle made it seem like she was..." Auldwine's shadow struggled to finish the thought.

"Already dead?" A chess piece finished, bathing in the waterfall of gold. "You saw him?"

"Mhm," the shadow answered. It moved closer to Hanna. She wanted to say hello, but when she tried to speak, the bloody face was choking her again. She was forced to watch as Auldwine's black hand went to greet the bloody face but the monster plunged its teeth into Auldwine's neck, sucking the life from him. Hanna shrieked. No sound came out. The face smiled at her. An invisible hand closed her eyes...

Hanna gasped and looked around her. She was in a bedroom. She recognized some of the furniture in the room, but not the people. She lifted her head and looked down her chest. It was rising and falling without any trouble. Her throat was dry, but nothing was choking it. Hanna wiggled her toes. They moved well enough. Hanna let her head fall back upon her pillow. She blinked and realized a man was staring down at her.

"Hey kid," a dark-skinned man smiled at her.

Hanna stared at him. *What a weird thing to say.* She went to say, "*I am not a child,*" but the words did not come out. Her mouth hardly opened at all. Her tongue slid to the side of her cheek. Her lips popped and whistled. She strained, thinking of where to put her tongue. *God, this thing gets in the way.* At the foot of the bed, a tall boy was watching her. He seemed confused. Beside him, a little girl was staring at her with a mixture of horror and surprise. Hanna focused intently and questioned, "Am I..?" Her words fizzled.

Another man answered, "You are Hanna Gardner, born in the capitol of the West, the Castle Rock. You married the innkeeper of Auberdine and reside there now."

Hanna blinked again. *Reside? Does he mean rest?* She had never heard that word before. A flood of memories suddenly made her very tired. She struggled to put words to the images. She saw towers of steel, odd symbols, pens, and parks. She turned her head and stared at the dark-skinned man. He had a name and she had known it. She was sure of it. *Esterman? No, that is not him.* She closed her eyes and tried to recall. Perhaps he was a mathematician... Hanna gasped, realizing who the man was. She rolled her eyes, embarrassed for having forgotten such a simple fact.

"You is the innkeeper," she nodded at the dark-skinned man. She added, confidently, "My h-husband."

Her husband chuckled. He shuffled closer to her and reached for her hand. He tilted his head, and then it seemed like he was in sudden pain. He pulled his hand back and examined it, as if checking for a splinter. He scratched his eyebrows and took in several sharp, deep breaths. He cleared his throat and looked at their children. "Uhm, no."

"Oh," Hanna blinked. She covered herself in blankets.

He leaned in closer and raised his brow. "We joked about it, though." He quickly added, "Marriage, that is." He shook his head. "I am Charles Eastmont. Your friend. Arthur's friend." He asked the tall boy, "Speaking of which, where is that bastard?"

Arthur, Hanna repeated. *That his name? Why do I not remember?*

A man in a white uniform answered, "He left just before the operation-"

Surgery! She remembered snow, a grim man, and a gun. She was filled with terror and put her hand on Charles. "You was lost."

Eastmont nodded. His cheek twitched and he tilted his head at her. He responded with a crack in his voice, "I was."

Is he asking a question? "Arthur... Y-you?" Hanna asked, forgetting the words which linked the two men.

"I'm afraid not," Charles frowned, turning away from her.

"Can someone," she paused, weary from the excitement, "Him. Upstairs?" Hanna asked. They looked at her as if she had spoken a foreign language. She clarified for them, "Husband?"

"He's not here," the tall boy replied.

Hanna yawned. There was so much excitement, so much to take in. She closed her eyes and took a few deep breaths. When she opened them, Charles was sitting beside her. *Charles!* Her husband had found him at last. Hanna felt a wave of energy and she asked, "W-where is A-Arthur?"

The man in white put his arm around the tall boy and the little girl. Hanna watched them watch her. They did not understand.

"Not here," the little girl whispered.

Why not? Hanna heard the wind howling. The covers were not enough. It was cold and she needed her husband. "G-gone?" Her lips shook. She was afraid. *Dream again. Must be. I know it.* Her husband was *always* beside her. "He went to war again?" She did not wait for a response. She knew that was what he had done. The muscles in her chest began to shake. She thought she might vomit. The little girl began to cry and Hanna followed her lead. Hysteria took over and Hanna tried to slide under the covers. But she could not hide. A huge paw had put itself onto her lap.

A large dog looked at her, tongue drooping to the side. Hanna looked away from it, afraid. "Off it. Get get," she muttered. When she dared to look again at the huge thing, it was staring at her like a person might. The dog's eyes moved with Hanna's. It wiggled closer to her, getting within petting distance. It wrapped its body around Hanna's, head resting on her lap.

Husband, she began to panic.

The dog looked up. Their eyes met once more. Slowly, the great dog stretched its head toward Hanna's, paused, and gave her a giant lick. Hanna suddenly felt warmer, calmer. She giggled and wiped the spit from her face.

The little girl walked up to Hanna. She was shaking. The girl handed her a small, green teddy bear. "This will protect you, mama." She scratched the dog's ear, "And Izzy, of course."

Mama, Hanna realized. *Of course, my children.* "You are," she paused, forgetting her words. She licked her lips. Her brow collapsed in concentration.

"You may find it hard to speak for a while," the man in white said. Hanna was sure *he* was not her son.

But the others in the room—she knew they were family. She smiled at the girl and spoke, not knowing if the words were coming out properly. "Very sweet, Emilia." The name came to her easily enough. It was moving her mouth right that was hard. *People do this always time,* Hanna reminded herself.

She asked the dark-skinned man who he was, "What is you?"

Before he replied, Hanna shook her head. "Sorry, sorry. Who is you?" The man at the foot of the bed looked at the tall boy. *Aeric,* she remembered. *Why do they look worried?* Aeric shrugged and smiled at her. Hanna felt embarrassed and avoided looking at him. The dark-skinned man finally replied,

"Charles Eastmont—"

He is quite polite, Hanna noted.

"—We met at the university. You studied mathematics."

"I did?" Hanna asked, stunned someone like her could do something so smart.

Emilia nodded rapidly, her excitement evident. "Yeah, yeah. You said everything else was too boring."

Eastmont agreed, "It is true."

The dark-skinned man beamed at her in a strange way. His hand floated over to hers and she instinctually grabbed it. She was not sure why her husband was so timid with her, but at least he was there with her.

"You are the smartest person I know," her husband complimented.

"You're flattering me. Just flattering. No n-need. I'm strong, Arthur."

Her husband pulled his hand away so fast, Hanna jumped a little. Then, he bowed his head and would not look at her. He tugged at his shirt collar and snorted a weird, unhappy laugh at her two children. "I am not your husband," he smiled. He blinked a dozen times and wiped his face, though there was nothing on it.

Then who? Hanna waited impatiently. Who was this strange man on her bed?

"Charles Eastmont," he finally introduced himself. "When we met, you were the brightest lady in the capitol."

Are they making fun of me? She focused on moving her mouth in the correct pattern, determined to speak properly. She made sure to put the words together correctly before speaking. "Very thanks you good." They looked at her strangely. *Oh, gosh. Manners.* Hanna corrected herself, "Sir."

Aeric and Charles looked at her with the same sad smile. Hanna remembered the word. *Pity.* Her daughter was staring at her too, but not with sadness. The little girl's pupils were wide with fear. Hanna could feel her lip starting to twitch. She followed Emilia's stare toward her scalp, brushing her hand hesitantly across her head. Her hair was gone. She moved her hands across her head in a panic. *Not all of it,* she sighed. Hanna put a finger on her bald spot. The slightest pressure made her wince. Fluid oozed onto her finger.

"Please," the man beside Aeric said. "Refrain from touching the site."

Doctor Yang! What does he mean about my sight? Stunned, her finger floated in the air.

"Do not touch that," he rushed over, moving her hand for her. He sighed, wiping the sweat from his brow. He stepped back from the bed.

Hanna licked the backs of her lip. *Smartest person he knows...* She shook her head. *What a joke.* She felt her cheeks getting wet. She tried to hide her eyes behind some pillows, but the little girl—Emilia—stopped her. She took her hand, saying, "Hold on, mama."

Her daughter hurried out of the bedroom. Hanna heard clangs and thuds from a nearby room. Yang and Aeric sat down beside her dresser and waited, both with a bent back. Yang crossed his legs and stared at the floor. Aeric rested his chin on his hand, his eyes darting between Eastmont and her. A moment later, Emilia returned with a piece of cloth, a pencil, and a huge book. She got onto the bed and crawled up to her mother. Isabelle gave the cloth a sniff.

"Paper, pencil, book," Emilia smiled, shooing away the hound's snout and handing the items to her mother.

What? Clearly, she was supposed to know what to do with the items. She took the heavy book and placed it on her lap. *Encyclo-, Encycloped-*

"What does it say?" She shrugged.

"Encyclopedia Mathematica," Aeric whispered.

Hanna looked at the book and then at her daughter. Emilia nodded.

Hanna analyzed the symbols adorning the cover. She knew one of them. "That's a four."

"That's right," Eastmont agreed, getting up and joining Aeric and Yang. He leaned against her dresser, nearly hitting his head on the candle-hanger above him.

Maybe they are right. I can do this. "That's an adder sign next to the four. And a taker!"

Isabelle looked at her, coughing.

"Your guess was good, too, big girl," Emilia told the dog, scratching her chin. "Those do things to the numbers."

"They do," Hanna confirmed, proudly. She opened the big book, skipping the introductions. She remembered not caring for those. "Ah, yes," she said, putting her finger on the first page of the first chapter. "Ar-Arithm..." Hanna rolled her eyes, smiling, "We know that." She flipped through more pages before finding a bunch of numbers. They were spaced between adders, takers, growers, and slicers. "Twenty take ten." She licked her lips. *Twenty is a ten,* she understood. *But what does that mean?*

"Two tens, one ten. One ten?" Hanna looked around the room. Their expressions did not tell her if she was right. She decided that she was. "Eleven, of course," she declared hastily, hoping nobody else did the problem. "Check the n-next page, sugarbear." Her heart was beating hard and fast. *Yang said I couldn't.* She was terrified. *But I can. I can,* she pleaded with herself.

"Um," Emilia sniffled. "If one square foot of a dam can hold back thirteen cubic feet of water, what is the area a dam has to be to confine a water system of three-hundred thousand cubic feet?"

"Emilia, dear," Hanna scowled, "Don't swear."

"Huh?" Emilia squeaked.

Charles raised his finger, "A dam, Hanna. A barrier, a dike."

"Oh, right," Hanna nodded quickly. "Obviously." She laughed and looked around the room, "Mind goes too fast, you know?" Nobody else was laughing. *Okay, slow down.* "Can you say more once? I use the paper this time."

Hanna waited, but her daughter did not speak. She looked up from the paper. Emilia wiped a pair of red eyes and put the book in front of her face. She repeated the question loudly.

Why is she sad? Hanna dwelled, not hearing the question very well. She cleared her throat and began writing down numbers. When she got to the total amount of water, though—she struggled writing down the correct number of zeroes. *Three-hundred thousands. Do I grow three by a thousand? How much is a thousand?* Hanna swallowed and looked at her paper. Her eyes returned to earlier numbers. *What does this thirteen mean? Why do I...*

"Ratio, ratio," she said, biting her pencil. *What is a ratio?* Sweat dripped down her forehead. Her hands were tightening around a pencil she did not know how to use. Her fingers trembled. The tool fell onto the bed, rolling to the floor. The quiet fall echoed loudly in her mind.

Hanna could not bear to look at the paper. This was simple. She knew it was. Children her daughter's age excelled at the stuff. She slammed the awful book and heaved it off the edge. She crumpled the paper and cast it away. "I am tired," she told them all, fighting tears.

"Misses Gardner," the doctor began. "Your capacities will return in due time."

"I am *entirely* c-capable," Hanna barked. She did not want to seem angry, but she did not want them to see her crying either. "Can I rest in peace?"

"Of course," Yang said, nodding stoically at her children.

Aeric rose. His knees cracked. "Love you, mama."

"I love you both," she said.

"Can't we stay longer?" Emilia pleaded. She had another piece of paper in her hand.

"What you has?" Hanna asked.

Emilia lifted her arm slowly and handed her a wrinkled white sheet full of scribbles. Hanna took the scribbles and squinted.

"Read it," Emilia smiled, standing proud over the scribbles. She was excited and very happy to have made the thing.

Hanna choked. She did not want to disappoint the girl. A lump formed in her throat.

Aeric launched forward and grabbed her sister's arm. "It's okay, Emilia."

"NO," Emilia snatched her arm away. "I want her to read it! She will like it! I had to use a dictionary."

Hanna blinked at the scribbles. "Fth, sch... The?" She hid her lips behind her teeth.

Aeric groaned, picked Emilia up, and took her away. Isabelle barked madly, demanding the girl be put down. She jumped on Aeric, gnawing on his arm. The dog's spit flew onto the walls. Aeric dropped his sister and mumbled some words. Hanna assumed they were the bad kind.

"I WANT TO STAY!" Emilia screamed, tears dripping off her face. Isabelle licked them from her cheeks before they fell.

"No, your mother needs rest," Yang told her.

"It's okay," Hanna assured him. *My little girl can stay*. Nobody seemed to hear her, though. Hanna was frozen. Everything was happening too fast and she was thinking too slow. Emilia left. Aeric left. Charles left. Yang started to shut the door.

"Izzy," Emilia called for her hound.

The dog did not budge.

"Come on, big girl," Hanna heard Emilia pat her legs.

Isabelle raised her head toward the sound. She tilted her head, thoughtfully. Then, she got up onto the bed. The dog ignored Emilia's calls, lying down as close to Hanna as possible.

The girl peeked her head back into the room. "I suppose mama could use the company."

The comment reminded her of her husband. Her mind raced as she tried to form the proper string of words. Hanna asked her daughter as she turned, "Can you bring daddy up? This bed is cold, even with big girl here."

Her daughter frowned and bowed her head.

23
Grove-keeper

The door closed quietly. Charles followed Aeric down the stairs, trying not to make a scene of his wounded leg. He would rather not make a fuss over a scratch when it seemed so many needed healing. They had hardly stepped into the tavern when Emilia turned from them all and ran away toward the inn's lower levels. Charles watched her go, listening to her stifled crying until he could no longer bear it.

"What the hell has happened?" He asked. *Why are my comings and goings always so gloomy?* Charles flinched at his self-pity. A few tavern-goers looked at him as if he were a ghost. He made a point to let them know he saw them staring. Their eyes met his and, realizing they were caught, they averted their gaze.

Young doctor Yang explained. "You were aware of her headaches?"

"I suppose so," Charles tried to remember.

Yang pointed at the table. "Well, they were symptoms of a greater sickness. She needed brain surgery." A slight, nostalgic smile crept onto his face.

Charles questioned, "And you did this surgery, then? With the assistance of your uncle?"

"No," Yang's smile faded. He looked behind himself and then wiped his shoulders of whatever dust had accumulated. "He thought it was impossible." He adjusted his belt and sat down to the right of the innkeeper's seat. "Forbade me to operate, actually."

Aeric took his father's tall seat. "Kicked him out for disobeying him." He poured himself a glass of water from a nearby pitcher and sipped it loudly.

Charles sat across from Yang. A silence ensued. Yang folded his hands on the table. Aeric looked at the ceiling and wiped his eyes.

"So," Yang's voice cracked. He stopped and continued in a lower voice, "You saw my uncle?"

"I did," Charles said, not wanting to upset the young man. "He seemed, uh, preoccupied." He did not feel the need to go into detail about how Yao Yu told him Hanna was dead and his nephew was to blame.

"Hm, hm," Yang cleared his throat. "I am sure he told you all manner of lies." He leaned onto the table, "He is a prideful man."

"He is," Charles nodded, glancing at the innkeeper's son.

Aeric was watching them intently. Charles thought he had aged considerably.

"What was the diagnosis?" Charles wanted to know.

"Headaches," Aeric answered in a weary tone.

Headaches, Charles echoed. His mother had complained about headaches as well. "Muscle spasms? Vomiting?"

Aeric tilted his head and removed the fingers from his lips. "Yes," he replied with surprise.

"Trench Rot," Yang declared, as if the information was of no importance. "An affliction of the brain." He gestured upstairs, "The taint was removed, though. Now—she must heal."

Charles looked up at the wooden columns and scratched his hair, "That new disease? The one soldiers got in Tanglewood?"

"We were shocked to find it in her," the young doctor admitted.

Charles spoke rapidly. "Well, we will need to study this fu—"

"What happened to *you*?" Aeric interrupted. "My father went searching for you days ago."

"Yes, yes. Whatever for?" Charles asked, finding it easier to continue asking questions than detailing all that had happened to him.

"We found your horse," Aeric said. "Then, we found your luggage—all filthy and washed up."

It was the young doctor's turn to ask a question, "What came over you? To travel during a blizzard?"

Slightly offended, Charles replied, "There wasn't a storm when I left."

"And what of your mother?" Yang pointed out. "Will she be alright?"

Charles scratched his cheek and glanced upstairs, thinking he heard Hanna call for them. Soon, he realized nobody was speaking. Both Aeric and Yang were staring at him. *Best be frank. It will be easier, that way.*

"She died. Just after I arrived." Charles blinked. They looked at one another, clearly hoping the other might respond.

"I'm sorry," Yang mumbled just as Aeric declared, "That's terrible."

Charles felt the urge to frown as well. Their condolences reawakened his old sorrow. It was as if Cora had just died that day. He bit his lip while his leg began to bounce up and down. He looked away from them both, afraid of what their sad faces would do to his resolve. Charles was sure he was one sympathetic gesture away from crying. *Not here,* he grimaced. He raised a smile like an anchor. He addressed the doctor, determined to do more for his mother's memory than mourn.

"My mother had a terrible cough, muscle spasms... She said it started with headaches."

Yang's right eye twitched. The young doctor froze. Finally, he lowered his head in understanding. "Hm."

Silence spoke next. Charles started to fidget, moving his fingers while his thoughts drifted. *Mama could have been saved,* came the painful realization. *But would she have turned out like Hanna?* She was his oldest friend and he no longer knew how to speak to her. The thought saddened him more than his mother's passing.

"Will she," Charles tried to be delicate. Aeric raised his brow and waited. "Hanna, I mean. Will she ever?" It felt wiser to leave his question unasked and let each person's own euphemisms speak for him.

"Perhaps," Yang shrugged. "She will require support, of course. Teaching, too—where applicable."

"I wish Arthur were here," Charles sighed. "What terrible luck we all have had."

"He will be back soon," Aeric put on a happy face. "He'll set things right. You know it."

Charles did not. "The forest is treacherous. I was nearly mauled by a pack of wolves after Atlani fled."

"Atlani?" Aeric questioned.

"The horse," Charles replied. He glanced behind him, addressing the exit, "I would like to see her." He returned toward the table, "If you'll pardon my absence?"

Aeric raised his brow, "You've been gone for weeks. A minute is hardly an offense. Actually, I'll go with you."

Charles grinned, holding the door for him. Aeric had grown and not in height. As they trudged down the Hill. Aeric inquired, "Why did you come back?"

Charles shrugged, "You all were the only family I had left, with my mother gone."

Not knowing what to say, Aeric scratched his ear and then put his hands to his hips. He replied, making his voice more manly than it had any right to be, "My father will love having you back." The lowness of his voice caused it to crack.

"I know," Charles grinned. "I intend to take him up on his offer."

"What was that?"

"Grove-keeper," he answered. Both gave a passing regard to the decaying cottonwood and then continued toward Atlani. "Lots of work to be done."

The stables were a lonely, cold place. There was a perpetual draft where broken planks had rotted away. Though dozens of animals could be accommodated, only two currently resided there. One was a lame donkey with a missing eye, the other was Atlani. When they entered the stables, the mare lost herself in excitement. She circled her stall, kicking her legs and whinnying. Then, she trotted up to Charles and licked his cheek.

Charles kissed her snout. Then, he pointed a finger. "You don't let me wander off again, understood?"

Atlani responded with an odd array of snorts and whinnies. Then, she turned and munched on a pile of hay.

"What *exactly* does a grove-keeper do?" Aeric questioned.

Charles left Atlani to her hay. "I suppose what your uncle used to do. Clean the granary, trim tree branches, pull weeds, water plants." Aeric's face was scrunched in thought. He periodically rubbed his chin or nodded to himself. Charles went to open the door.

Aeric beat him to it. He let Charles go first. Then, the boy stepped lightly through the doorway, gently shut the door, and paused with his head bowed. The wind whistled by. Aeric turned around like a top being spun. He said, breathily, "You uh-" He cleared his throat. "You think there will be more cases of Rot?"

Charles raised his cheeks. He was not frowning, but he was not smiling either. "Probably. Problem is, nobody knows where Trench Rot comes from. Just that it started during the War."

Aeric nodded. Then, he rubbed his hands together, and ushered him back up the Hill. The wind was opening and closing the redwood door. It creaked against its hinges. They were the only people outside, and aside from the breeze—only the quiet knocking of the door could be heard. Charles thought it might have been peaceful, had the innkeeper been home.

I hope he is okay, Charles worried. *Hanna asked about him every chance she got. She could never bear to lose him.* A petulant thought added, with a disgusting amount of hope, *She would have to rely on you more than ever, if it happens.*

Charles shook his head, refusing to think such unfriendly thoughts. "Let's move on."

"Hm?" Aeric asked.

Charles corrected, glad Hanna's son was not paying particularly good attention, "Go in, sorry."

The heat of the fire was a welcome change from the wind's bite. Charles scanned the tavern happily. The wooden pillars were as strong as ever, the smell of the kitchen as overwhelming. Charles saw two little girls playing on the floor. The scene reminded him of when he and Arthur used to terrorize the inn as children. He rolled his eyes as he thought about all the times Auldwine scolded them for misbehaving. His eyes went up to the rafters and down to a dark, tavern corner.

"You met Wenton, right?" Aeric questioned.

"Once or twice." The chef was one of the first to be injured in the war and had come to Auberdine seeking employment. Charles had few interactions with him before going to the front. Rumor was he fought for the Redfeather, but nobody really cared about the fact once they tried his cooking. "His food's good."

"Damn good," Aeric agreed, walking into the kitchen. Charles followed. The smell was hypnotizing and Charles immediately thought of his mother's cooking. Spices lofted through the air and into his nose, bringing nostalgia with them.

The chef appeared from behind a large pile of pots and plates. Wenton winked at Charles, "Smells like home, don't it?" He had a cage in one hand, and tongs in the other. Within the cage were at least a dozen crawfish. "We gon' have ourselves a boil." He put the items down and shook Charles' hand. Wenton's teeth were the yellowest Charles had ever seen. "I heard you was back, so I went and prepared a lil' homestyle meal."

"It smells like my mama's cookin', I'll tell ya," Charles replied. He saw Aeric's shock from the corner of his eye. "It's gon' be a good one."

"You know it," Wenton said, positively elated. "I tell ya, it is so refreshin' havin' another Redfeather here. 'Sides Laverne, it's just been me."

It was true. Charles' race was poorly represented in Auberdine. Often, he was mistaken for a dark-skinned Muhali. "I hear ya." Charles smirked at Aeric, who was clearly wondering where the eloquent Eastmont had gone.

"Well," Wenton rubbed his hands and took a hot sauce bottle. He poured the sauce into a measuring cup. "Now I gots an excuse to put some heat on in this-" he cleared his throat and looked at Aeric. He put his hand behind his back.

"Bitch?" Aeric finished with a wry smile.

A massive grin formed on the chef, "You god damn right."

Wenton opened the crawfish cage and grabbed his tongs. He started to whistle as he pulled out a live crustacean. He spun around with the creature as if he were dancing with it. Then, he dropped the animal into the pot of boiling water.

Charles could not stop staring at the pot of water. He tried not to think of the poor devil being boiled alive. The meal was a kindness, but one he would not wholly enjoy. He was a vegetarian.

Wenton's tongs froze in mid-air. A moment's deliberation passed and then he tossed the tool away. He grabbed the entire cage and dumped all the crawfish in at once. The cook smiled at them and bobbed his head proudly.

Charles might have said something courteous, but then the crawfish began to hiss. The kitchen was filled with their shrieks. The whistle of their roasting bodies sizzled his eardrums. Charles had heard the same pain in men. He imagined their organs melting, the pain they were enduring. He saw their little bodies rolling with the boiling water. They rose to the surface and plunged to the bottom, unable to control their fate. Charles saw drowning sailors.

"Excuse me," he said to the innkeeper's son. If he did not leave, he was sure he would vomit. He departed stoically, trying not to make a scene. He pushed the kitchen door away from him like it was assaulting him. The door smashed against the wall and fell limply shut. The screams faded. He went to the dark corner of the tavern and sank to the floor. His hands shook and his chest spasmed.

Aeric followed a moment later. He smiled at him, unaffected by the crawfish. *They both must think I am quite stupid.* Charles felt embarrassment warm his cheeks. He returned to his feet. Pain shot through his thigh. Charles ignored the pain. *This is nothing to being boiled alive.* He bit down on his cheeks to distract himself.

Aeric scratched the back of his head, looking around the inn. "Was that, uh, because of the war?"

"What?" Charles played dumb.

"Come on," Aeric knew better. "I've seen plenty of soldiers." He sat beside Charles and leaned toward him, whispering, "This was a war hospital, you know?"

Charles rolled his fingers through his hair. It was growing wild. The curls had become thick knots. Loops of hair at least an inch thick made his entire head feel larger. He rubbed his forehead and admitted, "Yeah, I know. You're right." Charles looked at the boy from his periphery. He was staring straight ahead. Charles did the same. They did not speak, instead listening to Wenton's singing from inside the kitchen.

Finally, the innkeeper's son cleared his throat. "Well, I admit... The shrieks were a bit much."

"They reminded me of sailors drowning," Charles said flatly. He stared blankly at his memories.

Aeric's cheek twitched. He blinked and scratched his temple. "All the other soldiers say the same type of thing, or they laugh at grotesque things. My mother always said I was lucky to not have gone."

"You are." Charles narrowed his gaze and looked Aeric in the eye. "Nobody likes war. Not by the end."

Aeric scratched at the tips of his fingernails. He tapped the ground with his foot. "My uncle used to say my dad was happiest on the front. When they were still offering shore leave, my dad refused."

Charles acknowledged the fact with a slight tilt of his head. He unfurled his bottom lip and lifted his shoulders. He joked, "Well your dad is crazy."

Aeric closed his eyes and let out a stuttered breath. He rubbed a finger along his stomach, tracing an odd pattern. "I would have taken all the shore leave I could get."

Charles smiled. Whatever had happened to the patriotic Aeric, the battle-loving boy—he did not know. He put an arm on the young man's shoulder. "Me too."

24

Ultimatum

"Are you sure?" Laverne probed. She was always fretting over his health. Galahad hated and loved that about her. "Mhm," he answered.

"I don't want you suffering on account of some manly pride," Laverne scolded him.

"It is not pride," Galahad almost laughed. "I think I am doing a little better." He smiled. Laverne did not return the gesture. Galahad frowned. *I need to be firm.*

"A little." Laverne tilted her head. "What that mean, hm?"

"Just..." In truth, he had no idea what it meant, because he did not know what he wanted. He bargained with his two desires, clearing his throat, "I just want to try a day without."

"Okay," Laverne agreed. She shook her head and swam closer to Galahad. "You finished gettin' clean?"

"Yes," Galahad replied. "Now I am."

"Good, good," Laverne got out of the baths. She wrapped a large towel around her chest, handing Galahad one in the same color. She made for the stairs, saying, "It's okay for a man to be in pain. Don' be a fool. You need medicine, ain't no shame, oka-"

Laverne froze. Charles Eastmont stepped into the baths. Galahad's eyes went from Laverne to Charles, and to Laverne again. It was an odd look she was giving Eastmont. That same look was usually reserved for him. Galahad walked closer to Laverne, hailing Charles with a small wave. "Well isn't this a shame," he joked.

"What?" Charles muttered, obviously taken aback.

"Arthur leaves to find you," Galahad clarified. "Yet here you have come."

"Yes," Charles coughed and wiped his hands on his pants. "How are you?"

"Not unwell," Galahad answered, politely. "I suppose his offer on the train brings you? Or you've been hiding in the weeds all this time?"

Eastmont raised his brow in surprise. "In part," he said. The man looked overlong into Galahad's eyes. The stare was piercing, like good Eastmont knew of every bad thing Galahad had done. He had given him the same regard on the train.

He does not like me, Galahad suspected. *Well fine, I don't like me, either.*

Eastmont directed his attention to Laverne, bowing his head slightly. "Ma'am."

191

"Oh, look at you," the plump woman eyed him up and down. "You look the spittin' image of my husband. How's your mama?"

Galahad surged with disgust. *She and this man are the same age and she acts as old as myth.* Galahad had half a mind to tell her off, to say she ought to be a mother to actual children. He held his tongue.

"Dead?" Laverne shrieked.

Galahad blinked and looked at Charles. *Dead? Is that what he said?* He rubbed the back of his ear. "Your mother?" He gasped, hoping a sympathetic voice would hide the fact he had not heard Eastmont the first time.

"That's what I said," Charles grunted.

Galahad's cheek twitched as he swallowed several indignant remarks. He forced a smile and waited for the conversation to fizzle out.

"You all alone, then?" Laverne inquired, stepping a great deal closer to Eastmont.

Galahad stepped forward, ahead of Laverne. He asked, "What happened?"

"Same thing Hanna came down with, I think." Charles smiled, "If you would excuse me."

Ever the child of malchance, Galahad shook his head. He started back to their room. Yet, Laverne remained fixated on Eastmont. She stared as the unfortunate soul descended toward the library.

"You just come and knock if you's needin' anything," she called. Only once the man had left her view did her attention revert to Galahad. "You tighten that towel," she ordered. Then, she cast a look of concern in the direction of Eastmont. "That's a boy that loved his mama."

"I think I may have been hasty," Galahad coughed. "I feel a tinge of nausea."

"Yeah?" Laverne replied, predisposed.

Galahad gritted his teeth and stared at her. *The man may well be older than her,* he perseverated. *She is wasting her time.* He burped, "Headache, too."

Laverne finally turned around. "Well, hon," she said, firmly. "I know you wanted to stop takin' your medicine. I won' force ya."

Galahad flinched, not expecting the response. "I think you are right," he said, weakly. Laverne watched him passively, so Galahad finished with a cough.

"Well I gots to respect your wishes," she pinched his cheek.

Don't, Galahad wanted to shout.

Laverne sighed, "Though my motherly instincts tellin' me to keep medicatin' ya."

Galahad rolled his fingers along his thigh like he was playing the piano. He sucked in his upper lip and made a popping sound. He suggested, looking down at his feet, "Those instincts, they're right a lot of the time."

"Oh, hon, I know it."

He looked up at Laverne hopefully.

"But part of helpin' others is lettin' them choose their path."

Galahad uttered, "M'yes," through his teeth.

Laverne asked, "What you gon' do today?"

He scratched his neck, contemplating taking some of Yang's powder. *Nobody would notice.* Galahad started deliberating, thinking of all the things he would have to do to make his ruse successful. Above all, he had to take the leaves without being seen. *And only take a little,* he noted. Then, it would be best if he was away from people for the peak of his high. That way, he would not raise suspicions...

Galahad winced. He answered, casually, "I'll go for a walk." He needed time away from the inn. That was the only way he would stay away from Yang's leaf. Nearness was a temptress.

Galahad tried his best to occupy his mind with other thoughts. Yet, he felt he was stuck in a cycle. *When I am sober, everything is about getting high; Yet, every time I get high, all I can think about is getting sober.* Had his father dealt with a similar torture?

The prospect frightened him. *I have better things to think about,* Galahad reminded himself, entering Laverne's bedroom.

The Oleander is waiting, he reassured himself. *I'll be too far from town to be addicted.* He put on a white shirt. There was a smudge that neither he nor Laverne could scrub clean. He ignored that.

I cannot leave yet, Galahad reprimanded himself. He put on pants which were a size too large. He strapped on boots he had yet to break in. Eyeing the coat Laverne had crafted for him, Galahad got shivers. *Too warm,* he decided.

He glanced at the mortar and pestle. At least, he had intended to. A quick glimpse became a long stare. He walked toward the tools; he stepped back. He thought yes and was filled with loathing. He thought no and was left void. Galahad pocketed his hands. His fingers twitched. His mouth filled with saliva. He swallowed his spit and immediately coughed it back up. He swallowed again; he coughed again.

"This is intolerable," Galahad groaned. He swiped the herb pouch containing Yang's leaf and buried it deep in his pockets. He clenched his jaw so tightly his cheeks began to hurt. Every time he got the urge to open the pouch, he bit down harder.

He marched through the inn. For all he knew, the tavern was empty. He did not stop until he was outside. Standing atop the Hill of the innkeepers, looking down onto Auberdine, he threw the herb pouch.

Yang's leaf tumbled down. Galahad lurched forward after it, but the farther he saw it go—the less he was inclined to chase. His eyes followed the pouch while it remained visible, trailing after it like a bloodhound toward prey. Finally, it disappeared underneath the shadow of the hedge gate. Galahad smiled, but he wanted to cry. He rolled his jaw, letting the muscles relax.

Galahad espied another object upon the Hill. It was ascending, though. He knew what the object was. It was a man. A man Galahad had been waiting for. *So, the time has come. At last, at last.* He debated retreating into the inn and hiding until the bastard departed. Before he had the chance, the constable addressed him, "Galahad, son of Cambyses?"

Galahad said nothing. *Look relaxed, like you were simply enjoying the air.* He leaned onto the patio railing and smiled down at the constable as a simpleton might.

"I've here a letter for ya."

Galahad tried to make small talk, to appear amiable. "How noble of you to take over after the postman's disappearance."

The constable coughed.

Too arrogant, he winced. "Well, thank you for delivering it."

"I need yo' signature," Goodwind demanded, not a hint of humor in his voice.

"Of course," Galahad cloaked himself in a joyful face. He grabbed the letter from Goodwind and swiped his pen, eagerly. "Where do I sign?"

The constable pulled a piece of parchment out of his back pocket. He clicked a pen and pointed at the bottom of the page, "This indicates ya received the letter."

"Oo," Galahad acted ignorant. "I do hope I've received some money."

Goodwind's eye twitched as he stared at Galahad.

Can he see through the charade? Does he believe the rumor or is he duty bound to be a statue? He signed and delivered the acknowledgement. Goodwind nodded, took the paper, and tipped his hat. "Good day."

"And you," Galahad waved. *You plump cunt.* He watched the dumb bastard until he was out of sight. His eyes turned toward the letter. *I could simply ignore it.* Galahad chuckled, *but they've already thought of that. I signed. I may as well read it.*

"Alright, you cruel bitch," he ripped open the envelope:

Galahad, son of the late Cambyses:

PLEASE BE ADVISED that this document serves as official notice that official inquiries are being made into your person. In question is the disappearance of Mister Frederick Kinsfeld. There is reason to suspect that you made threats against Mister Kinsfeld preceding his disappearance. Solicitors and investigators from the Castle Rock will conduct a thorough investigation into your dealings with the Kinsfeld family, the innkeeper, and any other relations.

YOU ARE HEREBY COMMANDED to remain within the Auberdine township until further notice.

Franz Hofstadt,

Magistrate, Castle Rock 4th District

Galahad read the letter a second time. He read the last sentence a third time, then a fourth. He was bound to town. *I will never leave. I will die in this pauper's paradise.* He wrinkled his nose, twisting his face. He glared down at Carolyn's little estate. Air billowed from his nostrils. He clenched his fists. His knuckles faded to white. In the span of a second, he smashed the patio railing, kicked over a rocking chair, and punched the inn wall. Splinters littered his hand. He seethed, staring at the blood trickling down his fingers. Pain came in pulses, as did his anger.

Luckily, nobody else was around. All he wanted to do was destroy something. He paced around the patio, fingers wrapped around his cheek. *I could leave, they would never find me. I could go west, only the Gardners and Laverne would know—and they would never tell a filthy solicitor.* But if he left, everyone would assume he was guilty. The thought renewed his fury. *Oh, how they would gossip. They would tell their children little stories about Galahad the grim. I would become a bedtime story to frighten children...*

A little squeak drowned out his thoughts. Soon, it was all Galahad heard. He listened. Galahad homed in on the faint squeaking, moving toward the other end of the patio. A tiny mouse was trapped. One leg had reached for a piece of cheese and one leg had been smashed by the trap. Now, the critter squirmed and cried.

Galahad watched as the vermin tried to pull away in vain. "Serves your gluttony right," he mocked the mouse. A smile formed on his lips for half a second. Then, he realized his words were just as much for him as the mouse. Fresh fury surged like lava up his spine. He raised his leg and thrust down like a meteor.

Galahad savored the crunch, grinding the ball of his foot. He lifted his boot. Fur wrapped around jelly was all that remained of the little critter. His anger suddenly vanished and the longer Galahad looked at the mess—the more he felt ashamed. He shuddered, "Y-you should never have been trapped in the first place."

His hand twitched. Galahad grimaced. He curled his fingers. The joints popped and rolled. His blood dripped down onto the mouse. Galahad rubbed an eye with his uninjured hand. He glanced behind him. *Just what I need during an investigation, evidence of violent tendencies.* Galahad kicked the mouse trap onto the grass and set the rocking chair upright. There was nothing to be done about the dent in the patio railing, nor the splinters jutting out from the wall. Hopefully, no one had seen. He reached for the redwood door.

The door swung open, nearly hitting his face. Galahad shrunk back, biting down on a couple choice words. He glared at the mindless oaf, intent on receiving an apology. When he saw Laverne step forth obliviously, he coughed to alert her. Laverne continued ahead as if he were not there.

"Where are you going?" Galahad inquired, doing his best to appear unperturbed.

Laverne gasped. Her eyes widened when she saw him. "Galahad, don't sneak up on me like that."

He heard a hint of annoyance. Galahad stifled his own. *She was only startled. I would be embarrassed, too.* Galahad waited, anticipating a soothing word and a caring smile.

"Just goin' to the market." She stared past him, "Eastmont must be in such pain, losin' his only parent. An' a mother at that! No one should have to suffer like that."

He could think of nothing to say. He simply echoed, "No one."

"Well, I'd best be off," Laverne hastened ahead.

He swallowed as much of his pride as possible. His voice cracked as he called, "I'll tag along." He wanted to be hugged, though company would suffice.

Without so much as turning around, Laverne yawned, "Nonsense... You're sick. You stay right here."

She could not care any less about me, now. Galahad watched the woman fade away. As her image grew fainter, Galahad felt colder. He tried to reassure himself. *I was going to leave. People drift in and out of my life. She is no exception.* The thought made him shiver. He wrapped his arms around his chest, stating, "Laverne was a temporary convenience."

The wind whistled by.

Galahad sighed. His anger had made him tired. His body ached. He longed to sleep, but he was not tired. A dreary emptiness took hold of him. *My father rots because of me. Latrell rots because of me. Terrell rots because of me. I rot because of myself.* They were cruel truths, but ones Galahad yearned to feel. He longed to feel worse. *Laverne loved me like a hobby. I was an idiot to want more.* He began walking slowly down the Hill. *My mother died when I was young, my father died when I grew old.* The sadder he got, the better he felt. *I don't need her. I don't need anything.*

His stance weakened. His legs and back bent. Galahad scanned the hedge gate and walked toward his quarry. He picked up the herb pouch and put it to his nose. His mouth filled with saliva. The nearness gnawed at him. He shut his eyes, unable to look at his medicine any longer. He folded his bloody fingers over the herb and shoved it into his pocket.

Galahad turned toward the western peak. *If others can make a fortune, why can't I?*

The question was met with another. *Why do I need a fortune?* Galahad scanned the western horizon. *A few marks never hurt. People wouldn't walk over me, at least.*

Another thought came to him which was more alluring than any dream of striking riches. *Nobody knows me up there. I could blend. Have a new life.*

It was hard to argue with that fact. Oleander Mountain might be cursed, but so was he. The peak was swarming with idiots looking for a fortune, but fortunately, those idiots were not looking for him. If there were ghosts on that mountain, at least they haunted everyone. *Carolyn's curses and Cambyses' ghost would have to climb a great height to reach me there.*

        Yes, it was time to go.

25
Remembrance

"He is stayed gone over a week, hasn't he?" Hanna lamented. She twirled a spoon around her teacup. The winter cold came abruptly and departed just as quickly.

Charles looked at his old friend, in a dress meant more for summer than early winter. It was flowery, elegant, and looked entirely different from how Hanna must be feeling. He had thought the grove would be his greatest challenge, but keeping Hanna from wallowing was proving more difficult. *She misses her husband and herself. I would be sad, too.* He tried to lift her spirits, "At least it is warm now. He won't have to deal with the cold."

Hanna closed her eyes...

She was frequently drifting off. Yang explained to them that she would have to sleep often to relearn what she had forgotten. Usually, she was only out for a few minutes. Sometimes, though, she had to be carried to bed. Charles usually made Aeric help him with that. It felt less intrusive and out of line to have Arthur's son help carry her.

Charles waited for a minute. He did not mind her napping. Indeed, he had quite forgotten how much he enjoyed spending time with Hanna. Most of his days were spent caring for her in some way. Even when they parted for the night, Charles found himself planning out the next day. Everything had become part of healing Hanna. Aeric had suggested taking some time for himself, that he did not have to be the only person caring for her. Charles shrugged off the suggestion. He craved to care; it felt good to nurture something besides plants.

Soon, Hanna yawned, stretched, and opened her eyes. Hanna put her elbow on the table and rested her head on her hand. Her cheek stretched upward, making her look more bored than tired. "It feel like I being young again," Hanna commented.

Charles ignored her error. Such slips in her speech happened regularly and correcting her would only hurt her. The woman's insecurities were already running rampant. "Yang said you wou-"

"Not like that," she stopped him. She stared out at the grove. Every branch was barren. Not even the snow remained. "I feel without point. Reminds me of before I gone to u-" She licked her lips and bit her tongue. "Un, universa-" Hanna sighed. After a brief rest, she tried again, emphasizing every syllable, "University."

Charles thought he knew what she meant. He asked her to explain, thinking it would do her some good to vent. "In what way?"

"It all feels no-meaning now, all of it. Like I eat and sleep only to delay..." Hanna drifted off. "You know?"

"I do," Charles nodded. He had felt the same despair when his mother had died.

"I wish Cora is here," Hanna muttered. "She always has something good to say."

He winced. He had still not told Hanna about his mother. "Always."

"We should ask her to visit," she thought. The idea lit up her face.

Hanna's smile was too much for Charles. He looked at the sky, unable to tell her the truth yet incapable to look at her and lie. "We should."

"She is the one woman I ever liked," Hanna reminisced. "Teached me all I learn about motherhood, if truth be said."

"Not your own mother?" Charles feigned ignorance. He knew well that Hanna disliked her mother. The old woman had been obsessed with beauty. She always wanted her daughter to wear whitening cream, lose weight, and find a rich man to marry.

Hanna squinted and looked at Charles very seriously, "She was a stupid woman."

"Taught you how *not* to be," Charles continued, paraphrasing a long conversation he had once had with her.

Hanna bobbed her head and said, "Yes," like it was the first time the conclusion had been drawn. She brushed her finger along the surgery site, rubbing the tiny hairs which had just started to grow. "She be so ashaming to see me as this," she chuckled. Then, she looked at Charles with a piercing gaze. "Cora would have said how strong I is, how pretty."

"You are," Charles affirmed. He sniffled, adding, "Very strong."

"Oh," she curled her hand in a show of vanity, "I know." She giggled, "I always been confident. Strong." Hanna scratched her temple and gazed down at the table. "But it been your mother who teached me I can be strong *and* a woman."

"You were always a woman," Charles laughed.

"Well... Yes," Hanna conceded. "But I runned from that t-tru..." Hanna rubbed her palm over her fist as she controlled her stutter. "Truth." She pointed a finger at him, "You know, I nevered like math, not at first."

"No?" Charles appeared surprised.

Hanna nodded, "I just want to be respectful. Respected! Everybody respects math. Cause not lots of peoples can do it." She rolled her eyes and leaned her chair back. "Now look at me. Just like the rest."

"You'll get there again," Charles encouraged.

"Wanted to be a mathematician, once," Hanna scoffed. "Now, I need to count f-f-f-fingers to do addition. Fingers!"

Charles did not know what to say to her self-pity. He would be a hypocrite to give a motivational speech, an enabler to add fire to the feeling, and a liar to disagree with her. He crossed his legs and poured them both some more tea. *She is remembering, even if she doesn't see it.*

Hanna took her cup and sipped it, loudly. "Guess it good I did not get a work in mathematics."

"You could have," Charles was quick to tell her. *She needs to hear some words of encouragement.*

Hanna shook her head, "Nah. Wasn't for me."

"No?" he asked, taking his teacup. He drank quietly while Hanna spoke.

"I just... did not want to deal with it." She paused, wanting Charles to complete her thought. When he did not, she continued. "The snooty looks, the quid pro..." Hanna's eyes scanned upwards, pursuing the missing thought. She waved the idea away. "I wanted to do math, not men."

Charles curled his bottom lip toward his chin. He bobbed his head and set his cup down.

"And I knowed Arthur wanted to go back home after school." She added, nostalgically, "Have a family." She peered past Charles. He looked over his shoulders. Emilia was laying with Isabelle, just far enough to not be eavesdropping but close enough to keep an eye on her mother. Noticing the adults were watching her, Emilia started cooing at her dog and tickling her belly.

Charles returned to the table and raised his brow. "You hated children when I first met you."

Hanna continued to watch her daughter, a smile creeping ever higher up her face. "I was, hm. What is the word for feeling big but being small instead?"

"Arrogant?" Charles posited.

Hanna smiled. "Arrogant. I thought mothering was... was a death sentence."

Charles laughed, "You called motherhood the walking womb."

"I thought it was the walking tomb?"

Charles wrapped his finger around his chin, trying to recall the specifics. "Eh, I don't remember."

"That makes two of us," Hanna joked. She folded her hands and looked at Charles. She did not speak for a second, wrangling her thoughts and preparing to speak. "Then, I meet your mother. I saw how she carried herself, even after all she goed, uh—went—through." She took in a deep breath and waved at Emilia. "Suddenly, motherhood did not seem such a bad deal."

Charles grinned, "Not the consolation prize for failed ambition you thought it would be, huh?"

Hanna raised an eyebrow, looked to her sides, and gave Charles a knowing look. "Those is my words."

"Mhm," Charles hummed.

"Oh, I miss her." Hanna put her hands to her lap and exclaimed, "Let's send a letter and ask her to visit!"

I have to tell her. Charles tilted his head, hiding one side of his face as if there was a blemish upon it. "Hanna," He sucked in his upper lip and tapped his finger on the table.

"Charles," Hanna batted her eyebrows, mocking his seriousness.

"When I went home this last time," he began to cough. He pounded his fist against his chest. Charles hacked up a glob of phlegm and spat it beside him.

"Lovely," Hanna commented.

"As I was saying, when I went home, my mother was really sick."

Hanna tilted her head, waiting for more information.

Oh, don't make me continue. Understand. Charles gulped, "She cannot make a journey. She had, I think she had... Rot."

Hanna's eyes opened like a gust of air blows curtains. "So she will rest and *then* visit?"

"She will rest," Charles swallowed. He shut his eyes, "But she will not visit."

Hanna blinked. She still did not understand, "But Cora Eastmont is stronger than me—and I be, uh, is... damn..." She whispered, staring at her feet. "I am fine now."

"*You* had surgery. My mother was alone."

Hanna's eyes swiveled. Her breathing intensified. She brought her hands to her forehead, cupping her eyes. "I wish I seen her more."

"I had a similar reaction when I saw—" He froze, unable to breathe new life into that terrible meeting. "Don't beat yourself up."

Hanna closed her eyes.

Charles began to think the information overloaded her senses. Seconds became minutes and Hanna remained silent. Charles debated taking her to bed for another nap. He got up to look for Aeric. He walked several steps before Hanna asked, quietly, "Where are you going?"

Charles raised an arm to point behind him, stuttered, and then sat back down. It was his turn to close his eyes. *At least she is not crying, yet.* If she started, he would never stop. To his surprise, Hanna did not seem particularly perturbed. She started speaking and seemed perfectly content.

"I have this funny thought in my head. I think it was something I used to, erm... believe, back during the war. I know I believe it, but I don't really understand it anymore. This s-s-s-," Hanna massaged her forearms. "Surgery and all..." Hanna scratched her scalp, "I know I *would* feel sad. Or, uhm... I should, but I don't."

Charles started to see what she was getting at. "If this is your infinity idea, you are in good company. I think you are the only one who understands that."

Hanna continued, puzzled by her own mind. "I have the thought in me, but... What does infinity mean?"

"Timeless, limitless," Charles defined. "Unending."

"It's the sideways eight, right?"

"Mhm," Charles confirmed. "You use it in calculus, I think."

Hanna grunted. "It is so strange, but when you told me about-" She let the sentence conclude on its own. "I wanted to cry, but then it was like I was dreaming. I thinked up something and I got happier."

"Share it with me," Charles smiled. "Maybe I'll feel better, too."

Hanna squinted as she found the right words. She took another sip of tea before starting. "Well, the university," she stopped abruptly, muttering, "No, no, that's not right."

She began anew, "The *universe* is talked to be infinite. That's what astrono-astro... People tell." She shook her finger at the sky, "And this is the part I don't get, but I s-still believe." She spoke her thought like a stranger reads a new book, carefully and hesitantly. "If time never stops, then the dice rolls forever." Hanna smiled, immensely happy, "The many probab-," Hanna paused. She rotated her head like her neck had a kink in it. "Prob-ab-il-is-tic outcomes that smushed together t-to make your mother..." She shrugged, "Well they are really, really low. Almost impossible to happen again. So much has to go exactly the same for Cora to be born. And not just Cora. All things before her, too."

Hanna stopped. Her eyes drifted up as she probed her mind. "This is the happy part, I think. Because the clock never stops ticking, no matter how long it takes—

Someday, the same dice rolls that builded Cora will build her new." She beamed at Charles, "One dice roll could even be a little off and the War, the Rot—all of it... It never happens." Hanna panted, completely exhausted.

Charles smiled at her. He had heard her explain her quirky religious belief before, her mathematical reincarnation. He knew she was building from the idea that organisms evolve somewhat randomly, and that the universe seemed to have no beginning or end. He still did not understand it very well. He lied, "That does make me feel better."

Hanna yawned. She stretched and got up from the table. Despite looking dreadfully lethargic, she spoke rapidly. "Now, if I kn-kn-knew what this business with prob-," Hanna rubbed her hands together, "Prob-ab-il-istic outcomes means with infinity... I gonna check the encyclopedia."

Charles got up. "Are you sure? You seem awfully tired." *Every time she looks at that damn book she gets horribly sad.* He went to follow her, but she had halted.

"Oh, hello," Hanna said. Two people were standing before her. One was a woman, dressed in glimmering purple. The other was a small girl, about Emilia's age. Charles quickly assumed the girl was the woman's daughter, as she was garbed in a smaller, identical dress. The girl was holding a bouquet.

"Misses Gardner," the woman shook her hand.

Hanna analyzed her.

"You don't remember me, do you?"

She shrugged, "Afraid not."

"Well, don't feel bad," the woman giggled. "We've only properly met once." The woman grabbed Hanna's hand and shook it. "Lilian Vellencourt."

"Nice to meet you," Hanna smiled, politely. "This is my friend, Charles Eastmont."

"Oh, I know about you." Lilian waltzed forward. Her hips swayed left and right with every step. Charles extended his hand. She looked up at him knowingly. Then, she gently took Charles' hand and kissed it. Some of the whitening powder from her face fell onto Charles' fingers.

Castle Rocker, Charles prepared himself. He chuckled at Hanna, hoping she did not get the wrong idea about his relationship with the mysterious woman. He wiped the whitening powder off his hand and smiled, "Sadly, I know nothing about you."

Lilian turned, one foot facing away, the other toward him. She spoke softly, "We can change that."

Charles choked on his tongue. *This is not the kind of talk a gentleman pa—*

She tilted her head sympathetically, pressing her lips, "When I heard about you and your mother, I must confess I wrote to her. I told her she could always have a place in my household." She laughed, "Miss Eastmont was quick to refuse."

"Yes," Charles grinned. "She was an independent woman."

Lilian furrowed her brow and nodded, "I respect that. Quite a lot. Still, a lot of women who share her circumstances are not. I like to help them." She glanced at Hanna and then back at Charles. She shrugged.

Charles flinched and then cleared his throat. Hanna was looking at him like he had stained his clothes or stepped in a puddle. He walked past Lilian and knelt to greet her child. "And who might you be?"

Vellencourt glided over and put her arm on his back.

Charles shivered and suddenly felt very grimy.

"My daughter, Elizabeth."

"Hi," the girl muttered.

Charles could see that the girl was intimidated by him and probably did not want to be there. He immediately stood up and gave the girl her space. He stepped back and tripped over Vellencourt. They both stumbled back. Vellencourt nearly fell, grabbing Charles' bicep at the last second. Charles regained his balance. The woman held on to his arm for a moment more, waiting for him to look at her.

"Those are," he chuckled nervously, hoping Lilian might relinquish her grip on him. "Quite beautiful flowers."

"Yes," Vellencourt said, releasing him. "Now give them to the nice woman, Eliza."

Her daughter raised a limp arm and gave the flowers to Hanna. She marched to her mother's side and whispered, "Can we go home, now?"

"No," Lilian muttered through her teeth. "We are going to spend some time together before we go up the mountain."

"Why couldn't Greta come?"

"Not here, darling." Vellencourt gritted her teeth, smiling. She patted Hanna on the back and stared at Charles, "We are making a trip to Oleander. Perhaps when we return, we can speak again." She bowed, "Do get better, Hanna. I would hate for this place to lose a woman's touch." She rolled her fingers in a wave, grabbed her daughter's arm, and led her down the Hill.

"She likes you," Hanna stated.

"Like seems a bit of an understatement." He wiped his hands on his pants. "She the one who bought the promontory fort from Buchanan?"

"I, uh." Hanna shrugged, "Maybe? I don't remember."

She's the one. "I remember her from the harvest feast. She scolded the old dockmaster, Degory."

"Hmm," Hanna hummed, continuing without him.

Charles caught up to her. She handed him the bouquet, "You is the grove-keeper."

It felt odd accepting the flowers. Charles laughed nervously. "Right. Yes, I'll find a spot for them." He changed the subject. "Her daughter seemed nice."

"Disfriendly, I thought."

"Only shy."

They went up the patio where Emilia was waiting. The child had her hands to her hip and looked down on them with disapproving eyes. "What did she want?"

"Gave me flowers," Hanna yawned.

Emilia glared at the bouquet, "Then why does Uncle Charles have them?"

Hanna laughed, pushing him, and then ruffling her daughter's hair. "Because he's in love."

"I am not," Charles denied. *Oh, just what I need. The town will love that gossip. Child of malchance and rich philanthropist sneaking about... The Inner Ring would gobble that up.* He said, emphatically, "That woman scares me."

"Mister Galahad hates her." Emilia pouted. "I heard him say so." She pulled her mother's dress, "And you said she was mean."

"No," Hanna shook her head. "You disremember, sugarbear."

"I do not," Emilia protested. "I watched when she came last. You made her leave." Isabelle began licking her hand and coughing. "Come on, big girl. Mister Galahad will tell them."

The girl ran off. Hanna smirked at Charles and let out a mighty yawn. "Too much excitement. I'm sleepy."

"Me too," Charles said sarcastically, glancing behind him. He guided Hanna up the stairs and brought her to the bedroom. He lingered at the door while she changed into a nightgown. Charles heard her open a drawer, swear, and a moment later open the same one. When the opening and closing of drawers was over, she went to her closet and muttered instructions to herself. It took Hanna several minutes to get ready.

Finally, she called. "Charles, come help a minute."

Charles entered the room and stared at his feet. After a few seconds, he realized there was no need for precautions and opened his eyes. The Gardner bedroom was disheveled. Blankets were strewn upon the floor. Pillows had tumbled onto the ground. Dirty and clean clothes littered the corners of the room and lurked underneath the bed. Hanna was sitting on the bed with her legs crossed, leaning over something.

"That," she sighed, "was difficult."

Charles suggested, "Place the gown in plain sight, after you're done."

"I did," Hanna waved him over to her. "I mean these." She gave him a handful of letters. "I kept seeing them whenever I looked for socks. Every day I meaned to give them back and-" She frowned, "Every night I forgetted."

"Well not this night," Charles beamed. *I thought they were destroyed. What luck.* He took the letters and, seeing Hanna was still sad—reminded her, "You remembered tonight, Hanna. Things are getting better."

"Yeah," Hanna nodded. She rolled onto her side, "You are right."

Charles went to the light, "I'll turn this off."

"No," Hanna lurched up. Her eyes were wide.

"Okay," Charles stepped back, "I'll leave it on." He took his leave. "Sleep well."

As he was descending, Emilia was running up. She went into her parent's bedroom, "Why is Galahad gone, mama?"

"I did not know he was," Hanna yawned.

"He is. And a bunch of people are saying mean things about him."

"People always saying mean things," Hanna dismissed.

Emilia shot a look at Charles which was both sad and angry. He shrugged. He had never liked Galahad. *The man always seemed selfish. Seems perfectly in character for him to disappear without a word.* "Come on, Emilia," he beckoned. "Let's play with Izzy."

"No," Emilia stomped past him. "You'll just leave, too."

26

First Steps

"I am not a child," Hanna reminded her children.

"I didn't say that," Aeric insisted.

Hanna folded her arms. "I hasn't left the inn since my surgery."

Her son pointed his palms at his chest and lowered his voice. "I know, I know." He opened his palms out at his mother, "All I am saying is that I should go with you. Just in case-"

"Just in case what?" She interrupted.

Aeric stuttered and looked at his sister.

Hanna tapped her foot.

Charles answered for her son, "In case it's all too much." He came up behind Hanna and put a hand on her shoulder. "You've still not recovered."

Hanna decided not to respond to that. She was going outside. She was not going to be trapped. Her nose wrinkled, "You smell awful."

Charles grunted and tucked his hand into his pocket, "Sorry. I was cleaning the stables."

Aeric rubbed his hands together, "Think you could do something else?" He paused just long enough for Charles to begin to nod. "The mouse traps need checking. And that dead cottonwood needs felling." He glanced to his side and rubbed his neck, "I would do it..." The boy shrugged and looked at his mother.

"I am *not* a child that needs watching," Hanna groaned. *I feel better. I can talk can't I?* She pointed her finger at him, "I breastfed you." She eyed Emilia. "And you, little lady."

Charles wrapped a hand around the back of his head. He looked down. "Not me, I am afraid..."

Hanna could tell he was trying to sound friendly. His normal, deep voice was raised in pitch. His smile was as non-threatening as ever. She waited for her old friend to agree with them. He seemed embarrassed. *As he should be! Arthur would be mad at him. I am not one of his trees.*

"... And I agree with Aeric."

Hanna knew she had lost. "Of course you do." She threw her hands into the air like a wanted man. "Alright, you can come."

"I get to come, too!" Emilia pouted.

"Fine, fine. We'll have a family outing."

Aeric excused himself and marched upstairs. Meanwhile, his sister scrunched Isabelle's face and asked, "Ready for a stroll, big girl?"

The dog tilted its head, knowingly.

Hanna was glad her daughter wanted to leave the inn. *Even if it is only to babysit me.* Emilia had isolated herself after Galahad had disappeared. She thought the girl was going to hide for days. After that first day though, she did not seem angry. *She seems a little sad, but that's normal, isn't it?* It was becoming a puzzle to piece together what she thought was true, and what was actually true. As her girl cooed at Isabelle, Hanna whispered to Charles, "Did you talk to her?"

"About?"

"Galahad," Hanna said, even quieter. "She liked him. Maybe thought of him as an, uh, uncle, I-I don't know."

Charles scratched his nose. "Not a word. Not about that, anyways..." He rubbed his ear, "Uncle, huh?"

Hanna tilted her head and smirked, "Jealous?"

Charles scoffed. "I'm not going to answer that. I am getting back to work."

Hanna giggled. She sat on the floor beside Emilia and put an arm around her. Her daughter glanced up and half-smiled. Then, all her attention went back to the dog. She tickled Isabelle's belly.

"How are you holding up, sugarbear?"

Emilia replied mechanically. "Good."

I may be dumb, but I know a lie. Hanna started, "You s-sure?"

"Mhm."

Hanna scratched Isabelle's head and smiled at the dog. It appeared to know what was going on, as its eyes followed Hanna's back to Emilia. "You don't seem very good."

Emilia paused and stared ahead. She shrugged and flashed a sad smile at Isabelle. The hound winked at her and coughed. Emilia resumed petting her and mumbled, "I'm happy."

"Even with Galahad gone?" *Your father?*

Emilia's lip twitched and she hid her neck behind her chin. She stopped petting Isabelle, leading the hound to raise a head lazily from the floor and cough. After another series of coughs, Emilia resumed petting the hound. Isabelle's coughs grew fainter as she lowered her head. She let a tongue fall lazily to the floor. Emilia sighed, "It doesn't matter."

Hanna leaned in closer and massaged her girl's back, "Him leaving, you mean?"

"All of it," Emilia stated, a touch of anger in her words.

I remember this... When her daughter felt sad or anxious, one little problem would become a hundred. *She's flooding.*

Emilia repositioned herself and looked at her mother, "I don't care that Galahad is gone. Or daddy."

That surprised her. Hanna shook her head, "W-what do you mean?"

"They are always gone," she shrugged. "I am used to it."

Hanna swallowed. "D-daddy be here if he is able, you know that."

Emilia shrugged again.

Don't do this, sugarbear. Hanna did not want to feel sad. It was so exhausting. "The w-war is over. He will come—" Hanna stopped abruptly, unable to find the words she wanted. She bowed her head, hoping happier thoughts would replace the bad ones. Was her husband dead? Was he lost, starving, or freezing? Hanna wrapped her arms around her chest.

Aeric marched down the stairs, his footsteps echoing throughout the tavern. The eyes of several guests turned toward the noise and widened. Hanna turned and immediately knew why. Her son was holding a rifle.

He marched up next to his mother and said, "We ready to go?"

She whispered, not wanting to cause more of a scene. "What you doing with that thing?"

"Protecting us," Aeric answered, using his I-am-the-dad voice.

Her son was probably the only one more affected by Arthur's absence than her. Aeric had been working tirelessly. When Hanna asked him why he was not sleeping, he answered, 'Dad doesn't sleep.' When she scolded him for smoking a cigarette with Wenton, he simply grunted. Then, later that night—the boy had apologized for his behavior, calling himself an idiot boy with no good sense. *He is so much like Arthur,* Hanna rubbed her eyes. *Too much like him.*

"Isn't there a smaller one?" Hanna asked.

"Dad took all the others. This was uncle's."

Hanna sighed. "Your..." she lost her train of thought. The barrel of the rifle intruded into her mind. She stared at it, fearfully, "Emilia d-does not need an, uh, an armed export." She winced. "uh, e-escort."

"Mom," he stared at her. "I was shot, remember?"

Hanna blinked. She had no response. She cleared her throat, froze, and then nodded. *I did not forget that, did I?* She was sure she had that information stored away somewhere. It did not seem new. The fact had simply not seemed relevant for a walk to the market. *But does that mean I forgot it?* Hanna moved her arms to her pockets. *He's afraid. That's all.* Her cheeks were warming. *I would never have been so stupid before. I knowed his mind. I did. Maybe this is just him growing older, getting more distant from his mother.*

Another thought spoke, louder and clearer: *Or, maybe it is proof I will never get better.*

Hanna swallowed. She swung her head back and forth and erased the idea from her mind. She ushered her children along, yelling enthusiastically, "Right, off we go."

The tavern watched them leave. Hanna hoped Charles would at least try to mingle with the guests. He and Wenton were the only ones left managing the inn and Wenton tended to swear. *Charles is a far better face for the public.*

"Misses Gardner," a voice quivered.

Hanna arced her neck, "Yes? L-Laverne?"

She was sitting in a dark corner of the tavern. The woman rose from her seat. As Laverne approached, it was clear she had been crying. Hands placed on her belly, she said, "Have..." she grimaced, "Have you seen him?"

"We have not," Aeric answered for her.

Laverne continued, "But if you have, w-will ya..." The woman stopped and breathed deeply.

"We will tell you," Hanna smiled.

"No!" She whispered a shriek. "I don' want to know. He is safer if I'm ignorant."

Aeric moved in between his mother and the grieving Redfeather woman. "What do you mean?"

Laverne was barely audible. Fear poured out of her wide pupils. "A man come ta see me t'day, askin' all manner a' questions." She cleared her throat, "Bounty hunter."

"Lord," Hanna gasped. "The town is really fussing over him."

"Carolyn is a liar," Emilia growled, her face wrinkled in disgust. "Frederick was mean."

"I don' doubt it. Mmmhm," Laverne hummed, "I don' doubt it. Still, if anyone asks where Galahad gone—don' tell 'em."

"Not a problem," Hanna told her, "I can't remember... Well, just about anything."

Emilia scolded her mother, "Don't say that, mama."

"What?" Hanna asked, unaware of what her daughter meant.

"I'll leave y'all be," Laverne bowed. She went back to her dark corner and began sobbing quietly.

The Gardners left their inn. Hanna asked again, "What was that about, Emilia?"

"You were being self-defecating," Emilia said, sternly.

"Deprecating," Her brother corrected.

"Whatever," Emilia stuck her tongue out at him. "Mama, if you say you can't remember, you will make it true."

"Sugarbear," Hanna defended, "You have to joke about things sometimes."

"Well it isn't funny," her daughter folded her arms.

Hanna smirked, snorting a gust of air out her nostrils. *She's so precious.* "Okay, I hear you."

They passed through the grove. The dead cottonwood was blindingly white. Isabelle trotted beside the three of them, her long tongue drooping down as her ears stood at attention. Aeric's rifle clanked with every step. Emilia gripped Hanna's hand tightly. When they got to the hedge gate, she let go of it and insisted she and Aeric go first. Then, she grabbed her mother's hand and led her through the Inner Ring. The district was empty. Everyone was in their homes, at the market, or on the Oleander. Their footsteps echoed against the stone. Aeric turned suspiciously toward every sound. Isabelle stayed so close to her, Hanna felt like she was riding the great hound.

Hanna had missed the smell of the air and the feeling of the wind. She did not have the urge to speak. Aeric was silent as well. Emilia talked, but only if there was something she wanted her mother to know about.

"There's a crack up ahead mama. Careful."

"You too sweet," Hanna smiled. *She is going to be a good mother one day.* She skipped over the crack. A pile of leaves filled the gutter and she and Emilia grinned at one another. Then, they each leapt into the street and began stomping their way through the leaves. The snow had made them wet, but it was still just as fun to smoosh them. Aeric watched from the sidewalk, disapprovingly. They jumped for several paces before Hanna had to stop.

She put her hands to her knees and panted, "Oh, my. I am not as young as I... Should be." She wiped her brow and tried to hide the wheezing coming from her chest. She stepped back onto the sidewalk.

"Mama, you should rest for a moment," Emilia said, her feet submerged in leaves.

"I has rested for lots of moments," Hanna recalled, doing her best to sound energetic. *I don't want them thinking mama can't leave home ever again.* She walked on, making her children follow. Aeric grunted and Emilia grumbled. They both stayed by her side.

When they got to the Muhali Islet, Emilia took hold of her mother's hand. Her palm was sweaty. Hanna whispered so her brother would not hear, "Baby, are you scared?" Emilia shook her head defiantly. Her eyes probed the market stalls. Her free arm pulled Isabelle closer.

They strolled through the market looking for nothing in particular. Fishers were selling trout, bass, and baubles. Hunters sold venison, furs, and fanged necklaces. Potters sold vases, mugs, and pots. Every stall had something the other did not. Yet, the same Muhali jewelry hung from posts and across booths.

Hanna knew she had seen it all before. Yet, when she saw the ruby circlets and the silver miniatures—they were as new to her as ever. The lines and designs fascinated her. Her children did not seem as amused. Indeed, Aeric seemed tired. His eyes drifted lazily to each stall, never staying long on any object. *Well, they insisted on coming. They can wait until I am done.* Hanna approached a woodworker's stall. The Muhali man bowed his head, "My lady innkeeper. Have my wares caught the eye?"

Hanna scanned his little shop. Behind him were several pieces of furniture, a chair, a bench—boring things. She was more intrigued by the tiny toys he had for sale. She pointed at a wooden horse and rider.

"Ah yes," the salesman gave the toy to Hanna. "Press the rider down onto the horse."

Hanna took the toy and did so. She heard a click.

"Now, push the horse's tail."

Hanna pressed. The rider was ejected from his mount and flew several inches up. It fell onto the road in a wonderful leap. Hanna chuckled happily. *How clever,* she thought, going to retrieve the device. As she bent down, a man walked by. He arced his head to look at her. She grabbed the toy and faced forward. The man's neck was straining to stare at her behind. She ignored the man's obvious staring. *He'll move on.*

"Eyes up front," Aeric ordered.

The gawker faced ahead and bobbed his head, "They're up front."

Hanna warned her son, "Don't start anything."

Aeric laughed and pointed at the man. He was retreating into the crowd. "He's a coward."

Her son was right. *This time.* She did not want him getting hurt again. *Still,* she allowed herself a smile, *that was very kind.* "I'll take this," she told the salesman. "How much?"

"Free," he answered. "May it bring joy as you recover, my lady innkeeper."

Hanna did not know how to respond. "Oh, well th-"

"You are too generous," Aeric interrupted. "Does five sound reasonable?"

"I insist," the woodworker put his hands behind his back.

"No," Aeric told the man, "I insist." He took out several bronze pieces from his pocket and thanked the man for his generosity. Then, he placed six coins onto the stall.

"That is not necessary," the woodworker smiled.

"Come on, mama," Aeric began walking away. He waved at the man, "Thank you, sir."

They started down another crowded stretch of stalls. Hanna watched her son, tall and proud, walking with his rifle strapped to his back. *My little bodyguard,* she smiled. The shiny, metal gun did not scare her so much anymore.

"Are you hungry?" She asked them.

"We can eat at home," Aeric responded. "We have food."

"But when was the last time we ever ate at one of these saloons?"

"Probably when uncle was alive," Aeric replied.

"That's too long," Hanna shook her head. "Emilia, darling—pick a place for us to eat. Whatever you want."

"I don't want to eat here." Emilia blinked at the clothing lines above her. "I like Wenton's food."

Hanna threatened, "You want your brother to pick?"

Her cheeks puffed up and Emilia pointed at the nearest saloon. "That one."

"Fantastic," Hanna smiled. She put an arm around both of her children and walked happily into the restaurant. It smelt nice in there. Candles and incense were burning. There were no seats except for cushions and pillows. A Muhali with a bejeweled beard seated them. When he saw who his patrons were, he bowed low and immediately brought them complimentary tea.

He poured them each a cup, "I am Rashif, son of Smerdis. How may I welcome you to my father's saloon?"

"What is *your* favorite dish?" Hanna inquired.

"Ah, yes." Rashif thought for a moment. "Anchorage soup has always held my fancy."

Hanna was quick to declare, "I will have that."

"Aaaah," Rashif wiggled a finger. "I cannot allow this. In better days, perhaps. But lately, the lake has been producing, hmm... Bad clams, bad fish, bad turtles. Until the Anchorage improves, I suggest the elk. We get it fresh from local hunters and season it with traditional desert spices."

"I'll have the elk," Aeric decided.

"And me," Hanna said, happily. "Emilia?"

Her daughter gazed up at the tall Muhali. She asked, "Do you have cake?"

"Ah, perhaps. Perhaps." Rashif leaned in and grinned, "But what kind does the young innkeeper want?"

Emilia pondered for a while. Finally, she stated hesitantly, "Chocolate?"

"At once!" Rashif nodded. "Chocolate for the princess of Castle Gardner!" He shuffled off through a cloud of smoke.

Hanna looked around at the colorful tapestries. "This place is cozy."

"Mhm," Aeric hummed. He lifted a red curtain and peaked outside. "The Yao have been going to the Anchorage. Some kind of sickness, down there."

Hanna's eyes went from a shiny candelabra to her son. "Hm?" She caught a whiff of incense and smiled, "We should burn some of this at the inn."

Aeric tapped his fingers against the old rifle resting on his thighs. He shook his head pensively.

"You look like a monk," Emilia laughed.

"You look like a zookeeper," Aeric replied. He gestured at Isabelle, who was taking up most of their table's cushions.

I think I am improving, Hanna thought. *I'm chatting like a social butterfly.* Three days ago, small talk would have exhausted her. She still had to think about the muscles in her mouth before she spoke, but it was not such a strain. There were some words she avoided, mostly ones with lots of Rs. Some of her words still escaped her, but they were just the large and academic ones. *This is not too bad, just like waking up groggy.*

Rashif approached with a platter of food. Their server kneeled, handing Aeric and Hanna a plate of meat, rice, and vegetables. "Two Elk steaks," he reached for a slice of cake. "And one sugary delight."

That is a large slice. "Emilia," she warned her daughter, "Eat slow."

Her fingers were already coated in chocolate.

Lord, Hanna rolled her eyes. *She is going to get sick.* She addressed Rashif, "Right. How much do we owe you?"

Rashif rose. "No charge. Complementary."

"Oh, come on," Aeric groaned, positively annoyed. He took out his coins. "Fifteen? Two steaks, a slice of cake—that's worth at least eighteen, yeah?"

Rashif backed away slightly. He bowed his head, "With the innkeeper missing, I would consider it bad luck to charge his wife. Bad luck, indeed."

"You are charging his son," Aeric scowled. "I want you to have this," he extended an open palm.

"The future innkeeper," Rashif corrected the young man. "Perhaps if your father returns, I might host you all once more. Until then, I must do what I can." Their server retreated into the incense cloud.

"When," Aeric snarled. The man had already disappeared when he looked at his steak with disgust. He muttered, "When he comes back." He grabbed his fork and began poking at the meat. "Who does he think he is, giving *us* a free meal?"

"Generosity isn't something to fuss over," Hanna said with a full mouth.

Aeric snatched his knife and cut into his elk. "Bastard."

They ate almost entirely in silence. Aeric had lost any willingness to communicate. He focused on his chewing, taking minutes to swallow the smallest morsel. Meanwhile, his sister was ravenous. Her cheeks were covered in chocolate. Cake crumbles tumbled from her lips. Hanna tried to make small talk where she could, but soon gave up. *They both miss him, even if they won't admit it.* Hanna looked down at her steak. Her husband had liked to bring game home to her. *When he was younger, at least...* Hanna sighed and folded her hands. *I may never hear him again...* She might even forget what his voice sounded like. Hanna shook her head forcefully. She cut a piece of meat and smiled, "Lovely food."

"Mhm," Aeric grunted.

Hanna put her silverware down. "S-sometimes I wonder if it is you who forgot how to speak."

Her son's eyes darted back and forth from his mother to his plate. Aeric licked his lips and bobbed his head. He grabbed his knife and cut several mouthfuls. He skewered one with his fork, chewed his meat quickly, and took another bite.

"There we are," Hanna grinned. "Bad manners to not eat a free meal, after all."

Aeric's attention drifted across the hazy room. Rashif was approaching, this time with another person. Her boy chewed even quicker than before, strained to swallow his food, and then—much to Hanna's displeasure—placed a hand near his rifle.

"Countless apologies due," the server bowed. "This man claims to know you."

Hanna had never seen the man before. His face was mean, unwelcoming, and scarred. He wore an old army uniform. It was quite dirty and the blue dye had been worn to a dull grey. His hat was flat. His face was cleanshaven. At the man's hip was a pistol.

"I've never seen him," Aeric stared at the stranger.

"I take my leave." Rashif bowed his head and hurried away.

The mystery man pulled a cushion from a nearby table and sat in front of them. Hanna did not like his military uniform. Emilia scooted closer to her mother. Hanna took her hand and massaged it. Meanwhile, Aeric tapped his rifle and Isabelle put both paws on the table.

The man smirked, "The dog looks like it wants to order a drink."

Hanna ignored the joke, "It is bad manners to sit at a table uninvited."

He folded his hands and placed them below his lip. Then, he pointed his index fingers at her, "I thought it was custom to allow anyone to sit at your table?"

Hanna swallowed. "What you d-want?"

The stranger rubbed the slight stubble below his nose. "Galahad, son of Cambyses. You know him, yes?"

Hanna heard her son beginning to speak and started before him. "As much as any in this little town."

"You are aware he is accused of murder?"

Emilia shook free of her mother's hand and glared at the stranger. "That's a lie. Frederick was a bully. Galahad did nothing wrong."

The stranger smiled at Emilia. "Perhaps, but he remains accused."

I don't like that look of his. Hanna leaned in front of Emilia. "We have nothing to say about Galahad."

Emilia did. "Only that he is innocent." She folded her arms in defiance.

The stranger's smile widened. "If he is innocent, little girl—then why has he fled town?"

"Alright, bounty hunter," Aeric stood his rifle up for all in the saloon to see. He curled his fingers around the weapon, "It is time to leave."

The man looked at Hanna, smirked, and raised his eyebrows. He took out his pistol.

Aeric put both of his hands on his rifle.

The bounty hunter put the pistol on the table and nudged it closer to Aeric. "If you want me to go, take my pistol."

Aeric eyed him warily.

Don't, Hanna pleaded silently. She mouthed the word to her son, but his attention was fixed on the bounty hunter. *Don't.* She looked over at Isabelle. The hound was at attention, baring its teeth.

"My brother isn't scared of you," Emilia taunted.

Aeric tossed a frustrated look at his sister.

The hunter continued, "He should be. He is." He took his pistol and holstered it. Leaning in, he asked, "You know the look of a killer, don't you?"

Aeric replied, not a hint of emotion in his voice, "You look like my father."

That made the hunter laugh. He clapped his hands and looked around. He wiped an invisible tear from his eye and all humor faded from his voice. "Not here, is he?"

Aeric's face was hateful. Nobody spoke. The other townspeople in the saloon stared at their tables. Everyone was quiet.

The stranger turned to Hanna. "Now, back to the matter of importance. The magistrate has placed a bounty on Mister Galahad."

He pecked his head at Aeric and Emilia like a bird eating feed, "Don't worry children. He's wanted alive." The bounty hunter stretched his arms, "I only want to know where he might be. If he is innocent, I will bring him back and clear his name. If not... Well, you have had hangings before, yes?"

Hanna spoke slowly, making sure not to stutter. "I have nothing to tell y-you." She scratched her wrist. "I know nothing about it."

"I don't doubt that," the stranger winked. "I hear the townspeople talking about you." He frowned, "*'Can't even pick up a spoon, let alone remember her name'.*"

Hanna clenched her fists and replied, "You the only who one t-t-t-" Her speech became silence. She could picture what she wanted to say and yet, the words did not come. Everyone in the saloon was staring at her. She lowered her head in shame. They all saw her for what she was. *I should never have left home today.*

The bounty hunter folded his arms and began speaking. "I heard a few rumors—"

Just then, the constable entered the saloon. He pointed a shotgun at the bounty hunter's head. "If ya mean to insult the innkeepers all day, by any means—stay. If ya want questions concernin' yo' bounty, leave."

"Ah, a fellow lawman," the hunter turned around and arced his head.

The constable's shotgun bumped his nose. "You ain't a lawman, Belmont."

"Tell me, Edric," the bounty hunter stood up. "If I ran, think you could catch me?"

Goodwind eyed the barrel of his gun, "This bullet could."

"Hm." The bounty hunter took off his hat, swung it to his chest, and bowed. He addressed the crowded saloon, "If anyone has any information 'bout the fugitive, I'll be staying in the Anchorage."

The man spoke with dignity and looked at the Gardners once more. "As I s'pose there's no room for me at the inn."

Hanna did not raise her head until the wicked man had left. Everyone looked at her, either with pity or curiosity. *They don't respect me. If I were not Arthur's wife—they would be laughing.* She was sure the moment she left the saloon, all the townspeople would begin gossiping about the idiot lady living at the inn. *'She can't speak. I hear she needs help getting dressed.'* She wanted to curl up and cry but did not want her children seeing their mother both dumb *and* weak.

Hanna stood up, thanked Rashif for his hospitality, and waved at everyone present. She marched home stoically, greeted the guests in the tavern, told Aeric she loved him, assured Emilia that everything would be alright, and went to her bedroom.

Then, she cried.

27

Homecoming

Auldwine,

Charles left today.

Laverne's boy ran off to the Overgrowth with some other Crofters' sons. I knew when her husband died, she would struggle—but I only thought she would lose her land. I never thought the boy would form a gang.

I would be devastated.

Young men can be so impressionable. It is why I wanted Charles away from all that. I raised him as far as I could from the mockery and hatred, hoping that if nobody could call him malchance, he would not turn mean. I hoped if he was far from the Pale, then nobody would ever call him mudpuppy. That is how boys turn bad—when all they have around them is badness. I thought I had succeeded, too. He was educated, toured the country. I tried so hard to hide him from violence, to protect him from the forces that make little Latrells form a gang. The forces that made Charles' father do the things he did. And now, just this morning, I waved my boy off as he joined a gang.

At least it is just the navy. Hanna tells me that Carolyn's husband, Siegfried, has not seen any combat since joining. I suppose no side wants to risk losing their expensive toys. But men are cheap. Expendable. Well, fine. Let Charles sit on some ship, fire big, phallic weapons, and wait for all the captains to come to their senses. I shudder to think about that man and the gas mask. But please, Auldwine, do not think of yourself as a villain. Anyone would have done what you had and if they say differently—they are liars and would have done far worse. I know I cannot convince you, so here—I will distract you.

Auberdine has been quite lively, despite the absence of almost all the men. A wounded soldier came to the inn, a Redfeather. Hanna says he is a fantastic chef. She wrote that he makes an excellent boil. If that is true—well I may just have to move closer to town! There are rumors he fought for the other side, given his race. I don't much care.

Several hikers went up the Oleander and found more black gold. A surveyor from the capitol came to investigate and concluded there were, indeed, great stores of oil... Well, any local could have told him that. That mountain has every mineral in abundance. Of course it had oil. There is talk of another economic boom, but nobody is too vocal. Most are too concerned with the war and many remember the old stories. I for one would never step onto the slopes of Oleander. Not while the bones of old Beauregard's fort lie in ruins. Not while the Overgrowth is still in shambles. I often wonder what this valley would be like if the Wanakha had survived the gold rush. What would it look like if there had been no Deluge? Who knows? Perhaps some other people will come for this black gold and make Wanakha out of us all?

In other news, Buchanan Bavar sold the old promontory tower. Sold it to some Castle Rocker. All the town is talking about is how the buyer managed to swindle Bavar out of his family holding.

My garden gave me the most excellent autumn harvest! I think it was because of your soil. Something about that Hill of yours. Also, I wanted your opinion on a matter. I saw the largest wolf the other day. Do you think another species might have migrated to Cottonwood?

Speaking of cottonwoods, the one you planted in your grove died. I suppose the heat got to it. The good news, though: Charles told me many animals prefer dead cottonwoods to living ones. Of course, you knew that. He said in a few years, you can remove it, and new saplings will take its place.

In short, all is as well as can be hoped in old Auberdine. I would much prefer to have my boys home, though.

Love,
Cora Eastmont

Charles folded the letter. He eyed the Overgrowth, unsure as to where home was now. He stared at the mossy, dilapidated mansions of a bygone age. Rutting elk tilled the fallow fields of forgotten farmsteads. Squirrels scurried over slipping shingles. He watched a wildcat wiggle into an open window. When the cat fled with a chicken leg, Charles chucked. He stretched his legs. *I should get back*, he told himself.

"Do you think he's gone mad?" A child asked her mother.

"I would not doubt it," the Pale woman replied. "He did fight in the war."

Charles caught himself glaring at the couple. *They talk like they are authorities on the subject.* He brushed the dirt from his shoulder and strode past the black walnut tree. When he crossed into the Inner Ring, he heard Evelyn saying to her sister, "Did you hear how he talked to Hanna?"

Carolyn pointed, "Where were the men that went with the innkeeper? That's my question."

Charles blinked a dozen times. He nearly fell over from how quickly he stopped. He stuttered over his words, asking Evelyn to elaborate.

Carolyn glared at him. "We were having a conversation."

Evelyn started, "The innkeeper, he—"

Carolyn swatted her sister, "Don't respond. It only encourages them."

Charles sped off, unable to be offended. Arthur had finally returned. *You have always had a problem with tardiness,* Charles would joke. *But this is just ridiculous.* He started jogging when he heard a cacophony of voices at the hedge gate. *What, did you go hunting while you were out, too? Go for a nice hike?* His pace slowed when he saw the crowd. He halted at the hedge gate.

The entire inn had spilled out onto the streets. The scene reminded him of before the war, when all the town watched Auldwine go. Though, nobody was cheering now and the only smiles came from snide gossipers. Scattered groups of townspeople pointed at the Hill. Aeric was speaking to a swarm of guests in a calming voice. Laverne and Wenton were chatting in a large group. Charles approached them. "What has happened?"

Wenton loosed a gravelly laugh. "Innkeeper came back."

"Well it is about damn time," he laughed. "So this... is a parade? A picnic?"

Wenton looked at Laverne with a smirk. Then, he hacked up a laugh. Laverne shook her head, "Son, this ain't no picnic."

Wenton bent over and swayed, his arms dropping low. "He came on in with his clothes tore up, went to see his wife, an' a minute later went 'round shoutin' that er'body had to go."

Charles wanted to smack him. *And this is funny to you?* He asked Laverne to clarify, "Permanently?"

The woman shrugged.

Something horrible has happened. Charles tugged at his shirt, suddenly feeling constricted. "I am sure he just wanted a moment alone with his family. I'll sort this out."

"An' you think you gonna just go in?" Wenton raised his brow and gave him a smug smile.

"Obviously," Charles grunted. He pushed forward, trying his best to ignore the sorry eyes of guests who did not know if they were homeless or not. Some tried to approach him. Charles just kept walking. He climbed the patio steps. He placed a hand on the door handle and took a deep breath.

The door opened.

Isabelle's brown eyes looked up at him. The dog coughed. A moment later, she coughed again. Emilia came up beside her. "Hi," she said in a voice that did not seem to care, "My daddy is back."

Isabelle coughed.

"Yes," Charles smiled. "I heard. Where is he?" An answer came before the girl could reply.

His voice reverberated throughout the tavern. Arthur Gardner was speaking to his wife. His voice started quiet, "How are you? Are you in pain?"

Charles assumed he was speaking to Hanna, but he could not hear her.

Arthur's voice cracked, echoing against the pillars. "I told you I do not want to talk about it."

Hanna whispered words too quietly and quickly for Charles to hear. Emilia and Isabelle started walking toward the back of the tavern, where the remnants of a fire were pulsating. Embers cracked and little flames rekindled.

The innkeeper simmered, growing quiet again. "I am sorry. I must remember you are more fragile now."

"Not that fragile," Hanna said.

"I think you should rest," Her husband said, not a hint of humor to be had.

"I'm okay, Arthur," his wife assured him. "The hunter scared me. That are all."

"Please?" He insisted, putting his arm around her. "It would make me feel better. I feel awful for my... entrance. If anything because it disturbed you."

"Arthur," she shook her head, "Y-you would not-" she paused, unable to find her words. "S-so, bloody."

"See?" Her husband interrupted. "Your brain is all scrambled."

Hanna stuttered. After a moment, she agreed. "You're right... Will you be up soon?"

"Yeah," Arthur answered wearily.

"Don't leave again," Hanna whispered as she went. "Please."

The innkeeper dragged a palm from his forehead to chin. He sighed and looked around the empty tavern. "Fuck," he swore.

Charles came into the light. "Welcome home." Embers flew and sparked new blazes in the obsidian fireplace.

Arthur's shadow twisted against the wall like a gnarled tree bending in the wind. "You bastard."

Charles took a step back. Arthur's clothes were tattered and stained with blood. His face was scarred with deep lacerations. Charles tried to joke, but his smile crumbled and his speech grew shaky. "You found me."

"So I did," Arthur folded his hands. He glanced to his side. "Should never have left in the first place."

"No," Charles agreed. He stepped closer and took a seat at the other side of the fireplace. "I uh, am glad you-" Charles stopped, unsure of what words were best to thank his friend.

"Yeah, you're welcome," Arthur grumbled. "What good it did. You get back, what... A day after we left?"

Charles frowned. The embers cracked and flew. He pulled his collar. "Well, we are both here."

Arthur's entire body nodded. His chair creaked.

Without warning, Isabelle began chasing her tail. She growled and twirled, chasing after her own self. Spit flew out in every direction. If Charles had not known better, he would have assumed she was being attacked by a wild animal.

Arthur barked, "Damn it Emilia, control your dog."

"She's just excited is all," the innkeeper's daughter replied. She did not mind the mannerism, nor did Charles.

Her father scowled. "It is embarrassing. What if a guest were to see?" Arthur folded his arms. "The thing is deficient and far too old to be so stupid."

Emilia moaned, "But da-"

"Put the creature to bed," Arthur shouted. He did not blink until his daughter and the dog slogged up the steps, away from sight.

The two were left alone. Charles sniffled. He had to sneeze but held it. The floorboards shuffled. Critters skittered underneath. Mice chirped.

Charles raised his brow. *He is overloaded. Needs a few days to recuperate, that's all.* He tried soothing the innkeeper. "Hanna is doing a lot better."

Arthur stared at him silently.

"She was much worse," Charles emphasized. *Even if she were mute, would that be so bad?* He said positively, "She'll get better. In time."

Arthur shrugged and flashed a faint smile. He snorted, "Think you're funny, do you?"

Charles did not immediately hear him. "What?"

Arthur cleared his throat. He reiterated, speaking as if the topic was casual small talk. "Two gravestones."

Charles' breathing stopped. Slowly, he realized what he had done. "Oh no."

Arthur's entire body was shaking. His chair rattled. His voice skittered and scratched like the mice beneath his feet, "I thought you were dead."

Charles swallowed. "I am so sorry."

Arthur looked at the dried blood coating his hands. He howled, "Why? Why make two? Do you have any idea what you did?"

"She—" Charles scratched his head, struggling to defend his actions. *I cannot believe this. I was so, so stupid.* He apologized twice more, doing his best not to make Arthur uncomfortable with his tears.

"And to leave during a blizzard!" The innkeeper snarled.

"It wasn't snowing when I left," Charles defended. He reprimanded himself, *All the same, I should have known. It was stupid.* All this unpleasantness could have been avoided if he had not been so hasty. *If I had not let my grief get the best of me.*

Arthur continued, "When we got to the cottage, I-I lost it. I thought something had happened to you both." His eyes twitched. His watery eyes lost no tears as his stern voice quaked, "I should have known. How could two corpses dig two graves?" Arthur's tongue patrolled his mouth. He whispered, shaking his head pitifully as he raised his mangled, muddy hands. "I thought I'd lost you."

"Yeah," was all Charles could say in his defense.

"What happened?" Arthur pleaded. "Cora was so healthy before the war."

"We all were," Charles remarked. "It was Trench Rot. Same as Hanna's."

Arthur scratched his cheek. "Where the hell did they get it? War's over."

Charles tugged at his collar. Arthur grunted. Charles nodded. Without a word, each agreed to change the subject.

"So," Charles gambled a grin. "About those guests?"

The innkeeper stretched his arms. "I made quite a scene."

Charles Eastmont raised his brow, waiting to hear the full story.

Arthur folded his upper lip toward his nose. "I don't know, Charles. When I saw Hanna… She could not even say my name without stuttering. I just stormed downstairs and told all those fuckers to get out."

Charles suggested, "I think we ought to let everyone back in. Quite a scandal, already."

The innkeeper nodded slowly. "I believe it." His tone shifted suddenly and for a moment, Charles thought Arthur was about to vomit. Instead, he belched and shook his head. "Let them talk all they want. There's much worse in the world."

Charles did not catch his meaning. Arthur did not elaborate. Instead, he got up—went to the bar at the right corner of the tavern, reached over the counter—and pulled out two cigars. He threw one at Charles. He bit down on the cigar, swiped a pack of matches, and walked briskly toward the exit. "Come on, let's herd the cattle."

They went out. Arthur leaned against a wooden support beam and bellowed, "Alright, get inside. It's going to be a chilly night."

The crowd did not move. Arthur repeated, "Or freeze. That's your prerogative."

The guests started to move.

The innkeeper giggled to himself. Yet when Charles looked at his friend, the humor was matched with bloodshot eyes. His forehead had deeply etched wrinkles which made it seem as if the man always had a furrowed brow. His muscles cracked and popped whenever Arthur moved. Wounds large and small littered his body.

One by one, the guests came trickling back. Laverne looked pitifully at them both. Wenton smiled and strutted back without the slightest hint of negativity. The chef even gave the innkeeper a handshake and promised him his favorite meals for a week. Then came the orphans, fear oozing from their eyes. Finally came the Redfeather refugees, the Muhali traders, and the Golden River folk.

Charles scanned the Hill long after the procession finished. Several guests were unaccounted for. He asked, "Where is Momed? And the others?"

Arthur grunted, "Hm?"

"Momed and the rest of those boys that went with you?"

"Yes," Arthur murmured as he scratched a scab on his arm. He spoke as blood started running again. "Dead."

They had been gone too long for good news. Charles swallowed. "How?"

Arthur tilted the cigar in his mouth, inhaled, and sent a gust of smoke from the side of his cheek. "Wolves."

Charles did not speak. *Yes,* he looked at his thigh, *I know a thing about Cottonwood's wolves.* He stared at the innkeeper, waiting for the man to elaborate.

Arthur exhaled a cloud of smoke, obscuring his face. He coughed as he continued, "Came on us in the night. They took the little Redfeather cunt... What was his name?" Arthur dwelled on the question for half a second and then waved his head and grunted. "Dead now." He inhaled his cigar. "We knew we were encircled. Before I knew it, Momed was shrieking at me and I was alone."

Charles shook his head. *I did this, this is my fault,* and other thoughts of blame began to beat his brain. He banged his fist against the railing. The wood had splintered from some other impact. Charles inquired as he picked out a splinter, "How did you escape?"

Arthur giggled and scratched the back of his head. He sniffled. "They, uh. I... They just left." He went on, "I was firing like mad, you know? Must have been too much trouble than I was worth." He looked at Charles, who had no words. Arthur continued, "Damn near ran out of ammunition." He coughed and pointed, "I hear Galahad went off."

"Mhm," Charles said, omitting the part of him being a wanted criminal. *Too much bad news,* Charles decided.

"Idiot," Arthur smirked. "Oleander is the epitome of roses and thorns." The two smoked as the sun set. Arthur's skin always had a pink tint. On that night, however, Charles noted his skin was more red than pink.

Charles did not quite understand. He asked quietly, "Did you run? When you saw the wolves?"

Arthur glanced at him out of the corner of his eye and scoffed. "Of course not. I fought in the trenches. I know not to flee."

Charles had finished his cigar. The smoke was already getting to his head. He wrapped his hand around his chin. *Wolves never pursue prey unless it flees first.* Charles asked if Arthur noticed anything odd about the pack.

"They were just wolves, Charles," Arthur replied, more annoyed than usual.

"Did you have any wounded in your group?" Charles asked, quite sure a new species of wolf had come to Cottonwood.

"We were all in great health," Arthur retorted. "I would not be so dumb as to bring unhealthy boys into harm's—" The innkeeper drifted off. He gestured down the Hill, "Look."

Charles did so. A man in a tattered army uniform was ascending toward them. He looked to be an officer. *One who had just climbed out of the trenches.*

"Tanglewood is up north," Arthur joked.

The stranger laughed politely. "I thought army men like yourself might appreciate it."

"Not in the slightest," Arthur replied. "What do you want?"

"I work for the magistrate," the man began. "Do either of you know where I might find a Mister Galahad?"

"Son of Cambyses?" Arthur asked. "Why?"

"He sold his father's property recently. I have important documents pertaining to the sale that he must sign."

Charles had a hard time believing him. "Why would Cambyses let his least favorite son sell his shop?" *Why is a government official wearing an old army uniform?*

Arthur put a hand on Charles' shoulder, "Cambyses died while you were away. Drank himself to death."

"Ah," Charles said, slightly embarrassed. The official nodded at him. He cleared his throat to apologize, though Arthur spoke first.

"He went off to Oleander."

The stranger's smile floated higher and higher. He bowed low. "Thank you, gentlemen." Then, without a word, he walked away. His shadow disappeared into the night.

"I don't like him," Charles judged.

"Me neither," Arthur nodded. "Probably a fucking tax collector."

I doubt it. Charles readjusted his collar. "Galahad is..." Charles paused. "An uh," he cleared his throat. "He's wanted for, well not murder exactly, but he left town. He was ordered not to leave while the investigation-"

"This about Frederick?" Arthur asked, casually.

"Mhm. Carolyn finally went to the authorities with her accusation." Charles had not wanted to ask Arthur, on account of his friendship with the man. Yet here the innkeeper was, smoking and smirking. Charles wagered he could speak openly. "Think he did it?"

Arthur looked up at the moon. "I don't know." He wiped his nose. He began to mindlessly pick another scab. "I do know that he's different from me. Us."

"Well," Charles nodded to one side, half-grinning.

"No, not his love of men. Not his race." Arthur looked behind him. "He was the only soldier I ever saw who… Who seemed happiest when he was fighting." His eyes went blank as he recalled, "He enjoyed killing, I think."

Charles blinked. He had nothing to say to that.

28

Flower of the Mountain

The wind sheared the stone walls. The water trickled along the chiseled canyon. Pink blossoms floated leisurely along the stream. There was no hint of any great deluge, nor any miner's ghosts. No sign of flooding remained on those walls. There were no water-logged ruins. All his life he had lived under the shadow of the western peak. All his days he had heard the stories of the cursed mountain, the floating corpses of greedy men, and the Wanakhan spells that kept the mountain pure. *What myths, what lies.*

The beauty of the gorge had slowed his pace. As the mountain air flowed through his hair, Galahad sighed. *I don't need to go fast anymore. I've rushed through my whole life.* He played with the idea of exploring Beauregard's haunted fort, of hiking to the top of the mountain, of starting his own business. He had no idea what he would sell. That did not seem important right now.

Galahad had yet to see anyone in the canyon. It seemed as if there was no oil at all. In fact, the gorge seemed so perfectly untouched, he was skeptical Beauregard and his miners ever rushed for gold at all. Had it not been for the smell of black gold and the occasional Wanakhan cairn, Galahad might have thought no one had been west at all. He enjoyed the isolation. It meant he could get high wherever he wanted, whenever he wanted. He felt as free as ever.

"I am on vacation," Galahad told the gorge. He removed a damp ball of Yang's leaf from his mouth and tossed it into the stream. He rubbed a finger against his pocket. He would have to ration the remainder of his herb. *I will run out before I reach town.* Galahad leaned back and played with the idea of going without for the rest of tomorrow. *It will make the next high even better if I lower my tolerance. Then, I could use less leaf and have two highs instead of one.*

Galahad sniffled and shot up to his feet. Yes, he would ration it. Perhaps he could squeeze three more highs from his supply.

He followed the river along its many bends. There were no cottonwoods so high on the mountain. The only trees were towering pines and crawling spruces. Some trees oozed down the rocks like green lava, others stood tall, and some were burnt to charred husks. Trunks walled off the tiny path, needles carpeted the way, and wind-warped branches pointed forward. "The Crone's Corridor," he remembered.

"And why you think they call it that?" Laverne had once asked.

223

"*Because the Wanakha thought the whole world was their sacred garden,*" he had responded. A surge of frigid insecurity shot through him. He should have been friendlier to her. Laverne had shown him so much love, and he had run away from it. He eyed the creeping plants with their green fingers. Galahad wrapped his arms around his chest, "She left me."

I do not have enough herb, he bowed his head. Upon thinking of his medicine, saliva began pooling in his mouth.

Like a wolf shaking a rabbit, Galahad's head suddenly shook back and forth. He was already high, even if he could not remember. He focused on the awesome landscape and its history. He narrated as Laverne might have, "Ooh yeah, the crone was a lovin' woman. Too lovin'. She cared for er'body. No matter what."

The wind blew a gust of sooty air in his direction. A spindly spruce stretched toward him. Galahad recoiled, sneezed, and coughed. Then, he continued. "Whole valley took advantage of her love. She didn' care. The woman had a lazy eye and couldn' see badness: she was bein' sucked dry. Like a buncha vampires."

The hands that had begun fidgeting in his pockets froze like a burglar caught in the act.

Galahad removed his groping hands and swatted his temptation. He focused on his distractions, "She couldn' see the badness in people. Only the good. So," Galahad hoisted his hands over his belly as Laverne might have, "People saw her as a good opportunity. 'Ventually, the Crone's back broke from the weight and she was eaten alive, ripped open like a pig on a feastin' table."

Galahad rolled his lips, realizing all the ways in which the story related to him and those he knew. He bit his tongue, searching for more distractions. He scolded himself when he found nothing, *You are in the most pristine place for miles and you—*

The twisted trunks and jagged branches had been replaced by a palisade of rotting wood. Crows hopped from post to post. Beyond the ruined wall, a stone fortress loomed. It resembled the promontory fort, though its stones had a muddy tint.

Galahad passed Beauregard's famed palisade and entered a courtyard. As he passed a brazier, he shivered. There was no heat coming from the flame, or Galahad could not feel it. As he stepped on the rocky ground, he felt numerous cracks and snaps. He glanced at his feet and saw what his childhood stories had always claimed: the skulls of the Wanakha were the pathway of the Pale. A pebble fell down the canyon wall. The tumble made the mountain hum with a deep resonance, like a Redfeather army chanting before battle. Galahad cleared his throat and sped toward the muddy fort. The bastion seemed like it was from a different time, with a drawbridge and a moat. The drawbridge was lowered, but a portcullis barred his entrance. Galahad peered between the bars.

"Hello," he said, putting on his best, non-threatening voice. He felt like something was watching him, but he dared not turn around. "Hello?" He asked, trying his best to not seem afraid.

A man with a tall hat walked by. He was eating a sandwich and spoke with his mouth full. "Oye," he pointed at Galahad. The man looked around, waited for a moment, and then cursed. "Damned watchmen went off to lunch." He then blinked and declared, his mouth full of food, "Find a horse and hold it." He clamored out of sight. The Portcullis was raised.

The man returned and scanned Galahad from head to foot. He raised his brow. "You're not one of my drillers. Nor one of my loggers."

Galahad gulped. "I'm not." *I have nothing to hide.* He belched and went to shake the man's hand.

The man picked his nose and wiped it on his pant leg.

Galahad's arm fell to his side.

The gate-keeper finished eating his sandwich and licked his teeth clean. "What brings you to Oleander Springs?"

Galahad answered quickly. "I wish to start my own business."

The man looked at him with quaint curiosity. He chuckled. "You are sure you are not here to be a driller?"

Galahad narrowed his gaze.

"Ah, whatever. I don't care." He disappeared. A second later, he reappeared with a ledger. "What's your name, then?"

Galahad almost choked. "Name? Why?"

"For the census," The man rolled his eyes. "Oleander Springs will be just as big as Auberdine soon, perhaps bigger." He laughed, "The Rock is going to want to send tax collectors. Best be prepared."

Galahad burped. If the Rock could send taxmen, they could send lawmen. "Cyrus. Cyrus is my name."

"Cyrus," The Pale man scribbled onto the ledger. Without looking up, he asked, "You are Muhali, yes?"

"What of it?" Galahad responded.

The man raised his brow.

"Fuck me," Galahad laughed at himself. "Sorry, it has been a long journey." He bowed his head, "Son of," he coughed, "Marius."

"Marius," he scribbled. He shut the ledger. "Welcome to the Oleander, Cyrus." He then grabbed a great book. Its pages sprawled out from the frayed bindings like a jaw of crowded teeth. "So—and do forgive my brevity—what was your profession before coming to the mountain?"

"Shop-keep," Galahad replied quickly. *Craftsman, woodworker, tailor, fishing supplies...* He prepared to answer more specifics. The man did not pursue the topic. He scribbled the detail onto the page and continued.

"So..." The man adjusted his hat and trailed off uncomfortably. "Fight in the war?"

Galahad had half a second. He debated lying. He weighed the benefits of telling a half truth. Finally, he simply nodded.

The recorder drew a symbol next to his prior markings. He then froze, frowned, and readjusted his footing. He questioned, "What side?"

"Ours," Galahad grunted. *Does he ask all newcomers these same questions?* "What exactly is this? A survey? More details for the census?"

"Oh no." He laughed nervously. "Just uh, procedure. Required by the Rock... You know, can't have oil reservoirs in the wrong hands." He giggled. "Can't give away gold to every man before we find out on what side of the trench he sat."

Galahad stared at him.

He giggled again. When the man saw that Galahad was not humored, he acted like he was coughing, pounded his chest, and quickly changed the subject. "Sorry, where was I? Right. Okay. Will your family be joining us?"

"Yes," Galahad blurted out.

The fact was recorded.

Why did I lie? He had not needed to lie. It was just going to be another thing he would have to remember. "Gonna be coming up next month," Galahad continued.

"Noted."

Son of a bitch. Galahad blinked, horrified that his mind and mouth could not agree. He burped and tried to think of something funny to say, something to quickly change the subject. *Something about the weather, or about general politics. Is he from the Rock?* Galahad did not detect any whitening powder on his face. *If I knew where he was from, I could insult his local sports team. Men love that.*

The man tossed the book haphazardly. It landed with a thud. He put an arm around Galahad's shoulder and welcomed him beyond the portcullis. "My name is Albert. Lord Albert, actually."

Galahad went through the hollow formalities Albert would be accustomed to, "Do you work for the census, then? Or are you in the oil business?"

Albert bobbed his head, "I am-"

A woman interrupted him, "The chief foreman for Best Oil and Gas."

When his ears recognized the voice, his eyes closed. He heard the quiet approach of heels and the slithering of a silk dress. Galahad's eyes remained shut. He acted like he was yawning and tried to hide his face. He wrapped his arms around his head and tilted his jaw toward the ceiling. The footsteps continued getting louder. Then, they stopped. Galahad ended the charade, opened his eyes, and shrugged.

Lilian Vellencourt was smirking at him. "We are in the presence of a celebrity, Albert."

"Indeed?" The Lord's cheeks sagged and his eyes widened.

Vellencourt nodded excitedly. "Oh yes. This is," she waited half a second and grinned at Galahad. She looked into his eyes and raised her brow slightly. "Cyrus, son of Marius. He and his father kept a food stand outside the parliament building, don't you remember?"

Lord Albert shook his head, "I do not." He stretched his neck and analyzed Galahad. "But I suppose that is a failing memory."

"I suppose so," Vellencourt agreed. She raised her arms like one offers a magnificent gift, "Welcome to the Springs, Cyrus." Lilian put her fingers subtly to her lips.

Galahad nodded. "Thank you."

Lilian hugged him. "It seems our paths are the same of late."

"It seems," Galahad said, voice cracking. His legs shook.

"Albert," Vellencourt barked, pulling away. "Does this man have lodging?"

"He did not come to drill..." Albert answered, uncomfortably.

"Oh," the foreman's master frowned. "That's a pity. Well, do see that he receives a mask." She stared at Galahad, "I like him."

What do you think you are doing? He was tired of Lilian's game of cat and mouse. *She blackmails and belittles me, tricks and manipulates me—and then turns it all around with mercy and generosity?* Galahad blinked. *Does she think herself a god?* Galahad bit his bottom lip. *Probably.* He spoke, though his throat was suddenly sore.

Vellencourt put her arm on Albert's shoulder and said, quietly, "Do make your way up when you have finished. Elizabeth is bored."

Lord Albert bowed his head. "Of course."

Lilian Vellencourt wiggled her fingers at Galahad in a wave. "Enjoy the Springs, Cyrus."

It looked to him quite like how a witch might cast a spell. Galahad watched her go, unwilling to give her a goodbye.

Lord Albert readjusted his collar. "That's the boss," he declared. "Lilian Vellencourt. I knew her husband before the war. We were good friends." He laughed nervously, stood up straight, and marched forward. "I am sorry I do not remember you, but I am pleased to meet you again."

Galahad scratched his head, "Likewise." He could hear chatter ahead. He turned around and looked at the quiet canyon. A pink blossom from some unknown flower flew onto his face. Galahad removed the gossamer petal slowly and stared at it. The shape was beautiful, the color was ornate, and Galahad wondered where it had come from.

"Ah," Albert said. "I remember my first time passing through the Crimson Gorge. You never forget it."

Galahad stared blankly at the Crone's Corridor, at the shattered skulls of the Wanakha. He could hear the sounds of the town. Bells, wheels, laughing. He was so close. Yet, he felt strange stepping closer to his goal. He was not as happy as he thought he would be. He felt worse, actually. *What the hell do I do now?* Now that his dreams were close to becoming a reality, Galahad did not really care to pursue them. He did not think he could. *Vellencourt, that bitch. She has ruined everything.*

Albert continued, pointing at a flower growing between a boulder. "They're beautiful, aren't they?"

"Very much," Galahad agreed. He had not seen the plant until it was pointed out. The stem sprouted between a thin crack in the stone and its petals rested atop the rock like a lounging cat.

"They have medicinal properties, I'm told. The Castle Rock outlawed them years ago due to the side effects, but I hear certain doctors still carry the leaves for extreme cases of pain. The boss does not mind them."

"Hm," Galahad hummed.

"I've tried it myself," Albert laughed. "Made me feel drunk."

"That so?" Galahad asked, quite preoccupied with his own thoughts. *What am I going to do?* He had put off deciding his fate until he reached the Oleander. *Well, I am here... I am free.* Galahad rubbed the money in his back pocket. It was not enough to start a drilling company, nor to build up a shop from scratch. Besides, he was sure anything he did would soon carry Vellencourt's shadow. *What is worth doing when one has no goals?*

"Indeed," Albert said, leading him to the other side "I chewed a few leaves and lost my head."

Galahad stopped. His melancholy mood shifted shape. "You chewed them?"

"I know," Albert let loose a mighty guffaw. "How barbaric."

"Very," Galahad said. A panicked excitement took hold of him. Hope bubbled up his body like boiling water. It seared his chest and burned his throat. He gazed at his palm just as a gust of wind swept the pink blossom from his grasp.

"It's actually a species of Oleander plant," Albert continued. He put his hand on a lever and pulled it down. Another drawbridge opened before them. "The Wanakha named the mountain after the plant, it is told. They said the plant gave all one wanted and took all one needed."

His words entered and left Galahad's ears without any notice. He was busy planning. He dug his fingers into his pockets and caressed the last of his leaf. Over and over he thought, *Not the last. Not the last.* He could find more. That was what the old man was implying, of course. He glanced at the gorge behind him. That gate had already closed. The gate of the mountain was opening. Galahad squinted.

A thick brown haze obscured the bustling town only paces ahead of him. Outlines of people hurried down a crowded street. Workers carried planks of wood. Etchings of shops loomed. In the distance, billowing buildings belched black smoke.

"Don't mind the smoke. Comes and goes. Just the weather," Albert said cheerfully. He covered his face with his sleeve and offered Galahad a mask. "A house-warming gift, if you will."

Galahad reached mechanically and placed the mask over his face. He had half a mind to turn back. He sniffed the sulfurous air and was reminded of the Great War. The towering depots and factories which littered the mountainside even looked like battlements. Galahad blinked. *It is okay*, he assured himself. *There are no artillery barrages*, he persuaded himself. His lips twitched and he stifled a cough. Just as he turned back around—the gleam of a pink flower caught his eye.

"Well," Albert coughed. "Hope you find what you're looking for."

Galahad did not reply. His eyes were fixed on pink blossoms, spindly stems, and those very familiar leaves. The rations in his pocket seemed a meager trifle compared to the bounty of a fully grown plant. He did his best to bar his brain, to lock down his mind, to ward against his wants. "It was supposed to be the last time," he lamented.

He reminded himself, *It still could be the last time*, but he did not believe it. Even as he tried walking away, he inched closer. First, he only wanted to inspect it. Then, he wanted to feel it. Finally, he just wanted to hold it.

Galahad uprooted the plant and held it to his chest, sniffing in the familiar and foreign aromas of the full plant. He felt a surge of weightless happiness. A depressive self-hatred followed. His heart plummeted. He scowled at the plant as he carried it down the polluted road.

Five bells tolled in Oleander Springs. Men wearing various levels of filth emerged from the woods. Galahad found himself following the mass as they wandered. Their black faces dripped oil onto the road. Their hands were brawny, but their eyes were sunken.

29

The Forbidden Tree

Charles found the first trap with ease. A mouse's rigid leg poked out from mechanical jaws. The lifeless limb looked like a leafless branch. He reached down and delicately placed the trap at the bottom of the bin. He was glad he did not have to see the creature's face. The second trap he found was made of a sticky substance, a sort of glue. A mouse struggled and cried as Charles approached.

He had hoped they would all be dead. He peered down at the mouse like a hawk. *Get it all out, come on now.* He closed his eyes so only the outline of an animal remained. Charles touched the trap. The snared animal tried to pull its body from the glue. Every action the mouse made only ensured his grave was deeper. Charles swallowed. He tried to retrieve the trap, but the glue had spilled out onto the edges. Every spot was coated in the substance. He got to his feet and retrieved a broom.

Charles poked a bristle onto the glue and hoisted the trap up. The mouse dangled. Charles put the garbage bin down and maneuvered the edge of the broom over it. He flicked the trap off his broom and into the refuse. The mouse shrieked and then was silent.

The next trap was also a sticky one. The mouse caught atop it was large. *Probably the male of a harem,* Charles decided. He stuck his bristles down onto the trap, but they did not stick. He plunged it down like a sword. A great clump of bristles attached themselves. Charles hoisted the screaming rodent up. As he turned the broom toward the garbage, a stray bristle poked the mouse. A shiver crawled up the critter's spine. It squealed and tried to claw its way from the glue, gnawing on its own foot.

Charles looked at the squirming animal and bit his tongue, curling his lower lip back into his mouth. "Damned thing is kind of cute." Charles closed his eyes and flicked the broom over the bin. When he opened his eyes, the trap remained. Charles flicked it again. The trap would not budge. Charles sighed; the mouse cried. He shook the broom again to no avail. He exerted more force, hoping the trap would not fly up and hit him in the face. He shook it back and forth. The trap remained glued to his broom. All the while, the little mouse cried and cried—its brain being scrambled and tortured by the motion.

Charles looked at his broom and at the mouse breathing rapidly. He placed the bristly edge of the broom onto the ground, leaned onto it, and put his foot on the edge of the trap. He tried to yank it free. Instead, Charles slipped and crushed the mouse's tail. It yelped and moved what it could away from the man.

The motions of terror and the sounds of the critter's crying was too much. Charles had heard and seen that mouse many times before. Dying soldiers sounded quite the same. He glanced up at the great redwood roof, covered in a layer of frost. Charles shook his head, bit his lip, and kept his foot placed on the mouse's tail. He yanked the broom free. Blood sprayed from the bristles. Mechanically, Charles lowered the bin and kicked the mouse into it.

Charles gazed at the garbage. They might not have been the smartest or strongest things, but Charles hated seeing them at the bottom of a waste bin. *I have seen a beautiful painting and marked it with a red 'X'.* Charles shivered, disgusted by his actions. He had placed a living thing in the trash, no better than a dirty rag. *Millions of years of continuous evolution and life ended by janitorial duty.*

Charles circled the rest of the inn. Whenever he found a trap with a living mouse, he tried his best to free it. If he could not, he stabbed it with the handle of his broom. It was the only form of mercy he could grant. By the time the sun was directly overhead, he had cleared the Hill of traps. He looked at his container of corpses.

He tossed the contents into a larger disposal and thought, *I wish there were still owls in the granary.* He rested for half a minute before going inside to start on the indoor traps. He had acclimated more to the cold, but the warmth of the fire and of friendly faces was a nice change. Aeric hailed him over to the petrified table.

"Charles," he smiled, "Don't worry about the traps. I'm on it."

He blinked. "Oh." Charles glanced at Isabelle. The hound sat below the table, waiting patiently for Emilia to share her scraps. "I just finished with the outdoor traps."

"Ah," Aeric shrugged. "Well, I just finished the ones inside. You get the Cottonwood yet?"

Charles shook his head. "No, I was actually about to start on that."

Aeric rubbed his hands together. His plate was nearly full but he grabbed it and slid the food into the trash. "Nasty business, those things. I think we need a cat."

Charles scanned the table, "Where is your father?"

Aeric looked at Emilia and said quietly, "He and Wenton were having a disagreement over, uh, seasoning."

"Seasoning?" Charles smirked.

"I don't know," Aeric scratched his cheek, "Dad just got up and stormed into the kitchen, roaring about the proper amount of salt."

Emilia chimed in. "I wouldn't bother him." Her legs were swinging from the seat. "He's unstable."

Aeric barked at his sister, "You don't know anything. You're still a little girl."

Emilia argued in a sing-song voice, not bothering to look up from her plate. "You didn't hear him last night."

"What happened last night?" Charles inquired.

Aeric answered hastily, "Nightmare. That's all."

"He's always having nightmares," Emilia said, feeding a morsel to Isabelle.

"No he is not," Aeric gritted his teeth. He muttered, "You don't remember before the war."

Emilia glared at her brother. "I'm going to check on mama."

"Don't bother her," Aeric protested. "She's sleeping."

"She is not a child," his sister told him. The siblings glared at one another.

Charles cleared his throat and said, "Say, Aeric, where's the axe?"

The boy stared at his sister and answered Charles. "Leaning against the granary."

Emilia patted her hip and her hound trotted happily behind. She marched upstairs toward her mother's room, stomping with every step. Aeric dragged two weary fingers down his nose and over his eyelids.

As he did so, his father emerged from the kitchen. Arthur smiled at Charles like a stranger might, raising his cheeks and lips slightly, almost like a grimace. Then, he pressed his fingers to his temple, glanced at the Gardner residences, and jogged upstairs.

Charles decided he'd best stay out of everyone's way today. *They need to find their routines now.* He went back outside and to the old granary. It felt strange to not hear the occasional flapping of wings, or even a lazy hoot. The axe was waiting for him against the door. The forlorn structure made Charles sad. He did not linger there long.

The cottonwood in question had been the first one planted on the Hill. Unlike other trees growing in the grove, the cottonwood had not been placed to bear fruit. Instead, Charles wagered Auldwine had expected the tree to die. *Even hoped for it.* Now, Charles espied old bird nests nestled in the trunk. Between cracks and hovels of crumbling bark, squirrels and even mice made their high homes. Fungi had started to eat away at the base of the tree, leaving a large opening. Charles had seen a fox take shelter there several times.

Now though, the tree was diseased. Charles could see patches of red and green on the white branches. Little animals and fungi were not the only benefactors of the tree's bones. Bacteria and other miniscule things were spreading like a fire across the topmost limbs. Before long, the disease would spread to other parts of the tree and then perhaps to the whole grove. The cottonwood's time had come and gone.

Charles swung the axe. He swung it again. A cavity began to form in the trunk and the wood groaned under a new center of gravity. The branches swayed, though the trunk remained strong. *I have a lot of swings yet,* Charles sniffled. He wiped the sweat from his brow before it had time to freeze.

The deeper he cut into the tree, the harder the wood became. The axe began to chip less and less of the wood. Charles could feel the muscles in his back straining as he put more effort into his actions. His forearms recoiled every time the axe plunged into the wood. Charles swung once more. He was hardly making any progress. It seemed like the tree was felling him more than it. Charles left the axe embedded, rolled his shoulders, and walked back to the patio for a break.

He found Hanna sitting there. She grinned as he neared.

"H-h-," her legs bounced up and down. "Having fun?"

Charles took a seat next to her. "You are great moral support."

"I know," she admitted. "Wanna go for a—" she searched for the word, "walk?"

"Maybe tomorrow," Charles panted. "This tree is stubborn."

"Ah," Hanna replied. She rocked in her chair and started speaking.

Charles had already begun, "Arthur has been having nightmares?"

She stopped and interlaced her fingers. "Uh huh. Since he come home from the war, actually." Hanna wiped her nose. "They got worse, though. Since this last time. He kicks lots now."

"War dreams," Charles shrugged.

"He doesn't like to sleep," Hanna said. "Tries to avoid it long as he can."

Charles understood. He thought of a new topic, a happier conversation. He crafted a question. *All things aside, it's nice to have him home, isn't it?* He made his tone a carefree one and said, "All things-"

"What are *you* doing out here?" Arthur scrambled toward his wife. "No coat, either. Do you want to get sick again?"

Charles placed his hands on his lap and smiled. He looked away and felt Arthur's eyes probing him. "And what are you doing?"

"Just working on that tree," Charles pointed.

"Yes," Hanna looked up at her husband. "He's clearing out that dead cottonwood. It's funny."

The innkeeper's face twitched. "Clearing out?"

Charles stood up and went back to work. "Yep. Diseased. Got to get rid of it before it spreads." He waved at Hanna and nodded curtly at Arthur. "Shouldn't be too long now."

Arthur ran in front of him. "No, no, no." His voice rose and he spoke frantically, "What the hell, Charles?"

"What?" Charles asked, perplexed by the innkeeper's response.

"I wanted you to keep the grove, not kill it!"

"The tree is already dead, Arthur." Charles gestured at the ground beneath the trunk. "Besides, think of all the new growth there will be once space is cleared."

"I don't want new growth," his friend glared. "That was my brother's tree."

Charles bowed his head. "I know, but it's diseased."

Arthur misunderstood. "Chop off the deceased parts." His every word cracked like brittle metal. "Come on, you fought in the war. We amputated wounded soldiers—we didn't gut them!"

Charles snorted surprised laughter and tried to explain. "The disease will spread and besides—there are saplings ready to grow."

"Damn it, Charles," Arthur grabbed his forehead. "Please."

Charles looked at his friend and listened to the pleading in his voice. *Maybe the disease will slow. Or it'll just remain on this tree.* "I'll just trim the branches," Charles whispered.

Arthur looked away. "Okay," he shook his head. "Thanks." Suddenly, he turned back—new life into his face. He asked, "I didn't give you your letters, did I? The ones from your trunk?"

"Uh, no," Charles replied. Hanna had, though.

"Okay, I thought so." Arthur marched toward his wife. "Do you know where I left his letters?"

Hanna scratched her head and smiled, "N-not a clue. I could help you look?"

"Fuck. I was hoping to go fishing, but this is just going to annoy me."

She doesn't remember. Charles stopped his friend just as he was jogging back into the tavern. "Hanna gave them to me a few days ago."

Arthur turned around slowly. "She did?" His attention was thrown at his wife. "You weren't going to tell me?"

"I-," Hanna rolled her shoulders nervously and scratched her cheeks. "I don't remembered," she admitted quietly.

Arthur's upper lip twitched. "Course not." He groaned, "Hanna, you cannot be outside without a coat."

"It's not that cold anymore," Charles suggested.

The innkeeper raised his hand. "I'm talking with my wife. Thank you."

Charles took a step back. *I've known her longer than you have,* he simmered. He grabbed the axe and returned it to its resting place at the granary. He was quite aware he was angry when he thought, looking at the derelict building, *He is just ruining everything. His brother would be ashamed.* Charles paused. His thoughts made him uncomfortable. They felt like betrayal. *He is my friend. A loyal friend that nearly died trying to find me.* Charles said a silent apology and returned to the porch. When he got back, a door had just been slammed and Hanna was staring at the horizon blankly.

"Hi," Charles said awkwardly. He sat next to her again. "You okay?"

She kept staring.

She's too fragile for this. Charles glanced to his side, contemplating if and how he should talk to Arthur.

"He's so... shaky," her voice quivered. "This morning, he yells to me for folding the wrong side of the…uh… blanket. I-I try to speak at him how I is thinking, feeling. He j-just interrupts. He don't let me talk."

"Hanna-" he began.

She exclaimed quietly, "I know he means good. He love me. That is why he so fr-frustrated. I just wish he..." She rubbed her wrists. Her head twitched and she winced. "I-I can't help it that I'm retarded now." She sounded angry, sad, and ashamed.

"You aren't retarded. It has hardly been-"

"I am," Hanna nodded. "Allbody knows it." She spat, tears flying from her face, "The whole town is l-laughing."

"They are not." At most, people talked about how they pitied her. *But they aren't shaming you.* Charles reached to put his hand on her shoulder.

Hanna brushed it off. She wrapped her arms around her chest. She raised a smile at him, "Just leave me be."

Charles did not want to. He wanted more than anything to hug her and make her see her worth, to give her back her sense of pride. Nevertheless, he nodded and reluctantly got up. *If she wants to talk, she knows she can. She just needs an hour.* He pulled open the door and found Emilia with her ear to the wall. Charles raised his brow and closed the door.

"Eavesdropping, are we?" he whispered.

Emilia put a finger to her lips. After another moment of listening, she took her ear from the wall and pouted, "I could hear him yelling at her." Her chest rose intermittently. Arthur's complaints about unclean plates echoed in the tavern. Emilia scooted closer to Charles, her eyes wide and hands wet.

"It's okay," Charles tried to soothe.

"He's a mean person," Emilia glared. "A-a, an asshole."

"Hey," Charles said sternly. He kneeled. "Don't say that."

Emilia watched Arthur as he scrubbed the petrified table. "Things were fine when he was gone."

"Your father is struggling," Charles said softly. "Things will get better and no matter what—he's your dad."

"I've never had a dad," Emilia grunted.

He did not know how to respond to that. He wanted the Gardners to be happy. He remembered them being happy. Charles coughed and merely said, "Me neither."

Emilia tilted her head questioningly. She analyzed him, not like a child might—but as a deep thinker. Isabelle was at her feet, staring up expectantly. Not liking the girl's attention directed at anything but her, the hound coughed and put her head directly under Emilia's hand. The girl petted the dog methodically. Her eyes bounced between her father and Charles. She swallowed, "I'm scared he's gonna hurt her."

He might, Charles wanted to say. "He won't," he assured the child. "He loves your mother more than anything."

"Okay," Emilia replied. She licked her lips several times. They were red with irritation. Then, she put her ear back to the wall and looked at him from the corner of her eye. "You probably have work to do?"

Charles looked down, bemused. *Typical Gardner.* "I suppose so, little lady."

30

Itch and Scratch

"**W**hy'd ya leave the Rock, Shyrus?" slurred one of the homeless men.

Galahad wrinkled his nose and rubbed his lips together. *I cannot believe there is no inn here. What a shell of a town.* He sniffled, "Well, uh." His bottom lip stretched toward his cheek as he thought. He settled on a partial truth. "Had an itch to be greater, I suppose."

"Like Wanakha fisher," Huang Shiungdi interjected. He looked at his empty glass in a daze, mind spinning. Like his friend, Andre Levingston, that unfortunate sot had been kicked out of company lodging for indecent behavior. Now, they were squatters on Galahad's dirt.

"Yeah," Andre rolled his eyes. He belched, "Whatever you say."

Shiungdi put his finger in the air and waved it, "No, I mean." He aimed the finger at Galahad. "Wanakha story tell of fisher who had-a itch."

Galahad was quick to remind the man, who was not as well versed in native stories as he thought, "Yes, but the fisherman's itch could never be scratched." He leaned back, confident the distinction between himself and the story was quite clear. Yet seconds after he had finished speaking, Galahad slowly realized the meaning of his words. The side of his lip twitched. The sensations of insects skittering along his skin sent a shiver up his spine. Galahad held his arms at his chest and slowly, covertly, began to itch them.

The uprooted oleander plant laid beside Galahad. He picked a few leaves, not realizing his hands were roaming. Blinding light slashed into the alleyway. The town bell tolled six times. *It's only dawn,* Galahad realized sadly, removing his hands. He hated mornings. *If I have unlimited supply, I must limit demand.* He dropped his medicine and waited for Shiungdi and Andre to stumble to work.

Huang Shiungdi shrugged. He glanced at his empty glasses and shook his head, "It-a like paper and rock. Itch always beat-a scratch." He put his palms on his knees and vaulted upwards. "I get-a more drink before I go to rig. You, Andre?" He swayed unsteadily, put a fist to his mouth, and belched. Fear filled his eyes as more than air filled his mouth. He squinted and swallowed. "Just-a one more."

"I'ma wait," Andre Levingston answered. "I like gettin' drunk more 'an bein' drunk."

Shiungdi staggered off. Andre lingered in their communal alley for a time, squinting at the sunlight. Then, with a belch, he stumbled to work. Galahad sighed,

235

relieved. Now he could have some solitude. He hated how wretched his fellow homeless were. All they did was drink, shit, and work. In some ways, their gluttony reassured Galahad. He had times of sobriety. He was not a *true* addict.

The reassurance twisted into a form of permission. *They are gone. The image is maintained. Now, you can use and still keep your pride!*

Galahad's mouth watered. He peeked out from the shadows. Main street was as hazy as ever. The sun's rays stabbed through the smoke with a red hue. The hungover populace meandered to their respective duties, soot on their faces. Automobiles with tinted windows sputtered down the street toward Beauregard's Palisade. *That is Vellencourt's base up here,* he had surmised. *Best Oil and Gas. B.O.G. A fit dwelling for such a vampirous bitch.* Like the ancient miner, her company would exterminate a people for profit.

Galahad loosened his mask and retreated into the shadows. He could not stand the town without a little extra help. Besides, he had waited an hour before taking his medicine. *I have remembered sobriety and now—*

"Do you plan on participating in my town, or are you simply looking for a suitable tomb?"

Galahad popped his lips and removed his crawling fingers from a stolen mortar and pestle. Unlike the rest of town, Vellencourt wore no mask and had no soot on her face. She wore a white shirt tucked into a red skirt. The powder on her face had been set and not a flake had fallen. A team of servants trailed behind her and were busy sweeping.

"Miss Vellencourt," Galahad answered dourly.

"Cyrus," Lilian began in an inquisitive tone. "What brings a shop-keep to my drilling operation?"

Greta stepped ahead of the other servants, "And when the change to Cyrus?"

Vellencourt responded with multiple blinks. Then, she gazed at the servant in unrelenting silence.

"Right," Greta declared. "I'll just get to work."

"Thank you." Lilian dusted off her shirt and applied a new coat of lipstick. "Cyrus. Come with me."

Galahad swallowed. *If I pushed her, she might hit her head.*

"Greta, you and the others may leave."

The servants obliged, though Greta gave Galahad a knowing, hateful look.

Great. A scene. Galahad walked into the light, annoyed. *I should have stayed in the forest, away from eavesdroppers.* Lilian was waiting for him, her arms crossed. She spoke in a leading tone, "I was just on my way to inspect my newest asset."

Galahad heard some irritation in her words. He warned himself, *Don't provoke her.*

"And yet here you are, like a shadow," Vellencourt whispered. She approached him and looked to her sides. "Should I worry about you?"

"No. I worry enough about myself for both of us."

Vellencourt giggled. She relaxed into her usual, smug self. "You're far too clever to be a wanted man."

"I am sure," Galahad paused to admire the Oleander's snowcapped peak, "I won't remain wanted for long."

"Don't sell yourself short," Lilian fawned. She walked beside him and took his hand.

Galahad wanted to recoil, but knew it was futile. *Let her do what she wants.* She had his secrets, all of them.

Lilian bent his index finger and twisted it. Galahad ground his teeth and ignored the pain. She took each finger in succession and proceeded to pull and rotate it. She held his pinky. "Did you murder him?"

Galahad looked her in the eye. He could see the individual brushstrokes that had applied her whitening powder. "Not the child."

Vellencourt wiggled his pinky and patted the back of his hand. She relinquished her grip. "I suspected as much. Walk with me. I just must show you my town."

"That is the tavern," she pointed. "I have an arrangement with Hinry, the barkeep there. I support his enterprise and my men get *nearly* free drinks."

"Every slum needs a carnival," Galahad muttered, now unbearably sober. He snuck a leaf through his mask and slipped it below his tongue.

"That leaf you suck on. It is potent, yes?"

Galahad coughed.

"That there is the fortune teller," Vellencourt changed the conversation. "He is never open when I come by. Sole business I have not bought out, actually." She pointed at a stone ruin, "That is the brothel. One of few buildings with enough private rooms for fornication, I am afraid."

"Why are you afraid?" Galahad inquired, now playing the part of eager tourist to distract from the other leaf he was putting in his mouth.

She peered at Galahad's mouth like a dentist. "Are you an addict, sweetie?"

Galahad grunted, "We are all addicted to something." The sweet, earthy taste of his medicine transformed into a sizzling sensation. It crawled up his brain stem and, instead of feeling his normal relaxation, Galahad was suddenly paranoid. He clawed his flesh with his dirty, sharp nails. *She knows me. I am dead. I should not have admitted my weakness. Oh, I am just my—*

Vellencourt breathed sharply, eyed the brothel, and said, "It is an old Wanakhan tomb. It was so overgrown, nobody knew it was a mausoleum until we cut down the trees. They were growing right out of the caskets, some of them! Don't worry, the madame exhumed the bodies before business began."

What a disgusting place. A hall of prostitution and death. His tongue sizzled with embers of ecstasy. A jolt of energy shot to his toes. His paranoia gave way to perversion. Suddenly, he quite wanted to try out the brothel. *How devilish,* he noted. Within seconds, he felt ashamed of the thought and believed himself the chief villain of all the town. He bowed his head and thought of good words to loathe himself with.

"Come now, Cyrus," Vellencourt had veered from main street and was standing at the alpine forest's edge. When Galahad approached, she feigned sensitivity. "Would you prefer Cyrus when we are alone? I understand that was your elder brother's name."

"Mudpuppy, whatever the case," Galahad repeated. *She is turning me in, I can feel it.* The woman played with him at the liquor store. She played with him at her tower… *I am a chew toy to her.* He contemplated running into the forest. His toes turned toward the tangles.

Only, the blue needles of tall spruce trees were no longer present. As they traveled, the foliage had been replaced with fallen trees and barren branches. Galahad peered through the skeletal assortment of dry brush and sickly spruce.

Shades of brown mixed with shades of grey. A massive chimney rose beside lanky pines. Stacks of eye-watering smoke soared into the sky. As they continued, Galahad glimpsed grinding gears and automobiles thundering through the thicket. The *chug-chug-chug* of a vast machine echoed among the dead trees. "Charming," Galahad quipped.

"Pollution is a natural byproduct of wealth," Lilian did not turn. "As an overabundance of that herb should have taught you. As your father should have."

Galahad squirmed in his filthy clothes, suppressing a shiver. "I am not my father."

"No, you have several redeemable qualities, I fear," Vellencourt said with indifference.

No one was out here. He could kill her. A swift bludgeon to the skull. "I have control."

"Oh you intoxicated sweetling."

I could hide her body in a log. "I am not an addict."

"That's a shame."

I could even dismember it so nobody would reco— "What?"

"Sugarplum," Vellencourt turned her head slightly. "I watched you in Auberdine. I have seen you in that alley, congregating with my most degenerative samples. You live and act like the most deplorable of characters. But fear not! Your dependence on that leaf is the only thing keeping *me* from turning you in."

Galahad blinked. Every sensory organ of his face swiveled in confusion. *This does not make sense.* "You've been," he burped, "studying me?"

"Oh poo," Vellencourt strode ahead. "I am no scientist. I enjoy the human mind, that is all."

And she enjoys mine, Galahad understood.

She pivoted and stretched her neck like a crane. "Looking at your father's lifeless body." She tapped his nose, "Bet that felt good, didn't it?"

That was the moment this wretched existence started, a dormant part of him would have said. *He looked so familiar. So childlike.* "Mhm," Galahad lied. "It did." He continued his epiphany in silence, *Oh that bastard. He exacted lifelong pity from me the moment he died. And the vengeance! What a marvelous hypocrisy I now live with.* He could not bear his words and openly tossed another intoxicant into his mouth.

Vellencourt eyed the crimson sky mischievously. She threw her hands up as she walked through the dead forest, "I murdered my husband!" She giggled to herself, "Oh what terrible fun you are. I should miss you if the hangman comes to collect."

"And what is the likelihood of that?" Galahad shivered. He looked back at the dead forest, wary of the shadows which infested it, even at high noon. Vellencourt had led him out. *But where are we now?* A murky, alpine lake stretched from the thicket to the bottom of a mighty glacier. He asked impatiently, sure of his impending doom, "And what is the likelihood of that?"

"Tut tut," Vellencourt replied, leaving the question unanswered. "This lake is the Adawakan's Sorrow. The glacier above that feeds it is called Niwot's Tear."

"I don't care about geography," Galahad growled. *What if she is leading me to a bounty hunter? I saw how Greta sneered. Her servant bitch must have been in the know. I should run.* He threw two leaves into his mouth. They stung his cheeks with familiar flavors, but all he gained from them was guilt. "Is that my prison?" Galahad pointed at a towering, black structure floating in the center of the Sorrow.

"You did not want to drill, so no."

A drill rig, he covered his eyes to see the shape better. A rickety pontoon bridge led from the beach to the operation. Men like insects scurried up and down the rig, heaving buckets and other supplies. Their ringing hammers echoed on the water. Fish slopped through the thick water.

Suddenly, the men stopped and looked at a single spot on the rig. They began counting down. Their voices carried over Niwot's Tear. The shoreline began to recede. When they reached one, the Sorrow shivered. Glacial ice plunged into the water. Waves lapped against the shore with force. The pontoon bridge swayed. Finally, a fountain of black gold shot up from the drilling platform. Cheers erupted as the men bathed in tar.

Meanwhile, fish floated up, gasped, and smacked their bodies against the surface. Their gills were clogged with oil. Their futile flopping only made them easier prey for opportunistic gulls.

Galahad pitied the fish. "How long before you collect?" He whispered.

"Collect?" Vellencourt questioned.

Don't play ignorant with me. "I am sure the bounty is handsome."

"It's cute," Vellencourt answered. "Not handsome." She grabbed ahold of a long strand of Galahad's hair. "You've been growing this out for quite some time?"

"When the war started," Galahad muttered. His hair was a few inches below his shoulders. His father hated it and had threatened to shave it off more than once.

Lilian dragged her fingers from root to end without regard for knots. "It's quite beautiful, though I would suggest more frequent bathing. The roots are too oily."

Galahad spoke through gritted teeth and blinked at the water. "Can't bathe down there."

"No," Lilian quickly agreed. "The water would kill you in minutes, just like those fish."

It was Galahad's turn to play. "Is that why you gorge your workers on the, uh, happy juice?"

Vellencourt took her hands from Galahad's hair and put them on his shoulders. "Was your father happy with his position in life?"

She could push me down if she wanted to. "No," he replied.

"Neither are those vermin," she said loudly.

She doesn't care who hears her. Why would she? Galahad wished he could be so reckless.

Lilian got closer. Her hips touched his. "Neither are you."

Galahad snorted. "Obviously."

"Neither am I," she said, the air from her lips tickled his ears. Lilian pulled away suddenly. She waited by the stairs, "I'll fill you in on a secret, if you want."

"Your secrets have yet to do me any good."

She covered her mouth and giggled. "Oh, how perfectly clever you are." She curled two fingers to her palm. "Come now."

Galahad scraped his tongue along his upper teeth. His gums were bleeding. He sighed and followed the woman onto the pontoon bridge. Passing drillers were careful not to look at either of them.

"They are like dogs," Galahad remarked. "Never daring to look their master in the eye."

"Indeed." Vellencourt shrugged and looked at Galahad curiously, "Which is why you fascinate me. For here you are, looking me in the eye."

Galahad smiled at his arbiter. "What is your little secret?"

"We are all insatiable." She pointed at the drillers heaving long lines of rope or carrying large boxes of supplies. "I quench two thirsts by providing for their drink."

"You keep them docile," Galahad grunted. *They are just as pathetic as my father.* He spat, "Can't be too unhappy when you're always drunk."

"The idea came to me when I saw your little Overgrowth."

Galahad chuckled in disgust. He did not know at whom. He pocketed his hands and fidgeted.

Vellencourt put her hands to her hips. "And yet, you and I get drunk off of something else, don't we?"

Galahad let out a quiet burp. "But it is me who will be hanged."

"Perhaps," Vellencourt rolled her fingers, intertwining her hands. "But perhaps not." She smiled placidly. "I would harbor you as Cyrus, if you would so kindly share your," she relished her proposition with an arrogant pause, "Proprietary knowledge."

"The leaf grows wild here," Galahad scoffed. *She is getting my hopes up, only to lie or extort. She swindled me once, she will again.* "You do not need me."

"The thing with beasts is sometimes, they cannot be made to drink without a lead." Vellencourt wasted no time, adding, "You are one of few I have ever noted to enjoy the raw quality of Oleander leaf. Moreover, you are the *only* person I know to think of refining it."

Galahad's heartbeat raced without his permission. His drool oozed out the corner of his mouth. In that slavish moment, he was glad the mask obscured his slavering.

Lilian pointed at a driller, leaning on a railing atop the drill rig. He was vomiting into the water. "Impurities like his diminish my profits, you understand?"

Galahad faced the owner of Best Oil and Gas and sniffed, "It is *quite* smelly out here."

"Dangerous, too," Lilian raised her brow. "The life expectancy of a worker in my company is twelve years younger than the pre-war average."

Galahad watched two drillers toast their waterskins. They chugged the hidden liquid and stumbled out of view. "I see."

"The issue I have found with grog," Vellencourt stared at her workers with motherly disappointment. "Is the fighting. The sickness. A rusted part tarnishes the machine."

My father was always too unpredictable, too wild. Galahad nearly fell for the woman's plan. Then, he tossed his greed aside and let his caution lead. "You need me to refine Oleander leaf? It is simple mortar and pestle work. You could dissolve it in water, though—" he looked at the polluted source and then at Lilian. Reluctantly, he stated. "It is ape work. Anyone could do it."

Lilian stared, "Shall we walk to the hangman together, then?"

The playful buzz of his high again became a drumbeat of panic. Galahad stuttered. "I j-just do not understand why you need *me*."

Vellencourt took several stray strands of her hair and set them where they belonged. She smiled warmly. Galahad was sure that smile had killed many lustful men. He had half a heart to heed it; however, he also had half a mind to murder the woman that wore it.

"This country and I have always had a tenuous relationship. It seems whenever I acquire something shiny, the Castle Rock wants to tarnish it."

Galahad stared at his sooty hands, scratched his muddy hair, and spat out a glob of sticky leaf. He laughed at himself, "And I am shiny?"

"The Rock always takes my toys," Lilian pouted. She bopped his nose. "But I do not share willingly."

Galahad cleared his throat. *Better a well-fed dog than a stray,* his survival instinct said. So beaten by paranoia, his pride did not object.

Vellencourt's fingers flew onto his forearm. Her painted nails scratched his skin. When she reached his palm, she tickled it and then, with a strength her petite hand hid well, shook his hand. "The Rock has outlawed Oleander Leaf but not its products. I want you to refine a new intoxicant for me. Not so potent as to weaken my quarterly earnings, but not so weak as to give my men idle thoughts. I want them in the medium." With her other hand, she pinched Galahad's cheek. "I want a million of you."

Galahad pulled away. *You cannot get comfortable,* he warned himself. *There is betrayal in this.* Galahad sniffled. He would be needing a new mask. His was not nearly as comfortable as he would like and the pollution was leaking through. *I will have to use her in return. When I have the capital, I will show her to toy with me.* He imitated his most servile stutter, "A-a-and w-will I get a p-place to sleep?"

Vellencourt dusted off her top. "Does that routine work often for you?"

Galahad choked. After an unbearable second of shame he would remember for the rest of his life, he nodded.

Vellencourt repositioned her breasts and rolled her neck. "For now, you lodge in the Palisade with my staffers. If you work well, I will give you Hinry's tavern. You'll be the town herbalist. That will be a quaint title to display when those damn inspectors and taxmen come." She walked along the pontoon bridge. When she noticed Galahad was not following, she clicked her tongue. "I would never trade a man for money."

A boat was docking beside the drill rig. The waves from its movement caused the bridge to rock slightly. Galahad's pride had one last quip, "Your husband would disagree."

Vellencourt laughed. She did not cover her mouth. Instead, she held her belly. "Yes, I think he would. Though, *he* was useless and I quite like you."

"That's odd," Galahad remarked. "I am not sure if I hate you."

"I remember thinking the same thing about my hus-" Vellencourt stopped. A little girl was jogging across the bridge toward them. She wore the same outfit as Lilian.

"Miss Vellencourt," the little girl panted. She addressed the woman with perfect posture and an air of formality. "The boring logs from site C are ready for you."

Vellencourt adjusted her shirt and tapped her foot. "Eliza," she growled. "Mommy is busy. Talk to Albert."

Galahad could not help but smile at the scene. He relished the slightest disruption to Vellencourt's bravado. *That unfortunate thing,* he thought, watching the little girl sway hesitantly. Lilian's daughter put her hands behind her back.

"When can we go home?" the girl asked. Her formalities had been replaced with a childish longing.

Galahad pitied the girl. He knew better than the child, arguing with Vellencourt was futile.

"You have to learn the business, Elizabeth." Lilian got onto one knee, reached into her pocket, and pulled out a tube of ointment. She applied a dab to her fingers and rubbed it across the girl's cheek. The redness in her cheeks faded behind a wall of reflective white. "There we are," Lilian smiled. "Off you go."

"Greta was teaching me fine," the girl complained.

Vellencourt got to her feet and glared down at her daughter. "She taught you *well.* Do not argue with a superior, young lady."

"I want to see Greta," her daughter argued, pausing between every word.

"You have not accrued any holiday time," Lilian answered simply. "Now get those logs to Albert before I have to write a reprimand."

The girl hid her face and shuffled off toward the drill rig. Galahad could not tell if the girl was screaming or crying. He licked his lips and blinked at Lilian.

The ever-composed Vellencourt snarled, "Every family loves differently," and stormed past him. "Have Greta fix you a room."

<h1 style="text-align:center">31</h1>

Out of Bounds

Hanna crossed her left hand over her right. She stared at the edges of the sheet. There was something wrong.

"You folded your arms," Arthur chuckled. He let his side of the sheet fall and walked over to her. He took Hanna's hands and unfolded them. He moved her arms toward the right position. He kissed her neck and said softly, "There we go." He went back to his side of the sheet. "Now," he began instructing slowly, his voice tender like one speaking to a child. "Come on up with your side like we are about to have a really wide hug."

Hanna did as he said. It had taken a few days, but Arthur was starting to return to normal. He was acting as sweet as ever to her, speaking in baby-talk often. Hanna did not mind the tone of his voice. It was better than yelling.

"There we are," Arthur encouraged. He took hold of the sheet and folded it one last time. He placed it on the bed and sat down, patting the spot beside him.

Hanna scooted next to him. Her husband wove his head left and right like a snake. "Uh oh," he played. He neared her forehead, paused, and kissed her.

"You've been so sweet today," Hanna noted. She rested her head on his shoulder.

"Well, you deserve it." Arthur put his hand on the back of her head and coursed his fingers through her hair. He rubbed the incision. "I know I haven't been good to you the last few days."

"No," Hanna was quick to say. She waited for Arthur to speak and half a second later, corrected herself. *I don't want him to feel bad.* "You lost all those boys in the woods. You almost lost me. I don't blame you at all."

Arthur held her head tightly. It was almost too tight. Hanna scooted closer to him. He whispered, his voice shaky, "I don't deserve you."

"Nope," Hanna attempted to joke. "You got lucky."

Arthur grunted a laugh.

"What are you going to do today?" Hanna asked.

Her husband groaned. "You know I hate that question."

"S-sorry," Hanna buried her head. "I just wanna talk."

"Well," Arthur bobbed his head and blinked. "What do *you* want to do today?" He did not let her speak and pointed, "See! Hard to answer, huh?"

"Not at all," Hanna told him confidently. She got to her feet and put her arms to her hips. "I want to read."

Arthur's face changed. He did not seem as happy. A moment passed and then he smiled. He stood up and put his arm around Hanna. "I can read to you."

Hanna put her hands behind her back and leaned in, shaking her head. "I remember a certain grumpy boy not liking math."

Arthur blinked. He looked at his feet. "You want to try the encyclopedia again?"

Hanna knew why he was worried. She tried to assure him, "I-I won't get frustrated that time. This time!"

"You don't seem too sure of yourself," Arthur said. He tilted his head. "Isn't there something else you could do? Something easier on your mind?"

"Well," Hanna started to think. *I have to practice or I won't learn. That was how it was the first time. I remember that, at least.* She sighed. *I did make an awful scene last night.* She had been in a perfect mood and went to practice Algebra. *Algebra...* Even thinking the word made her sad. *Why would you put letters in numbers? They are different things.* Hanna winced and glanced at her hands. They were fists. She took a deep breath and suggested, "I could go for a walk?"

"That sounds good," Arthur beamed. He hugged her, kissed her cheek, and guided her out of the bedroom. He held her hand as they went downstairs. He motioned toward the kitchen. Aeric was sitting beside the door installing a new hinge. "Why don't you take him with you?"

"Oh," Hanna pouted. *I would rather be alone. And Aeric is too protective.* "Look at him, Arthur. He's busy. See?" She added, "And he l-loves to work."

Arthur looked at her disapprovingly.

"I could bring the dog?"

Her husband rolled his eyes. "Isabelle is a coward." He shook his head and bit his lip, "Eh, maybe you shouldn't go after all."

Oh Arthur, you sweet dummy. She might have been annoyed if he were not so good-hearted. "I walked these streets for more than a..." She searched for the right word. All the while, she tried to make it seem like her pause was intentional. She did not want Arthur overreacting. She finally said, confidently, "Decade."

Arthur brushed his finger across her eyebrows. "Yes, well..." He traced his finger around her ear. "You aren't yourself now."

Hanna flashed a smile and wrapped her arms around her chest. Arthur took them and kissed both her hands.

"Besides," he looked down at her. "Look at the, uh-" He coughed and pounded his chest. "What the, uh, bounty hunter did." His face changed and he leaned in.

Hanna thought he seemed scared.

"You *sure* it was a bounty hunter?" He asked.

"Uh huh," Hanna nodded. *He said so.*

Arthur stepped back. He let Hanna's hands fall limply to her side. "I don't know-" Arthur twitched, "You don't know what you see anymore." He changed the subject. "Cold out. Don't want you getting the flu in your condition."

Condition. Hanna hated that word. Before she could make her case, though— her husband had gone into the kitchen. "My condition," she repeated. She sniffled. *It is quite cold.* She blinked at the redwood door. Her husband meant well but he could be just as stupid as her. *I may be retarded but my legs work good.*

"Still," Hanna whispered. *I don't want to go against him.* The last thing Arthur needed was for his wife to worry him senseless. Aeric was busy fixing a door hinge. So, she approached Charles. "What'ya doing?"

"I was going to clean the granary."

"Sounds fun," Hanna lied. "Can I help? I need to stretch my legs anyways."

"This could take all day," Charles insisted, pocketing one of his mother's letters. "Besides, you used to like solitary walks, didn't you?"

The question stung. *I don't know.* Hanna nodded, not sure if she was lying. "Arthur, uh, won't—" She could not put the words together. *Breathe, relax. The words will come.* "He don't want me to go any place without..." She shut her eyes and felt the blood humming about her head. "He would get mad if I went outside alone. He won't let me."

"He won't let you?" Charles' face got angry.

Hanna stepped back. *I shouldn't be too pushy. Why do I do this to men?* She felt the dry skin around her fingernails and started scratching it. *I need to work on being more polite.* She didn't want Charles to think she was complaining, or that she was angry with Arthur. "It's just, he gets all annoyed by stuff. I don't wanna stress him out if I can help it. He's always frustrated by this, that, or the other."

Charles snapped off his gloves. He waved his hands frantically, "Not the other!"

Hanna tried her best not to grin. She was being serious. "I mean it-"

"Fine, fine." Charles interrupted. "Forget the granary. Let's go."

The Inner Ring is as quiet as ever, apart from Carolyn's home. Strange people always seemed to be coming and going there. Men with old army uniforms, men in tailored suits, men in fancy hats. Presently, Galahad's accuser was sitting on the porch. Constable Goodwind and several other lawmen were speaking to her. When they saw Charles and Hanna, they quieted.

"Rude," Hanna whispered.

Charles informed her, emphasizing his first word, "*Some* people think the inn is harboring Frederick's killer."

She scoffed. "They can search for Galahad if they want. If Laverne cannot found him, he's gone."

Charles stopped. "Are you sure you want to go out today?"

"I am not a child."

Charles' face was stern, but it was not angry. "I did not say that."

Hanna looked up at him. He stood at least a foot taller than her, maybe more. *He's lucky he has dark skin. It will be harder to see his wrinkles.* She bit her lower lip, grinning. "Then stop being a little killjoy and let's go."

Charles looked her up and down. "Little?"

Hanna raised her brow, inched forward, poked his chest, and repeated, "Little."

Charles stared at her. She stared back. He restrained a smirk. Hanna did not.

"Okay," Charles rolled his eyes. "Where are we going?"

"Want to go to the Anchorage?" She quickly added when Charles began shaking his head, "We can just sit on the cliff. Don't gotta go down."

Charles eyed Carolyn's home. He bobbed his head, "Fewer people that way."

So, they made their way to the most abandoned neighborhood of Auberdine. Hanna wished she got to go there more, but the poor Pale folk that lived on the lake did not like the innkeepers, foreigners, and probably themselves. Hanna and Charles sat by a trickling waterfall. They stared at the houseboat village in the middle of the lake. *I think they were old settlers,* Hanna found herself remembering. She prepared a question for Charles, thinking about the sentence before speaking: *Too proud to go away after their neighborhood flooded, right?*

"Think he did it?" Charles muttered.

"Hm?" Hanna blinked several times. "Galahad?"

"Yeah," Charles nodded.

"Arthur says so," Hanna repeated. "That he always liked fighting."

Her friend turned his head back toward the street and bowed it slightly. "He told me that, too."

"He didn't seem that violent to me," Hanna shrugged. "Troubled. But sweet, too." *What a foolish thing to say of a wanted murderer.* "I probably just can't remember."

"Emilia liked him," Charles shrugged.

A hundred pictures flashed through her mind. Hanna blinked at them all, watching a life in motion. "She did, didn't she?" She gasped. "Yes, he defended her from Frederick's bullying."

"Guess he did too good of a job."

Hanna smacked his shoulder, "Oh, stop that."

Charles grinned. "Don't lie. You are not missing Frederick."

Hanna could feel her whole face warming. "You are *awful.*" She leaned in and hid her smile, "But maybe I am, also."

Charles shook his head, "No. You aren't awful."

Hanna looked at him and suddenly, felt like she did not know him. A burning question took over her brain and without thinking, she asked, "Why don't you have a wife?" When her friend looked at her strangely, she wondered if she had once known the answer. "Sorry," she raised her hands. "I knowed the answer. Just being silly."

Charles' tongue pushed his lower lip forward. He stared at the houseboats as he spoke, "You've heard the names people have for me?"

It was Hanna's turn to look away. She recounted, reluctantly, "Mudpuppy. Goblin. Trogg. Malchance."

Charles began to fidget. He grabbed some nearby pebbles and began tossing them. "You remember what 'Malchance' means?"

Hanna's jaw moved left and right. It did not open. She grabbed a few pebbles for herself.

"I am the son of a rape," he said flatly, like people said those words every day. "Hence, child of malchance. Or just malchance."

Hanna bowed her head. "Oh. Okay. Yeah." She exhaled nervously. "Sorry."

"Don't be," Charles said. When she did not respond, he dropped his handful of stones. He spoke in the calming voice Hanna was used to, "All part of the recovery process. Right?"

"Right," Hanna swallowed. She let go of her own handful and crisscrossed her legs. It was nice to finally be away from the inn. She popped her lips. "Did you ever know him?"

"Who?" Charles asked in his I-do-not-want-to-answer voice.

Hanna stared at him with an empathetic smile. *I may not remember much, but I know when you are playing dumb.* She waited for Charles to drop the act.

He sighed and scratched his neck. "No. My mother never told me who it was."

"Is that why," Hanna felt her cheeks warming. She debated stopping the conversation right there, but she had held her tongue for weeks. Nobody was around to scold her. "Is that why you don't want a wife? Because of him?"

His cheek expanded and deflated like a balloon. "*Want*," he repeated. "What a crude word for an ornate feeling." Charles cleared his throat, dusted off his pants, and turned his back on the conversation. He curled his legs and rested his head between his knees. "Kind of cold."

"Want to go back?" Hanna asked, wondering if she had offended another person. She picked at her cuticles.

Charles ground his teeth.

"I'm sorry," Hanna got up, anticipating another scolding. "I'll just go back."

Before she could take a step, Charles blurted, "When you are like me, you fear you are a burden. No, that's not quite it..." He stood and pocketed his hands. "I thought it was inevitable that I would become him. I'd never met him, but I was sure I would become the same twisted creature. The same monster. That if I let myself, I would commit the same atrocities."

Hanna felt ashamed for bringing the conversation up. With his hands hidden and his head bowed—big, tall Charles looked small and frail. She opened her arms. "Come on," she said, as if the man were her own child.

"No," Charles waved. "We should be getting back."

Hanna's arms fell to her sides. "Offer's on the table. You lump."

Charles responded, defiantly, "I am not a lump."

"Lump," Hanna said, popping the 'p.' She was glad she had not offended him. She rubbed peeled cuticle skin over her lip, wondering what Arthur was up to.

When they got to the hedge, Charles exhaled long and hard and then smiled. "Hot chocolate?"

That sounded good. She nodded excitedly. She grabbed Charles' hands, "We have to get Emilia. She loves sweets!"

He laughed, "Sounds good to me. I'll round up Arthur and Aeric. We'll make it a little dinner party."

A little family dessert. She waved Charles along, "Well hurry up then. I would think those long legs moved faster than a slug!"

They ended the walk by racing up the Hill. By the end, they were both far too tired to move at more than a slight jog. Charles panted, "That is one steep hill."

Hanna agreed. Her legs burned from the climb. A cup of hot chocolate was just what she needed after that. Charles took her hand and helped her up the porch. She was so exhausted, she did not notice the figure sitting on the porch.

"Arthur!" She exclaimed, running up to him. He was taking up two seats. "Scooch over. We're going to have some hot choc—" Hanna saw that she should not be speaking.

Her husband was frozen. His eyes were dark with shadows. When he spoke, his lips barely moved. "Gone for a little walk, have we?"

Charles walked forward. He spoke in an I-am-in-charge voice which Hanna rarely heard. "She wanted some fresh air."

Arthur ignored him. "You went out. Even after I told you not to." His chest rippled and his voice was shaky. "Why do you treat me like this?"

"Y-you," Hanna swallowed. *I had company.* "You said I gots to bring someone."

"I said," Arthur stood up. His eyes were wide and he spoke like one does to a baby, but not kindly. He spat, "You *gots* to bring Aeric. Your son."

"He had b-busy, Arthur," Hanna reminded him. "Charles offered-"

"You sought him out!" Arthur roared.

Birds flew from the branches. Ravens cawed. The grass whispered with the wind. Hanna did not like the silence that followed. She dared not step back from her husband. She could not see Charles and knew it would be bad to look back at him. She heard a floorboard behind her creak.

Charles stepped forward. His I-am-in-charge voice was gone. He sounded like Cora, like a mother trying to reason with her child. "Arthur, what are you saying?"

Hanna knew it was a mistake. *He is going to make things worse.*

Arthur's nostrils flared. "You mistreat me, Hanna. You lied."

"I did not!" Hanna pleaded.

"Deficients are poor liars," Arthur laughed bitterly.

Calm down, Hanna told herself. Her heart was thumping. All three of them were friends. *What has gotten into him?* "I knowed Charles longer than I… knew you. He is my f-f-friend."

Arthur chuckled and his voice got high. "So there it is." He brushed past Hanna and gazed up at Charles. "Explains that smug look of yours."

Smug? Charles had lots of faces, but smug was not one of them. Hanna put a hand on her husband's shoulder. "It was a walk."

He did not look at her. His command was short and stern. "Go inside, Hanna."

She stood her ground. *He's being dumb. Charles is his oldest friend.* Neither man moved. Hanna stood her ground, too. At least, she had intended to. She noticed in that awful calm, two heads poking out from the porch. One was furry, the other had hair like her own. *Oh, Emilia. Why must you always be watching?* Hanna closed her eyes. *A child should not see her parents like this.* She turned her attention away from Emilia and Isabelle, hoping Arthur would not notice them. She was careful with every word as she whispered to the innkeeper. "You risked your life to save this man." Hanna bowed her head and walked through the redwood door.

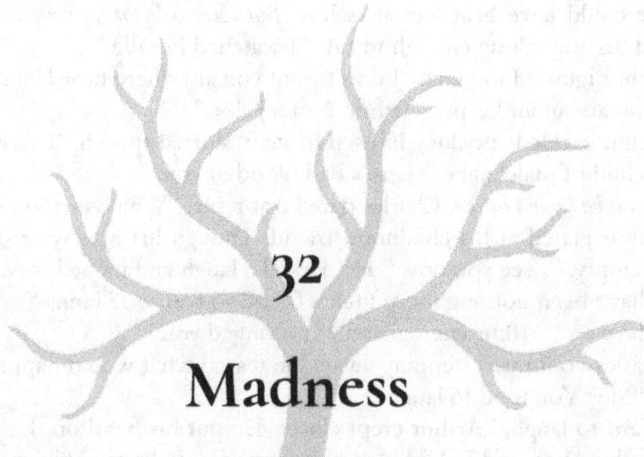

32

Madness

The door shut.

"And what a mistake that was," Arthur murmured. The innkeeper paced from one end of the porch to the other. He was like a shark circling its prey. *Be calm*, Charles told himself. Just as he did so, his fingers formed fists.

At that moment, Arthur froze. He glared down at Auberdine. He spoke happily, like a person recalling a joke. "I've been so irritable lately. Intangibly so." His eyes wandered madly.

Charles did not wish to have an extended conversation with the man. It was no use arguing with Arthur when he was angry. "Evidently."

Arthur pointed toward the sky as if having an epiphany. "And it hit me today. I realized I am your *only* male friend." He tilted his head and blinked at Charles curiously. He inched forward.

Charles stepped back, nearly tripping down the patio stairs.

"The rest are women." Arthur's voice went high, his tone questioning. "I asked myself, *Why is that? He is not like Galahad, and even that one had many male friends.*"

Charles thought the answer a simple one. "I have few friends in general."

Arthur's eyes were dead upon him. His voice was a cold monotone. "And fewer soon, with the way you treat them."

Charles stepped further down the Hill. "The way I treat them?"

Arthur's arms shot upwards. He looked to his sides and bellowed behind barred teeth, rabid as a wolf. "Why does everyone assume I am blind? Do they mistake the innkeeper's hospitality?" He spat, "You've always been jealous. Ever since she chose *me*."

Charles did not mean to laugh. He knew as it was happening that he had made a mistake. He swatted the smile from his face. "I never wanted her. Hanna has always been my friend." He repeated what he had always claimed. "She is too much like my mother."

Arthur simply stared at him.

Charles felt trapped between a truth and a lie.

Wicked wrath crept up the innkeeper's face. He snarled, "The mother whom you claimed to love dearly."

The knuckles in his fists cracked. Hot anger surged up his spine. "Claimed?" Charles could not believe the shriveled man standing atop those steps. He could have yelled. He could have beat him senseless. *But then, he's got no sense to start...* Charles swallowed his anger long enough to say, "I watched her die."

Arthur ignored the fact. "I don't want you anywhere near Hanna."

"You are an innkeeper, Arthur. Not a jailor."

Arthur cackled, mocking himself in swift, slurred speech. "I should never have trusted a child of malchance. There's bad blood in you."

And a bad mind in you, Charles dared not reply. "What is wrong with you?"

Arthur glared at his childhood friend. Though his eyes were on Charles, his stare was empty. "I see you now." He barked a laugh and inched forward.

"I have been nothing more than a friend to you. To Hanna."

"The war," Arthur encroached. "It changed you."

Charles continued stepping away. He feared what would happen if he turned his back. "Me? You used to laugh."

"Hard to laugh," Arthur crept closer. He put his hand on the rail. "We were raised together. You and I. And here you are, trying to be my children's father—"

Someone has to be, Charles' contempt nearly quipped. He took several more steps until he was safely off the stairs.

"My wife's lover," The skin on Arthur's gaunt face rippled as he shook his head. Spit flew from his mouth as he declared, "I know men, Charles." He raised his hand as if he held a decree. "Every man—"

Charles interrupted like a charging bull. His brow was raised. His voice was low. "Every man is not me." He watched the innkeeper's shaking knees as they left the last step. Charles looked anywhere but at his oldest friend, "Walk like a man, talk like a man, act like a man. Why must we be like our forebears?"

Arthur waved his raised fist as if he were a judge or king. "Forebears! Yes. Yours was a thief. A flesh-crazed assailant."

Charles retreated several paces until his back collided with the skeletal cottonwood. The hollow wood reverberated. "Why do you..." He risked a laugh, "You used to fight people that mocked me." Humor proved a mistake.

"And now you mock me," Arthur shuddered as a red hue took over his eyes. The bloodshot veins pulsated and when he spoke, it seemed to Charles he should have been crying. "I have done so much for my family. My friends."

"Nobody denies that," Charles said, as calmly and soothingly as he could. He relaxed his muscles and tried to reason, "You have served your family most of all. But now, you're hurting them. You're hurting yourself."

Emotion left Arthur's face, save for an occasional, sorrowful glance at the dirt below Charles' feet.

Charles took the cue and pointed at the Cottonwood. "You have a good heart, Arthur. I know you miss him."

"Stop it," Arthur whispered. "You don't know anything."

"You are pushing everyone away," Charles pleaded. "We were practically brothers. I would never come between you and Hanna. You know that." He tried once more to lighten the conversation, "I introduced her to you, after all."

Arthur licked his lips. His stomach growled. "Are you proud of yourself for that? Or angry?"

Charles flinched. He ignored the comment, instead saying, "When is the last time you had anything to eat? A good meal will do us both some good."

"Stop it!" Arthur shouted. "I can see past your lies. Your games. You want to roll me over. Why else would you dig two graves?"

"I was grieving," Charles groaned. He could not stop his eyes from rolling. He wished he had.

"No," Arthur rubbed his arms furiously as he started sweating. "I can't believe it. I won't believe it."

"Why not?" Charles raised his hands in surrender.

"I can't believe it," Arthur said again. He approached, took a deep breath, and rushed forward with more strength than the frail figure ought to have had. He pushed Charles backward, "I will not!"

Charles fell, hitting his head on a discarded shovel. The metallic ring echoed for a time until all that could be heard was the innkeeper's troubled breathing. "Get off my shovel," he ordered.

Charles blinked at the tool. He got to his feet and cautiously handed Arthur the rusted shovel. As he did, he realized the freshly upturned dirt around the dead tree.

"Fertilizing," Arthur snapped, although he did not sound angry. He sounded hopeless, scared, and above all—sad.

Charles inhaled suddenly. Now, he understood. "You can't bring it back." He felt an envelope in his back pocket. It was the last one he had taken from the cottage. In a way, he wanted to keep it shut. It would be his last true conversation with Auldwine and his mother. After that, the words would just be memories. "You can't bring him back," he said again.

"Charles," Arthur finally looked at him, not simply through him. His fingers twitched and tapped on the tool's handle. "I promise you." His eyes slammed shut and he swallowed, clearly pained.

"What do you need from me?" he asked. *I cannot treat him the same way I did before the war. He's just like Hanna.* He approached with a delicate tone, "How can I be a better friend to you?"

Arthur's knuckles tightened on the shovel. His head bobbed backward and forward. His lips quivered.

"Hey," Charles smiled. "We're home. You're home. Auldwine may be gone, but—"

"Go."

Had an artillery shell landed beside him, Charles would not have heard it. Had the two mountains suddenly crumbled, Charles would not have seen it. Had he been stabbed, he would not have felt it. "What?" He finally asked.

Arthur shivered. He blinked a dozen times and stomped his feet. He scoured the sides of the Hill fearfully. "Please," Arthur cried. "Just go."

Charles opened his hands like a beggar, "Go where?"

"STOP!" Arthur shouted, but not at Charles. His entire body shook. "STOP!"

"Arthur," he tried. *He needs the Yao.* He tried to intervene between Arthur and whatever ghosts he was seeing, but the innkeeper would not allow it, smacking the soil with his shovel. "Arthur!"

The innkeeper froze. "You." He stabbed the dirt with his spade. "Need to go."

"Where?" Charles questioned again, his blood rushing to his heart.

Arthur Gardner seemed to cower and only half of his face could be seen. One eye looked at his friend. He mouthed, *"Get away from me."*

Whether directed at him or his illusions, Charles did not stay to find out. He turned his back on the innkeeper, his family, and faced the sooty sky of Auberdine. Into the stable he went.

Atlani seemed to know what was on his mind, as she bobbed her head in agreement. Charles rested his head on hers and let several tears fall. "I am sorry," he told the aged animal. "We can both retire after this, I promise." He whispered, "I am sorry." The animal raised its great, silver head. Then, with joints cracking, Atlani laid down.

"No going off on our own," Charles told the animal.

Atlani snorted.

Charles wiped his nose and patted the mare's back. He held onto her neck as the mare slowly lifted them both up. They left the stable. Charles looked up the Hill.

Arthur's silhouette paced around the dead cottonwood.

Charles's chest rose and fell. "Treat her kindly," he said, knowing the innkeeper could not hear him. He clicked his tongue and Atlani trotted through the hedge gate. There were no storm clouds on the horizon, but the sky was brown and ashy. Charles dared not think what omen that entailed. As metal clanged against wood and specks of soot fell onto his face—he felt he was a soldier again.

33
Foul Fog

Galahad stared down the long table at Vellencourt's paupers, puppets, and miscellaneous people. *One-armed impotents, worn whores, and broken spirits all of them. The countess in her castle collects*—he became aware of his drooling and wiped his mouth. He stared at Lilian's women servants, all with whitening powder on their faces. *It is like she seats ghosts at her table.*

Galahad eyed the clock. Though he had broken his rule of using before the evening, he would *not* be breaking his second-most important. *No using until you have come down. The second one is hardly a high if you do not wait.* He suffered his growling stomach and eyed his platter of uneaten food. Meals prepared by Vellencourt's serfs always seemed to be missing something. Galahad had eaten enough breakfasts to know, the eggs were cooked fine. The bacon was crunchy. The potatoes were seasoned well and *not* mushy. Nonetheless, every bite was a fight to keep down.

Presently, Lilian was staring down the long table. Her eyes were fixated on him.

Galahad played his part and bit into some bacon. He wished there was a dog to give his scraps to. *But then again, I am the dog.*

"Cyrus," the boss's voice quieted all conversations. They looked at him and then at Vellencourt. "How is the mechanical grinder working?"

"Very well. The leaves take the finest form I have ever seen."

Lilian smiled sadly. "Good. Raw leaf is illegal in the Rock and I do not want to deal with an inspector's ambitions. Have you done some quality control?"

"It is quality," Galahad replied.

Lilian beamed. "Good. I am sending two of my worst drinkers your way as preliminary studies. Hinry is not to serve them alcohol and their superiors are to monitor their work. Cyrus, do not overindulge them."

She is never one to overindulge, that Lilian. Galahad gave his plate to the nearest serving woman and departed.

The stuffy palisade was replaced by the sooty promenade. Main street was as noxious as ever since the new drilling rig struck oil. At times, Galahad felt as if he were swimming in a viscous fog. Even with a mask, his breathing was slow, his chest was heavy, and his muscles randomly convulsed. Indeed, the first time his body spasmed, he thought it was the new form of Oleander plant he had refined. Yet, all but Vellencourt displayed the same shakiness.

When I get my fortune, Galahad plotted, *I will clean this place up. And Auberdine. I'll show them 'mudpuppy.'* He waved his hand through the haze. He had not yet peaked, he could feel it. The high surged to his brain stem, tickling it like a teasing lover. Then, his nerves tightened, squeezed, and sputtered with sweet bodily sensations. Shapes and smells merged into a behemoth of awareness. His walk was independent of the passage of time. His feet moved independently of space. He walked as the Oleander. He was the mountain.

Drool leaked onto Galahad's pants. He raised his brow at the many stains, wondering which the spittle had made. "I am gonna need to look proper!" He declared. He saluted a logger, trudging into a forest everyone said was haunted. "G'luck, sir."

The logger stared at him as if he were the devil himself. His eyes sank into their sockets as he sped away like a frightful girl.

"Oof," Galahad declared flamboyantly. He made a kissing face and held his belly. A series of thoughts began with a rooster; they ended with a stamp collection. Galahad chewed the air, "That—" he raised his index finger. He exaggerated his every word, "That was the greatest moral achievement of any man. Where now shall my intellect a-spire?" After a pause, he chomped his teeth in a laugh. "Gah gah gah gah!"

Galahad basked, waiting for Vellencourt's minions. He was sure, within only a few months, the entire mountain would feel as he did. A minute feeling of dread accompanied that knowledge, though Galahad refused to acknowledge it. He loved mornings.

Galahad scanned his environment. "Bup," he moved his head. "Bup," he moved it again. "Bup!" He declared, finding a suitable scene to pick apart. The westerly edge of main street was dominated by strange architectural ruins, quite unlike the log and brick structures nearer the Palisade. Greta called them 'garden-homes,' but Galahad found that name laughable.

The garden-homes contained old stone terraces, mossy foundations, and lichen roofs. Withered corn stalks grew in the dirt and debris of fallen foyers. One home had an uprooted berry bush with the skeletons of berries still hanging from its branches. Another had a row of smelly squash swarming with slugs. Most had peach trees, though the only fruits growing were long, messy mosses.

"Lots of spiders in those," Galahad commented.

He watched one of the homeowners as she watered. The bucket in her hand tipped over onto a corn stalk. The water moved like molasses. It came out like a tongue and slowly licked the side of the stalk, before settling like pudding at its base.

I'm not an expert, but that is not water. Galahad rolled his eyes. The woman gardened like one who should be starving. And yet, she was plumper than she had a right to be. She returned to the porch, put down the bucket, and picked up a large, glass bottle containing brown liquid.

Galahad pitied the woman. She had grown more of a husk than any of her corn. *Vellencourt knows their nature too well. It's that one who is the gardener, not this husky whore.* He cleared his throat and spat a glob of sticky spit onto the street.

The woman looked up from her alcohol and, seeing him standing in front of her fence, waved stupidly.

Galahad smiled like a friend and said, as happily as he could stomach, "Good morning!" He bowed his head and muttered to himself, "Stupid creature."

The Oleander Springs was no different than the Overgrowth. The people were famished, the properties were forlorn. The few bunkers of prosperity were nestled near Beauregard's Palisade. Those who lived there were employed exclusively by one woman.

Just then, Galahad decided to deviate from his instructions. "'Cuse me, ma'am." He removed his mask, needing all the friendliness of his face to convince her.

"I didn' mean to invite ya," the woman said gruffly, sheltering her liquor beneath her bosom.

"No need to worry over your liquor. I do not drink." The corner of Galahad's lip twitched into a smile, "In fact, that is why I come. You see, I have a certain stimulant. Works like alcohol but with *none* of the side effects."

The woman glared, unconvinced.

"See here," Galahad took a jar of greenish white powder from his pocket. "Dip your finger in there and give it a sniff."

Slowly, reluctantly, a fat finger dove into the substance.

How easy to market to addicts, Galahad awed. *They've already been bought.* "Now sniff," he encouraged, seeing her staring at her fingertip. *Hurry up, you fucker, this haze isn't a bubble-bath to breathe.* He stifled a cough as he said, "I am Muhali, my good woman. You have my oath on the desert. You shall not come to harm from this herb. Only the opposite."

At the invocation of his race, and the associations the Muhali had with trading, the oafish woman took off her mask and sniffed. She immediately sneezed.

You wasted all of that, you little—Galahad stopped himself. *There's those wide, red eyes.*

"And this don' make me feel sick?" She asked.

Galahad simply grinned.

"H-how much can I buy f-for…" She wiggled a ring from her finger.

How much indeed? Galahad had never considered such an important question. He waved his hand casually, "First purchase is free. Take another dip, ma'am."

"So generous!" The stinking finger plunged once more into his powder.

Galahad then turned and waved, "Name is Cyrus. I will be in front of the fortune-teller's from morning until…" *Give yourself time to relax.* "The early afternoon!"

"Thank you!"

Galahad pivoted, bowed, and before he knew it, a strangeness said, "And to you, a thousand gratitudes."

He sniffled, blinked, and scurried away. *I have never been to Muhal.* He put his mask back on before the pollution overwhelmed him. *I have never said that.* What had gotten into him that he would act like such a caricature?

"Cyrus, son of Marius?"

"Camb—" Galahad stopped himself. He leaned against the fortune-teller's window. "You must be Vellencourt's drillers."

"Andre Levingston," the homeless Redfeather introduced himself, forgetting that he had slept on the same dirt as Galahad only a week before.

"Pleasure," Galahad replied.

"We-a know," Shiungdi scolded the other. "Now. Boss-a say you have new drink."

"Yes," Galahad nodded. "Not a drink, though." He revealed the jar and explained some of the best ways to ingest the herb. "But for now, powder will do." The degenerates dove their greedy fingers into his herb, stretched their masks off, and snorted.

Andre's stomach compressed; he exhaled sharply. Then, again. "Woah. Mo' poten-an-a day's whiskey."

Shiungdi's head began to float like a buoy on his neck. He curled a finger at the jar, stared at Galahad, and then questioned, "This is-a medicine. Hm?" As the words flew from his mouth, however, a fly began buzzing around his head. It pestered the Golden man as if he were the only creature around.

Galahad tilted his head. *An odd symbol for this exchange.* He inspected the sky for grey clouds, cleared his throat of any stray pebbles, and folded his arms.

"Medicine… Or what?" Shiungdi asked again.

Galahad tore his eyes from the fly. He burped, "Just medicine."

Andre pointed at the tavern, "If you at the tavern, I can buy more? Boss said you charge similar prices as Hinry."

That controlling, presumptive bitch. Galahad swallowed an indignant remark and remembered he could have been a dead man hanging by now.

Shiungdi's finger darted into the jar and swiped another swab. Before Galahad could register the theft, he had snorted. The Golden man stood on his toes and shook his head wildly. "F-f-f," he frothed. "Yes. I see you at-a tavern tonight."

Maybe you need to take it slow, Galahad almost said. Instead, a voice resembling his father's croaked, "Whatever you want, sir. Thousand Gratitudes."

Shiungdi and Andre practically skipped to their grimy labor.

Galahad watched them go with apprehension. He peered into his sampling jar morosely, scolding himself for what he had just said. *Thousand gratitudes?* Galahad shivered at an unvoiced thought. He could still hear the buzzing of that damn fly, though he did not know where the sound came from.

He followed the fly's buzzing. *You come down here. I will end your miserable life. Fucking vermin, getting fat on people's leavings…*

Galahad fixed his posture. He stared at the polluted town with its ambling population. He muttered, "I'm not fat." He glanced at his watch, an abominable gift from Vellencourt. *Not even close to the evening…* He had been so very diligent about following his second-most important rule. *I am still coming down.* He repeated aloud for strength, "Just before dinnertime and not a moment sooner."

Still, everyone else was using throughout the day. *But you are better than them,* came his pride. *You are better than him,* added his loathing.

I am not my father, Galahad thought defiantly. His temptation wove its familiar web, distorting the defiance. He stared at the darkened shop of the fortune-teller and told the emptiness within, "It *is* the afternoon." *I had not used at all this mo—*he corrected his praise and his temptation morphed. *I only used once.* It had been several hours. He was practically sober. Besides, he would soon make more money than anyone from Auberdine, his father included. He was a success. *I deserve a reward.*

Like lightning strikes, his finger plunged into the jar. When two tips were coated with powder, he decided his *new* rule would be more forgiving. *You can run this business and have some fun,* he told himself. *Mornings are time for dealings; the afternoons are time for me.*

He snorted all the powder and shook his head madly. "Woah," he moaned. *This might be the best high yet.*

Galahad had not felt very slow or sleepy, but now he knew he must have been. He eyed himself in the fortune teller's window. He tutted his tongue and shook his head at the reflection. "So rustic, so provincial." His clothes were worn, ugly, and lacking. *I must find something more suited to this success.*

The midday sun was heating the road. For some reason, the Oleander was not experiencing a winter. All the inhabitants of the Springs seemed to disregard the anomaly. Endeavoring to fit in, Galahad had not mentioned the sweltering heat. If it were a worthy conversation starter, he would have heard more discussions. So, he ignored the sweat on his brow and jaunted to the tailor.

Automobiles rolled down the road. Galahad looked up at the men and women riding in the steel contraptions. He eyed them as equals and did some quick math. Even with the prices Vellencourt set for his product, he just needed to be patient. *I only need to keep up this level of business for a few months and then... Well, perhaps I will have two automobiles.*

He swung open the tailor's door. A bell rang and an old man appeared from behind a row of suits. White clumps of hair protruded from his ears and nostrils. Breadcrumbs littered his beard and his breath stunk of soup. "Ye' caught me eatin', sir. Apologies f'the mess."

"Apology accepted," Galahad smiled. "How much for one of your suits."

The tailor eyed him and frowned. "Too much f'you, I am sure."

Galahad relished the assumption. He had expected the reply and soaked it in. Then, once the tailor was clearly about to show him the exit, he flashed the money he had earned from selling Cambyses' store.

"Ah," the old man began to cough violently. His back bent and he readjusted his collar. He ushered Galahad to the back of the store and acquired a measuring tape. "Do excuse me. Your garments did not—"

"What is your name?" Galahad interrupted.

"Millhouse, sir," the old man answered. "Millhouse Niemeyer."

Galahad might have burst out laughing, had he not seen another opportunity in the man. His head was abuzz when he played, "Are you a prejudiced man, Niemeyer?"

The old man stuttered an incoherent reply. He was hardly able to hold the measuring tape to Galahad's chest.

"Do not be ashamed, good man. I understand." Galahad chuckled, "But my fellows may not. They tire of your Pale assumptions and may well import their clothing in protest."

"Your fellows?" The tailor whispered.

Galahad rolled his eyes. "My associates!" He exclaimed. "You do not think we Muhali do business alone?"

"O-of course not," the tailor bowed his head.

"Perhaps a discount on one of your fine suits will help me forget this lapse in decency."

The tailor hesitated as they both eyed the same, ornate garment. "I can give you ten percent off."

Galahad patted the tailor's shoulder. "You're a finer man than first impressions betray. May I change into the suit now? It will be good advertising if I walk out sharp."

The wrinkled idiot bobbed his head. "Of course, of course! I have a room just there you can use."

He had never worn a suit before. It took Galahad several minutes to figure out how to button the trousers over his undershirt. Moreover, he had never worn a shirt with so many ruffles. *Why would a designer intentionally make folds in a shirt?* Galahad thought it silly. However, he assumed the flowery pattern was typical of high society.

It reflects prestige, he told himself. Galahad eyed himself in the clean, resplendent mirror. A smile formed on his face as he equipped the final addition, a purple suit jacket. The garment glimmered whenever light bounced off its many silken threads. *There we are,* he winked at the handsome man before him.

Galahad left his old clothes piled in the tailor's dressing room. He left nine marks on top of the dirty rags, thanked the idiot tailor, and strolled out of the store. He folded his hands behind his back and walked down main street. He passed by all the familiar shops, whistled all the tunes he knew, and even tried to have his fortune told. No teller was home and the lights were off.

"Pity," Galahad frowned. The fortune teller was one of few establishments he had yet to visit.

His walk continued aimlessly. He poked his head into stores, peered at their wares, and even played at buying some curiosities. However, he soon became bored. Moreover, his body was alight in the leaf's effects and he felt he was wasting a valuable high.

He thought about another business he had yet to visit—one which frightened and excited him. He thought about whether it was a good idea to make an appearance there, if he was the kind of clientele that was served. He feared he would be mocked or worse. Yet, an unignorable tingle was in his toes. Excitement swelled within him.

Galahad walked casually toward the town brothel. He paced around the entrance several times, making sure nobody was around to see. When he was sure he could escape inside without detection, he darted down a dark corridor. He knocked against the door. A slit opened and two eyes stared at him.

"Business or play?" asked a woman.

"Both?" Galahad responded.

The slit closed and the door opened. An older woman with a bare chest welcomed him. "Hello, darling."

Galahad peered past her for signs of any male workers. He burped, "H-hello."

The woman took his hand and rubbed his fingers, "What might I do for you today."

Galahad pulled his arm away. "D-do you have any men?"

The madame puffed her lips and said, like a mother talking to a baby, "Oh sweet boy. No need to be nervous." She smiled and took his hand once more, "We have your vintage."

Galahad sighed with relief. "I was not sure how you would react to, uh, differing tastes."

"No need to fear," the madame guided him to a back room. They passed walls of bas-relief stonework. Though eroded, Galahad could make out the Wanakhan style. "We accept all types of business."

They crept further down the old mausoleum. Galahad could clearly see the honeycombs in the walls where the dead were once stored. Paintings and tapestries sought to obscure their enclaves. Behind hidden walls, men and women grunted and groaned. Their echoing pleasure made Galahad shiver. *These sounds might well be haunting ghosts. This is not a whorehouse.* The madame guided them to a large chamber. A tomb stood in the center, covered in red tablecloth. Women rolled dice upon it while several men lounged, smoking from a waterpipe.

The madame barked in a Muhali language and three men stood at attention. They were scantily clad with only undergarments on. She turned and asked, "Which pleases you, darling?"

Galahad quickly decided. One man looked far too strong. The other was too small. The third was rather average. "The one on the far left," he pointed. The unimpressive worker stepped forward and the other two went back to smoking. Then, the madame guided them to a room filled with incense and candle sconces. The only piece of furniture was a neatly made bed.

The madame blew a kiss. "I leave you to your play."

Galahad eyed the man. He looked a little younger than Galahad and from the lack of scars on his body, had escaped the war. His hair was neat, his face was cleanshaven. Galahad removed the rest of his clothes and eyed his lower body. *That* was well-kept as well.

Galahad leaned back and gestured at his pants. "Careful not to get them dirty."

The man frowned and said, dumbly, "Not speak good."

Just my luck, Galahad groaned. "Not dirty," he reiterated, wiggling his sleeves as a display. He kicked off his trousers and arced his back. The whore removed his pants. He reached for Galahad's purple suit jacket. "No," he raised his hand. "Keep on."

The whore blinked, nodded, and wrapped his fingers around Galahad's penis. Excitement coursed through him and for a second, he was on the verge of pleasure. Then, familiarity set in. The tugs, pulls, licks, and kisses only stretched his skin. His penis softened.

"If I wanted friction I would have stayed home," Galahad growled. He was glad the room was dark, as he was surely blushing. "Bend over."

The whore knew that phrase. Within moments, he was on all fours and awaiting his client.

Galahad positioned himself behind. He gazed down at the features which usually excited him most. He played with the whore's genitals and his own. He stiffened just enough and quickly placed his penis. He tried to penetrate. He softened.

"Fuck," Galahad swore. He gazed down at the whore with repulsion. *He is nothing. He is boring. I need someone exciting. Someone with charm, who can... who can...* "Any others who can speak?"

"You want speak?" The whore looked back.

"Yes," Galahad muttered. *He was forced into this work, I am sure of it.* He frowned at the young prostitute. His pity turned to annoyance. "Get dressed. I am done."

"You pay madame?"

"Sure," Galahad sighed. He would pay at the very least for wasting their time. He put his trousers back on, not bothering to neatly tuck in his undershirt again.

He strolled out of the bedroom and strutted like a man who had just been satisfied. He wiped his brow and smiled happily at the madame standing in the parlor. "Thank you kindly, madame."

"No luck, then?" she said, knowingly.

"What?" Galahad acted the fool.

"You are not the first man who did not know what the body was saying." She waved her hand dismissively. "Mountain is full of your type. Half a mark for the trouble, please."

Galahad licked his lips, not sure if he felt better from the knowledge or worse. He hastily exited the deathly brothel. As he shambled out of the shadowy corridor, an immense loathing filled him.

I knew the leaf does this to me. Why did I make a fool of myself? He shook his head and spat. *I can't be so weak.* One moment, he had been shopping as a respectable man.

The next, he had lost all willpower and sought only the most carnal feelings. *I must have some control, or I...* His thoughts drifted to their conclusion. He felt ashamed for how high he was, and how bright it had been when he had consumed. *Sure, I waited for the second high, but—but so did Cambyses.*

Feeling akin to his father lit a fire under his feet. Galahad charged into the road, intent to do a good deed. Or, at the very least, to lead a normal life for the rest of the day. He looked to greet the nearest stranger with a 'good afternoon.' He saw nobody on the street. Indeed, he could not see the street.

Instead, the typical blanket of brown had intensified. An oozing fog rolled down the road. The town was cloaked in a smog. Sulfurous scents filled the air. Galahad grunted his annoyance and tightened his mask. The thin cloth barely helped. He wrapped his arm around his chest, clenched his shoulder, and buried his nose between his forearm and his bicep.

Galahad hoped the dirty air did not stain his new suit. He joined the many others on the road, their faces buried in their arms or hidden behind masks. The town waded through the thick haze. Visibility was poor; they all squinted and groped their surroundings. Doors opened and were quickly shut as people hurried home.

The smoke burned Galahad's eyes. They began to water and blur his vision. He wiped the tears. The soot from his jacket dragged across his face. The urge to itch became like a balloon growing larger and larger. Finally, Galahad could not bear the sensation. Not wanting to put more pollutants through his pupils, he smooshed his forearm against his eyes and rolled his head. For a moment, Galahad forgot about the groping smog all around him. He rubbed his eyes and groaned as the searing itch was whittled away.

His eyes opened. Galahad peered through the haze. He tilted his head. A little girl stood in the middle of the dirt road. She made no effort to hide her face. Indeed, she was starting to cough. Galahad waited. The child swayed and gagged on the air. Still, she did not move. The little girl planted her feet and opened her mouth wide. She inhaled a great amount of haze, held it, and fell to the ground. Her limbs twitched as she heaved and hacked.

Galahad leapt forward. He swept his arms under the child. He lifted her while she violently kicked. She thwacked his chin, though he did not feel the pain. His head swiveled in every direction. He could barely see the outline of the tavern to his left. He barreled forward and practically threw the child indoors.

Her convulsions took a minute to stop. When she regained control of her muscles, The girl's face became bewildered. She stared up at her savior with a mixture of awe and fear. Dry, white flakes fell from her dirty face. Galahad gasped. *Vellencourt's daughter?*

He whispered annoyedly, "What the hell were you thinking?" His fists were shaking.

The girl turned her cheek, unable to look at Galahad. A tear fell from her face, soaking her whitening powder and turning her skin a muddied grey. "You weren't supposed to be there," she sniffled.

"You could have suffocated!" Galahad yelled.

The little girl cowered behind her hands. She could hardly speak. Her body was shaking as if from a personal earthquake. "I was t—trying..." She paused, gulped, and whispered. "I was sad." She shook her head. Spit and tears flew in every direction.

Galahad growled, "What does a child know of sadness?" He scoffed. *This little cretin has more privileges than anyone. Little ignorant shit.* "Your mother is walking gold. You can have anything you want."

Elizabeth Vellencourt's face shriveled into a hundred wrinkles. The whitening powder on her face dripped down onto the dirt. She shrieked, pointing at the puddle of tears and chemicals at her feet, "She won't even let me call her MOM!" She held her chest, shivering. As quiet as a mouse, she added, "She *hates* that word." Her tears came coursing back and she cried, "Everything is worse since daddy died."

Galahad found her sadness revolting. "Your mother has more money than everyone else in this town combined." He analyzed her immaculate dress, torn and frayed by her fall. Her makeup had irritated her skin, covering it in sores. Galahad turned, unwilling to give her any pity.

"She never uses it!" Eliza pleaded. "At least, not for fun."

"No?" Galahad inquired.

"She w-won't even give me an allowance." She glared, "Every child gets an allowance! It's the rule!"

"Not quite," Galahad rolled his eyes. He had only been allotted weekly beatings.

"I have to," she altered her voice to one of mockery, "*Work or starve.*" She ripped the sleeves from her dress. "She wants me to be just like her. In every way. Even the bad ones."

Galahad cleared his throat. He was starting to pity the creature. As much as he would have liked to hate her as he did her mother, he did not like hearing a child cry. It sounded too familiar. He rubbed his cheek. "I uh," he cleared his throat again and began playing with a lock of hair. "I hated my father..." *And I killed him,* Galahad almost said. He checked himself at the last moment. He admitted, as honestly as he could bear, "And hating him has been the worst thing I have ever done."

Eliza wiped her tears and asked, carefully, "Because he was good after all?" Her question was full of disbelief.

"Oh no," Galahad answered frankly. "He was a piece of shit."

The little girl giggled.

Galahad ignored the fact Eliza's giggle was the very same as her mother's. He sighed, "You hate someone or something long enough, you just end up hating yourself."

Eliza scrunched up her face, biting back bitterly, "I wanted her to feel guilty."

"She will," Galahad told her. "Or, uh, would..." He took a deep breath. "Point is, if you can stomach it." He paused, wincing. "Just let it go."

The little girl spoke with an air of innocence, "Then what?"

Galahad shrugged. He looked at Eliza out of the corner of his eye, "A lot of little children have little to nothing to eat. Nowhere to sleep. I would start by thanking your mother."

Eliza sucked in her top lip and she nodded mournfully.

"Let's get you up," Galahad sighed. He strapped his mask to her face and shepherded the little girl through the haze.

34

Fertilizer

When Charles left, things changed. Whenever her husband spoke to her, Hanna wondered if there was a second meaning to what he said. Or perhaps she was overthinking everything. Arthur did say women tend to overthink. *Or maybe I underthink?* Arthur always had to explain things twice and repeat things. *I would be frustrated if I had to live with me, too.*

Hanna could not be sure. That was the problem. *I thought I was getting better. I could speak okay.* Now, it was like everything before her husband's return was a dream. Each morning felt like her first day after the surgery. She was close to giving up math for good. If she could give up speaking, she would do that, too. It was all so hard. She would think of a word, lose it, and say some other word instead. Or, her mouth started twitching and said nothing at all. It did not help that she was so aware. Hanna could see the faces change when she started to stutter. That only made it worse. Some faces felt sorry for her. Most probably wished she would just get to the point.

"Stop it!" She hissed at herself. She refused to spend yet another day feeling sorry for Charles or herself. He wanted to go home and she needed to get better. "Now, where are you?" She asked the unfamiliar study. Her books were scattered, her compass was missing, and no matter where she looked— the encyclopedia mathematica was missing. She had checked her bedroom, she had searched the stables. Now, she was rummaging through her old office for the second time. She opened the drawers to her desk. Nothing. After a second, she mistrusted her eyes and opened the drawers a second time.

"Hanna," her husband said, leaning against the doorway. "I threw it out."

She stopped. "What..." She shot a gust of air up her face and tossed some hair behind her head. She asked, casually, "Why?"

Arthur frowned a smile. He went to embrace. Instead of hugging her, however, he ushered her out of the office. "I want to turn the room into a nursery."

Hanna did not understand. "We have kids."

Arthur held his belly as he chuckled. "Can't have too many. I love kids."

Well that is nice to hear. Maybe he will start spending time with Emilia. She blinked and remembered how their conversation had started. "I want to t-teach the kids ma—"

Arthur put his hands on her shoulders. "Don't get worked up." He kissed her cheek and told her, lovingly, "You struggle when you are under stress. Let me help."

"I want you to," Hanna admitted.

Arthur pecked his head forward and smiled. "Then let me, okay?" He took her hand and massaged it, "I am the only one that really knows you."

Then you would let me know math, Hanna instantly thought. "I know," said the innkeeper's wife. She was pulled closer to the man. Lips touched hers. She smiled and pecked Arthur on the cheek.

The innkeeper wrapped his arms around her and guided her to their bedroom, "Is it okay that I defend you?"

Hanna thought he sounded sad. She nodded, though she added, hesitantly, "B-but you scare me when you shout."

"I..." Arthur trailed off. He folded his hands around his belly and stared at the ceiling. "I get so angry." He glanced at Hanna and smiled weakly, "It's like a revolving door of irritation. One slight just echoes and echoes until I am seething. I can't forget anything."

Well since he is being honest, Hanna gulped. "I get afraid and I don't know w-what to do for you. Or how to help."

Arthur chuckled hoarsely. "I don't know what to do or how to help, either." His voice cracked like he was crying, but only for a second. "I used to get in so many fights."

Hanna massaged his arm and took his hand. She had to ask. If she did not, she would question what she did and did not know forever. "What did Charles do?" Hanna asked in her just-a-caring-wife voice.

Arthur glared, but only for a moment. He closed his eyes, leaned in, and kissed her forehead. "Women are simpler creatures. More innocent." He paced around the bedroom, his hands behind his back. "Men are brutes. We steal, lie, and lay." He started fidgeting with his fingers, "Me especially." He tapered off before quickly adding, "Which means I know men. I know the tricks of the trade, so to speak."

"I loved Eastmont like a brother," the innkeeper went on, shaking his head. "When I returned..." His nostrils twitched and Arthur slammed his fist down onto the sheets. His jaw hardly moved when he said, "From trying to save him."

Hanna was paralyzed. She waited for some sign that it was okay for her to speak. It took a few seething breaths for her husband to finally look at her. Seeing her fear, Arthur frowned. His face filled with guilt. "He was taking advantage of you, Hanna. He saw a woman without the ability to say no."

Hanna did not agree. She risked saying so. "H-he seemed normal to me."

Arthur smiled, "Of course he did, darling." He arced his head and reminded her, "But you could not remember before the surgery. He took advantage of having a fresh start with you."

What an awful thought. The realization made her shiver. Had Charles really tried to lure her? "I never thought of that," she whispered. "So, he was lying to me?"

Arthur nodded. Hanna saw how hard it was to talk about a man he once loved. "He was hoping I had died, I think. He wanted my family and my inn for himself."

Hanna squinted. "Arthur... P-please explain. Because I am," She laughed anxiously, "just too slow to understand this." She recalled foggy memories. "Charles used to f-flinch when we—you and me—kissed. W-when anybody kissed. He never h-had a lover. I think."

Arthur did not reply for a time. After some moments, he closed his eyes, unable to look at his wife. "He did flinch when we kissed. I am sorry, my sweet thing—but you misremember the facts. He wanted you as a lover from the moment he saw you."

Hanna massaged her wrists. The conversation made her feel too many emotions at once. She was horrified by the secrecy of it all. She also felt guilty. If Charles had loved her and he was casted out because of his love... *Isn't his bad luck my fault?* Hanna thought the blame belonged to her. Still, she wondered about the man's intentions. "I hate this, Arthur." She held her head and braced for a headache that never came. "I just want to be sure. I want to be—" she searched for the words, "normal again."

Arthur outstretched his arms, "Sshhh," he soothed. "You will be. I'll make sure of it."

Ruff, Ruff, Grrrrrr!

The innkeeper revoked his hug. His tone reverted to the grim, monotone one. He glided to the window and glared down.

Ruff, Ruff, Grrrrrr! Came Isabelle's playful noises.

"That beast makes too much noise," Arthur muttered. "Emilia needs to take it on more walks, I—"

Hanna blinked. There were two reasons her husband had cut himself off. *Has he realized he has not acknowledged or spoken to his daughter in weeks?* Hanna gulped. *Or has he seen something upsetting?* Her answer came quickly in the form of stomping boots. She dared not deter him as he left. When he was gone, she went to the window, hoping Emilia would hold her tongue.

Isabelle's hind legs stretched into the air, her front paws were digging around the dead Cottonwood. Many barren patches of dirt lined the tree, and Hanna knew Arthur would not like uneven soil. *She is going to track in so much unwanted mud.*

Emilia was squatting beside her furry friend when her father stormed out. His yell was a faint grumble from her high-up window. Hanna worried for her daughter. She did not have the same mannerisms as her mother. *If she talks back, that hound is going to get hurt.* She hurried down the stairs. As she crossed the tavern, she made sure to loudly say hello to as many patrons as she could. *Please don't hear him, please don't hear him, please don—*

"Misses Gardner," a voice squeaked.

"Evelyn?" Hanna asked. She talked over her husband's nearby tantrum, hoping nobody would hear him if she was loud. "Why are you out and about?"

"I've told you brats not to play by this tree," droned the innkeeper's lesson. *"If I see that dog digging here. I will turn it into glue."*

Evelyn took tiny steps. She walked hesitantly, as if afraid of landing on a nail. As she neared, Hanna realized that her son, Wilhelm, was hiding behind his mother. They both wore black. Evelyn had a pink bow in her hair, but that had gotten dirty. When the widow reached Hanna, she froze. Her eyes went left and right and toward her feet. Her lips wiggled with unsaid words. *Is this what I look like when I talk?* Hanna found herself wondering.

"I," Evelyn squeaked. She clenched her son's hand and pulled him beside her. "I just want to apologize for my sister."

Hanna's heart welled. Everyone was worried about Frederick's disappearance. Hanna was especially worried about the boy's mother. Carolyn had stirred up quite a lot of anger among the Inner Ring.

"She has been cruel," Evelyn added, insecurely.

"It is just a dead tree. Just dirt. Mama would let us play."

Hanna had the urge to offer her a cup of coffee. When Emilia's upset words entered her ears, she answered distractedly. "You are too sweet—"

A deep voice rumbled from the corner of the tavern. "You did no wrong." Laverne had her hands at her hips. She swayed toward them. The rest of the guests acted as if their conversations were too important to interrupt, but Hanna saw their eyes drifting over to the three women. "'Cept maybe by bein' too complacent."

Evelyn started to bow. "Galahad did not—"

Laverne roared over her. She did not sound angry. She did not sound friendly. She sounded prideful. She sounded meek. Her voice cracked. Her voice carried. Hanna's skin got goosebumps. "Your apology ain't nothin' to me. All it do is fix your guilty conscience."

Evelyn looked at Wilhelm. "I do feel guilty," she whispered. "My husband hurt me when he was alive. I'm sure you knew that." Wilhelm squirmed uncomfortably. Evelyn's voice grew a little stronger and she looked up at Laverne for a moment. "But, I don't know if I would have survived that man if the whole world made assumptions of me. If it treated me like Gerald did."

Laverne stared at the Pale woman. "And how Gerald treat ya, hm?"

Evelyn bowed her head again. "That..." She wiped her hands against her dress as if they were dirty. "Like I was beneath him. L-like I was insolent for having my own opinion."

Hanna swallowed. The argument between her husband and Emilia seemed over. The one between Laverne and Evelyn seemed just beginning. *Arthur will not like this conversation.* She wished the ladies would find somewhere else to talk.

Laverne barked a quick laugh. "So you think you's a mudpuppy, do ya?"

Wilhelm whispered, "Let's go, mama."

"Hush, child," Evelyn snapped. She folded her fingers and stood up straight.

Laverne remained like a stone tower. Her hands were fixed to her hip. Her head was tilted toward her shoulders and her nose was wrinkled.

Evelyn's tongue pushed against her cheek. After a moment, she admitted, "A little. Yeah."

Laverne squinted. "Sayin' ya suffered, too..." She paused and took a deep breath. "That don't comfort me." She pointed, "It shouldn't comfort you, neither." She hummed to herself and shook her head. She went on, "Sure don't atone for yo' sister and it—" she bit down on her words. "Damn sure don't make that boy free."

The tavern stared at her. Laverne sniffled. She wiped a tear from her cheek. Hanna had never seen a woman cry with so much dignity before. She clearly had a few bad words loaded into her lungs. When she sighed, they disappeared. Laverne swatted lazily at the floor, shook her head, and sat back down. Evelyn licked her lips, rubbed her forearms, and quickly trotted away.

The tavern received a second of silence. Then, the redwood door slammed shut. Arthur was panting and Emilia was nowhere to be seen. Hanna thought of a way to ask what had happened. *I should slap you for talking to her like that*, Hanna wished. The innkeeper's wife intentionally fumbled, not wanting to sound aggressive. "W—"

Her son came from the shadows and spoke over her. "Isabelle digging up that fertilizer you put in?" He shot a look at his mother. It was the same warning look she gave to calm *him* down.

What a lot of nerve, mothering me, she might have smiled. "You fertilized a dead tree?" Hanna said flatly. She would not spare her husband's mood where her baby girl was concerned. *I may be dumb, but I'm a mom, too.*

"Shut up," Arthur snarled. He shoved past his wife and disappeared into the kitchens.

Hanna stared blankly, unsure of what bad emotion to feel. *So much for kind words and kisses.*

Her son nudged her with his shoulder. His hands were full of empty mousetraps.

"Hi," Hanna gave her son her best smile. She rubbed his back and to her surprise, there was no boyish flinch from her embrace. In fact, he pocketed his traps and hugged her.

"This isn't like my l-little, soldier," she joked.

Aeric pulled away, slowly. He looked out the east window and admitted, "Only kids *want* to be soldiers."

Hanna heard the words and should have danced. "Oh, what I would have done to hear that during the war." She hugged him again. "What is this about fertilizer?"

"Dad was burying old meat around uncle's tree. Said it was a Golden River fertilizing technique."

Hanna did not think you could revive a dead tree with spoiled meat. "Maybe he learned it from Charles?"

Aeric's face smooshed into an expression of doubt. "Dad's not a gardener." He swallowed, disturbed by something, "I am going to put some mousetraps around the granary. It smells awful."

Hanna nodded, eyes fixed on the kitchen. She could hear her husband slamming cupboards shut. Pots and pans clanged. *Oh, Arthur Gardener,* she shook her head. *You cannot cook all your problems away.*

35

Pyrewood

An oozing feeling crept up his back as if worms were wriggling within him. He squirmed. *Are his accusations true?* His heartbeat quickened. Charles could not deny that he did love Hanna, though not in the crude ways Arthur accused him of. *At least, I do not think so.* He wondered if he was blind to his own feelings.

'*Your only friends are women,*' Arthur's voice echoed in his mind.

Charles shook his head. He recalled his response, that he had few friends. He remained discontent and another thought quickly overwhelmed him.

You have few friends, but you gravitate toward women.

Women, Charles reminded his anxiety. *Not just Hanna.* He preferred female friends. He had never thought to question the habit. Now, it seemed a quirk bordering on perversion.

Charles argued against his insecurity, *It is not perverse.* He walked through his thoughts, reintroducing them to his actions.

I was raised by a woman. It seemed obvious that this would make him friendlier with females, more able to strike up conversations with them.

But I was not raised in isolation. I had Auldwine. This realization stumped him and Charles paused for a long while. Finally, he explained to himself. *Auldwine was not like other men. He was a gentler, more thoughtful sort. And then, there was his brother.* Charles rolled his eyes, angrily. *Arthur really thinks we were having an*—He released an uncomfortable snort and choked on his breath. He thought of his faceless father.

"If lust makes a man, call me a toad," he scoffed. Charles glanced at his lap. He eyed the crease in his trousers like one reading a foreign language. He squinted and tried his very best to think an awful thought about Hanna. He pictured her naked body, her breasts. Several convulsions crept up his body and he writhed in a painless agony. "No, No, no," he said, disgusted.

Charles sat there, panting. *This should not be hard for me.* His heart raced and a feeling of irrevocable guilt filled his chest. He did not blame Arthur for his mistrust. *All men feel lust. All men seek pleasure.* Charles swallowed. *But not me. I am a child of malchance. I am my own creature...* He breathed in and a depressed wave plummeted into his lungs. He let out a quiet, "Ribbit."

Atlani sniffed the air. Her ears were forward. Alert.

He quieted his thoughts. Charles was not taking any chances. With one hand on the reins, he readied a pistol.

Atlani's ears began to swivel madly. Anxious.

Charles scanned their surroundings. The trip had been more than uneventful. The eastern way was devoid of elk, deer, bear, cougar, and even wolf. The only howl he had heard was on his first night, and that must have been in the Overgrowth. The lack of animals only made him more wary, however.

Atlani stopped and raised her head. Aware.

Charles clenched the reins and watched his mare's next action. What the horse did next was critical. He whispered soothingly, "Hey, big girl. Don't you worry."

Atlani spread her front legs. She leaned back slightly. Afraid.

"Hey, hey," Charles intervened, foregoing his reins for a tender touch of the mare's mane. "No need to run. We are almost home." He cooed, "See that? Ash and spruce are all intertwined. Means we're almost at the cottage. You remember the cottage, right?"

Atlani stomped and snorted. Annoyed.

Charles relaxed and took the reins. He chuckled, "Okay, take your time. See what you need to see."

Despite not eating, Atlani was chewing. The mare cocked one eye back at Charles. To him, it seemed the animal was asking forgiveness. When the mare bowed her head and slowly trotted forward, Charles felt she regretted where next she took him.

Charles stretched his neck. Anxious.

They passed under ash and spruce. A lone gust blew. A stream of aspen leaves flowed with the wind. The babbling brook was muted by a thick layer of ice. Atop the eastern peak, a large boulder broke from its ancient spot. It crashed down the slope, singing a deep dirge as it went. When it finally stopped, the mountain of riddles rumbled. The quaking aspens quivered. The sky was dark, though not from the night.

Then, Charles saw.

Cold ash dusted the ground where his mother's home once stood. The door was singed off, open forever. The roof was the sky. Columns and archways of reinforced stone were all that remained of his home. A chipmunk saw the new arrivals and darted out of view, crawling up the splintered remnants of Charles' armoire.

Another boulder tumbled down the mountain of riddles, singing its dirge as it plummeted into ice.

Charles smoldered. Without thinking of his safety, he leapt from Atlani and charged into the ruin. *What has happened to you?* He asked the wreckage. He passed the grave of his mother. While her stone was still erect, the one he had made from himself was toppled. *Arthur…*

Charles' eyelids twitched as he stared at what remained of his past. He shut his eyes and clawed his forehead. He breathed in, letting a mélange of emotion pool in his lungs. His eyes burst open. He stomped the stone meant for himself. "You god damned—"

His eyes read his mother's initials, now carbonized in black. He melted to the ground. His rage became guilt, his guilt became regret, and the regret became sorrow. He hugged the tarnished stone and begged his mother, "Don't be mad at me, mama. Please don't be mad." He had the urge to bang his head against the stone but stopped when he felt it would disturb his mother further. Instead, he stood up and promised frantically, "I can rebuild this. You'll see mama. The same r-red…" Charles' wavered and wept.

His sorrow became rage.

"If those damned wolves had never come upon Arthur," Charles clenched his jaw, recreating the scene from infernal scraps. *Yes. Arthur said they were attacked not long after finding the stones… The wolves must have cornered them. Maybe one of the younger men threw their lantern. That would explain the ruins…* Charles moved from grave to garden. The fertile, silty soil had a grey layer atop it. He scanned the dirt for pawprints, hoping to find the direction the strange wolves went. *I will kill every one of those beasts, even if I must break that damned croft apart.* He saw several animal tracks, but they were mostly small game.

Charles passed over where a wall once stood. He gazed at the cluttered piles of debris which he had so wanted to leave in peace. Now, his mother's memory was truly erased. Her notes, her letters to Auldwine, her poetry books, her entire life—all gone.

"How did it happen?" He asked the devastation, speaking as if it were a witness. Something else had happened here which Arthur's story could not account for.

Charles placed his hand onto the waste, staining his hand with the grey powder of his mother's ashen letters. *All gone,* he frowned. *She's truly gone.* Charles braced his knees and stood slowly. As he moved, he heard a ruffle amongst the silence. It came from his back pocket.

At once, he let out a series of short, elated sniffles. His heart slowed and he pulled an envelope from his back pocket. *A letter.* It was the last of the set he had taken with him to Auberdine. He looked westward, realizing Arthur may well have destroyed the other letters he had left. *I hope Hanna can save those…* He stared at the dirty envelope, thankful at least to have one family memento.

He set to read it but was suddenly overcome by a stench. It was a familiar, fetid aroma that made Charles instantly think of the sunken glade. *A wolf and its prey had died there, too.* Charles marched out of the razed structure and pointed a commanding finger at Atlani. "You hear anything, run to me. Otherwise, you will likely die."

Atlani chewed the air, thoughtfully.

Charles followed the source of the smell. The western mountain's shadow stretched out. Dusk was approaching and there would be no warm bed tonight. *There will be no rest for many nights ahead,* Charles prepared himself. He left the burn scar and waded through a sea of frozen cattails until he found what he was looking for. A body, submerged in the frozen stream. Its hands held the arms of a weeping willow.

Charles knelt beside the body and realized the face had belonged to Momed. Charles sighed. *I lost a house—but you lost your life.* He kissed his thumb and pressed it against the willow. "The Wanakha believed it was good fortune to die underneath a tree."

He pulled the corpse from its icy tomb and laid it on the sandy embankment. Charles was struck immediately by a dismembered limb, a missing foot. *Now that's uncharacteristic of wolf feeding.* Indeed, aside from the missing foot, the boy was utterly unravaged. Charles squinted, wondering what hungry predator would choose such a meager trophy.

Charles frowned. *Does this new wolf hunt for sport?* Charles strained, sitting Momed with his back against a mighty lodgepole pine. "I cannot bury you, but this tree," he pointed at the towering goliath. "This was once considered a royal tomb for the Wanakha. Perhaps, if they are right—you will be reborn amongst giants."

Charles wondered if the other bodies were nearby. *I need more information. What were these wolves up to? Why do they behave so strangely?* He frowned at Momed and, recognizing the callousness of his thoughts, said aloud, "I'll give them a proper funeral."

Despite his search, though, Charles found no other bodies. *That would explain why Momed was left alone. Why pluck him from the ice if other bodies were easier pickings?* He sat beside his toppled headstone and grunted at the initials. Then, he retrieved the envelope from his pocket. He unfolded the oily edges and gasped. There were two letters stuffed together. A stray tear trickled down his cheek as the moon rose over the Oleander. The first letter was clearly from Auldwine, as the army paper showed; however, his mother had annotated it. Her comment, written on the top of the page, read: "*Auldwine's last words.*" Charles swallowed.

Cora,

The war has now gone on so long, the dreaded day has come. Arthur has joined me at the front. He came joking, but I fear his humor will not survive this Tanglewood. We talk often about home, of the inn, of hunting together, and of little Aeric and Emilia. Do you know—I have never seen my brother so saddened as when he spoke of leaving his children?

I saw him kill his first man. The change that washed over him in that instant... One should never see that pain etched onto a brother's face. He joked about it later, but I know it scarred him. Yesterday, I told Arthur if I die, I want my bones brought back home. I don't want to feed these worms and rats. I want to be buried under my tree. The one you said that died...

Nobody talks to me anymore. I suppose I understand. At home, I am the innkeeper, a friend. Here, I am their leader. The one who must shoot them for cowardice. The one who orders them to die. They cannot talk to me as they once did, not even poor Arthur. I understand.

At the same time, I wonder if this war has created a casualty of my character. I cannot lie, Cora. I am angry and slow to forgive—especially myself. I still care for my men, even the enemy's men... I just can't bring myself to show it. It is like the slightest affection or happiness is the heaviest burden. It has become routine to be irritable. I cannot break from the habit.

I worry for you and Hanna, for my niece and nephew. It is to you we soldiers give a ruined world. Once we are all shot and dead, it will be you who shall inherit this Tanglewood.

Bah! Damn this despair. I am not dead yet and I will not act as if I am. If we are all to live in Tanglewood, so be it! Trenches are cold and wet but at least you cannot get a sunburn.

My time is up. I have only a few minutes before I lead a sortie over the line. Have to take some useless village from the Muhali.

I love you, Cora. I wish I had said it more when I was still around. I look back on all the times I could have told you and did not, the little goodbyes and the late nights, the mundane mornings and the boring afternoons. I should have said I loved you like they were the only words I knew. When I return, I will devote myself to those words. I will give up the inn and join you at your cottage. I should have done so years ago. I should have left it all the second you told me you were cold at night.

I am sure Hanna would take over if you asked her. She's smarter than me, at least. Will you bring it up, the next time you two visit? If she will not keep it, don't pressure her. It is a big responsibility, but she has managed thus far, has she not? And that would not prick my brother's pride too much, I think. Oh Arthur... He needs a long rest and a quiet retirement. I am sure the weight of keeping the inn would kill him.

Should Hanna refuse the position, maybe Charles would take over? Arthur would be fine with his childhood friend running things. After all, he joked about it when they were children.

It is time. I must go.

Love,
Auldwine Gardner

Charles reread the letter, as well as his mother's annotations. He could feel her rage in those little quips of, "You are damned right, love-lost moron, oaf..." He also read her pain in the stains across the page, where her tears had fallen. He folded the letter and took the second. He hoped this was his mother's reply, that some soothing words had reached Auldwine before he died. Yet, he quickly realized that the letter was not written by Cora Eastmont. The paper was also army-issued. The penmanship was familiar, but not his mother's.

Cora,

By now, that damned quartermaster has told you about Auldwine. He has shared his indifferent words of sympathy and delivered his belongings. But he has shared only half-truths. You deserve the full truth, as it will be you who is left alone by my brother's passing. So, I will share just this once what is unfolding at the front.

On our sortie, a shell landed directly on us. Many men were obliterated, their skin sheared away, their bones cooked off. No remains. Auldwine was among them, but he was not destroyed.

Now, understand—Auldwine and I made a pact. We promised one another we both would come home—regardless of our fates. If one of us died, we swore to bring the other back.

Understand also that the Tanglewood is worse than letters, newspapers, and the like are permitted to describe. This letter alone is contraband. But I will not lie to you, just as I will not break a brother's bond.

I have his foot in my pack. It is all that remains of Auldwine. I will spare you the details, as I can hardly bear them myself. Even thinking about my grim duty is enough to shake my wits and get my men killed. Yes. My men. I have inherited my brother's responsibilities, of which feeding starving men is now the most pressing. My men are mutinous, Cora. The whole front is bordering on anarchy. I had to lie. To them, the quartermaster, the captains.

The Muhali dreadnoughts have cut off our shipping. We have no rations, Cora. I cannot let anyone know how many calories I carry. Even if the flesh belonged to a beloved man... hunger blinds honor. The sanctity of the dead no longer applies to soldiers. If a man dies, his meat belongs to the regiment. But I have hidden him, our Auldwine. I will sooner die than let these heathen soldiers boil his bones in carrion soup. Let this demented army starve, as far as I am concerned.

I am sorry for telling you all this. It is in part so that you may know: Auldwine *will* come home. He will have his grave. I will survive this war no matter the cost. I am bringing my brother back and he will have his Wanakhan burial. Though, he will need no great tree to lay beneath. He was already a giant. The best of men.

Bound by one we love,
Arthur Gardner

A sentence echoed in his mind. *"I have his foot in my pack."* The muscles in Charles' chest tightened. He folded the two letters without blinking, neatly tucked them back in their envelope, and pocketed the documents. He stood and approached Momed's lifeless body. Charles turned his head curiously, examining the corpse's severed ankle. The cut was clean, made by a knife. The tightness in his chest grew, causing his body to vibrate with adrenaline, dread, and something else. He searched the body for any toothmarks, stray blood, or strangulation. He followed the coagulated blood up the stomach, toward the left breast, and without thinking—tore Momed's clothes. Frozen chunks of flesh broke from the cloth, revealing a small hole in the skin, only millimeters in diameter.

The tension in his body released. Charles staggered to his feet and fell onto his back. He skittered away from the glimmering corpse. There had been no wolf attack. Momed was shot.

As Charles processed the horrible facts—recalling shovels, freshly dug dirt, and a dead tree— Atlani walked toward him, waiting for the man to look at her. When he did, chilled tears wetting his cheeks, she gestured to the west.

Charles wiped his eyes. He looked at the sun setting behind the Oleander. That shadow stretched far into the heart of Cottonwood. The tip of darkness stabbed into Auberdine and when the light finally faded, a distant wolf howled.

36

Tongue Bite

The pestle rolled around the mortar. The driest part of the leaf broke apart into smaller clumps. The wet stem smeared the powder into a type of paste, gluing the choicest powder to the pestle. The tool rose toward a careful nostril. It savored an inhale and exhaled with delight. The morning light shot onto the substance as the nostril tensed and a gust swept up the dazzling shards. Loose flakes flew toward twitching eyes.

Galahad's bedroom door suddenly opened. Vellencourt never bothered to knock. She ordered with a tired voice, "Get dressed."

Galahad's hand remained on the pestle for a moment.

Lilian rubbed her eyes, smearing the greyish tint of stained whitening powder. "Go on, then. Take another whiff."

Galahad had not waited for her sentence to conclude. He took a sharp inhale off the pestle and scraped the rest of the powder into a small jar. He rolled out of bed and sprung to attention.

"You wore that suit to bed?" Vellencourt snorted.

"Wanted to break it in," Galahad answered hesitantly. *You must have to break in suits. Why else would they be so tight?*

Vellencourt stared blankly. After her silent judgement, she offered a hand.

Galahad took it warily, wondering why she was allowing him so many decisions this morning. She guided him through the servant's quarters and into the great hall. Many women and a single man were eating breakfast. One, however, was not. At the head of the table, where Lilian usually sat, was Greta. The crone's head and hands were locked in a pillory. Her mouth was gagged.

Galahad grinned, savoring the irritating woman's punishment. All the other servants, however, dared not look at anything but their plates. "What'd she do?"

Lilian snarled, "Disobedience."

Galahad's back straightened. *Does she mean to threaten me?* Had Lilian found out about his extra business? *Of course she has. She is making a point of Greta. Everyone is a servant. Everyone must perform their role.* Lilian was marking her territory, simple as that. *She is a beast in fashionable clothing. A pretty-patterned python. I cannot let her strangle me.*

Vellencourt pulled Galahad out of the dining room and into a shadowy staircase, illuminated only by the red hues of a crimson sun.

"I should let you know—" Galahad began to come clean about his extra dealing.

"Elizabeth has been saying good night to me." Lilian gave him a look that must have been a smile. Though, her cheeks hardly rose, her eyes barely happy. All that queenly pride had left Lilian. "Even said I love you of her own volition last night."

Galahad nodded before he knew what to say. He tried to recall. *Lilian's daughter… Oh right, yes. The little suicide attempt.* "You're wel—"

"I underestimated you," Lilian interrupted. They took to the top of the stone fort which overlooked the rotten battlements of Beauregard's palisade. The Crimson Gorge was dark with smog as an easterly wind blew.

Most people do, Galahad quipped. He had already met the woman's requirements. He had refined a great deal of Oleander plant, given her and her men detailed information about the use, side effects, and dosages, and overall—he was proving himself. Yet, as he watched the looming sky, he still felt unfulfilled. The brown clouds moving toward Auberdine looked like fangs. *Or ghosts.*

"You clearly have more to offer B.O.G."

Galahad caught Lilian looking at him from the corner of her eye. Neither turned. They watched the procession of ghostly smog as it sailed eastward.

"I should have assigned you to Elizabeth. You are a useful item."

Galahad licked the backs of his teeth and popped his lips, not enjoying being called an item.

"A useful *person*," Lilian put a hand on his shoulder. Her grip was not its usual strength. In fact, her touch was unsteadily gentle.

This is no game, she does not know about my extra business. Vellencourt lied well with words, but she was horribly honest with her emotions. *I am safe,* he realized. Reassured, he questioned openly, "What did Greta do to get such a… poetic punishment?"

Finally, Lilian looked at him. "She forgot she was a servant." Lilian patted his back forcefully, briefly unbalancing him. "A fact she will remember before the day's end."

Galahad clicked his tongue. *I will break her walls before long.* He grinned at the rotten palisade, *I will charm her and that brooding daughter.*

"Your refined herb—it does not look or smell like the parent plant?"

"No inspector would suspect it came from an Oleander," Galahad replied quickly. As their conversation progressed, his heartbeat thumped in his ears. Their voices grew muffled. No matter how loudly one talked, it always seemed quieter than other sensations and thoughts. He studied Vellencourt's face and continued reassuring her, "Though, if they did… Just buy them off."

Lilian's mouth moved, but the words were voiced in an unfamiliar rhythm. The sounds of individual consonants became words unto themselves; he could not recognize a single sentence in the woman's speech. He stretched his eyelids in a variety of poses, distorting and exaggerating Lilian's many expressions. He suddenly could not grasp his native language. Lilian paused frequently, stared off, and moved her hands. She was talking about something important, but Galahad was only able to focus on the last part:

"The law kept at a distance is the lifestyle kept safe… Have you summited yet?"

Galahad shook his head. He was completely lost in the conversation. He suggested, "You can mix it, snort it, smoke it."

Lilian glared at him, but something quickly overcame her annoyance. She persisted. "I will market it as a form of tobacco perhaps. That does not matter right now. Have you been to the Oleander peak yet?"

Galahad swallowed his saliva, though he did not know why he was drooling. "Uh," he fumbled, getting distracted by the smog sailing toward Auberdine. *Like little ghosties,* remarked his wayward mind. "Uh. I've been meaning to. Haven't had the time, though."

"You should reach the peak," Lilian declared. "Even if it is just once." She gave him that same, sentimental look that so unnerved him. Lilian was sad about something.

Always perceptive, Galahad tried to gain more favor by stating, "When I return, I could talk with your daughter."

Lilian's weak smile accompanied a single nod. Then, she ushered him away. She wished him luck on his journey, gave him more praise for his work, and then shut the door. Galahad found the entire conversation uncomfortable. *That's a woman with an odd sentimentality.* He would have to pay attention to her daughter. Elizabeth would be instrumental in duping Lilian. *Tricking the trickster,* Galahad smiled.

He eyed the white spear-tip of the Oleander. The summit was a good several miles above the Springs. Feeling a bit intimidated, Galahad looked back. A trapper sat outside the hunting lodge. The building was like all others in the Springs, ancient and smelly. The hunters and fur-trappers had yet to renovate and the door hung by its hinges, drooping lazily toward the ground. The windows were empty vessels, the wood was rotten, and birds nested on the chimney. A foul smell came underneath the lodge's foundations. Galahad saw a fat worm wriggling below the trapper's feet.

The man did not seem to mind and was plucking the strings of a massive theorbo. A melody of high notes followed a resonating low note. Galahad waved at the man; he tipped his hat and plucked a booming low note. The sound resonated across the walls of main street. A cheerful melody followed and drowned away the low drone.

Galahad's hand groped his pocket. He sniffed. The wind blew his hair in front of his face. A blacksmith's hammer clanged against an anvil. Metal screeched against a grindstone. Galahad snorted his medicine and whistled the musician's melody. He could not hit the high notes, but he hit the low notes just fine.

The climb took him past the lumberyard. Fearful loggers shuffled through the eaves, ever wary of something Galahad could not see. They whispered as he walked, all pointing and crossing their hearts. One logger bowed his head as he passed, "Woe is the man who walks the Wanakhan wood."

Galahad's left cheek sagged. His eyes sank with indifference. *Superstitious folk. They deserve a menial life.* Galahad whistled his way up the Oleander. Whenever he heard rustling in the brush, he assured himself it was a deer. Whenever he heard a strange bird, or the fluttering of frantic wings, he told himself that he was too important to be deterred. *I have a mission to fulfill here.* Galahad panted, climbing the mighty peak. *If there is a god, he has seen me to my successes.* He wheezed, "Baptism by fire!"

When he was halfway up the mountain, his knees started shaking. "Fuck me." Realizing he needed some more stimulation, he retrieved his medicine jar. Only wanting a fingerful, he saw that there was not much left. *Only some powder along the sides. I might as well use it all. One great high.* Intoxicated by the idea, he gathered all the medicine. He exhaled forcefully, preparing his lungs. When they were empty, he snorted all the powder into his nostrils.

Galahad's body twitched. "F-f-f," he frothed. His toes stretched and pulled. His eyeballs vibrated. His entire body churned, alight in sensation. For seconds or minutes, he sat in the dirt, unable and unwilling to stand. Finally, however, his body settled into a pleasant hum. His senses acclimated to their heightened awareness. He stood.

The Oleander peak was only a few steps away now! *That great blue…grey…red…chromatic peak! Look at how it shimmers. Now those Wanakha had it wrong. This is the mountain of riddles!* Galahad skipped up the tiny mountain, thinking it no steeper than the Hill of Auberdine. Sweat dripped off his brow as he reached the melting glaciers. Boulders lined the last hundred feet in an organized way. Galahad's reason told him the Wanakha had put them there. His medicine knew it was a sign. "This will be a climax in my autobiography!" He shouted gleefully.

Galahad had peaked. The Oleander was his. He was the Oleander. Auberdine was beneath him. Vellencourt and her Springs were beneath him. The smoking sludgeries were like gnats to him now. The haunted alpine forest was a bed of twigs. Galahad breathed with fulfillment. It had been so long since he had felt the calm of contentment, he nearly cried. He did not have the chance.

"Morn'," said a voice.

Galahad pivoted, nearly falling down the mountain from surprise.

A man wearing an army officer's uniform was sitting on a boulder.

"War's over," Galahad jested. *Ruined my summiting, you…*

"I beg to differ," said the military man, rolling his tongue in a detestable drawl. "Galahad, I presume?"

His eyes retreated in their sockets. Galahad froze. He dragged his tongue across his upper teeth and mulled over the man's word. *He has no proof. I will not concede.* He adopted a rustic accent. "Don' know anyone by tha' name."

The bounty hunter smirked and his chin dropped to his shoulder. "Do you think everyone is as dumb as they look?"

Do not admit. Do not submit. Galahad's cheek twitched. "Dumber."

The hunter rasped a quick laugh, clapped, and declared, "Funny. I like that. You'll be good company on the road."

Galahad feigned uncomfortable politeness and spoke as if denying a dinner request. "I'm afraid our paths won' be convergin' for too long. Ifin you headin' to the Palisade—"

The man slowly blinked. Then, a large, modified blunderbuss swung into view. The gun had been ancient before the war. Now, it belonged in a museum. The man leaned on the weapon, bit his lower lip, and smiled wide.

As old as his gun was, Galahad was sure it functioned well enough. He puffed out his chest and postured, "I am a citizen of this country." His voice had changed and now he spoke like a person of privilege and prestige. "If you are accusing me of being a criminal, I shall need a judge."

The bounty hunter took something out of his pocket. It was a corn cob pipe.

A bead of sweat trickled down Galahad's forehead.

The bounty hunter struck a match. He set a fire to the tobacco within and took a few puffs, popping his lips loudly. Finally, he took a deep breath, froze, and exhaled. Smoke steamed from his nostrils as he spoke, "Y'ave a tamper, son? No? More's the pity. Alas, tongue bite it shall be... Now, there is a judge in Auberdine. Nice lady. Kinsfeld."

Galahad's legs twitched. He watched the man as his chest rose and fell. His pipe bobbed around the corner of his mouth. He blinked; the bounty hunter stared. A hawk called. Mountain goats foraged. Pebbles shifted. Wind blew. Galahad crouched. His heels lifted off the ground. A burst of energy shot through him as he leapt away.

A sharp pain stopped him. He saw a blur of stones. He felt the grinding of gravel against his cheek. A rock shaved his lip, slipping inside his mouth. All he could do was choke on it. Only one arm moved when he tried to push himself up. The other wiggled, spurted a foul liquid from the elbow, and fell limp. Galahad bit the rock in his mouth and spat it away. He crawled forward, dragging his dangling arm with him.

The bounty hunter's boot landed on his hand. Galahad felt the pain in his fingers shoot up his body. The boot rolled along his knuckles, grinding them into the mud. The joints in his hand popped. His forearm spasmed. A numbness took hold of him... The shadow of a man looked down, knelt, and began moving his body... Galahad felt the thumping of his body against a new surface, walled and wooden. *My coffin*, Galahad figured. His arms slid into shackles. A sliver of fabric surrounded his bleeding elbow. His eyesight shimmered. He saw silver streaks, swarming shadows, and then nothing. He slipped from consciousness...

When Galahad awoke, he was cold. He opened his eyes slightly. A brown maw loomed above him. The clouds like specters hurled themselves down. Then, they flew back up with the howling wind. Sticks and twigs broke under him. The rocks did not. His back bounced and bumped against a wagon bed. The chains around his wrists tightened and squeezed his skin. A groan escaped him. "I have money."

The hunter agreed, happily. "Yes. I thank you for the contribution."

He robbed me... "That's my money," Galahad tried to rise. The chains stiffened.

"Refrain from moving too much," said the bounty hunter. Galahad stretched his neck and looked at the man. His lips were pinching on his pipe.

"You shot me," Galahad rasped. He eyed the stain on his shoulder. *My poor, poor suit...*

"I did," he replied. "Not Brigadier General Belmont's finest shooting, but..." He popped his lips and exhaled a cloud of smoke. "I *am* retired now."

Galahad tried to sit up. The chains reminded him of his place. The rocks followed suit, lifting the wagon into the air and knocking his head against the bed. He stifled a groan and tried to be still.

The wagon stopped. "Here," said Belmont. He unhorsed, reached into a satchel, and came to Galahad with a darkened bottle. "This is for the pain."

Galahad recognized the liquid immediately. *God damn me*... He shook his head and pulled at his chains. *I cannot. I won't.* The smell of liquor made him gag; his intoxicated mind swelled within itself. Galahad rattled his chains and shut his mouth. The hunter clasped. One hand pried his jaw open. The other gorged him.

The bounty hunter watched him gag. "You did this to yourself," he deemed.

Galahad tried to spit. He choked as the liquor slipped deeper down his throat. He bit down and tried to stop himself from swallowing. But it was useless. His will was shattered. The powder in his brain welcomed the liquor like an old friend.

He felt sick; he had failed himself. *I die a weak husk. A Cambyses.* "I have succumbed," he grieved.

The bounty hunter chuckled, "Do not get torn up. You had no chance."

I meant about... Galahad rethought the words and decided he agreed with both meanings. Indeed, after another thought—he realized it was *not* his fault. He did not choose to drink. He was forced into the act. *Just like...* Galahad shuttered. He would not think that simile through. He was just like himself and that was all. *Fuck Cambyses. This has all been his fault.*

Galahad shivered. A trickle of stomach acid shot into his mouth. It was infused with the taste of liquor, further sickening him. He swallowed, groaning.

The killer of an addict becomes one himself. Galahad snarled at the sky. *This is all some bored God's theater. The clouds, this barbarian, and now this.* Galahad spited the blue hue emerging from the grey. *Fuck the noose. This is my ultimate trial.* "Oh yes," he mocked. "I see your cruel metaphors."

Belmont quipped, "Oh joy. A killer and a lunatic. Pinch me or is it my birthday?"

Galahad ignored the jest. He muttered, "The wagon, the liquor, the chains. And what if I am not in control? Neither is this Pale cunt!"

The wagon wheels shrieked to a stop. Galahad waited for a thunderbolt. Instead, a hand wrapped itself around his chin. Galahad giggled, unwilling to show weakness. "It is not pain! It just tickles!" His mouth was forced open once more.

"This will shut you up."

Galahad choked on the alcohol. "A wise move, oh heavenly One! Use him and teach me! Ha!" He swallowed and gagged simultaneously, mixing the liquor with his bile. When his jaw ached too much, he swallowed in spite. "I am the master! I have the control!"

Belmont turned his head and eyed him suspiciously. He nodded to himself and turned back around. "I may have to stick around for your hanging."

Galahad blinked several times. *My Lord, listen to me. I cannot have snapped this quickly. I sound as insane as a bumbling boy after a bombardment. Is my will so weak?* Galahad grappled with his chains, searching for some weak point.

"Don't bother, kid. That chain is as sturdy as a trench line."

Why did he say that? Am I speaking aloud? Galahad eyed the sky. *Fine, play your games with me. I can play, too.* Galahad laughed hysterically, "I just need a war drum, then." A familiar weightlessness wrapped itself around his head. *Ah finally. Now this is a good way to go.*

"No drums here, mudpuppy. And they did not help you or your Redfeather allies in the war, either."

Galahad debated arguing, informing the general that he fought for the Rock. He decided it would be more fun to agree. "Muhali trenches were always well rationed. Even without our stores, we always had Pasty Pale prisoners to pick at."

Belmont laughed, "That explains your touched head. Cannibalism rots the mind."

Galahad gnashed his teeth, "Nom nom nom!" He awaited the bounty hunter's sarcasm eagerly. He hoped he had disturbed him. When the man did not speak, Galahad frowned and tried to relax.

I wonder what way is best to die. He did not like the prospect of a firing squad. Guns did terrible things to bodies. Yet, a bullet in the head would probably be the most painless. Beheading would be the most memorable for the town, but too grim. Hanging would likely be his fate and in a way, that saddened Galahad. He would just be another neck. No pomp, no flair. *Though that was Terrell's fate. It could be a fitting comeuppance.* He spat, "Yes, that would right the cosmic scale." His eyes roved madly through the sky. The maw of smog had moved farther eastward. The alpine forest was empty of sound, save the creaking of wheels. Galahad grinned triumphantly. *I am in control.* The only power a fat god could have was what people gave it.

Galahad swam in his happy head. He thought joyfully about all the interesting people he would meet in damnation. *I hope I meet the cunts who started the Great War. Yes, I have some questions for them.* He hoped he met Beauregard. *What went through his head when he exterminated an entire people?* Galahad supposed it was a little like how killing his father felt. Galahad's nose surged with sensation. He sneezed violently. *That will be a fitting torture for us both. The father and the son who hated each other, forced to roast in the same fire.*

His eyes began to struggle with their surroundings. A pit formed in his stomach. He was dizzy. A knot tightened in his throat. He pushed it back down. "Slow down," Galahad muttered. Nausea washed over him, stronger than any physical wave. The urge to vomit overtook him. Galahad shook his shackles and resisted the feeling. *Too much…* Panic overtook his pride. "I can't breathe."

"Altitude sickness. You'll be better when your head is not so high in the clouds."

Galahad might have laughed at that. *Damn you,* he glared at the sky. A chunk of vomit came oozing up his throat. He swallowed it. His pride reminded his panic, "I will not. I am in control." As the words left his lips, his tongue tasted vomit. The sense overwhelmed him. The sickness swelled into his mouth. Vomit spewed despite Galahad's resistance. He choked on the chunks that remained between his cheeks. His throat narrowed. He coughed madly.

"Your bounty is not that much," Belmont groaned. "Do not make a mess back there."

Galahad struggled to speak. His pride had shriveled. "Please. Just stop."

That amused the hunter. "Ah, the begging starts early." The wagon halted. Belmont dismounted and rounded the wagon. He informed his prisoner, "Lucky for you, then. We need to wait for the gatekeeper."

Galahad sniffed up his leaking snot. The vomit in his nose leaked back into his throat. "Ugh," he moaned. *Beauregard's Palisade.* He was near now. His sojourn was over. *Death is not an idle concept for me. It is not some theologist's theory.* The madness of moments ago lingered only as embarrassment, shame, and fear. He wanted to weep. His body convulsed. He shivered. "Fine," Galahad moaned. "I am not in control. I am not."

The bounty hunter laughed and strolled out of sight. "Of course not. And I must confess. Begging in your state is quite disingenuous." Galahad heard him strike a match. "Oh, how I pity the damned."

Galahad dry-heaved. The remnants of vomit left his mouth. A partially digested clump of leaf was coated in bile; it reeked of death. He rasped, spitefully, "The damned are your livelihood."

Belmont ignored the comment. He hailed another, "Ah, my friend. Do open this gate. Brigadier General Belmont requires passage to turn in his bounty." Footsteps thundered down a corridor. The gate remained shut. The bounty hunter barked, "Girl, are you deaf? Belmont says to br-"

New footsteps rang against stone floors. They approached slowly. The back gate of the palisade creaked open. "Thank you, Walcott," came a woman's voice. "You may go now."

Galahad groaned. *Lilian Vellencourt, here for one last laugh.* "Enough games," he muttered, loud enough to protest and quiet enough to perhaps be ignored. *Or has she come to retrieve me?*

Vellencourt remarked casually, "Mister Belmont. I hear you have found your bounty?"

Laughs it is, Galahad realized. She had betrayed him, just as he had foreseen.

Belmont clicked his tongue. "Was roaming about, just like your servant said."

That is why she was in the stocks this morning. She betrayed Lilian, too. Galahad made a note that if given the chance, he would strangle Greta.

Vellencourt inquired, "What is the prize for this one, then?"

There was no response.

Vellencourt laughed, "Belmont, you silly boy—I am not some flesh-monger like yourself. I do not partake in the sale of men. You can divulge your business secrets with me."

The bounty hunter grunted, "Fifty marks."

I could pay that. Galahad found himself offended at how meager a sum his life was worth. *I thought I would be worth at least two hundred marks. I am a murderer, after all. Very dangerous.*

Lilian spoke loudly, "Alive?"

"Dead." Belmont laughed. "Live catch is worth double."

Lilian Vellencourt looked down at the wagon, "He's bleeding out."

The hunter scrambled to the wagon bed and peered at the wounded arm. Galahad would have taken pleasure in seeing his panic, but the pain was too great. Moreover, his body was going numb. He watched motionless as Belmont paced around the wagon. He had his finger to his chin.

Vellencourt stared. "You know, Belmont. I don't think you will be getting a hundred marks for this one."

The hunter lashed out, "I don't need a woman lecturing me."

Vellencourt rolled her eyes and glanced down at Galahad. "Oh, and here I was going to offer my services to you."

The bounty hunter was silent. Galahad gulped. He heard more footsteps and the folding of paper. "How much?"

"Twenty-five marks," came Lilian's reply. She interrupted Belmont's attempt at bargaining. "You still make an extra twenty-five."

The bounty hunter grumbled. It seemed he could do the math. Seconds later, Galahad heard the clanking of keys. Faces congregated above his body. "What?" He asked them. Was he free? *What is Lilian doing with me?* Exhaustion took hold of him. He breathed heavily and his eyes struggled to stay open.

Lilian frowned at him. Her dress obscured the sun and turned its light into many different colors. "Walcott," she called, "See that he is bathed and ready for supper."

"Should I prepare him a bed in the servant's quarters?"

"No," Vellencourt replied. "That will not do."

"Not too comfortable," Belmont grunted. "His irons stay on."

37

Exodus

Hanna watched her husband mop. The dullest activities had become so difficult for Arthur. *Why?* Her husband made a pass around the petrified table. She looked away. He did not like it when people stared and had cursed several orphans for what she was doing. As he lapped around the hall for yet another cleaning, she peeked out. Many guests had scarfed down their food and departed, wary of her husband's behavior.

So strange. Can he not see the sparkles on the floor? Hanna gulped. He had hardly noticed her this morning. They woke together, but she had been a ghost. *Or him…* He floated out of bed, stared at his reflection, and then proceeded to clean.

The slightest creak was a crash. The sole light of the room, a roaring fire at the end of the hall, casted the innkeeper's shadow. Hanna could not help but stare at the distorted limbs dancing on the walls. They unnerved her. *Is this anticipation? Am I being stupid? Why does he keep looking out the window?*

Hanna sniffled. Her husband froze. He glanced around and then, rolled his shoulders. Hanna wondered if anyone else saw the action, and if they did—if they thought he was nervous, too. *Maybe I just don't read people well.* That could be. *I can't read books… People are more words than books.* Hanna's chin gave way to that familiar weight of hopelessness. She bowed her head.

Her fingers bled constantly now. Even after the comforting roughness of picking her skin gave to pain, she continued scratching. She needed something to distract from her thoughts. *Why am I anxious? He is cleaning. Cleaning. Cleaning. Emilia. Emilia. Anger. Anger.* Hanna rubbed her scaling fingertips against her lips.

The redwood door opened. Her son slipped through noiselessly. His pale skin was colored by that awful haze that had come down. His clothes were stained brown.

That might be why Arthur's nervous. We never have smog here. That's a city thing. Hanna smiled at her son, consoled by her rationalizing.

Aeric did not see the gesture. He had something in his hands, something silvery. His steps were careful, but as he neared the Gardner stairs, he sped up. The floorboards creaked. The now-familiar scurrying of mice sounded beneath him.

Arthur's ears focused on the mice. He pivoted, cutting off his son. "Where did you set those traps again?"

Aeric froze.

Hanna straightened, alert. After his behavior with Emilia, she worried about Arthur's temper.

Her son's eyes looked everywhere but at his father. "Just outside."

Arthur squinted, "Just outside. So, the stable? The hedge perimeter? The granary."

Hanna blinked. *Why didn't that last one sound like a question? Is that some way of speaking I forgot? That sounded like*—she did not have time to think. Her son had sat down beside her.

"I put some by the granary, yeah. Just outside though."

Aeric continued a moment later, talking about the useless building and how he did not go in. "Should just demolish it," he said, just as his fist slipped covertly over his mother's folded hands.

His hands are clammy. What happened in that haze? She felt his finger unfold on hers, dropping a metal object into them. *A spoon?* Hanna stopped herself from asking her son many questions. However, she could not stop from looking at him curiously.

Aeric shot up. He pushed himself from the petrified table and declared, talking to Arthur more like an acquaintance than a father, "That haze is thick. I don't suggest going out there."

Hanna swallowed. Arthur heard it, too. The innkeeper tilted his head. "That bad?"

"Yep," Aeric's throat seemed to tighten.

"Ah, well," Arthur hugged his son, tightly. "Don't go back out. Get some rest."

Aeric's arms rose heavily and patted his father's back.

The innkeeper released. "Do you need me to get the Yao?"

"No, no. Just tired."

"Okay," the innkeeper shrugged. He peered out the browning window, stained with smog.

Aeric quickly trotted out of sight.

Hanna waited several minutes. Her husband began cleaning the windows furiously, ignoring the haze and his coughs. Hanna thought it was a waste of time, as the smog would just stain the glass again. She did not voice her opinion, of course. She glanced at the spoon. She sniffed it. *Soup?* She left the hall, intent on asking Aeric some questions.

"What was that about?" She prepared her words. She knew when she was stressed, her mouth did not always cooperate. *"You're going to make your father worse."*

She went down the hall. She stopped outside her daughter's bedroom, hearing Emilia crying. She bit her tongue, thinking. Quickly, she went up to her son's closed door and slid the spoon under. "Come see me soon," she said to the door.

Hanna entered her daughter's room. Emilia was sitting on the floor, her legs raised and her arms curled around her body. Isabelle was licking the girl's ankles.

Hanna sat next to them. "What's the matter, sugarbear?"

She grunted that her mother already knew. When neither of them spoke, Emilia then whispered, "Everyone else has a good dad. It's not fair."

"Not everyone," Hanna smiled. It seemed an odd thing to be smiling about.

"Uh huh," Emilia argued. "Dixon wouldn't shut up about his daddy all through breakfast! They were gonna go on adventures and be farmers."

Hanna bit her cheek and glanced at the floor. "Isn't his daddy missing?" She could not remember.

Emilia's face formed annoyed wrinkles. "Whatever," she muttered. She raised her nostrils and looked down at her lap. "I wish my daddy was missing."

"You don't mean that," Hanna said, hoping she was right. She added, trying to be the girl's positivity, "You've hardly had a chance to get to know him. The war stole him from you."

Emilia's lips trembled. Her quiet voice cracked, "Why do you stand up for him?"

Hanna swallowed. She said the first thing to come to her mind. "That's how l-love works."

Tears came to her eyes. She squeaked. "I know that, mama. I know it..." She wiped the tears away and threw her fists to the ground. "It's why I hate him. He is mean to you."

Isabelle stood up and walked behind Emilia. She licked her ear. When Emilia did not respond, she curled her body around the girl like a coat.

Meanwhile, Hanna struggled to respond. She wished nobody else saw Arthur's tantrums. They did not understand him as she did. They only saw the outside of things. "He is not—"

Emilia's eyes welled. She wailed, "He's gonna hurt you..." She swatted her mother's hands away. Her body and voice shook. "Every day is w-worse. I wake up in the n-night to check on you. B-but even after I check, it-it isn't enough. I feel like I have to stay up all night or else he will do something."

Oh, my sweet girl. Hanna wanted to say that Arthur would never hurt her. Something told her not to. So, she listened.

"I can't sleep," Emilia cried. "I always see bad things when I do."

Hanna immediately thought of her nightmare with the bloody hand. "What kind of things?"

Her daughter sealed her lips and shook her head. "Uh uh. If I talk about them, they might become real."

I know, sugarbear. I know. Hanna started to say everyone thinks like that at one point. As she took in a breath, she stopped. She rolled her head up and down, as if she had a kink in her neck. She rubbed her arms as she spoke, "I think t-that talking... makes them less real." When she finished, embarrassment shot up her spine. Her eyes twitched open and shut. *Why would she listen to me? Why should she?*

Emilia scooted closer to her mother. "What if it turns out they are crazy? If I am crazy?"

She massaged Emilia's back and said, warmly, "I have crazy fears, too." A second later, the child fell into her mother's arms. Hanna continued, feeling a little surer of herself. "They don't make me crazy."

Emilia nuzzled up to her mother. She asked, her voice muffled. "How do you stop them?"

Hanna smiled, frowned, and strained. She did not know. "I am n-not an expert," she began, borrowing the voice of someone who was. "But I think everyone is afraid. Your daddy has nightmares every time he tries to sleep." She smiled down at her daughter, hoping that might make her feel better.

"Good," she replied.

Hanna blinked. "About everyone being afraid, or ab-about daddy?"

"Both," her daughter mumbled.

Don't be mean, sugarbear. She patted Emilia's head lightly and looked at the room for a new topic.

She found one in her daughter's dog. Isabelle had crawled even closer to Emilia. When the animal realized Hanna was looking at her, she coughed and wiggled closer. She put her head on Emilia's lap and began licking any bare patch of skin she could find. Emilia giggled and pushed the hound's head away. Once she had removed her hand, Isabelle rebounded back like elastic, coughed, and licked Emilia's chin. Finally, Emilia crawled to the side of her bed and patted her legs. Isabelle trotted over and flopped onto Emilia, panting happily.

Hanna grinned, "Izzy is sure at-" She scowled at the missing word, squinted, and finally said, "Attentive."

Emilia tickled the dog's belly and rubbed her chin, "Yeah. She knows how to help."

Hanna leaned forward, "I think that is cause she is a lot like you."

Emilia kissed the dog's head. She repositioned herself, pausing her petting for just a second. Isabelle protested with a cough until the girl continued. "When she gets nervous," Emilia started, "Usually during storms. I just give her a pet and she's okay. She still shakes. Doesn't howl, though."

"And you?" Hanna tried, "What makes you better during *your* storms?"

Emilia rolled her bottom lip over and under her top lip. She thought for a minute. She looked at her mother; she bowed her head. She looked again; she hid her face again. "I get all confused when I'm scared... I get shaky like Izzy... A-and I wonder if I am getting anxious. I hope that I am not, because it gets so bad. It's gotten worse, too. Sometimes, I think I am more scared of being scared than anything else." Emilia gulped.

Isabelle had raised her head up and was staring at the child. The two looked at one another. Emilia looked at her mother out of the corner of her eye. Then, Izzy nudged Emilia's hand and slid it down her fur.

"She's petting herself," Hanna smirked.

Emilia nodded. "When I am really bad, she puts her head on my hand like this." She put a finger to her chin, "Something about touching her puts me back together." The little girl tilted her head and stared at her mother. "You can't touch fear. But you can touch Izzy."

Hanna lost her next breath. She got to her feet and rubbed her eyes. "You're awfully smart, you know that? You make me so proud."

Emilia grinned. "More than Aeric?"

"You are my favorite daughter," Hanna answered.

"You only have one!" Emilia told the hound, "That's cheating! Big girl, get her!"

Isabelle lifted her heavy head lazily. She looked at Hanna, then at Emilia.

"You'll just have to catch me," Hanna teased the dog, scratching her ears. She grinned at the pair and darted downstairs. Naturally, Isabelle saw someone running and sprinted after them. Hanna was relieved as the paws pitter-pattered in pursuit. *Good. She won't mope without her Izzy.* Sure enough, Emilia followed behind.

Arthur was nowhere to be seen. Hanna was glad of that. She did not want to aggravate her husband and it seemed that was all Isabelle could do. *He just needs some space from Emilia,* came a calming thought. It had not settled long before Hanna grimaced, *He's had years of space.*

"Come on, mama," Emilia pressed. She was waiting at the redwood door.

Arthur is out there. He's working. "I don't like it out there, sugarbear. It's all smokey." She suggested, more for Arthur's good than her daughter's, "What about playing downstairs? The library could be fun?" *He never goes down there.*

Emilia pointed, "Izzy wants to run!"

Hanna debated. Fear and family were so intertwined now, motherly love was becoming as complicated as her math book. "Let's teach the big girl how to swim!"

Fortunately, Emilia liked the idea. She patted her thighs, "Izzy!"

Ruff. Ruff. Ruff. Claws scratched against wood.

"Izzy!" Emilia yelled.

Hanna took a deep breath. She heard it again: *Ruff. Ruff. Ruff.* The scratches were coming from her left. *The granary.* In an instant, she thought of Aeric's odd behavior, the weird spoon, and her husband. She jolted outside and heard her husband's growl. A pit formed in her stomach.

"God damn it, Emilia." Arthur gave his girls no time to react. A silhouette charged the sounds. The dog saw the innkeeper approach, barked excitedly, and nudged the granary door. Then, Izzy sniffed the ground, her tail wagging furiously.

"Get away from there," Arthur snarled. He pushed her out of the way. He stood in front of the moldy, damaged door. He kicked the dog's snout. Izzy jumped back, stared at the innkeeper, and then began chasing her tail.

"You settle down," he said behind his teeth.

The dog began spinning. Like a screw driving into a wall, she grounded herself.

Hanna reached the scene just as Emilia began arguing with her father. She was helpless to stop what happened. Her words did not come out.

The innkeeper grabbed the animal by the neck. Isabelle yelped.

"I said settle down," he said behind his teeth. He smiled bitterly, "Or I will turn you into glue."

"Stop it!" Emilia pushed her father's legs. He did not budge. His hands remained on the dog's neck. The animal did not move and looked up at the man fearfully. Emilia squeaked, "Stop! She didn't mean it!" She sank to her knees. "Don't hurt her!" Her voice cracked. "She's my only friend," the girl pleaded.

"Bad choice of friends," Arthur muttered. Izzy coughed. Her eyes were wide with pure fear. The mighty animal's tail was tucked between her legs. She whimpered, but the sound only infuriated Arthur more. The innkeeper shook the animal.

Emilia rammed her father's knees. The unsteady grip loosened. Isabelle sprinted away.

"Izzy!" Hanna called, but it was no use. The animal was frightened and only fear could be heard.

That did not stop Emilia from shrieking and sobbing. The cries struck Hanna like a knife, but her husband did not feel similarly. Arthur grabbed Emilia's face, squeezing the cheeks. "You do not hit your father. Understand?"

Emilia spat.

Arthur wiped the spit from his cheek. He raised his other arm and flattened his palm.

"Arthur Gardner!" Finally came the mother's voice. He glanced at her. Hanna suddenly felt a fear in her chest. She tried to keep her voice raised. "Don't you dare!" The command sounded more like begging, but luckily—her husband responded to that.

"Your mother is frail and scatter-brained. If she were not here, I would teach you proper manners."

"She is *not* frail," Emilia cried.

"Speak when spoken to." Arthur released the girl and stormed away.

That's your daughter, the mother seethed. The innkeeper's wife cried, "I-I putting her to bed."

The redwood door slammed shut.

Emilia immediately ran after her dog, crying, "Izzy," for everyone to hear. Hanna followed, calling, "Emilia." When she finally caught her daughter, she had slipped into the stables. The child wheezed and wiped sooty tears from her eyes. "Emilia," she hugged her daughter. The girl kicked, pulling away, "See? He is—" She was cut off by a series of hoarse coughs. "Awful!"

The mother nodded. The wife changed the subject, "You're coughing, sugarbear."

"I don't care," Emilia sniffled. "Izzy is lost."

And she already has a cough. Oh… This haze isn't good for her. Hanna sighed. "Cover your face with your shirt." *This will give Arthur time to settle down.*

Emilia did as her mother said. Then, she grabbed Hanna's hand and they went into the smog. The muffled calls went unanswered. The Inner Ring remained silent. The Overgrowth remained indifferent. Finally, when the smog began to bite their eyes, Hanna picked her daughter up and carried her away, sobbing. They went back up the Hill, and back into the main hall.

They never went back home.

38

Koi and Carp

Galahad awoke with a dry throat and cracked skin. *And yet, why does it feel so humid?* Had he woken in a jungle? Yellow flowers like lanterns hung like suns from green vines. Galahad wondered what he should think of them. *What lesson should I learn from you?* Galahad groaned, weary of the game. *This is my own mind, of course.* His paranoia had him debating the wind and decrying the sky.

A waterfall trickled placidly. Next to it were exotic plants, colorful rocks, and a decently sized pond. Galahad laid on his back. Sunlight pierced through a glass dome. His bed seemed perfectly placed within some sort of greenhouse. *It smells fishy.*

"The koi garden," came Vellencourt's voice. "An odd place for hospice, I know."

Galahad arced his head. The woman left two armed guards at the entrance of the greenhouse. He was shocked to see she was not wearing any whitening powder. Indeed, she was only wearing pants and a plaid shirt. She sat beside his bed in a bamboo chair. It looked incredibly uncomfortable.

"I had no beds to give away, save for servants." Lilian frowned. "Those accommodations would not be right for you."

Galahad scoffed. "No. I have earned the Overgrowth in miniature." He had the urge to itch his scalp. When he raised his arms, iron kept them in place. The shackles chafed his wrists. He sighed at the sight of scratches and stains on his suit.

Vellencourt's frown wiggled itself into a pitiful smile. "We got off poorly, Galahad."

He closed his eyes. He had no fight left. She had shot, skinned, and mounted his pride.

Lilian Vellencourt shuffled in her seat. Galahad peaked at her. She crossed her legs and looked away from him.

"Where is the hunter?" He inquired. "Waiting outside?"

"Belmont will collect you this evening," the woman replied. She cleared her throat. "I have given Greta a scar to remember you by." She glanced at the pond, "I would have kept you hidden."

Galahad was too angry to respond. She was lying to him and it was giving him an awful headache. *Is this how sobriety feels? Or mortality?*

"But I cannot risk harboring a *known* fugitive. Even if Elizabeth seemed to like you. Bad for business. And her future."

Galahad felt an eyebrow throb. His toes were numb. He coughed, "Elizabeth?"

"Well," Vellencourt brushed her pants and pulled out a small mirror. Uttering a quiet, "Oh my," she quickly reached into her pockets and pulled out some lipstick. She lined her lips with red and popped them. She finally looked at him, "I won't bore you with the specifics. I know your attitude toward family."

Galahad cackled in cold anger. "Oh, the arrogance." He winced as the pain in his arm shot up to his head, "You would have murdered Cambyses before your first birthday."

Vellencourt seemed startled by his frankness. A second later, her composure and calm returned. She leaned in and spoke softly. "I suppose we have reached the point in our friendsh-"

"We are not friends," Galahad corrected.

Vellencourt rolled her eyes. "Association... Where we may be blunt." She folded her hands on her lap. She sighed, smiling the kind of smile that was both sad and glad. "I know what it is like to be hated when all you want to be is loved."

Galahad spoke carefully. "So you offed Mister Vellencourt because he hated you?" He waved his finger, "Temper, Temper."

Vellencourt's smile snapped. "I am not talking about that filthy pig." She rolled her shoulders and for a moment, Galahad thought she might leave. Then, she mumbled reluctantly, "I am talking about Elizabeth."

Galahad could see her tongue roving around the roof of her mouth, pressing against her cheeks and between her teeth.

"I know she wishes I were not her mother," she finally said. "That she had some poor peasant life with hugs, kisses, and hungry bellies." She sniffed, slapped her thighs, and stood. "Point being, after your interaction with her, she says she loved me."

"How touching," Galahad grunted. *This bitch will thank me and condemn me in one breath.*

Her response was quick, her tone was annoyed. "You would not be alive without my intervention, you ungrateful—" She ended her insult prematurely.

Galahad pretended ignorance. "Oh. You were talking to me? I thought your daughter was near."

She smirked at him with the same smugness Galahad was well acquainted with. Then, her brow twitched and she settled into a seething silence.

Galahad grinned placidly at her, content with his small victory. He would have liked to enjoy it longer, but Greta came in moments later. She waddled toward Vellencourt, the muscles in her crooked back popping as she walked. She bowed her head and hunched down even lower. Only a stained bandage remained where her right ear used to be. She asked, "Now that the murderer is awake, may the general fetch it?"

Lilian stood. She eyed the crone with disgust. Greta's face contorted with misgivings, fear, and shame. Then, just before her servant spoke, Lilian smacked Greta's wound. The bandage sagged and the gaping wound was revealed.

The servant shrieked in agony but within seconds, had regained her dignity. The ugly fool folded her hands behind her back. "I did what I thought was best, ma'am. It was not safe for us. I-"

"Yes, yes," Lilian raised her hand. "Let's not pick our scabs. That conversation is over. Tell Belmont that he may have his prize when I am finished."

Galahad had thought that perhaps Lilian had bought him from Belmont. *Why else would she pay to store me here?* He had assumed, wrongly, that Lilian could not give up her plaything. *She has used me for her experiment and now, I'm off to the garbage.*

When Greta had left the greenhouse, Lilian apologized. "A good servant, albeit damaged beyond repair."

Galahad again acted ignorant. "Your daughter?"

"Oh please," Lilian retorted, folding her arms. "You murdered your own father. Do not pretend that there is not a void where your heart should be." Before Galahad could reply, she continued, "When you saw other children playing at the park, did you yearn to switch places with them?"

Galahad snapped. "I am *not* a toy."

Vellencourt beamed. She unfolded her arms and glided to the side of his bed. She put a hand on his leg. "But you want to be."

Galahad laughed. *At least I am not the only one going insane.*

"Why else would a grown man allow himself to be treated as a child?" Vellencourt asked. "To lodge with a woman like Laverne and then with—"

Galahad's face became grim. "Laverne was a kinder woman than you'll ever be."

Vellencourt's eyes widened. "Don't mistake me. I respect her little charity. Few people take an interest in the war's wounded, fewer still the orphans." She looked at the Koi pond and drifted off into silence. A man was stooping by the water and throwing pellets into the pond. She smiled and her gaze returned to Galahad. "You know," she began, "I am not unlike Laverne."

She looked down at Galahad with such benevolence, his legs lurched from her. The shackles scraped his shins. His legs slid to a stop.

Lilian's voice lost its low resonance. She spoke kindly and in a higher pitch. "I have many broken beings under my wing."

"And I am not to be one, hm?" Galahad asked, feigning apathy.

She put a surprised hand to her mouth. "Oh, no." It was her turn to wave a parental finger. She frowned, "You are a danger to my success. And you *did* overstep when you started peddling that drug on your own. Oh, don't look surprised." Lilian shooed the notion of freedom away like a pestering fly. "Besides, some beasts are so broken, it would be best to let nature run its course."

So it was only a goodbye, a last humiliation. *Well, at least I will retain some sense of dignity.* He scowled at the shambling gardener and shook his head at his sorry existence. *Being her pawn would kill me quicker than a noose.* He looked up at the glass ceiling. *Still, I could better suffer her gloating if I just had some Oleander powder.*

Galahad winced. The craving and the shackles created a hopeless hell within his mind. He glared at Lilian Vellencourt, determined to not take his eyes off her.

"Consider Greta," Lilian started. "When I found her during the Great War, she was walking the Castle Rock whoring herself out to any cripple with a cock." She opened her arms toward the gleaming glass, "Now, she is thriving. I've done that for many women."

Galahad did not think public torture and mutilation was thriving. He pointed at the man by the pond. "What about that one? I thought you hated having men in your household."

Vellencourt clicked her tongue. The man let the last pellets in his hands fly onto the water's surface. He turned toward the noise. "Sampson," she ordered. "Come."

The man obeyed. Sampson was a pale and grimy creature with a long, ragged beard and a homely face. A row of tooth marks had scarred one of his hands. "Sampson fought in the war," Lilian explained. "Same as you."

Galahad commented suspiciously, "In awfully good shape, aren't we?"

Lilian answered before the veteran had a chance. "Sampson was wounded in a less visible area." She leaned toward Galahad, "You see, he is not truly a man."

Sampson bowed his head.

Galahad snorted. "Clearly. He will not speak for himself."

Vellencourt shook her head. She clicked her tongue and the servant immediately left them. Once out of earshot, she elaborated. "Sampson's lower half was damaged by a shelling. His penis was blown to bits."

Galahad was glad someone else in the room was as damaged as he was. *Fuck Sampson. He gets to live his life.*

Lilian continued, "After the shelling, Sampson was left to die in no man's land, just feet away from his fellow soldiers. He screamed for help. Being good-hearted men, his comrades leapt from the safety of their trench to save him. One by one, they were mowed down."

Lilian blinked, frowned a smile, and continued. "Well, Sampson kept screaming, men kept leaping over the trenches to save him, and men kept dying." Vellencourt glanced over her shoulder. The veteran was watering several potted plants from a tin pitcher. "Eventually, the pain of seeing his friends dying overwhelmed the pain of his wound." Vellencourt glanced at Galahad from the corner of her eye. "I am told he stuffed his fist into his mouth to stop himself from screaming."

"That would explain the bite marks," Galahad muttered.

"He lost the ability to speak after that," Lilian finished. "I found him begging in your Overgrowth and just had to save him." She shifted her position on his bed and leaned back onto her hands. "See? He is no threat. He takes care of my garden and I take care of him."

Galahad analyzed her. *Her husband is dead but not forgotten*, he was sure about that. He recalled how eager he was to do a good deed after murdering Cambyses. *She is not so dignified. Not so strange.* He supposed she had some lingering guilt. Why else would such a wicked woman take such pains to watch over the wretched? *She must think I am wretched, too.*

"I liked you." Lilian inhaled, saying, "I liked our chats. Even if they were a bit contentious. I enjoy that."

Galahad chuckled. He eyed her complexion, bare of all whitening powder. A shred of his pride returned to him. Lilian Vellencourt, the wealthiest and most successful person he had ever known, was lonely. He presupposed, "So you have delayed my death for one last conversation?"

Lilian was quick to answer his question with another. "You will agree good ones are hard to come by?"

Annoyingly, he also wanted to have one last conversation with the bitch. *She robbed me of my property, my business, probably my life...* Galahad rolled his eyes and sighed. He pointed a finger toward the water, "Am I right in assuming this bed has wheels?"

Vellencourt followed his finger, nodded, and rose. She wheeled him to the water's edge, grabbed her own chair, and positioned it beside the bed.

Galahad scanned the garden. It reminded him of the innkeeper's grove in spring. *I wonder if I will get to see the inn one last time...* He doubted it. Carolyn would want retribution for her boy. They would sentence him the very day he was returned. *The Pale will poke and prod me. They will parade me like an animal, exaggerate what I have done.* Galahad frowned. *Better than being remembered for parricide.*

"Well," Lilian groaned after several minutes. "Are there two mutes in this greenhouse?"

Galahad was fixated on the koi pond. "I was thinking," he began. "About my life up to this point."

Vellencourt extended her arms and folded her fingers toward her palms, like a cat pawing at mice. "Oh, do tell."

"Only..." He looked down at all the beautiful fish swimming in the pond. They were magnificently colored in reds, oranges, and yellows. They swam as little sunrises beneath the surface, or perhaps as sunsets. There were no dull fishes in that pond, only the most splendid were allowed to swim in that little paradise. "I am sure if I was born with your privileges," he glanced at the woman. "It would be me in that seat."

Vellencourt removed her shoes and dipped her toes into the pond. "You know what lives in this pond?"

"Koi," Galahad answered.

"Mostly," Vellencourt agreed. "Sampson put some crawfish, too. A few frogs came from outside several months ago. I think they will become permanent residents."

"Well," Galahad tried to articulate how he felt. He found the task taxing. "They, uh, are beautiful." They were more than beautiful. Those fish swam with some beauty Galahad had been lacking all his life.

"They are really not that impressive," Vellencourt chuckled.

She pretends at humility. "How much did they cost you?"

"Not much. Sampson did most of the work and if he spent anything, it was time." Vellencourt turned, "You see, you cannot *really* breed koi."

"Why is that?" Galahad asked, preoccupied with a crawdad crawling along the mud carpet. The fish swam above, sprinkling their shit down onto it.

"Even the prettiest koi do not produce beautiful offspring," Lilian informed him. "The patterns and colors are more sporadic, random." She leaned toward Galahad, saying quietly, "You see, koi are just common carp."

"Indeed?" Galahad asked. He was still transfixed with the crawdad. It was moving scraps of uneaten food toward a burrow.

"Yes. That is the dirty little secret. The rich keep koi and the poor eat carp."

Galahad saw her point, but his brain was not in union with his mouth. Out of the corner of his eye, he saw a pink flower. Thinking of a response became a maze, his mind bound by the confines of his craving. Every quip, comment, and crass remark was drowned out by the drumming of his want. It was within reach, yet he could not reach. He could not grab the plant himself. He would have to ask. Galahad was nauseated by the thought.

The leaf held his eye, but something else held his tongue.

Lilian went on, "The rich spend ludicrous amounts on varieties of koi. All the while, they merely buy into a system, a game. The koi in this pond are no different than the common carp. Their colors are meaningful because we made it so."

Galahad lurched from the leaf. He latched onto her point. "I see. Color and worth are in the eye of the beholder."

Lilian giggled, "I went to some fishmonger's stand and asked if he could capture some carp. He came back with a dozen ugly brutes. In two years, I had raised up a batch of the most beautiful fishes this side of the Golden River. I could sell them and buy the Anchorage, people and all."

Galahad snorted. "You don't think," he paused as he momentarily forgot his thought. "That, uh..." He recaptured his thought and spoke before he could forget it again. "That it is a weird thing we all do, selling living things?"

Vellencourt leaned back and buried her hands in the mud. "This is why I could not let you go to the gallows just yet. You've too much to say."

His eyes drifted to the Oleander plant. His fingers tapped against the bed. Saliva pooled in his mouth. He shut his eyes and muttered, "I'm glad you think so."

"As to your question, I have no answer." She shrugged, "If the fish came out as their forebears, ugly and dull—I sold them to be eaten. If they came out beautiful, they earned a lavish life."

Galahad had her. "So the colors *do* matter."

"Oh, for now," Lilian agreed. "But koi are a fashion. Colors and patterns go in and out of style." She pointed at a huge, black fish with orange spots, "He is my oldest one. I could have sold him for thirty marks before the war. Now, due to changing tastes—he is worth next to nothing."

Galahad could not get a good look at the fish. He sympathized nonetheless. "A pity."

Vellencourt pulled her hands from the mud, leaned forward, and washed her fingers in the water. She stood up and brushed off her bottom. "If Sampson were to stop influencing the spawn, the whole school would be washed away. The same dull color would return, the same old fish."

"I always thought koi were distinct types of fish," Galahad admitted. He allowed himself a glance at the Oleander plant. Saliva quickly swelled back into his mouth.

"As common as they come," Lilian reiterated. "Just carp."

Galahad found her point lacking. Moreover, he did not want her to think she was smarter than she was. As he began to argue, the saliva in his mouth fell down his throat. He coughed. Mucus spilt down his cheeks. Unable to wipe his face, Galahad muttered, "Yes, well, humans are a different beast."

"Without a doubt," Vellencourt agreed. "Plotting, prideful, prickly, and-"

"Prejudiced," Galahad muttered. "Hateful, horrible, and-"

"I've never understood the Pale prejudice," Lilian blurted. She caught his eye, "Truly."

Galahad stopped. She was lying, of course. "It is quite easy to understand. One's heritage merits mockery-"

"Yes, yes," Lilian groaned. "Anyone who lives a day in our country can hear a thousand slurs. The Pale people with their mudpuppies, troggs, and the like." She sighed, brushing her hair behind her head. "It is all so antiquated."

"Antiquated?" Galahad was on the verge of losing his temper. How could this woman say such things when she had lived in the Overgrowth? *The blindness*, he rolled his eyes. *She used the same prejudice to cheat me out of my father's property! My life!*

"Yes, yes. I hear the words, the name-calling." Lilian shook her head, "Your Inner Ring's contempt of outsiders is so cartoonish. They hate other peoples like old Beauregard hated them. They act like little caricatures." She stared into Galahad's eyes. "The modern prejudice is not personal."

"Oh? Then how is it you acquired my father's store, then? Was that an impersonal arrangement?"

Lilian paused to take a deep breath. She licked her lips and replied, calmly, "I can give it back to you, if you wish?"

Galahad's face flickered and for a moment, he thought he might vomit. He glowered at the pink blossoms and finally, turned back to Lilian. He grinned. The movement became a chuckle, and then a hearty guffaw. The dried saliva on his cheeks cracked and a drop of snot meandered into his mouth. Galahad was glad, as the repulsive taste distracted him from the Oleander plants. He looked away from the herb.

"I used you, I admit it." Vellencourt put her hand on Galahad's cheek, forcing him to look at her. "But I did not manipulate you as an individual. No, I used the presumptions of your neighbors against you. I utilized the stupidity of your neighbors against you. I did not simply bark at you like old Beauregard. I used the lingering suspicions he left in place. The latent misconceptions and the gnawing fears."

Vellencourt wiped Galahad's cheek. "I do not need to call you a mudpuppy. It is redundant. Dead men's words echo the name all across our country." She smiled, "I am hungry. Are you?"

"No," Galahad replied instinctually. He did not want to agree with her on anything, and yet—his stomach growled.

Vellencourt eyed his belly and smirked. "My, my, mister. Are you trying to prove a point?"

Galahad caught himself grinding his teeth. *Fuck it...* He licked his lips. "I'm famished."

Lilian Vellencourt beamed at him. "Let's fix that." She rang a little bell and remarked, "One of my cooks came down with a terrible headache, so we may have to wait a while for our meal."

Galahad lifted his shackles and frowned. "But I am in such a rush to finish my errand."

Greta entered the garden.

Lilian requested politely, "One last dinner for the doomed, please."

Greta's lips wiggled with an unsaid thought. She then murmured, "For two?"

Lilian rolled her eyes. "Obviously," she scowled, as if the answer should have been self-evident.

39

The Den of the Beast

Charles fidgeted. He glanced at deputy Northington. He was staring out a smudged window, squinting at the haze. He, like the constable, was distracted by news that the fugitive had been caught. Outside, the Pale were preparing for Galahad's trial.

What will they do for Arthur's? Charles could not bear the thought. He had come to terms with Arthur's actions, but he could not yet come to terms with his own. *I am condemning them as much as him.* Hanna, the kids, the inn itself—all would be shaken. *I may be destroying centuries of tradition with this claim. Oh, how the gossipers would talk. The innkeeper…* Charles straightened, reassuring himself. *I am not sharing the letter. No one needs to know the full truth.*

"And this, uhm," Goodwind's question devolved into a series of hoarse coughs. "Damnable smoke." He tried again after taking a swig from his flask. "This tattered cloth. It from one of those lost souls?"

"The boys that accompanied Arthur into the woods," Charles reiterated impatiently. "The stain is from a bullet wound to the chest." He pointed, "That water-logged rifle belonged to another young man. You can see the aspen leaves lodged in the barrel. Clearly, it was near the eastern mountain, where elevations permit aspen to grow."

"Clearly," Northington rolled his eyes.

Charles did not bother wasting words on the constable's deputy. While Goodwind *did* have a penchant for pride, the young man seemed to have a prerogative.

"I admit," the constable finally stood. "It's an interestin' story."

"A terrible story," Charles corrected.

"Indeed," the constable sniffled. He hoisted his trousers and tightened his belt. "But, I ain't have the men to verify yo' claim. Let 'lone bring in the innkeeper."

Charles quipped, "You have the men to fetch Galahad. Is Carolyn's word worth more than—"

The constable raised his fat hand, "I can go west and not east," he wheezed. "Because the son of Cambyses disregarded a magistrate's order."

Charles saw the constable's point, but he could not give up that easily. "I saw that noose. Awfully preemptive."

"Carolyn's stirrin' a hornet's nest. But she ain't able to lift the gavel an inch."

Charles bit his tongue. "So you will not, at the least, bring the innkeeper in for questioning?"

The constable turned his head and ordered deputy Northington, "Make sure that mare got 'nough hay. And tha' she stays outta the haze."

Edric then frowned at Charles, "I'm doin' alls I can, Eastmont. I'm lettin' tha' horse use our stables. I jus' can' bring him in. If this town gots a king, it's the innkeeper. Hearsay and miscellaneous items ain't enough to bring ruin down on the Gardners."

Charles felt a sense of relief that he had failed. At least for a day, Hanna would not be remembered for her husband. For a day, those children will grow up as children ought to. Charles swallowed. *But what if Arthur acts again? I am delaying only to worsen the pain...* He stormed down the jailhouse steps.

"Consider any new evidence," Charles heard the constable whisper to his deputy. "But keep this case quiet."

A haze thicker than any he had experienced in the Castle Rock bathed his skin. Charles covered his face with his shirt and walked around the Inner Ring. The marble homes were coated in muddy hues. The Pale, however, did not seem to notice the smog and hived around the walnut, now a hanging tree. Buchanan Bavar stood on a ladder, tightening the noose.

I wonder if Galahad underwent a similar torture as Arthur. What horrors did he have to bear to kill little Frederick? Charles shook his head, hoping the Muhali found peace.

Charles casted a cautious look at the Hill. *What evils men must endure to act as Galahad and Arthur do.* He frowned, *We do not call the War great because it turned us into gentlemen.*

Suddenly, his cautious look became a curious one. A Pale silhouette outlined in brown tumbled out of the granary. Charles watched the figure fall onto his back and skitter from the door. He squinted at the scene:

That's Aeric. With those long legs and no finesse in using them. What are you doing, son? Aeric laid on his back for only a second before leaping to his feet and glancing to his side. A moment later, he tiptoed back to the granary's entrance. *Why the hesitation? Close the door, then.* Yet, Aeric lingered there for a second too long for Charles to forget. *That's an odd action.* Aeric finally shut the door. *He's trying to be quiet. Doesn't want someone to see him.* Aeric stared ahead and kept his hands glued to his sides. He walked mechanically into the inn.

Charles clenched his jaw. *"Consider any new evidence,"* he recalled the constable tell his deputy. Charles sniffed and patted his side. Reassured by the cold metal of his weapon, he reluctantly crept up the Hill.

The door to the granary opened with a quiet creak. The haze was less thick in the ruined building, but a cold draft carried stench all the same. He probed forward, stepping onto a dirty rug. Despite seeming flat, his next step stopped short. He stubbed his toe against something underneath the rug. Charles grunted from the pain, but otherwise kept silent. He knelt to investigate, pulling the rug to reveal a handle.

A cellar? Charles guessed. He began pulling open the hatch.

Just as he started, the innkeeper's voice hissed through the stone. Charles held his breath.

"Dixon, little fella. What are you doing out in the cold?"

Charles' body stiffened and his eyes widened. He lowered the hatch and returned the rug to its original position. His ears followed the voice as it paced around the granary.

The innkeeper tutted his tongue. "You'll be missing out on supper if you stay out too long."

"I'm not hungry," the orphan answered indignantly. His voice was unnervingly close.

Arthur let a disappointed, "Oh," escape him. His footsteps grew louder and when he spoke next, he was dreadfully close. His voice carried through cracks in the cobbles. "That offends me."

Charles could see his shadow shifting.

"I—" Dixon began. "It's just, I heard sounds and I got curious."

Charles turned silently toward the door. He debated going upstairs, but did not think the stairs would silently bear him.

"Voices?" The innkeeper nodded. "I seriously doubt that. This place is condemned."

"B-but," Dixon argued.

Arthur interrupted. "Listen, my boy. I know your papa is dead and you have no discipline."

Charles could see his shadow bend down. A crooked, black hand attached itself to a smaller figure. He heard Dixon's hair rustling.

"*But*," the innkeeper continued. "When your benefactor tells you something, you don't argue."

Dixon shoved off the shadowy hand. "I have ears, mister. I heard something."

"Maybe you're going crazy," Arthur suggested. "Maybe your father's death has turned your reason to rot."

"He is not dead," Dixon glared.

Charles thought of the postman's body in the sunken glade. *Oh, you poor boy.*

Arthur's voice rose in pitch and his shadow slid backward. He leaned against the cobbles. Dust rained down from the rafters. Charles stifled the urge to cough.

"Your papa delivered mail to the crofters, yes?" Arthur asked.

"Yes," Dixon growled.

Arthur's cruel smile peeked through the wall. "Well, that means he probably got lost in the east, between the mountain of riddles and here. Am I right, my boy?"

Dixon answered nervously. "Yes."

"Ah," Arthur blurted out, acting as if he was having an epiphany. "It so happens I just travelled eastward myself."

That bastard, Charles clenched his fists. *He is enjoying this.*

"So?" Dixon scoffed.

"So," The innkeeper continued. "Ah, well—I should not be presumptuous. Let me first ask: How long has your papa been missing?"

Don't do this Arthur. Charles could tell where the conversation was going. *Do not be like this.* His old friend was fond of jokes, but this was not humor. This was torment.

Dixon spoke eagerly, even hopefully. "He went out to tell Miss Cora the war was over. He said it was going to be his last delivery to the mountain, but he didn't say why." The boy paused and he asked, "Did you see him?"

"I did. And I must say, it was the man's last journey. He did not lie to his son."

Dixon's shadow stood triumphantly. His happy eyes shone through the stone slits, saddening Charles even more. "I knew he wouldn't."

"But why hasn't he come back?" Arthur's voice was soft and naïve. "That is your next question, no?"

Dixon bobbed his head excitedly. "Uh huh."

"I cannot say for certain. I wish I had asked him, but I was in a hurry and he was in no mood to talk."

Charles could feel his heart thumping. His blood flowed hotly. His hands shook and his mind went still. He felt both calm and wrathful, as if he were preparing for a battle.

"But he is so far east," Dixon suddenly cried. "How will he get to me?"

"I do not know," Arthur pretended to care. "Perhaps it would be best for you to go to him?"

Dixon stayed silent.

"I have an idea," Arthur declared excitedly. "How about you think on it over some food, get some rest—and in the morning we can decide what to do?"

Dixon strayed away from the granary. His voice grew quieter, "I guess that's okay..."

"Perfect," Arthur said. He was now irritable and impatient. "Now off you go, before adults decide what is best for you."

The boy's footsteps faded. A minute passed before Arthur's shadow moved. He snorted, "Fucking kids," and moved toward the door.

Charles stepped back, praying the stairs did not betray him.

The door began moving.

Charles stepped onto the first stair. They had retained some sturdiness and did not groan from his weight. The door whined as it opened, giving him just enough time to reach the top of the staircase.

Two boots stepped inside. The door creaked and closed. It was as silent as the starless night is black.

Charles' forehead was glistening with sweat. The beads raced down his face toward the floor. He put his hand out and caught them before they fell. He wiped his forehead.

The granary groaned. Dust shivered and fell like snowflakes down from the ceiling. Charles felt a sneeze building in his nose. He tensed all the muscles in his body and denied the urge. Down below, footsteps fell like hammers to an anvil.

Then, all sound stopped again. All except the thumping of his heart. In that moment, Charles suddenly smelled something strange. The scent of biscuits, vegetable soup, and roasted chicken filled the granary. He did not have time to analyze the smell.

The innkeeper's knees cracked. Several strange sounds permeated the granary. As they did, Arthur chuckled, "There we are. Now, what did I say about making noise?" The man's voice was reverberating. It sounded like he now stood in an amphitheater. "Bad listener, tut tut tut." The innkeeper clapped his hands. Charles heard a thump and a ring, Then, all was silent once more.

Yet, he was certain the innkeeper would catch him if he descended now. Five minutes elapsed, testing his calm. Finally, the foreboding footsteps fell again.

Arthur whistled quietly. His lips must have been chapped, as the tune was airy and without melody. He grunted and sighed. There were two dull thumps. The door opened. The door closed.

A cellar. Charles had thought he knew everything about the inn, but he had never known about a cellar. *I suppose Arthur did live here. I only visited...*

Charles peeked from a hole in the mortar work. Arthur passed through the redwood door. The grove was silent and the haze obscuring. He returned to the rug where a hidden hatch laid. Charles rolled up the rug, bound by curiosity. He took the handle and opened the hatch, torn by his duty. He smelled vegetable soup and something else. The something else halted him.

The innkeeper has a secret. It may be enough to take him from Hanna. Feeling slimy for his thought, he added, *and the guests. The kids.* He put his foot on the top rung of a rope ladder. He peered down. *10 meters,* Charles estimated.

At the bottom, he was relieved to find an electric lantern. He flicked the switch. The darkness washed away with a buzzing electrical hum.

Once his eyes adjusted, he immediately noted a dirty plate. Napkins and silverware were laid neatly beside it, though they were oddly clean. He bent over and sniffed the messy plate. *Chicken,* he realized. *That would explain the smell from earlier. He was carrying a plate.* He pulled away and peered at the silverware. *What is Arthur doing bringing meals down here?*

With what he did to those young men, Charles decided, *I may never know what his motives are. I guess it explains where he has been eating…* Except, Charles saw, all the food was uneaten. Week old soups had coagulated. The fresh chicken had cooled. The silverware was dusty.

Charles probed the cellar. Curiously, it seemed too meticulously sculpted to be entirely natural. Each wall was flat and the room itself was perfectly square. Charles walked the perimeter. He felt the limestone for any other clues, coating his hand in cobwebs.

He turned a corner and his fingers brushed a tattered tapestry. The colors were worn, but the ornate weaving still told the old tailor's tale. He tilted his head as he analyzed the old ornament. *Seems to be from the settlers' time.* The scene depicted an old fable: A man with a musket stood below a hill, pointing up at several wooden shelters, lodges, and other structures. The heads of other people loomed at the foreground of the tapestry, their eyes following the commander's finger.

The Wanakhan cleansing, Charles remarked, leaning forward to inspect the work. As his weight redistributed onto the tapestry, however, the cloth began to fold in on itself. The sensation of falling overwhelmed him and he straightened. When the feeling passed, he hesitated. He gazed at the tapestry suspiciously. He poked the drape; it glided backward, revealing an emptiness directly behind it.

Charles blinked and bowed his head. He pushed past the tapestry and entered a hidden enclave. Worn cots were spaced evenly throughout the long hall. The sheets and pillows were all decayed and gone—but the frames remained. The vacillating darkness flickered. One by one, Charles inspected each bed. Every decayed cot was similarly abandoned except for one at the end of the chamber.

Charles knew at once who slept in that final bed. His lantern clanked; his hands shook. Unsteady legs brought him forward.

Frederick Kinsfeld had been laid delicately atop the dusty cot. A blanket covered his chest. *That's from the inn,* Charles noted begrudgingly. *The guest rooms have that same pattern embroidered on their sheets.* To Charles' horror, the smell of chicken came surging back. He sniffed. *Vegetable soup, too.* He eyed the nightstand beside Frederick's bed. A fresh plate of biscuits and vegetable soup laid uneaten.

Charles saw that the corpse's mouth was ajar and, after pulling his sleeve over his hand, nudged Frederick's rigid jaw. A fresh chicken wing fell out of the corpse's mouth.

Charles covered his own mouth and wretched. *Arthur… Oh no, Arthur.* He pulled the blanket back to reveal what he already knew: Frederick's corpse contained only one foot. The other was merely a pustule of rot. Seeing the dismembered body, he felt sorry for Arthur. *He relives that time during the war. He's too…* He looked at the fresh plate.

"He's still just trying to be a good innkeeper," Charles lamented quietly.

His legs had never felt so heavy. *This was no misfortune. No misunderstanding. He killed this child in cold blood.* His head had never been in such disunion with his heart. *How could he have changed so much?*

The stink of death mingled with the polluted fog. Charles sniffed the concoction of hazy decay. *He would have let Galahad take the blame for all of this.* He did not particularly like Galahad, but he felt sorry for the man. *All his suffering because of a supposed friend…* He would have to hurry to catch the constable. *Galahad cannot be condemned for this.* Yet, Charles found it difficult to condemn Arthur. Tears filled his eyes. A heavy weight made his head bob slightly. He was nauseous. If it had not been so dark, he was sure he would have been losing his eyesight. Ten seconds or ten minutes passed. Charles could not know how long he lingered there.

Every memory he had of Arthur Gardner began flooding back to him.

Charles recalled the years he had spent with Arthur in the capitol. A happy memory surged out of his nostrils as a nostalgic snort. The young fool used to come to him every night to ask him what Hanna thought of him. *'Okay, okay, Charles—say she doesn't like me? What then?'*

'You will just have to accept that,' Charles had said to his insecure friend.

Arthur shook his head, *'No, I could never do that. I love her.'*

Charles had tiptoed around his own feelings in that time. All he had wanted in that moment was to be a good friend, to Hanna and to Arthur. He stifled his own emotion and said, *'Then, we will just have to convince her you are the best man for her.'*

Charles had never forgotten the young man's reply. It had haunted him in his darkest moments and lifted him up in his best. *'Let's just hope she doesn't find out the truth.'*

'What might that be?' Charles had asked naively.

It had been one of only a handful of times when Arthur had hugged him. *'It is you, not me, that is the best man.'*

Charles had replied with some incoherent, humble nonsense. Whatever he had said, Arthur was having none of it. Tears came to his eyes as he remembered his oldest friend's words. *'None of us could ever hold a candle to you, Charles.'*

He had replied to Arthur's rare sincerity with a joke, some embarrassing quip about romance he had forced his mind to forget.

Charles squeezed his eyes shut and stifled his memories. They would only debilitate him further. *That is not the same Arthur. She is not the same Hanna.* Suddenly, he noticed that he was picking at his cuticles. Glancing down at the bloody, peeled skin, he was reminded of someone with that same tick. Charles' anxieties then halted. All his worries became melancholy rage.

"Some people die in the war and keep on living," Charles whispered to himself. He did not know where he had heard the words, or if he had just made them up.

Charles did not hear the granary door open.

Hanna is the smartest person in this entire, forsaken town. His tears seethed down his cheek as his head grew hot. *And Arthur will make her think she is the dumbest.* "Damn me," he muttered.

The footsteps above were nothing but the breeze knocking against the stone. Charles hoped the foundation was stronger than the haze.

I should never have encouraged Arthur. She is too good for him. And he is too bad for her. He sniffled and wiped his nose. *I need to get her away from his poison.* Even if she loved Arthur Gardner, her husband did not love her. *Not like he should.*

Charles flinched. *I am being selfish. Just like him.* His anxieties surged back. He was just like his father. He was going to ruin a marriage. He was going to take whatever he wanted, same as that vile monster. Charles' body vibrated. Indecision and incapacitating dread welled up until he thought he might convulse. His heart was beating harder than it ever had, even during the War.

Suddenly, the calm voice of Cora Eastmont came and quelled all his worries. It spoke not of hope, but of something vaguely like it. Charles nodded to the thought. *It is precisely when one most needs a friend that friendship is the hardest to give. Do not go back for yourself. Do it for her.*

This is not selfish, Charles said, with his mother's memory amplifying the thought. *Arthur was a friend, but my friend is gone. So too is Frederick Kinsfeld, and all the young folk Arthur murdered in the woods...*

"I cannot let Hanna," he winced, knowing if he continued the thought he would reveal too much. *If the town learns the full truth, Hanna's life will be over. Her children will grow up worse than if they were malchance.* Even Arthur, damn the man, did not deserve to be remembered as a lunatic. Charles swallowed the lump in his throat.

It can be framed as just a murder… The Gardners will be spared some of the aftermath…

Charles heard labored breathing behind him. Before he could turn around, a blunt force collided with his skull.

<h1 style="text-align:center">40</h1>

Deposits and Withdrawals

The eaves of Cottonwood loomed. Dark clouds had gathered over the forest. The naked, twisted branches wore a thin coat of snow. Belmont dismounted and reached into one of his storage containers. He equipped a large overcoat. He approached Galahad and took one of two water skins from his belt. One he reserved for himself—the other he used for his prisoner.

Galahad shook his head. He did not like the taste of the hunter's water. *He filled it on the mountain. I can taste it.* "I'm not thirsty."

"We are not stopping once we enter the forest," the bounty hunter pressed. He waited for a response. "Have it your way." The wagon rolled on.

That is exactly what I have not had, Galahad commented. He had a business. A life. Now he had business with death. He fought the urge to gag. The only thing that stopped him was the mask strapped to his face. If he vomited, there would be nowhere for the mess to go but back down his throat.

Belmont spoke as if replying to Galahad's thoughts, "I hate it when you lot resign to your fate."

"I am sorry I have not proved a better sport," Galahad mumbled. He glanced up at the darkening sky. The haze had ended dusk prematurely. Night swarmed as they travelled further into Cottonwood.

The hunter lit his pipe. The glow of embers illuminated a small circle around his head. Snow fell onto the bowl and simmered into vapor. Belmont blew a puff of smoke into the cold air. "You act as if you have already been tried."

"Haven't I?"

"Well running away *has* tarnished your case," Belmont agreed. "I think it obvious you are a murderer."

Galahad found that funny. "Do you, indeed? What is my tell?"

"Besides fleeing an investigation... It is your fascination with god."

"I don't believe in God," Galahad reminded. His nausea surged back. The warmth left his body. His muscles rattled to keep warm. A sharp pain stabbed his brain. He was sure all he needed was leaf. "Do you have any Oleander herb?"

Belmont sucked several gusts of air threw his pipe. The embers grew hot and cackled. "Of course not."

He's toying with me.

Galahad swayed in his seat. The shackles on his ankles sliced his skin. Sweat dripped down his throbbing forehead, leaking through his mask and into his gaping mouth. The nausea ebbed and flowed. "Leaf," he muttered. "Leaf."

Belmont grunted, "I'm doing you a favor."

Galahad dry-heaved. His arms were so, so itchy. Yet, he could not scratch.

"I'm like a divine intervention," Belmont laughed.

Galahad writhed, hating his body for being so weak. Since dawn—a headache had been patrolling his brain like a devouring worm. Currently, his forehead throbbed. If the pattern replayed itself, soon his ears would be thumping. The pain brought him to seething silence. Galahad had never been so angry in all his life. He quaked with a bodily hatred. Chills became sweats, sweats became chills.

Several minutes of travel elapsed before their silence broke. Neither Belmont nor his captive was responsible for breaking it. The wagon stopped. "Do you hear that?" the hunter asked. He pulled out his pipe and pointed in the direction of the sounds.

"Drumming?" Galahad thought immediately. *Bandits, perhaps?* Galahad hoped beyond hope he would get to see the bounty hunter murdered.

Belmont did not think so. He hopped off the wagon and peered into the vast darkness. "We still have several hours until we reach the outer ring," he claimed.

Galahad had trekked through these woods before. The journey might take all night. He commented, "If we have no incidents, perhaps."

"Belmont fears no wolf or lion."

Galahad rolled his eyes. He had known many officers like his captor. They were an arrogant breed prone to gallant displays of idiocy. He had no doubt that Belmont loved every moment of the Great War. *The bastard probably volunteered.*

His captor stared down the road. He scanned the pathway and pointed his weapon at any sound.

"Not going to make very good time like this," Galahad commented. Liquid trickled out his nostril and into his mouth. *Bloody nose.*

"Awfully eager to die," Belmont snorted.

"I am already dying," Galahad croaked.

Belmont grunted a reply. He gazed into the gloom. Finally, the wary hunter hoisted himself back onto the wagon. The fire in his pipe died away and he did not rekindle it. He kept his blunderbuss close, propping it up as a warning to any unfriendly eyes.

As the pair pierced deeper into the penumbra, it became clear there *were* unfriendly eyes watching them. Cries and calls crackled and crashed through the thicket. Large beasts bugled and bellowed. Eyes like crimson stars stared at them from the canopy. All the while, the faint drumming sound persisted.

The bounty hunter muttered to himself, "Like the damn Muhali war drums."

Galahad did not fear the terrors of the night. What could a beast do that his own body was not already doing to itself? He let his head hang forward and he closed his eyes. The bum-da-dum-da-dum of the drum lulled him into a conscious sleep.

He dreamed of the tangled roots of ghastly trees. He saw men with long hair like his, looking down from the glens with disgust. They carried bows and decorated their bodies with trophies and other oddities. Galahad assumed they were Wanakha. *Aren't you dead?* He asked one of the figures. It bowed its head and pointed for Galahad to continue. There was a look of sadness in that one's eyes. Other Wanakha were less sad. They were angry. Their arms drooped at their sides. They were long and tendril-like and at the wrists—the hands devolved into swirling, liquid gold.

Galahad opened his eyes. Only a biting cold told him that he was awake. He prepared for the nausea and the headaches. His body aches returned and his temperature rose. He began sweating. He shifted in his shackles, trying to find some way to stretch his wretched legs.

Belmont was chewing on the stem of his pipe. Though it was unlit, a red glow tinged his shadowy face. Galahad sighed and tried to go back to sleep. Instead, the wagon stopped. His body was jolted forward. Flakes of bloody skin were shaved off his wrists. Galahad groaned and glared at the hunter. He then saw why they had stopped.

A lantern barred the wagon's way. "Welcome ta' Auberdine," said a voice.

"I have come to deliver a bounty to the local law."

"As that'd be me, I would say you've come far 'nough," replied the constable.

"Do I detect resentment in your voice?"

Goodwind grumbled, "I sure hope so," and waddled to the wagon's side. "Y've spoiled yo' catch, hunter."

The constable's fat face was a prism of different colors. Galahad's teary eyes, as well as the pain in his temple, blinded him to the man's expressions. Galahad turned away as a thousand, invisible knives stabbed his body. He managed a few tired groans and a frothing, "Leaf."

The constable walked away. "What'd ya do t'him?"

The bounty hunter and the constable began to argue. There were mentions of Tanglewood, honor, reparations, atrocities, and other big words that had no meaning for a dying man. Galahad moaned, wishing the affair could just be over. As the two men transacted his life, he saw his father's face in the canopy. *Were it not for Frederick,* he snarled at the hallucination.

Galahad gnawed on his tongue, distracting himself from his thoughts. Yet, he could entirely ignore the fact that he was being punished. *Punished for my father!* He asked his hallucinations, *How mechanical could you be?* The crimson-eyed canopy collectively blinked.

He would not bear it. As the constable lifted his twitching body, he rationalized his fate. *This is not a punishment. Not for him. This is something else. Some other crime.* Galahad glared at the constable's pudgy face. Pink hands locked chains around his wrists and ankles. A thick arm guided him into a box welded atop an automobile. The constable closed his mobile jail, circled around, and climbed atop the smoking vehicle.

Galahad analyzed his new quarters. A row of iron bars acted as a window to the Cottonwood. At the head of the automobile, another set of bars gave Goodwind a view of his prisoner. He inspected the bars between him and the constable. He put a hand on the cold metal and nudged the bars slightly. Galahad thought he felt them move, but just then—a wave of nausea hit him. Like a reluctant vassal before its lord, he knelt. A slight trickle of vomit came from his mouth. The taste quickly triggered more. He gagged until he could not breathe, and his tongue seemed to hang by a thread.

The constable asked his prisoner, though his eyes were not open. "You sick? I know Misses Gardner had something. You catch it?"

"Huh?" Galahad rasped. The question had been muted by his heaving.

"Ya sick with the Rot?" the constable asked again.

"Not with Rot," Galahad shivered. "Just get me some," he gagged. His chest convulsed. A pain shot up his arm. *Is this what a heart attack feels like?* Blood leaked from his nose into his mouth. He swallowed the droplet and spoke, not attempting to hide the quaver taking over his voice. "The plant. Oleander."

"Ya cannot go back to the mountain until ya have yo' trial," the constable said in a tone of boredom. He looked near to falling asleep.

"Leaf!" Galahad pleaded. He was not sure if the tears in his eyes were from gagging or from longing. Regardless, he felt he would die without his medicine. He made no attempts to wipe his tears, knowing they might stir the lawman to getting him some leaf.

"Leaf?" The constable repeated.

"Damn you," Galahad bit down on his tongue. Fighting the urge to scream, he gritted his teeth. "Get me Yang. He knows."

The constable rubbed his eyes. He wheezed into a handkerchief. He glanced at the cloth and uttered, "Oh dear." He tossed the soiled item into the thicket.

Galahad scratched his face. *Maybe he is in withdrawal, too… He must be hiding the leaf!* Little bits of skin started to shave off but itching felt so good—Galahad could not stop. When his fingernails started to turn bloody, Galahad simply licked them. He sucked each finger and bartered, "Then anyone." He slurped, excited by his new, most convincing argument. *He just doesn't want to share. But he doesn't want to be a fool, either. I will call his bluff!* "I-It is a little pink flower. Prettiest flower. Medicine in the leaves. When we get to town, you can find—"

The automobile halted. The constable leaned forward and put his hands on his thighs. "I won't be that easy to get rid of." Goodwind turned and saw Galahad's lips begin to quiver. He shook his head and said sympathetically, "And trust me. Ya don't want to be alone. Not with Kinsfeld in a rage."

His feigned sorrow and disgusting pity were too much. Galahad stormed toward the bars and rattled them. "I am dying!" He groped for the man's keys dangling by his waist.

The constable flinched in time. He gave his prisoner a disciplinary look.

Galahad prepared a slew of insults but choked on all of them. He fell to the floor, gagging. Nothing came from his stomach except a small, solid substance. It looked quite like a pebble. Galahad blinked at it and prepared to vomit again. As he waited, though, he found he was no longer very nauseous. He gazed at constable Goodwind, now standing at the doorway. His eyes were saucers of sympathy. Galahad quickly looked back at the floor. He did not feel sick anymore. *But he does not have to know.* Galahad groaned. He laid on his back and cradled his stomach.

"Oh dear," the constable frowned. He shook his head and muttered, "I blame the father…"

Galahad interrupted his writhing and snarled, "What!?"

"For yo' defect," Goodwind answered delicately. "A crop's only 'sgood as its field." He placed his arms behind his back and bowed slightly. "I think I know what ya need."

Galahad licked his lips. He went to the perimeter of his enclosure and kissed the ground. "They are little pink flowers. Not the blossoms. Leaves. Thank you, thank you. The leaves. Just enough." He looked up at the constable and tried his best to smile, "To help with the pain."

The constable left. He must have had some on hand because it only took a moment for him to come back around.

Galahad was on his knees, wiping his tears. He thanked the constable once again and held out his hands. Yet, as Goodwind approached—he saw something funny in the lawman's hand. "That is not my medicine," he realized.

The constable opened the prison door. "No, but it always helps when I detain a drunkard."

Galahad fell backward and skittered to the edge of the enclosure. "No," he spat. "I'm sick. They are little, pink plants."

"I know, son," the constable replied quietly.

Galahad's lips twitched. His cheeks rolled and sagged. His fists trembled. His body surged with adrenaline. His mouth began to froth.

"Y'ain't dying," the constable approached warily. "I know what y'are going through. This will help with yo' cravings. Y'll be able to sleep."

Galahad rose. "I will not be taken for a fool anymore." He lunged at the lawman's throat. Then, as sudden as lightning strikes, a pleasant sensation shot into his leg. A numbness washed through his body. Galahad tilted his head in surprise, opened his mouth, and fell to the ground.

He awoke feeling restless. His chest was heavy and the prison was thick was dirty air. The automobile did not bounce as much, leading him to think they had finally reached the Overgrowth. *Still dark,* he noted. He rubbed the back of his skull and recalled the past events. He could not recall what had happened after the constable had taken him. *I must have been very tired.* He stretched.

Then, he shuttered. Galahad shivered and fell forward onto the nearby chamber pot. His tongue felt like it was being yanked from his throat. His stomach spewed out. Green chunks and coagulated blood filled the waste barrel.

The constable chuckled, "There we go. Get that outta yo' system."

Galahad turned his head and wiped his mouth. "Get what?"

Goodwind waved a dismissive hand. "Never mind. Feelin' better?"

Galahad gagged. He swallowed the acid in his throat and growled, "Fantastic."

"Thought you had Trench Rot at first," the constable stated.

Galahad sniffled. His stomach roared. He managed a grin, "Perhaps I do."

A smirk flashed on Goodwind's face. "Hungry, I bet."

Galahad blinked several times. "Yes," he quickly replied. A few seconds later, he continued his thought. He spoke slowly, "But, I am fine. I think, that—do you have any leaf?"

"Empty belly it is," the constable shrugged. "Suit yourself."

I did suit myself, Galahad sighed at his disgusting, purple vestment. *I was on my way toward success.* For the first time in his life, he was reaching his goals. *I would have made my first million.* He glanced at the dozens of undigested stems floating among the rest of his stomach contents. He scratched his neck and quickly lost all interest in thinking about the mountain. He got to his feet and approached the constable.

Galahad leaned forward, pushed the iron bars, and said, "You know, I could probably break these before you could even stand up."

Goodwind replied with slight grogginess, "Go 'head." His voice was airy and weak. He rolled his shoulders, "But I'm the only thing keepin' that mob from ya once we pull into town."

Galahad chuckled and shook the bars. They clanged and the hinges heaved slightly. He retreated to the corner of his cell. He pressed his cheeks against the rear-facing bars, staring at the outer ring. They passed a group of men gambling in the street. From what Galahad could see, they were not betting money. Only loaves of bread, potatoes, and some fruit had been placed in the pot. An old Pale man shrieked and threw his cards, "I have been cheated. How dare you dupe Degory? My granddaddy's daddy was the fourth duke of Aubourg! Deromir the Valiant!"

Galahad remarked wearily, "The Overgrowth is particularly wild."

The constable leaned forward. "Nothin' can be done 'bout them 'till the Inner Ring sobers up."

Sobers up, Galahad repeated silently. He sniffed. Auberdine stunk of the Oleander's refineries. *Why must this haze hound me?* He rolled his tongue between his upper and lower jaw. He licked the inside of his cheek as he thought aloud, "The constable consumed by the mob."

"Consumption is indeed a problem," the constable coughed.

Galahad raised his brow and told him, "I will not have a fair trial. I don't ask you to change that," he pressed his tongue against his canines, "But if they are drunk off emotion, can I be wasted on my preferred intoxicant?" In the silent second that followed, Galahad smelled and tasted the leaf. He spat, "Little leaf with a pink flower. The Yao have some."

Goodwind said nothing.

"Oh come," Galahad groaned. "At least let me choose my last meal. Will you take that from me, too? That and a fair trial?" He waited for the response. *I have him. That fat fuck cannot argue with my logic.*

Goodwind would hear none of it. As dumb as the constable was, it was clear to Galahad that the fat man was an idealist. He thought of the law and of justice like a man thinks of a crush. There were no imperfections in law. The process was perfect. Guilty men went to the gallows, innocent men were acquitted. "We will follow the law," he said.

Galahad grinned but he wanted to shout. He muttered, "Whatever you say." He paced up and down his bouncing prison. There was an energy in his legs that made it impossible to stay still. He wanted to slice the muscles in his thighs just to relieve the energized feeling. *Is this what sobriety feels like?* He coughed, "Overrated body high."

The constable ignored the remark.

I suppose this was the only way I would quit, he chuckled. *Perhaps I will. If this fat cunt is right, I may be in jail for a few months.* He snorted, "Had to get chained to get free. Fuck me."

While the constable again ignored him, his symptoms did not. Galahad's sight shimmered into shards of watery light. Nausea nudged its way into his head. His throat swelled and contracted while his tongue stretched out. Galahad winced and restrained his sickness. His muscles ached and a deathly cold nestled itself in his bones. The withdrawal convulsions continued for many minutes. Galahad closed his eyes and focused on his breathing. Whenever he felt the urge to vomit, he took a deep breath and held it. He could do nothing about the chill and tried his best to ignore it. He only had to wait out the storm.

When the pains subsided, Galahad smiled. He was learning the motions. *I can get through this.* What was more, he no longer had any opportunity to succumb. The bodily hurt of his symptoms was nothing compared to his mental symptoms. The constable was a firm man. He would not yield.

So, what is the harm in trying again? A faint voice chimed. Galahad turned his ear at the voice. It sounded vaguely like his own. He nodded to himself. The suggestion was quite logical. No harm in asking. "Mister constable, sir. Please. If you could just call on the Yao?"

"Yao Yang is busy. His uncle has a terrible cough and wants no visitors."

Galahad seethed. "You could fetch some strapping young boy, then? I am *sure* it grows wild."

"I don't do favors for prisoners."

Galahad blinked, tilted his head, and remarked to himself, *As long as I am imprisoned, I am free.* "Hm," he grunted. *What a curious turn of phrase.* Driven by an intense hope, Galahad felt he had to speak. "You know, Edric—may I call you Edric?"

"Consider it a last rite," the constable chuckled. "If death is, indeed, yo' fate."

It is, Galahad knew. He looked around his cell, as dull and dark as any waiting room to hell ought to be. He was sure it was dawn, but the sun's rays were a tinted darkness. "Well," he began, "I don't really mind the cell." He started to laugh, only stopping when a piercing cough interrupted him. Once his throat was clear, Galahad continued, "Call me crazy if you want, I certainly do—but knowing I am barred from the world has an odd comfort."

Galahad blinked at Edric. The constable did not speak and so, Galahad replied to himself. *The world and its temptations are moot in here. The din is muted.* He bit his lower lip and beamed up at the ceiling. The drumming was getting louder. The droning rhythm was for him.

Goodwind grunted a laugh. The muscles in his body clicked and clacked. "With that racket," he rolled his eyes, "I can see why." He tapped the thin iron posts of his mobile jail. "These here bars keepin' horrors on both sides away."

Galahad feigned offense and frowned. "You think I am a horror, Edric?" It felt good to joke. He had forgotten who he had been, this 'Galahad.' *I used to be so funny,* he remarked. *So fun.* Everything had gotten so serious, so dark. Between his ambition and his addiction, he had stopped finding time for Galahad. Even during the war, he had found time to make light of things.

Goodwind struggled to reply, stifling a quiet cough.

"I think I am a horror," Galahad remarked casually. "How could I joke on the eve of my own hanging, otherwise?"

The constable shook his head, as if he were sad to see a criminal hang. "Ain't no goblin that ain't a human first."

Galahad pouted, "Fine. Be polite." He tilted his head, smirking. "Do you think I did it?"

The automobile stopped. The engine sputtered a sneeze of fumes. The constable stood tall and declared, "I do." He clicked his belt a deal tighter and looked directly at his prisoner. "I knew the moment I served you that letter."

Galahad raised his arms in a futile gesture. "Well," he coughed. "You're right... In part." He coughed again, "I am a guilty man." He sighed and soaked in the constable's shocked face. He breathed so freely, he wondered if he had gained a third lung.

The constable waved a finger and shook his head. He shuffled toward the stairs and muttered, "I'll pretend I didn' hear that outta curtesy f'our customs." He heaved a heavy leg onto the first of many steps. He lumbered off the automobile.

"I am a killer," Galahad called after him. His lips formed around another confession, *I am an addict.* That truth, however, never made it through the locks in his throat. Some particularities of Galahad would only be his to know. An annoying lump lodged itself in his chest. He coughed, but the feeling remained.

"If called to testify," the constable recited, "I will be forced—"

Galahad snapped. Before he had time to think, he rushed his bars and rattled the iron. "Damn the trial." He shivered and wished he had some company in his cell. He wished he had something to drink, eat, or do. *Maybe they will give me a last supper, or some other request...* The prospect of being free, however, suddenly terrified him. He shivered again, but he was not cold.

"It will not be fair," he whispered a shout. "It has *never* been fair." He coughed and wiped the water in his eyes, "So to hell with me." Galahad skittered to the back corner of the room. He wanted to be as far from the outside world as he could be.

"They will take me away no matter what," Galahad whispered for his own sake. "Or it will take me away."

The constable eyed him with curiosity.

"I don't want to become a circus."

"Your trial will not be a circus," the constable said proudly.

Galahad let him think the trial was what he meant by his comment. The drums continued beating, reminding him of the war he once fought. *I never left the front...*

Edric cleared his throat. "I am goin' ta settle'm down. This drummin is a heresy. I'm sure, as a veteran, those drums remind ya of evil... D'ya want some water?"

"No," Galahad barked. "No food, either." His hunger was a devil that did not deserve any satiation.

Edric narrowed an eyebrow at him and nodded. A strange appreciation was in his look. Then, he sighed and hoisted his belly above his belt. The lawman left him in the muddy darkness.

When the constable was out of sight, Galahad's belly roared. He spat a glob of saliva as he called, "For pity's sake! Leaf!"

The constable grunted.

What does that mean? Galahad eyed his shoulders. God, he was itchy! He dragged his long nails down the length of his legs. He shuddered, "Oh, yes. A grunt. Too prideful to give in to me, but too genial to deny me."

The drumming ceased.

Galahad hobbled toward the front of the cell. He sat, crossed his legs, and leaned forward onto a raised arm. He wrapped his chin around his hand and stared at the bars. He noted the familiar fog lazily sinking and rising like airy waves. Galahad thought about the haze and for the first time in many months, his mind did not wander. A gust of exasperated air rolled through his lips.

Galahad remarked to his cell, "Cambyses should have gotten arrested... Would have made him a better man." He placed his palms on his thighs and annunciated with relish, "Rehabilitated." He giggled and stomped his feet giddily.

"He is here?!" Galahad heard a shouting voice. Another voice declared, *"Well, let's be done with him here and now!"*

Galahad nodded mournfully. He wondered if they would hang him in the same place as Terrell, or somewhere different. He hoped they spruced the event up a little, added some flare. Galahad did not want things to be dull. *Perhaps we could paint the gallows a fun color, or a—*

A moment of clarity came to him. *Am I really fawning over the details of my execution?* Galahad scratched his neck and joked with his cell, "All this planning, people are going to think I am getting married."

Suddenly, a thought flew into his head. Galahad bent his neck up at the ceiling, observing the idea like a soaring bird. Sure enough, his execution would end his life. Galahad popped his lips and sent a gust of air rolling from them. "Poof," his eyebrows flared. *But that is not all it will accomplish.*

Galahad stood up. He began pacing from one end of the cell to the other. *I killed Cambyses and on that same day, I stole his medicine. After that, I became the same wretch my father was. All his weaknesses and faults became mine. He wanted success but only ever found the bottle and—*

A chill settled in his heart as he recalled his last few months: reveling with his medicine, climbing the mountain, and starting his business. He was tempted to be sad. Then, Galahad remembered Vellencourt's manipulation, the back and forth of his cravings, and the ruin of his dreams. He remembered the lack of sleep, the paranoia, and the end of many friendships.

"*That* was my punishment," Galahad surmised. That conclusion excited him and he scoffed, "Not a hanging!"

Galahad burped at the silence that followed. He scratched his neck. "An end to misery," he announced. And it had been misery. *If there is a God, I hope I gain some visitation rights to ask him about this.* Galahad eyed the ceiling and as more Pale cried out for his death, he wondered about his fate. *How many coin flips have there been to get me to where I am? What are the odds I kill my father, become an addict in turn, and am forced to live in his shoes?*

If there was a God, he was a damn good writer. Galahad folded his hands and swallowed. He tugged at his collar. Cambyses was still an awful man. *He deserved to die.* Galahad licked his lips and admitted, *like father, like son.* A dreadful cough took hold of him. He spat and convulsed and when his throat was as dry as a desert—trickles of blood flowed from his mouth. Coagulated blood splattered onto the floor. Galahad rasped, gasping for breath. The coughing subsided, leaving him light-headed and gazing down at his feet.

The taste of blood in his mouth, the moistness around his lips, and the pain in his chest—they made Galahad giggle. He resembled his father on the day he died. Galahad tickled his arms and wheezed. *And so the metaphor is complete.*

"But not quite," Galahad noted. He looked at the ceiling accusingly, "How come *daddy* got to go with his drink and I have to go without? Playing favorites, hm?"

"Oh, fuck it," he rolled his eyes. He wiped the blood around his lips and rubbed it on his forearm. He nudged the metal walls like an old drinking buddy. He opened his mouth to joke about his execution, but his jaw simply hanged. An image of all the people who had ever loved him came to mind. He imagined what their reactions would be to a rope around his neck. He pictured Laverne weeping, little Emilia hiding her face, and Arthur shaking his reserved head. He wondered how they would take the news. *Galahad, son of Cambyses, was a murderer.* Galahad swallowed and quickly decided he did not want to think about his death. He fidgeted and tried to distract himself.

Luckily, it was not long before Goodwind returned. "Y'all stay back. I am taking the prisoner to jail. We gots to be civil. Stay back!" The constable whispered to his prisoner, violently, "Y'ill get a fair trial if it takes all winter."

Galahad chuckled awkwardly. *I would rather not be paraded from court to cell.*

The constable gave a gravelly cough that ended with a muffled groan. "Damn fog. Damn inn. Damn mob." He wheezed as he waddled to the door. He reached for the keyhole. "It's my own damn fault. Weakness." The constable let out a few more, muffled coughs. He rubbed his forehead and unlocked the cell. Then, he took in a deep, squeaking breath. "Not anymore," he finally said. "I am the law and I will maintain it."

"You've had an eventful morning," Galahad quipped. He noted the eerie silence slipping through the ceiling. "Sounds like you muzzled them."

The constable wheezed. He seemed to be slowing down. His normal drawl was like molasses slipping out of a toppled jar. "Told 'em... They were disturbing..." He trailed off and his eyes rolled back.

"I have never met a man as tired as you," Galahad shook his head.

The constable's chest rose and as it fell, his body trembled. A series of small coughs turned into a perpetual hacking.

"You aren't a smoker, are you?" Galahad inquired. "Terrible irony if so, I would say..." He recoiled when he saw the constable's face. Edric Goodwind's cheeks were turning blue, his eyes were crimson, and his neck was a throbbing purple. His sweaty hands slid from their roost and the constable tumbled backward.

The haze! Galahad shouted, "Get up! Let's get you inside!"

Edric groped at his neck and foul brown tears poured from his eyes. He glanced at his prisoner in terror.

Galahad leapt from prison. He vaulted to the constable's side. He took hold of the man's hand. The fingers like a slithering snake slipped from his grasp. "Edric, you have to breathe," Galahad growled. "You fat fucker, just breathe," he shouted.

It was no use. A wisp of air escaped his windpipe. His tongue wriggled like a worm squirming up from the soil; it straightened and stiffened. Then, his tongue, his hands, and the rest of his body all went limp.

Galahad stared at the scene in disbelief. He licked his lips and bit his tongue. He glanced at the open cell. He eyed the foul liquids on his hands. Sickened, he hobbled away. He glanced over at the dead lawman. It seemed like mud was oozing out of his eyes. The veins in his hands crisscrossed his flesh like bloody streams. *God, he looks like Cambyses.* Another spat of nausea overwhelmed him. Galahad lurched. He inhaled the fumes of his sickness and gagged.

Finally, when he thought he too might choke if he stayed bent over, he lifted his head. He dared not look at the constable. So, he stared at the eaves of Cottonwood.

I could leave, Galahad realized. *I might even escape.* Galahad tilted his head and bobbed it in acknowledgement. *There would be no bounty hunter this time.*

Galahad shook his head at that idea. *Not for a while. But they would come. Even more now.*

I wouldn't go back to the mountain. Not with Vellencourt there. He would have to go somewhere else, somewhere nobody expected him to go.

Redfeather. Galahad smirked. *Yes, nobody would think I would want to return there. Nobody would want to visit that ruined country.* Galahad stepped toward the stairs. He closed his eyes and bowed his head at the constable. "I am sorry, sir."

He jumped up. *I wonder if there are any Oleander plants that far north?*

Galahad swallowed. He scratched his fingers and belched. He glanced back at his cell longingly. He sucked in his lower lip.

I cannot leave as I entered, Galahad decided. He eyed the constable's corpse. *That will be how you end up. All dirty and foul.*

A hateful tear fell from his eye. It seemed no matter what he did, he would die for it.

I will go somewhere safe from the plant, Galahad reasoned. The idea lasted for a few moments before he dismissed it. He could not be delusional anymore. Galahad sighed and said, "I inherited my father's talents." Like Cambyses found his bottles, Galahad would find his herb. *I cannot lie to myself. Not now.*

He closed his eyes and slowly began to nod. He lifted his foot to make his decision, stay or go; suffering or *suffering,* freedom or *freedom.* Just then, he heard a shout. Galahad froze. A stampede of footsteps stormed toward the constable's automobile.

"I don't care about the process, Edric!" Several pairs of feet stomped into view. Carolyn Kinsfeld's voice rang, "I am sorry, but—"

The cruel widow homed in on the lifeless figure.

On the other side of the corpse, Galahad stared at her. He sighed at the forest, glad the decision was not his to make.

Buchanan Bavar and deputy Northington halted in disbelief.

Galahad's arms fell to his waist. He relaxed his posture and strode toward his accusers. They yelled at him to stay put. He ignored them. He walked back into his cell and, once sufficiently behind bars, greeted them. "Hello, gentlemen."

Carolyn's nose twitched. Her head darted left and right to try to understand what had happened. She glanced at Goodwind and then, from the corner of her eye, at Galahad. She might have been grinning.

Buchanan Bavar declared, gruffly, "He's a murderer after all. Jus' as filthy as the sire."

Northington rushed over to the constable's side and took hold of his hand. He wiped his brow, which seemed quite dirty to Galahad. His voice trembled, "Let's hang him and be done with it."

Carolyn stepped into Galahad's cell. Her tongue roved along the side of her cheeks, prodding the flesh. She spoke only from one side of her mouth, as her tongue was predisposed. "Well..."

"Let's get this over with," Buchanan said sluggishly. "I don't want to miss breakfast."

"No," Carolyn said. "Edric's dying wish was for this little troglodyte to have a trial." She raised her brow triumphantly, "We must honor that request."

41

Husband in a Haze

The tavern was a great deal colder. Though the fireplace was blazing at the end of the hall, nobody sat by the fire. The side booths were vacant. There was only one person at the petrified table. Arthur slouched in his seat. He hunched over his soup and stared at it with a changing mixture of disgust and horror.

Despite the hall's emptiness, Hanna felt claustrophobic. She frowned at the windows. The freezing fog had still not lifted. Now, it seemed to have changed colors. It had taken a muddy hue. The little wisps that licked the windows stained the glass with dirty streaks. The sunlight scattered, turning the morning into a bloody sunrise. Hanna hated it. *It's cold, it's stinky, it's ugly, and my husband won't eat.*

She smiled at Arthur. He did not notice. He had not said anything to her since last night. Nor had he slept. Instead, while Hanna pretended to sleep, Arthur paced around the bedroom, muttering to himself. Occasionally, he would stop and just stare at her.

Hanna tried to joke, but her frustration overtook her tone. "For someone not eating their food, you spend a lot of time looking at it."

Arthur scowled at his bowl.

Hanna felt he was scowling at her. *He hasn't forgiven me.* She tapped her toes on the floor. *Well I haven't forgiven you.* Her knees bounced as she searched for something to say. She leaned forward and tried to sound as enthusiastic as she could. "Maybe when the fog goes away, you can go fishing?"

Arthur licked the side of his teeth. A little bump swiveled across his cheek. He grumbled, "I haven't caught anything noteworthy since—" he rolled his lips in a wavy pattern and sighed at his soup. "Since I can't remember when..." He sighed, scratched his forehead, and smiled.

The smile was so forced, Hanna would have preferred he had frowned.

He pushed his soup away, "I'm okay. Besides, that fog is putrid. Bet it is killing all the fish." He blinked a few times and his smile shivered. He got up and pocketed his hands. "Have you seen Aeric?"

He asked the question with an unsettling, worried tone. Hanna shook her head. She had not seen him since last night. *He's acting as strange as you lately,* she might have said in another life.

Her husband walked to the window. He stared into the dirty storm. "Don't go to the granary. I am doing some maintenance."

"Okay," Hanna quickly agreed. It was always best to answer him quickly when he got into one of his bad moods.

Hanna hoped the creeping fog did not get inside the inn. It sank and stayed wherever it went. It swam like something living and left like something dying, shaking and squirming up the sky like spirits. And an awful chill remained wherever the fog went. She walked over to the fire. It did not seem as warm. *It's all this empty space,* Hanna reasoned.

She started to pace but stopped when the thudding and thumping of her footsteps made her feel insecure. Though he did not move, she felt that her husband was annoyed by her. All his smiles were a lie, a scream teetering on the edge. *I just need to avoid him for the day. He's gonna brood, that's all.* She stopped pacing, shivered, and rubbed her hands. The sliding of her skin sounded like a stampede in the silent hall. She heard her husband sigh and promptly froze.

I'll just go check on Emilia.

Upstairs was even colder, though the echo was not as bad. Hanna sniffled and, when she heard her daughter do the same, paused at her door. She heard her sniffle again. *She's crying,* Hanna determined. She quietly took a few steps backward. After a moment, she stomped forward and knocked on the door.

Emilia sniffed. She sucked up her snot and said with a congested drawl, "Come in."

Hanna stepped in and smiled at her daughter. She did not mention the girl's red eyes or tear-stained shirt. Knowing, she asked, "How's my sugarbear?"

Emilia was sitting on her windowsill, looking out the circular pane. She did not look at her mother and stared at the oozing fog instead. "We shoulda gone with Charles."

Hanna felt a force wrap around her neck. When she spoke, only the slightest sounds squeaked out. "This is our home..." She cleared her throat.

Emilia turned her head and gave her mother a nasty look. She flared her nostrils, "He left us." A moment later, she bowed her head and wiped her eyes. She stuttered, "H-he left you." She cried as she whispered, "E-even th-though he knew—" she rocked back and forth and let out a sharp cry. "T-that you needed help."

Hanna took a step to console her daughter. "I wish people would stop saying I need help."

"B-but," Emilia started. She shook her head and after a second of silence, her lips trembled. Little gusts of air were all the words her daughter could manage. "You were f-fine w-when Charles looked after you."

It sounded to Hanna like her daughter's throat was being squeezed. She looked at the redness around her cheeks and felt the fresh wound on her own thumb. She frowned and approached her daughter.

"I wish he was my daddy a-and Arthur was dead."

Hanna interrupted her stride so quickly, she nearly fell backward. A fearful eye darted toward the open door and blinked at the empty corridor. Hanna tugged at her collar and muttered, "Don't you say that. Ever again." She felt a surge of embarrassment. Her body stiffened as a wild twitch went through her.

Emilia eyed her mother. Then, she closed her eyes and hid her face.

Hanna anticipated the girl's tears. She hesitated and stood dumbly between the corridor and the window.

Emilia petted the sill mechanically.

Hanna took her hand and massaged it. "I'm sorry, sugarbear. I should not have snapped." She hesitated, knowing her apology was not well received. "Emilia?"

"H-he wants to shoot him," came her daughter's muffled voice. "Charles."

"He does not," Hanna said lovingly. "Your father isn't happy with Uncle Charles, but he would never—"

"I *heard* him," Emilia persisted. She left the sill and leapt onto the bed. She hid behind her sheets.

She was dreaming, Hanna knew. She sat on the edge of the bed and put her hand on Emilia's leg.

The girl's leg twitched and retreated further up the bed. She threw the covers off her face, "He is *always* yelling! He's so mean. A-and Charles is so nice! W-why can't you see?"

An unbidden thought replied, *I can see, sugarbear.* Hanna washed the response away before it could do any damage. She replied, hopefully, "I don't like the anger, either... B-but he'd never hurt anyone." Hanna leaned forward and said, quite proudly, "'Specially not with me around." She beamed at her daughter, feeling *that* might console her.

It did not. Emilia sniffled and brooded for a moment. She sucked in her bottom lip and stared at her mother. Finally, she furrowed her brow. The girl spoke with a seriousness that shocked Hanna at first. "Being a woman is a mix of wanting to feel safe and not wanting to be afraid."

Hanna gazed at the ceiling. "Well, I suppose that's true... You're such a smart girl." She was quite sure a compliment would turn around the girl's bad mood.

It did not. Emilia's lips reverted to a familiar tremble. She curled her legs up to her chest. With her face hidden between her knees, she whispered, "You said that. To Aeric and me."

Hanna tilted her head as she tried to remember. Vague memories of benches, boys, and trees zipped through her mind. Her hands floated up; her arms wrapped around her own chest. She saw her son and daughter looking up at her. She heard the taunts of local boys. Hanna bowed her head. "Oh..." She admitted, shame filling her sorry heart. "I did not," she struggled for the word, "remember."

The sheets shuffled. Emilia crawled over to her mother and rested her head on her shoulder.

Hanna let out a pained sigh and closed her eyes. *I haven't recovered at all. I am still the same idiot I was the day I woke up.* She shook her head, denying her tears. *I can't even remember how to be a mother.*

"It's okay not to remember, mama."

Hanna snorted, smiled slightly, and put her hand on Emilia's head. She held her daughter closer and admitted, "I don't feel okay."

They sat in silence for a long while. Both had no idea what to say. Hanna thought they had come to the end of their conversation, with neither quite able to make the other feel better. When one of them sighed, the other did as well. Hanna looked at Emilia. Her daughter stared at the wall, making no attempt to speak. So, Hanna looked at the wall and stayed silent, too.

Emilia lifted her head and scooted in front of her mother. She crossed her legs and gulped. She scratched her head and slowly started to speak. "It's okay not to remember..." She sniffled and bowed her head. "But it's not okay to not feel safe. It's not okay to always be afraid."

Hanna smiled. Her chest felt like someone was stepping on it. She whispered, "I did say being a woman was a mix of the two... Feeling safe and feeling afraid."

Emilia looked up. "But it isn't a mix," she cried. "You aren't yourself anymore."

Hanna shrugged off her growing defensiveness. She said, trying not to get annoyed. "Honey. The doctors cut my brain open. Of course I—"

Emilia interrupted her. "You were still you when Charles took care of you."

Hanna opened her mouth to disagree, licked her lips, and looked away.

Her daughter continued, speaking rapidly, "Now, it is like you aren't even a, a—" Emilia froze, as if not wanting to continue her thought. She squeaked a quiet, "Mom."

Hanna swallowed and nodded. She did not want to remember Charles Eastmont. So, when the unwanted memories came, she was both terribly angry and horribly sad. She recalled the days where he sat with her outside, patiently helping her read and speak. *He never raised his voice at me*, she thought she remembered. Hanna recalled how he had always tried to keep her happy and to make her laugh. *I haven't laughed with Arthur in a long, long...*

Hanna stopped herself. She rotated her head and popped the kinks in her neck. She got off the bed and stood as tall as the weight on her shoulders allowed. She spoke as loudly as the tightness around her neck allowed, "You're stressed. We all say stuff we don't mean when we're stressed."

Emilia did not say anything else as she left. Hanna was glad. She loved the girl, but she needed a break from her daughter. She walked to her office and stared at the door. A brewing guilt began to boil. Hanna reassured herself, *Even the best mothers need alone time*. She nodded at the thought, tried to stay calm, and went into her office.

At first, she thought she had taken a wrong turn. Her desk and her books were all missing. Then, she recalled that Arthur had turned her study into a nursery. Hanna approached Emilia's old crib. She felt ashamed as she touched the mobile hanging above. She felt not even the slightest nostalgia seeing the old furniture. *I guess this proves Emilia right. Real moms feel something when they see this stuff...*

"There you are!" Came her husband's happy voice.

Hanna turned and flinched a smile. *Well, he seems happier.* "Hi."

Arthur strolled in and embraced her with a wide hug. "I guess we are both feeling the same way."

I doubt it, Hanna knew. She smiled a tad wider. She looked at where her bookshelves had been and wondered where her textbooks were.

"I'll miss Charles," Arthur sighed. He hoisted his hands around his hips. "But he made his choice."

Hanna raised an anchored smile. *Why are you bringing him up?*

Arthur's eyes got wide with pity. He saw through her façade. He pointed his wife's chin up and said lovingly, "Hey, don't you look like that." He added, positively, "We could have another kid, soon."

Hanna humored him by keeping up her smile. *Don't ruin his mood*, she told herself.

Arthur touched her waist and said into her ear, "We *should* have another."

Hanna brushed him off, "Not now."

Her husband grazed her cheek and circled her. "We aren't getting any younger. You especially."

If this was seduction, Hanna could not tell. "Thank you for that," she said, trying her very best to not sound as annoyed as she was getting. *How can his mind go to this so soon? How can he think about it at all?*

Arthur let out a sagging, exaggerated frown. "I didn't mean it like that."

"I know," Hanna continued smiling. She said, trying her hardest to sound pleasant and positive, "I am just not in a mood."

Her husband stepped backward. Then, his nostrils flared. He crept closer and took her hands. He smiled, baring his teeth. "Sweet sugarbear," he began in a tone Hanna did not think belonged to her. "Don't you want to be a mother?"

Hanna took back her hands and folded them around her stomach. "I am a mother." *And don't call me sugarbear. That's not your word.*

Arthur narrowed his eyes and said with a clenched jaw. "Aeric will leave you soon."

Hanna breathed deeply and fought with her emotions. "As grown boys—" She winced and took a deep breath. "As they do." She gestured at the door, "Your daughter is still young. Emilia and I talk every day."

Her husband ignored the mention of his daughter. He closed in on her and grabbed her breast.

Hanna shook him off and stepped even farther away. Her back touched the wall. Her heels froze against the floor.

Arthur's nostrils flared again. His cheeks danced up and down. His lips twitched and his eyes became dark slits. He spoke as if unable to catch his breath, "I thought we were past this."

Hanna's guilt surged. She took a step toward the innkeeper. "Past what? I-I only... Not right now. That's all."

Arthur's head rolled left and right. His nostrils rose higher and his eyes sank beneath his brow. "Now, tomorrow, next week." He lurched forward and looked down upon his wife. "Admit it. Charles got into your head."

He was so close to her, Hanna felt the pounding of his heart. She did not reply. *Why must he always be so afraid? So angry?*

Arthur spat, "What else has he gotten into?" He grabbed her waist and squeezed her body against his. A stranger's eyes stared at her with both repulsion and want.

Hanna thought quickly. She said, with not a hint of untruth, "He could never change my opinion of you." *You, on the other hand, are doing a good job.*

Arthur's chest fluttered and he let out a series of hiccup-like breaths. He glowed with happiness and leaned in for a kiss. "Thank you, thank you."

Hanna stood still while he kissed her. She pressed her lips slightly but could hardly manage to move. Her body was immobile.

Arthur tilted his head to its side. He said in a voice Emilia often used with her dog, "That's all I wanted." Yet even as he said the words, it was clear it was not all he wanted. He groped Hanna's bottom.

Hanna had enough. She pushed her husband off. She stared at the man in anticipation.

He looked at his hands and then at her. He squinted, as if staring at some object which was far away.

Hanna stared right back at him. She had her limits. *I don't care if I am being a bad wife. A bad mother. Any of it. I want to be a good me.* Even as the thoughts formed, she felt awful for having them. She stuttered and felt awfully cold. "It doesn't f-feel right."

A wave of anger surged up her husband's body. He scowled at her and said in a low voice. "And when will it? When Charles Eastmont stands in my place?"

Hanna snapped. "You're delusional."

A shred of humor washed over her husband's angry face. "Why must everyone say that?" He asked with a gritted smile. Quickly, he launched his body at the crib and shattered it. The frame crumbled and the sheets sank sadly to the floor. His hateful eyes went from the ruined furniture to his wife. He shouted, "Maybe I am the only sane person left!"

He did not wait for a reply. Her husband was done talking. He grabbed Hanna's arm and pulled her out of the nursery. The man dragged her through the corridor and past the children's bedrooms. He kicked open their bedroom door and hurled her onto the mattress. He unbuttoned his shirt and growled, "No gratitude. After all I have done for this family. This town." Arthur's hands rushed to his pants.

"We are all grateful," Hanna tried. She did not believe her words.

Arthur's hands reached for his shoulders. His shirt slid off.

His quiet wheezes and slobbering stare came from a face Hanna did not recognize. She closed her eyes.

"Even you?" Arthur asked. Hanna could tell the question was not for her.

She opened her eyes reluctantly. His head had turned. Arthur looked with bored cruelty at his daughter, standing lonesome in the doorway.

Emilia did not look at her father but instead gazed at her mother. "Izzy is gone and you…" Her cheeks were wet and her brow was sweaty. She hardly opened her tearful eyes and said, choking on every word. "I hope you are happy. I hope you are." Emilia tore her eyes from her mother and ran away.

Arthur rolled his eyes. "We'll get the bitch a new dog. That one was retarded."

Hanna had never felt so angry. "Our daughter is not a bitch."

Arthur rolled his eyes and muttered dismissively, "Of course not, of course not." He eyed her with an interrogating look. "You think I don't love her?"

Hanna swallowed. She did not want to answer that. She wished she had just stayed silent and let his anger subside. She closed her eyes again. "Sometimes I don't know."

The room was silent. Hanna opened an eye. Arthur had come closer and was leaning forward. He stared at her with mad, wide eyes. His thin body shook. His bony arms vibrated as he whispered. "You are deficient." He chewed on his tongue and peered out the window, "So, I don't blame your forgetfulness. But I will not be called a bad father. I am a good father." He paused and then shouted at her. "Look at me!"

Hanna's eyes burst open. Her husband was smiling without a trace of happiness on his face.

"I think it an awfully stupid expectation of me, that I should care for all people equally." He paused and narrowed his eyes, "Don't you?"

Hanna nodded dutifully.

"I don't think it makes me immoral to love my family more than others. Don't you?"

Hanna nodded. *If this is his love, how does he act around everyone else?*

He grabbed his heart and said as if wounded, "Don't say I do not love my daughter. I am a man. I love like a man."

Charles is a man and he never once yelled at me. Hanna twitched. She nodded loyally. Her tongue travelled along her cheeks as she weighed the benefit of speaking her mind with the harm of angering Arthur.

"When I heard... That little fat shit... Well, I can throw stones, too!" He laughed, "And you say I do not love her!"

In the span of a single blink, Hanna found her husband unrecognizable. Without thinking, she slowly crawled away from her husband. "Y-you."

"M-me," Arthur mocked. "I will not tolerate disrespect or meanness. Especially not from idiot children," he paused. His nostrils flared, "Or a braindead, retarded womanchild." He put his hands on the edge of the bed and crawled toward her like a beast.

Hanna had never felt more afraid and disgusted. She kicked her husband and vaulted off the mattress. Arthur stumbled back to the wall and fell to his knees with a cry. In that second, she was overwhelmed with pity. She hated seeing him like that, all wretched and thin, all angry and mean. She stared down at him in revolt. "Everyone is retarded except you." She looked toward the door. The last of her reservations shattered as she heard Emilia outside, shrieking for her dog to come back.

Hanna muttered, "I am not retarded," and left her husband. She sprinted down the stairs. She grabbed the only coat she could find, a big parka, and stormed out the tavern. She could hear her daughter crying, but she could not see.

The freezing fog was all around her. It smelt of sulfur and sizzled her nose. She followed her daughter's frantic calls. "Izzy! Izzy!" She circled the Hill, crying out her own, "Emilia! Emilia!"

Soon, her daughter's calls grew quieter. Whether from the distance or from something else, her daughter's voice seemed to grow sickly and hoarse. She heard a final, "BIG GIRL!" Then, all was silent.

The brown haze surrounded Hanna. She called for her daughter, "Emilia! Sugarbear!"

A gunshot replied. Arthur rasped a rabid roar, "Enough games, Hanna! Come back inside before you catch a cold."

Hanna did not answer. She crawled through the gross haze. She thought she saw her daughter and the dog in every wisp. When she reached out, the taunting fumes simply shriveled around her skin and sizzled her with tiny burns.

Her husband's voice had overtaken her. He was already down by the hedge. "Hanna, please. I am so—" A fit of coughing overtook him.

Hanna struggled with her own urge to cough. Hanna could not be found; she needed to do the finding. Her brain squeezed in on itself.

Her husband shot his gun madly and yelled hoarsely. His calls were frantic and pitiful, but Hanna could not hear them. She would not.

Hanna did not respond to the man's shrieks and cries. Her daughter was her priority. Her family was her priority. She struggled to keep breathing. The tightness around her windpipe seemed total. Her throat swelled. She could not breathe. She could not see. Her daughter was lost and she could not find her. *My sweet little girl.* "EMILIA!" She shrieked as her knees trembled.

She plummeted to the ground. Hanna glanced at her chest. There was no hand around her neck. No bloody face held her brain. So why was she choking? She strained to see, but all around her was white. She gripped the sooty grass and tried to sit up. The heavy haze resisted her attempts and pushed her back down. She slipped away.

Seconds or minutes later, she awoke with a shiver. *So cold... But why am I sweating?* She sniffled; her nostrils had frozen shut. She cupped her hands around her mouth and tried to warm them with her breath. She only managed a few sputtering gasps. Moreover, what little air came from her lungs was cooler than it should have been. Hanna rolled onto her sides and got into a fetal position. Her chilled bones creaked. *This is not part of my dream.* She waited for the bloody face to make it all better. Once he took her brain, she could wake up. *I know this dream,* she smiled hopefully. Fog like a mound of dirt was covering her body. *Blankets,* she remarked snugly. She slipped away.

As quick as contentment came to her, it dissipated. Her eyes shot open. *This is not my nightmare,* she remembered. *Emilia.* She jumped up. The haze tried to keep her down. Undeterred, Hanna staggered to her feet. A new heat filled her heart. "Emilia?" she asked the fog.

She can't hear that. Hanna had hardly made a sound. She cleared her throat and tried again, "Emilia!" Only hoarse whispers came out. She was voiceless.

I will find her. Hanna set off into the blinding white, burying her nose and mouth in her shirt. She reached with one arm to feel her surroundings. So dense was the air, it felt as if she were dipping her hand through murky seawater. The little dust particles zipped down her arm and coated her fingers. After several paces, her outstretched arm began to freeze. She shifted and used the other arm.

"Emilia!" She croaked. Hanna blinked and waited. She saw nothing ahead.

"Hanna," whispered a voice.

Hanna turned around, "Emilia?"

"No, you bumbling—"

The wind whisked away the words.

Hanna stood there, no doubt only several feet from the voice. It let out a pathetic cry. Hanna stared into the shapeless smoke. Was the figure there? Or there? The voice growled and spat. "Pick me up," it demanded.

Hanna knew to whom the voice belonged. Still, she was reluctant to grant it a face. Moreover, she did not have time to waste on it. Her family was her priority. *Emilia needs me.* She began slowly walking backward.

"Hanna," the voice hissed.

Hanna would not listen. She kept walking. *My family is my priority.*

"You retarded, cheating—"

An easterly wind zipped past and quieted the voice. Hanna did not hear it again.

When she was certain it could not hear her, she called out for her daughter. The words came up her windpipe like slicing blades. She choked and grabbed her throat. Suddenly, it seemed her mouth was less dry. Hanna swallowed and shuddered. Droplets of blood oozed down her chin as she tried to call for Emilia. She managed a short, shriek. Then, her tongue numbed and coiled around her words.

Panic slithered down her spine. *Emilia has been out here longer than I have. She must be s-so...* Hanna licked her lips. Her tears burned her face, but she could not help crying. Her daughter was scared, sick, or worse. Hanna twitched and turned in circles, hoping a miracle would bring her child to her. She scoured the smoke. She searched for a second before stumbling upon a huge object.

It was a tower of twisting, writhing smoke which rose like a great wave. It was darker and denser than all the surrounding haze. It seemed to suck at its surroundings, leaching the air until it was many stories tall. It then paused and eyed her like a boot eyes an ant. Just as Hanna went to put her shirt over her mouth, the pillar of pollution plummeted. The plume pummeled her like a giant's fist.

The remnant of clean air in her lungs shot out. Her back cracked against the frozen dirt. Iced blades of grass slashed her skin. Broken, the innkeeper's wife did not even have the strength to choke. The pillar coiled around her body. The searing soot gnawed on her clothes. A thousand burns lacerated her face. If she were bleeding now, she could not feel it. The weight of her arm was too much. Her legs wobbled unresponsively.

Her final sight was of her child. As her eyes closed, a brightness blinded her. Hanna seemed to float upward and for a moment, her chills left. With one final breath, all the tension in her chest released. Her lungs relaxed. Her thumping heart slowed and quieted. Her limbs fell limp.

A pale arm coiled around her leg.

42

A Fair Trial

The haze had come down the mountain. The little men and women scurried through the Oleander's murk. Their faces were obscured by the morose mist. Flakes of soot fell from their cheeks like autumn leaves from trees. Yet, they hardly noticed the oozing fog and only commented on it in passing. They pointed and gossiped about it like they pointed and gossiped about the condemned.

They had been Galahad's neighbors, though he hardly recognized them. *I've never seen many of these people. The very definition of reclusive...* He squinted at the Pale townspeople. The bone-chilling smoke was beginning to paint everything black and brown. The white faces looked more like his with every passing minute. *I wonder if I might find a metaphor in that,* the damned man wondered. Galahad smiled amiably at the haze, stifled a cough, and awaited Carolyn to speak his fate.

The widow huddled with her dogs. She whispered with Buchanan Bavar, a man named Goldman, and the constable's deputy, Northington. They fancied themselves makeshift judges. Galahad found them amusing. They had not even bound Galahad's arms and legs properly. *I could hop away if I wanted to...*

He did play with the idea. He could escape into the Overgrowth and hide in the haze. Visibility was poor, the Overgrowth was large, and he was strong. He smiled at the idea as if it were an old friend he would rather not converse with.

Galahad closed his eyes and swallowed. He raised his bound wrists and clumsily brushed the soot off his suit. He frowned at the sanguine stains on his jacket. *I suppose it is fitting,* he remarked. The branches of the black walnut creaked in the wind. A gust of powerful wind came from the west and caused the entire tree to sway. It looked like it was nodding.

The haze grew thicker as Carolyn deliberated with her men. A gale was crashing down from the mountain. A dark plume was plummeting toward Cottonwood. The clouds like tidal waves swelled into the air and rushed east. The wind broke upon the stone houses. The trees shivered and leaned into the road. Their trunks bent and their limbs swayed.

Even the trees are eavesdropping, Galahad grunted. Dried leaves fluttered past his face; they were the only things still flying in the muddy fog.

At last, Carolyn spoke. The wind swept up her words and carried them away. Galahad heard a faint, distorted, "Bring him out!"

Northington and Goldman brought a limp corpse indelicately to the crowd. From the way the two bore the body, one might have thought the lawman had been unloved. Each held one of the constable's hands and pulled the heavy husk as if it were a sled. The road sheered its stomach, forming a bloody trail to Carolyn. They dropped the body between the widow and the condemned. Galahad found the whole affair theatrical and tasteless.

The wind quieted as Carolyn knelt beside the constable's corpse. Stray conversations concluded amongst the crowd. Carolyn lifted Goodwind's head and shook her own. Galahad could not see well, but he could tell that Edric's face was now completely black. Carolyn let the corpse's face fall back into the dirt. She tutted her tongue regretfully. The widow addressed Northington to her right and Buchanan to her left. "We found the constable dead, did we not?"

The two cretins nodded. Buchanan said, proudly, "Found he had choked. Or been choked."

The townspeople turned toward one another, voiced an opinion if they had one, and then turned back to the judges. Far in the back, Evelyn chimed, "I think we should have the Yao's opinion. They are the doctors, not us."

Galahad found the request completely reasonable. They would know instantly what had happened. *Bring them out,* he wanted to say. A glimmer of unwanted hope was followed by a nagging idea. *They have leaf. The Yao gave me my first leaf. I could get some. They have leaf.* While he salivated, a quiet, convincing, 'Run into the fog. Be free,' pestered him for his attention. Galahad groaned and rolled his head in anguish.

The crowd watched. Several gruff men declared loudly, "He knows the Yao would find him guilty. Bring them out, I say."

Carolyn silenced the crowd with a slicing shriek, "We do not have time for distractions." She glared at her sister.

Evelyn's tone seesawed between conviction and fear. "I should feel better if Yao Yu gave a cause of death. We are dealing with a man's life, after all."

Carolyn snarled, "I would feel *better* with my son next to me." The wind picked up as she lost control of her voice. She spat, "But he is dead. Killed by this vile creature!"

The trees lurched forward. Several small branches slid into the street. Buchanan held his hair in place as he yelled, "We found him in the act. He was fleeing even as the constable's body cooled." His hair flew in his face as he said to the skeptic, "Goodwind..." Suddenly, he was overtaken by a cough. He beat his chest, grunted, and finished, "The constable was strangled. Plain as day."

Galahad looked around. Despite being midday, it was dark as dusk. A smug smirk formed on his face. The sun was bloodred. *What is plain as day is this smoke.* Galahad was sure the constable had suffocated. Though, he was quite content with that truth being his own. He chuckled gleefully at the Pale's ignorance.

Carolyn turned wrathfully, "He mocks us even now." She pointed at her sister. "We are dealing with an animal. Not a man."

Evelyn bowed her head sadly. She voiced no further objections. Strangely, Galahad was relieved. He wanted things to go smoothly. He felt an unwavering itch to scratch his arms, but in chains he could hardly do that. His nausea was as much a part of him as his fingers or his eyes. His stomach groaned, churning an empty bile. His legs spasmed and his chest convulsed. *I am a failing specimen,* Galahad told the grey sky. *No hiccups, please,* he prayed. The sooner this grim business was over, the sooner he might be freed.

It would be best if he stayed silent and let the crowd have their way. Still, he could not completely quell his old inclinations. He taunted the mob, "If I am an animal, why have you all gone into a frenzy?" He puckered his lips and said, sadly, "I've got no food today, ducklings."

Carolyn flew at him and struck him with the back of her hand. The pain was not great; the embarrassment was mild; the rage was rampant. Galahad struggled with the urge to break from his meager bonds. He could kill her and ease the process along. *I could even give these beasts a story to tell their grandchildren. Wouldn't that be charitable?*

"I want to hear his story," a little boy said eagerly.

Galahad had not planned to speak his case. In truth, he feared what would happen. He did not want to lie; nor did he want to tell *all* the truth. *Still... One last hoorah could be fun. That would give these cunts some gossip.* Galahad blinked at Carolyn playfully. *Go on, then. What shall it be?*

The widow sniffled. She coughed and waved a weary hand. "Fine," she acquiesced with annoyance. "But do not be swayed by pretty words. This thing is a murderer."

Galahad spoke comfortably and softly. "I am touched that you think my words are pretty."

Carolyn shot him a nasty look.

Galahad flinched a smile and addressed the watchers. The air scratched his throat as he inhaled. He raised his bound hands like one offering a libation. "Before we begin—a toast to Frederick's good health, wherever he may be."

The crowd launched a collective, nervous look at Carolyn. Galahad also glanced at her. The widow lowered her hateful gaze and put her shaking fists behind her back.

Galahad swallowed. His throat was far too dry for a speech. His body quaked with nervousness. He almost wanted to laugh. Here he was, with a chance to clear his name, and he had not the slightest want to be free. The return to normal—a fresh start—that seemed more a punishment than any hell. He licked his chapped lips. His empty belly growled. *God, how I just want to escape this all.* He rubbed his chilled hands along his dirty suit. The devil in him voiced its typical opinion, *The truth sets you free. Isn't that the cliché?* Galahad flashed a half-grin. His belly roared. *You murdered your father, but not Frederick. Tell them that. People knew Cambyses. They would be more sympathetic toward your circumstances. He was a drunk. Frederick was a little boy...*

Galahad squinted, trying not to see double. He cleared his throat. *The truth sets good men free. But I have been free and it is not good.* He spat. The wind swept up his saliva and turned it back around. The spit landed on his suit and slid to his shoes. Galahad nodded, finding something special in the scene. A sudden vigor made him gleeful. He shot a look at his father's old landlord.

"Buchanan Bavar!" He said in a confident, ecstatic voice. *This has all been a stage, anyways. Props, actors, stories, tragedy...* He smirked, *And comedy.*

The landlord's eyes filled with suspicion. Galahad watched the anticipation build in him. *Are his eyes red?* He wondered. The speechless buffoon muttered an incoherent word which Galahad immediately overpowered.

"Do you know—I have missed your visits to the family shop?"

Buchanan paced around Carolyn and growled nervously, "We are not discussing your late father."

Galahad rolled his eyes. "Yes, indeed. I particularly miss how my *late father—*" His heart skipped a beat as he mentioned his father aloud. "Took advantage of your illiteracy."

The mob's murmurs mixed with the wind's whispers. Buchanan's eyes were empty horror.

"Oh—" Galahad beamed at the dumb bastard. He cooed and shook his head sympathetically, "Don't be so embarrassed." He cooed as if to a baby and addressed the captivated crowd, "It is no secret."

Buchanan gripped his pockets. His head twitched at Galahad like a woodpecker. He covered his mouth like he was coughing.

Galahad swung his bound hands like a pendulum. He then saw Buchanan's eyes *were* red. *Oh, how perfect,* Galahad thought. *I might even see him cry.* He breathed deeply, though the muddy air scratched his chest. Oddly, he felt like he had finally returned to himself. He looked up fondly at the noose and smiled. "Well, the war is over," he remarked. "My father is dead," he pointed his bonds at Buchanan. "And you have been swindled out of many years' rent."

Buchanan bellowed hoarsely, "He's a liar! J-just like his muddy progenitor!"

Galahad grinned. "If I am a liar," he said slowly and articulately. "Haven't you proved me truthful?" He beamed at Bavar innocently.

"Enough," Carolyn growled. "I will not have my son's memory mocked. Are you going to make your case, or make a fool of yourself?"

Galahad blinked at the blackening haze and shrugged. Then, he smiled at Carolyn. "Why not both?"

Several restrained laughs came from the crowd, though they were masked quickly as coughs.

Carolyn glared at her fellow townspeople. "Enough," she hissed. The widow walked to the hanging tree. She paced around Galahad, her hands placed pretentiously behind her back. "Are you a murderer?"

Galahad scoffed. *That's not a yes or no question...* He belched and felt an odd, burning sensation wash over his tongue. He shook his head and cleared his throat. He smiled at Carolyn dismissively, hoping she did read his mind. A glance at his gallows filled him with dread. This was not a game. This was not a game. He was going to be executed. His neck would snap and his lungs would fail. The end. His mind began preparations. He felt a cold grip around his neck. He reached for the phantasmal noose and sank under a ghostly weight. He hunched over and told himself this was not reality. *I am on the train. My father is alive. My mind is my own. My mind is—*

"Of course he is!" Buchanan shouted, finding some resolve at last. "Bad blood, bad associations. Did he not fraternize with that flesh-mongering murderer? That draft-dodging trogg from th'Overgrowth?"

The wind had shifted. The trees reached for the condemned; their limbs groped toward the walnut. The last leaves of Fall shivered and flew into Galahad's gaping mouth. He choked and hacked. His throat tightened and burned. *At this rate, the haze will kill me before the hanging.* He frowned morosely at Evelyn. He shook his head and turned away from that devil's advocate.

The wind swept up Carolyn's cries and amplified them. "Are you a—"

"Yes," Galahad suddenly blurted out.

"What?" came a vindicative screech.

Galahad closed his eyes. "I have murdered." He quickly opened his eyes and readied a qualifying, *As all patriots have. Of course, I murdered. I fought in the war.* He gazed at young Northington, whose family doubtless paid to keep him safe. Galahad envied his youth, his immaculate, unscarred self. He twitched a smile and bowed his head in defeat. He could lie, but it seemed so unnecessary. He could drag this on and struggle to live...

Even as he thought of living, he pictured a nice concoction of Oleander plant. *The two are inseparable now...* The thought put an end to any final lying. He would not give in. He shuddered and said, "I am dead already."

Carolyn and Buchanan looked at each other questioningly. A snort of disbelief precluded a triumphant cry. Carolyn rushed up to Galahad and grabbed his chin. "There we have it! A confession!"

The widow's fingers tightened around Galahad's throat. She looked at him with a tilted gaze. He recoiled; was she salivating? *She looks positively hungry.* He hid his fear and postured, "Are you to be the noose?"

Carolyn's eyes flashed with loving hate.

"Or perhaps—" His taunts ended prematurely. Carolyn's fingers slid away. A real rope took their place. Galahad took a deep breath and savored the feeling. The air coursed into his nostrils and tickled his nose hairs. He ignored the burning sensation of soot traveling into his lungs. His diaphragm expanded and filled with calming coolness. He breathed out.

He had intended to smile at the hangman beside him. Instead, his neck rubbed against the rope and an animal instinct overtook him. His heart pounded and his eyes widened. "I have not confessed entirely!"

Buchanan Bavar scoffed and pushed the hangman out of the way. He swiped the executioner's hood and placed a crate below Galahad's feet. He placed him on the precipice. Northington took the other end of the noose and tied it around a thick, onyx branch. Galahad felt them tightening and began to cry. "I have not told my truth!"

Carolyn crept back toward him. "Go ahead, then."

Galahad shook with relief and wanted to kiss her. The feeling faded when Buchanan and Northington continued tightening his noose, talking about 'Proper noose-craft.'

"Why did you take him from me?" Carolyn interrogated quietly. She was not asking for the crowd's benefit.

Galahad twitched. He had wanted to speak his truth. He let out a choppy sigh and sniffled. He winced and looked away from the widow. *I hope, if you're an omnipotent kind of God—that you will forgive me for this.* He swallowed. *Because I will not be forgiving myself.*

"WHY!?" The mother cried.

Galahad pitied her in that moment just as he pitied himself. She was not asking out of malice. She was begging out of desperation. And he had no answer to give her. As the seconds went on, her sorrow began to simmer. She eyed him with the type of hateful disgust Galahad might have given to himself. *She can no more move on from his disappearance than I can abandon my addiction.* He frowned at her and confessed as much as the barriers in his brain allowed. "I suppose the same reason you are going to hang me from this tree."

Galahad bowed his head and twiddled his thumbs. Buchanan plucked the taught rope. "That's craftsmanship, Northington. Can't ask for a better execution."

Carolyn twitched a maddened grin. "And what reason is that?"

Galahad's face wrinkled in anger. Nevertheless, he stayed silent. He was too afraid if he spoke, even to insult someone, that he would reveal his misdeed. He clenched his teeth and began to grind his jaw, wary of what would come if he were allowed any more words.

Northington patted Carolyn's shoulder before joining the rest of the townspeople in the road. Buchanan lingered beside the tree and eyed the noose proudly. He turned his attention to Galahad, relishing his position.

Wilhelm complained to his mother, "It's stinky out here. Can we go inside?"

"Let's," Buchanan wheezed and looked away briefly. "Get this over with."

Carolyn stepped in front of Buchanan and said in a shaking monotone, "No. I want to hear him out." She faced Galahad and pulled his chin up. She dragged her long nails against his facial hair, drawing blood. "Go on, you devil. Why is my son dead?" She sniffled and her hand retreated. She fanned herself and wiped her tears. After waiting a minute, she let out a choppy sigh. Carolyn swallowed and leaned into Galahad's ears. She lifted her blouse and revealed a silver blade. "I can make this easier if you just tell me."

Galahad analyzed her. *I hate you, that's for certain. But...* Was that a glimmer of hope in her voice? *A mother's love.* He wanted to compliment her. He might have, had he indeed killed Frederick. The fat boy was nothing to him, though. He hid behind his humor and his hatred. He smirked at the shining steel, "I murdered for my own reasons. Same as you will."

Carolyn rolled her lips and flashed her teeth. Her nose twitched like a hound on a scent. She barked, "Go on, Buchanan." She lifted her head high. "I am not a murderer." Finally, the widow joined the rest of the Inner Ring.

His rope stiffened. The noose tightened. Galahad stood on his toes to give the rope some slack. The walnut branch holding the rope sighed and cracked. The crowd talked amongst themselves, all waiting for the tolling moment. Galahad turned his head as if draining water from his ear, hoping to relieve some of the pressure around his neck. He stared sideways at the vigil. He had expected the Pale to look at him hatefully or proudly. To their credit, apathy was the predominant emotion on their faces. However, a few people seemed saddened. Several children were not watching at all and tugged at their parent's shoulders to leave.

"I can't breathe," Wilhelm whined. Evelyn nodded. "Me neither," she said.

Me as well, Galahad smiled sorrowfully.

That mother and son departed. Many more stayed and it seemed the vigil grew ever more jubilant. While Buchanan prepared to be a hangman, the rest of the Pale uttered jokes, complimented each other's outfits, and shared snacks.

"There we are," Buchanan announced, fitting a dark hood over his head.

Galahad thought he looked foolish and would have said as much had his organs not all plummeted. His heart sank, like it too was being hanged. Galahad averted his eyes from the hangman and stared ahead.

Then it seemed that the wind began to wail and the air took on an eerie, choral hum. The gusts surged through little holes and crevices. Black air billowed out, blowing like notes from a flute. Buchanan put his boot upon the box with a thunderous thud.

The easiest things became the hardest. Galahad gulped for air and held the breath. He begrudgingly exhaled and pockets of air seeped from him. His eyes shimmered and filled with tears. They mixed with the haze and burned his cheeks.

Galahad glanced at his tattered suit and for one last time, he felt the urge to escape. He swallowed, but there was no moisture left. His mouth was desiccated.

The weight of Buchanan's boot moved the box slightly.

He's toying with me. Like I did with him. Galahad rolled his lower jaw and pressed the teeth forward in their sockets. He glared ahead, resolving not to show any fear or sadness. He opened his eyes wide and let the soot dry his tears. He watched the Pale watch him and made sure to remember their faces. He hoped a few would go to the same hell.

Galahad found it odd that strangers he had never seen were deciding his fate. The Inner Ring hardly left their houses, and here they were—judging a man they only knew from an accusation. He did not think the circumstances a fair one... Galahad squinted. Was there someone he recognized in the mob? *Yes, I know that face. Where have I seen it—*

Galahad blinked a dozen times and quickly looked away. He stared up at his noose and began to hyperventilate. His father was among the crowd, staring emotionless at his son. In his hands were two glasses. Had he been alive all this time? *No, no. NO!* His father was dead. *I watched him die. I buried him.*

"Do it," Galahad whispered. His heart stopped beating briefly and he winced. After a few seconds—he realized the crate had not been kicked. He glared at Buchanan, "Do it!"

Buchanan cleared his throat and tugged the noose, inspecting it for quality. He smiled at Galahad, obviously savoring the dead man's anticipation.

Galahad's face flashed a hundred different emotions. Finally, his eyes sank and his cheeks sagged. His voice was regretful, "Will you bury me in my suit?"

Buchanan's eyes were empty. The whites were red and his face was covered in muddy soot.

Galahad peered into the hangman's eyes and tried to be amiable. *Don't take my suit. Please.* "It's a small thing," he snorted a smile. "But it's a trifle for you, right? A last plea from a damned man."

Buchanan's eyes surged open. He looked positively horrified.

Galahad glanced at the crowd and back at the hangman. "What? A murderer can't want his dignity?"

Buchanan retorted with a rasp. He shook his head, though it did not seem the movement was conversational.

Galahad stretched his feet as vertically as he could and crept an inch closer to the hangman. Something was amiss. Galahad analyzed the man. Both their chests rose in staccato. Both their eyes were full of fear. "I am sure the knot is fine," Galahad assured. "No one will judge you if you botch your first hanging... Now about my suit."

Buchanan raised his lips and his cheeks widened.

"There we are," Galahad grinned. "Got to make a good first impression down th—"

A glob of blood spewed onto his suit. Galahad blinked at the fluid.

The crowd was deathly silent, save several coughs that would not be quieted.

Galahad waited on Buchanan's boot. *Go on, you illiterate fucker. Kick the box and go inside before you suffocate. You stupid, insufferable idiot.* "Just be done with it," Galahad groaned.

Buchanan seemed not to hear him. His eyes were full of fluid. The man's legs swayed unsteadily. His head jerked forward like a woodpecker. Little, inconspicuous hiccups leaked out of his closed lips.

Galahad stared at the sorry fool. He spoke frantically, "Go on. Before the smoke..."

Buchanan Bavar's chest rose. When he exhaled, a screeching wheeze came forth. His chest stayed erect for a second. Then, a fountain of blood erupted out of his mouth and nose. His foot tumbled off the crate, pushing it slightly. The hangman fell with a force, dashing his head on a gigantic, exposed root. His blood coated the black walnut's wood.

The crowd was filled with dread. The sharing of snacks ceased. No one laughed. No one talked about the weather. The smoke was no longer a novelty to adorn a grim day. It was the grim. The crowd began to disperse. At first, all was orderly. Then, as young Northington rushed toward the walnut, ready to finish the deed, he fell to his knees and groped his neck. When the Pale saw that, they took flight. As they ran, many more fell to their knees. Others simply could not muster the strength and choked where they stood.

Galahad watched in disbelief. It was like the smoke had pooled in each of them and waited for an opportune moment... The many emotions competing for Galahad's mind suddenly vanished. They gave way to a gleeful, madness. He made no attempt to contain his jubilant craze. He gazed up, past the walnut and the haze, and laughed at the sky. "Hah!" He said, triumphantly. "YES!"

He gazed at the little rats fleeing their execution. He could not follow them fast enough. The haze had blanketed all and Galahad saw only a few feet ahead. His ears, however, worked well enough. The chaos was like a choir to him. He giggled and called out, "The metaphor, eh? The metaphor!"

"Not so innocent, not so guilty," he told the hanging tree. He frowned and as if staring at himself, mocked in a deep voice, "Why so blue?" He cackled, "Swim fishy, swim!"

"NO!" Came Carolyn's terrible cry.

Galahad smirked at the figure shambling from the muddy shadows. She covered her mouth with one arm.

It is too perfect! A Godly ending! "Justice," he hissed. "OLD... ROTTEN... JUSTICE!"

Carolyn stepped closer, her eyes focused on one thing. She did not look at Galahad. It was like he was not there at all. "No," she croaked.

"Yes!" Galahad roared. He relished the thick, polluted air. The smoke entered his lungs. His chest burned. His neck tightened, but not from the noose. "A gift from Lilian Vellencourt!"

Carolyn's face contorted. She turned her head and fell flat.

"That'll be a hard stain to wash out!" Galahad giggled madly. He felt a jolt of energy. They were all dying. All of them. "And we'll all go together," he sang in a joking baritone. "To pick—" A violent cough interrupted his song. His own blood leaked onto his suit.

Carolyn's arms surged. She pulled her body forward, crawling with such conviction, Galahad praised her, "What strength!" He pressed his lips and shook his head at the hangman's corpse, "You take notes, Bavar."

Carolyn threw her arms onto the crate. Her fingers coiled around Galahad's shins. Then, he felt a tightening. One foot fell from its roost. The rope creaked and

Galahad's body began to rotate around his big toe. Carolyn adjusted her grip and looked up at the man she so hated. Galahad smiled at the wretched woman. Her eyes were red, her skin was brown, and her hands were ready to murder. Galahad nodded at the crate.

Carolyn wheezed. Blood trickled out her mouth. Her limbs twitched and though she had a firm grip on the crate, she could not move it. Her fingers curled toward her palms like a dying insect. She glared up at him.

Galahad had just enough strength to smile down at her as he too choked. The rope was taut, but he did not hang.

43

Eastern Winds

The wind roared above the cellar. Ethereal bass voices reverberated in that haunted cellar. Charles languished there, nursing his head. Arthur's assault had been vicious, but the man did not have the strength his deadly weapon demanded. Charles' skull pounded in pain. He took in data blankly, unable to form a single sentence. *Soup bowl smashed, liquid strewn, heaviness atop the hatch, my pistol gone, extra blanket on top of the corpse.*

Arthur had bludgeoned him in a panic. He had left him in the cellar without a plan.

Arthur. The name no longer brought its many memories. The attack had awoken an animal mind in Charles, one which viewed his childhood friend as nothing more than nostalgia. *When he comes back down, I will overpower him. He is too emaciated to fight me.*

The depths of his brain still squirmed with association. 'He has been starving himself. Pity him,' a muse whispered.

Charles took to the ladder like a spider on a web. He climbed to the top. Just below the hatch, Charles lurked, listening. He stared at the hatch. He pushed on it, knowing it would not budge. *What has he dragged atop it? A crate?* Charles relaxed his eyes and limbs. He listened to the wind and the voices upon it. A cacophony of voices had gone quiet, no longer the stadium clamor of just an hour ago. *They must have brought Galahad back. He's probably sitting in some jail. Just like me.* Charles grunted at the commonality.

Other voices began to crescendo. The sounds traveled loudly in the thick air. First, he heard Hanna. She called after her daughter, but the words were distorted by the haze. Charles could not pick them out. Next, he heard Arthur's wild yell. A hundred tones called his wife's name, each of them twisted by Arthur's gravelly shriek.

The silence which followed was most distorted of all. It would not break but for the bass groaning of the viscous wind. Charles' ears swelled with pressure, deafening him slightly. Thinking of Hanna caused Charles to convulse. He pushed against the hatch again. As he did, he heard the quiet closing of the granary door. Charles froze. *Footsteps.*

Charles slowly climbed down the ladder. He hid his body against the wall, Arthur would not see him if he stared down the descent. At least, that was his hope. The muffled groan of moving furniture echoed from above. Charles tensed.

Four eyes focused fearfully on the hatch. Five fingers coiled around the handle. Three hinges whined and rotated. Two shadowy figures peered into mutual darkness. One thin man crept down the cellar. *That's too large a man to be Arthur*, Charles realized. *But that face—it is so… misshapen. Monstrous.* He stilled his breathing and prepared to lunge at the figure.

A twisted hand rose. Light emanated from it. The lantern's brightness blinded Charles. A voice spoke, further disorienting him. "I knew it," Aeric Gardner whispered.

Charles shielded his eyes, squinting. The young man was wearing a Tanglewood mask. "You knew I was down here? In this haze?"

Aeric turned. The bug-eyed lenses of his gas mask fixed on Frederick's cot. "I… I…" He started and stopped, sputtering like an automobile's engine. Eventually, the innkeeper's son went silent. He walked over to the cot, where many of the inn's silken sheets hid the brutality of his father. With a swift action, Aeric threw off the sheets. "I was checking mousetraps when I saw several vermin skitter under a rug. I tried to capture them underneath it, but they had disappeared behind a hatch."

Aeric took off the gas mask, revealing a beaten brow and entrenched eyes. He tossed the old gas mask to Charles. The soldier in him shivered, remembering the touch of an army-issued item. "Where did you get this?"

"It was my uncle's. He sent it to me during the war, saying he would never wear one again… Never said why, either."

Charles felt he knew why, but there was no time to share. He asked, "What about you? That haze is worse than city pollution."

Aeric smiled. He bowed his head before the smile could reveal a crippling frown. "I was watching from my window all day yesterday. You seemed okay sneaking around with just a shirt-mask… Besides, we have to make sure my…" A pained sigh escaped him. He continued, "Mother is okay."

Charles' antipathy toward Arthur now became immense pity for his son. There seemed no way to wash that hollow, defeated look from Aeric's face. As the young man glanced at Frederick's empty face—his own was similar abandoned. "Here," Charles took several letters from his pocket, "When we are not trapped in this craze—read these."

"What are they?" Aeric quickly took them. He grabbed the wrung of ladders and began climbing.

Charles followed, glad to be leaving the cellar but in no way relieved. He struggled to respond until they were in the cloaking haze. Now doubly distorted by the air and his mask, his voice sounded mechanical. "Auldwine's and Arthur's last days."

Aeric put his shirt over his face, not probing what Charles meant by 'Arthur's last days.' Instead, he pointed ahead, "That was where I last heard my dad. I think he was near my mother, but I could not investigate. I knew I had to reach you."

Charles nodded. He bent his knees in a fighting posture. Around him, individual columns of smog swayed with the breeze. It looked and sounded like two armies vying against one another. The wind clashed and crashed against the smog. It slashed and smashed like artillery shells. The gale zipped and the smoke roared.

More and more, Charles felt he was caught amidst a terrible melee, as if two colossi were battling for territory. He closed his eyes and though he was not religious, prayed to any god that might be listening. *Let them be safe. Let them come home. Even Arthur. Yes, even him, if that is what it takes.*

Dense pillars of smoke crowded the grove, licking the branches and resisting the easterly wind. Aeric and Charles looked at one another, wondering where to search. Aeric glanced at the silhouette of the inn, where a black sheet of grime flowed from the roof to the foundation. A red sun shone onto the tainted wood. He began to speak but was interrupted.

"Pick me up," Arthur demanded.

Charles swirled around, seeing no body to accompany the speech. He walked in the direction of the sound, but Aeric stopped him. The innkeeper's son shook his head, lowered his shirt from his face, and mouthed, "My mom first."

They continued into the tangled grove, listening for Hanna but hearing only the innkeeper. "You cheating woman… I love you… Please, don't leave me alone… I cannot handle this new world without my old."A pained cry silenced Arthur Gardner. Neither Aeric nor Charles looked back.

The haze began to irritate Aeric's eyes. The young man squinted, stumbling more and more.

"You get inside," Charles told him, "I can keep searching."

Aeric did not hear him. Rather, he pointed and began to run.

Charles followed when he saw the forlorn body in the grass. Hanna Gardner's nails were sunk into the soil, her legs bent in a crawling pose. They turned her body around. Dirt and soot had stained her face black. Her mouth was full of debris.

Without thinking, Charles took off his mask, cleaned off Hanna's face, and strapped the device to her. They then lifted Hanna up and, with Charles guiding Aeric—brought Her inside. The patrons had all gathered around the windows and gasped when they entered.

Charles hardly saw them, nor heard their questions. He tried to discern if Hanna's chest was rising—or if it was still. He debated swiftly, wondering if she should be brought to her bedroom. *Too much bad has happened there. She won't want to wake there.* "Laverne, would you mind if we used your bedroom? We wouldn't have to go up any stairs."

Laverne responded shortly, "Whatever ya want, honey."

Hanna's body was brought to the kitchens. Charles resisted the urge to listen for a heartbeat. He could not bear the worst. Wenton stayed out of their way as they wove through the narrow spaces. He offered to bring the three of them some herbal water. Charles saw no need to respond, though Aeric called for a clean washcloth. When they reached Laverne's room, Aeric placed all the pillows into a mound. They laid Hanna down.

Charles could no longer avert his eyes or postpone the necessary. He placed his hand on her wrist and waited. Charles swallowed some despair and sighed some relief. *A pulse.*

Aeric was now sitting on a rocking chair. He was leaning forward, his hands folded under his chin. When Wenton came into the room carrying three glasses and a damp washcloth, the young man did not seem to notice.

Charles swiped the washcloth. "Put the glasses down wherever there is space."

Wenton did so and hurried away.

Aeric cleared his throat and asked, quietly, "How is she?"

Charles tried to smile, but he could not lie much more than that. It was like someone had dumped a bucket of black paint on her. As he brushed his finger along Hanna's cheek—he was moved to tears. He went to wipe his tears and smeared the same soot on his skin. "She will be just fine," Charles prayed. He gazed at his dearest friend with a deep feeling of guilt. Her clothes were tattered; her blouse was frayed. Her skin was stained.

"I…I'm going to take Auldwine's mask… And get Emilia."

Charles bit his lip and shuddered. "Okay," he whispered. "Be careful out there." He took Hanna's hands and washed them clean. Her shining white skin soon shone as pale as a specter. Much of the washcloth was now a muddy hue, forcing Charles to use the other side for Hanna's face. He gently applied the cloth to her cheeks. Streaks of white skin emerged under the pollutant. Charles could not help thinking, as the layers of dirt and worse were removed from her motionless face— that he was exhuming Hanna's body. *If her skin looks like this, how is her heart? Her lungs?*

Hanna wheezed. Her chest rose a centimeter and sputtered back down. Her legs twitched slightly.

He could not help it. Charles grabbed hold of Hanna's hand and clenched it tightly. With his elbow, Charles wiped his tears. With his cloth, he washed the rest of her face.

Hanna stirred slightly. She muttered unintelligibly and rolled onto her side. All the while, she kept a tight grip on Charles' hand. Her foul, frayed clothes were ruining Laverne's sheets. Indeed, her clothes were worse than her skin had been. The pollutants had reacted with her clothing, searing many little holes into the blouse. Charles ignored proper conduct and peered through the gaps in her clothing. Her skin was not white, it was not black. *Red.*

"We need to get these clothes off," he told her. "You're having a reaction."

Of course, Hanna did not respond.

Charles paused, a life of panicked decency culminating in necessity. Charles was more than uncomfortable but he did not let his misgivings show. He begged the woman's forgiveness and then shouted, "Wenton, can you please fetch some of Misses Gardner's clothes?"

The chef obliged readily.

Charles turned to his task. He started by unbuttoning her blouse, though he did not need to do much. Most of the buttons had already been ripped off. Next, he focused on her undergarments. At first, he tried to be respectful and keep his eyes shut. However, he found no luck removing Hanna's brassiere. Indeed, he accidentally touched her skin in the process. Her body was pocked and hellishly hot. Charles opened his eyes and cursed his prudishness. He removed Hanna's brassiere and the rest of her underwear.

Then, he placed his hands upon Hanna's shoulders and lower thigh. He carefully maneuvered her so he could remove the stained sheets. Then, he quickly placed Hanna Gardner's head on the pillows and wrapped her as tight in the remaining covers as he could. Just as he finished the task, Wenton returned.

"Just put them on the nightstand," Charles panted. "Good. She will need them when she wakes up."

Wenton bowed his head respectfully and left. He shut the door gently. Then, callously, he began talking with Laverne in the kitchens. *"It was bound'ta happen."*

"Mmhm," Laverne hummed. *"Innkeeper in name only. Man done lost his mind. Y'see his son lately? Not right."*

"Aeric's a good kid. Bu' tha' father a'his… Redfeather has whole hospitals for people like him. Wards."

"Wonder how he treats Hanna in priv—"

Charles did not listen to another word. He could not. Arthur had hurt so many people, that if he heard one more word against him—he would have forsaken him. Yet, even after all that had happened, Charles could not forget the friend he once had. *If he dies, would I be a murderer?* The decision was made. He thought, hopefully, *He will probably be unconscious. I'd be able to bring him inside without a struggle. The constable can decide what to do, after that.* He hurried through the kitchen with haste.

When he entered the tavern, he halted. All the orphans were gathered around the windows. Two merchants were speaking a foreign language; Charles did not need to be fluent to know they spoke excitedly. No one seemed particularly perturbed save Charles. "What is going on up here? Why is that door open?"

No one cared to reply. Virginia simply stated, "You can see it going west now!"

Charles licked the perimeter of his mouth and bit his lower lip. Then, he covered his face. He stormed the front step. He stopped immediately.

Charles squinted. The haze had lifted. It had been pushed back to the west and the faint outline of Oleander peak was now fainter. Charles tilted his head and gazed toward the east. His jaw fell slightly. He scratched his head. Though still far away, it seemed that the mountain of riddles had come closer to town. It was as if the peak had picked up its roots and walked. Charles rubbed his eyes and after another moment of awe, turned away from the eastern spire.

He returned to the ruin of Auberdine. The haze had hurried away, but it had done its damage.

A blackness blanketed the Cottonwood. The granary was an obsidian peak. The stables were an onyx mausoleum. The town was an ebony vein. Every inch of town was soaked in soot. The marbled estates of the Inner Ring were painted anew. The grove was grey; the hedge was stained. Even the skeletal cottonwood was now black.

And underneath that long-dead tree, Charles concluded his search. A still figure was slumped against the blackened cottonwood. After a quick debate, Charles approached. He jogged down and knelt before the body.

Arthur Gardner's eyes were open. His mouth was agape. Blood had flooded down his chin and onto his chest like a long, ghastly tongue. His twisted visage stared past Charles. The many bags under his eyes had shriveled into one. Layers of soot coated his face.

Despite all that had happened, Charles was moved by the scene. He could not cry, but he knew he would not be happy for a long time. He stared at the body. His oldest friend looked positively horrified. The widened eyes gazed at something far beyond Eastmont.

Charles closed Arthur's eyes and wiped the blood from the body's chin. "I will try to remember you as were," he promised the corpse. He wiped the lips of dirt and blood. He brushed the blackness off the cheeks. Even in death, the face muscles naturally remained in a slight grin. He cleaned the eye sockets so the smile lines were not hidden.

"Goodbye, Arthur."

The town was still, save for a person at the base of the Hill. Aeric ducked beneath the stable doors. He threw off the gas mask. He gestured for him to come down. Charles looked at the ground, where so many of Arthur's troubles were buried. He lifted himself up by the skeletal tree's branches.

He jogged down, "You found her, then?"

Aeric bowed his head. "All safe." He swallowed. "Do you think… I could, uh, get a moment with him alone?"

"I won't go back up there for as long as you want," Charles affirmed.

"I mean… Keep the guests away for me? I want to say goodbye to a father… Not to, uh—what he was."

"We don't have to tell them the entire story?" Charles risked his morals. *This would destroy you all. The inn might never recover from such a scandal.*

Aeric wiped his brow. He bit his lip and smirked sadly, "You don't believe that." He walked warily toward his father's body.

Charles sighed. *No, I don't.* He glanced at the redwood door, the granary, the roof, the hedge, and finally—the stable. *No use dwelling on hypotheticals.* He pushed the stable doors open, revealing two entwined figures.

Emilia's face was muddy. Isabelle's fur was filthy. With their eyes closed, they seemed like unpainted sculptures. With a groan, Isabelle laid on her side. The hound curled around the child and put a protective paw around her chest. The hound blinked at Charles and then began licking the child's face. Emilia stirred and wrapped her arm snugly around Isabelle.

Epilogue

"It's not like you have to go to town. Not exactly a trek," Aeric pestered. "And it has been such a nice day. No clouds, no haze."

Hanna glanced at the window. "Whose morbid idea was it to put the memorial here? Not mine."

Aeric popped his lips.

His mother stared at him. Everyone had agreed except her, though she played ignorant to the fact. To the rest of town, the old granary had served no purpose. It had valuable stone and many poor people needed headstones. Besides, many thought the inn was the rightful recipient of so many homeless dead. Some thought it was the innkeeper's penance. Hanna thought so too, albeit silently. For the most part, she thought it was cruel to keep so many painful memories nearby. She turned from the window and sat on the edge of a new, smaller bed. "I am not ready to see him yet."

Aeric was quick to reply, "Then don't go for dad. What about Galahad?" He did his best to sound joyful and awe-inspired, "They built a beautiful mausoleum for him. Tomb for a king."

"A poor recompense," Hanna snapped. She remarked, *I hope they cleaned that suit before burying him in it.* "If our family had not used him, he wouldn't need a tomb."

Aeric was quiet for a moment. Then, he raised his brow, "Recompense?" Her son grinned, "You've been reading again."

Hanna flinched a disarmed smile, "I might have been."

He leaned against the dresser, "I'm glad. You really do sound so much better."

"I just needed time."

Aeric paused before responding. He scratched his ear, "So you won't go?"

Hanna was so exhausted by his prodding. She would not go like a beast on a lead to visit some ghastly graveyard. She kept her mouth shut while her tongue roved along the roof of her mouth. Finally, she admitted, "I can't, Aeric." She knew she sounded tired and exaggerated the weariness to her benefit. "I don't even know who to mourn, or if I should mourn at all."

Aeric shrugged. The joy in his voice was starting to strain. "Don't mourn then, Ev—"

Hanna said, soft but stern, "I am happy for Evelyn. I really am." She closed her eyes and paused for a deep breath. She had no idea how to continue her argument. She pursued a tangent, "If my nephew were murdered and eaten by—" She sniffled. "Well, I would not be wearing *pink*."

Of course, Hanna did not mean her meanness. She was glad Evelyn was no longer a prisoner of grief. She looked at her son, waiting for him to say she was not being sensitive. She blinked, expecting some harsh criticism of her callous demeanor.

Aeric did not make her feel bad. At least, he had not intended to. He scratched his head. A hint of hope attached itself to his words. "Charles wants to see him."

Hanna suddenly became worried and excited. Her heart sank and soared. *Charles was supposed to be at the capitol for months. Have they finished already?* She asked as if uninterested, staring at the ceiling, "He's back, then? All the way from the Rock?"

Aeric turned and opened a dresser drawer. It had been one of his father's. Hanna peered past his shoulder suspiciously. *I should have cleaned those,* she chastised herself. The boy turned around and opened a tiny bottle of whiskey. He pulled out a shot glass from the same drawer.

How long had Arthur had that, there? Hanna's eyes widened. *How many secrets did he have?* She shook her head rapidly and focused on her son.

Aeric poured himself a shot and swigged it down. His mouth twisted with disgust. He wrinkled his nose and squinted.

Hanna stared at him disapprovingly.

Aeric coughed slightly and covered his mouth. He set the whiskey and the glass on the dresser and opened his palms. "What? Visiting his grave isn't easy for me, either."

Hanna rolled her eyes. *We are forced to visit every time we leave the inn.* She pressed the prior subject, remarking casually, "I didn't think we would see much of Charles, anymore."

Aeric rubbed his hands and went to depart. "Well, he should be here any moment." He paused with one foot in his mother's room and one foot in the hallway.

The words echoed. *Any moment.* Hanna stood up and demanded, "Why didn't you warn me?"

Aeric's upper lip rolled toward his nostrils as he lied, quite smugly, "I thought it would be a nice surprise."

"It is not," Hanna decried breathlessly. She put her hands on her hips. "Go on, then. Much to do! Shoo! I will see you at supper."

Aeric was taken aback. "Even with Charles going, you won't visit him?"

"Especially so," Hanna whispered in horror. She waved off her son and spent the next several minutes pacing around her room. There was a lot more room to walk without such a large bed taking up space. Her little one was nice, and warmer, too. Still, she could not stay in her bedroom forever. Not with Charles Eastmont and the Yao returning. The whole town would expect her.

Oh, they already gossip so much. Cannibal's widow locked in her room. She snarled at her sheets, "Perfectly tragic. Forlorn princess tucked away in the tip-top of some tower." She glanced at her closet and felt a surge of indignation. *We're some haunted house now, a tourist attraction… Fine. If I must make an appearance.* She strode up to her wardrobe and analyzed her clothes. "Repugnant, ridiculous, revolting, revealing…"

Hanna narrowed her selection to two very different choices. She laid two dresses on her bed and stared with disgust at both. One was beautiful, as blue as the ocean. The other was a black, drab thing with a veil. She had never made such a fuss over her choice of clothes. So why was she so indecisive now? The decision overwhelmed her and she walked to her window.

Hanna gazed down at the cemetery. She sighed at the several mourners pacing around the graves. Aeric kept insisting she be one of those sorry lot, but he had no idea. She probably looked at those headstones more than anyone else. She may not have stomped on the fresh dirt like the rest of the mourners, but she knew to whom every stone belonged.

The grand mausoleum at the center of the cemetery belonged to Galahad. It was at the highest point of the Hill, just lower than the inn. Laverne was the first to suggest he get a memorial, seeing as he was murdered by a mob on false accusations. Evelyn quickly agreed, along with some of the more penitent Inner Ringers. *The ones who survived, anyway.* Hanna did not disagree with the monument. Galahad *had* deserved better. But why in her backyard? She was careful not to show such feelings around Laverne, but she could not help how she felt.

Presently, Laverne was standing beside the mausoleum. That was typical. She was usually at the cemetery, nowadays. The only other people that paid respect to Galahad were Emilia, Aeric, and some cloaked woman. Hanna did not recognize her.

Momed and the other men Arthur had murdered were buried beside Galahad. They had above-ground caskets crafted of granary stone. Due to the group's superior misfortune, Charles had argued they should each receive a superior monument. Both Laverne and Aeric had been quite specific about their placement, too.

A few feet down the mausoleum, a wide ring of white stones began. It stretched the perimeter of the Hill. It was the first of two circles that wove between the grove. It belonged to those souls, named and nameless, that had perished in the Overgrowth. Some had suffocated from the smoke, others had been murdered. Some families chose to bury their dead in the Wanakhan tradition. Most preferred a stone. Further down the Hill, the outer ring of graves was dominated by Inner Ringers. Most of those dead had taken part in the hanging of Galahad, save Frederick Kinsfeld who was buried beside his mother.

Yet, one grave she refused to notice. Apparently, it contained Auldwine's remains. The remains that, according to the letters she would not read, were a reason for Arthur's change. She felt a tinge of guilt for not visiting her brother-in-law. Her guilt was violently diluted by her repulsion from that tree. *All those… remains… With the toothmarks and the…* Hanna groaned. By everyone's insistence—they had chosen to bury Arthur there as well. Even if she had wanted to visit him, it was such a gruesome monument. She risked a glance at that terrible stump. *Will they bury me there, too?*

She returned to the dilemma of the two dresses. *If I wear black, people will think I miss him. A cannibal.* Yet, if she wore colors, people might assume she had moved on. Apathy or agony. Hanna wished it could be one or the other. Stuck between the two dresses, she felt as if she were in purgatory.

"Guh." She scowled and snatched the blue dress. People already snickered behind her family's back. *Better they think I am glad.* As she dressed, she heard Aeric greeting the travelers. She resisted the temptation to spy from her window. Nevertheless, she heard Yao Yu speaking. As the men walked around the cemetery, she tuned out Charles' distinct voice.

Once dressed, she waited as long as possible before going down. It took Emilia charging up to her room to finally rouse her.

"Mama, come on! Charles is here!"

Hanna smiled reflexively. Her daughter's demeanor had improved day by day. Now, it was impossible to mope with her in the room. Her newfound energy was infectious. "I'm coming, sugarbear," she called, quickly walking up to her mirror. "Just doing some makeup."

Emilia waltzed in and inspected her mother's face. She eyed her foot to head. "Did you just start?"

Hanna swatted at her daughter, smirking all the while. "Get out of here, you little miscreant."

Emilia jumped back, giggling. "Only if you promise to hurry up."

Hanna groaned, "Okay. I promise."

Emilia put her hands to her hip, mimicking her mother. "Good." Finally, she scurried off.

Hanna stared at the woman in the mirror. She wove her fingers through her hair and touched her scar. Nobody could see it now. Still, she did not feel like the woman from a year ago. The old Hanna would have been excited to see Charles. Yet, she felt afraid. She wanted to greet the man warmly, but she feared herself. *What if I see him before I see Arthur? What if I look at Charles and instantly feel better? Will Arthur have been right all along?*

Hanna shuddered at the thought of seeing Charles before seeing her husband's grave. *What an awful wife I am.* She scowled one last time at her reflection and assumed a dignified look. She did not have to ruin anyone's night; she did not have to be the life of the party, either. As she walked down the stairs, she whispered, "There are more people at the table than Charles. You can do this."

Indeed, there were *many* more people at the table. Hanna thought it strange so many folks wanted to stay at the inn after what Arthur had done, but here they were. Orphans, outcasts—the Overgrowth had practically moved in. *I suppose after a natural disaster, the homeless can't be picky...* A few survivors from the Inner Ring were also present at the table. A Pale man and his child had escaped the fate of most of the mob, but the smoke had destroyed their home, nonetheless. Most of their furniture and mementos were forever stained with soot.

Hanna sat at the head of the table. The food on her plate was cold. On her left, Emilia and Josephine were giggling about something. On her right, Aeric was conversing with Yao Yu. The stubborn old doctor was nodding his head as her son spoke.

"So what did the capitol say?" Aeric asked.

Yao Yu twirled an unlit cigarette. "We have-a secure more medicine, investigators, equipment..." He licked his lips and tapped the cigarette on the table.

"And?" Her son pressed.

"Inspectors sent-a-to west mountain," Yu replied. He bit his lower lip, raised his brow, and returned the cigarette to his shirt pocket. "I tell about haze," he continued.

"Mhm," Aeric responded, now wary of what the doctor was preparing to say.

"I tell also about inn-keeper." Yu and Aeric shared a brief, silent exchange. Then, the doctor glanced at his nephew. He placed his palms on his lap. "Arthur Gardner not first-a soldier to go mad from-a war. But-a profession has developed, so to say. We can treat-a soldier like him."

Aeric's cheek twitched. Before the conversation could continue or fizzle, he steered it along. "Did the Rock agree to send masons? Carpenters? We have a lot of rebuilding to do."

Yao Yu nodded, "Not many. But some."

"And the Inner Ring?" Aeric asked. "We have a lot of vacant homes. The Ring is practically empty." He pointed his spoon down the line of patrons, "I say give them to these families here." He then shrugged and acknowledged several legal questions.

Hanna pretended to be listening. She searched the petrified log for that specific person. *Where is Charles?* An empty seat beside Emilia soon answered her question. She wiped her clean mouth and rejoined the conversation.

Yao Yu was patting his nephew's back and beaming proudly.

Hanna blinked at the two doctors. She rubbed her scalp, sniffled, and started to ask Yao Yang a question.

"That so?" Aeric muttered. He interrupted his mother and called down the table, "Rashif!"

The Muhali fumbled to his feet. "Yes, Sir Gardner."

Aeric folded his hands and pointed two fingers at the man, "You once served my family a free meal. That debt needs repayment."

Hanna felt a wet and furry nose brush up against her arm. As the table erupted with cheers and clapping, she rubbed the dog's neck. "Big girl," she scowled. The large hound sniffed and stretched her snout toward Emilia's plate.

Hanna acted perturbed. She said, loudly, "This is no place for an animal. I'll just get her out of here." No one, not even Emilia, seemed to notice.

She guided Izzy. As they neared the stairs, the dog became harder to lead. Then, as Hanna went up the first step, the hound darted away. With a groan, Hanna followed. She hurried past the petrified table, acting as casual and calm as possible. She reached Izzy after only a moment. The dog was sitting beside an open, red door. Her tail thumped.

"Come on, you little stinker," Hanna ordered.

Izzy tilted her head and then bolted outside.

Not again, Hanna fumed. *I will just have to get her a leash. A short one.* She stomped after the dog. After several paces, she realized she had inadvertently wandered into the grove-cemetery. She stopped at Galahad's gleaming mausoleum just seconds before colliding with someone.

"Oh," Laverne greeted her. "Evenin', Miss Gardner."

Hanna sniffled and thought of correcting her. She was not divorced, after all. The title did not seem worth the effort. She smiled politely. "Hi."

"He was just a child," Laverne stated. She turned and stared at the circle of headstones. "All of 'em was."

Hanna cleared her throat, not knowing what to say to that.

Laverne rested her hands on her belly and faced the mausoleum once more. She shook her head. "That mountain killed him."

Hanna agreed as she thought to the contrary, *Carolyn's mob killed him.*

"I'm glad the Rock sendin' up inspectors. Tha' place is lawless."

"Me too," Hanna said, itching to go back inside. She did not feel like she belonged among the mourners. *I am trespassing*, she swallowed. Feeling a need to remain cordial, she tried small talk. "I hear there was a monopoly up there."

"Mhm," Laverne replied. "Workers on strike, still."

Hanna sighed. She was not very thrilled by current events and would rather not take on the world's burdens. She had her own.

It seemed Laverne felt similarly. She put a hand on the mausoleum and bowed her head. "Silly boy. I tries to tell him." She muttered, "The self the only thing ya can search for and get more lost."

Hanna did not feel she was the one being spoken to. Just as she stepped back, Laverne gestured, "There's yo' dog."

Hanna scanned the Hill. Sure enough, there was Isabelle. She marched toward the animal, who was oblivious to the trouble she was in. The hound was wagging its tail excitedly and pawing at the ground. Hanna's brisk pace was slowed when she saw the hound beside a lonely tree stump. She abruptly halted when she saw a man sitting there, too.

"Charles," she gasped. He was sitting by the Gardner graves, staring at the tree stump with a sad smile. Hanna ignored the inscription carved into the bark, gulped, and pointed inside, "You're missing the feast," she noted.

Charles grunted. He lowered his chin and stared at Arthur's grave marker. "Auldwine loved this one. I remember when it was a little sapling."

Hanna smiled, her fingers scraping instinctually at her cuticles. The smog had stained the wood black. No one could wash it off. "Yeah," she fumbled, "I, uh, it's nice." She glanced at the night sky.

Charles stood up. He looked down at the graves and pocketed his hands. A cool winter breeze blew past, ringing several chimes on the porch. He shivered.

"You d-don't have to do this, you know," Hanna finally said. "Nobody would shame you if you just walked past."

Charles smiled, "Likewise."

Hanna was speechless. She pretended to cough, hoping Charles might continue speaking or she might find a way to get back inside. Her eyes darted to her husband's grave. She wondered what Arthur looked like down there—if he was still recognizable. She shivered and joked, "I should not have worn a summer dress," as if her chill were from the cold.

Charles said nothing.

Hanna hated that. She wished he would just lead the conversation. She had nothing to say. Not about him. Not about Arthur. After an unbearable second of silence, she defended herself. "I was meaning to see him... Eventually."

"No need to explain yourself," Charles replied quietly.

Hanna took a deep breath. "I should get going," she smirked and rolled her eyes. "Head of the table and all." She started toward the porch.

"Or you could stay with us?"

Hanna smiled and frowned. She had heard him. She had not heard him at all. She choked as she whispered, "You and Izzy?"

Charles looked into her eyes. "No."

Hanna could not help herself. The first tear came without warning. She felt it trickle down her cheek. When it fell from her face, a dozen more took its place. Her lips quivered and she nodded several times. Charles walked up to her and gently guided her toward the two graves. While she felt such immeasurable sadness, she also felt relief. It felt good to finally grieve. For the first time, she mourned the man she had lost. Charles took her hand and together, they read the words on the grave.

"The Innkeeper and the Cannibal."

9 789898 590950